"... a tale throbbing with full-blooded, heroic men and women and chilling, malevolent villains..."
—*Rave Reviews*

"*Defy the Eagle* by Lynn Bartlett is another amazing historical paperback.... This is her third book and her most ambitious to date."
—*Minneapolis Star-Tribune*

"This is a glorious and sensuous love story that I promise will be a great reading treat."
—*Affaire de Coeur*

"A wonderful, wonderful novel... Don't miss it."
—*Romantic Times*

Lynn Bartlett

Defy the Eagle

WORLDWIDE

TORONTO • NEW YORK • LONDON • PARIS
AMSTERDAM • STOCKHOLM • HAMBURG
ATHENS • MILAN • TOKYO • SYDNEY

DEFY THE EAGLE

Worldwide Library Trade-Size Paperback July 1986
Worldwide Library Mass-Market Edition May 1987

ISBN 0-373-97050-1

This book is dedicated to
Neil Meyer,
my agent and friend.

THE DREAM

A SOFT RAY OF SUNLIGHT filtered through the leaves of the sacred oak trees, clothing the woman who knelt beside the stream in a mantle of light. A doe and her fawn, having drunk of the refreshing water, approached the woman and trustingly accepted the grain she held in her outstretched hand. She laughed, a gentle sound which floated through the grove and brought a smile to the lips of the man who stood watching her from the concealment of the trees. He stepped from behind the oak and walked toward her quietly, utilizing the stealth which had been handed down from his father and his father's father. The woman did not hear him, did not sense his presence—not until he stood directly behind her and grasped a handful of the loose, flame-colored hair which lifted in the breeze.

She turned and regarded him through wide, violet eyes. The doe and her fawn scampered away but she appeared not to notice. "Briton." Her voice was soft, musical.

"Roman." The word should have been a curse, but instead it fell lovingly from his lips. "I have waited overlong."

"As have I." She rose and was willingly enfolded by his arms. He drew her against him and kissed her deeply, hungrily; when they parted, her eyes, now a fathomless purple, trapped him and held him prisoner while time flew past unheeded.

HE AWOKE AND LAY for several minutes beneath the pelts which sheltered him from the night air, staring at the sky. The same dream. By the gods, the same dream! Would he never be free of this vision, this torment which had plagued him for nearly two decades? With an oath he threw back the pelts and left his bed. There would be no more rest this night, not for him. The mighty warrior brought low by a dream of a woman, he jeered silently as he picked his way over the sleeping forms of the half-dozen men who had followed him from the village. The sharpness of the night air cleared his head, cooled his inflamed senses. He needed a woman, that was all. And not a woman of Rome, but one of his own tribe. An Iceni woman. He would take a wife as he should have done years before. She would cool this fever in his blood, the ache in his loins which came over him with the dream.

"You have risen early, Caddaric. Or has your sleep been disturbed?"

The voice brought Caddaric up short and he turned to face the man who had materialized from the trees. "As are you, Clywd. Have you been speaking to your gods?"

The mocking tone drew a laugh from the older man and he pushed back the hood of his black cloak, exposing gray-streaked hair to the firelight. "They are your gods as well and I know you believe in them, so why do you beg their wrath?"

Caddaric motioned impatiently. "I am not a Druid; the gods do not speak to me."

"They speak," the Druid countered. "You do not listen. That is the difference. Come, share my fire and tell me of your dream."

Caddaric's eyes narrowed suspiciously, but he followed Clywd and seated himself at the small fire. "What dream?"

"The one which shadows your face and heart," Clywd replied easily.

"Do you peer into men's souls, old one?"

"When the need arises." Clywd fixed Caddaric with an unwavering stare. "You are my son. Is it so strange that I

should know when the flesh of my flesh is troubled?''
Caddaric did not answer and Clywd added several twigs
to the flame before he spoke again. ''You are a warrior, a
source of pride to me and your people. Do you fear the
truth more than battle?''

''I fear nothing.'' Caddaric glared into the flames. The
fire reminded him of the woman of his dreams and with
a low groan he relented. ''A woman—I dream of a
woman, Father.''

''Ahh.'' Clywd nodded. ''She is beautiful, I trust, and
will bear you strong sons. Have you offered for her?''

''Nay.'' Caddaric answered in a tortured voice. ''We
have never met, except in my dreams. And in my dreams
she is Roman.''

''Ahh,'' Clywd said again and pulled a pouch from his
robe. He extracted a handful of herbs from the leather,
placed them in a beaten copper bowl and eased the bowl
into the glowing embers. Brightly colored flames leaped
upward in a dazzling display and Clywd nodded, satisfied. ''She has been with you a long time, my son. Since
you first became a man. I saw her birth eighteen sum-
mers ago, but I was not certain until now why the gods
chose to show me the birth of a Roman girl-child.''

''If I dream of her again I shall go mad,'' Caddaric
confessed, accepting without question his father's
knowledge. ''I was twelve when I first dreamed of her,
and then she was but a child, a babe. I have watched her
grow, become a woman.'' He shook his head. ''She does
not exist; she cannot. This is but a punishment visited
upon me by the gods because they knew I would betray
our people and fight for a time for the Romans.''

Clywd's face turned grim. ''There was no betrayal—
that, too, was destined by the gods. What you learned as
a Roman auxiliary will soon be put to use against the Romans themselves.''

''It will come then, wise one?''

''Aye. As surely as day follows night. And that presents you with a problem, my son.'' Clywd added more

herbs to the copper bowl and studied the colors which arced forth.

"If she is indeed of Rome, then there can be only one solution," Caddaric ruminated when his father remained silent. "When the Iceni rise to throw off the Roman yoke, the land must be cleansed completely of the Empire and its people. If this woman exists, she will perish. There is no other course."

"Nay. The woman must not die," Clywd announced with sudden vehemence. "Some will be spared, this woman among them."

Caddaric frowned. "Why?"

"Have you not guessed?" Clywd replied in a voice as soft as the wind rustling through the oaks. "She is your destiny, Caddaric."

The old man still gazed blindly into the fire and Caddaric leaned forward to grip his arm. "There is more. Tell me what you see, Clywd."

"In time—all in good time, my son." Clywd shook off his son's hand and rose. "Her destruction will cause yours as well, that much I will say. Guard your future well, young warrior." He turned and with a whisper of his robe disappeared into the grove.

Caddaric watched him go and then plucked the copper bowl from the embers. With a long forefinger he poked at the contents of the dish and snorted derisively. "Ashes—only ashes."

Chapter 1

JILANA AUGUSTA BASILIUS—first daughter of the merchant Marcus Basilius—drew her mount to a halt in the clearing of the forest and dropped lightly from the saddle. She allowed the horse to graze and, laughing, raised her arms above her head and twirled delightedly in the first rays of the sunlight.

"Free! I am free," Jilana cried, her voice caroling through the wood. But only for a time, a treacherous voice in the back of her mind mocked.

Her smile faded and, sighing, Jilana allowed her arms to fall to her sides. It was true; in a matter of days she would wed the Tribune Lucius Quintus and the time she spent here would be ended. Lucius—ever ambitious—would have no tolerance of her early morning rides; he expected Jilana to remain in the city and court the wives of those men who could further his career. Lucius did not, as he so often said, plan to remain a tribune forever. Even now his family in Rome was thinking of ways to hasten his return to that city. His father was a senator and one day Lucius would take his place. Hopefully Lucius would find a way to cover himself with honor before that day came, and what better path to glory than through service in the military. Lucius had already proved himself a leader of men and a skilled soldier—unlike so many other senatorial tribunes. To be chosen as his wife was no small honor. Jilana shuddered at the thought and bent to pick the wildflowers she loved so well. She did not mind marriage to Lucius—after all, she was eighteen, well past the age when most women were already married—and the fact that she did not love him bothered Jilana not at all. What did claw at Jilana's heart was the knowledge that Lucius would some day take her from this island which was her home. Unlike Claudia, her younger sister, Jilana had never been to Rome. She had been born in Britannia and her parents had lived here and traded with Britons for several years before the Emperor Claudius had led the final assault upon the barbarian inhabitants. They had fled Britannia for a short time and lived in Gaul, so her mother said, but Jilana had taken her first steps on Britannia's soil. This was home; Jilana spoke the Briton's language with the same ease she spoke her own, and she loathed the thought of living in Rome where all things would be unfamiliar to her.

"Oh, Juno," Jilana sighed aloud. "Why did Lucius not choose Claudia in my stead?"

Claudia, newly returned from Rome, would have made Lucius the perfect wife. She had ambition enough to match his, she could charm with a glance, and she was totally ruthless. A year in Rome had honed her characteristics to a fine edge and Jilana shuddered to think of living out the rest of her life in the company of a hundred Claudias. Tears of self-pity pricked her eyelids and Jilana hastily blinked them away. She was, in spite of everything, a Roman; and while hers was not the blond, dark-eyed beauty of Claudia, Lucius often said her pale, flame-colored hair and violet eyes were captivating. For the present that would be enough, and in time Jilana would learn all that Claudia had learned. In Rome.

"Greetings, mistress."

Jilana left her thoughts and the ground with an alarmed gasp and found herself staring at a tall man who stood watching her from the edge of the clearing. He wore the uniform of a centurion and he spoke her tongue, but that did nothing to alleviate the frantic beating of Jilana's heart as the man bore down upon her. Trembling, Jilana clutched the wildflowers to her breast and retreated a step when the stranger halted in front of her. Sheer terror chained her tongue and Jilana regarded the hard blue eyes fearfully.

Caddaric stared at the pale, oval face which was at once familiar and unknown, and felt his senses reel. His dream had become reality and, as in his dream, Caddaric heard himself say, "Roman."

Jilana started at the sound of his voice, colored with some unnamed emotion, and half-turned, poised for flight. For several moments they stared at each other; Jilana suddenly aware of the vulnerability of her position and Caddaric struggling to suppress the urge to crush her against him. Witch, Caddaric's mind screamed. Roman! You are the one who torments me so. You are the one who haunts my dreams and makes peace elusive. *She is your destiny.* Clywd's words cleared Caddaric's roiling thoughts and he studied the woman in front of him. She was delicate, far more delicate than his dreams had led him to believe, and her red-gold hair was bound up in the Roman fashion. But it was her eyes that held Caddaric— they were a deep violet, fathomless, more enchanting than any Caddaric had ever seen. The blood pounded in his temples, threatening his self-control. How he ached to take this woman in his arms, to twist his hands in those silken curls and kiss her until she begged for mercy. Jilana paled beneath the bold, appraising stare, unexpectedly intimidated by the overpowering presence of this man. Every fiber of her being cried out to Jilana for escape, yet she stood as if rooted to the ground because her legs refused to obey her commands.

Seeing the fear in the wide, violet eyes, Caddaric gentled. "I did not mean to frighten you, mistress, but rather to offer my help. Are you lost?"

"Oh, nay!" The gasped-out denial brought a smile to the centurion's lips and Jilana relaxed as the blue eyes lost their wintry haze. "I come here often, Centurion. 'Tis you who must be lost, for I know of no one else who has come here before."

Caddaric laughed. "A soldier must know the land he protects, mistress. My friends and I visit these woods to hunt the wild boar and today my path led me here. For your own sake, 'twould be best if you gathered your flowers some other day, Lady..."

"Jilana." Jilana gave her name readily but curiosity danced in her eyes and she forgot her fear. "You have deceived me, Centurion; you are not Roman." The man's face darkened and Jilana hurriedly explained, "While you speak my language quite well, you have the faintest trace of an accent."

"You are most astute, Lady Jilana," Caddaric answered smoothly. "I am of the auxiliary, not the legion."

"I was not aware that the auxiliary forces were stationed here." Jilana frowned. "Are you new to the town?"

"We arrived only a few days ago."

"Strange, Lucius did not mention that auxiliaries were being sent here." Jilana pondered that for a moment and then shrugged. The day was too beautiful to be spoiled by thoughts of Lucius. Smiling, she looked up at the man who towered over her. "I bid you welcome, Centurion. I think you will find Venta Icenorum pleasant duty."

Caddaric bowed, then glanced meaningfully at the forest. "Part of my duty includes protecting young maidens such as yourself from harm. I should never forgive myself if the boar we were hunting came across you. If you will permit me, Lady Jilana, I will see you safely from these woods."

Sighing, Jilana assented and followed the centurion to where her mount was grazing, but when he made to lift her into the saddle she shook her head. "Come, we will walk together."

"As you wish, lady."

They fell into step, one on either side of the horse, and as they wound their way through the forest, from time to time Jilana stole a glance at the centurion. Absurdly, he reminded her of the oak trees—tall, sturdy, with arms and legs which were powerfully muscled, he seemed a part of

"We do not know Queen Boadicea's situation. Catus Decianus, the Roman procurator, may reconsider and allow our Queen and her daughters to rule. If that happens, we shall return to our village and bury our weapons once again and the Romans will not know how strong the Iceni are."

"And if the Romans make good their threat to strip Boadicea of her authority?" one of the warriors questioned.

"You know the answer," Caddaric said grimly. "We are Iceni—we will not go willingly into Roman slavery."

"Caddaric speaks wisely," the older man at Caddaric's side spoke up. "He knows the Roman ways; we do not. We would do well to follow his advice. If Roman blood is to be shed, Caddaric will see that your battle-axes spill their share."

"Will you never cease protecting me, Heall," Caddaric asked wryly when the men fell to discussing Heall's words.

Heall shrugged and examined the buckle of his cuirass. "You said yourself that if we must do battle with the Romans we must learn to obey orders if we are to win. I sought only to lend the weight of my years to your sound judgment."

"Then you believe my way is best?"

Heall grinned, his silver beard parting to expose twin rows of white teeth. "If I did not, I would never have allowed you to persuade me to wear this hated uniform. We will be in and out of the town before the Romans know we were there."

Caddaric nodded, then faced his men. "Go back to the forest and wait, my friends. Word will reach you soon enough." Without further argument the warriors disappeared and a moment later Clywd came forward from the trees. "Greetings, wise one. Have you begged protection for us from your gods?"

"Always you mock the gods and still they favor you." Clywd shook his head despairingly. "Did they not deliver the woman into your hands?"

Caddaric went white with shock, all too aware of Heall's curious eyes upon him. "Your gods confound you, Druid."

"Nay, my son, I see most clearly. 'Tis you who are confounded." Ignoring Heall, Clywd halted in front of his son and asked bluntly, "Why did you let her go, Caddaric? She was yours for the taking."

"The time was not meet," Caddaric snapped, effectively ending the conversation. He adjusted the baldric—from which hung the *gladius*, or short sword—to a more comfortable position on his shoulder and motioned to Heall. "Come, 'tis long past time. We do not want our entry into the town to attract unwanted attention." In his fury Caddaric did not notice that he ground the wildflower under his heel.

Clywd gazed after his son and old friend, a haunted look coming into his eyes. "Oh, my son, it would have been kinder to claim her now! Why did your defiance of the gods not extend to this woman?" Heavy-hearted, Clywd turned and melted into the trees.

"WHERE HAVE YOU BEEN?" The sharp words halted Jilana upon her entrance into the villa and, turning, she found Claudia regarding her angrily. "We have all been waiting for you," Claudia added waspishly. "Even Lucius."

Jilana swallowed convulsively. "Lucius? Lucius is here?"

"Lucius is here," Claudia mimicked acidly. "By the gods, Jilana, you act more like a barbarian than a Roman!"

"I act like myself," Jilana retorted hotly. "What I do is none of your affair!"

"We shall see." Claudia turned and ran toward the front of the villa. "Father! Mother! Lucius! Jilana has returned."

Sighing, Jilana trudged after her sister, oblivious to the richly tiled, mosaic floor over which she moved and the furnishings that had been imported from Rome by Augusta. Her meeting with the centurion weighed heavily upon her and Jilana strove to order her chaotic thoughts. She must surely be wicked to allow a chance meeting with that man to disturb her so. She would be Lucius' wife soon—it was to him that her allegiance would be given, as well as that brief flare of passion the centurion had brought forth. I will not think of him, Jilana told herself fiercely. I will not!

"Jilana!"

Jilana gasped, the bouquet of wildflowers trembling in her grasp as her father's voice jerked her rudely from her thoughts. Without realizing it, Jilana had started up the steps to the second story of the villa and she blushed furiously as she turned and met the four pairs of eyes staring at her.

Marcus Basilius took a step forward and waved his daughter down from the stairs. "Come here, Jilana." Jilana meekly obeyed, following her family and a glowering Lucius into a spacious room littered with couches, pillows and low tables. She stood stiffly in front of her father while Marcus seated himself on a couch, arranged the folds of his toga, and fixed Jilana with an unwavering gaze. "You will now explain, daughter, where you have been and why you did not see fit to tell anyone of this house that you were leaving."

"Father, I—" Jilana gulped and lamely held out her bouquet. "I went riding and stopped to gather these flowers. I fear I lost track of the passage of time." Claudia snickered and Jilana sent her a quelling look.

"What are we to do with you, Jilana? You have been ordered again and again not to ride outside the walls of the town alone, and yet you persist in defying me! Why?"

Jilana lowered her eyes to the flowers. How could she explain to him that she was more at ease in the forest than she was in the villa? What words could she use to describe the peace the oak groves brought to her heart? "I do not mean to defy you, Father."

"But you do so, nonetheless," Marcus said gravely.

"And she rides in those disgusting tunics the barbarian women wear," Claudia put in with obvious relish. "Just look at her, Father, she—"

"That will be quite enough, Claudia," Marcus interrupted. The warning flashing in his dark eyes sent Claudia back to her pillows where she glared at both her father and sister.

Jilana's cheeks flamed as Lucius' eyes dropped to her short tunic and then to the gleaming length of leg below.

"Well, Jilana," Marcus questioned. "Have you nothing to say?"

"Nay, Father." Jilana bowed her head over the flowers.

"Is it your wish, then, to continue to humiliate your family with your behavior?" Her stricken look was answer enough and Marcus softened. "I have been harsh with you, Jilana, and I did not intend to be; but you must be aware that you are no longer a child. 'Tis long past the time when you should accept the responsibilities of your position."

"You frightened us all, Jilana." Her mother, Augusta, joined the conversation for the first time, her quiet voice carrying more rebuke than Marcus' harsh words.

"Forgive me, Mother, such was not my intent." At the pleading look in Jilana's eyes, Augusta opened her arms and Jilana flew into them. "It will not happen again, Mother," Jilana whispered. "I promise."

"Tell your father," Augusta whispered in return.

Jilana did so and Marcus nodded, a forgiving smile on his lips. "'Twas not such a large mistake, for all we have made of it. Go now and change, we must leave shortly."

"Aye, Father." Casting a wary glance at Lucius, Jilana ran to do her father's bidding.

"You are far too lenient, Marcus," Lucius said when Jilana had vanished into a room on the second level. "Jilana is beautiful but she must learn where her duty lies."

"Would you have me whip her, Lucius? Or mayhap shackle her so that she cannot indulge in the freedom she holds so dear?" When Lucius made to speak, Marcus gestured him to silence. "Jilana will be your wife soon enough—I will wager you fare little better at managing Jilana than I have. Claudia, take Lucius to the garden and wait for us there.''

When they were gone Augusta went to her husband's side and took his hand. ''Lucius Quintus may be a fine soldier, but I fear he will make Jilana unhappy. At first I thought the marriage a wise decision but now—''

''Hush,'' Marcus commanded. ''All will be well.'' He rose and brushed his lips across Augusta's forehead. ''Jilana is very much like her father, is she not?''

Augusta nodded, her violet eyes clouding in remembrance. ''Her spirit is his, and her need to be free. Oh, Marcus, had I not been so young, so angry with my parents for marrying me to a man who would take me away from Rome, Jilana would have been your child instead of—''

Marcus placed a finger over her lips. ''Our first years together were not easy for either of us. We were married to cement an alliance between our families, but the passage of time has brought us more and we should be grateful. From the moment Jilana was born I claimed her as my own and, I confess, I found her far easier to love than our Claudia.''

''We should tell Jilana,'' Augusta worried. ''She has a right to know, Marcus.''

''Nay.'' Marcus glanced up the stairs and then guided Augusta toward the garden. ''Jilana did not come from my loins but from my heart, and I have long since forgiven you your Briton lover. The truth of Jilana's conception you and I will carry with us to our graves.''

Augusta bit the inside of her cheek to keep the full truth from escaping. One other knew of Jilana's true parentage; he had, in fact, known of the child she carried before Augusta herself had been certain of the fact, had seen the subtle changes in her body and been overjoyed. But his joy had changed to disbelief and then rage when Augusta had told him that she was staying with her Roman husband and would raise the child as a true citizen of Rome.

His rage had been terrifying, all the more so because he did not give vent to it. Instead, he had withdrawn into himself, the only sign of his anger the waves of tension radiating from his hard muscled body. She had been afraid he would beat her, but he had not. He had looked straight at Augusta, and the agony in his eyes had torn away the shield she had built around her heart. Augusta had realized then that she loved this incredibly gentle man who was her lover, the father of her child, but she could not leave all that she knew and make a life in some remote village with this Iceni warrior. 'Twas impossible; she was not brave enough. And he had seen the determination in her face and known that arguing would avail him naught. So he had turned his back and walked away from the woman he loved and the unborn child he had already come to cherish.

Did he still live? Augusta wondered now. She had never seen him again and after a few years she had stopped fearing that one day he would reappear and shatter her well-ordered life. And if he appeared now, 'twas possible he would not recognize Augusta and he certainly would not recognize Jilana as his daughter for she bore no resemblance to her father, only a striking resemblance to her mother. Aye, Augusta rationalized, Marcus was right. 'Twas best to leave the past buried, undisturbed. Marcus need never know that a third person was privy to their secret, for that third person posed no threat. Marcus spoke and Augusta raised her face to him and smiled, relegating her thoughts to a far corner of her mind.

It was a breathless Jilana who joined her parents and Lucius, but none could fault her appearance this time. Every strand of red-gold hair was neatly braided and coiled and her white toga fell in graceful lines from her shoulders to her ankles. Even Lucius, for all his ire over Jilana's behavior, could not resist her incandescent beauty and the pleading in the depths of her violet eyes, and he unceremoniously left Claudia's side to go to his betrothed.

"I hope I have not inconvenienced you, Lucius," Jilana said quietly as Lucius bent over her hand.

"Nay, Jilana." Lucius' dark eyes burned as he gazed at Jilana. "To see you thus is worth the delay."

Jilana colored. "Did my appearance cause you concern as well, Lucius? If so, I do apologize."

"I have no wish to humble you, Jilana," Lucius replied gently. "But to choose today of all days to go riding alone—" He shook his head. "When you are at last my wife, I will see to it you do not place yourself in needless jeopardy."

"You confuse me, Lucius. I was in no danger this morning."

"Jilana, you are such an innocent," Lucius sighed in exasperation. "Yesterday Catus Decianus disinherited the widowed Iceni queen and her daughters and claimed authority over the Iceni. Had you been present, you would have seen how the Britons reacted, how angered they were by the loss of their queen. We may be forced to bring the Iceni to heel if they do not accept Caesar's will."

"Must they bow to Caesar," Jilana asked sadly, remembering the times she had seen Queen Boadicea riding with her husband across the open plain near Venta Icenorum. "Can we not leave them their pride, at least?"

"Do not be absurd," Lucius replied crisply. "There is pride enough to be found in being part of the Empire."

"For us, perhaps, but for the Britons?" Jilana spread her hands eloquently.

"You do try my patience," Lucius snapped. "Were I you, I would not be so hasty to question the Empire and Caesar. Caesar's wrath is great and it has been known to extend to disloyal Romans. Guard your tongue, Jilana!"

"I am not disloyal," Jilana cried, quickly lowering her voice when her family turned as one to stare at her.

"You will be able to prove that soon enough, Jilana. Come." Keeping Jilana firmly at his side, Lucius steered her to her waiting family. "We are ready now, Marcus."

"Where are we going?" Jilana demanded when they stepped through the garden gate onto the street.

Claudia, walking in front of Lucius and Jilana with her parents, heard Jilana's question and called over her shoulder. "The Britons are about to feel the might of Caesar's word. By sunset the entire island and all its wretched natives will have learned to listen when Rome speaks." She would have said more but Marcus clamped a firm hand on Claudia's arm and gave her a warning look.

"I do not understand." Jilana looked at Lucius, truly seeing him for the first time that day. Instead of a toga he wore an iron-plated cuirass, from his left shoulder his gladius hung in its baldric and a dagger was suspended from the right side of his belt. His helmet—the detachable earpieces menacingly in place—was slung over his shoulder, and Lucius' black hair glinted in the sunlight. Suddenly afraid, Jilana stopped and placed a hand on Lucius' arm. "Why are you in full armor, Lucius? There is no battle to be fought here."

"But there is, Jilana," Lucius countered. "We go now to see Boadicea cast down. This is Caesar's will. In a matter of hours she will be stripped of her title, her palace, and her possessions. When that is done she and her daughters will be sent from the town to return to the mud and wattle hut from which they sprang. All that was hers will be Caesar's. So it has been so ordered."

Jilana paled. "And if the Queen resists?" The foreign centurion's words suddenly took on menacing proportions.

"The orders will be carried out," Lucius repeated softly. "No resistance will be tolerated."

Jilana looked about her, all thought of the unknown centurion fleeing as she saw other Romans making their way to the Iceni part of Venta Icenorum. Now her ears were open, as well as her eyes, and in the distance she heard women's screams, men's harsh shouts, and the sound of children crying.

Lucius heard the sounds as well and he tenderly framed Jilana's ashen face in his hands. "'Tis Caesar's will, my heart. All the land in the city is to be taken from the Iceni by any means and delivered into Caesar's coffers."

"This is not just," Jilana whispered.

"'Tis not for us to decide, Jilana. I follow orders and so must you."

"Nay!" Jilana shook her head. "I will not see this—I want no part of this vile deed!"

Lucius' face hardened, all tenderness evaporating. "Virtue of your birth has made you part of this. You will go and witness Caesar's might, Jilana, though I needs must carry you to the Iceni palace!" He clamped an iron arm about her waist and forced her back into the pedestrian traffic.

Jilana resisted Lucius' efforts with all her might, but to no avail. He was far stronger than she, and when at one point she refused to walk, Lucius fairly dragged her forward. "How can you be so cruel?" Jilana gasped, a sick knot beginning to form in her stomach. "Let me go, Lucius!"

"Nay," Lucius said grimly. "Your father has indulged you overmuch, Jilana. You are a Roman, though you seem to forget it, and this is one time you will behave as such. No one will say my wife refused to see the sentence of Rome carried out upon the Britons."

"Lucius, I beg of you, do not force—" Jilana's protest died abruptly as they entered the Iceni portion of the town. Horrified, Jilana halted and gazed about her. To her right lay the body of a man, his tunic stained with blood. A woman crouched beside the body, her anguished wail sending an icy prickle up Jilana's spine. Farther ahead a young woman was crumpled in the doorway. Her short tunic had been torn to little more than a rag and there were ugly bruises on her arms and legs. Jilana knew, instinctively, that the woman had been used most brutally, and Jilana cried out softly at the sight of a dagger plunged up to its hilt in the woman's chest. Wherever she looked Jilana was greeted by scenes of carnage, and the violet eyes filled with tears.

Silent, inwardly shocked by the havoc Roman troops had visited upon the helpless and defenseless, Lucius pulled Jilana forward. Blood—Iceni blood, Lucius did not doubt—pooled in the streets and more than once Lucius caught Jilana when she stumbled and nearly fell. 'Tis not this Caesar meant by his order to reclaim Iceni property, Lucius thought as he hurried Jilana past the devastation. What had these Britons done that had caused them to be put to the sword? They found Marcus, Augusta and Claudia waiting at the palace gates and with a sob Jilana wrenched away from Lucius and threw herself into her father's arms.

"I know, child, I know," Marcus murmured soothingly. Over Jilana's head he met Lucius' eyes. "Did you not skirt the Iceni quarters?"

"Nay. We were borne along by the crowd." Lucius had the good grace to look sheepish when Marcus shook his head in disgust. "I will leave Jilana with you and be about my duties."

"Young fool," Marcus muttered when Lucius disappeared into the crowd, then he turned his attention to Jilana.

Claudia watched bitterly as her father's golden head bent to Jilana. It had always been thus—Marcus cared more for Jilana despite her outlandish behavior than he did for Claudia with her perfect, Roman manner. Maliciously, Claudia noted, "One would think Jilana sympathizes with the Iceni, the way she carries on. How can you tolerate such an outburst, Father?"

"I tolerate it because I can imagine quite well what your sister has seen," Marcus replied, his low voice lashing Claudia into silence. "Mayhap we should return the way Jilana came so we can see how you fare."

Claudia sniffed and turned to her mother. "Let us enter, Mother, for if we tarry longer because of Jilana's weak constitution we shall miss seeing the barbarian queen humbled."

Augusta regarded her golden-haired daughter with well-disguised distaste before looking to her husband. "Marcus?"

Sighing inwardly, Marcus nodded. "Go. Jilana and I will follow shortly." When the two women had passed through the battered-down gate, evidence that the Iceni had tried to keep the palace inviolate, Marcus lifted Jilana's head from his shoulder and gazed into the clouded violet eyes. "I would have spared you the sight of the Procurator's vengeance."

"Is it Caesar's will to rape and murder," Jilana asked tearfully. "The Iceni are—were—our allies. Is this how Romans treat their friends?"

Jilana was fast losing her innocence, a loss Marcus deeply regretted but was helpless to prevent. "We shall speak of this later, Jilana, in the privacy of our home; but for now we must obey the order to see Boadicea dispossessed."

"Father, I cannot," Jilana implored, her voice breaking. "I beg you, allow me to return to the villa."

Marcus shook his head. "For good or bad, you are Roman. I will not have any say my daughter is disloyal." He gripped Jilana's shoulders tightly. "Look, but do not see. Hear, but do not feel. And remember always that I love you. Now come."

Jilana walked numbly beside her father into the courtyard of the Iceni palace, barely noticing the press of people. Augusta's dark auburn hair was like a signal beacon from the forefront of the crowd and Jilana smiled wanly as her mother slipped a comforting arm about Jilana's waist. "'Twill not be so terrible, Jilana. The Procurator will read Caesar's command and Boadicea and her daughters will leave the palace, that is all."

"Oh, nay! Surely there will be more," Claudia exclaimed breathlessly, her dark eyes glittering. "Defiance such as Boadicea displayed yesterday, and today by ordering the palace gate barred, is not tolerated; I learned that much in Rome. Catus Decianus will undoubtedly make an example of this upstart barbarian. Look! The soldiers come!''

Jilana swallowed the bile which kept rising in her throat and turned with the rest of the spectators as a squad of soldiers detached itself from the main body and marched to the doors of the palace. Words were exchanged between the Roman centurion and the Iceni guards—harsh words, for a moment later the unarmed guards were ruthlessly slain by the soldiers. A gasp went up from the crowd, then a cheer as Catus Decianus stepped forward from his personal guards.

"Romans!" The Procurator's words rang clearly through the courtyard and Jilana felt herself grow light-headed with fear and self-loathing. "Behind these walls is a woman who has defied Roman law and mocked our Divine Emperor Nero! She has named me liar when I told her of Caesar's will concerning the Iceni people. While we mourn the death of our friend and ally, King Prasutagus, we also realize that he left no male issue to succeed him. We reject the harlot queen's argument that Iceni royalty flows also through her veins and that she should, therefore, enjoy the same rights the Empire so generously bestowed upon her husband. There is no male heir! The ruling line of Prasutagus is ended!" Catus Decianus paused and fixed the waiting crowd with a feverish stare. "Britannia was subdued and brought into the empire eighteen years past. We were generous; we did not behead or crucify those who had fought against us. The Empire did, in all good faith, conclude treaties with the barbarian kings, and see how our generosity is repaid! We are mocked, ridiculed. The temple dedicated to the Divine Emperor Claudius, he who dealt so faithfully with the Britons, falls into disrepair at Camulodunum because the barbarians will not part with a single coin to do honor to his memory!" Outraged murmurs went up from the Romans at this, and Catus allowed them time to whip up their indignation.

"He lies!" From their place at the courtyard wall, well behind the true Roman legionaries, Heall made the accusation through clenched teeth.

Caddaric nodded imperceptibly, filled with the longing to bury his sword into the back of the Roman Procurator, the only target available from their position. "Men have been beggared for that temple," he replied in an equally hushed voice. "This we know, but the Romans do not care for truth. Catus does but justify his actions."

"We are not helpless," Heall ground out. "We have seen royal guards slain and we do naught. Are we cowards?"

"Nay, but we are only two." Caddaric subdued his terrible wrath with an effort. "Our deaths now would serve no purpose, but our time will come to repay tenfold what we have seen. Be silent now, draw no attention to us."

The grumbles of the Roman citizens had grown to a low roar and now Catus Decianus raised his hands for silence. "My countrymen, hear now Caesar's will and see how the Empire deals with traitors. The land of the Iceni is no longer an ally but shall henceforth be only a province of the Empire. The chieftains of the Iceni are hereby stripped of all lands and possessions. All relatives of King Prasutagus will be gathered up and sold into slavery, including the woman Boadicea and her two daughters, and their ancestral holdings will revert to our Divine Emperor Nero. But first, the Empire will show all of Britannia how it deals with miscreants and troublemakers. The woman who calls herself queen will be scourged so that she may carry Caesar's mark with her into slavery!" At Catus' signal, the squad of Roman soldiers shouldered a battering ram and attacked the wood of the palace door.

The thunderous sound of wood hitting wood flayed Jilana's nerves and she bit her bottom lip to keep from crying out. About her people were laughing, cheering the efforts of the legionaries, and a feeling of deep shame coursed through Jilana. She had believed, in her ignorance, that Roman soldiers fought only other soldiers, that an unarmed populace had nothing to fear. So this is how slaves are made, Jilana thought dully. While their friends owned slaves, her father employed only freemen, but until this moment Jilana had never spared a thought toward the source of those slaves.

"Father?" Claudia's voice drew Jilana's attention and she watched as Claudia went to Marcus and laid an imploring hand on his arm. "Father, will you purchase an Iceni for me so that I might have a maid to attend only myself?"

Marcus shook his head. "You and your sister have an attendant, Claudia."

"One that we must share," Claudia replied emphatically. "Father I am fully grown, far past the age when I should be allowed my own maid. In Rome, Aunt Cyrilla insisted I have a woman of my own."

"This is not Rome," Marcus said, exchanging a look with Augusta. "Your mother's sister lives differently than we."

"But how shall I face my friends when I return to Rome," Claudia wailed. "They will have heard of the upstart Iceni and will want to know why the house of Basilius would not buy so much as a maid!"

Marcus started to answer, but the crack of the palace door giving way stopped his words. Claudia gleefully clapped her hands and started forward, taking up the cry of: "Bring forth the harlot queen! Let the Iceni taste Roman justice."

The massed citizenry surged forward and Jilana found herself separated from her parents and unwillingly pushed to the very fore of the spectators. Her heart pounding, Jilana forced her eyes away from the splintered palace door and gazed at the sky. She would not watch this spectacle—not even if Nero himself so ordered!

"Jilana? Jilana?" Claudia's high voice forced Jilana to survey the crowd and she discovered her sister some distance to her right. Smiling proudly, Claudia pointed to the wood-framed palace and screamed, "'Tis Lucius! He has the honor of dragging the harlot forth."

Pale, Jilana turned violet eyes to the door and beheld the sight of her betrothed escorting a tall, red-haired woman from the building. Once he reached out and placed a hand on her upper arm, but she shook him off with haughty disdain. Boadicea! Looking every inch a queen, Boadicea walked past the assemblage to the place where Catus stood and stared at him coldly. 'Twas obvious Boadicea had no intention of humbling herself before the Roman Procurator, and a hush descended as the people strained to hear what was said.

"You have come early, Roman," Boadicea stated in a rich, clear voice. She tossed her head, sending the long, red hair flying like a defiant pennant, and glanced at the silent crowd. "Are your lives so empty that you take pleasure in seeing a defenseless woman beaten?"

"Silence," Catus roared. "You are here to be punished, woman, not to mock these loyal Romans."

Boadicea's hands clenched into fists, her only outward show of emotion. "You have slain my guards and battered your way into my palace. What has happened to my people outside these walls I can only guess. I am powerless to resist what you have planned for me, but I will not hold my tongue because you so order, maggot. No Roman commands me!"

An angry hiss went up from the crowd and Catus stiffened. "You would have done better to beg mercy, harlot."

"Mercy? From you?" Boadicea threw back her head and laughed.

Enraged, Catus turned to Lucius. "Bind her, Tribune. Take her to the scourging post." The post in the courtyard was actually the weapon-stone, a tall column of sharpening stone. Its presence was traditional in every Celtic chief's forecourt: anyone wanting to sharpen a weapon was free to use the weapon-stone. For Boadicea, being bound to the stone must have been doubly painful, for the Iceni had long ago surrendered most of their weapons to the Romans. And, unknown to the conquerors, what few arms the Iceni had retained were buried in the earth, of no use to their Queen.

Lucius saluted and obeyed, no flicker of emotion touching his face as he and his men marched the bound Iceni Queen to the scourging post. Nor did he glance at Jilana, though he passed directly in front of her.

Try as she might, Jilana found she could not obey her father's instructions to neither see nor feel. When Boadicea's dress gave way beneath a soldier's rough hands so that her back might be bared for the whip, Jilana barely suppressed a dismayed gasp; and when the whip sang through the air to crack sickeningly against the Queen's bare skin Jilana sank her nails into the palms of her hands. Boadicea bore the scourging silently, her head cradled against the cushion formed by her upraised arms. From the sound of the first lash until the whip at last fell silent, Jilana did not look away from the tall, proud woman.

"Cut her down," Catus ordered finally. When the command was mercilessly carried out, a cry escaped Boadicea's lips as she sank to the ground and the Procurator smiled. Ignoring the fallen woman, he commanded, "Tribune, take your men into the palace and remove from it any object of value."

The soldiers departed, as did some of the citizens, but the majority of the Romans hurried forward to laugh and jeer at Boadicea as she struggled to her feet. Jilana was buffeted from one side to the other by her impatient countrymen but she felt it not. Glancing toward the palace, Jilana saw a dozen weeping women being held against the palace wall by the drawn swords of a squad of legionaries. They had to be Boadicea's ladies in waiting, Jilana realized, for they were gesturing toward the Queen and talking rapidly. Jilana looked to Catus Decianus and was revolted to find him laughing, obviously relishing Boadicea's futile attempts to rise.

Of their own volition, Jilana's legs carried her forward and she rudely shouldered people aside until she stood in front of Boadicea. The Iceni Queen slowly raised her head until her brilliant, blue eyes locked with Jilana's violet ones. For a long moment they stared at each other, Boadicea awaiting the fall of yet another Roman insult and Jilana searching vainly for words to express the sorrow which filled her heart.

"Jilana, nay," Marcus whispered, somehow knowing what his daughter would do.

Augusta had seen her, too, and she lunged forward. "Marcus, we must stop her!"

Marcus caught his wife before she had taken two steps and held her firmly in his arms. In a horrified voice he told her, "'Tis too late, Augusta. The gods must protect her now."

Caddaric, unable to see what was taking place because of his position, had had his fill of Roman abuse. "No matter what befalls me, Heall, return to the others before the gates of the town are closed. The Queen's chieftains must be told what has transpired here today."

"Caddaric!" Heall lurched forward but the young warrior was far out of his reach.

Unaware of the tumult, Jilana extended a slender hand to the fallen Queen. "Come, let me help you." Boadicea eyed her warily and, in spite of the insults her fellow Romans were shouting, Jilana bent and drew one of Boadicea's arms around her shoulders.

Boadicea came to her feet with a small cry and Jilana struggled under the woman's weight. The crowd refused to yield and Jilana, a grim set to her jaw, pushed at the human wall with her free hand. Vile epithets followed Jilana's every step but she ignored them as she doggedly cleared a path for herself and her awkward burden. Though she was tall by Roman standards, Jilana was far smaller than the Iceni Queen and Boadicea was forced to bend in order to accept Jilana's aid, an action which caused even greater pain to her raw back.

"Let me go, child," Boadicea groaned softly. "When he has humiliated me to his satisfaction, the Procurator will have me carried inside."

"Nay," Jilana panted, shuddering when a glob of spittle splattered against her toga. "I would have you know at least one Roman here today is not lacking in courage."

They had advanced only another few inches when the crowd abruptly quieted and parted, and Jilana stared straight into the narrowed eyes of Catus Decianus. "You flaunt Nero's will, woman," the Procurator said in a menacing voice. "This Iceni is bound for Rome, to serve the Emperor himself. Nero will not take it kindly when he learns of your interference."

"Will he take kindly the fact that you allowed his newest slave to wallow in the dirt so that her wounds became infected?" Jilana retorted, although her heart thumped wildly in her breast. Lucius stood at the Procurator's side and Jilana avoided his censorious stare. "Only a fool would allow Caesar's prize to court destruction, Catus Decianus."

The Procurator's face turned an ugly shade of red and Lucius hastily stepped forward. "Jilana, your concern for this woman is misplaced. Her wounds—"

"You know this woman, Tribune," Catus inquired angrily.

White brackets appeared at the sides of Lucius' mouth, but he answered steadily, "Aye, Excellency. She is my betrothed."

"Ah, I know her now. You are the daughter of Marcus Basilius, are you not?" Without waiting for Jilana's reply, Catus added, "You are young and therefore allowed a mistake in judgment. Leave the barbarian and return to your home. We will see to her care."

Jilana's violet gaze did not waver. "Will you give the order now, Excellency, within my hearing?"

For a moment it seemed Catus would strike her, and Jilana braced herself for the blow. Catus raised his hand but then, apparently, changed his mind. Glancing about the crowd he spied a grim-faced legionary and motioned to him. "You, Centurion! Come here." When the centurion halted behind the woman and saluted, Catus ordered, "Take the Iceni into the palace, and be quick."

Catus turned and stalked off, Lucius following him, and the crowd, sensing that there was no further sport to be found here, dispersed.

"I will take the Queen now."

The familiar, deep voice sent Jilana's heart racing and as Boadicea's weight was taken from her, she gazed wordlessly into the centurion's blue eyes.

Caddaric gently pulled his Queen's arm across his broad shoulders. "Queen Boadicea will be cared for, lady."

Jilana nodded and wrenched her eyes back to Boadicea's strained features. "I will have a salve made for your wounds, Majesty, and my father's own physician will tend you."

Sadness filled Boadicea's eyes and she shook her head. "Nay, child. There is no need for you to do more. For your kindness I give you thanks."

Jilana watched until they were inside the palace before she turned and left the courtyard. It struck her, as Jilana wound her way through the streets to the villa, that barely two hours had passed since sunrise.

Boadicea did not speak until the centurion had carried her through the ransacked Iceni palace to her chambers. The Queen's chambers were untouched—at least for the moment—and Caddaric tenderly lowered Boadicea to her couch and then touched her hand to his forehead in a gesture of servitude.

"The Roman uniform suits you well, Caddaric," Boadicea commented in a strained voice. "I nearly mistook you for a true centurion."

"Forgive me, my Queen." Caddaric went down on one knee before her. "I would have served you best by impaling the Procurator on my sword."

"Nay, Caddaric. Such action would have brought your death, and my back would still have been laid open. You chose the wisest course."

Boadicea had winced at the mention of her wounds and Caddaric hurriedly rose. "I shall bring your women, Highness, so they may tend your wounds."

"Hold, Caddaric." Boadicea forced her pain away and motioned Caddaric back to her. From outside her chamber came the sound of Roman feet tramping over the wooden floors as the soldiers carried out the Procurator's order to sack the palace. Tears started to Boadicea's eyes as pain, humiliation and visions of the scene outside her chamber threatened to overwhelm her. "Am I so much a threat to Rome that they could not leave me what was rightfully mine?"

Caddaric strode to the door and, after assuring himself that no one was within hearing distance, closed the portal and returned to the couch. "Our people have answered your call. By nightfall our force will be large enough to take you and your daughters from Venta Icenorum and protect you until the rest of the warriors are roused. In a month we will be strong enough to meet the Romans, defeat them, and spirit you safely to the northern part of the island."

"Nay, Caddaric, I will not run!" Boadicea leaned forward, her eyes flashing. "Have I enough warriors to avenge myself here, this night?"

Caddaric hesitated. "Tonight, Majesty?"

"In two days they will take me to Londinium and from there to Rome. I have no time, Caddaric!" Boadicea lowered her voice. "Have I warriors enough?"

"Perhaps. Your chieftains will begin arriving in the forest with our force by afternoon." Caddaric paused, considering. "What is your plan?"

"Surprise—total surprise. Tonight the Romans will be celebrating. They will be drunk on wine and the shedding of Iceni blood; they will not expect us to attack." Boadicea took Caddaric's hand. "Go to my chieftains, Caddaric, tell them what I desire."

"And if the Queen's wish is impossible?"

"Then I will go north. But I would rather die fighting the Romans than running from them." Boadicea released him. "Go now, Caddaric. I know you will find your way back with my answer."

"If it please you, Majesty, I will send Heall in my stead and I will remain here to guard you."

Boadicea shook her head. "You must both go. The Romans can do no more to me than what has already transpired. My women will tend me while you and Heall learn the enemy's weakness and rally my warriors." Caddaric started to protest but Boadicea silenced him with an imperious look. "Go, my brave warrior, and return to me with glad tidings."

Caddaric bowed and left his Queen. The palace was alive with Roman soldiers and Caddaric surreptitiously made his way past the growing piles of confiscated royal belongings to the courtyard where Heall waited. Wordlessly Caddaric gripped Heall's upper arm and steered him toward the palace gates.

"I thought you had been taken," Heall growled; then, noting the direction they took, he questioned, "Why are we leaving? Should we not stay with the Queen?"

"She bids us leave," Caddaric answered, and he quietly explained Boadicea's orders to the older man. "We must locate the barracks and armory and determine the strength of the Roman garrison. Then we will wait with Clywd for the Queen's chieftains and tell them what we have learned."

While Caddaric and Heall set about learning the enemy's defenses, Jilana stepped inside her parents' walled garden and, with a slight squaring of her shoulders, walked to the villa. The servants looked at her askance and Jilana sighed inwardly—the news of her indiscretion had spread quickly. Over the tiled floors Jilana glided, the soft click of her sandals echoing hollowly as she passed through the hall. Claudia's enraged voice carried from the far side of the villa's lower floor and Jilana increased her pace. Character assassination was Claudia's first love and Jilana did not intend to allow her sister a clear field on which to hone her skills.

"How could Jilana behave as she did," Claudia was shrieking as Jilana entered the room. "How could she? 'Twas bad enough she went to that...that barbarian's aid, but to be recognized by the Procurator as well! I do not know how I shall bear the humiliation."

"Why should you be humiliated," Jilana asked, her quiet tone a vivid contrast to her sister's. "'Twas not your hand which raised Boadicea from the ground, Claudia. The responsibility is mine to bear."

"As well you should," Claudia snapped. "But we will suffer as well. Catus Decianus will surely mention you in his report to Rome—Father's business will be hurt and my chances for a perfect marriage will be ruined."

Jilana wrinkled her nose. "We are a long way from Rome, Claudia. I doubt anyone there, including the Emperor, will take too much notice of what happens on this island." She glanced around the room. "Where is Mother?"

"In her bedchamber, where you have driven her," Claudia jeered.

"The morning was too much for your mother, I fear," Marcus put in, a warning eyebrow lifted at Claudia. "The Procurator's guards escorted us home but would not allow us to wait for you. Your mother was sick with fear that the Procurator had taken you."

"I am sorry, Father." Jilana's cheeks pinkened beneath her father's gaze. "Not for helping the Iceni Queen, that I do not repent, but for causing you and Mother needless fear."

"She is not a *queen*," Claudia screeched. "She is a slave! Caesar's slave. You risked our name and good prospects over one who is less than a piece of offal. I shall never live down the humiliation, and if my friends in Rome learn of this I shall die of embarrassment!"

With an exclamation of disgust, Jilana rounded on her sister. "A nation died today, Claudia. An entire people were stripped of their land and made slaves. Surely that is of far more import than the vaulted opinions of people at the other end of the Empire!"

"You will see how important those opinions are when Lucius takes you to Rome," Claudia spat. "People in Britannia may tolerate your uncivilized ways, but those in

Rome will not. Your comeuppance is long overdue, dear sister, and I pray that I may see it delivered."

"We know well your opinions, Claudia; you have voiced them often enough," Marcus sighed. "Leave us now; I have matters to discuss with Jilana in private."

Claudia was not to be denied a parting shot. "Lucius will not be pleased with you, Jilana. He will reprimand you even if Father does not."

When Claudia was gone, Jilana walked slowly to a place in front of Marcus. "Will you beat me, Father?"

"Do you feel you deserve a beating," Marcus countered.

"Claudia thinks so, and so does Catus Decianus, and probably most of your friends," Jilana replied thoughtfully, but her violet eyes showed no trace of remorse. "For myself, I followed the dictates of my conscience, but I am willing to abide by your decision."

A smile flirted with the corners of Marcus' mouth. He had taught his children that inner peace would be achieved only through being true to themselves, but he had also counseled compromise when their conscience ran opposite to the rules of the Empire. Claudia had taken only the advice on compromise to heart whereas Jilana, more often than not, was so true to her conscience that Marcus feared she would die a martyr to it. "When was the last time I struck you, Jilana?"

"The day I released your prize falcon," Jilana answered promptly. "I thought it cruel he was allowed to fly only when you so willed...but I was only six at the time," she added, remembering quite well her abused posterior when Marcus had learned of the act.

"So now instead of my falcons you offer yourself as shield to Nero's scourged slave. Caesar would do more than redden your buttocks if you earned his wrath. Remember that, Jilana, and take my warning to heart."

Jilana bowed her head meekly, obediently. "Aye, Father."

Frowning at this sudden change in heart, Marcus lifted Jilana's chin and forced her to meet his gaze. "I regret what happened to the Iceni people and their Queen, Jilana, but nothing you or I do or say can change Caesar's will. For good or bad we are Romans, daughter. We must make concessions to our citizenship. One day, perhaps when Lucius gains the power he desires, you and he will be able to change our government and curb its excesses, but the time is not yet ripe. Do not sacrifice your life without purpose."

Jilana stared at her father with new understanding. "Was Claudia right, Father? Have my actions endangered you?"

"Claudia exaggerates," Marcus said gently. "Eyebrows will be raised and a few tongues may wag but that is all. In time, all will be forgotten."

"Will Lucius forget?"

Marcus smiled. "Aye, if you do not remind him." He sobered. "The first step toward erasing people's memories will be taken tomorrow evening. The Procurator is to dine with us." Jilana recoiled in horror but Marcus held her fast. "Claudia is delighted; your mother and I are less enthusiastic. You need not fawn over him—that will be happily done by your sister—but you must at least be civil. Keep Lucius at your side throughout the evening; he will deal with any devious questions the Procurator puts to you. Follow Lucius' lead in conversation and you will be safe. As soon as you decently may, contract a blinding headache, beg the Procurator's forgiveness, and go to your bedchamber."

"Aye, Father," Jilana whispered. Marcus released her and she walked to the door. She paused and turned searching eyes upon her father. "I did not expect the compromise to begin so soon."

"Go and see your mother," Marcus ordered. "Discuss the evening with her. There is no one better at avoiding compromising situations than Augusta. And, Jilana," he called when she took a step forward, "I was proud this day to call you daughter."

NIGHT CAME GENTLY to Venta Icenorum, as if denying the violent forces Catus Decianus had that morning set in motion. In the Roman portion of the town, homes were well lit and the sound of laughter and animated conversation filled the night air. In the Iceni quarters, however, the homes as well as the mood were dark, forbidding. Not even the sounds of mourning were heard and a sentry at the Iceni palace tried vainly to overcome his uneasiness at the unaccustomed silence. The sentry pivoted and began retracing his steps along the outside wall of the palace. At the same moment the Roman back was turned, a figure detached itself from the sharpening stone and dashed noiselessly across the shadowed courtyard and into the palace.

Boadicea heard him first, and signaling one of her women to open her chamber door, she drew herself stiffly upright on the Roman couch, the only piece of furniture the soldier had allowed her to keep. "Enter, Caddaric," she said in a hushed voice, "and tell me what news you bear."

Caddaric obeyed, his tall, broad-shouldered frame filling the doorway before he strode into the room and went down on one knee in front of his queen. "Forgive me, Majesty, but our number is too small to accomplish your wishes this night. We require one more day in which to grow strong enough to bring the Romans low."

Boadicea sighed. "So little time, Caddaric, and yet the morrow seems an eternity away. My heart screams for vengeance and you say I must wait." The royal features contorted with thwarted need as Boadicea came to a decision. "Then tell my chieftains to fill the streets with Roman blood. Tell them also to bring to me the Roman Procurator and his personal guards. I will see their deaths with my own eyes."

"'Twill be as you command, Majesty."

For a moment the Queen was silent, contemplating the shadows cast by the room's solitary lamp. In a harsh tone Boadicea said, "They outraged my daughters, Caddaric. Stripping my daughters of their inheritance was not enough, the Romans had to take their virginity as well. Tell that to my people."

Caddaric closed his eyes, rage heating his blood. "All will be avenged, O Queen. None shall escape our vengeance." He touched her hand to his forehead and went to the door.

"Caddaric." Boadicea's voice swung the warrior about. "The young woman who helped me today—do you remember her?"

"Aye, Majesty." Caddaric's hand tightened around his sword hilt. How could he forget Jilana when she had been in his thoughts throughout the day? She and the man who claimed to be her betrothed.

"She is to be spared along with her family, if such a thing is possible. You will see to it, Caddaric." Before Caddaric could think her lenient Boadicea continued, "They will be made slaves—the girl will be given to the warrior who brings Catus Decianus to me."

"As you command, Majesty." A wave of the royal hand dismissed him and minutes later Caddaric had left the town behind and melted into the forest beyond.

He felt the presence of warriors and warrior maids all about him, but not even Caddaric's practiced eye could discern their positions. The forest was alive with his fellow tribesmen and though Caddaric was loathe to consider what the following day would bring, his pride in the Iceni nation swelled his heart. Clywd—once again swathed from head to foot in black—stepped from the trees directly into his son's path.

"Rebellion?" At Caddaric's short nod, Clywd appeared to shrink under the voluminous folds of his robe.

"There is no other choice, wise one. You better than anyone should know that we are powerless to fight what the gods decree."

Clywd turned. "The chieftains wait. I will take you to them."

Caddaric delivered the Queen's orders to her chieftains and then detached himself from the waiting Iceni force and made his way to the clearing where he had discovered Jilana. *Jilana*. Caddaric's heart hammered painfully as he remembered his first glimpse of the woman who had haunted him for so long. His dreams had not done justice to Jilana's beauty—she was more incredibly delicate than Caddaric had imagined, her eyes such a remarkable shade of violet that to gaze into them was akin to drowning. He had not expected the unbearable yearning of his soul to possess Jilana, nor had he anticipated Jilana's bravery in the face of Roman justice. A faint smile curved Caddaric's lips and he stretched out full length on the ground and contemplated the moon. By the gods, but Jilana's courage had stirred him! Iceni women—the warrior maids—were as fearless as their male counterparts, more than willing to die a glorious death on the battlefield. But to encounter that same quality in Jilana, a Roman, kindled a flame in his soldier's heart. When Caddaric had beheld the fierce, uncompromising gleam in those violet eyes he had known that Jilana was his intended mate.

Blue eyes narrowed thoughtfully, Caddaric allowed his mind to consider the morrow. Since Jilana would be given to the warrior who captured Catus Decianus, Caddaric would have to make certain he was that warrior; but first he would see Jilana safely out of reach of the fighting which would take place. As for Jilana's family and betrothed . . . Caddaric's jaw set in a hard line as he remembered the man who had laid claim to Jilana's hand. In spite of the Queen's command, Caddaric could not allow Jilana's betrothed to come with her into slavery. To accept as her mate an Iceni warrior, she must forget her Roman heritage—she must begin life anew, at Caddaric's side, with no lingering traces of the Empire to mar their time together. Jilana's family must be eliminated from her life.

Abruptly Caddaric sat upright and stared at the surrounding forest. He knew that in all probability he would not live out this revolt against Rome. Caddaric was a soldier and a soldier's lot was to die in battle; it was a fact which, until now, had neither worried nor elated him. He would die one day and he preferred a clean death on a battlefield to that of a lingering death of illness. For that reason Caddaric was the perfect fighting machine, and because his utter contempt for death was tempered with an excellent grasp of timing and strategy, Caddaric had risen to the rank of centurion in the auxiliary. Yet now a feeling of desperation touched Caddaric's heart as he realized why he had not fallen in some earlier battle. The gods had spared him and tormented him with dreams of Jilana so that he might recognize the woman who would bear his son. Hopefully, Caddaric thought with his usual touch of mockery, the gods were foresighted enough to allow him a leisurely space of time in which to plant his seed within Jilana.

Chapter 2

THE MORNING FOLLOWING Boadicea's dispossession dawned chill and overcast, fitting Jilana's mood perfectly. She slipped from her bed before the other members of her family awoke and donned her short riding tunic. As she belted the wide leather girdle around her waist, Jilana's conscience twinged painfully. She was, again, in direct disobedience of her parents' wishes, as well as Lucius'. After the scene she had created at the Iceni palace, Lucius had given strict instructions that she not set foot outside the villa until Catus Decianus left Venta Icenorum and her parents had reluctantly agreed. Jilana sighed, silenced her guilt, and wrapped a long, warm cloak about her shoulders. She would be trapped in the villa for the better part of the day, preparing herself for the Procurator's visit, and Jilana needed some time alone to forget the horror of yesterday.

Only a few of the servants were stirring at this hour and Jilana neatly evaded them as she made her way from the villa. The separate kitchen was the place Jilana ran the greatest risk of discovery, but since her grumbling stomach loudly protested the idea of by-passing the source of the delicious smells wafting toward her, Jilana veered toward the kitchen and positioned herself by an open window. Despite the early hour the cooks were busy preparing for tonight's feast and Jilana's mouth watered at the sight of cheeses, wheat cakes, fruit and the earthenware jars filled with assorted preserves Marcus had imported from Rome. Jilana's stomach howled indignantly at such temptation and she waited impatiently until the two cooks disappeared into the storeroom of the kitchen. The instant her path was clear Jilana left the window and dashed through the door. With a minimum of wasted motion, Jilana snatched up a cold leg of mutton which had caught her eye, a half dozen wheat cakes, and two loaves of freshly baked bread and placed them in a small, woven market basket. Before the two women could return, Jilana fled, darting across the courtyard to the stable.

Jilana's mount, a gentle bay mare, snorted eagerly at her mistress's arrival and Jilana lovingly stroked the soft nose before turning her attention to the saddle and bridle. Jilana readied the mare with a careless efficiency which would have disgusted Claudia, and led the animal through the stable and the arched gateway which was hidden from the villa. Once in the street, Jilana sprang into the saddle and sedately walked the mare to the east gate of Venta Icenorum. The sentry knew Jilana well, but this morning his usual smile was missing. Instead of a hearty greeting the sentry briskly motioned her through the gate with a look of studied contempt that cut into her heart. Sighing, Jilana tapped her heels against the mare's sides and galloped across the plain which stood between the town and the forest.

Without consciously planning to do so, Jilana headed straight to the glade and dismounted at the precise spot where she had been standing the day before when the mysterious centurion had come upon her. For some reason she did not comprehend, Jilana found herself hoping the centurion would appear, even while her sensible self chided her heart for its foolishness. She continued to hope, nonetheless, as she set her confiscated meal on the ground and then slowly surveyed the towering oaks.

Jilana pivoted gracefully, violet eyes searching the undergrowth. "Centurion," she called softly, willing him to materialize. Eerie silence met her call and when the wind freshened, lifting Jilana's cloak in billowing folds, an unexpected chill touched her spine. He is here, an inner voice whispered; yet Jilana sensed another presence as well, and this second presence left her mouth dry with fear. Today hatred emanated from the forest, destroying the serenity of her secret place with devastating thoroughness. I dare not stay here, Jilana thought wildly, but it seemed an eternity before her legs regained enough strength to allow Jilana to return to her horse. The wind sighed through the trees, but to Jilana the familiar noise had an ominous ring: the breeze sounded to Jilana's ears like the screams of a host of dying, tortured souls. With a choked cry, Jilana mounted and sent her mare crashing through the trees.

Caddaric, flanked by Heall and Clywd, stepped into the clearing and watched Jilana disappear. Passion flamed in his blue eyes as Caddaric plucked the abandoned basket from the ground and studied its contents.

"A most beautiful woman," Clywd murmured appreciatively. "You should have answered her call, Caddaric."

Caddaric snorted in disgust and cut himself a generous portion of mutton. "To what end, Druid? 'Tis not my wish to find a dagger in my back before I have had a chance to avenge our Queen." Both Clywd and Heall chortled over his words and Caddaric shook his head. "'Twould not be so amusing had your footsteps been shadowed for the past few hours." His reprimand did little to extinguish either man's mirth and with a resigned sigh Caddaric glanced at the spot where he had hidden. "Come forth, Ede, the wicked Roman is gone."

The taunting note in Caddaric's voice brought a low cry of outrage from the trees and a moment later a tall, lithesome young woman followed her voice into the clearing. "Wicked Roman! Bah!" Ede glared at Caddaric. "She is little more than a child—an easily frightened child as well."

Caddaric shrugged and handed Ede the basket. "Eat."

Ede tossed her head, sending the loose mass of moon-silver hair shimmering defiantly. "I will starve before

Roman food passes my lips!'' When Caddaric shrugged again, totally indifferent to her outrage, the flecks of green in Ede's eyes snapped to life. "Who is she, Caddaric? Why does a Roman woman ride from the safety of the town and call for you?"

"So you admit she is a woman." Caddaric grinned, finding Ede's jealousy amusing. "It gladdens my heart to know your eyesight is so keen. Had you named her child again you would have remained behind tonight. I want none to fight who cannot distinguish child from adult or post from Roman."

Ede was not to be diverted. "Who is she, Caddaric?" she hissed.

"A Roman. The same Roman who yesterday extended her hand to Queen Boadicea and earned her life," Caddaric said calmly.

"The same Roman who gave our brave Caddaric flowers," Heall put in gleefully.

"By the gods!" Ede's hand fell to her dagger. "I shall kill her with my own hands."

"Nay." Clywd, too, entered the conversation. "By the Queen's own command this one is to be spared and given to the warrior who captures the Roman Procurator."

Ede's face glowed with malice and she eyed Caddaric as he leisurely bit into one of the wheat cakes and handed the basket to Clywd. She waited impatiently until the two older men retired some distance away to share their meal before continuing. "Then I shall capture the Procurator. Does that suit you, Caddaric?"

Caddaric raised a mocking eyebrow. "Do you ask my permission, Ede? Or do you but toy with the idea of having a slave? In truth, I doubt you would find Jilana of little help in building a fire or sharpening your battle-axe."

His knowledge of Jilana's name added fuel to Ede's jealousy. "You would use her well, no doubt!"

"Enough." Caddaric's patience and amusement had reached their limits.

"Nay," Ede spat. "I know you well, Caddaric. You want this woman for yourself. I have seen the hunter's

gleam in your eye often enough to know what it fore-
tells." A sad catch colored Ede's voice. "Why do you take
such delight in causing me pain?"

"You cause your own pain," Caddaric told her bluntly.
At the tears which welled in Ede's eyes, however, Caddaric softened. "Ede, 'tis over between us. We parted
nearly six months ago."

"You loved me," Ede protested, her chin trembling.

"Mayhap, for a time." Caddaric took her strong hand
in his. "Brave as you are, glorious as you are, I could
never take you to wife. In the time we shared together
your jealousy ate like a canker at my mind and soul."

"But if you took me to wife in front of our village and
your father—"

"Nay, Ede." Caddaric interrupted as gently as possible. "You would not change, nor would I. Choose another, Ede; any warrior in our village would die of
happiness if you honored him as you have done me."

Ede pulled away from Caddaric. "I will have no other!
From the time we were children I have sworn you would
one day take me to wife and you shall. If I must destroy
your Roman slut then—"

Caddaric delivered a calculated slap to Ede's cheek and
when she fell into sullen silence he warned her coldly,
"Touch one hair on Jilana's head and you will earn my
hatred as you have just earned my wrath. She will be
mine, Ede, mine. I will tolerate none of your interference!"

Caddaric watched as Ede fled, sobbing, into the forest. He had not meant to be cruel but it was the only
choice Ede had left him. Caddaric ran a hand through his
hair, shrugged off the unpleasant scene with Ede, and
joined his father and Heall.

NIGHT CAME AGAIN to Venta Icenorum and as the
strengthened Iceni force crept from the forest and scaled
the walls of the town, Lucius strode from the villa to the
garden and found, as he had been told, a slender woman
seated on one of the marble benches. As he covered the

distance between them, Jilana turned and the breath caught in Lucius' throat. Here, in the moonlight, Jilana was more startlingly beautiful than she had been during the preceding hours. Her hair—artfully threaded with seed pearls—had been swept up to reveal the slender column of her neck and the right shoulder was bared by her toga while an ornate brooch held the fine linen in place over her left. She had clung to him tonight, deferring to his opinions in all things; and though Lucius knew her changed behavior was due to the presence of Catus Decianus, he still hoped Jilana had at last accepted the responsibilities of her position. Lucius stopped in front of the bench, smiling when Jilana rose and looked at him hopefully.

"The Procurator is gone," Lucius told her. "He and his guards left some time ago; by now they are on the road for Londinium."

"The gods be thanked." Jilana breathed a sigh of relief and returned his smile. "All is well."

Lucius nodded. "Will you come inside?"

"Nay—not yet." Jilana took his hand. "Come, Lucius, enjoy the garden with me."

"I must report for duty within the hour," Lucius began, only to be silenced by Jilana's quiet laugh.

"Must you always be a soldier, Lucius?" Jilana twirled away from him, and, overcome by relief at Lucius' good news and the heady wine she had drunk at the meal, struck a pretty, teasing pose. "A maid likes to be wooed, Lucius, not told of time limitations. Why is it you have never wooed me with honeyed words?"

"I—" Lucius hesitated. The glib ease with which he addressed other women was conspicuously absent with Jilana.

"When you first sought my company, my father was most concerned," Jilana teased, sensing his discomfort. "'Twould seem, beloved, that you have a reputation for seducing women with your sweet tongue. Father even went so far as to warn me that I must not allow you to touch more than my hand."

"Jilana, we will speak no more of this," Lucius ordered harshly.

"*You* have not spoken of it at all," Jilana impudently reminded him. "At first I feared you to be a great, lusting animal who would tear off my clothes if I but smiled at you." She grinned. "'Twas soon obvious your appetite was much curbed where I was concerned."

Lucius reddened, grateful for the distance which separated them. He loved Jilana with an intensity bordering on reverence, but that did not diminish the physical desire she engendered within him. "Come inside, Jilana."

"Nay." Jilana walked back to Lucius, hips swaying seductively. Placing a forefinger squarely in the middle of his chest she began to circle him, drawing her finger across chest, arms, and back as she walked. "I am yet a virgin, Lucius. Did you know?"

"I expected no less," Lucius croaked, fighting the heat searing his blood.

"Many women my age are not," Jilana continued matter-of-factly. "Even Claudia had a lover—in Rome. She told me."

Lucius choked, not knowing how to respond. Now instead of her forefinger, Jilana's hand was making a path across his upper torso and the blood pounded in Lucius' temples.

"We will soon be wed, Lucius, and still I do not know the feel of your lips against mine." Jilana stopped walking and gazed at Lucius. "Claudia told me of the joys she found in her lover's arms. Is it so with all women?"

"I—I do not know," Lucius replied. "Mayhap."

"Did your women find pleasure in your bed?"

Lucius groaned and, keeping his arms rigidly at his sides, met Jilana's gaze. "So they claimed."

Smiling, Jilana pressed herself against Lucius, her mouth only inches from his. "Will you deny your betrothed what other women have known?" Abruptly her teasing manner fell away and Jilana whispered, "You are to be my life, Lucius. Will you not at least kiss me and tell me that while we may not love each other we will at least share passion? I must know, Lucius; 'tis important to me."

Lucius took Jilana in his arms. "We will share more than passion, Jilana, that I promise." He touched his lips to hers.

Jilana closed her eyes, willing herself to feel the shiver of delight she had experienced when the centurion had touched her yesterday. Lucius' kiss was not unpleasant, but it stirred no flame within Jilana and she was vaguely relieved when it ended.

Lucius stared at Jilana, his dark eyes blazing as he drank in her beauty. He dared not touch her again, not while his blood ran so high. To preserve her honor he must take Jilana inside, deliver her safely to her father, then leave and find a woman to assuage his need. "Will you come inside now, beloved? My time grows short."

Jilana shook her head. "Bid my parents farewell and then I shall see you to the gate." As Lucius walked to the villa Jilana contemplated his retreating figure and sighed inwardly. Why could she feel nothing for the man she would wed when the mere touch of a mysterious centurion sent her heart racing?

"Lady Jilana!" Jilana started and, turning round, probed the shadows for the source of the whisper. "Here, lady. In front of you—by the garden wall."

Jilana gasped. "Centurion?" Surely her mind had conjured the image of the man half concealed by shadows!

"Aye, lady, 'tis I," Caddaric answered softly. Relief washed through him when, after a hasty glance over her shoulder, Jilana hurried to where he stood.

"I thought never to see you again," Jilana said. She came to a halt just inches away from the tall soldier and found it impossible to control the mad leaping of her pulse. "How did you find me, Centurion? Why have you come?"

"Finding you presented no problem, lady; I had only to ask directions of one of the citizens of the town. Your father is well known."

Jilana studied the grim set of his jaw and her heart sank. "Are you here to chastise me as well?"

"For what reason, lady?"

"My actions of yesterday. Family, friends, Procurator—all have wagged their tongues over me. 'Twould seem all of Venta Icenorum has a personal interest in charging me with my duties as a Roman citizen. Were you sent to do the same?"

"Nay, lady." Caddaric looked at the villa and then back to Jilana. "Has your betrothed also rebuked you?"

Jilana nodded. "Do you know Lucius Quintus?"

Caddaric shook his head. "I heard him tell the Procurator you were betrothed."

"Aye—five days hence I shall be made his wife." Sudden desolation engulfed Jilana and she smiled wanly. "When his duty here is ended, we shall go to Rome. For me there will be no more early morning rides to the meadow."

"The world changes, lady." Over the top of Jilana's head Caddaric watched four men enter the villa. Boadicea's revenge had begun. "Forgive me, Jilana."

Jilana's confusion at his words changed rapidly to fear as she realized he had spoken, not in Latin, but in the native tongue of this land. "You are Briton!"

"Iceni," Caddaric clarified softly. "This night the world cracks apart for both of us, Roman."

The centurion's eyes were filled with the promise of death and Jilana reeled backward. "Father! Mother!" Her scream was joined by another from the villa and Jilana turned to flee only to find herself caught in the centurion's arms.

"Do not cry out," Caddaric warned. "As you value your life, Jilana, do not fight me. You are to be spared."

"My family," Jilana sobbed, struggling to free herself. "Foul traitor! Let me go!"

Annoyed, Caddaric shook her roughly. "When it is time, death will find you; do not tempt the gods."

"Nay!" Without thinking, Jilana rammed her knee up into the centurion's groin and found herself instantly released. Not sparing the groaning man so much as a glance, she turned and ran into the villa before the centurion could recover.

Carnage—absolute and complete—greeted Jilana. Throughout the house servants lay dead or dying and Jilana fought back a scream as she stumbled through the halls. Where were the soldiers? Surely by now their neighbors had heard the screams and given the alarm! Jilana flew from room to room, her horror growing with every step. Where were her parents, and Lucius and Claudia? Had they escaped? When her search of the lower floor proved fruitless, Jilana picked her way over the bodies lining the staircase and searched the bedchambers.

"Jilana!"

In her own bedchamber Jilana froze, recognizing the centurion's voice. "Juno, protect me," Jilana murmured. Moving to the door, she pressed an ear to the wood and strained to hear the approach of the centurion.

"Jilana, hear me. There is no place to run, not for you. Should any Iceni happen upon you, you will be put to the sword. The Roman garrison has been taken—only I can protect you now." On the first floor of the villa, Caddaric paused, alert for any sign of movement. The sight of the dead servants touched him not; his concern was purely for the Roman witch of his dreams. He had to find her and place her under guard until he found Catus Decianus—for her sake as well as his own. Minutes passed with no response and Caddaric grew angry. "Jilana, come to me! Do not be so willing to court your own destruction."

"Better death at the hands of my enemies than shame," Jilana whispered. She dropped the bar into place across the door as quietly as possible and ran to the second entrance to her room, a door which opened onto the colonnaded gallery at the back of the house. The other bedchambers opened onto the gallery as well, but Jilana shrugged off the thought. The centurion—the Briton—had not left the lower floor, so she still had time for flight.

Once on the gallery, Jilana hid behind one of the columns and peered cautiously at the courtyard below. No bodies here—praise the gods!—nor any sign of movement. A feeble ray of light came from one of the stable windows to her right and a spark of hope flared in Jilana's heart. Surely her family was there—they had managed to escape the villa and now were planning a way to find refuge from the senseless slaughter. Keeping a watchful eye on the courtyard, Jilana unstrapped her sandals and slipped them from her feet. If any Iceni still prowled the villa and its grounds, no sound must give her away. Silent as a wraith she ran from pillar to pillar, the sound of her own breath roaring in her ears. The gallery's staircase loomed out of the darkness and Jilana offered up a silent prayer of thanks to Juno, the guardian of women.

"Jilana." A hand on her shoulder spun Jilana around and she came face to face with the Briton. "I told you there was no escape. Now come—"

With a despairing cry, Jilana raised her arm and swung, striking Caddaric full on the side of the face with her sandals. Caddaric stumbled backward, regaining his balance just as Jilana reached the bottom of the stairs. A low growl escaped his lips as Caddaric charged after her. Her heart pounding, Jilana raced toward the stable, all too aware that the Briton was coming closer with each passing step. Still, she was ahead of the Briton, and if all else failed, once in the stable she could find a weapon with which to defend herself. Jilana glanced over her shoulder to determine how far the Briton lagged behind. The next moment her foot connected painfully with some object on the ground and Jilana found herself sprawled on the paved courtyard.

"Little fool!" Caddaric reached down and pulled Jilana to her feet.

"Let me go," Jilana pleaded. There was no escape for her now, for the Briton had twisted both her hands behind her back and was holding her tightly against his chest, but some primitive instinct forced her to ask for her freedom. A sob caught in her throat when, glancing down, she saw the body of the gardener. Raising terrified eyes to the Briton's grim face Jilana whispered, "If I am to be spared, as you say, then why not free me? No one need know! Allow me a horse and by morning I will be far away."

"Nay. I am ordered to bring you to Queen Boadicea." Tears slipped from her eyes and Caddaric steeled himself against the tug of his heart. "Even if I could free you, I would not. As a Roman, alone in Iceni territory, you would be killed by the first warrior who stumbled upon you."

Jilana shook her head miserably. "Why are you doing this? My father was ever kind to your people. Why have you killed the servants and my family?"

Caddaric's face darkened. "Are you so lacking in wisdom that you cannot guess what is happening, Roman? 'Tis not your villa alone which has been invaded." Jilana shook her head once again, this time in confusion, and Caddaric cursed softly. "The Iceni are in revolt; by first light Venta Icenorum will belong solely to my people."

"Revolt!" Jilana's voice was a horrified whisper. The Romans feared rebellion and slave uprisings above all else, especially in far-flung provinces like Britannia where the full might of the Empire's military could not immediately be brought to bear. Roman civilians bore the brunt of such insurrections and Jilana remembered with sickening clarity the tales of rape and atrocities which occasionally took place at isolated villae. But not here. Surely not here!

Caddaric knew the tales as well, and he understood the fear which drained the strength from Jilana's limbs, but he was not prepared for her next words.

"Then kill me now, I beg of you," Jilana said weakly. "If there is any mercy in your heart, you will draw your dagger and put a swift end to my life. You shame me by allowing me to live when all I love is dead."

In that instant Caddaric forgot that her parents and sister had existed—he saw only Jilana as she had looked in her betrothed's embrace while he stood watching from the shadows. Her struggle to escape him, her subsequent request to be allowed to go free, these had not been unexpected; but her plea to follow her betrothed to the grave drove Caddaric mad with some unnamed emotion. Unable to bear the sight and touch of her any longer, Caddaric thrust Jilana away with such force that she fell to the ground.

Too shaken by the night's events to rise, Jilana stared at him. "What will you do with me now?" She asked the question not out of fear of death, but out of fear of the unknown.

"I will not kill you," Caddaric said tersely. "Much as I would like to slit that lovely neck of yours, I shall obey the Queen's command." He turned toward the stable. "Clywd! Come out here, Druid, I have need of you."

Jilana's heart skipped a beat when the stable door opened and a man came forth. Hoping against hope that either her father or Lucius had overcome the Iceni and disguised himself in the flowing black robe, Jilana could not help the small cry of disappointment that burst from her lips when the Druid reached them. The man was unknown to her and Jilana felt the last of her hope crumble.

"Take her to the villa," Caddaric ordered harshly. "Keep her there until I come for her."

Clywd nodded. "The work is nearly finished in the stable."

Caddaric stiffened, aware of Jilana's sudden interest in their conversation. "Take her—I will complete the task."

The Briton stalked toward the stable and Jilana scrambled to her feet and ran after him. "What task? What lies in the stable?" Ignored, Jilana grabbed the Briton's arm and pulled at it until he was forced to stop and look at her. "The gods curse you, Briton, answer me!"

"I go to finish what my men started," Caddaric replied, a muscle working in his cheek.

"That tells me naught," Jilana cried.

"You may accompany me," Caddaric offered. Then, with utmost cruelty he added, "This night we found many Romans cowering in their stables. They ran like sheep, leaving their servants to defend their homes, and we treated them as such. Do you wish to see the fate your family met?"

Jilana blanched, understanding quite well what the Briton was saying. Her family and Lucius were dead, victims of the Iceni revolt. Neighbors, friends, they too were dead, or would be when the warriors found them. Her world was gone, shattered by the Procurator's greed and Boadicea's revenge. An ever-growing weakness stole through Jilana and as she crumpled to the ground, the last thing she saw was the Briton's mocking face.

Caddaric sprang forward, catching Jilana as she fell. With unexpected tenderness he lifted the Roman woman in his arms and carried her to Clywd. "Hers is the corner bedchamber—keep her there until I return."

"Was it necessary to be so cruel with her," Clywd asked as he took the slight burden in his own arms. "You could have spared her much grief, my son."

Caddaric's lips thinned angrily. "I do not tell you how to speak with the gods, old one. Do not tell me how to deal with this woman."

"You risk much," Clywd warned. "With this one deed you may lose your destiny and earn the Queen's wrath."

"Enough! I will do what I think best." Blue eyes blazing, Caddaric stood his ground until Clywd retreated into the villa. While it pained him to have disobeyed the Queen's command regarding this Roman family, Caddaric did not regret what had transpired here tonight. Jilana would bear the yoke of slavery well enough, but to see her family also enslaved would have been intolerable. A determined set to his jaw, Caddaric turned and entered the stable where Heall and two other warriors waited for him. This business must be swiftly accomplished so that he could find Catus Decianus and win Jilana for himself.

NOT UNTIL MORNING did Jilana recover from her faint, and when she opened her eyes to gaze about the room, she believed that she had been the victim of a nightmare. In the iron brazier in the center of her bedchamber a fire had been lit and Jilana stretched languorously, secure in the knowledge that she was warm and in her own bed. Surely no Iceni would have taken such pains to ensure her comfort! In a few minutes her maid would enter the bedchamber to dress her hair and help her into a fresh toga, and then Jilana would break her fast with her parents, Claudia, and, possibly, Lucius. From the lower floor came the sound of laughter and movement and Jilana smiled. All was well—the Iceni rebellion existed solely in her mind.

Tossing aside the bedcovers, Jilana sat up, swung her feet to the floor—and froze at the sight of the blood-stained hem of her toga. Scenes of the night past tumbled through her mind and as Jilana unwillingly touched the ruins of her once-elegant hairstyle a feeling of utter desolation ravaged her heart.

"Drink this, child."

A drinking cup was held in front of her and Jilana recoiled with a gasp, then forced herself to look at the man who had spoken. He was tall, spare, with light blue eyes which viewed her—not unkindly—from an ageless face.

"Drink," Clywd said again, understanding her fear. "'Tis only a draught which will give you strength."

Jilana violently shook her head and scrambled to the far side of the bed. There she knelt, the bedcovers clutched protectively to her breast, and eyed the man fearfully. She remembered him now—this man was a Druid, a priest of the Britons. Druids offered human sacrifices to their gods and Jilana trembled inwardly. She would accept naught from this man!

When his prisoner did not move, Clywd sighed and retreated to a chair at the side of the bed. Once seated, he set the drinking cup aside and smiled gently. "I will not harm you, child. You have been spared for a reason and I neither question nor defy the gods' wishes. Do you understand?" Jilana gave no indication that she either heard or understood his words so Clywd repeated what he had said, this time in the Roman tongue.

Jilana did not believe a single word the Druid had spoken. She was a prisoner, with no hope of escape, and she knew well enough a prisoner's fate. She would be killed, or passed from man to man until her body and soul were so ravaged that some man would finally kill her because she displeased him. Better death than to be so ill-used, Jilana thought wildly. She must either find a way to force this priest into killing her now or discover a means of opening her veins if she was left alone for a time.

To that end, Jilana rose and stared haughtily at Clywd. In a clear, challenging voice she said in the Briton's language, "I spit on your gods, priest! Only weak-minded fools serve them and only faint-hearted cowards follow those fools."

Clywd stiffened angrily and then, unexpectedly, gave a short burst of laughter. "You must share your opinions with Caddaric upon his return. In truth, child, you hold much in common."

"Caddaric?" In spite of herself, Jilana's curiosity was pricked. "Is this Caddaric the one who masquerades as a centurion?" Clywd nodded and the violet eyes filled with hatred. "You are a fool, old man, to think I will share so much as a word with that dog. I shall curse his name throughout eternity."

"By whose gods will you curse him—yours or his?" A knock sounded at the door and, chuckling over Jilana's defiance, Clywd rose and lifted the bar from the door.

The door had barely opened when Caddaric strode into the room and Jilana took an unconscious step backward. Gone was the centurion who had so bewitched Jilana in an isolated glade and in his place stood a fearsome Iceni warrior whose bleak expression turned Jilana's blood to ice. At some point in the night past, the centurion's uniform had been discarded in favor of the rough woolen tunic he now wore and the clothing, as well as Caddaric himself, was spattered with blood. What drew Jilana's attention, however, was the fresh gash which marred the Briton's left cheek. The bloody line cut diagonally from the hairline at his temple, across the cheekbone, to end at the jawline.

The dark blue eyes never left Jilana's face as Caddaric spoke to Clywd. "The Queen plans to address the people. Go below and tell the warriors and warrior maids to assemble at the palace."

"You are hurt," Clywd noted anxiously. "Your wounds—"

"Are not serious," Caddaric interrupted. "Go, Clywd. Leave us." With a last glance at Jilana, Clywd departed. Caddaric waited until no sound issued from the hall beyond the door and then, in slow, deliberate movements, he unstrapped his baldric, leaned his sword against the wall and advanced upon Jilana. Halting at the foot of the bed he coldly surveyed his captive. "You seem to have survived your swoon well enough. Have you eaten?" Jilana stared at him balefully and Caddaric checked a flare of irritation. The drinking cup caught his eye and he picked it up and sniffed at the contents. Satisfied, he rounded the bed and offered the cup to Jilana. "Drink this first and then we shall see about getting food for you."

Jilana turned her head aside and gazed out of the window. She would not countenance speaking to this man, let alone accept nourishment from him. If all other resources failed, Jilana would starve herself to death!

"'Tis not poison," Caddaric said, thinking he understood her refusal. He took a sip of the liquid and once more extended his hand. "Bitter, mayhap, but not deadly. Come, drink—"

Jilana's arm struck out, sweeping the cup from Caddaric's hand. Clywd's draught spattered them both and with studied contempt Jilana brushed at the droplets on her toga. Anger flashed in the Briton's blue eyes but she refused to give in to her own fear.

Caddaric glanced first at his tunic, then at the mess on the floor, and finally at Jilana. "You are a foolish woman," he said in a deceptively soft voice.

Jilana tossed her head defiantly and presented her back to her captor. Juno, let him kill me now, Jilana begged as a vision of her family and Lucius appeared before her.

"Since you will neither drink nor eat," Caddaric told the slender back, "you will tend my wounds when I have bathed. I would not have my Queen see me thus."

Jilana swallowed the enraged retort which came to mind. Calling upon every Roman god, she silently rained curses upon this Briton's head and pleaded with the gods to give the barbarian a long, torturous death.

Caddaric's temper rose with each moment that passed and he felt the last vestiges of control slipping away. When Jilana's shoulders resolutely squared themselves, Caddaric clamped a hand around her left wrist and spun Jilana about. "Though you hate me with every fiber of your being, you will obey me, Jilana."

"Nay," Jilana spat, unable to remain silent any longer. "If Caesar himself so ordered me, still I would not obey you."

"Your Emperor is in Rome, surrounded by Praetorian Guards and no doubt dining on honeyed fowl," Caddaric ground out. "You, however, are here. Alone."

"Aye, alone," Jilana echoed bitterly. "You saw to that, did you not, Briton?"

"I am Caddaric."

"I know well your name," Jilana hissed. "That shriveled priest told me. You are no brave soldier, Briton; you are a murderer who slays innocents in their beds! A true man faces his enemy squarely but you hide in darkness and revel in the slaughter of women and children."

Caddaric's eyes darkened. "Do you still court death so eagerly? You are a greater fool than I had thought. Worse still, you are a danger—not only to me but to every Iceni."

"A threat!" Jilana laughed incredulously. Then, a venomous expression on her face, she added, "Aye, I am a threat, Briton, for given the opportunity I will kill you and yours as carelessly as you dispatched all those I held dear. This I vow.''

Her words held the ring of truth and an icy finger touched Caddaric's spine. He was, above all else, a soldier, a veteran soldier of not inconsiderable experience, and he was possessed of the soldier's intuition which told him that the most dangerous enemy was the one to whom you showed mercy and then took into your own camp. Caddaric released Jilana's arm, drew his dagger from its sheath, and slowly pointed it at Jilana's breast.

Jilana's heart lurched painfully against her ribs and then she sighed softly. The gods had heard her prayers. Jilana drew a deep breath and closed her eyes. ''A clean stroke I beg you, Caddaric.''

For what seemed an eternity Caddaric gazed at the delicate face so close to his own. Fascinated, he watched the point in Jilana's throat where her pulse beat, even while he steeled his arm to drive the dagger into her heart. Caddaric was no stranger to death, yet he found his hand refused to obey his commands when it came to this woman. She was his enemy; she had sworn vengeance against him—and she was his destiny. No matter what his soldier's instinct told him, Caddaric could not kill Jilana. With a snort of disgust over his own weakness, Caddaric sheathed his dagger and watched as the violet eyes fluttered open and filled with dismay.

''Why?'' Jilana asked pitifully. ''Why?''

''Your life is not mine to take.'' Caddaric pivoted away from Jilana and crossed the room to reclaim his sword. When he spoke again his voice was oddly strained. ''Queen Boadicea has commanded that you be given to the warrior who captures Catus Decianus. You and the Procurator are the reason for the assemblage at the palace, Jilana.''

''But the Procurator—'' Jilana started to protest.

''Be silent,'' Caddaric ordered curtly. His failure to find Catus Decianus during the past bloody hours weighed heavily upon Caddaric. Soon he would be forced to turn this woman over to another man. What then would become of his destiny?

"Where are you going?" Jilana asked when Caddaric opened the door.

"To bathe," Caddaric replied shortly. "We shall leave for the palace when I return. Prepare yourself."

Fear and sorrow threatened to overwhelm Jilana the moment the door closed behind the Briton and she brushed at the tears which flooded her eyes. Denied an honorable death, she was to be made a slave to whatever man lied and claimed credit for capturing Catus Decianus. The Procurator had escaped the massacre—Jilana clearly remembered Lucius saying the Procurator had left for Londinium—so how could a warrior offer proof of what was impossible? Jilana swallowed the lump in her throat and gathered her fragmented thoughts. She was alive—and terribly alone. Her fellow Romans were undoubtedly dead, or, with luck, had been able to flee. Jilana was isolated from all which was familiar and surrounded by those who hated what she represented. But she would not treat the Iceni to the spectacle of a broken, whimpering Roman, Jilana resolved. She would meet her fate with as much pride and dignity as Boadicea herself had shown.

To that end, Jilana stripped off her soiled toga and cleansed herself as best she could with only a ewer of water, a basin, and a piece of soft linen. The water was cold, but Jilana ignored her protesting flesh and, placing the basin on the floor, she stepped into it and poured the last of the clean water over her shoulders. Shivering, Jilana hastily toweled herself dry and arrayed herself in the finest toga her chest held. The snowy material fell in graceful folds from her shoulders to her ankles and was edged at the hem with interlocking green rectangles, the color of her father's house. *Her father's house.* Tears started once again to Jilana's eyes and she shook her head violently. She would weep later, when there was no possibility of some barbarian intruding upon her grief. Trembling inwardly, Jilana seated herself at her dressing table, unbound her hair and carefully removed the strand of pearls from the red-gold curls. Methodically, Jilana drew a brush through her waist-length hair until the heavy mass crackled with a life of its own and then she struggled to braid the willful tresses and wrap them around her head. The result was disastrous, as Jilana saw when she looked into the polished metal of her hand mirror. The braids were helplessly lopsided. Jilana pulled the combs from her hair and untwisted the braids. She must try again.

The door flew open and, with a gasp of dismay, Jilana turned to watch Caddaric stalk into the bedchamber. He spared Jilana a brief glance before crossing the room to deposit what appeared to be a roll of clothing into his own chest. Still clutching her brush, Jilana rose and eyed the Briton uncertainly as he strapped his baldric over his shoulder. At least he was clean now, Jilana noted. The soiled tunic had been replaced by a fresh garment and his short hair glistened with droplets of water.

By the gods but she is lovely, Caddaric thought as he adjusted the baldric. Visions of his dream sprang to mind and the need to take Jilana, to make her his, overpowered all else and without conscious thought Caddaric crossed the room to stand in front of Jilana. "Witch," he murmured.

Jilana swallowed convulsively at the word and stood breathless as Caddaric's large hand twisted through her hair. He has taken leave of his senses, Jilana thought wildly, for she could think of no other reason for the madness dancing in the dark blue eyes. Undoubtedly Caddaric meant to violate her, to punish her for the crime of being Roman. Caddaric's lips touched her own, but instead of meeting with violence Jilana discovered an unexpected gentleness in the Briton's kiss. A strange lassitude crept through Jilana's veins, and when Caddaric deftly parted her lips for his questing tongue she made no protest. Reality spiraled away from Caddaric as he circled Jilana's waist with his free arm and crushed her against his chest. Though Jilana gave no response, neither did she resist and with a growing urgency Caddaric devoured the sweetness of her mouth.

Wave upon wave of pleasure surged over Jilana and for a time she forgot that Caddaric was her sworn enemy. A longing she had not known existed surfaced in Jilana—a longing which filled her with a sweet ache and left her weak and breathless when Caddaric at last released her. How she yearned to lean against him once more! To know the pressure of his lips against her own, to run her fingers through the damp brown hair. Even the jagged wound upon his left cheek did not repel her for— Jilana's thoughts ground to a stop and a mortified blush spread across her face. What was she thinking? This man was not Lucius, nor even a Roman. He was a Briton, murderer of her family! A sob caught in Jilana's throat. She wrenched herself away from Caddaric and ran to the far side of the room where she pressed herself against the wall and regarded him through wide, bewildered eyes.

Sanity returned to Caddaric as he gazed sadly at the forlorn yet undeniably enchanting figure Jilana presented, and he cursed himself for his actions. She was his destiny—if Caddaric had doubted Clywd's prophecy before he did so no longer, not after having held Jilana in his arms. The knowledge that he would soon surrender Jilana to another now clawed at his vitals and Caddaric seethed with impotent fury.

"Put on your sandals," Caddaric instructed in a tight voice.

Jilana obeyed, taking care to stay out of Caddaric's reach, and followed him from the bedchamber. As they walked through the villa Jilana saw, to her astonishment, that the bodies had been removed and the floors cleaned of their bloody evidence. Jilana bit her lip to keep from asking about the disposition of the dead but as they walked to the Iceni palace, carts laden with the corpses of the town's citizens rolled past Jilana and her captor and she found it impossible to chain her tongue.

"Briton?" The intense blue eyes fixed upon her so abruptly that Jilana paled, but she forced herself to continue. "Did you murder all my countrymen?"

Caddaric stiffened. "Nay, not all. A few escaped."

"And the children?"

"Those young enough to forget this place and their Roman parentage were spared—they will be raised as Iceni. As for the rest—" Caddaric slowly shook his head.

"You killed them," Jilana cried. "They were but children yet you slew them!"

Caddaric stopped and grimly faced Jilana. "The Queen's daughters are little more than children, yet they were outraged by your noble Roman soldiers," he informed her.

Jilana paled. "I—I did not know."

Caddaric clamped an unyielding hand on Jilana's upper arm and pulled her forward. "War is not pleasant, Jilana; everyone suffers, including those who are not soldiers. 'Tis a fact I cannot change."

Forced to take two steps to Caddaric's one Jilana struggled to retain her balance while committing to memory the scenes of destruction of Venta Icenorum. Did the sight of such devastation leave Caddaric unmoved? Jilana wondered. He did not glance at the carts, nor at the corpses which could be seen from time to time. What a change one day had made in the town. Today it was the jubilant Iceni warriors and their women who filled the streets, not the Romans. Today Roman blood washed the earth, not Iceni. Suddenly, without warning, the desire for revenge surfaced in Jilana and a hard core of resolve formed within her. The Iceni would pay for all that had happened—Caddaric, in particular. Jilana did not see the quickly concealed flare of anguish in the sapphire eyes, and she misunderstood the expressionless mask which had settled over his features as they neared the palace.

Caddaric's uncaring attitude—as well as the curious looks she received from the Iceni they happened to meet—stung Jilana to the quick and when she and Caddaric entered the palace grounds Jilana angrily jerked her arm from Caddaric's grasp. "You do enjoy this, do you not, Briton?" Jilana panted. "You revel in death; you delight in humbling me when you know I am powerless to defend myself!" As soon as the words were spoken Jilana realized the gravity of the mistake she had made in acknowledging what had transpired in her bedchamber. Caddaric's eyes snapped with derisive laughter and before Jilana could guess what he planned, Caddaric curled a muscular arm around her waist and lifted her upward along his body until their eyes were level.

"I did not hear you scream in outrage, or bite, or scratch. 'Twas only when the deed was accomplished that your Roman conscience plagued you." Jilana blushed furiously and with a short bark of laughter Caddaric returned her to the ground. "Chain your tongue, Roman. The warrior who receives you will not be as patient with you as I." The words flayed his already bruised spirit, creating an inner pain so great that Caddaric wondered he did not die of it. He had failed to find the Procurator so relinquish Jilana he must; but the memory of her sweet mouth tortured him so that in retaliation he lashed out at her, as if his action would deny his pain.

Subdued—at least for the moment—Jilana walked beside Caddaric through the crowd of Iceni. A dais had been raised in front of the palace and Caddaric elbowed a path through his countrymen until he and Jilana stood at the fore of the crowd. Frankly curious, even hostile, stares were directed at Jilana and some of the bitter defiance drained out of her. Never had she felt so alone, so completely unprotected. Until yesterday Jilana's world had been kind and gentle and now she was surrounded by those who hated her. Blinking away tears of self-pity, Jilana was more than a little alarmed to see a fair-haired Iceni warrior detach himself from the crowd and stride toward them.

"Caddaric!"

Caddaric groaned inwardly and inclined his head to Jilana. "Say naught to this man, Jilana. Keep your eyes downcast and your bearing meek. I will answer the questions he is certain to ask." Something in Caddaric's voice told Jilana she would be wise to do as he said and she hastily lowered her gaze to the ground as the strikingly handsome Iceni drew near. Grateful for Jilana's unexpected cooperation, Caddaric turned his attention to the approaching warrior. "Greetings, Artair."

Then two men grasped each other's forearms and Artair grinned engagingly. "You look well, Caddaric, despite the rigors of last night. Your leg is not painful, I hope."

Caddaric felt Jilana's startled glance fall upon him but he steadfastly ignored her. "The leg will heal, Artair, do not concern yourself."

"Still, you were injured because of my clumsiness," Artair persisted, brown eyes filled with concern. "Had I not stumbled backward, your opponent would never have laid his sword upon you."

"Clywd will see that the wound heals," Caddaric replied stiffly. He knew well enough Artair's reason for approaching and it had nothing to do with his injury.

"So this is what Clywd spent the night guarding," Artair commented. "Ede will not be pleased." The warrior eyed Jilana speculatively, confirming Caddaric's suspicions. Before Caddaric could stop him, Artair seized a handful of red-gold curls and jerked Jilana's head back so that he could see her face.

Violet eyes met brown and Jilana forced herself not to move or cry out when Artair's free hand casually explored the curves of her body through the toga. Two bright red spots of humiliation burned on Jilana's cheeks and as Artair's mouth curled into a leering smile, the metallic taste of hate sprang to Jilana's tongue. She knew, instinctively, what Artair was thinking and she longed to plunge a dagger into his black heart.

Artair guessed her thoughts and, laughing, roughly caressed Jilana's jawline with his knuckles. Looking to Caddaric, Artair inquired, "Have you bedded her yet, my friend?"

"Nay." Caddaric had unconsciously closed a hand on the hilt of his sword during Artair's performance and his grip tightened at Artair's words. "The Queen's order was to keep her safe. That I have done."

"You have more control than I," Artair said harshly, speaking for all the world as if Jilana were deaf. "I would not turn over such a prize without first sampling its charms."

"Mayhap that is why I was entrusted with her care and not you," Caddaric rejoined as calmly as was possible.

Artair greeted the ponderous statement with laughter. "Always so staid, Caddaric, so grim. This is a time for rejoicing, for celebration. We have won a great victory, my friend; I would think that would raise even your spirits." Artair's eyes slid back to Jilana. "Did Caddaric tell you? You are to be given to the warrior who captured the Procurator."

Jilana looked at Caddaric's stony profile before she nodded. "I have been told," she said bitterly.

"She speaks our tongue," Artair exclaimed, delighted with his discovery. He did not notice that Jilana's fluency came as a surprise to Caddaric as well. "I could ask no more in a Roman slave!"

Jilana's violet eyes widened in shock and Caddaric felt himself pale. "*Your* slave, Artair?"

"Aye, Caddaric, mine." Artair lifted a handful of the soft, fiery tresses to his lips. "The gods were with me last night—they guided me straight to the Procurator."

Caddaric surveyed the crowd through narrowed eyes. "I do not see Catus Decianus, Artair," Caddaric challenged bluntly.

"I was forced to kill him," Artair shrugged carelessly. "Still, I believe our Queen will give me this woman, Caddaric. 'Tis not my fault the Procurator chose to fight rather than surrender." With a satisfied sigh, Artair released Jilana and turned his overly handsome face to Caddaric. "I will take my prize now, Caddaric."

"Nay." A muscle worked violently in Caddaric's jaw and he pulled Jilana against his side. "Until Queen Boadicea decides differently, Jilana remains with me."

"Jilana? Ahh, Jilana." A knowing smile lit Artair's face as he glanced at the Roman woman. "Very well, Caddaric, carry out your orders, but remember she is mine. Let naught happen to Jilana while she is in your care."

Jilana watched Artair return to his friends with a sinking heart. His easy manner and purported concern for Caddaric's health had not deceived Jilana—she had looked into his eyes and seen the ruthlessness there. Artair would use any means, fair or foul, to obtain whatever he desired and at the moment it was obvious he desired Jilana. Jilana shuddered at the thought of becoming Artair's slave and stole a look at Caddaric from beneath her lashes. Would Caddaric believe her if she told him Artair was lying about the Procurator?

"Caddaric—"

"Be silent," Caddaric snapped impatiently. A rustle of movement at the palace drew a murmur of appreciation from the assembled Iceni and then a great shout went up as Queen Boadicea strode into the sunlight. Beneath the din of the cheering Caddaric warned Jilana, "When the Queen calls for you, go forward and kneel in front of her. Remain kneeling until the Queen says you may rise. Do not speak unless the Queen so orders, and if you do speak, your tone must be respectful. If the warrior who inherits you believes for a moment that you treated Queen Boadicea with the slightest contempt—" He allowed his words to trail off and fixed Jilana with a fierce look.

Jilana swallowed to ease the constriction of her throat and turned away. There was no need for Caddaric to complete the thought—she was painfully aware that within minutes her life and well-being would be of concern to no one. Her new master—Jilana cringed inwardly at the word—could use and abuse her as suited his whim. This was, Jilana suddenly imagined her father whispering in her ear, a time for compromise.

Boadicea mounted the platform and, in stiff movements that reminded Jilana that the Iceni Queen's back had been laid bare, gestured for silence. "My people, victory is ours! This day we have taken the first step in driving the Romans from our land. Our efforts will not cease 'til the last enemy has nurtured our soil with his blood!" The Iceni battle cry rose from a hundred throats and bloody weapons, as well as the heads of Roman victims which had been impaled upon pikes, were lifted in the air to show support of Boadicea. Jilana wrenched her gaze away from the gruesome sight and found Caddaric viewing the proceedings silently, his sword sheathed. As if sensing her gaze, Caddaric turned and Jilana was taken aback by the sadness which filled his eyes. He should be as excited as the others, Jilana thought in confusion, yet he looked as if the Iceni, not the Romans, had been defeated.

"My people," Boadicea cried again when the tumult subsided. "Today was but the first of many battles yet to come. In the course of our rebellion Iceni lives will be lost, but those of us who remain behind will sing praises to the memory of our dead. To die in battle is a gift bestowed by the gods—every Iceni knows this to be true. When the hated Romans are gone, your children and your children's children will boast of your courage and feats of valor." Boadicea paused, her eyes coming to rest upon Jilana. "Not all rewards need be so intangible. For the warrior or warrior maid who has made a prisoner of the Roman Procurator, Catus Decianus, there is a special prize." The Iceni Queen motioned to Caddaric and the tall warrior escorted Jilana to stand before Boadicea.

Caddaric went down on one knee and in the face of the ensuing silence, realized that Jilana had remained firmly on her feet. "Kneel," he commanded in a horrified whisper. "Quickly, Jilana!"

Jilana barely heard him. Boadicea's words had driven all thought of compromise from her mind and her fear had been replaced by calm determination.

One of the Queen's advisors stepped forward and pointed his sword at Jilana. "You will kneel, Roman, and do honor to our Queen."

"Nay, I will not." Outraged shouts followed Jilana's quiet statement and she imagined she heard Caddaric groan.

The advisor advanced, his sword lifted menacingly. "On your knees, Roman, or you will taste my sword."

"My parents are dead. My sister and my betrothed are dead. My friends are dead. Think you I fear the bite of your blade?" Ignoring the furious man, Jilana defiantly raised her eyes to the woman above her. "Do with me what you will, Majesty, but I will not kneel. You are not my sovereign or my sovereign's *foederatus*. You are Queen of a nation in revolt and I will not bow to my people's sworn enemy."

Cries of "Kill her" and "Behead the Roman slut" rang in Jilana's ears and she was vaguely aware that Caddaric had risen to stand at her side.

Boadicea raised her hand and in the deafening silence which ensued asked loudly, "Why do you defy me? Two days ago you raised me from the ground and offered some small comfort from your people's wrath. In return I ordered you and your family spared. Do you display your gratitude thus?"

"'Tis impossible to be grateful when my own life serves only to remind me of death."

Boadicea's face lost its look of irritation. How like her own daughters this Roman was, begging for death rather than a life of shame. The Queen's heart twisted as she signaled her advisor to resume his place. She could no more sentence this agonized young woman to the sword than she could grant her bewildered daughters' pleas for a draught of poison. She suddenly felt older than time. Boadicea turned slightly. "Come forward, Artair, and claim your prize." While Artair obeyed, Boadicea told Jilana. "I regret the loss of those you held dear. I have been told how your family, when they were offered their lives, chose to fight rather than surrender."

Jilana slanted a glance at Caddaric. He had to be the source of the Queen's information and it pained Jilana to have learned of her family's fate in so public a way. Boadicea was speaking again and Jilana dragged her attention away from Caddaric.

"I had hoped to personally avenge myself upon the Procurator, Artair. Were those not my orders?"

"Aye, Majesty." Artair bowed his head in a fine gesture of humility. "I sought to obey your command, yet when the Procurator came at me with his sword I was forced to defend myself and could not stay the blow which killed him. Forgive me, my Queen, for having failed you. I am not worthy to receive your generous gift of this Roman slave."

Jilana's stomach churned at Artair's fawning tone. He was, indeed, unworthy, but who would believe her if she named the Iceni warrior as liar? Boadicea was conferring with her advisors—no doubt debating the wisdom of bestowing Jilana upon the warrior who had, however unwittingly, disobeyed a royal command. The Queen had spared Jilana twice, 'twould be folly to risk Iceni wrath a third time. Still, she must try, Jilana decided. Her lips parted to voice her protest and immediately an excruciating pain gripped the right side of her neck. Turning, Jilana found Caddaric's large hand on her shoulder and when she made to speak the pressure of his fingers increased. Pain lanced down Jilana's arm and the muscles of the right side of her torso, and Jilana bit down on her bottom lip to keep from crying out.

The agony Caddaric was inflicting upon Jilana was no less than his own inner pain, but Caddaric was determined to keep Jilana from tempting death again. What she might say Caddaric could not begin to guess, but he knew she had to be silenced for her own protection.

Boadicea had reached a decision and she motioned Artair to rise. "The Procurator's death was no fault of yours, Artair. The life of one of my warriors far surpasses the life of the Roman Procurator. Therefore, because you did find Catus Decianus and sought to obey my wishes, the woman is yours." Artair grinned broadly as Boadicea addressed the rest of her people. "Messengers have been sent to our distant villages to tell of our victory. Within a fortnight our number will increase a hundredfold and we will march south upon the enemy. Rest and fortify yourselves, my people, for our success is dependent upon the strength of your sword arms!"

Amid riotous cheering, Boadicea turned to leave the dais and Caddaric gladly released his hold on Jilana. Artair hurried to where they stood, eager to claim his possession. Jilana saw him coming and before either Artair or Caddaric could stop her she lunged forward and ran to the steps of the platform.

"Queen Boadicea! I beg a word with you!" One of the guards—thinking the Roman a threat to his Queen—seized Jilana's arms and placed a dagger at her throat.

Boadicea paused, her eyebrows arched in surprise, and then slowly descended the steps until she stood in front of Jilana. Caddaric and Artair had reached Jilana by this time, apologies for the Roman's impudence already spilling forth, but the Queen silenced them with an imperious glare. "Release her," Boadicea ordered her guard. The glare did not abate as she turned her attention to Jilana. "Speak."

Fear dried Jilana's mouth and her voice emerged as little more than a whisper. "I—I cannot go with Artair."

"What you wish does not signify," Boadicea replied impatiently. "My command will be carried out. You belong to Artair—"

"But Artair did not slay Catus Decianus," Jilana interrupted desperately.

Artair turned red with anger. "To name me liar before my Queen will not better your fate, Roman!"

"I did not call you liar." Jilana's tone was sharper than she had intended and she lowered her voice to a softer level. "I wish only to know how you can be certain the man you slew was Catus Decianus."

It dawned on Caddaric as Jilana spoke that Artair had not set foot inside Venta Icenorum until last night. Artair had not witnessed Boadicea's humiliation, and therefore had not seen the Roman Procurator—but he had seen Jilana, Caddaric remembered. Only a fleeting glimpse, as Clywd carried her into the villa, but enough to know that the Roman woman was beautiful.

"I will not answer to a slave," Artair was saying.

"Then answer to me," Caddaric said menacingly. When Artair rounded on him, Caddaric lifted a questioning eyebrow. "To my knowledge you have never seen Catus Decianus. How then did you identify the man?"

Boadicea watched the two men closely. One slave—no matter how beautiful—was not worthy of such an uproar. In a few weeks' time there would be Roman women aplenty for all the Iceni warriors, yet Boadicea doubted another woman would satisfy either of these two men. Artair was a bit of a braggart, but Caddaric was painfully honest. Caddaric would not lightly question Artair's honesty unless he had good reason, of this Boadicea was certain. Boadicea sighed—her back smarted painfully beneath her gown and her daughters had great need of her. She wanted the business of the Roman woman settled quickly. "I would like an answer as well, Artair. How do you know you killed the Procurator?"

Artair, affronted pride evident, drew himself up to full height. "The man was at the garrison, dressed in the robes of a high-ranking civilian, and he carried the seal of office. But you need not believe me. I took the Roman's head."

"Show it to me," Boadicea commanded.

As Artair hurried to comply, Caddaric glanced at Jilana. Her face was as white as her toga, her violet eyes dark, haunted. Did she know something he did not? Was that why she demanded proof of the Procurator's death? Or had the events of last night deranged her mind? Artair returned, triumphant and gloating, and held his prize aloft on a pike, an expectant look on his face.

Artair's proof was greeted by three different reactions: Jilana, though it hardly seemed possible, grew even paler; Boadicea allowed her vexation to show; and Caddaric barely contained a shout of joy. The head was not that of Catus Decianus, but his assistant!

"Artair," Boadicea began angrily, then shook her head as Artair's smile faded. "This is not the Procurator." She turned to Jilana, her eyes burning. "Where is the Procurator, Roman? Where have you hidden him?"

Jilana raised her head, reveling in this small victory. Bitter hatred welled up in her and she threw caution to the wind. "He is gone, O Queen of the Iceni. To Londinium. You and your warriors murdered everyone save the man who wronged you. My congratulations—" Before Jilana could seal her death warrant with her harsh invective, Caddaric stepped forward and slapped her with such force that she fell to the ground. She stared up at Caddaric through tear-filled eyes and knew for the first time the salty taste of her own blood in her mouth.

Boadicea nodded approvingly, her sympathy for the captive gone. At least one of her warriors knew how to deal with this arrogant Roman. "Take her, Caddaric. She is yours for the services you have performed for me of late." She silenced Artair's protest with a look. "'Tis only just, Artair. Do not argue my point." With that the Queen swept past them and into her palace.

"I will have her back," Artair told Caddaric bitingly. "No matter what the Queen says, this Roman is mine!"

"Upon my death, mayhap, but not before," Caddaric replied mockingly.

"She will be mine," Artair repeated, his face rigid with determination. Artair's gaze fell to Jilana and he added with a sneer. "I would have treated you kindly, Roman, more kindly than Caddaric will. In time, when he tires of you or dies, you will come to me and then you shall learn how I deal with those who so carelessly dishonor me."

Eyes flashing contemptuously, Jilana struggled to her knees. "I will open my wrists rather than belong to you!"

"But not before I have opened your thighs. Think on that, slave." Artair laughed harshly and swung away, leaving Jilana shaking with fury.

Caddaric watched Artair depart, his blue eyes thoughtful. Even when they were children Artair had been given to thoughtless promises and rash threats, yet Caddaric sensed a new resolve in Artair this day. Had Jilana been an ordinary slave, a common prize of war, Caddaric would gladly have shared her with Artair as he had done so often in the past. Caddaric shook his head. Jilana was his destiny, the mother of his still-unconceived child. He could share her with no one, not even Artair.

A certain amount of trepidation filled Jilana as the tall Iceni turned back to her. His eyes, indeed his whole face, were unreadable. In her blind panic to be free of Artair's ownership, Jilana had not thought to be so casually handed back to Caddaric. Surely now, after the scene she had caused, Caddaric would beat her! Or have her wagging tongue torn from her mouth! She was the enemy and Jilana knew instinctively that Caddaric was far from tolerant of those who opposed him. Her own injured cheek bore witness to that. Caddaric's large hand swooped toward Jilana and she braced herself for another blow. Surprisingly, Caddaric's hand stopped just at her shoulder and Jilana stared up at him in confusion.

"Come. I will take you back to the villa."

Some of Jilana's courage returned and, ignoring Caddaric's offer, she gained her footing under her own power. She was, however, powerless to prevent Caddaric taking her arm and leading her from the courtyard into the street. They walked silently, Caddaric thinking of ways in which to overcome Jilana's resistance and Jilana plotting revenge upon and escape from this loathsome Iceni. Another cart of Roman dead rumbled past, diverting Jilana's thoughts. The body of a woman possessed of dark auburn hair lolled dangerously near the rear edge of the cart and Jilana halted abruptly. A strangled cry escaped her lips as the hair fell away from the woman's face, revealing features unfamiliar to Jilana.

"What is it?" Caddaric asked impatiently, his temper flaring at what, he was sure, was Jilana's deliberate defiance.

"My mother—" Jilana choked out. "I... I thought I saw my mother."

Caddaric glanced at the receding cart and then at Jilana. "Come." Jilana obeyed automatically, only to bring both herself and Caddaric to a stop before they had taken a dozen steps by the simple method of digging her heels into the ground and refusing to move. A fierce gleam in his eye, Caddaric jerked Jilana to him. "You try my good nature overmuch, Roman. Continue in this manner and you will learn how I treat disobedient slaves!"

Barely conscious of his ire, Jilana raised her eyes to Caddaric. "I must find them, Briton. My parents, Claudia, Lucius—I cannot allow them to go to their graves without being properly prepared."

Caddaric's face shuttered. "Impossible."

"Why?"

"Jilana—" Caddaric shook his head. "Mass graves have been dug. There is no way of knowing in which one your family lies or if they have yet been buried. They may not even be together, Jilana."

"I do not care!" Jilana said wildly. "I must find them and I will, though it means searching every grave! You have killed them, is that not enough for you? Must you also deny me the comfort of seeing them purified before the gods?"

"What you wish is not possible," Caddaric replied. "I understand your sorrow, but 'twill serve no purpose to hunt through the bodies."

Jilana blanched. "Are they beheaded, then? Dismembered, so I cannot recognize them?"

"Nay." Caddaric's voice gentled. "You do not realize the enormity of what you are asking, Jilana. I watched you in the courtyard; you nearly fainted at the sight of the heads on the pikes. How will you be able to sort through the dead?"

"I am stronger now, and prepared for what I must face," Jilana added quickly at Caddaric's grunt of disbelief. "In my place, would you not beg exactly what I have?"

Caddaric appeared to soften, briefly, but the next moment he clamped an iron hand on Jilana's arm and propelled her along. In a harsh tone he muttered, "You have begged naught, either from myself or Boadicea. For a slave you are too full of yourself and a life that was. If you do not lose your pride and accept your fate, I shall resort to unpleasant methods to make you tolerable."

Jilana shivered, aware she had pushed the Iceni warrior to his limits, yet she could not abandon her family and Lucius. For their immortal souls Jilana would do what she had not done before—humble herself to the man who had killed them and enslaved her. She would do as her father had advised—oh! how long ago it now seemed—and compromise. Quickly, lest her pride overrule her heart, Jilana put her free hand over Caddaric's and, having caught him off balance, pulled him into one of the deserted buildings they were passing. If she must be humbled, 'twould be in private.

"By the gods, what—" Caddaric's roar died as Jilana fell to her knees in front of him.

"Forgive me, lord, for having angered you. Henceforth I shall chain my tongue and seek only to please you and obey your every command. Only have patience with me, I pray you, should my manner lapse, for I am unaccustomed to the role of slave."

Wary of this sudden change of heart, Caddaric placed a hand under both of Jilana's elbows and raised her so that he could gaze into her eyes. "I am neither a child nor a fool, Roman. You speak these sweet words only so that I will allow you to search for your family."

Jilana stared into the hard blue depths of Caddaric's eyes, feeling her toes brush the floor. His hold upon her did not waver and while Jilana knew Caddaric could easily crush her if he so desired, she also sensed he did not mean to harm her. "'Tis true, lord; I wish to find my family. Yet should you grant my boon, I swear you shall never find a slave more devoted to you nor more obedient to your wishes. I beg you, lord, for this one thing."

"You are mine, Roman, given to me by the Queen. I can do with you as I please."

"Aye, lord," Jilana replied softly, her mind turning—as she knew Caddaric's was—to the kiss they had shared in her bedchamber. "But would not a willing slave be more to your liking?"

After a long moment Caddaric nodded and slowly lowered Jilana to the ground. "Very well. I will take you to the burial sites, but I will not aid you in your search."

"That you allow me my search is more than enough," Jilana answered. She took his hand and placed her forehead against it. "You are most generous and I give you thanks."

"Enough!" Caddaric roughly reclaimed his hands and gestured to the door. "By the time the sun has set this night you will not think me generous, you will think me cruel."

True to his word, Caddaric led Jilana out of the city to a small hill, the nearest burial site. Without a word Caddaric left her at the perimeter of the bodies and retired to the side of the hill to watch Jilana's progress. She stood, unmoving, for a long moment and although her face was hidden from Caddaric's view he could well imagine the horror and revulsion her violet eyes must be mirroring. With a slight smile Caddaric saw the resolute squaring of Jilana's shoulders just before she bent and rolled the body nearest her onto its back. She had courage, Caddaric grudgingly admitted, a desirable trait in the mother of his child. Not for a moment did Caddaric believe her act of humility and contrition back in the town—come morning, when her search was ended, Jilana would bare her claws once more. Satisfied with the turn of events, Caddaric stretched out upon the grass and allowed weariness to overtake him.

Jilana—her heart stopping each time she turned over another of her countrymen so that she might see his face—worked at her grisly task with fearsome determination, unaware of the passage of time. She ignored the taunts of the Iceni warriors who were so efficiently and unceremoniously disposing of the dead and concentrated instead upon choking back the sobs which tightened her throat when she happened across bodies of friends or merchants she had frequented. *So much death!* The waste numbed Jilana's brain as she moved mechanically through the piles of dead. She began, after a time, not to see the horrible wounds or the faces of those who were not her family. She could look and not see; and Jilana experienced the strangest sensation of standing apart from her body and watching a different Jilana sort through the dead. The girl in the blood-stained toga would not find her family, the dispassionate Jilana realized. Too many of the dead were put into the grave before she could look at them, and more carts deposited more bodies atop the ones she had previously searched.

Still, Jilana persisted. The warm spring sun beat down upon her, its promise of renewed life a terrible mockery in view of the tragedy of Venta Icenorum. Jilana's arms ached from the unaccustomed strain and she found herself growing lightheaded as the day wore on. Cursing her weak body, Jilana paused and straightened, trying to ease the sharp cramp in her lower back. She looked over her shoulder to measure her progress and found, much to her dismay, that she had covered less than half the length of the grave. Tears of frustration fell unheeded from her violet eyes and Jilana sank to the ground, defeated. Not caring if the Iceni saw her and laughed at her weakness, Jilana drew her knees up to her chest, buried her face in the stained folds of her toga and wept.

Far from being the object of scorn, Jilana was regarded by the Iceni warriors with a mixture of sympathy and respect. Word had spread of this woman—not only had she, a Roman herself, defied Rome for the sake of their Queen, but when she had been made a slave she had refused to go submissively into captivity. The warriors might have believed her actions foolish, yet they could not help but admire her courage. Ordinarily hardened to a woman's tears, the men now turned to the one who possessed the Roman survivor and silently implored him to put an end to her suffering.

Caddaric felt the warriors' looks. The lengthening of the sun's rays had wakened him in time to see Jilana crumple to the ground and now he shook his head sadly. Had Jilana heeded his words she would have been spared this ordeal. A fellow warrior offered Caddaric a pouch containing dried meat and a skin of wine, and while Caddaric ate he considered the woman who was now a part of his life. Caddaric rose and, after speaking briefly with one of the Iceni, made his way to where Jilana sat.

The first Jilana knew of Caddaric's presence was when a gentle but insistent hand capped her elbow and drew her to her feet. She stared silently at Caddaric through tear-filled eyes, her entire frame trembling as she fought to control her weeping.

"'Tis enough, Jilana," Caddaric said quietly, remorse plucking at his heart.

"N-nay!" Jilana desperately tried to shake off his hold. "You did promise me that I might search—"

"And search you have, to no avail." Caddaric peered into her averted face. "The day is gone, Jilana, and the dead must now be put quickly to rest before the wild creatures can feast upon their remains." He felt her shudder and added gently. "You will not find them, Jilana, though your heart is set upon your task."

"Help me," Jilana begged in a raw whisper. "Together we—"

"Nay, Jilana. I said I would not aid you and my decision has not changed. Now come, before you cause me to lose my temper."

They entered the town through one of the gates now guarded by an Iceni warrior but when Caddaric made to turn onto a side street Jilana held back. "Ahead lies the temple of Astraea. I would go there."

Caddaric's lips thinned. "The goddess of justice? What need have you to pray to that one?"

"That she may intercede with the other gods and see the souls of my family fairly judged," Jilana answered, her hopes sinking at the mocking gleam which entered Caddaric's eyes. "Please, lord, this one last boon I would beg of you. 'Tis not such a large thing."

"'Tis large enough," Caddaric said roughly, but the pale oval of Jilana's face gave him pause. Would it do so much harm to allow Jilana to mourn in her own way? If speaking to her gods would bring Jilana some portion of comfort, Caddaric would grant her that much. Without giving voice to his opinions of the gods—Roman or Celtic—Caddaric nodded his consent and accompanied Jilana to the temple. He did not set foot upon the stairs, however, and when Jilana was halfway up the steps she turned back to him with a questioning look. Caddaric inclined his head slightly. "Go, make your peace with your god. I will not intrude."

Jilana stared at Caddaric, snared by the clear, sapphire gaze, and he permitted himself a tight smile. Haggard and disheveled as she was, Jilana presented a most alluring picture. Her unbound hair caught the rays of the setting sun, creating a halo of pale flame about her head and shoulders, and Caddaric longed to twine his hands in the silken tresses. Desire flooded Caddaric and through no conscious will of his own, he took a step forward. Jilana must have read his intent, for with a small cry she turned and fled up the steps into the temple. Caddaric sighed. He must bring all his patience to bear on Jilana. She did not know, as Caddaric believed he did, that they were destined only to bring the best of their separate worlds together in a child. 'Til Jilana understood and accepted their fate, Caddaric would have to exercise caution—distraught women gave birth to distraught children.

Her heart pounding as she remembered the look in Caddaric's eyes, Jilana threw herself before the altar and sobbed out her plight to the idol of the goddess Astraea. "My family is beyond all earthly care, so I can but pray that the gods have judged them fairly; but the Iceni Queen has given me to a fierce warrior. 'Tis not enough that this Caddaric took the lives of all I held dear, now he seeks to claim my virtue as well! He will have me, Astraea, whether I fight him or not, so I beg of you a way to bring justice to the Briton. Hear me, O mighty Astraea! Let me be the instrument of your will. Give me the privilege of righting the wrongs done against my house.''

Jilana lifted her eyes to Astraea, then blinked rapidly to clear her vision. On the altar, barely visible in the light of the guttering torches, lay a dagger. Scarcely daring to breathe, Jilana struggled to her feet and cautiously ascended the three steps of the raised altar. Had she gone mad? Was her mind, unaccustomed to the brutality of the last hours, playing tricks upon her? Jilana's fingers closed around the hilt of the dagger and she gasped softly. 'Twas not her imagination! That the weapon was small did not alarm Jilana, for its size made it perfect for concealment. Jilana's spirits rose as she turned the dagger over in her hands. Astraea had heard and answered her prayer! By way of experiment Jilana pressed her thumb over the point of the blade. A trickle of blood instantly appeared and formed a rivulet which ran the length of the blade. A smile of satisfaction touched the depths of Jilana's eyes as she thoughtfully sucked the blood from her wound. No longer was she defenseless against Caddaric's might. When he sought to claim her virginity Caddaric would meet with a nasty shock, Jilana thought as she studied the ornately worked ivory hilt.

"Roman!" Caddaric's voice, coming from the entrance behind her, caused Jilana to start and as she turned Jilana instinctively hid the dagger behind her back. "Curse you, Roman! Do you worship your gods in darkness," Caddaric demanded as he blundered into a marble plinth.

"Your people no doubt killed the priestess and her attendants," Jilana called in a voice that trembled. "No one remains to light fresh torches." Even though Jilana's eyes had adjusted to the wavering light she had difficulty seeing Caddaric clearly and she breathed easier. If she could not see him, Caddaric certainly could not have seen the dagger in her hands.

Caddaric frowned at the white cloth in front of him, all that was visible of Jilana. "Have you made your peace with the goddess, Roman?"

"Only a few moments longer," Jilana answered. When Caddaric made no move to leave she added waspishly, "May I not have privacy for my worship, Briton? Or do you fear I shall call down the curses of the gods upon you?"

Caddaric snorted. "I have been cursed before, Roman, and as you can plainly see I still live. My life is charmed." He pivoted on his heel. "Be quick, Roman, or I shall leave you to the mercy of the guards who patrol the streets."

When she was alone Jilana quickly tore a strip of linen from her toga and, after a moment's deliberation, tied the weapon to her inner thigh. Having arranged the folds of her toga, Jilana prostrated herself once again in front of the marble altar and its idol.

"My thanks, O wondrous Astraea, for delivering unto me the means to mete out justice. I shall not fail you or my family. The Briton shall pay, I swear it." Jilana gained her feet with ease and ran headlong from the temple, eager to be about her task.

Caddaric's eyes narrowed as Jilana flew down the temple steps and knelt before him. "What is this, Roman? Some new trick you have devised in order to gain yet another favor?" He drew Jilana upright but the violet eyes remained downcast, as befitted a slave.

"Nay, lord," Jilana gasped out. Afraid Caddaric would feel the wild excitement coursing through her veins, Jilana carefully withdrew herself from Caddaric's touch and knelt before him once again. "I shall ask naught of you for Astraea has shown me the justice of what has transpired. Though my heart longs for my family and decries the slaughter of innocents, still will I serve you well. Your people, too, have been wronged. 'Tis my fate to stand as redress for the ills done to you and your Queen by my countrymen. This Astraea has told me and this I do believe."

Caddaric, accustomed to those who laid the blame for their defeat at their gods' feet, gave vent to a harsh burst of laughter and strode away, leaving Jilana to follow as best she could. Puzzled by his attitude, Jilana scrambled after Caddaric, her eyes fixed on his broad shoulders. She had hoped to allay his suspicions of her by attributing her change to Astraea's will but still he seemed doubtful. Had she overplayed her role? Jilana wondered as she quickened her step in order to keep a distance of three paces between herself and Caddaric. He must be lulled into a false security if she was to have a chance to use the dagger now riding securely against her thigh. Would a show of temper or fear achieve her end? Mayhap Caddaric thought her capitulation untimely and wondered what plot now tumbled within her mind. Do not appear too eager to please, Jilana cautioned herself. My fate has been sealed by the Iceni but Caddaric may still escape my dagger if my haste makes him wary. I must draw him slowly into my coil until he believes me totally cowed by my slavery. Then, when the Briton least expects it, my blow will fall. So lost in her thoughts was Jilana that she failed to see Caddaric stop and turn just outside the villa. Jilana plowed straight into the Briton and would have fallen had Caddaric not wrapped an arm about her waist.

"What are you planning? I wonder," Caddaric murmured as he gazed into the startled violet eyes. "Vengeance? Retribution?"

"Nay, lord," Jilana whispered, fearful that the press of their bodies would reveal to Caddaric her precious weapon. "Release me, I pray you."

Misunderstanding the anxious note which entered Jilana's voice as their bodies touched, Caddaric said, "I shall not abuse you unless you fight me. You have known enough men to understand that we prefer compliance to resistance. Do not be alarmed," he continued as Jilana's lips parted to give voice to a denial which Caddaric would never hear. "Though I would have wished you a virgin, that you have known a man's touch will not affect your purpose."

Defy the Eagle

"My purpose," Jilana sputtered, only to be silenced by Caddaric's mockingly arched eyebrow.

"You will find me a tolerant master, Jilana," Caddaric informed her airily. "And if you please me, a gentle bed mate. Mayhap in time you will be free to return to Rome and be none the worse for your experience."

"I have never set foot in Rome," Jilana spat, her temper igniting under the Briton's casual assumption of her lack of chastity. "Nor am I likely to do so since only your death will put an end to my slavery."

"Do you wish my demise?"

"Aye, most heartily," Jilana answered wildly. "'Twill save not only my life but my virtue as well." Caddaric laughed softly and Jilana quivered with indignation. "That you find my situation amusing I do not doubt. I expect nothing more from a barbarian!"

A smile lingered on Caddaric's lips and he nodded, pleased with Jilana's response. "You are a vixen, Jilana, admirably suited for what must be." At her confused look Caddaric's smile broadened and he bent so that his mouth was only inches from Jilana's. "Now retract your claws, dream witch. You may rail at me in private, but not in front of my men."

Jilana's eyes widened at the order delivered in such a soft voice. "I shall not—"

"You shall obey me," Caddaric interrupted in his deceptively mild manner. "I welcome your spirit—indeed, I feared you had lost it to your goddess—but the continued well-being of your exquisite body depends upon obedience."

Her anger simmered restively but the thought of her dagger comforted Jilana. Let the Briton believe he had won. Jilana lowered her gaze. "I hear and obey, lord."

Caddaric took her chin and forced Jilana to meet his eyes. "I dislike it when you do not look at me when you speak."

Jilana met the now-cold sapphire eyes and shivered. "I hear and obey, lord," she whispered. "Thy will is mine."

Caddaric nodded shortly and, with one arm draped around Jilana's shoulders, pushed open the door to the villa. The scene which greeted Jilana rendered her speechless and she stood numbly beside Caddaric. The villa, her home, had been turned into an Iceni camp. Torches crackled in their wall holders, small oil lamps flickered on the low tables and braziers had been set at intervals throughout the reception hall. Iceni warriors and warrior maids—engaged in the various pursuits of cleaning their weapons, eating, and generally ransacking the villa—welcomed Caddaric hurriedly and eagerly returned to their tasks. From the other rooms of the villa came the excited babble of voices and a sick feeling washed through Jilana as she realized her family's treasures were being gleefully discovered. A silver goblet—one of a set Augusta had brought from Rome as part of her dowry—rolled crazily at Jilana's feet and she fought the impulse to pick it up. Caddaric walked forward into another room and Jilana dazedly moved with him, stepping over serving platters, heaps of clothing and scattered, inexpensive jewelry. Claudia's cosmetic box lay discarded upon the mosaic floor, its jars of creams, rouges, scents and dyes haphazardly opened and then discarded. Oh, Claudia, Jilana thought wretchedly, how I wish you still lived so that I might tease you about your vanity.

"Greetings, Caddaric." Jilana blinked away her tears and watched coldly as Artair, the Druid and another man Jilana did not know came toward them. Jilana recognized her father's new cloak swinging from Artair's shoulders and her hatred of the man increased a hundredfold. He, too, would feel the kiss of her dagger, Jilana vowed.

Though he gave no outward sign of his emotions, Caddaric inwardly seethed over the sacking of the villa. He had hoped to spare Jilana this sight, and while he would not deny his force their right of plunder, Caddaric had given orders that the looting be done in an orderly fashion.

"This could not be stopped," Clywd explained softly, understanding the flame in his son's eyes. "When the blood is fevered naught will cool it, though Heall and I did our best."

Caddaric nodded and turned a disdainful eye on Artair. "You wasted little time in adding to your coffer, Artair."

A knowing gleam entered Artair's eyes. "You like it, Caddaric? 'Tis yours." He unclasped the cloak and offered it to Caddaric. "I willingly share all that I have with you," he added softly, but the generosity of his act was diminished by the fact that Artair looked, not at Caddaric, but at Jilana as he spoke.

"I have clothes enough," Caddaric replied easily. He thoughtfully fingered the material before smiling at Artair. "'Tis a sturdy bit of cloth which will keep you warm during the nights to come. A wise choice, Artair."

Artair's face reddened with anger. "You, of course, will have no need of material for warmth."

"Nay." Caddaric glanced at Jilana's flushed cheeks. "I shall be warmed in ways most tender." Jilana shot him a look of pure loathing and Caddaric chuckled. "Patience, my pet, the time grows ever closer."

Jilana would have shrieked in outrage had not a tall, lithe woman hurled herself against Caddaric's chest at that moment. Thrown off balance by the unexpected embrace, Caddaric was forced to release his hold on Jilana and, stepping away, she watched in amusement as the Briton and the woman crashed to the floor.

Spread-eagled, his efforts to escape effectively hampered by the arm which curved behind his neck and the other around his waist, Caddaric had no choice but to remain motionless as a pair of soft lips fastened hungrily upon his mouth. Ribald laughter filled his ears and, looking up, Caddaric swore silently as he saw the corners of Jilana's mouth quirk. When at last his lips were freed Caddaric stared coldly at his attacker. "Have you done, Ede, or shall I complete here what you would have started had it been within your power?"

Caddaric spoke so softly that only Ede heard the taunting words. Her face turned bright red, then deathly pale as she rose and waited for Caddaric to do the same. "The day was long in your absence," Ede ventured timidly. "What kept you from us?"

The mocking expression Jilana was beginning to know so well appeared on Caddaric's face. "We are in revolt, Ede. Had you forgotten? I have several duties which now require my attention."

Ede's eyes narrowed wickedly. "I do not believe *duties* required you for an entire day." She stared at Jilana with ill-disguised hostility. "Artair said you found a way to claim this creature but I did not believe him. I shall carve your beating heart from your breast, Roman," Ede threatened.

Jilana regarded Ede curiously, thinking that the Briton would be incredibly beautiful if her features were not twisted with malice. Jilana shrugged. "Do as you wish, I certainly cannot stop you. My life is held in the hands of the one who owns me and if he wishes my death, so be it."

The placid response caused Ede's mouth to work soundlessly while Caddaric bestowed a warning frown upon an uncaring Jilana. Clywd hid a smile and Heall shifted uncomfortably when Caddaric's gaze fell upon him.

"I warned you Ede would not be pleased," Artair put in, his good humor restored. "Apparently two women is one too many."

A muscle worked in Caddaric's jaw. "Were I you, Artair, I would see to my own affairs."

"Aye, Artair, 'twould be a blessing not to hear the air whistling through your empty head," Ede agreed vehemently. "The Roman will merely make our lives easier when we march through the land."

A hoot of laughter from the bystanders greeted Ede's pathetic rationalization and, despite her stature, Ede appeared to shrink in front of Jilana's eyes. "The Roman will make Caddaric's nights easier, 'tis true," came a shout from somewhere behind Jilana. "Our only hope is that he has enough strength left to march and fight!"

Even Caddaric laughed at that remark and without sparing Jilana a glance, he steered Ede away from the circle of prying eyes to a place of relative privacy.

"Do I embarrass you?" Ede asked spitefully, jerking her arm from his hand.

"You embarrass yourself." Caddaric's voice was cold. "Where is your pride, Ede? To throw yourself at me in front of those who know us both is unworthy of you."

"I do not care!" Ede pushed distractedly at the mass of pale hair. "I saw you this morn with the Roman—you treat her not as a slave but as a treasure. Your eyes soften when you look at her and I can sense the fire in your blood. Beware, Caddaric, lest you become possessed by her!"

Caddaric pursed his lips. "Does Artair please you, Ede, or do you but use each other?" Ede gasped at this sudden change of conversation and Caddaric smiled slightly. "Did you think I did not know? There are few secrets in our village and, in truth, it gladdened me to know you had chosen another. Artair will treat you well if you but allow him the opportunity."

Ede shook her head. "Nay. Artair is besotted by your Roman slave. Last night, when the fighting was ended, he spoke of nothing else." To prove her point Ede gestured to where Artair stood apart from the rest, his eyes never leaving Jilana. She stole a glance at Caddaric. "He knows well how to please a woman when darkness falls, yet 'tis you who brings happiness to me in the light of day."

"Do you think to make me jealous, Ede?" Caddaric's fingers tangled in Ede's hair, recalling briefly the pleasures they had shared. In spite of everything he wished to spare Ede more pain.

Ede raised her eyes to Caddaric, delighting in his touch. "Our nights were pleasant ones, Caddaric. Much ill will would be laid to rest if you gift Artair with the Roman."

Suspicion entered Caddaric's mind and with a cruel deliberation his fingers tightened in Ede's hair. Ignoring

her cry of protest Caddaric drew her hard against him.
"'Twas you who plotted that Artair should claim Jilana,
was it not?" He gave Ede a rough shake. "Tell me, Ede,
and quickly, or I shall strip you of what little pride you
still possess."

"The woman is a plague," Clywd sighed. "As long as
she clings to Caddaric he will find no peace."

Jilana unwillingly looked at Caddaric and smiled as he
embraced Ede. So the Briton had a jealous wife who obviously had no intention of sharing his dubious favors,
Jilana thought with relief. The threat to her virginity faded
and she turned her attention to the Druid and his com-
panion.

"This is Heall." Clywd performed the introduction
when Jilana's violet eyes lingered on the warrior. Heall
inclined his head to Jilana beneath Clywd's undisguised
interest.

Heall's stare was disconcerting but Jilana met it
steadily. He studied her face with bright, brown eyes, intent upon its every line and then, as an afterthought,
considered the gentle curves beneath her toga. Jilana
stiffened in outrage. She had been leered at enough for
one day. "You seem bent upon the same course as the
noble Caddaric. When two minds are so alike there is
generally a tie of blood. Am I to be shared by father and
son, graybeard?"

"Though I love Caddaric as a son, he is not of my line.
You mistake my intentions," Heall replied in a raspy
voice. One of his large hands came up to stroke the sil-
very beard that flowed down his jaw to his chest. "I noted
only that you appear fatigued and your gown is soiled.
Clywd and I managed to preserve your bedchamber
against destruction, so if you wish, I shall take you there
so that you may change and rest."

This unexpected kindness took Jilana aback and she
stood in silence for several moments. "I—I thought—"
she stammered and then shook her head. "The Brit—
Caddaric will be angry if I leave without first begging his
permission."

"Will he indeed?" Clywd's blue eyes snapped with amusement and he glanced at his son. "Do you now fear his wrath when only this morning you called upon all your gods to curse him?"

Jilana's chin rose. "I fear him not!"

"Good." Clywd smiled. "Then go with Heall and allow your soul a brief respite from its pain."

Jilana allowed Heall to take her arm and lead her through the villa to her chamber. "Is he a seer?" she demanded of Heall as they ascended the steps.

Heall spared her an almost gentle look. "Clywd is . . . Clywd. He listens carefully to the gods and they in turn grant him special powers. At times he has been known to look into the future and see what awaits us there, and on occasion he sees into a man's mind and heart."

Jilana shivered. If what Heall said was true, Clywd would be a dangerous man to be with when thoughts of her vengeance upon Caddaric were so strong in her mind. Heall opened the door to her bedchamber and to her dismay Jilana saw that torches and lamps had been lit here as well.

"We arrived too late to prevent Ede from going through your possessions," Heall apologized gruffly. "I fear she took some of your clothing and a few pieces of jewelry before Clywd and I—"

"It matters not," Jilana interrupted bleakly. "I am certain Caddaric will give Ede the rest in time. She is, after all, his wife."

Heall started to clarify matters for Jilana but the expression in her wide, violet eyes halted his explanation. The proud defiance she had shown at the palace this morning and again in the villa was rapidly fading as the numbing shock of the day and night past set in. Jilana swayed on her feet and with a muffled exclamation of concern Heall wrapped a thick arm around her waist and guided Jilana to the bed. "You must do as Clywd said and rest."

Jilana shook her head. "When I close my eyes, what will I see? What dreams will torment my sleep? My family—" her voice broke and Jilana doubled over as a terrible ache seized her heart. "'Tis not to be borne, old one. Would that I had died with the others."

Uncertain what to do or say, Heall awkwardly patted Jilana's bowed head and surveyed the bedchamber. This room, like the rest of the villa, had been searched and all possible weapons confiscated. At least, thought Heall gratefully, they need not fear that Jilana would find the means to end her life.

"Ah, see here," Jilana cried. Oblivious to Heall's efforts to comfort her, she slid to the floor and, kneeling, lifted a length of flame-colored material from its resting place. "'Tis my bridal veil," she whispered. The diaphanous cloth fluttered through the air and came to rest about Jilana's head and shoulders. She touched the material lovingly, remembering her mother's excitement when the ship carrying it had arrived from Rome. "Better now to use it as a shroud."

"Nay." Heall knelt and framed Jilana's face with his hands. "There is always a reason for living, though you may not think so now. It takes more strength to live, when you are torn from all you love, than it does to die."

"I have no such courage," Jilana murmured, drawn by the gentleness in Heall's dark eyes. "Your Iceni women have the strength, but I was gently raised. I am Roman, not Iceni."

"Yet you have the courage." Heall placed the flat of his hand on her left breast in a gesture curiously devoid of passion. "Here, in your heart, lies all the strength you will ever need—you have only to discover and use it."

"How can you speak with such certainty?"

"I know," Heall stated, a smile crossing his features for the first time. "When you would not bend to the Queen I saw the might of Rome as I have never seen it before. 'Tis a fool's mistake to believe you weak."

"And a greater fool comforts the enemy," came a mocking voice from the doorway. Caddaric stood behind them, his eyes narrowing when he noted where Heall's hand rested. With apparent unconcern, Heall bestowed a final smile upon Jilana, took his hand from her person, and rose to meet Caddaric's icy stare. "I will gladly share the woman, Heall. When I am done with her."

Heall drew himself up proudly. "She is little more than a child, Caddaric."

"Nay, a woman," Caddaric contradicted, his eyes fixed on Jilana's bent form. "Come here, Roman."

Jilana quailed at the harsh command, but she obeyed. Remembering Caddaric's anger when she failed to meet his gaze, Jilana forced herself to look into the hard sapphire eyes.

"Did you bed Heall?"

Jilana gasped and Heall's features stiffened. "You do both Jilana and myself a grave injustice, Caddaric."

Caddaric ignored his old friend. "I will have an answer, slave."

"Heall did but seek to ease my sorrow," Jilana said defensively.

Caddaric gave a noncommittal grunt and nodded curtly to Heall. "Leave us now, Heall."

"Aye, Caddaric, but first—" Whatever appeal Heall planned to make died a quick death beneath Caddaric's dangerous look and he silently left the room.

"Am I not to be shown kindness by anyone?" Jilana asked when Caddaric did not speak. "Why were you so cruel to Heall?" It did not occur to her to wonder why she spoke up for the older man.

"I will not have my warriors lusting after you when they should be occupied elsewhere," Caddaric ground out.

"He did not lust after me!" Jilana cried indignantly. The fleeting peace she had known in Heall's presence was gone now and her heart felt raw again. "Heall was kind, nothing more. Do not accuse him of your own rutting ways."

"And Artair? Was he also kind?" Caddaric caught Jilana's chin between his thumb and forefinger. "Raise not your voice to me, slave. You have caused naught but trouble since this morn and tonight you left my presence without asking permission—for that alone I should beat you!" Something snapped inside Jilana and with a hissed intake of air she raised her hand to strike, only to be brought up short by Caddaric's silken warning. "Do not tempt my wrath, Jilana, for only you will suffer should I lose control."

Jilana slowly lowered her hand and backed away, relieved that Caddaric did not follow. Instead he kicked aside the litter on the floor and, crossing the room, seated himself on one of the two remaining chairs. The hard, blue gaze leisurely traveled the room, then settled upon Jilana with such intensity that she felt compelled to speak. "Where is your wife? Ede, I believe you called her."

"I have no wife."

"But Ede—"

"I have no wife," Caddaric repeated calmly. His eyes caught and held on Jilana's veil. "And you will have little use for a bridal veil. Remove it."

Jilana pulled the veil from her hair and draped it carefully over her arm. "How did you know this is my bridal veil?"

The tremor in her voice apparently amused Caddaric for he smiled insolently. "The same way I know that if I search hard enough I will find a pair of saffron shoes and a tunic of finest linen. On your wedding day you would have been crowned with a garland of flowers. I have spent much of my life in the company of your countrymen. In fact, I even lived in Rome for a time. I know your ways, Jilana; you have no secrets from me." He glanced once more about the bedchamber and shook his head. "We left you little enough, but 'tis just as well. Now you will learn the Iceni ways."

"Never," Jilana retorted. "I am a Roman, not an uncivilized barbarian! Slave or not I shall never decry my customs."

Caddaric raised a mocking eyebrow. "We shall see."

A knock sounded at the door and at Caddaric's answer a procession of Iceni entered, Clywd at their head.

Two men deposited a large wooden tub a short distance in front of Jilana while another built a fire in the brazier. Steaming water was poured into the tub by the other Iceni warriors and the two women in the group placed food and wine upon the low table just to Caddaric's left.

"Enjoy this night's revels," Caddaric instructed coldly when his people were finished. "On the morrow you will set the villa in order—tell that to those who are seeking their sport below. Tell them also that I have claimed this chamber and everything in it as mine. Now go." The speechless Iceni filed out of the chamber and Caddaric turned to Clywd. "My order included you, wise one."

Clywd smiled. "As soon as I have tended your wounds I shall depart."

"I will look to them myself, as I did in the legion." Caddaric sighed at Clywd's pained expression. "In a day, two at the most, we will begin training for the battles to come. At the moment, however, I crave only peace and a great deal of privacy. Give me your medicines, Clywd, and be on your way."

"Artair told me of your injuries," Clywd sniffed. "If infection sets in you may lose both leg and life."

"Have done, Clywd," Caddaric growled, his impatience showing. "If I have need of your powers I shall call for you. 'Til such time, have the goodness to grant my request."

After a fruitless debate with his son Clywd left, muttering under his breath, but his pouch of herbs and salves rested at Caddaric's feet.

Jilana glared at Caddaric. "Why bother to stop the looting? Venta Icenorum is in ruins. All those who could possibly care about their homes and possessions are dead."

"Your Roman treasures are of no concern to me," Caddaric heartlessly explained. "An army must have discipline. That is what enables your legions to win their battles—even when the situation appears hopeless they unquestioningly obey orders. My people must learn to do the same and their education begins now, before they reach a battlefield.'' The corners of his mouth twitched into a travesty of a smile at Jilana's wide-eyed gaze. "Surely your betrothed—the brave tribune—discussed the need for discipline with you.''

"I am a woman, not a soldier, and Lucius treated me as such. I leave the business of war to men,'' Jilana said stiffly. "You have no right to laugh at the dead.''

A strange look crossed Caddaric's face. "I would not have you find me lacking when compared to the noble Lucius.'' With a slashing motion of his arm he indicated the tub. "The bath is for you, Roman.''

Jilana spared the tub a disparaging glance. "I will cleanse myself as I always have—in a proper bath.''

Caddaric chuckled. "Mayhap you have not noticed that no hot air flows through the hypocaust. The fire has burned down, which is why the rooms are heated by braziers. Unless you can stoke and fire the furnace, Roman, I advise you to take advantage of my generous gift, no matter how crude it may seem.''

"While you watch?'' Jilana demanded incredulously. Mixed bathing was prohibited by Roman law but Jilana's consternation stemmed from another source. Stripped of her clothing, her only weapon would be discovered and all would be lost.

"A fine display of maidenly virtue,'' Caddaric applauded in a less than admiring tone. "Unfortunately, your outraged sensibilities are of less concern to me than the possibility of contagion from the dead. Disrobe, Roman, and rid yourself of the stench of death.''

Jilana's eyes darted about the room, seeking a way to shield herself from Caddaric's avid gaze. At last, when her search yielded naught, Jilana asked in a quivering voice, "Will you at least turn your back?''

"And deny myself the only pleasure this day affords?'' Caddaric laughed mirthlessly. "Nay, Roman, I think not. Imagine me to be your beloved Lucius if 'twill make the deed easier. You willingly shed your clothing for him, I have no doubt.'' Caddaric's voice hardened. "Do as I say or I shall strip you with my own hands.'' When

Jilana's terrified eyes glanced toward the door he added, "A guard stands beyond the portal and the door to the gallery has been barred on the outside. Will you obey me, Roman, or must I make good my threat?"

Trapped, alone, Jilana decided upon the only course of action left to her. That she would most certainly die at the hands of the Iceni guard outside the door Jilana instantly accepted; but she would die happily, with the knowledge that her dagger lay buried in Caddaric's heart. Accordingly, Jilana presented her back to Caddaric and began to disrobe. The cloth fell from her shoulders, leaving her back exposed to Caddaric, and Jilana held an arm to her breast to keep the material from slipping further. Her free hand, hidden from the Briton's view, crept beneath the folds of the toga and closed around the dagger's hilt. The dagger slid easily from its sheath and Jilana silently called upon Mars to guide her aim.

"Cease your dallying, Roman," Caddaric called out imperiously. "You have been told—"

With a low cry Jilana allowed her clothing to fall to the floor and, turning, she flew across the chamber to deliver a mortal blow to her enemy. A look of disbelief crossed Caddaric's face when he found himself attacked by a naked madwoman armed only with a sacrificial dagger. Had it not been for the blood lust shining in Jilana's eyes, Caddaric would have laughed at her pitiful attempt at revenge. As it was, Jilana's arm arced downward with terrible surety and Caddaric effortlessly parried her blow by simply bringing his own arm up to meet hers.

The delicate bones of Jilana's wrist connected with Caddaric's well-muscled forearm with a loud crack, and Jilana gasped at the numbing pain which tore up her arm. Caddaric's free hand closed around her throbbing wrist and the next moment the hand which had thwarted her attempt on his life wrenched the dagger from her hand.

"You are mad," Caddaric growled. He tossed the dagger to the floor and released Jilana. He had not reckoned on the extent of Jilana's determination, however, and Caddaric grunted in pain as a dainty foot landed a telling blow against his right thigh. Snarling, Caddaric wrapped an arm around Jilana's waist and easily hoisted her over his shoulder.

"Put me down!" Jilana shrieked. "You insolent barbarian—" Her words dissolved into a scream when the palm of Caddaric's hand smacked across her exposed posterior. Tears stung Jilana's eyes but before she could voice her outrage at this latest abuse, she was all but hurled into the bathwater.

"Now you will bathe," Caddaric thundered, blue eyes dark with fury.

Anger and pain merged, turning Jilana into the madwoman Caddaric had already named her, and in that moment she knew only that she had to fight and go on fighting until Caddaric ultimately defeated her. Honor demanded no less. "I will not obey you," Jilana spat. Her hands had instinctively balled into fists and in a final, desperate show of rebellion she struck wildly at Caddaric. She saw nothing save Caddaric's mocking face, felt nothing save the wild, primitive need to hurt Caddaric in retribution for the destruction of her world. Her blow was ill-timed, for Caddaric had seen the gleam in her eyes and taken a step backward. Now he stared pitilessly down at her and laughed, but there was no humor in the sound. She had earned his wrath, this Jilana did not doubt, and even as she wondered what punishment would befall her, Caddaric's hand descended and she was pushed beneath the surface of the water.

"Do as I order, lest I change my mind and drown you for the trouble you have caused," Caddaric said harshly when Jilana came up sputtering.

The madness had passed, and the bedchamber and its furnishings suddenly came back into focus. Jilana bit back a sharp retort and looked away from Caddaric to the place where her dagger lay. She had failed. *Failed!* Her enemy still lived and she was now utterly defenseless—all was lost to this fearsome Iceni. Silently, hating the fact that she had no choice but to obey, Jilana scrubbed her flesh fiery red under Caddaric's watchful gaze. She stepped from the tub and faced the Briton defiantly, daring him to comment upon her nakedness.

Fully aware of what she expected, Caddaric merely offered Jilana a towel, and when she all but tore the cloth out of his hands he favored her with a taunting smile which belied his burning anger. "Mayhap I should cut out your tongue. You are quite bearable this way."

Something in his eyes sent a splinter of fear shivering up her spine and Jilana inadvertently retreated a step. She dropped her towel in the process, an action which seemed to amuse her captor.

Caddaric's amusement quickly vanished when the door opened and a group of six Romans, Artair at their head, entered the chamber. Artair's greedy stare rested solely upon Jilana and a mortified blush spread across her face. Ah, Juno, that these men should see her thus! Humiliated to the very depths of her soul, Jilana was surprised—and shamelessly grateful—when Caddaric snatched a *palla* from the floor and wrapped her trembling form within its folds.

Caddaric swung back to Artair and fixed him with a dangerous look. "What is the meaning of this, Artair?"

Slowly, Artair dragged his gaze from Jilana to Caddaric. "I am offering you the service of my slaves—as a gesture of good will. They will remove the tub and see to any of your needs." He shoved the first man toward the improvised bath. "Do as I say." The man looked fearfully at Artair but made no move to obey, not even when Artair prodded him with the point of his sword.

"He does not understand our tongue," Caddaric informed his fellow warrior. "I doubt any of them do. If you wish these men to be of service to you, Artair, either speak to them in their own language or teach them ours."

"By the gods, I will not," Artair sneered, a petulant look settling over his face. "I waste no time pampering slaves! If they cannot obey me they are useless and I will send them to join their countrymen."

As she realized what Artair meant, Jilana started forward with a low cry, only to be caught in one of Caddaric's arms. "You cannot let him do this thing," Jilana implored, her wide eyes searching the Briton's cold features. "Oh, please, you cannot!"

"The slaves are not mine. I have no part in their fate." Without so much as looking at her, Caddaric drew Jilana back to his side. "Artair! Since you plan to dispose of these Romans, do so elsewhere. I wish my chamber as uncluttered as possible."

Jilana shivered at such callousness and felt herself gathered more securely against the Briton's chest. Nor was the movement lost on Artair. Smiling slightly, he pointed his sword toward the Romans. "What say you to a trade, Caddaric? My six for your one. In this way we both have slaves who will obey us."

"Nay, Artair, but I will allow Jilana to act as interpreter if you desire." Caddaric's fingers tightened warningly on Jilana's shoulder through the folds of her cloak. "Tell your people what is required of them, Roman."

Jilana did so, in a trembling voice, and was vastly relieved when her countrymen obeyed without protest. "You see, they are willing," Jilana ventured to the glowering Artair. "If you would but show them what you want or allow me to teach them the Celtic tongue—"

"Be silent," Artair shouted, his face reddening. "The next time your wagging tongue insults me I will have your head on a pike!"

Jilana instinctively shrank against Caddaric, her only source of protection, and firmly clamped her lips together. If Artair claimed insult she would indeed be killed. Slaves had no rights—a bitter fact, but one Jilana knew she must accept if she wished to live and avenge herself and her family.

The male slaves were gone now and Caddaric allowed his full anger to show. "You risk much with such a weak ploy, Artair, including your life. I will neither trade nor sell this woman—yet. The next time you wish to see me you will present yourself courteously, not in such a brazen manner. Now go." Artair was nearly out the door when Caddaric added, "And, Artair, do not threaten my slave again. I alone mete out her punishment."

The words came hard, but when they were alone Jilana forced herself to say them. "Thank you, lord."

"Thanks from the same slave who tried to bury a dagger in my heart only a few minutes ago? Clywd's gods have performed a miracle!" Jilana's indignation at his mocking must have shown because Caddaric laughed and tilted her face to his. "If you are truly thankful there is a way you can show your gratitude. A way which Artair so rudely interrupted."

The Briton's words were soft, almost gentle, but they struck fear in Jilana's heart. So the time had come, she thought dazedly as she gave in to the pressure of the Iceni's arm and accompanied him to the bed. Just as her family and freedom had been taken from her, her virginity would now be the latest victim of the Iceni rebellion.

"'Tis not such a hard task I set before you," Caddaric explained as he seated himself on the bed and handed Jilana his dagger. "But it must be done quickly, cleanly. Put my dagger to heat upon the coals and we shall begin."

Jilana paled, her violet eyes staring into the Briton's calm blue ones. Great Juno, help me, she prayed desperately. The barbarian is mad! He means more harm than I thought. Simple ravishment was one thing, but to be left disfigured, physically scarred.... Jilana swallowed convulsively. Mayhap if she convinced the Briton that she would offer no resistance he would forego whatever cruelty he had planned. A maiden still, Jilana had only a vague idea of what transpired between a man and woman, but she was certain that heated daggers had no part of the normal act.

Caddaric frowned at her resistance. "Come, Jilana, it must be done. 'Twill be a relief to us both to have it finished."

"B-but, Lord," Jilana stammered. "Surely there is another way?"

"Aye, but it is longer and more painful for me." Caddaric lifted a questioning eyebrow. "Do you wish for me to suffer unnecessarily?'' Pure terror seized Jilana and it was all she could do to shake her head. ''Good. Now set the dagger to heat and—'' he surveyed the clothing on the bed, picked up a *stola* and draped it over Jilana's arm ''—put this on. The cloak will only encumber your actions.'' Impatiently, Caddaric closed Jilana's fingers around the dagger hilt and gave her a push toward the brazier. ''Bring Clywd's pouch back with you.''

A nightmare, Jilana thought as she obeyed the Briton's instructions. Trembling from head to toe, Jilana returned to the bed and found Caddaric had stripped off his tunic while her back had been turned. Clad only in a brief loincloth Caddaric watched her approach, his face surprisingly grim for one who had been so anxious to begin this entire business.

''I hope you are stronger than you look,'' Caddaric muttered as he took the pouch and sorted through the contents. '''Twill do me no good if you faint at the sight of blood.''

Such deliberate baiting stiffened Jilana's spine. ''Were I to swoon, Briton, I would have done so at the gravesite. Why you wish to torture me in such a manner I do not know, but I will die before I faint at your hands.''

''At my hands?'' Caddaric shook his head. ''You speak in riddles. Here is the balm you will need.'' He set the clay jar aside and pulled an unwilling Jilana between his thighs. ''First the bandage, so that I may see what damage you have done.''

Speech deserted Jilana; she simply stared as Caddaric unwound the cloth which covered his right thigh. He is wounded, Jilana thought, and needs my help. That she had misinterpreted his aim made Jilana giddy with relief. Concern over the loss of her innocence fled when the last of the bandage fell away to reveal an ugly gash that ran from the middle of Caddaric's thigh upward to the lower edge of his loincloth. Blood spilled from the wound to form a puddle on the floor and Jilana gasped aloud.

Seemingly indifferent to the injury Caddaric ordered, ''Bring one of those buckets of clean water.''

Jilana obeyed without hesitation. For the moment the Briton ceased to be her hated enemy. He was simply a human being, hurt, bleeding, and in great danger of dying if something was not done. Jilana tore several pieces of cloth from one of the gowns at her feet and knelt in front of Caddaric. "Let me." Brushing aside his hands Jilana pressed all but one of the cloths against the wound while her free hand wetted the remaining material and wiped the dried blood from his leg.

"'Tis not infected," Caddaric stated, and Jilana thought she heard him sigh in relief.

"I did this," Jilana asked weakly, assaulted by guilt. Undoubtedly in her desperate struggle, the kick she had managed to land against his leg had opened his wound.

"Do not apologize," Caddaric answered dryly. "Better a little blood than finding death at your hands. Get the dagger." He pressed his large hands over the rapidly staining bandage and managed a wan smile for Jilana when she returned with the red-hot dagger. "Draw the blade across both sides of the wound. This must be done quickly enough so that the flesh does not cling to the blade, but slowly enough to seal the veins. Once this is done, clean the wound, apply the Druid's balm, and then bandage the wound lightly but securely. Do you understand?"

Jilana nodded but weakly protested, "Should not the Druid or Heall do this? My hand could tremble . . . or my courage fail."

A strange glow entered the depths of Caddaric's eyes. "I know you well, Jilana. Your courage will not fail."

With that simple vote of trust Caddaric removed the bandage and closed his eyes, effectively placing his life in Jilana's hands. She wavered briefly. 'Twould be a simple matter to kill the Briton now and then open her own veins before his comrades discovered her deed. Jilana stole a glance at his face and felt something unnamed stir within her. Disgusted at her weakness, telling herself that only a sound opponent was worthy of her vengeance, Jilana placed the blade against the Briton's flesh and followed his instructions with amazing surety.

The scent of scorched flesh filled the chamber and Jilana's stomach roiled. She looked up to find Caddaric staring at her. "'Tis done, Briton."

Caddaric nodded, an odd pallor on his sun-bronzed face. "Excellent. The gods chose you wisely, my witch."

While Jilana watched, an emptiness veiled the Briton's eyes and he slowly toppled forward. Like a massive oak being felled, Jilana thought irrelevantly. The dagger fell to the floor as Jilana caught the Briton in her arms. It took every bit of strength Jilana had to lower Caddaric gently onto the bed. She managed to swing his legs onto the bed as well, but he lay perilously near the edge and, despite her struggles, Jilana could not budge his greater weight. In the end, Jilana was forced to seek help from the guard Caddaric had placed outside the chamber door.

Somehow it came as no surprise to Jilana that Heall and the Druid had made their pallets outside Caddaric's chamber, nor that no other Iceni stood watch. The instant she opened the door Heall sprang to his feet while the Druid rose in a more leisurely manner.

"Caddaric has need of you," Jilana said before either man could speak. Turning, she led them into the chamber and gestured wordlessly toward the bed.

Clywd assessed the situation at a glance. With a nod to Heall, he grasped Caddaric's legs while Heall braced one knee against the bed and slipped his hands beneath Caddaric's arms. With an ease which made Jilana all too aware of her own physical weakness, the two men centered the unconscious warrior in Jilana's bed.

Caddaric moaned once when he was being moved and before she could stop herself Jilana cried out sharply, "Have a care with him!" Two astonished pairs of eyes fell upon Jilana and she reddened. She could think of no plausible explanation for her reaction, so Jilana stayed silent during Clywd's examination of Caddaric. When the Druid reached for the balm to apply to Caddaric's wound, however, Jilana stepped to the bed and extended her hand. "I will see to this."

Clywd's eyebrows shot up but he retired gracefully, watching with great interest as Jilana dressed the wound. "You have a gentle touch," he commented when Jilana was finished.

Jilana shrugged and pulled a blanket over Caddaric. "I did but follow his orders—like any good *slave*." Bitterness colored her voice.

"Yet I think you would have helped Caddaric even had he not asked," Clywd said thoughtfully.

The Druid's words struck a chord of truth within Jilana and she grimaced. "As a slave I have no choice but to obey my master," Jilana maintained stubbornly. "Had the Briton not ordered me to help, I would have cheerfully watched him bleed to death."

A faint smile touched Clywd's lips. "Perhaps." He motioned to Heall, who was engaged in the pleasant task of studying Jilana. "Should Caddaric worsen, you must call us. We take our rest in the hall."

Jilana remained silent and unmoving until the men left and then she sighed heavily. Drained of all emotion save anger Jilana glared at the sleeping Briton, the source of all her turmoil. When he awoke Caddaric would doubtless believe as the Druid had—that she ministered to him because she bore him no ill will. Jilana's eyes narrowed and she drew a finger down the fresh gash which marred the Briton's left cheek. The need for revenge surfaced once again within Jilana and she plucked the now cold dagger from its place on the floor. She raised her arm, positioning the blade above the Briton's throat. How long she stood there Jilana did not know but some mysterious force stayed her blow and when, at last, her arm dropped back to her side, Jilana found her muscles weak and trembling from the force she had been exerting.

"Nay, I shall not kill you yet," Jilana whispered to the slumbering warrior. Her eyes dark with hatred, Jilana carefully cleaned the wound on the Briton's cheek and then applied the Druid's balm. "When you are as you were the night my family was slain, then shall I have my revenge. I shall care for you most tenderly, Briton, have no fear; but once you are well, not even the gods will protect you!'' Jilana bent and touched her lips to the Briton's in a mocking kiss—a kiss that promised, not passion, but death. Straightening, Jilana laughed silently and then, so that the Briton would know there was no room in her heart for mercy, she drove the dagger into the headboard of the bed with all her might. Turning, Jilana found the discarded cloak and wrapped herself in it. Her rest this night was taken on the hard couch the room afforded but Jilana did not notice her discomfort. Exhaustion blessed the Roman woman with a dreamless sleep.

''Will she not do Caddaric harm?'' Heall worried on the other side of the door. ''Caddaric's weapons are at her disposal, as well as your pouch of medicines.''

Clywd chuckled. ''Have you not yet learned to trust me, old friend?''

''I trust you,'' Heall replied solemnly. ''Tis Caddaric and Jilana who arouse my concern.''

Clywd reached out and grasped Heall's forearm. ''Better than anyone, you know how quickly hate fades in certain situations. No harm will befall either of them.'' He smiled reassuringly and quietly told Heall of Caddaric's vision and his own. ''Already they are bound to one another, though both would deny this truth. Their destinies are joined—henceforth they rise or fall together. You will see.''

Chapter 3

CADDARIC STRODE THROUGH THE VILLA which was his temporary shelter, his face grim. Nearly a week had passed since the Iceni had risen in rebellion and, while Caddaric had chafed impatiently, the Queen and her generals had dispatched messengers to the other tribes with offers of an armed alliance against Rome. Caddaric's soldier's mind knew that delay, for any reason, increased the danger of failure. The Iceni had to march, and quickly, before any survivors of Venta Icenorum reached a Roman garrison and told of the uprising. The Iceni's only hope of victory lay in surprise and speed—they had to oust both Roman civilians and soldiers from their island before Rome brought the might of its military to bear on the rebels.

At last, Caddaric thought without satisfaction, the messengers had returned, but their news was less than heartening. Queen Boadicea and her people, for all practical purposes, stood alone against Rome. The lack of complete support from the other tribes disturbed Caddaric but he accepted it philosophically. 'Twas the hideous tale carried by the Ordovician messenger which stirred disbelief and hatred in Caddaric's heart and occupied his thoughts. The news had to be imparted to Clywd and Caddaric dreaded the telling. How could he tell his father of this latest atrocity? How could he explain to a Druid that his mystic life's blood, his refuge, was no more? Caddaric paused before his chamber, one large, brown hand resting upon the latch. The indistinct drone of voices reached him through the wood panel and the line of his jaw hardened as he visualized the scene within. How could one slender girl—and an enemy at that!—beguile every male who so much as laid eyes on her? Heall and Clywd insisted upon treating Jilana as an honored guest, an act of insanity which scraped Caddaric's nerves raw. Jilana was, after all, a slave, not a royal personage from another tribe! At that moment the light laughter Caddaric knew to be Jilana's floated to his ears and Caddaric's face darkened. By the gods! 'Twas time to put a stop to this unseemly behavior before Jilana bent Heall and Clywd to her will. His anger had nothing to do with the fact that Jilana did not gift him with so much as a smile, let alone that musical laughter. Or so Caddaric told himself as he threw open the door.

The tentative smile on Jilana's face died when Caddaric burst into the chamber. Startled, Heall half-rose from his place beside Clywd on the couch—the same couch which served as Jilana's bed. Before the upward motion of his body had stopped, Heall's sword was out of its scabbard, its gleaming length menacing the intruder. Jilana, seated on the floor between the two men so that she might face them both, caught her breath at the sight of Caddaric. Positioned as she was—her back to the door—Jilana had been forced to turn her head in order to see who had entered. As always, Caddaric's sheer size amazed her and frightened her. Unwillingly Jilana remembered their first meeting. She had not been frightened then, at least not after he had spoken to her in a gentle voice so totally at odds with his size and rugged features. No. Caddaric had not been frightening then; he had been compellingly attractive. But he was no longer gentle, either in thought or in mien. For the briefest moment her wide, violet eyes met Caddaric's blue gaze before she slowly, circumspectly turned away. She had memories of the stable in which her family had been murdered as well and she must never forget that Cad-

daric had played a part in that act. Feeling particularly
vulnerable with both Heall and Caddaric looming above
her, Jilana remained motionless, afraid of drawing Caddaric's obvious wrath. Clywd, too, remained unmoving,
watching the reactions to his son's entrance with wry
amusement.

Heall's protectiveness served only to worsen Caddaric's mood. "Thus does an Iceni warrior pass his days,"
Caddaric sneered. "Pray do not let me disturb you."

Anger showed on Heall's face as he returned his sword
to his belt. "You bade me guard Jilana—"

"Guard, aye; not entertain," Caddaric snapped irrita-
bly. "While you closet yourself with my slave, rust covers our battle-axes and Iceni youths busy themselves with
the charms of women. 'Twill go badly for us when we
meet the Roman legions if the only blood our young men
have shed is that of virgins!"

"You have repeatedly drilled our warriors and warrior
maids," Clywd interposed smoothly, aware of the blush
which stained Jilana's cheeks at Caddaric's words.
"Naught is amiss."

Caddaric swallowed a harsh retort. The news he was
about to impart would cause misery enough this day.
"You are right, Druid." With a final glare directed at the
top of Jilana's head, he turned to Heall. Caddaric's
expression became less harsh at the look of injured dignity upon the older man's face. "That we are chained to
this place is no fault of yours. My words were hasty and
unjust. Forgive me, old friend."

Jilana's eyes widened. This was the first time she had
heard her Iceni captor apologize or admit he was wrong.
Usually he stormed about the villa with a black look upon
his face, finding fault with any of his people who were
unfortunate enough to attract his attention. Jilana nervously toyed with the long braid of red-gold hair which
draped across her shoulder to coil in her lap. Never had
she encountered a man as harsh and ill-tempered as Caddaric.

"Jilana, I thirst. Bring me wine."

The command brought Jilana's head up with a snap and she stared rebelliously at Caddaric. He had taken the one chair now left in the chamber, and as she watched he stretched his long, heavily muscled legs out in front of him and raised a questioning eyebrow at her. How dare he look so completely at ease, Jilana thought furiously. It crossed her mind to defy Caddaric's order but she quickly discarded the idea. She had no wish to bear the brunt of his mockery when others were present. Grudgingly Jilana rose, poured a cup of wine and offered it to Caddaric.

Caddaric sipped the wine gratefully, then set it aside and allowed his gaze to sweep Clywd and Heall. "Messengers arrived at the palace this morn." The atmosphere in the room altered so swiftly that Caddaric felt the hairs at the back of his neck stand on end. "We now have allies."

Relief washed over Heall's face. "At last! Who are they, Caddaric? The Silures? Ordovices? Brigantes?" Heall rapidly listed the tribes to whom their Queen had appealed.

"The Ordovices." Caddaric chose his words with great care. "Not the entire nation, Heall, but a few of the villages."

Some of the fire went out of Heall's eyes. "A few," he repeated, confused. "How many have joined us, Caddaric?"

"A thousand, perhaps a handful more." Heall's disappointment was as keen as his own; both men had harbored hopes for an alliance among the tribes.

"Traitors!" Heall cried bitterly.

"Nay, Heall, they are not. The western tribes have been nipping at the legions for years: they strike, then retreat to the safety of the mountains as Caratacus taught them. At present their chiefs see no reason to do battle on unfamiliar terrain, particularly since Rome has never fully conquered their territory." Caddaric shrugged philosophically and reached for his wine cup. "Do you not remember Claudius' invasion? We Iceni did not rise as one and join the Catuvellauni to repulse the Roman attack—now we are being repaid in the same coin.''

"Aye," Heall agreed, one hand scrubbing wearily at his craggy face. "Have any other tribes answered the Queen's summons, Caddaric?"

"The Trinovantes are with us." When his announcement was greeted less than enthusiastically, Caddaric reminded Heall, "Between our two tribes and the Ordovices we will number forty thousand, nearly equal to Suetonius' four legions. And, mayhap, we will gain more warriors when news of our victories spreads." Pure loathing curled his lips into a sneer. "And we will have to guard our backs. That Brigantian whore, Cartimandua, will betray us to Rome as she did Caratacus, if she learns of our plans."

Jilana, pale and shaken by the magnitude of the discussion, could nonetheless not resist asking. "Who is this Caratacus? You speak as if he is a god."

"I did not realize you were so ignorant," Caddaric mocked.

"I am not ignorant," Jilana flared back, a rush of color staining her cheeks when Caddaric snorted in disbelief. "I wish only to understand this revolt which has destroyed my life."

Caddaric stared at Jilana, his gaze resting insolently upon the curve of her breasts. Heat seared through his veins, threatening the rigid control Caddaric had imposed upon himself during the past few days. His eyes skimmed upward, pausing briefly on the pulse point in Jilana's slender throat before coming to rest upon the soft fullness of her lips. The warm invitation of her mouth brought a ragged edge to his breathing and when Jilana—unnerved by Caddaric's silence and the forbidding set of his jaw—moistened her lips with the tip of her tongue, Caddaric wrenched his thoughts back to Jilana's question.

"Caratacus could have been the savior of Britannia," Caddaric began in a clipped voice. "His people, the Catuvellauni, led the resistance against the Roman general

Aulus Plautus when he invaded Britannia seventeen years ago. When, in the end, the Catuvellauni were defeated and Caratacus' brother slain in battle, Caratacus gathered his family and fled into the west." Caddaric's eyes darkened as he recalled the epic tales which had reached every corner of the island. "There he welded the Ordovices, Silures and Deceangli into an army which threatened the legions' control not only in the west but throughout the entire island. For years Caratacus and his followers harassed the legions, nearly driving them out of the western territories. Then—although the gods alone know why— Caratacus changed his tactics and decided to fight a pitched battle." Caddaric's mouth twisted. "He was defeated, his forces scattered. His wife and children were captured by the Romans but Caratacus escaped into Brigantia."

"But the Brigantian queen is loyal to Rome," Jilana interrupted. "She is our staunchest ally."

"Even so." Caddaric's voice was flat, yet laced with contempt. "Rome's legions have long stabilized her throne, kept her secure from her people and the husband who knows she is unfit to rule. So, out of gratitude to Rome, Cartimandua betrayed Caratacus to the governor-general."

Jilana swallowed, unable to look away from Caddaric's hard eyes. "What . . . happened then?"

"Caratacus and his family were sent to Rome, where they were pardoned by the Emperor Claudius. A wise man, Claudius," said Caddaric wryly. "Why elevate an enemy to the status of martyr by killing him when, by allowing him to live, he becomes little more than an object of pity? Of course, Claudius' pardon came with the provision that Caratacus and his family remain in Rome as exiles." Caddaric lifted the cup to his lips and drained the wine. "Such is Roman mercy—what is life worth when one must live and die in a foreign land?" He shook himself mentally and thrust the cup at Jilana. "More wine."

Heall had been pacing the room during Caddaric's recitation but now he halted beside the young man and allowed his eyes to light adoringly upon Jilana's delicate form. "She is not responsible for Caratacus' fate. Do not berate her so, Caddaric."

"I did but answer the Roman's question," Caddaric growled. "Should I have been less than truthful?"

"She is but a child, Caddaric, alone and confused," Heall replied. "Should she be punished for events which were not her doing?"

"She is a Roman. Should I thank her for what has befallen this island?" Caddaric countered with a snarl. Jilana returned, offering the wine cup with hands that trembled ever so slightly, and Caddaric accepted it wordlessly. The barbed words of Heall's reprimand gnawed at his conscience, for Caddaric knew they were justified.

"And now, Caddaric, tell us the rest." Clywd's soft voice broke the silence of the bedchamber and three startled pairs of eyes flew to the Druid.

Caddaric inhaled sharply, feeling a part of his soul wither beneath the Druid's piercing blue eyes. Any reprieve, no matter how slight, would be welcome and to that purpose Caddaric raised the cup to his lips and emptied it.

When Caddaric did not answer immediately a cold dread enveloped Jilana. Juno, nay, Jilana prayed silently as she walked, unseeing, to the open gallery doors. Visions of the recurrent nightmare flooded Jilana's brain, rendering her immobile, and she knew with despairing certainty what Caddaric would say.

"Druid," Caddaric began and found he could go no further. He set the wine cup aside and clasped his hands tightly together, wondering how best to impart his news. At last, when the silence threatened to become deafening, Caddaric forced the words from his throat. "Suetonius Paulinus has overrun Mona. The priesthood is dead; the families who sought refuge there slain. The legions have desecrated the altars and are felling the sacred oak groves." Caddaric hesitated. "Shall I describe the Roman attack?"

"Nay." Clywd's eyes lifted from Caddaric to fall upon Jilana's rigid body. "You can tell me naught that I do not already know."

"Aah, I see." Caddaric's tone dissolved into mocking brutality. "I had forgotten your gift of sight. How kind of the gods to allow you to witness the decimation of your fellow priests!"

A spasm of pain contorted Clywd's face. "'Twas not kindness but rather torture. Being a Druid makes me no less a man, Caddaric! I see, I feel, with the same intensity as you. Do you think I enjoyed Mona's destruction? Do you think I laughed as I watched Roman swords render the Druids and innocent families into little more than bloody flesh?" He rose and in two swift steps stood over Caddaric, his thin frame trembling with indignation. "You were twelve when I was taken and sold into slavery; you bought my freedom when you were twenty-two. Know you what I did every day of those ten years? I used the gift you hold in such contempt to discover the fate of my family, and I gave thanks to the gods that they allowed one of my children to live. I saw you grow into manhood under Heall's care and I wept because I was not there. I saw you and your brothers taken by the legions; I saw their deaths and watched when you turned your face and heart from our gods. And I died a little with every passing day because I could not give you succor. Yet still I gave thanks that you were whole of mind and body. The gift of sight is not often kind, but for ten years it was my only comfort. On the day you bought my freedom I wept with gladness that my son, cold and grim though he was, had been returned to me by the gods." Clywd paused to draw a ragged breath. "Though I am allowed to see the future, Caddaric, I cannot alter what will be. That knowledge is my own private torment."

The gash on Caddaric's left cheek showed garishly red against the unexpected pallor of his face. Clywd's revelations—indeed, the tirade itself—were shocking considering the Druid's mild, unassuming nature. After a long moment Caddaric found his voice. "Father, I did not know."

"Only because you never thought to ask," was Clywd's harsh reply. "If you had—had you thought beyond your own mockery—you would have learned long ago that my gift offers both comfort and agony beyond compare." The anger drained from Clywd; he turned wearily and walked toward the gallery doors.

"Father, stay." So seldom did he address Clywd as such that Caddaric felt his tongue twist around the word. Yet, Caddaric now remembered a time when the name had been warmly familiar. "I . . . I would speak with you."

Clywd shook his head. "There is too much to be done; sacrifices and prayers must be offered up for Mona's dead." He paused beside Jilana and spoke in a voice so low that only she could hear. "The gift of vision is a sacred one, child. Open your mind and your heart—and do not fear what you will see."

Before Jilana could reply, the Druid was gone. I am no prophetess, she thought with a shiver of apprehension. I had no visions, only nightmares, dreams of Roman revenge upon the Iceni, and yet . . . Jilana forced her attention to the conversation Caddaric was holding with Heall and listened in growing horror as Caddaric described the Roman assault on Mona as he had heard it from an Ordovician warrior. Unbidden, the specters of her nightmare rose before her eyes; Caddaric's voice faded to an unintelligible drone. It did not matter. Jilana did not need words to know what had transpired upon the Isle of Mona. She had seen it all too often. Mona—that which was now a legend.

Black-robed priests lined Mona's shore, their wild curses mingling with the shrieked taunts the priestesses hurled at the Roman legions across the strait. Interwoven with the holy ones stood the warriors, spears and swords held aloft as their battle cries joined the cacophony which rent the thin shroud of fog surrounding the isle. The magnificent display of Celtic defiance sent a ripple of apprehension through the Roman troops who stood silent

*and unmoving upon the opposite shore. A barked order
came from the Roman officers and all traces of hesitancy
evaporated. The foot soldiers marched in perfect unison
onto the waiting flatboats; the cavalry took to their saddles and, with a counterpoint of creaking leather and
jangling harness, spurred their mounts to the water's edge.
There was a second, strident command and the legionaries surged forward.*

Jilana closed her eyes, her fingers curling into her palms
as she fought off the remainder of the vision. She would
not view the carnage again! Through sheer force of will
the images receded but the sounds remained: the sound of
sword meeting sword, the cries of the wounded, the terrified screams of the innocent children whose families had
sought refuge on Mona.

"Jilana! *Jilana!*" A pair of hands gripped her shoulders, roughly shaking her from the last vestiges of her
trance, and Jilana gasped at the pain Caddaric was unwittingly inflicting. "By the gods, woman, you try my
patience! I am in no mood for your defiance today!"
Caddaric released her so unexpectedly that Jilana staggered backward into the door frame.

"Your mood is all too plain," Jilana retorted, her anger flaring at his callous treatment. "You are fit company only for scorpions! I do not wonder Clywd has never
before claimed you as son within my hearing. How great
must be his shame at having spawned such as you!"

Caddaric's arm arced backward; his eyes darkened before the gathering storm of his anger. Jilana raised her
chin, rebellion snapping in the depths of her violet eyes.
They stared at each other for a long moment, the air between them charged with electricity until, grudgingly,
Caddaric lowered his arm. This woman sorely tried his
control and he would not allow her that weapon. "My
mood," he stated perversely, his lips curling, "is not your
concern. Nor is my father. You exist only to serve me, to
fulfill my wants."

Jilana flew at him then, her fingers curved to rake the
smirk from his face. Laughing, Caddaric caught her wrists

and twisted them easily behind her back. "Release me," Jilana hissed, oblivious to the fact that her body was intimately molded against Caddaric. "Release me or by all the gods I will—"

"Scratch out my eyes?" Caddaric chuckled mirthlessly. "I have sheathed your claws, little *wicca*, and this time you have no dagger."

The blunt reminder of the fate of her only weapon brought Jilana up short. On the morning following the Iceni uprising Caddaric had awakened first and found the dagger embedded in the headboard. He had risen, shaken Jilana out of her slumber and, while she watched, returned to the bed and casually snapped the blade at the hilt. Wordlessly, Caddaric had dropped the useless dagger hilt onto her lap and quit the chamber. Though Caddaric had never spoken of the incident, from that time forward no weapons of any kind—save the sword Heall carried for Jilana's protection—were allowed within the bedchamber.

"I will not always be defenseless," Jilana spat. "One day, Briton, you will pay for the way you have treated me."

"Have you been treated badly?" Caddaric mockingly inquired. "I think not. Your meals are brought to you here in this room, as are your daily baths."

"Baths which you insist upon watching!"

Caddaric grinned and nodded. "I am certain others, including Lucius, have viewed you thus, so you need not pretend shyness with me." Jilana's indignant gasp passed unnoticed as he continued. "In truth, little wicca, your life is hardly changed, save for the fact that you no longer pass your days gossiping. Although," he added, recalling the scene upon which he had just intruded, "even that may not have changed."

Jilana's voice, when she finally found it, shook with rage. "Do not expect my gratitude, Briton! I repay your *kindness* every night by changing the dressing on your leg."

"Hardly an odious task." Slowly, Caddaric released Jilana's wrists and slid his hands up her back. "I could banish you to the kitchen to work beside the other captives during the day and take your rest in the stable at night."

"Then do so," Jilana challenged with false bravado. She had encountered the other captives only once, when Caddaric had at last allowed her the freedom of the courtyard. Recognizing one of her mother's dearest friends in the bedraggled group of slaves, Jilana had rushed to greet her fellow countrymen, only to find herself the object of scorn and derision. Whore, the Romans had named her in their hatred. Iceni harlot. A slut who clung to her worthless life by gracing the enemy's couch. The taunts had grown uglier, hands had yanked at her hair, and when Jilana had sought to explain her situation she had been shoved to the ground. Jilana shuddered to think what might have happened had Heall not come to her rescue. Heall's low growl and menacing look had sent her attackers scurrying away and Jilana had fled to the safety of her bedchamber without a word of thanks. Since that day she had ventured into the courtyard only when the other captives were occupied elsewhere.

Caddaric studied the set of Jilana's jaw, irritation mingling with admiration. He knew full well what had happened between Jilana and the Roman slaves and he silently acknowledged the courage it took for Jilana to calmly issue such a challenge. "Nay, Jilana, I will not. Lovely you are, but I doubt you could bake so much as a wheat cake without reducing it to a cinder."

With a furious exclamation Jilana twisted away and paced about the room. "If I am so worthless, then give me up. Let another deal with my inadequacies." The slender back she presented to Caddaric stiffened resolutely. "Or set me free."

"Never!" Caddaric's bark spun Jilana around and a few strides of his long, powerful legs brought him within inches of her. "Understand this, Roman: you are mine until I decide otherwise. Neither tears nor pretty entreaties nor shrewish behavior will sway me—they will only anger me.'' He paused to allow Jilana to take his words to heart while he casually wound the thick, red-gold braid around his hand, drawing her ever closer. ''Beware, my dream witch. I could break you, snap you with my bare hands as if you were nothing more than dry kindling.''

The breath caught in Jilana's throat; her eyes darkened with apprehension when her breasts brushed Caddaric's lower chest. She realized, suddenly, that at some point Heall had left the chamber, and she was alone with Caddaric. That realization and Caddaric's strangely taut expression sent a premonitory chill through Jilana.

The faint tremor brought a raised eyebrow from Caddaric and he allowed his gaze to wander from Jilana's face to the hollow of her throat. Her pulse fluttered wildly and Caddaric succumbed to temptation and touched a forefinger to the sensitive spot. How delicate she is, Caddaric thought as his hand easily circled the slender column of her throat. The image of Jilana rising in damp splendor from her bath flashed into Caddaric's brain and sent a sharp pang through his loins. Desire flared within him, a desire he knew must be carefully controlled. He had held himself in check during the past few days, allowing Jilana as much time as could be spared in which to adjust to and accept her new life. But time, that most precious commodity, was no more. Boadicea would march soon and battles would follow and he would once again face death. Jilana's reprieve had ended with the return of the Iceni messengers.

Jilana understood, instinctively, the resolve which hardened Caddaric's features. Panicked, she turned to flee only to be brought up short by Caddaric's hold on her hair. Tears of pain and humiliation welled in the violet eyes as Caddaric slowly, inexorably, drew her across the room to the bed.

''Briton, nay,'' Jilana managed to whisper. Caddaric was systematically unbraiding her hair and Jilana frantically sought to divert his attention. ''What if Heall returns?''

"He will not," Caddaric stated with such confidence that Jilana believed him.

"The gallery doors—"

"The villa is empty, as is the courtyard." Caddaric combed his fingers through her unbound hair, glorying in its color and texture.

"Then you should be with your men—" Jilana's voice died as his fingers skimmed the flesh at the back of her neck. Against her will, tiny bolts of lightning danced across her skin at the contact. Praise the gods her back was to Caddaric; Jilana could not have borne his mocking laughter had he seen the color which now rose in her cheeks.

The electric spark raced through Caddaric as well; it tautened the muscles of his arms into iron bands and tripped the steady rhythm of his heart. "My men," Caddaric murmured in reply as his hands fell to Jilana's shoulders, "grow weary of my biting tongue, and I seek sweeter company than they afford."

"Then go to Ede," Jilana returned in a voice that was far less emphatic than she would have wished. "You will find no comfort here."

"Shall I not?" An odd smile softened the line of Caddaric's mouth and his hands persuasively kneaded the stiff set of Jilana's muscles.

A soothing warmth flowed from Caddaric's hands, threatening the stability of Jilana's senses. "Caddaric, let me go." When he neither replied nor loosened his grip, Jilana swallowed back the cry of despair which rose in her throat. "I will not play your whore, Briton," Jilana lashed out in a strangled voice when Caddaric pulled her back against the solid wall of his chest.

"So ready to judge, to accuse. Your temper matches your hair, little witch." Caddaric lowered his face to Jilana's hair and rubbed his cheek against the soft, sweet-smelling tresses. With a muted sigh, Caddaric ran his hands down the slender length of Jilana's arms, then crossed his own arms beneath the swell of her breasts. "I do not ask you to play my whore." He briefly closed his eyes, savoring the feeling of Jilana securely enfolded against him. "You offered me flowers once."

Caddaric's breath danced across Jilana's cheek and a tremor coursed through her. "That was before I knew you."

Slowly, ever so slowly, Caddaric withdrew one of his arms and turned Jilana until she stood facing him. "And now, wicca? Do you know me now?" At her shaky nod, Caddaric placed his forefinger beneath her chin and raised Jilana's face toward his own. "What am I, Jilana?"

Jilana's mouth went dry. "My enemy," she answered, amazed by the gentleness in Caddaric's eyes and touch. "My enemy," she repeated, as if to reassure herself of the fact. In truth, she thought hazily, Caddaric appeared far less threatening than he had only minutes before.

"I would not treat my enemy thus." As he spoke, Caddaric's lips traversed her brow, her cheek, and then, with curious restraint, hovered only a breath away from her mouth. "Do you not weary of our constant bickering, of the barbed words we fling at each other?"

Jilana nodded. The need to be constantly on guard whenever Caddaric was near left her nerves in tatters but she had no choice. Caddaric held her as slave, subjugated her will to his and made a mockery of her pride. But 'twas the ghosts of her family which gave strength to Jilana's legs and drove her out of Caddaric's embrace.

"Jilana!" Stunned by her unexpected resistance, Caddaric watched in disbelief as she fled to the opposite corner of the room.

"Stay away from me," Jilana cried when Caddaric took a step toward her. Aah, Juno, how could she have allowed him to touch her so intimately? The blood of her family stained his hands!

"Nay, Roman, I will not." Blue eyes narrowed, Caddaric stalked across the floor toward his prey. The arm of the chair struck his thigh and with a savage oath he picked the chair up in one large hand and sent it splintering against the door.

Jilana's heart pounded erratically at the violence in Caddaric's face. She wanted to flee, to hide, to throw herself on the floor and beg his mercy, but she did not. To cower before the Briton was the coward's way and Jilana, the screams of her family crying out to her from the grave, was no coward. "I hate you," Jilana spat. "Murderer! Barbarian!"

The taunts were the final goad to Caddaric's temper. With a swiftness uncommon for a man his size, he snared Jilana's wrist and pulled her against him. "I am no murderer," Caddaric snarled, his eyes blazing down into hers.

"Liar!" Jilana twisted wildly in his grip, but to no avail. "My family's blood stains your hands."

"Your family is lost to you," Caddaric agreed harshly, "but not by my sword. And as for your hate," he continued ruthlessly, ignoring Jilana's cry, "I care not. You have exhausted my patience, Roman, and I will wait no longer for what is rightfully mine."

Before Jilana could protest his right of possession, Caddaric had scooped her into his arms, retraced his steps across the room, and tossed her carelessly upon the bed. Jilana struggled upright, fear coursing in icy waves through her veins as she took in the implacable lines of Caddaric's face. "I will never willingly submit to you." A muscle leaped in Caddaric's jaw and Jilana nearly fainted at her own audacity. Good Juno, I did not mean to speak those words aloud!

"Willingly?" Caddaric studied her curiously, his head tipped slightly to one side. Jilana's first thought was that he had reconsidered, that with Ede so close at hand and so obviously willing, he had no wish for an unwilling woman. Then Caddaric smiled. His was a nice smile, chiseled lips turning upward to reveal white, even teeth, but 'twas so devoid of warmth that Jilana's heart sank. His smile was oddly amused, like a god enjoying the feeble struggles of some hapless mortal. "Willingly," Caddaric reiterated. "You mistake me, Roman; I do not care whether you are willing or not. You belong to me and I intend to have you." To clarify his meaning, Caddaric pulled his tunic over his head and tossed the garment aside. Heedless of the color which rushed to Jilana's cheeks and the way she quickly looked away from his half-nude body, Caddaric leaned one knee on the bed. "Come here, Jilana."

I am lost, Jilana thought wretchedly. He means to have me and I cannot stop him.

"I said, come here." Impatience laced Caddaric's voice and Jilana uttered a brief prayer that he would not hurt her too badly. Reluctantly she rose to her knees in front of Caddaric, her eyes fixed on the bed linens. "Look at me, Roman."

This second command was even harsher than the first and Jilana forced her gaze upward. Caddaric's narrow waist flared into an uncompromisingly male chest thickly covered by a wedge of brown, curling hair. It seemed to fill Jilana's entire field of vision and she swallowed in an effort to relieve the sudden constriction in her throat. She pulled her eyes away from the disturbing sight and nervously glanced at the bronze torque which circled Caddaric's neck. The torque was intricately scrolled; the two ends, fashioned into wolves' heads, met in the hollow of the Briton's throat. The hollow was accentuated with each breath he drew and Jilana quickly finished her perusal and raised her eyes to Caddaric's. Blue, so blue, was Jilana's first thought as their gazes met and held. As turbulent, as ever-changing, as the sea surrounding Britannia—and filled with a sadness that clawed its way into her very soul. I will not soften to this man, she told her crumbling defenses. He is my enemy, responsible for the destruction of all I held dear.

"A little peace, Jilana," Caddaric murmured, entranced by the confusion reflected in her eyes. "Is it so much to ask?"

The quiet plea breached Jilana's defiance as nothing else could. She knew what Caddaric was asking, knew that she should hate him for it, but she could not. Her anger and defiance gave way to the devastating loneliness Jilana had kept at bay during the past days. *A little peace,* her mind echoed temptingly. "Nay, Briton," she sighed at last. "'Tis little enough to ask."

Her voice was so small that for a moment Caddaric was not certain Jilana had spoken. He searched her face, seeking some sign of treachery or the defiance she hurled at him like daggers. But no; even if he had imagined the words, Caddaric could not mistake the surrender in those violet depths. Victorious, Caddaric caught Jilana in his arms and crushed her lips beneath his own. She rested lightly against his chest, but the impression of her breasts burned through the fabric of her stola, searing his flesh. Blind to all else save the desire singing in his blood, Caddaric assaulted the fragile barrier of Jilana's lips and pushed beyond to explore the recesses of her mouth. By the gods she is sweet, Caddaric thought as his tongue probed and tasted. One hand cradling the back of Jilana's head, the other splayed across the small of her back, Caddaric slowly pressed Jilana to the bed. Off balance, Jilana instinctively clutched at Caddaric's shoulders and he groaned at the touch of her hands.

The heavy, masculine body came to rest familiarly upon her own and Jilana shivered. Caught in the bargain to which she had agreed, Jilana was uncertain as to what was expected of her. She lay quietly, allowing Caddaric an unhindered investigation of her mouth while her mind absorbed the impact of the way he touched her. His hand moved upward from the small of her back to the place between her shoulder blades and Jilana felt her breasts being lightly, repeatedly, crushed against the wall of his chest. The hand tangled in her hair held her still for the kiss, but when Jilana hesitantly turned her head aside, Caddaric allowed the movement. Abandoning her mouth, his lips trailed a warm path past her ear and down the slender column of her throat until they reached the neckline of her stola. Tiny darts of pleasure raced along Jilana's spine but when Caddaric's tongue touched her flesh, her eyes flew open. Her surprised gaze collided with Caddaric's inquiring one and she felt a crimson blush spread upward from her neck to her forehead.

With the deliberation of a master strategist, Caddaric slowly withdrew his hand from Jilana's back and raised himself from the delightful cushion she provided until there was enough space for his hand to lay claim to her ribcage. Beneath the heel of his hand Jilana's heart fluttered unevenly. Deliberately, provocatively, Caddaric brushed the tip of one breast with a callused fingertip and felt Jilana's heart leap against his palm. He repeated the action and Jilana gave a smothered gasp and tried to shield herself with her arms.

"Nay, wicca, you will not deny me," Caddaric growled. His eyes narrowing slightly, he parted the flimsy defense and drank in the sight of her hardened nipple straining against the fabric of the gown. Before Jilana could guess his meaning, Caddaric's lips closed around the sensitive point while his hand surrounded the fullness of her breast.

A bolt of pleasure so intense she thought she would die of it shot through Jilana. Her breathing seemed suspended, her body tortured by some inner flame that found its way from her breasts to the center of her loins, and then Caddaric turned his attention to her other breast. A soft cry escaped Jilana's lips and her fists curled fiercely into the bed linens as she fought her body's urge to writhe within the embrace. Not for the world would she have Caddaric think her defiant, for then he would cease this strange magic in which her newly awakened senses were delighting.

Caddaric nibbled his way back along Jilana's throat until he once again claimed her mouth. His kiss was long and deep, brimming with the same intense need that sent his hips arching reflexively into Jilana's. One of his hands slid down to cup a buttock and hold her still against the intimate contact while his lips traveled to the sensitive spot just below her ear. "Jilana. Jilana," he whispered thickly. The way she trembled beneath his touch aroused Caddaric even further and he nipped sensuously at her earlobe. "Why do you not respond to me? Why do you not touch me?"

Jilana—soaring in a world of pure physical pleasure—struggled to make sense of the words he spoke. Respond? Touch? Caddaric's hand stroked the length of her thigh and the caress was another shock to her already spinning senses. Jilana forced her eyes open and met Caddaric's dark blue, turbulent gaze. "You wish me to touch you?" she asked breathlessly as he feathered a kiss across her mouth.

"Aye." All the yearning in his soul was contained in that one word, for at this moment—seeing the wide, violet eyes so soft and yielding—Caddaric wanted nothing more than the touch of Jilana's delicate hands.

Hesitantly Jilana reached out to the broad shoulders. Her fingertips skimmed across flesh which was forcefully stretched over bulging musculature and, intrigued, she investigated the prominent biceps of Caddaric's upper arms. Muscles tensed and rippled beneath her exploration and Jilana found herself remembering the incredible strength of his arms. How warm he is, Jilana thought as she traced Caddaric's collarbone from his shoulders to the base of his throat. Even the torque was warm, radiating the heat of its owner.

Caddaric went still beneath Jilana's touch but the pounding of his heart seemed to vibrate through his entire being. The very nature of Jilana's caress spoke of her innocence and Caddaric willed himself to move slowly, to be patient with any fears—Jilana's hands flattened themselves against his chest and he groaned as they blazed symmetrical trails down his torso, only to stop when they reached the barrier of the loincloth.

Jilana's exploration ceased with Caddaric's harshly indrawn breath, but her fingernails curled into his chest when he rolled to his back, carrying her with him. The skirt of her gown twisted upward around her thighs and as she lay with her legs firmly trapped between his, Jilana reveled in the feeling of his hair-roughened legs rasping against her softer flesh. Strong hands circled her waist, drawing her upward over that long, hard body until she was uncomfortably aware of the surging masculinity which only his loincloth held in check. With one hand at the small of her back, Caddaric pressed Jilana against the blatant evidence of his arousal and she gasped at the fiery spear of longing his action produced.

Caddaric framed Jilana's face between his hands. "Kiss me, wicca."

Mesmerized, Jilana obeyed. Her lips softly molded themselves to his, and this time, when Caddaric's tongue begged entrance to her mouth, Jilana shyly welcomed him. Swept along by mutual passion they clung together, their bodies melting against each other in a vain attempt to deny the material which still separated them. Caddaric's hand found and massaged the back of Jilana's knee and continued the sensuous motion along her leg until he reached the juncture of her thighs. The nest of tight auburn curls teased his fingertips and he brushed against it. The low sound issuing from Jilana's throat delighted him and he probed further, initiating her into the joys of the flesh.

Jilana shuddered at the pleasure splintering through her loins. She buried her face in the curve of Caddaric's neck as his fingers stole the breath from her lungs and the strength from her limbs. As though in a dream, Jilana heard Caddaric murmuring soft, unintelligible phrases that seduced her heart as surely as he was seducing her body. Caught in his own trap, Caddaric lazily opened his eyes—and froze.

There, silhouetted in the open gallery doors, the sun burnishing his fair hair into a golden halo, stood Artair. For several moments Caddaric lay motionless, stunned disbelief holding him in place on the bed; and then, with the sudden fury of a summer storm, outraged anger poured through him. Uttering curses that consigned Artair to the gods of the Iceni underworld, Caddaric flung Jilana aside and hurled himself from the bed toward the gallery doors. Grinning, Artair sidestepped the charge and drew his sword in one fluid motion.

Jilana levered herself upright just in time to see Caddaric skid to a halt with Artair's sword point only inches from his throat. Like figures in some terrible mosaic the two men faced each other, silently assessing the other's ability to continue the one-sided battle. Horrified, Jilana watched as the muscles rippled across Caddaric's wide shoulders and his large hands flexed, then curled themselves into fists which seemed to her every bit as lethal as Artair's sword.

"Nay, Caddaric," Artair warned as he gently pressed the metal point to Caddaric's throat. Jilana's low cry echoed through the room but neither man spared her so much as a glance. "I came at your father's request. The Queen has called for a meeting of her council and Clywd wishes you to attend."

"When?" Caddaric's voice was low, clipped. A muscle bunched in his jaw at the slow, impudent smile that curled Artair's mouth, but the blade against his flesh prevented him from wreaking havoc upon the other man.

"Clywd said immediately. But," Artair's gaze flickered to Jilana, "I am sure he would understand should you decide to tarry."

"I will be there," Caddaric ground out. His blue eyes glittered darkly as Artair nodded and slowly backed away. With a violent curse, Caddaric stepped back into the room.

The gallery doors slammed closed beneath the force of Caddaric's hands, accompanied by the sound of splintering wood. Jilana stared at the fissure which appeared in the once-solid panel of oak, allowing a slice of sunlight to carve its way across the floor. Caddaric's next words did nothing to alleviate Jilana's sudden resurgence of fear.

"Artair will pay for his intrusion. I swear it!" Caddaric swung on Jilana, eyes narrowing at the sight of her pale thighs. "Cover yourself—or do you relish the thought of being exposed to any man who happens by?"

Stung by his words, Jilana scrambled from the bed and nervously smoothed the wrinkled material over her hips. Her hands trembled and her knees threatened to buckle— a legacy of Caddaric's kisses, although she told herself otherwise. "I did not beg to be raped in the full light of day," she reminded him tightly. "If you remember—"

"Rape!" The single word was like a roll of thunder and Caddaric whitened beneath his tan. His hands came to rest upon his hips, startlingly dark against the white of his loincloth. "By the gods, you dare call it rape?"

Jilana swallowed convulsively, regretting her words, but too proud and stubborn to back down. "You threatened me, held me against my will...." Her voice trailed off at the look in Caddaric's eyes. There was anger there but something else as well. A brief flash of pain.

"Rape," Caddaric repeated, feeling as though Jilana had driven a spear into his vitals. He had shown her tenderness, more tenderness than he could recall showing any other human being, man or woman. And she called it *rape*! Without a word, Caddaric located his tunic and shrugged it on. Brushing by Jilana, he opened the trunk containing his possessions and removed a pair of soft leather boots. Seating himself on the edge of the bed, Caddaric pulled on the boots, then quickly laced and tied the thongs so that the leather was wrapped securely against his muscular calves. When he rose, the hurt twisting through him was well concealed beneath implacable features. When he finally spoke, his voice, too, was devoid of all emotion. "In my absence, Roman, you will put this room to right." Jilana nodded, her red-gold hair shimmering like liquid fire, and Caddaric fought the urge to bury his hands in the silken mass. Instead, he turned on his heel and quit the chamber before his actions turned Jilana's accusation into truth.

Warily, expecting Caddaric to reappear, Jilana approached the chamber door and peered into the hallway. It was empty, and from below came the sound of a door closing, marking Caddaric's passage. Relieved, Jilana closed her own door and surveyed the shambles of the bedchamber. The chair Caddaric had so easily tossed aside was irreparable, fit only for kindling, and the bed linens were draped accusingly over the foot of the bed until they puddled on the floor. Jilana made her way to the bed, her cheeks flaming when she noticed the indentation she and Caddaric had left upon the mattress. What insanity had possessed her? What madness had Caddaric brought forth with his touch? Pricked by guilt, confused by all that had transpired, she mechanically made up the bed and set about straightening the room. 'Twas easier to take refuge in physical labor than sort out her chaotic thoughts. And yet, she could not forget the tender strength with which Caddaric had held her.

CADDARIC HAD NO SUCH OUTLET. He sat beside his father in the great council chamber, listening to Boadicea outline her plans for the Iceni in a calm, strong voice, while a part of his mind conjured various means of exacting retribution from Artair. Such daydreams came to an end, however, when the Queen spoke of the upcoming march. That the Iceni must march and carry the revolt to the Roman legions was a strategy Caddaric supported, but a feeling of dread settled over him as he listened to Boadicea describe the composition of the Iceni column. Imagining the march, Caddaric's blood turned colder by degrees. His distress must have shown on his face, for Boadicea's eyes narrowed as she paced by him.

"This plan has been most carefully laid out by my advisors and myself," the Queen stated when she resumed her seat. "However, if any of you have concerns I will, of course, be willing to listen." Her gaze swept the room twice before finally coming to rest upon a frowning Caddaric. Carefully, Boadicea settled herself against the back of the chair. "Caddaric, your father was most insistent that you be allowed to attend this council. Have you any comment upon our course of action?"

After a moment's hesitation Caddaric nodded and rose gracefully to his feet. "The plan is sound, my Queen, but..." He glanced at the members of the council, then met Boadicea's suddenly hard stare with a cool one of his own. "'Twould be wisest, I believe, to leave the women and children behind." The protests Caddaric had anticipated erupted and he welcomed them. The delay gave him precious time in which to painstakingly choose his next words.

Two bright spots of color dotted Boadicea's cheeks. Clywd was her most trusted advisor, the only Druid she allowed to give counsel; Caddaric had earned her trust as well, but Boadicea was queen enough not to take his disagreement lightly. She raised her hand in a royal command for silence, and when the chieftains obeyed, Boadicea favored Caddaric with a brittle smile. "I trust you will explain yourself, Caddaric."

Caddaric nodded again, not missing the undercurrent of anger in Boadicea's voice. Not for the first time, he wished he were a gifted orator instead of a staid, plodding soldier. Perhaps then the Queen would give his words the importance they deserved. "We must move swiftly to engage the Romans, before they have time to summon reinforcements from Gaul."

"You state the obvious," Boadicea interrupted impatiently. "But since the governor-general, Suetonius, is off Britannia's western coast, raping Mona, I scarcely think he will have learned enough to send to Gaul."

"But the legate of the Ninth Hispana may have learned of our revolt and taken it upon himself to send for reinforcements." Caddaric shifted uneasily. "Because time is of the essence, it is vital that our march not be hampered in any way. To bring our women and children with us is folly. We must leave them behind. We must—"

"—fight like Romans?" A voice from behind Caddaric finished bitingly. Caddaric stiffened, but did not turn to face his accuser; instead he kept his eyes steadfastly upon his Queen. "We are Iceni; our women follow us into battle and some fight at our side and our children watch and learn what it means to be an Iceni warrior."

"And because of them we will travel at a fraction of the speed of the Roman force," Caddaric cut in. "This time we cannot afford that particular luxury."

"You were too long among the Romans," another voice taunted. "Have you forgotten our ways? Or has your

Roman slave softened your courage as well as your manhood?''

The reminder of Jilana tapped a primitive reservoir within Caddaric. This time he spun around, his hand falling to the hilt of his sword. His attacker, a tall, burly man, did likewise. Within seconds, space had been cleared around the two men and they circled each other warily, swords drawn and glinting wickedly. Caddaric moved first, his sword making a swift, downward arc to meet his opponent's blade with a harsh, metallic clang. He fought to disarm, not to kill, but the other man did not suffer from such motives. His sword flashed through the air with deadly intent and Caddaric was hard pressed to keep his defense harmless. Years of training as well as his own instinct threatened to take control and allow Caddaric to end what he knew to be an uneven contest, but he held doggedly to innocuous parries. Perspiration trickled down Caddaric's chest and back as he warded off blow after blow. Insanity, Caddaric's mind cried out when he glimpsed the battle lust in his opponent's eyes. *We fight each other instead of the Romans. If Iceni fight Iceni, how much hope is there for an alliance between the tribes?* The momentary lapse in concentration was nearly Caddaric's undoing. His guard wavered and even as he corrected his error, he felt a burning sensation along his right upper arm.

Caddaric fell back a step, feinted to his right and, when his opponent followed, concentrated all of his strength into a double-handed, reverse blow. His sword sang through the air in a wide, flat arc; blade clashed against blade with a numbing force that ripped the weapon from his opponent's grasp. Instantly, Caddaric drew back and pressed the point of his sword against the other man's heart.

"Thank your gods that I am not a Roman," Caddaric harshly told his opponent, "for if I were, you would be dead." The other man said nothing, merely glared and tried to rub some feeling back into his arm. An ominous silence blanketed the council chamber as Caddaric grimly lowered and sheathed his weapon. He turned back to face Boadicea, too aware of the burning ache of his wound and the blood running down his arm to worry about his lack of eloquence or to remember that he should couch his advice in tactful words. "When the legions come, my Queen, and they will, they will be unencumbered by children and baggage carts. Caius Suetonius Paulinus is a soldier first, a governor second. He may be occupied on Mona, but the moment he receives word of our rebellion, he will force-march his legions across the breadth of this island to crush us. To defeat him we must plan well and be quick enough to counter his every move. Otherwise we are doomed."

"We are not doomed," Boadicea replied in a voice so filled with royal hauteur that all eyes turned to her. "Already our number almost equals Suetonius' legions and when word of our victories spreads, more tribes will join our war band. By the time we face Suetonius, the sheer weight of our force will crush him." She fixed a blatantly skeptical Caddaric with a repressive stare. "Our final victory over the Romans will be remembered for generations, immortalized by our bards. Our dead and the dead of Mona scream for vengeance and we shall heed their cries. We have no need for doubters within our ranks, Caddaric."

Her challenge scourged Caddaric's pride. Stiffly, he moved toward Boadicea, his injured arm dragging his sword from its scabbard as he went. Caddaric heard the whisper of metal against metal and, without looking, knew that the Queen's guards had drawn their weapons. Was he *so* different? Had the years spent away from his tribe changed him so much that his loyalty was in doubt? The thought brought a bitter taste to his mouth. He stopped in front of Boadicea and, ignoring the pain his action would cause, hurled his sword to her feet. The gesture was time-honored: that of a warrior promising loyalty to his overlord. "Our law says that all may speak freely in council. Aye, I harbor doubts, my Queen, but they are of strategy, not of where my loyalty lies. I pledged my sword to your house upon my return. I am yours unto death—unless you forswear me.''

Boadicea allowed her gaze to wander slowly over Caddaric. Blood ran down his arm in crimson rivulets; it stained his hand and dripped from his fingertips to spatter the floor at his feet. Camulos, Boadicea swore silently, how can we wage a war against Rome when we come to blows in council? Rising, she snatched up Caddaric's sword and faced her chieftains with the weapon gripped in both hands. "This ends now," she said angrily. "Enough Iceni blood will be shed by Romans in the months to come—we have none to spill over petty squabbles and old feuds." Boadicea swept Caddaric's sword about her in a flat arc that encompassed all her advisors. "As chieftains, I will hold you responsible for the behavior of your people and for enforcing my will. The punishment for those who would indulge their tempers in spite of my command is banishment!" The heavy silence that followed her pronouncement told Boadicea that her command would be enforced, and she offered up a quick, silent prayer to the Earth Mother that she had not pushed her people too far. Banishment from one's tribe was tantamount to a living death sentence: a warrior's weapons were taken from him, his possessions confiscated, he was escorted to the tribe's border and warned, on pain of death, never to return. He would wander for the rest of his life, never truly accepted by another tribe and eyed with suspicion wherever he went. Word spread quickly among the Celtic tribes of Britannia. If only Prasutagus were still alive, Boadicea thought wearily. He, with his flair for diplomacy, would have known how to weld the Iceni and the Trinovantes into a cohesive war band without resorting to such dire threats. Boadicea had never missed her beloved husband more than at this moment.

Enough! Prasutagus was dead and she held the fate of her people in her hands. Boadicea carefully lowered the sword and offered it, hilt first, to Caddaric. "Take back your sword and keep your vow to my house. I have need of a warrior such as you."

Boadicea waited while Caddaric resumed his seat next to Clywd. As soon as his son was within reach, Clywd hurriedly examined the wound and dressed it with a wide strip of cloth taken from one of the pouches hanging from his belt.

Throughout the process—accomplished quickly and with a minimum of fuss by the Druid—Caddaric looked chagrined by the attention, and Boadicea hid a smile by settling carefully back onto her chair. Anger spent, she addressed the assemblage in a calm, sure tone. "Our women and children will come with us; in this we have no choice. The Ninth Legion lies to our north, at full strength. As Caddaric has stated, when the legate, Petilius Cerealis, learns of our revolt he will take action. Undoubtedly he will move against us, and we dare not leave the women and children behind to face his soldiers."

"What of our crops?" one of the chieftains wanted to know. "The fire of Beltane has not yet been kindled." Beltane, the "fire of god," celebrated the return of spring and signified the beginning of a new growing season. The Roman interdict against the Druids may have forced the priesthood from the occupied territories, but the tribes had not forsaken their religion. Instead, the royal family had assumed the responsibility for the three major festivals: Beltane, in the spring; Lughnasadh, in honor of the sun god Lugh, held in the summer; and Samh'in, the festival of the dead, celebrated in autumn. The Roman conquerors, wisely, had not objected so long as the Druids were not present. And in private, the people had continued to worship the gods of their fathers rather than the new Roman gods, and awaited the return of the Druids.

"We will observe Beltane," Boadicea assured the chieftains with a smile, "but not here, for we cannot spare the time. When Beltane arrives, we will be on the march; 'twill please the gods to have the Druids light the fire amidst the ruin of a Roman fort. As for the crops," she shrugged, as if the matter were of little concern, "again it is a matter of time. We cannot plant our fields, so we will empty our storehouses for the march and take what we need from our enemy's granaries as we conquer his cities. We will be well provisioned when we return, never fear." Boadicea rose. "Tonight we will celebrate our alliance with the Trinovantes. There will be a great feast upon the plain and later, with the rise of the moon, the Druids who have so recently joined us will offer sacrifices to the Morrigan, goddess of battle, to Camulos, god of war, and to Andrasta, goddess of victory."

It was the final break with Roman authority, this public worship of the old gods, and the chieftains and advisors were on their feet in an instant, shouting their approval. Boadicea left the council chamber on the buoyant tide of their voices. Caddaric bowed as she passed, then looked to his father. "You do not look pleased, Clywd. Surely you wish to see the people return to their own gods."

Clywd smiled. "The people have never forsaken the gods, Caddaric; our Queen's pronouncement changes only the manner in which they shall worship, not the substance." He took Caddaric's good arm and guided him from the chamber. "Boadicea is wise in using the presence of the Druids to her advantage."

"Boadicea use the Druids?" Caddaric snorted. "'Tis more likely the other way around."

"Think you so?" Clywd's face grew taut. "How long will it be before news of Mona spreads through the city and the allies' camp?"

"Not long." Caddaric winced as his arm was jostled by the crowd. "By the midday meal, mayhap; certainly by nightfall."

"And the reaction to it?"

"Outrage, anger." Caddaric frowned. "Why do I answer questions for which you have answers?"

"So that you may learn there is more to making war than following orders and killing the enemy," Clywd replied sharply. "Now then, our people are angered by the destruction of Mona, and with it the core of our priests, judges, bards, seers and teachers. Those lately arrived to the Iceni cause waver; they begin to wonder if mayhap they should not have stayed in their villages where the Romans might do no more than confiscate their food. Suddenly, Boadicea announces that there are, indeed, priests in our midst. These priests have dedicated themselves to her and will offer up sacrifices to her cause. What will happen to those who have doubts?''

Caddaric was silent for a moment and then replied thoughtfully, "They will see the war as twofold: to avenge Boadicea and the dead of Mona." The Roman attack upon Mona struck at the very heart of Celtic beliefs. As long as Mona existed, the tribes could pretend that they were not totally dominated by Rome, that one day the Roman invaders would leave and all would be as it once had been. Mona's fate had ended such pretense. The Romans had destroyed Mona to end the political unrest which sprang from the Druid priesthood. What Caius Suetonius Paulinus had failed to recognize, however, was the mystical reverence in which Mona was held by the Celtic populace. "There will be no doubters," Caddaric concluded. "The people will put aside the quarrel of tribe against tribe in order to wreak vengeance upon the transgressors."

Clywd nodded. "And when word spreads among the other tribes, Boadicea will have more allies flocking to her war band. Fate has given our Queen the only weapon which has a chance of uniting the tribes; let us pray she has the wisdom to use it properly."

Caddaric lifted his face to the sunlight as they left the palace courtyard and stepped into the street. "It is possible," he murmured.

"What is, my son?"

"That Boadicea may succeed after all." Caddaric looked down at his father and gave him a wild, reckless grin.

JILANA SAT on the edge of the bed, awaiting Caddaric's return to the villa. In his absence she had tidied the room and carried the pieces of the ruined chair to the kitchen to be used as fuel for the ovens. The hostility of the other

Romans she encountered had been expected, and Jilana had forced herself to ignore the lewd comments and openly resentful looks. 'Twas bad enough to fear the Iceni, she would not hide out of fear of her own countrymen. She was as much a victim of the revolt as they, even if they did not believe it. Back in her chamber, Jilana had taken up her brush and begun the task of restoring order to her hair while her mind pondered the drastic changes in her life. The hate which had bolstered her resolve to be avenged upon the Iceni had slowly dissipated as she came to know Clywd and Heall. They told her of their life before the Roman conquest, of their village, their ways. The invasion had taken much away from them, and not just in tangible things. Iceni pride had been dealt a hard blow when King Prasutagus had sued for peace with the Emperor Claudius rather than lift a sword against the invasion. But the Iceni would be free, the King had assured the chieftains; *allies* of Rome instead of conquered territories. Still, as a safeguard, Boadicea had ordered her people to bury their weapons in case the Romans went back on their word.

And, as the years had progressed and the Iceni saw what befell the Catuvellauni, the only tribe on Britannia to truly resist the Roman legions, the people began to accept Prasutagus' judgment. The people traded with Rome; the chieftains brought Roman furnishings into their homes. Some of the young people even went so far as to adopt Roman dress, speech, and ways, to become what the remnants of the once great Catuvellauni tribe had been forced to become in order to survive, Romanophiles: part Roman, part Celt, belonging totally to neither world. At first the Iceni had been grateful to be spared the destruction visited upon the Catuvellauni, but gradually, as their taxes rose, as their young men were impressed for service into the auxiliary Roman legions, as Prasutagus' wishes were more frequently overridden by those of the governor-general, as they endured the snickers and jibes of the retired Roman legionaries who settled on farms given to them as a reward for their twenty years of military service—farms whose land was rightfully Iceni property but whose true owners had no say in its confiscation—the Iceni people began to chafe beneath the Roman yoke. Their freedom was in name only; in truth they were little better than slaves. The first mutterings of revolt had begun more than a decade earlier, but while Prasutagus lived there was peace. When the King had died and Boadicea had subsequently been humiliated, the battered Iceni pride had risen to the fore and, as Heall had said, Jilana had lived through the aftermath.

Which brought Jilana full circle back to Caddaric. He was a hard man, frighteningly so to Jilana, and he lacked the spontaneity that was so much a part of the other Iceni she had observed. As Artair had said, Caddaric was grim, and even on those rare occasions when he relaxed with Heall and Clywd there was a bitter edge to his laughter.

Jilana drew the long fall of her hair over her shoulder and began braiding it. Yet for all his harshness Caddaric had treated her well. She was not physically abused and he protected her from the warriors and the women by bringing their meals to her chamber and making use of Artair's slaves so that she might bathe in relative privacy. Even his temper was rigidly controlled except on those occasions when he was provoked beyond endurance— and, Jilana admitted now, she took a perverse satisfaction in goading him. Forcing Caddaric to lose that iron control, even momentarily, made her feel less like the slave Boadicea had named her and made Caddaric more human. And in spite of their harsh words, he protected her; Jilana never felt as safe with an armed Heall guarding the door as she did with an unarmed Caddaric present in the chamber. Aye, he protected her, but the memory of his burning kisses reminded Jilana that Caddaric did not need to beat her in order to have his way. He need only caress her and a delicious languor would seep through her, leaving her as helpless as if she were bound with heavy chains. She blushed at the liberties he had taken and tried to whip up some measure of righteous indignation, but her traitorous mind insisted upon remembering the fact that she had enjoyed that time in his arms.

The chamber door opened to admit Caddaric and Jilana braced herself mentally. Until she settled the turmoil within herself and discovered whether his previous anger had been spent, the wisest course would be to draw as little attention to herself as possible. She studiously watched the progress of her fingers through her hair as she heard Caddaric cross the room and seat himself on the couch. She thought she heard him groan, and the sound was so reminiscent of the soft noises he had made when they had lain together on the bed that Jilana blushed. She risked a glance at him from the corner of her eye and found him stretched out upon the couch. His left leg exceeded the length of the couch so that three-quarters of his calf was unsupported and his right leg was bent at the knee and angled, his booted foot resting on the floor in front of the couch. The single, curved arm of the couch supported his head and shoulders, and his eyes were closed. He looked exceedingly weary.

Jilana cleared her throat. "If your leg pains you, mayhap you should take your rest upon the bed." He opened one eye, subjecting her to such intense scrutiny that Jilana shifted her gaze back to her hair. An uneasy silence filled the room as she resumed her task.

"'Tis not my leg." Jilana started at his words and Caddaric winced at the sight. He deliberately softened his voice before speaking again. "Where is the healing pouch Clywd gave me?"

"In my chest." Jilana did not look at him as she spoke, concentrating instead upon winding a bit of leather about the end of the braid and tying it in place. Movement flickered in her peripheral vision and she heard a chest being opened, then closed a moment later. Caution gave way to curiosity and Jilana turned to see what Caddaric was about. The sight of the new bandage on his right arm shocked her. "You are hurt!"

"Aye." Caddaric dropped the pouch on the floor beside the couch and went to the washstand to pour water from the ewer into the basin. "'Tis slight."

"Let me see." Jilana was on her feet and at his side before he could object.

"Are you so bloodthirsty?" Caddaric eyed her curiously as she picked up the basin and brought it back to the couch. "Or is it just that you enjoy my pain?" As soon as the words were out he damned them, but it was too late. He had meant to be kinder to Jilana, to make up for the way he had spoken to her after Artair's appearance, but his good intentions seemed to be as substantial as air.

Jilana looked at him in surprise. "I enjoy no other's pain." It was the truth. Once—a mere week ago—she would have enjoyed seeing Caddaric and any other Iceni writhe in agony, but no longer. The Iceni had reacted against Roman injustice and the Roman citizens of Venta Icenorum had borne the Iceni vengeance. 'Twas an anguished truth, but a truth nonetheless.

"Not even mine?" Caddaric asked when Jilana seemed to mentally withdraw from him.

Blinking away tears that welled in her eyes, Jilana answered his question with one of her own. "You said you did not kill my family. Is that the truth?"

Caddaric nodded, surprised by her tears. If she had wept for her family before, she had done so in his absence and concealed any telltale signs from him. A flicker of hope sparked in his chest. "I had no hand in their deaths, Jilana. I swear it." He would not swear by any of the gods, for he was no hypocrite. "I swear by my honor and my sword."

And with those words Jilana knew he spoke the truth, for Caddaric valued his sword and his honor as a man above all else. "I believe you." A part of her cried out that this was treachery, but Jilana did not listen. Whatever future she may have was with Caddaric; her family was dead but she was still alive and must start anew. With Caddaric. "Sit down." She gestured to the space next to her on the couch. "Let me tend your arm . . . lord," she added hesitantly.

Caddaric sat carefully, hardly daring to believe this unexpected change. "You need not address me as such, little wicca. My name will suffice." Jilana had accepted her fate, Caddaric thought triumphantly; she had tacitly agreed that she was his. And since she accepted it, there was no further need to bludgeon her spirit with the fact. Now he could afford to be magnanimous, to return to her a portion of her pride. He knew well how important an illusion could be to one's soul.

"I thought the Queen held council, not battle," Jilana softly commented as she unwound the soiled bandage and cleaned the wound. From the healing pouch she withdrew the salve she used on Caddaric's leg and applied it to his arm. Caddaric's breath hissed between his teeth at the unavoidable pain.

"One of the chieftains was offended by my strategy," Caddaric answered when he had unclenched his jaw. "We argued."

"With swords?"

"Within our tribe this is the typical way to settle a dispute." In an undertone, Caddaric added, "I wish it were not so."

"But the Iceni are peaceful," Jilana argued. "I cannot remember when . . ." Her voice trailed off. She had been about to say "when differences among the Iceni were settled with combat," but then had realized that during her lifetime the tribe had been forbidden weapons. Because they might rise against the Empire.

"None of the tribes of this island were peaceful," Caddaric explained, unperturbed by Jilana's slip, "until Claudius landed and put them under Roman rule. We would raid for cattle to increase our wealth, or in retaliation during a feud. We did not contentedly tend our herds or till the land."

Jilana shook her head, unable to comprehend a way of life in which raiding was commonplace. She took a strip of cloth from the pouch and carefully wound it about

Caddaric's arm. "You find that uncivilized," Caddaric hazarded, guessing the path her thoughts had taken.

Jilana glanced at the hard, blue eyes and quickly looked away. "I find it strange. Why risk your life and place your home and cattle in danger when there is no need? 'Tis childish."

"Mayhap," Caddaric conceded a bit too readily. "As childish, would you say, as a nation which insists upon conquering other nations so that it has a continual supply of slaves, gladiators and soldiers to serve, entertain and protect its spoiled citizens and greedy ruler?"

There was no answer to that. The truth stung and raised the color along Jilana's cheekbones. She tied the bandage in place and rose. "'Tis finished." Jilana turned, only to be brought up short by a firm hand closing around her wrist.

"You are angry." Caddaric looked up at her set features, enjoying the feel of the delicate bones beneath his fingers.

"What does it matter?" Jilana stood quiescently, not fighting the pressure. 'Twould serve no purpose; Caddaric's strength was far superior to her own; there was no need to demonstrate that fact yet again.

Caddaric smoothed the silken flesh over her pulse with his thumb. "Mayhap our ways are childish, even uncivilized to a Roman. But for all our raiding and feuding we do not hold life cheaply; it took the Roman legion to teach me how little the treasure of life truly meant—and how carelessly it could be taken away."

There was pain buried deep in his words, a torment Jilana could barely sense, but was there nonetheless. Caddaric was not, she realized with a start, as invulnerable as he pretended to be, and she found a part of herself wanting to reach out and soothe whatever ache still haunted him. His words the night of the uprising came back to her: do not be so willing to court your own destruction. How was it that a man who spent his life in such a violent profession came to regard life so highly? Jilana wanted to ask, but the truce between them was too fragile to bear such questioning. Instead she pulled away from Caddaric and replaced the medicines in her chest.

Caddaric watched her walk away, enjoying the way the material of the long, straight stola clung to her slender hips. A belt cinched the material at her narrow waist and the memory of the way Jilana looked rising naked from her bath sent a shaft of desire through his groin. She had donned the belt during his absence, and Caddaric wondered, with a mixture of amusement and irritation, if she thought the flimsy length of leather would prove a deterrent against his advances. Smiling inwardly he reclined once again upon the couch and followed Jilana's nervous pacing of the room. "There is to be a feast tonight, a welcome to our allies and the Druids who have joined us," Caddaric said when Jilana perched upon the edge of the bed. "You will accompany me."

Jilana swung toward him, her eyes suddenly dark and troubled. The thought of being put rudely on display again destroyed her new-found security. "May I not remain here?" As soon as the words were out Jilana winced at their pleading tone.

"Nay. There will be no one to guard you and I dare not leave you to your own devices." Their eyes met and Caddaric knew she understood. If Jilana remained behind she would be left alone for the first time, without a guard outside her door or other Iceni warriors milling through the villa and courtyard. She could not be trusted not to try to escape.

The troubled look on Jilana's face nagged at Caddaric's conscience, but he had no choice. "I *am* sorry, little one." The weak smile she gave him only made Caddaric feel worse. He had broken their fledgling peace, reminded her of her slavery. Now he must find a way to set things aright. An apology was unthinkable, of course, but as Caddaric cast about for a way to extend his own olive branch he hit upon an idea that would surely bring Jilana as much pleasure as it would himself. "Would you like to bathe?" The look Jilana gave him clearly asked if he had taken leave of his senses and his anticipation gave way to embarrassment. In a stiff voice he explained, "Artair's men are busy preparing for the feast; they will have no time to prepare your bath tonight. I thought that if you wished…" She regarded him in such an odd manner that Caddaric's voice trailed off.

Artair's men. Artair's slaves. Slaves, like herself. The familiar burning resentment flared for a moment and then disappeared. Caddaric had deliberately avoided the word slave. Out of consideration for her feelings? Jilana wondered. The possibility did much to dispel her nervousness and she offered Caddaric a small, but genuine, smile. "About my bath," she prompted gently when it appeared he would not continue.

Slowly, Caddaric expelled his pent-up breath. "Though not heated, the bath house is in good repair and the water in the *caldarium* is pleasantly cool. If you like, I will take you there."

If she liked? Excitement shone in the violet eyes as Jilana slid from the bed. 'Twould be wonderful indeed to enjoy the deep pool rather than the confines of the wooden tub. *If she liked?*

Her joy went through Caddaric like a spear and he turned quickly away. Such a little thing, this bath, to bring so much happiness, and he planned to use it to his advantage. He was a cur. "Gather what you need. I will wait for you on the gallery." He bent over his own chest and removed a change of clothing before leaving the chamber.

Jilana hardly noticed his actions or his retreat. Arms wrapped about herself, Jilana whirled around the room before coming to a stop in front of her chest. Opening the chest, Jilana sorted through its familiar, meager contents. The ransacking of her chamber had left her little enough. Three stolae—two of white linen, the third a soft wool dyed blue—a like number of short tunics of fine but undyed wool; a belt; a russet *paenula*, a heavy woolen hooded cape; a precious vial of rose-scented oil; one pair of sandals and one pair of shoes; and her saffron bridal veil were all that remained of her once extensive wardrobe and possessions. Dismissing the loss, Jilana chose the

blue stola and, as an afterthought, picked up her comb
and the vial of oil. Quickly now, lest Caddaric grow impatient and decide to forego the promised venture, Jilana
slipped her feet into the pair of soft leather shoes and all
but ran from the chamber.

Caddaric waited at the gallery railing, watching the activity in the courtyard below. The breeze ruffled the soft
curls on his head and when he turned to look at her, Jilana was pierced by the same attraction she had felt at
their first meeting. His free hand rested upon the wooden
railing and Jilana was assaulted by the memory of how
gently that same hand had caressed her. There was no indication that Caddaric remembered his earlier tenderness. He nodded once and started toward the stairs,
leaving Jilana to follow. And follow she did, until they
reached the courtyard and Jilana became aware that several men were openly staring at her. Instinctively, she
quickened her step so that she walked at Caddaric's side.

The frankly curious stares angered Caddaric. He knew,
as Jilana did not, the gossip that had spread through the
Iceni host regarding Jilana and himself. Everyone knew
that her life had been spared because of her kindness toward Boadicea, and that the Queen had sent Caddaric to
keep this one Roman safe—that much of the story, at
least, held fast to the truth, as did the part which dealt
with Jilana's confrontation with Boadicea the next day.
Thereafter, however, the truth was liberally sprinkled with
imaginings of the Celtic mind. Jilana, 'twas said, was a
sorceress. How else could she have lain naked in Caddaric's arms, and then produced the dagger to plunge into his
shoulder at the exact moment that his manhood pierced
her, unless by magic? And see Caddaric. Had he not
changed since the night he took the Roman to his pallet?
Did not his men avoid him? Aye, they did. Even Heall,
Caddaric's most trusted friend, was not trusted too long
alone with the red-haired witch. And, as final proof of
Jilana's sorcery, Caddaric bore no wound or scar from
Jilana's blade. Not even Clywd's most powerful unguent

could cause a wound to disappear. Aye, surely she was a sorceress, and her magic most potent.

Now a corner of Caddaric's mouth lifted in an unamused smile. The gossips did not consider the fact that if Jilana was truly a sorceress, she would use her powers to escape her enemies—an important fact to Caddaric but apparently not to the other Celtic minds. Mayhap they chose to believe that Jilana harbored a passion for him, but whatever their reasoning, Caddaric did not disabuse them of it. A potential sorceress was held at arm's length, a source of curiosity and not a little fear. All the better; for no matter how seductive a man might find Jilana, he would hesitate before laying a hand upon her. As for the rest of the gossip, 'twas to Caddaric's benefit not to correct the other misconception. If magic would not deter a man, Caddaric's sword arm and temper would.

The bath house lay just ahead and to their right, resting in the afternoon shade of the villa. It was a small building, erected not for its beauty but for its purpose. Augusta had missed the gracious baths of Rome so, to please his wife, Marcus had built one. Since there were no public baths in Venta, as there were in Rome, Augusta and her friends were quick to take full advantage of the bath. Here in the afternoon, the women gathered to immerse themselves in the rectangular hot bath, or caldarium, and then stretch out upon the marble benches while their attendants oiled their bodies and scraped their flesh with a *strigil*. Then, while the ladies relaxed in the heat and exchanged gossip, they were offered wine and fruit by the household servants. Since the bath lacked a proper *frigidarium*, or cold bath, with which to close the pores of the skin, the women would then retire to the *tepidarium*, or temperate room, to cool down and receive a second light oiling before dressing and returning to their homes. It was a ritual which Jilana had shared with her mother since the age of eight.

All these thoughts raced through Jilana's mind as Caddaric pushed open the heavy door of the bath house. There was an air of abandonment about the building, as though it had stood unused for months rather than a few days and Jilana's eyes burned with sudden tears. She led Caddaric through the hall with its exquisite wall paintings of bath scenes and stopped when she reached the point where a second hall intersected the first. Directly ahead, flanked by paintings of Venus and Hylas, stood the door leading to the caldarium. To the right and left lay the short passages to the changing rooms.

"May I change and join you in the pool?"

Her soft question brought a nod from Caddaric. Jilana turned to her right and walked down the hallway. Caddaric waited until the door closed behind her before turning to his left and entering the changing room.

The changing room was small but light flowed through the bank of long, rectangular windows which ran along the outside wall just beneath the ceiling. Caddaric paced the perimeter of the room, noting the marble benches, the ornate grills in the floor which signified the presence of a hypocaust—or furnace—and the mosaic floor, where the tiles captured the image of a horse stretched out in full gallop. The mosaic was beautiful and Caddaric allowed himself a moment's appreciation before inspecting the rest of the room. Shelves were spaced along one wall, and here Caddaric found clean towels, an oil flask, and a silver-handled strigil, the small instrument with a short, curved blade which was used to scrape the oil and dead skin from one's flesh. The strigil, undoubtedly, had belonged to Jilana's father, as had the oil. From the passage a door opened and closed, and then sounded again, closer this time. Jilana had entered the bath. Caddaric stripped off his tunic and loincloth and selected a towel from the shelf. He started to walk from the room and then paused, considering. After a moment he retraced his steps and picked up the oil flask and strigil.

Jilana reclined in the pool, her head resting upon the cool marble edge while the water lapped against her neck. As Caddaric had warned, the water bordered on cool, but it was heavenly just to be able to stretch out full length and feel the water invade her every pore. The caldarium door opened and so did Jilana's eyes, but they shut just as quickly when she realized Caddaric was nude. The door closed and Jilana turned her head aside, assuring Caddaric of complete privacy even though they would share the pool. She had deliberately chosen the far end of the pool for the same reason. The bath was twenty feet long, half as wide, and four feet in depth; once Caddaric was safely submerged, and as long as she did not stand up and they both kept to their separate ends of the pool, they should be able to share the bath without embarrassment. Embarrassment or curiosity? a silent voice mocked, and Jilana quickly brought a hand to her cheek to cool the blush there. Aye, she was curious. She had tended Caddaric often enough to be aware of the differences in their bodies and to wonder at them, and this afternoon had only heightened her curiosity. She wondered what would have happened if Artair had not interrupted them, and then pushed the thought away. 'Twas unseemly. But still, the memory of Caddaric's flesh beneath her hands sent a pang through her loins.

"Wicca."

The voice, so near, startled Jilana and her eyes flew open. He was beside her in the water, one arm stretched out along the marble edge behind her head. The water swirled as he shifted position, his leg grazed her hip, and Jilana realized that Caddaric had joined her on the submerged ledge carved out of the walls of the pool. Suddenly wary, she slid away but Caddaric did nothing other than tip his own head back against the edge and close his eyes. Jilana watched him for several minutes, every muscle tensed and ready should he try to repeat his earlier advances. Caddaric remained where he was, occasionally moving to cup water in one large hand and lave it over his chest. Intrigued in spite of herself, Jilana watched as the circular motion of his hand disturbed the pattern of his chest hair and then drifted lower, below the water line. She was seized by the urge to duplicate his movements, to allow her hands to drift across his chest....

Her fingers curled involuntarily and the sting of her nails biting into her palms brought Jilana to her senses. Striving for an air of indifference, Jilana forced herself to recline once more against the wall and close her eyes. She should be concerned for her modesty, Jilana reminded herself; for propriety's sake she should move further away, ideally to the opposite end of the pool. The water in the bath was clear and every line and curve of her body would be revealed to Caddaric if he chose to look, as would his to her. She found that thought disturbing, but not offensive. In truth, Caddaric had seen her nude so often she doubted her body held any secrets for him, but his, on the other hand ... Jilana firmly suppressed such wayward thinking. They were enemies; she was his slave. She had been strictly raised in the belief that she would go to her marriage bed a virgin; this wanton, reckless *curiosity* about Caddaric would simply have to cease. Jilana sank lower into the bath, raised her hands to her burning face and then trickled water over her exposed shoulders. The shocks of the past week must have been too much for her, she decided, and she was now succumbing to the strain and becoming ill. Why else would the water suddenly feel so very warm?

Cautiously, Caddaric opened his eyes and turned his head toward Jilana. Her eyes were closed, her neck delicately arched over the edge of the bath in a manner that seemed to invite his caress. The red-gold braid of hair was coiled around her head, but in several places wisps of hair had escaped the pins and now curled damply against her cheeks and nape of her neck. Did she know what a tempting sight she was? How the brush of his thigh against her hip had sent his heart hammering so heavily in his chest that he had been certain the ribs would crack? Nay, Caddaric decided as he watched Jilana's slender hands trail water across her shoulders, she did not. For a beautiful woman she seemed supremely indifferent to the reactions she produced in men. Caddaric regretted, fleetingly, the forces that had decreed Jilana should be his slave, but he shrugged the regret aside. How else would she have come to be his? Without Boadicea's rebellion Jilana would have married Lucius, and even if she had not, her family would certainly never have allowed her to be courted by an Iceni warrior whose only relationship with Rome was that he had deserted one of its legions in order to buy his father's freedom from a Roman general. A bitter smile touched his mouth as he thought of Jilana and her family. Aye, the fates had not been kind to Jilana, but they had brought her to Caddaric and he would not cavil with that outcome.

The bitter smile faded as Caddaric studied Jilana's profile, and had she been watching, Jilana would have been astounded by the softening of his features. When had it all changed? Caddaric wondered. Until this afternoon he would have sworn that all he wanted from Jilana was her body and the possible product of their physical union. A week ago he would have been content with her unresisting compliance in his bed but now, having tasted her passion, Caddaric knew that would no longer suffice. He wanted all of Jilana, willing and passionate or strong and defiant. Above all, he wanted to end completely the hate that had lain between them. He wanted her trust.

Caddaric turned his gaze from Jilana to his hands. Large and square, with long, thick, blunt fingers, they were the hands of a warrior, not a patrician, and they seemed to accentuate the differences between himself and Jilana. Women, especially Roman women, liked to be wooed and courted with words, an art at which he was far from skilled. In all his life, Caddaric realized, he had never truly conversed with a woman such as Jilana. He had talked to his mother, of course, and his sisters, but he had been a child then. The women he had known during his time with the legion had been more interested in his coin than his conversation. And then there was Ede, a warrior maid with whom he could discuss the quality of a blade during the day and take to his pallet at night without the ploy of pretty, meaningless words. Jilana was different from his previous women: he could not take her like some common camp follower and he could not treat her with the casual indifference which had been Ede's. In order to make Jilana truly his, he would have to have her mind as well as her body, and that would mean sharing a part of himself which he had kept inviolate since the invasion of Claudius. A feeling of sick dread settled in Caddaric's stomach; compared to Lucius he was clumsy and vulgar, a barbarian. 'Twould no doubt be amusing to Jilana to watch him struggle to string three words together in order to converse with her. Still, he had to try.

For what seemed an eternity, Caddaric searched for something to say and when, at last, he had found a subject he thought might interest Jilana, he carefully planned his sentence. Thus prepared, he turned toward her and, in what he hoped was a casual manner, said, "This bath reminds me of the public bath I visited in Rome." At his first word, Jilana had looked at him and the rest of what he had planned to say was lost in the depths of her violet gaze.

Jilana waited hopefully in the silence that descended once again, as anxious as Caddaric to put an end to the strange tension that seemed to hum between them, but for a different reason. There was safety in conversation. "Does it?" she asked helpfully. "I have never been to Rome."

Caddaric hurriedly pulled his thoughts together, thankful for her question. "There are differences. The hypocaust was working so the caldarium and *laconicum* were boiling hot, as they are supposed to be. I remember there were senators present, discussing Nero's obsession with his Greeks and his singing while the sweat poured from their bodies." He found it amusing, the memory of those senators gravely discussing Nero and his excesses as if they were holding forth in the Senate, and tried to share the humor with Jilana through a faint smile. She watched him expectantly, finding nothing odd in the senators' behavior. It was the Roman way of things; her father had routinely conducted business in his own caldarium. Caddaric nervously cleared his throat and returned to the subject at hand. "There was a frigidarium, of course, but I had done too much freezing when I was stationed along the Rhine to enjoy it." He stopped abruptly, remembering the bitter Rhine winter, and, following that, the transfer to the desert furnace called Judea. His time in the desert had ended with his brothers' deaths and his own desertion.

"Claudia often spoke of the baths," Jilana said quietly. She sensed his withdrawal, more marked now because of the effort he had made to establish a link between them.

Caddaric roused himself with an effort. "Claudia?"

"My sister." Jilana's lips trembled over the words and she looked quickly away. "Claudia went to Rome, with my mother, when she was thirteen. They had intended only a short stay, but Claudia fell in love with the city and its way of life. When Mother returned, Claudia stayed behind with an aunt. She was gone for three years and when she came back she was changed, different from the sister I remembered." Jilana sighed and trailed a hand through the water. "She ridiculed our bath; compared to the magnificent ones she had visited in Rome and Pompeii, I suppose this did seem inferior." Tears flooded her eyes as she realized the disloyalty of her words. In her sister's defense, Jilana added, "Claudia was not suited for life here. She was too delicate to endure the hardships of a frontier settlement."

Caddaric snorted his disbelief. "I saw her the day the Queen was flogged. She was not too delicate to scream for Boadicea's blood or relish the sight of it when the lash laid her back open." He fingered the scar on his cheek. "No doubt she relished the gladiatorial combats to be found in Rome."

"You know nothing," Jilana hissed. *"Nothing!"* But what he said was true; Claudia had described the gladiators and their contests with an excitement Jilana had not been able to fathom. That Caddaric dared to criticise Claudia was maddening—that he dared to be correct was intolerable. Tears, so long unshed, spilled over her cheeks, but Jilana no longer cared. "She was my sister! How dare you—" Her voice broke and Jilana reached out blindly for the side of the pool, intending to run from this barbarian and his hateful truths.

"Jilana, nay."

Strong hands captured her wrists and dragged her through the water to the warm, hard cushion of his chest. Immediately her wrists were released and his arms gathered her close so that her head rested in the hollow of his shoulder. "I hate you!" But the sobs that tore through Jilana's chest drained the venom from her words.

"Aye, I know." Caddaric stroked a gentling hand over her hair.

"She was my sister," Jilana repeated brokenly.

Her sorrow tore at him, opening fresh wounds in his heart. "I know." Caddaric held her fiercely, protectively, waiting out the storm. "I know what it is like to lose a loved one. My two brothers fell in battle while I watched, unable to help them. They were Iceni and they died fighting for the Roman legion that had been sent to quell an uprising in Judea. When it was over I took their bodies and washed and prepared them as best I could. There were no sacred oak groves, no Druids, and though I had money, no legion priest would allow me to purchase a sacrifice which would smooth their way to Annwn." Annwn, the Celtic land of the dead. The name sent a shiver through Jilana and Caddaric wrapped her closer in his arms. "I buried them beneath the sands of the desert—buried them deep, so that the jackals and hyenas could not unearth them and feed upon their flesh." Jilana's arms went around his neck, her fingernails digging into his shoulders, sharing his pain as he shared hers, returning a measure of the comfort she had received. "My mother and sisters had been killed when Claudius invaded our island; now my brothers were dead. My father was a slave to General Aulus Plautus. My family was no more."

Jilana's breath caught at the hollowness of his voice. "How you must hate Rome and me." She sought to move out of his arms, but Caddaric held her still.

"I bear no love for Rome, but you, little wicca..." Caddaric brought one hand to her chin and tilted her face toward his. "Nay, I do not hate you." Slowly, Caddaric lowered his head and brushed his lips across Jilana's.

Jilana stared at him, aware of the frisson of pleasure that curled through her at the touch of his mouth. There was tenderness in his touch, a gentleness which belied the dispassionate shell which was his armor. And there was pain—a pain Jilana recognized because it matched her own—and, incredibly, she wanted nothing more than to take away all the pain inflicted upon Caddaric by her countrymen and give him in its place...peace. The same peace Caddaric had offered this afternoon in her bedchamber. Was this what he had been feeling when he had taken her in his arms? Had he wanted, beyond all else, to give her comfort? Between them lay something of immense power; it shimmered in the depths of Caddaric's blue eyes, challenging her, daring her to reach out and risk being consumed in its depths. The unknown might consume them both, for Caddaric, too, seemed oddly reluctant to grasp what the moment afforded; yet Jilana knew, through some age-old wisdom in her heart, that this strange power also held the balm for their wounds. And much, much more.

Without conscious thought, Jilana's hands slid from Caddaric's neck to the damp curls on his head. Slowly, half-afraid, half-intrigued, her fingers tunneled into his hair and brought his head downward. His breath fell across her lips and Jilana closed her eyes. Their mouths met, gently, and the exquisite sensations produced by the joining elicited a soft sound of pleasure from her throat.

His mouth flowed over hers, softening the flesh, heating it; Caddaric's arms tightened, bringing Jilana's breasts teasingly against the dark mat of hair covering his chest. Her hands fell to his shoulders as Caddaric's tongue traced the outline of her lips and then explored their fullness. She wanted to move closer, to be absorbed by the strength and heat of his body, but Caddaric kept her at that same, teasing distance while his tongue seduced its way into her mouth. Caddaric deepened the kiss, his tongue seeking hers for a controlled, sensual meeting that made Jilana sink her nails into his shoulders.

The kiss grew in power, causing a riot of sensation within Jilana. Her breasts tingled and deep within her core an ache flared to life. At the small, unexpected pain she caught her breath, and as she did so her tongue withdrew and grazed the length of Caddaric's. This time 'twas Caddaric who gasped, and Jilana felt the powerful muscles beneath her fingers contract one by one until he seemed carved from sun-warmed marble. The pressure against her lips eased, as did the heady persuasion of his tongue, but the rhythmic throbbing of her blood left Jilana giddy. Caddaric's arms around her back and beneath her knees held her securely, but Jilana felt strangely weightless. Confused, she opened her eyes and looked at Caddaric. The blue of his eyes was dark, almost hidden by his half-closed lids, but pinpoints of light glittered in their depths. The arm at her back tightened, lifted, and Jilana knew the sensual abrasion of his chest hair against the side of her breast.

It dawned on her then that they were no longer in the pool. Her weightlessness had been caused by Caddaric carrying her through the water and up to the steps. Now there was no longer even the pretense of a bath with which to assuage her conscience's demand for modesty. Reality descended with the wrath of an avenging god and tripped Jilana's heartbeat. *This is wrong,* she tried to tell herself.

"Nay, Jilana." Caddaric sensed her retreat and spoke quietly, but the words vibrated through his chest and into hers. He brushed his mouth over Jilana's and a flame instantly surged through them both. If she refused him now... "'Tis meant for us, wicca. Fight me if you must; I will understand and do my best not to hurt you."

Jilana swallowed, aware of the drumming of her pulse. "You will rape me?"

A smile, sadly amused, touched his mouth and was gone. "Nay, Jilana, I will not rape you. I will not have to. Your pride, your strength, will exhaust themselves and then I will have only to kiss you, caress you, and you will be mine."

What Caddaric said was true and his blunt words, while not kind, were more welcome to Jilana than sugar-coated lies. He could easily have lied and perhaps she would have believed him in order to pacify the rigid Roman morality with which she had been raised. But his honesty touched her and took away the guilt and shame. Her life was different now, *she* was different. She must make her own rules for her new life, even as she sensed Caddaric had made his. He was a hard man, but an honest one. She could trust him. Reaching out, she traced his mouth with a forefinger. "I will not fight you," Jilana said in a soft but steady voice. His fingers dug painfully into her rib-cage and she gasped. "You promised not to hurt me, Caddaric." Immediately the pressure eased and she smiled gratefully.

"I will try to take more care with you," Caddaric murmured as he bent his head toward her once again. He carried Jilana further around the pool until they reached the discarded towels and then removed the arm supporting her knees. Her arm slid around his neck and when her legs brushed against his, Caddaric tightened the arm around her back while his free hand smoothed over her buttock and cupped into the resilient flesh. Jilana was suspended several inches above the floor, her breasts and abdomen molded enchantingly against the iron planes of his body. A shudder ran through Caddaric and he reluctantly lowered her to the floor. She swayed for a moment and when Caddaric reached out to steady her, he was nearly undone by the silken feel of her beneath his callused hands. "Jilana." She looked at him squarely then, those incredible purple eyes wide and unfocused with passion, and seemed to regain her balance. Trembling himself, Caddaric knelt and made short work of spreading the towels on the floor as a pallet.

Ah, gods, Caddaric chastised himself, to take Jilana upon a hard marble floor. He should stop, take her back to the bedchamber and lay her upon the soft bed— Caddaric's thoughts came to a jumbling halt as he felt Jilana settle next to him upon the towels and place a hand on his shoulder. He looked up and found her watching him, her expression trusting. Swallowing, Caddaric turned Jilana so that her back was to him and began removing the pins from her hair and setting them aside. The braid slipped from its coronet and he slowly untwisted the neat coils. Jilana's hair was a luxury in itself; like silk it flowed through his fingers, caressed his thighs, and fell in a fiery river down her back. Caddaric moved closer and massaged her shoulders. He would have to be careful, some rational part of his mind warned; he could so easily hurt her with his greater strength. He ran his hands down her arms. Jilana shivered and he instantly wrapped his arms around her, pulling her back to his chest. "Are you cold?"

"Nay." Jilana's voice emerged as a throaty whisper. It was the truth; Caddaric's touch sent out tongues of fire that stole her strength and gave it back again. Jilana twisted in Caddaric's embrace until they were face-to-face. A few strands of her hair caught in the dark mat covering Caddaric's chest and a wildness grew in Jilana's soul at the sight.

Caddaric followed her gaze and his breath nearly stopped at the erotic picture. While he watched, Jilana slowly raised a hand and began to dissolve the web between them. Deliberately, Caddaric grasped her hand and pressed it onto his chest, directly over his heart. She remained motionless for what seemed an eternity and then her fingers moved, threading their way through the fine hair, exploring its texture. With a groan Caddaric pulled her closer and claimed her mouth. This time her mouth flowered eagerly, welcoming his invasion. He sampled her leisurely, investigating the warm cavern with slow, languid strokes that drew a soft purr from her throat and quick, short stabs that invited Jilana to examine him in the same way. She was hesitant, her tongue retreating just as it met his lips. Impatience flared in Caddaric and he was tempted to frame her head in his hands and hold her immobile while he plundered her mouth. And then he remembered that she was a virgin, that the play between a man and a woman was foreign to her and that he had never imagined he would be the one to initiate her into this intimacy. Caddaric had never lain with a virgin and he realized, with a tremor of apprehension, that the presence of her innocence changed everything for him as well.

A fierce protectiveness swept through Caddaric and he gathered Jilana close, his mouth sliding from hers to trail across her cheek and neck. He would make this joining a sweet one—a precious moment to be salvaged from the present and savored in the future.

A thousand sensual explosions blossomed within Jilana. The heat of Caddaric's mouth on her throat triggered a vibration which ran the length of her body and she tightened her arms around his neck. His hands consumed her; they alternately massaged and caressed every bit of her back, then lingered over the swell of her buttocks. Caddaric spread his hands around her hips until his thumbs met and, with a light touch unusual in a man of his size, moved them upward. Every inch of her flesh was incredibly sensitized, her breathing ragged. She ached for something as yet unknown, and when Caddaric cupped her breasts and stroked her nipples to life she cried out softly.

Caddaric kissed her tenderly, the seductive stroke of his tongue an erotic counterpoint to the incessant manipulation of his hands. Jilana melted against him, her body as malleable as hot wax as he lowered them both to the towel. This time, however, when he started to withdraw, her tongue followed, teasing its way past his lips and into his mouth. From deep in his chest came a groan of pleasure, a sound which invited Jilana to venture further within. She explored timidly at first, uncertain of her actions, and then with greater confidence. He tasted like sweet wine, Jilana discovered, a rich, subtle flavor that went to her head. With the floor beneath her now, she released his neck and ran her fingers over the breadth of his shoulders and down the muscled ridges of his back.

"Nay," Jilana whispered when Caddaric released her mouth.

"I did not know a wicca was so passionate a creature," Caddaric teased, but his eyes were nearly black with his own desire. He pressed tiny kisses against her collarbone and his voice when he spoke again was hoarse. "There is more, little wicca, so much more." Bending, he rubbed his lips against the globe of one breast. Jilana caught her breath, her nails curled into his back and Caddaric smiled at the fine tremor which ran through her.

"Caddaric—Oh!" Jilana's words died as his lips closed around her nipple and drew it into his mouth. Her back arched, bringing Jilana closer to the source of such devastating magic. Her nipple was laved by Caddaric's tongue, then lightly scored by his teeth. She gave a tormented whimper as Caddaric diverted his attentions to her other breast and his hand slid down her stomach to the nest of auburn curls which guarded the juncture of her thighs.

Jilana moved restlessly and Caddaric stilled her by draping one thickly muscled leg across both of hers. His fingers penetrated her veil of curls to stroke apart the petals concealing the bud of her desire. Jilana stiffened in reaction and then her body shuddered with pleasure as Caddaric repeated his ministrations. Instinctively Jilana arched into his hand, allowing Caddaric's fingers to slip lower, to find that part of her that was unaccountably moist.

Groaning, Caddaric raised his head from her breast and took Jilana's lips in a long, searching kiss. Jilana was alive in his arms, an abandoned creature who threatened his control with the innocently seductive movements of her body and mouth until he ached like a green lad. Her legs twisted beneath his, opening, inviting his exploration. A wild desire burned through Caddaric and his fingers slid into her beckoning warmth.

All the strength seemed to leave Jilana and she could do nothing more than cling to Caddaric as he took her on a sensual journey. She felt weightless, disembodied, with Caddaric's hands and mouth her only chains to earth. His fingers worked a mysterious enchantment, assuaging the initial ache while creating a new, spreading tension that had its core deep inside her. Jilana moaned, felt his lips harden against hers until the kiss became wild and uncontrolled. Caddaric's tongue stabbed into her mouth and Jilana retaliated in kind; then she gasped when his full weight covered her and her breasts were crushed into the cloud of hair on his chest. His hand withdrew from her and moved to curve around her hip, then on to the swell of her buttock, and Jilana murmured a protest.

Caddaric's heart thudded painfully against his ribs as he kissed the line of her throat. "Lift your hips, Jilana." His voice was hoarse, barely recognizable, but she did as he asked and he slid his hand fully beneath her. Carefully, slowly, he guided himself into her, pausing only when he encountered the expected barrier. He felt her fingers tighten on his shoulders as he pushed experimentally at the membrane. What would cause her the least pain? Quickly? Slowly? His own slipping control decided the matter. Perspiration beaded his forehead and the tension in his groin was despairingly familiar. Gathering himself, Caddaric rocked forward and knew immediately the sting of Jilana's nails.

Jilana cried out at the sharp pain but Caddaric's mouth was on hers, drinking the sound from her lips. He was embedded within her and Jilana could feel herself stretching to accommodate his presence there. She tried to lever herself away but Caddaric held her firmly in place.

"Wait," Caddaric ordered in a voice that was both gentle and rough. "'Twill pass, I swear it."

Jilana opened her eyes and looked at his face, so close to her own. Caddaric's eyes were closed and his face was set in an almost grim expression. Curious, she whispered, "Caddaric?" Her pain receding, Jilana raised a hand and brushed her fingers over his cheek. Immediately his eyes flew open and she was lost in their indigo depths.

"Does it hurt badly?" Caddaric smoothed a curl away from her temple, relaxing when Jilana shook her head. "The first time hurts a woman, so I have been told." He moved slowly, testing her reaction. Jilana frowned slightly and he kissed her again, matching the motion of his tongue to that of his body. The frown disappeared and her eyes fluttered shut. He could feel the passion take control of her once more and began pressing warm kisses upon her cheeks and throat. "'Twill not hurt again, wicca... and after this... you will find..." His voice failed as Jilana tried to match his rhythm. His hands moved to her hips to guide her.

A fierce heat consumed Jilana as she found the rhythm. Everything faded save the seductive curl of Caddaric's tongue and the tension that heightened when Caddaric repeatedly sheathed his manhood in her softness. Jilana soared, borne upward by Caddaric's strength. There was a shifting within her, a shimmering pulse that stole her breath and left her panting. Caddaric's pace quickened and she followed, more than willing to go wherever he would lead. Higher she flew, and still higher, until that tension within her exploded and bathed her with a pleasure so intense she cried out.

At Jilana's cry of fulfillment, Caddaric cast aside the last vestige of control. Her legs tightened spasmodically around his waist, driving him deeper as he reached his peak. He shuddered with the force of his release and his hands locked her hips against his pelvis. How long Caddaric held Jilana to him he did not know, but gradually he became aware of his bruising grip. Despite the gentleness of his withdrawal Jilana caught her breath, and Caddaric rolled to his side and pulled her into his arms. Usually he did not hold the woman afterward, nor did he like it when she twined herself around him like some strangling vine. Caddaric lifted an eyelid and looked down at Jilana. She lay quietly, her eyes tightly closed and her arms crossed in the valley of her breasts, but he could see the heightened color along her cheekbones. She was not asleep. He extricated one of her hands, meshed his fingers with hers and brought their hands to the center of his chest. Better. Contentment stole over Caddaric and, in the heartbeat of time before he fell asleep, he wondered what Jilana was thinking.

Jilana lay quietly, listening as Caddaric's breathing became even and rhythmic, before daring to look at him. Asleep he looked younger, less stern. Jilana smiled and bravely allowed herself to look down the length of him now that he could not see. His arms, chest and legs were bronze, a fascinating contrast against her own white limbs. Only that part of him normally covered by his loincloth was untouched by the sun and Jilana caught herself staring at the dense thatch of hair below his waist. A warm curl of sensation ran through her and she dragged her eyes upward to their entwined hands. With his passion spent, she had been afraid that Caddaric would ignore her, or worse, make some cutting remark. She had never imagined the joining of a man and woman would be filled with such heart-stopping ecstasy. She closed her eyes, remembering the moment when she had exploded with pleasure. And he had been so tender with her, so patient, even when she had tried to withdraw from the pain he had had to cause. Jilana smiled and nestled closer to the warm strength of him, aware of a spurt of pleasure when his arm curled more securely around her waist. How safe he made her feel, protected. As she drifted into sleep, Jilana wondered how she could have feared this man who had been so gentle with her.

CADDARIC AWOKE FIRST, but not in his usual warrior's manner. Instead of coming from a deep sleep to instant alertness he drifted lazily to consciousness, pleasurably aware of Jilana's soft body curved so enticingly against his own. His hand drifted over the silken flesh of her back and came to rest upon the flare of her hip. The movement disturbed her and she pressed nearer with a tiny sigh that stirred the hair on his chest. Smiling, Caddaric opened his eyes and gazed down at the perfect oval of her face. Sable lashes dusted with gold lay like wings upon her cheeks and her mouth, swollen from his kisses, was temptingly parted. The memory of her fire and passion flooded his brain and Caddaric felt a stirring in his loins. He was hungry for her again, as hungry as if he had not yet lost himself in her delightful body, and that surprised him. Stifling a groan, Caddaric raised his eyes to the ceiling and watched the sunlight from the high windows play across the paintings there. Would Jilana be shy or willing this time? Caddaric wondered. He had given her pleasure their first time, of that he was certain, and the knowledge gave him a certain swaggering pride. But his pride quickly deflated as he remembered the pain he had caused. She had been a virgin, and glancing down, Caddaric saw that the proof of her virginity stained her thighs and his burgeoning manhood. Gradually his smile faded and his gaze returned to the ceiling. Mayhap Jilana would hate him for taking this last reminder of her life before the uprising—of her family and Lucius. And he could not blame her. His rekindled desire was extinguished as quickly as flame meeting water.

The sunlight turned golden, the shadows lengthened, and Caddaric became aware of the hardness of the floor and the passage of time. Reluctantly he disengaged his hand from Jilana's and shook her awake. Those breathtaking violet eyes opened slowly, blinked once, twice, then hazily focused on his face. And then, though Caddaric could scarcely credit such a thing, her mouth curved into a hesitant smile.

"Have I slept long?" Jilana was apprehensive beneath Caddaric's steady regard and a tremor crept into her voice.

The simple question, tinged with Jilana's own uncertainty, was a balm to Caddaric's own misgivings. Though he did not smile, his features relaxed and he pushed a lock of red-gold hair away from her temple. "Aye, wicca, long enough. 'Tis time to finish our bath and return to our chamber so we may prepare for tonight.''

Before Jilana could answer, Caddaric swept her into his arms and his strong legs carried them both into the pool. The water seemed cooler now, lapping as it did at her legs and posterior. She shivered, and in response Caddaric thrust his legs straight out and they both sank beneath the water. His arms loosened and Jilana twisted away and rose to the surface. Sputtering, pushing back the long hair plastered over her face, Jilana glared as Caddaric came to his feet with a great shower of water.

'''Twas a mean trick,'' she upbraided him as he tossed his head and sent a spray of droplets over them both.

''No trick,'' Caddaric replied, reaching for the wash cloths Jilana had placed at the edge of the pool along with her rose oil. ''You were still half-asleep—now you are fully awake.'' He tossed one of the cloths to her and then began to scrub himself with the other.

Jilana swallowed, watching the cloth make its way across the muscular flesh of his arms and chest. Standing, the water came to just below her breasts, but on Caddaric the surface was much lower. Blushing at the path her eyes had taken, Jilana scooped up her cloth and concentrated on her own ablutions. Little by little, as she moved through the water, twisting this way and that to clean herself, Jilana became aware of the soreness in certain areas of her body. Surreptitiously she worked at the stiffening muscles in her buttocks. She drew the cloth down over her stomach, intending to cleanse the part of her which hurt the most, and was horrified when the cloth came back streaked with red. For a moment she stood staring at the cloth, uncomprehending, and then embarrassment flooded her and she turned hastily away to complete her bath. But not before Caddaric had seen. With slow, thoughtful movements, Caddaric finished his bath and sank once more, briefly, under the water. Rather than use the stairs at the end of the pool, Caddaric placed his hands on the cool marble of the bath's edge and lifted himself out of the water. By the time he had wrapped a

owel around his waist, Jilana was approaching the steps.
Caddaric picked up the second towel and went to meet
ner.

"Thank you." Jilana took the towel from Caddaric,
but did not meet his eyes. Quickly she dried herself,
shielded her body with the towel and started for the door,
but Caddaric's hand on her arm stayed her.

"You hurt."

Caddaric's calm statement brought a fresh surge of
embarrassment to Jilana and she closed her eyes. "'Tis
naught," she managed in a strangled voice.

"'Tis a matter of some importance to me," Caddaric
said in a low tone. His hand began a soothing motion. "I
should have taken more care with you, little wicca. I did
not mean to take you on a marble floor."

Jilana's eyes flew open and she looked at Caddaric.
"You regret it then? You wish you had not..." She
choked, unable to finish the question.

"I only regret the manner, wicca, not the deed," Caddaric assured her. "Do you?"

A trembling smile touched Jilana's mouth and she
shook her head. Immediately she was enfolded in Caddaric's arms and crushed against his chest.

"You are mine." Caddaric's voice held a fiercely possessive note and his arms tightened, as if daring her to
disagree. When she did not, he released her and stepped
away. "Henceforth you will share my bed."

"If you so order."

Caddaric started, some of his confidence waning. "You
said you did not regret—"

"And I do not." Jilana interrupted. She drew the towel
tightly around her breasts and started once more for the
door. "Has it never occurred to you to ask rather than
command?"

Caddaric's anger flared. Did she think to control him
simply because he had bedded her? "You are impertinent," he bellowed as Jilana opened the door.

"Aye."

The door closed behind Jilana before he could respond and Caddaric swore loudly, summoning a few particularly colorful curses he had learned during his time in the legion. He grabbed the offending vial of rose oil and scowled at it. So Jilana thought he could be manipulated, did she? Caddaric snorted in disgust. A typical Roman woman's ploy—allow a man the use of her body and then exact payment afterward, when the man was sated and in an expansive mood. Oh, aye, he knew the Roman wicca's game, but she would find him less maneuverable than she had doubtless found the besotted Lucius. Caddaric had not forgotten that scene in the garden, when Jilana had deliberately teased Lucius; he had seen the rigid discipline the Roman had had to exercise and now Caddaric vowed that he would not allow Jilana that kind of power over him. It did not occur to him, as he strode from the caldarium, silently damning Jilana for the loss of his earlier contentment, that his oath was already broken.

Jilana was waiting for him when he emerged from the changing room, looking as if there was nothing amiss. While dressing, he had fanned his anger and now, seeing her standing so calmly, Caddaric's temper flamed out of control. He thrust the vial into her hands with a snarl. "I will not beg you to share my bed, Roman. You will do so, or not, at my whim, not yours. Fool I was to think you had truly changed, but I will play the fool no longer!"

Jilana's violet eyes widened in astonishment at the tirade, her faint smile vanishing. His voice was an angry roar, emanating from the very depths of his chest, and she automatically retreated a step. "Caddaric, wha—"

"I am no fawning Roman nobleman to be brought to my knees by the promise of your favors. You are, remember, mine for the taking."

"Oh, aye, I remember," Jilana hissed, her eyes shooting purple sparks. Her fear was gone, supplanted by her own anger. Furious, she hurled the stola she carried at Caddaric and derived a momentary satisfaction from the way the material wrapped itself around his head. "You remind me often enough, you clumsy, oafish *barbarian*!''

"Barbarian!" Caddaric extricated himself from the folds of the garment just in time for the vial Jilana threw to hit him squarely in his eye. He gave a brief grunt of pain and brought one large hand up to cover the injured area while he reached for Jilana with the other.

"You have broken it!" Oblivious to all else, Jilana stared in dismay at the remains of the precious Egyptian glass vial where it had shattered upon the floor. The scent drifted upward and the oil spread into a pool, surrounding them both with the fragrance of roses. There was the sound of glass crunching underfoot as Caddaric stepped toward her and her arm was seized in a vise-like grip.

"Forgive me," Caddaric apologized acidly. "Next time I will strive to catch your missiles. Unless you throw a dagger, in which case you may be sure that I will duck." He gave Jilana a one-handed shake that threatened to snap her neck. "Mayhap in the future you will refrain from telling me how to behave."

"I—did—no—such—thing," Jilana ground out. Her head spun and she saw two of everything, including Caddaric. And one Caddaric, particularly in his present mood, was more than sufficient.

"You did," Caddaric stated flatly. He released Jilana and tossed the stola back at her when she fell backward against the wall. "Consider yourself fortunate if the worst I ever do to you is give an order!"

His words penetrated her shifting world and Jilana blinked rapidly to clear her vision. The two Caddarics merged into one who was turning away and rubbing his eye. "Juno, is that what made you so angry," Jilana murmured in disbelief.

"I am not angry," Caddaric argued perversely. He probed the flesh around his eye and glared at Jilana over his shoulder. "Your aim is improving."

Laughter welled inside Jilana and bubbled forth before she could control herself. Caddaric's glare increased in ferocity and she shook her head. "I meant only to tease

you, Caddaric." He made a rude sound of disbelief and
Jilana straightened, her expression serious. "'Twas a jest,
Caddaric, truly. I thought you would see the humor in my
words and retort in kind."

Caddaric was silent, considering her statement. At last
he nodded and the sharpness anger had lent his features
abated. He reached out with one hand and cupped the side
of Jilana's face. "Did I hurt you?"

There was genuine concern in his voice and Jilana
smiled reassuringly as she rested her cheek against the
palm of his hand. "Nay, Caddaric. What of your eye?"
Caddaric uncovered his eye and Jilana stepped closer to
examine the damage. The skin surrounding the eye was
red and beginning to swell and an involuntary rush of
tears bathed both eye and flesh. Using the hem of the stola
she had thrown at Caddaric, Jilana gently dabbed away
this final evidence of her assault. "I am sorry," she apologized. And she was, but the humor of having injured
Caddaric with a vial of perfumed oil when she had once
had a dagger at her disposal and failed, caused her mouth
to quirk irrepressibly. "But, in truth, you did anger me
and bring this upon yourself."

"You *are* impertinent."

The repetition of his earlier statement sent a shaft of
unease down Jilana's spine, but when she looked directly
into Caddaric's eyes she relaxed. He was, in turn, teasing
her, and Jilana was vastly relieved that the famed Celtic
temper was once more in abeyance. "Aye."

Caddaric mused aloud, brushing her still-damp hair off
her face, "I think you will be a trial for me, little wicca."

"The names I called you," Jilana said quietly, "I did
not mean them, Caddaric."

"I am glad." He placed a kiss on her brow and, with
one arm draped around her shoulders, led Jilana outside.

Their peace was re-established and Jilana had to be
content with that, although she wished that her apology
had not gone unrequited. Still, she reminded herself, she
had learned a great deal about Caddaric. He could be
gentle or rough, at times heedless of his own physical

trength, but he had not hurt her even when his anger
eached its zenith. After the diffused lighting of the bath,
he afternoon sun seemed particularly bright and Jilana
hielded her eyes with one hand while she pushed at her
damp hair with the other. Her hair was badly tangled, Jilana realized. It would take time to work out the snarls to
her satisfaction.

"My comb." Jilana halted and half-turned back to the
bath. "I left it in the changing room."

"Stay here; I will find it." Caddaric was gone before
Jilana thought to protest.

Alone, Jilana wandered into the courtyard and sat
down on one of the sun-warmed benches there. The
breeze lifted her hair and she ran her fingers through it in
an attempt to comb out the worst of the snarls before they
could dry. Voices carried from the kitchen, but the words
were indistinct so Jilana ignored them. The fact that her
fellow countrymen, those who held her in such contempt, occupied the kitchen did not dampen her mood.
She was enjoying this relative freedom, her first since the
rebellion.

She closed her eyes and turned her face to the sun, relishing its warmth, and allowed her thoughts to drift. Thus
it was that Jilana did not notice the tall, emaciated man
in white cross the courtyard with a contingent of six warriors and enter the kitchen. Nor did she pay attention
when the voices in the kitchen rose and became shrill, took
on a pleading note, then fell silent. She thought of Caddaric, wondering if now he might allow her to visit the
stable and see her mare. Mayhap, if she asked, he might
also allow her to ride. Not far, to be sure, but perhaps to
the forest. Or would he think she was trying to manipulate him again? Jilana frowned at that thought but
brushed it aside. She would wait a few days before making her request; by then he would have forgotten the accusations he had made today.

Strangely, Jilana found that she was not concerned with
her future. She was Caddaric's; he could do with her as he
pleased. Caddaric's hints to the contrary, she was certain

the Iceni rebellion would burn out within a few weeks, certainly within a few months. Once informed, the legions would descend on Venta and the Iceni would retreat and she would be rescued. There was an odd pang in her heart at the possibility of rescue, but, Jilana told herself bracingly, that was what she wanted; and in order to see that day, she had to compromise with Caddaric. 'Twas all her surrender today had been, a compromise; she offered the free use of her body in exchange for his protection.

The thought left a bitter taste in Jilana's mouth and, without knowing it, her mind took the same path Caddaric's had earlier. How different things might have been without the rebellion, if she and Caddaric had met as equals. He might truly have courted her then, even won her father's approval. Mayhap they would have married and Caddaric would have taken her to his village to live. Jilana wrenched herself away from that treacherous daydream with a mute cry. Juno, she must not allow herself to think of such things, to allow her heart to be vulnerable to Caddaric in this way. She must remember that beneath all the compromises there lay one unchangeable truth: they were enemies. And hard on that thought came another shattering truth: if the situation had been different, Caddaric was the kind of man Jilana could have loved. That was why she had given herself to Caddaric, because her heart had willed it thus, not through any justification of compromise. Unfair, Jilana thought as her throat constricted with unshed tears. Unfair, unfair, unfair.

"Slave."

The voice which spoke that epithet was deep and melodious, and very close. Jilana's eyes flew open and came to rest upon a white-robed man standing in front of her. He was painfully thin, the flesh stretched so tautly across his face that it seemed the angular cheekbones must pierce the skin. His blond hair fell straight to his shoulders and glinted in the sunlight. A scrap of memory nagged at Jilana. This man was a stranger and yet she felt she had met

him before; his face was vaguely familiar. He was young,
no lines or furrows yet marred the lightly tanned flesh,
and his features were sculpted in such perfect detail that
he might have been Apollo come once more to walk
among mortals. Until Jilana saw his eyes. Bright green,
his eyes glowed with an inner fire that terrified her and
held her motionless. He was consumed by that fire, driven
by forces Jilana could sense but not comprehend. The day
seemed suddenly chill.

"Up, slave; come with us." He gestured behind him.

Jilana tore her eyes away from the man and saw, for the
first time, the Iceni warriors guarding the other Roman
prisoners. Her own terror was reflected in the faces of her
countrymen. Shaking, not wanting to obey but afraid to
defy this strange man, Jilana rose, her stola clutched in
her hands. "Wh-where are you taking us?" Jilana's
question was haltingly asked, and her voice died completely when the malevolent glitter in the man's eyes increased.

The malevolence, however, did not extend to his voice.
When he answered, his tone was as sonorous as before.
"To make peace with the goddess," came his reply, and
there was a gleam of grim satisfaction in his green eyes.

Something deep within Jilana cried out that his answer
was not what it seemed, but she was helpless to resist his
strange power. As if in a dream she felt herself take one
step forward, then another. And then Jilana heard Caddaric's voice; it was faint, as though it traveled a long
distance, but it was enough to make her pause.

"Nay, Lhwyd, not this one. She was given to me with
the Queen's blessing."

The green eyes left Jilana, swung to the intruder, and
narrowed viciously. "Greetings, Caddaric." Even though
Lhwyd was visibly annoyed, his voice never varied in its
sweetness. "How fares your honored father?"

"Well enough." Caddaric moved so that he insinuated
himself between Jilana and Lhwyd.

The instant she was lost to Lhwyd's sight, Jilana felt the
loss of his power over her. Her leg muscles trembled in

reaction and Jilana fought to stay on her feet. Never had Caddaric's harsh voice been so welcome! She cast a fleeting glance at her countrymen; they remained terrified and thoroughly cowed. But why? What was so frightening about going to the temple to worship their gods? Jilana forced herself to concentrate on the two men.

"Your father is a Druid," Lhwyd was saying. "You, better than most, must understand the importance of what we are about to do."

Caddaric laughed coldly, a laugh Jilana had heard so often before. "I understand nothing, Lhwyd; not your gods, not your ways, and least of all your rites." He gestured toward the group of Romans. "I care not what you do with these, but the red-haired one is for me, not your stone altars."

The muscles in Lhwyd's jaw worked furiously. "It is not for you to decide, Caddaric. This is a matter for the goddess and she has decided—"

"Nothing," Caddaric interrupted rudely. "You have decided, Lhwyd; 'tis your interpretation of the omens which sways the people."

"But not you," Lhwyd replied, and this time his sweet voice was tainted with mockery and something else Jilana did not recognize. "Never you. You will go your own way regardless of who you shame."

Caddaric stiffened. "The shame is in your mind and your sister's. I never lied to Ede." He heard Jilana's sharp intake of breath and willed her to remain silent.

"You gave her hope where none existed," Lhwyd countered. "Some might say that is a lie." When Caddaric's hand fell to the place where his sword normally hung, Lhwyd smiled coldly. "Druids do not fight."

"Aye, they satisfy their thirst for blood with sacrifices," Caddaric taunted in return. "Leave the girl, Lhwyd; you want her not as a sacrifice to the Morrigan but to Ede's vanity." For Caddaric, that was the end of the matter. He wrapped a hand around Jilana's upper arm and pushed her gently in the direction of the house.

"You cannot do this," Lhwyd shrieked from behind them. Gone was his soothing tone; his voice now reflected the depth of his anger. "I am a Druid now, Caddaric; not the lad who worshiped you upon your return. My word is the law!"

Caddaric stopped and turned back to Lhwyd. "And my loyalty is to the Queen; you and yours are here on her sufferance. Shall we take the matter to Boadicea?" The phalanx of warriors looked from the Druid to Caddaric as he waited for Lhwyd's reply. When, after several long moments, the Druid turned his back on Caddaric and walked away, the contingent followed and Caddaric propelled Jilana up the steps.

When they entered the bedchamber, Jilana's strength finally abandoned her and she collapsed upon the couch. "Is is true," she asked when she was certain she could speak without a betraying tremor to her voice, "that *man* is going to sacrifice my people to his god?"

"'Tis true," Caddaric answered gruffly. He carefully folded away his used tunic and withdrew a pair of *breeks* and garters from his clothes chest. "But the Morrigan is a goddess, not a god. Our goddess of battle; the face of the Earth Mother in war."

Jilana looked away as he pulled on the breeks with their gathered ankles and secured them around his waist. She was no longer comfortable with the intimacy they had established in the bath. When she looked back, Caddaric had smoothed the tunic back down and was sitting on the bed, cross-gartering the material to just above the knee. The horror of his answer formed a pool of despair within her. "He is Ede's brother?" Caddaric's reply was a curt nod. "Do you think Ede asked him to...kill me?" Silence greeted her question and Jilana's nerves finally shattered. "By the gods, Caddaric, answer me! Will this Lhwyd be satisfied with your ownership of me or will he come again?"

Caddaric said simply, "You are mine. I will protect you."

"How?" Jilana demanded. "Priests are powerful; even Caesar listens to them. How long do you think Boadicea will put your claim above one of a priest?"

Caddaric knotted the second garter and, at last, looked straight at Jilana. "I will protect you," he repeated solemnly. "Believe that."

Her heart believed his words and trusted him, but Jilana's mind knew the bleak truth of the matter. Lhwyd would eventually go to the Queen, complaining of Caddaric's stubbornness in the matter of his Roman slave, and she would be turned over to the white-robed Druid.

The despair on her face hurt Caddaric and he slowly crossed the room and gathered Jilana into his arms. With her head resting on his chest he murmured over and over, "I will protect you, little wicca; nothing will harm you."

Jilana burrowed into the warm haven of his embrace, wanting desperately to believe him but knowing that, eventually, not even Caddaric would be able to cheat Lhwyd of his prize. Caddaric stroked her hair with one hand and his lips pressed reassuring kisses against her temple, and for a few precious moments Jilana willed herself to ignore the idea crystallizing in her mind and pretend that they truly were two people who held each other in deep regard.

At last Caddaric pushed Jilana away and regarded her seriously. "Forget Lhwyd, little one. The Queen gave you to me and only she can take you away." He kissed her gently upon the lips. "And now, I think we must take care of your hair."

As Jilana sank back to the couch, Caddaric retrieved her comb from the top of his chest. Joining her on the couch, he turned Jilana so that her back was to him and slowly, patiently, began to work the multitude of snarls from her hair. Surprised at his actions, Jilana sat quietly beneath Caddaric's ministrations. Gradually she relaxed, finding the motion of the comb and his gentleness soothing. Behind her, Caddaric smiled, enjoying his work and the effect it had upon her. And while he worked, while Jilana remained physically relaxed, her mind raced as she sought an avenue for escape.

Chapter 4

ESCAPE. The knowledge of what must be done, once planted in her mind, had given Jilana no peace, and Caddaric's announcement that the war band would march tomorrow had nearly sent her into a state of panic. Escape. Walking beside Caddaric toward the plain which bordered the eastern edge of the oak grove where Boadicea's feast was to be held, Jilana fought against a rising tide of despair. How could she manage an escape in the few hours left to her? Caddaric, as a mark of his trust, had removed Heall as her watchdog upon their return from the bath and had left her alone while he went with a group of other men to help with the preparations for the feast, but neither man's absence had abetted her plan to escape. While they were gone, the Iceni had looted the villa—save for the bedchamber she and Caddaric shared—and vandalized what could not be carried off. Jilana had remained in her chamber during the looting, afraid to venture beyond its security after her encounter with Lhwyd. Then Caddaric had returned, and though his presence was a comfort it also dashed her half-formed plans of stealing a horse from the stable and getting away from Venta Icenorum.

Jilana sighed inwardly and wrapped the russet paenula more closely about her against the evening chill. It was dusk now, and the fires lit by the Iceni flickered a wan orange against the darkening sky and looming oaks. She had prayed silently to her gods, begging them to deliver her from Caddaric, and their answer was here, walking easily at her side with one arm around her waist. Perhaps the gods knew that she was torn, that part of her wanted to remain with Caddaric and explore the tender feelings he aroused while the other screamed that to do so would seal her fate. Or perhaps the gods could not give an answer until her own ambivalent feelings were resolved. Aye, that was it, Jilana told herself. She would have to harden her resolve against the inner man Caddaric had begun to reveal to her. What difference did it make that Caddaric had been gentle in taking her into womanhood, or that he had promised to protect her, or that he had worked so patiently over her snarled hair and enjoyed the task? Jilana blinked away the tears that formed when she remembered how he had worked the comb through her tangled curls, all the while admiring their color and texture. Nay, she would escape—had to escape! Her life was more important than the betrayed trust of this man! She must never forget that he was a warrior born and a soldier trained; if his Queen so ordered he would hand her over to that mad Druid, Lhwyd, without a second thought, no matter what his feelings might be. Jilana shivered at the thought and Caddaric's arm tightened immediately.

"Are you cold?" Caddaric looked down at Jilana and frowned when she did not lift her head to meet his gaze.

"Nay." Jilana kept her eyes fixed on the fires ahead. Isolated as she had been during the last few days, she had not realized how many Iceni had come to Venta Icenorum. At least a hundred fires dotted the landscape, which meant that the war band surely numbered in the thousands. Boadicea truly intended to have her war. "What is expected of me tonight?"

Her chill tone heightened the unease Caddaric had been experiencing since the encounter with Lhwyd and he drew Jilana to a halt. "You will sit beside me, share the fire and eat your fill. What else should you do?" Jilana continued to stare off into the distance and Caddaric impatiently turned her face to him. "Answer me, Jilana."

"Serve you and the others from your village. After all, tonight Roman slaves will be in short supply, at least for servants." Jilana held his gaze until anger blazed in the blue depths of his eyes and hardened the planes of his face; then her eyes slid away to focus on the center of Caddaric's chest.

"You blame me for Lhwyd's actions," Caddaric breathed, anger warring with a sense of loss. "'Twas not my doing, Jilana." Jilana shrugged indifferently and a sliver of fear embedded itself in the region of his heart. Eyes narrowed, Caddaric again used his free hand to force her to look at him. "What are you thinking?"

Jilana twisted out of his hold. "You may have my body, Caddaric, but my thoughts are my own. Did you think this afternoon would change that?" The breath hissed between his clenched teeth and Jilana resumed walking in the direction they had been headed. Fool! she chided herself. You should have remained soft and pliable; now you have reawakened his suspicions.

Caddaric followed Jilana, wrapping his fingers around her arm to steer her toward his fire. Jilana was wrong, though she could not know it. He was wary of her strange mood, but not suspicious. Caddaric believed she was afraid, and in her fear lashed out at him. As the days passed she would come to understand that he would, indeed, protect her and then she would open herself to him once again. As they walked, he silently cursed Lhwyd for having resurrected the wall between himself and Jilana.

Several people were gathered around the fire to which Caddaric guided Jilana. Meat was being turned on spits above the fires, including this one, and standing this close the smell of the roasting meat made Jilana slightly nauseous. Heall and Clywd smiled their welcome, a gesture Jilana could not find it in herself to return. Artair and Ede were present as well and Jilana was silently grateful when Ede sidled up to Caddaric and engaged him in some meaningless conversation. Unfortunately Ede's shift of attention also freed Artair, and he lost no time in imposing himself between Heall and Jilana.

Artair made a show of inspecting her, his brown eyes sweeping from head to toe and then intently examining her face. Annoyed, Jilana snapped, "What are you looking at?"

"You." Artair smiled a thoroughly engaging smile that Jilana was certain had melted many an Iceni maid's heart, but his eyes remained hard. "I see no bruises."

"Did you expect to?" Jilana inquired acidly.

Artair shrugged. "Caddaric is without equal as a warrior, but I wonder if his prowess on the battlefield is not a disadvantage in his dealings with women."

Jilana wanted to hit him. Instead she looked deliberately at Caddaric and Ede and then back to Artair. "He does not seem at a disadvantage." Gods! Did everyone know what had transpired in the bath?

Artair's eyebrows raised at her self-possessed tone. "I suppose Caddaric does hold a certain fascination for some women. I would not have thought you were one of them."

"As Ede is?" Jilana asked with mock sympathy. "Poor Artair. Have you nothing you can call your own?" She did not wonder at her own daring. Let Artair do his worst; if he killed her for her uncivil tongue it was likely to be a far swifter death than Lhwyd had planned. Artair stiffened beneath the verbal blow and suddenly Jilana knew the reason behind his interest in both Ede and herself. The breath she had inadvertently held sighed out of Jilana. "You are jealous of him."

A grin split Artair's face, but when he spoke his voice was strained. "Jealous of Caddaric? You have taken leave of your senses."

Wise enough not to press too hard, Jilana murmured, "As you wish," and moved away to sit on the grass just outside the circle of firelight. Looking around, Jilana watched the Iceni gathering around the fires. Embraces were exchanged, as well as some friendly insults which were quickly forgotten as the Iceni refilled their skins from the plentiful vats of mead and the more rare kegs of Roman wine which dotted the spaces between the fires. The last remnants of the sun were gone now and the moon and stars began to appear in the night sky. Around her Jilana was aware of the women unwrapping the rest of the feast as they gossiped about everyday subjects: their husbands, their children, the birth of a baby, their homes. And when they spoke of the future their remarks were prefaced by, "When we return from battle." Celtic voices swirled around Jilana; from the distance a bard sang the glories of bygone days and suddenly Jilana realized why the sound of the Iceni tongue, familiar from childhood, was now oddly changed to her ears. For the first time in her life, the Iceni were free, truly free in spite of the battles yet to come, and that freedom resounded in their voices and actions. Were these the sounds from Caddaric's youth? Jilana wondered, forgetting that she was hardening her heart against him. Was the loss of what she was witnessing what had driven him all these years?

Jilana pulled away from her thoughts long enough to acknowledge Heall when he left the fire and joined her. He appraised her much as Artair had, but his eyes were compassionate. Jilana felt a blush rise in her cheeks and was grateful for the darkness. Caddaric's friends apparently had no doubt as to what had transpired between the two of them.

Heall looked up at the heavens. "A pleasant evening." From the corner of his eye he caught the motion of Jilana's head as she nodded agreement. "There is a chill to the air, though. Each year I am more eager for Beltane."

"This year the celebration will be even more special, will it not, Heall? The Beltane fire will be kindled by a Druid," Jilana observed quietly.

"Aye." Heall's voice held an unmistakable note of reverence. "Too many years have passed since our priests have been present."

Jilana looked to where Clywd stood, the fire casting leaping patterns upon his black robe. He was as tall as his son, but not nearly as muscular, and their temperaments were so different that Jilana often had difficulty believing they were father and son. And yet in one way they were similar: both held themselves apart, as though an invisible wall separated them from the rest of their countrymen. Caddaric's aloofness Jilana understood, it was the way of a man who made a living through waging war, but she found Clywd's remoteness confusing when he so obviously cared for his people. Curious, she asked, "Where has Clywd been since Caddaric freed him?"

Heall left his contemplation of the heavens and looked at Jilana. "On Mona."

A chill ran down Jilana's spine and before she could stop it, a tear spilled from her eye.

Heall nodded sympathetically and wiped the dampness from her cheek with a finger. "He left barely a month ago. I woke up one morning—the day before Boadicea was flogged—and he was sitting at my hearth, staring into the ashes. When I asked why he had left Mona, Clywd replied that he was needed here."

"And you believed him?"

Heall chuckled softly. "I have known Clywd for all of my fifty years. The first I knew of his gift was the day thirty years ago." His voice grew soft as he traveled back to the days of his youth, and in spite of her own predicament, Jilana listened eagerly. "Caddaric had just been born, and in celebration Clywd and I formed a hunting party. My sister's husband was one of those who joined us and I shall never forget the look on Clywd's face when he saw Gawen. He knew, you see, that Gawen would not return from the hunt, but he hoped that his vision was wrong." Heall's voice trailed off and he had to clear his throat before continuing. "Gawen died, torn apart by the wild boar we were tracking. Clywd killed the boar using only his knife." Heall shook his head. "He was a madman, leaping from his horse and charging the animal before we could stop him. He should have been killed—no one takes on a boar with only a knife—but he emerged without a scratch, the only blood that of the boar. Clywd picked Gawen up, carried him home and then disappeared into the forest for a week. I was frantic, searching for him throughout the daylight hours, but his wife, Caddaric's mother, told me to leave him be, that Clywd would return. And he did.

"Clywd came to me and told me what had happened. This was not the first time the sight had come to him; he had been living with it since boyhood but had rejected it. He wanted to be ordinary, to live a simple life; Gawen's death had showed him that he could deny his power no longer. His wife understood, perhaps better than I, the pain he had been living with in attempting to deny the sight. Clywd left for Mona that same day and was gone for five years. When he returned he was changed but still my soul's friend. There was a sadness in him that permeated the delight he found in his wife and children. I do not know if he saw their fate, if he knew that he would have them for only a few more years, but I think he did. But for those few years they were happy; Clywd had learned the art of healing on Mona and he gave up farming and raising horses and cattle. Raiding was commonplace then, and on more than one occasion our village was glad of his art." Heall saw the tears brimming in Jilana's eyes and reached over to pat her hand. "I am sorry; I did not mean to make you sad."

Jilana shook her head. "I am glad you told me, Heall. It helps me understand why Caddaric turns so often against his father."

"Caddaric was without a father for the first five years of his life and when Clywd returned it was another year before his youngest son truly accepted him. And then Claudius invaded and Clywd and the other two boys were taken and Caddaric was left to me. Life has soured that young man, I am afraid."

"But not you," Jilana commented wryly and had the satisfaction of seeing Heall grin his agreement.

"Nay, not me," Heall laughed. "As long as there is mead to drink and women to love, life is never bitter."

Jilana's soft laughter joined his. "And why have you never married?" she asked when their laughter faded to smiles. "Surely one of those women you loved felt

slighted when the warrior Heall did not take her to wife?''
Heall's smile disappeared with alarming suddenness, and
Jilana hastily apologized. "Forgive me, Heall, I did not
mean to pry."

Heall remained silent for a long time, watching the fes-
tivities around them, and when he spoke his voice was
laced with pain. "Our ways are different than yours, Jilana. A woman may accept or reject a suitor as she
pleases, according to her wishes rather than her family's.
And she may share a man's bed freely without benefit of
marriage; there is no shame in that." He hesitated for so
long that Jilana thought he was finished, but then Heall
cleared his throat once more and continued. "I gave my
heart to a woman once, many years ago. I wanted, more
than anything, to take her to wife but there were entan-
glements, complications I could not overcome. To ask
another to be my wife would have been unfair."

Jilana would have pursued the topic further but at that
moment Boadicea, flanked by her two daughters and followed by warriors of the royal household, arrived in her
wicker chariot. A great cry went up from the Iceni as
Boadicea dismounted and walked among her people; the
sound built and swelled and the Iceni stamped their feet
and beat their weapons against their shields until the
ground trembled. Unlike Heall, Jilana did not rise in order to salute the Queen. She remained seated, watching.
Heall raised his voice with the tumult but Clywd was silent and unmoving while Caddaric merely nodded his
support as Boadicea passed by.

Boadicea's fire was at the heart of the roughly formed
circle of Iceni, and when she had reached it she raised her
hands and gestured for silence. Slowly the shouting subsided and her strong, confident voice rang out. "My people, the time has come! Tomorrow we march against the
Roman oppressors!" The Iceni shouted their approval
and Boadicea waited patiently for their silence. "Already
we number a thousand, and even now the rest of our nation rides to join us. The Ordovices and Trinovantes will
ally with us as well. By Samh'in we will have driven the

legions into the ocean and destroyed all traces of Rome in
our land. No more will our precious island be known by
the hated name of Britannia. As we take back our land,
so shall we take back the name of our country. Albion!''

This time the roar was deafening and looking up, Jilana found that Caddaric had lifted his sword high above
his head and was shouting along with the rest.

"And now, my people," Boadicea continued when she
could be heard again, "let us celebrate what is to come.
Lhwyd," she gestured to the Druid who stood respect-
fully behind her, "has blessed the herd from which this
night's feast was taken. With the gods watching over us
our success is assured!''

With a final, thundering salute the Iceni settled to the
ground and applied themselves to their food. Uncertainly, Jilana rose and stepped closer to the fire as people
swarmed around her and reached out with their knives to
carve off chunks of meat from the roasting haunch of
beef. Jilana stared at the meat, the bile rising in her throat,
and knew that she could not force herself to eat it. There
was a gentle touch on her arm and she turned to find
Clywd regarding her sympathetically.

"I regret there is no fowl, but Caddaric has said that we
must save them for the march since ducks and chickens
are easier to transport than cattle." Clywd smiled and
reached inside his robe to extract a leather bag which he
handed to Jilana. "I managed to save this from the
kitchen, but eventually, child, you will have to learn to eat
as we do."

Nodding, Jilana took the bag. "Thank you, Clywd."
Caddaric appeared at her side, a large piece of meat
skewered on his knife in one hand and a wineskin hanging across his chest. In his other hand he carried part of a
loaf of bread. Holding her own meal, Jilana followed
Caddaric to a small group of people and reluctantly sat
beside him. The only familiar face was Heall's and Jilana
braced herself against the expected abuse from the others. When it was not forthcoming, she dared a quick
glance around and was surprised when two of the women

greeted her with shy smiles. She responded with a tremulous smile of her own and then turned her attention to her meal.

The drawstring bag yielded two rounds of cheese, dried figs, a generous handful of almonds and a small pot of preserves—more than enough for one meal. Jilana crumbled a bit of cheese between her fingers and dropped it onto the ground as an offering to whatever gods inhabited and protected the plain before breaking off a portion of cheese for herself and returning the rest to the bag. Beside her, Caddaric was tearing into his portion of beef with obvious relish, the loaf of bread balanced on his breek-clad thigh, ignoring the conversation which flowed around them except to nod or shake his head when a question was directed to him. When the meat was gone, he wiped his knife clean and returned it to its sheath, then tore a piece of bread from the loaf. He was as methodical in his eating habits as he was in everything else, Jilana thought as she nibbled the cheese.

Jilana found it impossible to remain aloof from her eating companions for long. Gradually the women drew her into conversation by asking questions about her life before the revolt. At first Jilana answered hesitantly, uncertain of their motives and more than a little discomfited by the fact that the men would pause to listen to her replies. The women, however, were genuinely interested and their questions were without malice. They were simply satisfying their curiosity. Jilana could not help comparing this conversation with those she had had with Claudia, and immediately felt guilty because Claudia suffered by the comparison. Her appetite disappeared and Jilana returned the cheese to her bag.

"You could be Iceni," one of the women was saying, and Jilana looked up at her. Her name was Guendolen and she was a true warrior maid. A sword lay by her side in its sheath and her hair was obviously bleached and hung stiffly about her shoulders. She was also tall and the muscles in her arms and legs bespoke the rigors of her training and life. Jilana murmured her thanks for the compliment and the warrior maid continued. "I have often seen you ride outside the town; you ride well."

Jilana smiled weakly, embarrassed that this women recognized her while she could not remember ever having seen the woman. Until a week ago, Jilana realized, she had paid little attention to the Iceni. "Your hair is most unusual," Jilana offered in return.

Guendolen smiled with pleasure and Jilana found it hard to believe that she could be fierce in battle. "I wash it with lime, according to the old ways."

Jilana listened as Guendolen explained that once men and women alike had treated their hair with the bleach obtained from heating shells or limestone. It was as Jilana was reaching for the wineskin Caddaric held out to her that an unnaturally high scream rent the air. The sound froze her hand in mid-air and Jilana felt the fine hairs at the back of her neck stand up. The scream came again, followed by a wail of Latin words that was soon drowned out by Celtic voices. Slowly, carefully, Jilana withdrew her hand and placed it on her lap. There was no need to ask what had happened or stand, as the others were now doing, to see the event with her own eyes. She knew. Lhwyd had begun the sacrifice.

"Look at me, Jilana." Jilana obeyed the unmistakable note of command in Caddaric's voice. Her eyes flashed briefly, and in that instant Caddaric saw her fear and panic. And then it was gone, concealed, and while he admired her strength of will he wished it had not been necessary. "Do not be afraid; Lhwyd cannot hurt you. I am here. Trust me."

Caddaric had moved closer so that he could be heard over the din, and Jilana longed to throw herself against his broad chest and into the haven his arms offered. Pandemonium had broken out among the Iceni. They left the fires and dashed to the oak grove, eager to witness the homage being paid the Morrigan, and their excited shouts echoed inside Jilana's head. Their eyes locked, Caddaric drew Jilana to her feet and in that instant she knew what he intended.

"Nay, you cannot ask this of me," Jilana entreated. His gaze flickered uncertainly and suddenly Jilana knew that her prayers had been answered. She hurled herself against his chest with what she hoped was a pathetic sob, and was rewarded for her performance when Caddaric's arms came around her. "Let me go home, Caddaric. Please, I beg you—do not force me to watch Lhwyd put my people to death."

Jilana was trembling in his arms and Caddaric tightened his embrace in a gesture of sympathy and comfort. The victims' screams were becoming more audible now as the ceremony progressed and the Iceni watched in respectful silence. He wanted to tell Jilana that the screams were not caused by pain—that the sacrifice, the actual loss of life, was quick and merciful—that it was fear that caused those pathetic sounds. But he could not. She had endured so much already, and maintained her pride in the process, that he could not bear to have her witness the humiliating attempts the other Romans would make to save their lives. "Very well," Caddaric said at last. "Go back, but keep to our chamber." Jilana's head nodded against his chest and Caddaric tenderly kissed her hair. "I will return as soon as I can." Jilana slipped from his arms and ran toward Venta Icenorum. Sighing, Caddaric watched until she was swallowed by the darkness before turning to the oak grove.

Jilana ran as fast as she could, slowing only when she reached the east gate of the town. With only the moon for light, the paving stones were treacherous and Jilana stumbled several times as she raced through the streets to her home. Finally she was there, bursting through the garden gate and flying through the once beautiful garden. A small statute of Priapus, the god of gardens and fertility, tumbled from its plinth when she bumped into it, but Jilana paid it no heed. The only sounds were her own ragged breathing and the fall of her leather shoes against the stones of the courtyard. The stable loomed just ahead of her and then she was inside, leaning heavily against the door while she caught her breath and her eyes adjusted to the darkness of the building. Her heart was pounding, threatening to burst out of her chest, not from the physical exertion but from nervousness. She waited tensely to be challenged by a guard, but when several minutes passed and the only noises made were by the horses, Jilana relaxed. The stable was unguarded.

At last her breathing steadied and Jilana groped along the ledge by the door until she encountered a lantern and flint. It took several attempts to light the tallow candle within the brass lantern cage because her fingers trembled so badly, but the spark caught and the lantern spread a welcoming pool of light around her. The stable was unchanged; pitchforks and shovels were propped against one wall and in the back she could see a mound of fresh hay. The horses, at least, had been well cared for. Picking up the lantern, Jilana made her way past the stalls until she came to her bay mare. The horse whickered inquisitively when Jilana hung the lantern on a beam and opened the stall and slipped inside. She patted the mare's flank lovingly and reached for the bridle which, thank the gods, still hung from its peg beside the stall. Speed was of the essence, for she remembered Caddaric's promise to return as soon as he could.

It was when Jilana led the mare from the stall that she discovered the saddle was missing. "Nay," Jilana whispered. She could ride bareback, of course, but it would be far easier with a saddle. Lifting the lantern from its peg, Jilana walked the length of the stalls and found to her dismay that all the saddles were gone. Why? The answer came clearly out of her rising panic: the Iceni intended to exchange the Roman saddles for their own. They were the best horsemen in all of Britannia, of course they would use saddles of their own making. Undoubtedly the Roman saddles had been taken as booty or destroyed. The mare whickered again but Jilana ignored her. Perhaps she should take the time to inspect the small storeroom in the hope that a saddle could be found there.

"What are you doing, Jilana?"

The soft question spun Jilana around with a gasp. The light from the lantern did not extend to where the intruder stood, but he was silhouetted against the open door and even if she had not recognized his voice she would have recognized those massive shoulders. While she watched, the mare walked forward and nuzzled Caddaric in a friendly manner. The blood pounded in Jilana's ears and without realizing it she started toward Caddaric. "You must let me go, Caddaric. You must!"

"Nay." The word was flat, clipped, and when the light hit his face the anger sparkling in the depths of his blue eyes was obvious.

Jilana lashed out bitterly. "Why? Why did you let me go when you knew what I planned? Do you enjoy seeing me humiliated, defeated?"

"Nay," Caddaric said again, answering her second question first. "I came after you because I thought you were frightened. And I was worried that one of the warriors might have followed you." One large hand came up to gently stroke the mare's neck. "Until I saw the light from the stable I did not consider the possibility that you might be running away from me."

"Do you blame me?" Jilana demanded. She was trembling so violently that the lantern shook. "Let me go to my own people, Caddaric."

"To what end?" Caddaric regarded her curiously, as if her request made no sense. "The countryside is alive, wicca; Boadicea's people are moving to join their Queen. Even if I let you go you would only be caught again. This is a war and all of Albion is caught up in it. There is no safety to be found on this island."

"Except with you," Jilana retorted scathingly.

Caddaric's head came up at that and his gaze pinned her to the dirt floor. "Aye, little wicca, save with me." He caught up the mare's reins and turned her back toward her stall.

As Jilana followed him, her eyes fell on the tools leaning against the wall. She could not let Caddaric stop her! Her life depended upon getting away from the Iceni.

Carefully Jilana set the lantern on the floor and reached for the closest implement. Her hands closed around a shovel and she tightened her grip until her knuckles turned white.

Caddaric's eyes were focused on the mare, but he was aware of Jilana coming quietly up behind him. "I suppose I should be grateful that you no longer have a dagger," he said. A slight smile curved his lips as he turned his head to look at his spirited little witch. "Otherwise—".

Jilana brought the shovel down upon Caddaric's head with such force that the handle cracked. A groan escaped him and then he toppled forward to the floor like a felled oak. The mare whinnied in fear, rearing, and Jilana quickly dropped her weapon and snatched the trailing reins. Only when the mare had quieted did Jilana dare a look at Caddaric. He lay so pale and still that Jilana was filled with the certainty that she had killed him. She knelt beside him and touched his head. There was a large lump beneath the thick, curly hair that swelled beneath her fingers and she hastily removed her hand, then placed it against his mouth. He was breathing and there was no evidence of blood, and Jilana uttered a short prayer of thanks to whatever gods protected Caddaric. She was about to rise when she caught sight of the pouch containing the food Clywd had given her tied to Caddaric's belt. After a moment's hesitation she rolled Caddaric onto his back and untied the bag. She needed the food, Jilana told herself as tears stung her eyes, for she had no idea how long she would be traveling. And she would not feel sorry for hitting Caddaric, nor would she succumb to this insidious feeling of guilt that told her she had betrayed his trust. But the sight of him lying there, defenseless, made a mockery of her resolution to take the mare and leave without a backward glance. Instead, Jilana bent and pressed the gentlest of kisses upon his lips. Caddaric stirred beneath the pressure and groaned, and Jilana hurriedly rose to her feet.

Jilana led the mare out of the stable onto the villa grounds. Pausing to glance down the intersecting streets, listening intently for sounds that would mean the Iceni were returning from the feast, she traversed the town until she stood in front of the south gate. The gate was open and less than a mile away was the road built by the legions. Hitching her long skirt over her thighs, Jilana mounted and urged the horse onto the well-worn path that was beaten into the plain. When she reached the main road she hesitated, not knowing which direction to take. Jilana vaguely remembered that Lindum, where the Ninth Hispana Legion was based, lay to the north, but she had no idea how far away it was. Aside from accompanying her father south to Camulodunum on one of his trips, she had never left Venta Icenorum. Jilana drew a deep breath and turned the mare onto the paved road, heading south. Camulodunum was the capital city, the headquarters of the governor-general; it should be well defended and offer the protection Jilana needed.

HUNGRY, FRIGHTENED, and weary unto death, Jilana reached Camulodunum late in the afternoon of the third day of her escape. She pulled her mare to a halt in the concealment of the sparse wood edging the paved road and studied the city. There was a great deal of activity outside the city proper and she breathed a sigh of relief when she recognized the leather tunics and aprons of iron strips of the legionaries standing guard. The constant fear of the past three days fell away. It was over! She was free and safe. In the upsurge of emotion that followed, Jilana felt imbued with energy and she kicked her tired mount into a canter in her haste to reach the city. As she approached the city she forgot the strain and fear that had been her constant companions. She had ridden for three days, staying in the forest when she could, but never out of sight of the road for without it she would be lost. Her food had run out by the evening of the first day. The mare, fortunately, had had an abundant supply of food and had upon occasion, found small puddles left by the rain. Jilana had drunk alongside the mare, too thirsty to reject the muddied water. The worst times had been when she had to go deeper into the forest in order to avoid the continual flow of Iceni who were journeying northward to join Boadicea.

Fear had kept Jilana awake and alert, forcing her to continue when she wanted nothing more than to lie down on the carpet of leaves and sleep. Her mare had seemed to understand the need for haste. Whether it was to break into a gallop on those rare occasions when Jilana's fear drove her to use the road or pick a way through the underbrush in the forest, the mare's determination had equaled her rider's, and now Jilana patted her neck and murmured encouragements. At her approach a handful of soldiers had formed up, their short swords drawn, but in her excitement Jilana paid their odd manner no heed. She waved gaily, called her greetings, and failed to notice that when she reined in the mare the legionaries fanned out and surrounded her.

"There is a rebellion in Venta Icenorum," she burst out. "Queen Boadicea—" Her warning was interrupted when one of the soldiers grabbed the mare's bridle, causing her mount to sidle nervously. Before Jilana could control the movement, a second soldier had grasped her arm and she tumbled from the mare's back to land in a heap at the soldier's feet. "What are you doing? I am Jil—" The words died as Jilana confronted the sword pointed at her throat.

"What tribe are you," the legionary demanded. "What trick is this?"

Stunned, Jilana could only stare at the hard face above her. Trick? What did he mean? Her confusion grew as the flat of the sword pressed upward beneath her jaw and he ordered her to rise. Jilana obeyed, shakily, and the legionary circled behind her. The sword point bit into her back and the first tendrils of fear coiled in Jilana's stomach. Why were they doing this? she wondered desperately. Why? Something warm and wet trailed down her spine and Jilana realized the sword had cut deeply enough to draw blood. It dawned on her then that the legionary had prodded her because she had not obeyed his order to march. She started to protest, but thought better of that idea. The man would undoubtedly take her to someone in a position of authority—she could protest her treatment then. She stumbled toward Camulodunum, numbed by this newest threat from such an unexpected source.

Jilana was oblivious to the curious stares she attracted as she was marched through the city. Her legs were trembling and she had to concentrate upon putting one foot in front of the other. A small military post came into view, separated from the rest of Camulodunum by exceptionally broad avenues, and relief swept through Jilana. She would be taken to the *praefectus castra*, the post commander; he would explain this rude treatment. Her hopes were dashed when she was forced instead to a small, rectangular building with barred windows. A jail! Before she could form a protest she was through the front door and in front of a smaller, low door.

The legionary sheathed his sword and wrapped a meaty hand around her arm as the jailer came forward. "A rebel for you," the soldier informed the jailer as the latter unlocked one of the low doors. "Came riding up bold as you please and started jabbering in that damn native tongue."

A cold wave of despair washed through Jilana at the legionary's words. So that was why he had treated her so shabbily! She had become so accustomed to speaking the Britons' language during her captivity that she had forgotten to revert to Latin. Hastily, she tried to correct that mistake. "Nay, you do not understand. I come from Venta Icenorum but I am not Iceni!" Her stomach tightened at the wary look the two men exchanged. "Listen to me, I beg you. I am Jilana Augusta Basilius, daughter of the merchant Marcus Basilius."

"Aye, and I am Augustus Caesar," the legionary mockingly replied. Then he gestured to the other man. "Throw her in the cell."

"Nay, please!" Jilana grabbed the low lintel and dug in her heels, defying the jailer's effort to push her into the cell. "Call the praefectus castra; let me explain to him!"

The legionary ignored her plea. "Mithras, can you not handle one little girl?" he swore when the jailer's struggle to subdue the prisoner earned him a kick in the stomach.

Had Caddaric been present he could have warned the two men that Jilana was not one to meekly accept her fate. Winded and retching, the heavy-set jailer fell backward beneath the impetus of Jilana's foot, and the legionary stepped into the breach. Avoiding Jilana's well-placed kicks, he grasped her flailing legs in one strong arm and with his free hand began prying her fingers from the lintel. He succeeded in loosening one of her hands, and for his efforts received four gouges from her broken nails down his cheek. Swearing feelingly, he picked Jilana up bodily and moved backward until her fingers were forced to relinquish their hold on the wood. Jilana twisted and writhed in this brutal embrace, kicking ineffectually and then turning her nails and teeth on any piece of the legionary she could reach. How dare they treat her this way? Anger and despair overrode common sense and Jilana cursed them soundly, albeit breathlessly, first with the Roman gods and then with the Celtic ones. She was Roman, damn them! A citizen! She doubted she could say the same for either one of her attackers. *They* would not become citizens until they fulfilled their enlistment.

"Stop it, you little she-cat," the legionary growled when Jilana's struggles threatened to unbalance him. The next moment he howled in pain as Jilana's teeth sank into his wrist and hung on. He released her briefly in order to deliver a glancing blow to the side of her head.

Bright sparks of color danced in front of Jilana's eyes and she felt herself crumpling to her knees. Her mouth tasted salty and faintly coppery, and she realized she had bitten into the legionary's wrist hard enough to draw blood. Groggy from the blow, she raised her head and tried to focus on the soldier. "I am Jilana Augusta Basilius. I was taken prisoner at the outbreak of the rebellion. You must believe me!''

In response the legionary wrapped an arm around her waist and tossed her into the cell. The fall knocked the air out of Jilana's lungs and she could only shake her head feebly when the soldier stated, ''No refugee that has made it here has managed to do so on horseback, nor did they use the Britons' language. And even if I had been inclined to believe your story, the way you fight and curse would have caused me to change my mind.''

The cell door closed behind the legionary with a thudding finality that momentarily stopped Jilana's heart. The bolt shot home and she lay motionless, listening as the two men departed. Gradually she realized that the floor of the cell was damp and cold and she turned her head to examine the dim cell. In the far corner was a mound of straw and a wooden bucket, neither of them too clean if her nose was any indication; the air was heavy with the scent of urine, perspiration, and other odors she had no desire to place. The room was devoid of any other comforts. A weary fatalism overcame Jilana and, in spite of her aching head, she knew that in a matter of moments she was going to fall asleep. The last of her energy had been exhausted on the legionary and she needed to rest. She dragged herself to the straw pallet and sank into its prickly depths with a strangled sob. Her last thought was the hope that her mare had fared better at the legionary's hands than she had.

NIGHT HAD COME to Camulodunum, but darkness did not halt the furious activity of the legionaries and able-bodied citizens just outside the city. For the past four days they had worked day and night with shovels and picks in order to carve out a ditch and build an earthwall around the city. The vallation was barely halfway around the city, the progress slowing as the men grew exhausted from their labors.

Centurion Hadrian Tarpeius, his brown eyes bloodshot and red-rimmed from lack of sleep and hard physical work looked on as long, wooden spikes were embedded in the sides of the ditch. Which direction would the Iceni queen choose? Hadrian asked himself yet again. North, to engage the Ninth? Or south, to overrun helpless cities? Daily, Hadrian prayed that she would have the conceit to take on the northern Legion, but the feeling of dread in the pit of his stomach warned him otherwise. A fall from a horse had broken his leg, preventing him from accompanying his century to the battle for Mona. From his tent he had watched them march away under the auspices of his second-in-command and cursed the fact that he was to recuperate in Camulodunum as post commander of the token force quartered there.

He had barely accustomed himself to the crutches when the first survivors of Venta Icenorum had straggled into the capital. Their news of the rebellion had come as a shock, but he had not worried overmuch. He dispatched a messenger to Lindum, asking for reinforcements from the Ninth's commander, Petilius Cerealis, and had sent a similar message to the Procurator, Catus Decianus. As yet there had been no answer from Lindum, nor had his own messenger returned. Hadrian had to assume that the soldier had been killed before reaching his destination. From Londinium had come his messenger, an additional two hundred men to bolster the ranks of the eighty legionaries under his command, and word that Catus Decianus had fled to Rutupiae and taken ship to Gaul. At that moment, Hadrian would have sold his soul to Hades to have that greedy coward Decianus in his power. That worm had loosed the Furies upon Britannia and run to safety.

Would this meager attempt at defense succeed? he wondered now. Mithras, it *had* to! Two hundred and eighty men—perhaps a hundred more if he counted the veterans who had retired near the city to the plots of land given to them at the end of their service—to defend a city of several thousand. And the bulk of the male civilians would prove useless, even if he could equip them. They were government parasites; soft, fat men who would undoubtedly turn tail and run at the first clash of weapons.

The earthwall and the deadly ditch behind it would be the city's first line of defense. Once completed only a narrow causeway would connect the city to the surrounding plain and the Iceni would pay dearly for every foot of the causeway they took. Hadrian sighed and shook his head. His command would be spread too thin around the city's perimeter to stave off any concerted attack, despite the effects of the lethal spikes. It would only be a matter of time before the Iceni realized that they had to span the ditch, and once they did Camulodunum would be theirs for the taking.

Hadrian turned and hobbled back to the diggers. He would have to send another messenger to Lindum. And pray. Along the way, the centurion paused at some of the campfires to talk to his men and offer encouragement. His outward confidence was infectious and he left the soldiers in better spirits than he had found them. At the last fire, he overheard a conversation between several legionaries that brought him up short.

Turning as fast as his crutches would allow, he sought out the speaker and barked, "What did you say, soldier?"

The legionary paled and rose hastily to his feet. "Centurion?"

"What did you say about a prisoner, soldier?" Hadrian hobbled closer and pushed his face close to the other's. The man's cheek bore four, wicked scratches. "What prisoner?"

"Th-the Iceni woman," the legionary stuttered. Hadrian's temper and harsh discipline were legendary throughout the Twentieth Victrix Legion. He was the *primipilus*—literally, "first spear," the senior centurion of the first cohort of the legion. His authority was second only to the legion's commander. For all purposes, this man's word was law within the legion. All this raced through the legionary's mind as he sought to form his answer. "A woman—an Iceni woman who swears she is Roman—came to the town today and I took her prisoner."

Hadrian's face set in austere lines and when he spoke his voice was deceptively quiet. "You did what?"

The soldier's mouth went dry at the mild tone. He knew from experience that the quieter a primipilus became, the more trouble he was in. His voice cracked when he answered, "I took her prisoner and left her in the jail."

"When?"

"L-late this afternoon."

"And why," Hadrian asked mildly, "do you believe this woman to be Iceni when she claims to be Roman?"

The legionary gave his reasons but they suddenly sounded weak and unconvincing. If his judgment of the woman was wrong, he would be doing forced drills under the weight of his forty-pound field pack for the rest of his enlistment. With that thought in mind, the legionary grudgingly gave his name when the centurion asked it, and was reassured when Hadrian did nothing more than nod curtly and walk off into the night.

Because of the crutches, it took Hadrian longer than usual to return to Camulodunum, and with each step he cursed the misguided intentions of the young soldier with whom he had just spoken. Whoever the woman was, she was a valuable source of information—information that could affect his strategy; information that had been delayed for several hours. Upon reaching his office within the garrison, Hadrian ordered his subordinate—one of those useless tribunes sent by the Senate—to the jail to retrieve the prisoner, then sank wearily onto the hard chair behind his desk. Grimacing, he dropped the crutches to the floor and glared at them. His leg ached and he gingerly massaged the flesh that could be reached without disturbing the splints. A measure of opium would relieve the pain, but he dared not use the drug, not until he had interrogated the prisoner. Hadrian settled instead for a cup of wine from the supply his predecessor had left behind. The wine was Egyptian, dark and strong and sweet, and it eased the hollowness in his gut. Hadrian was refilling the copper cup when the office door swung open.

Jilana paused just inside the doorway and when the tribune shoved her impatiently forward she whirled and glared at him. She was angry enough at her treatment and frightened enough of her future to be arrogant when the man behind the desk—a centurion, judging by his helmet—ordered her to sit. "I need a bath," Jilana informed him haughtily. "My cell was alive with vermin. And I demand to know why I have been treated in such an appalling manner!"

Hadrian blinked in astonishment at the brazen display. The furious little creature in front of him was no Iceni, of that he was certain. Her clothes and speech were obviously Roman, her hauteur too clearly inbred to be feigned. Carefully, Hadrian replaced the jar of wine. "Who are you?"

The simple question shocked Jilana into temporary silence. For the first time in nearly two weeks she was being neither bullied nor harassed, and in the moments it took her to assimilate that fact she was aware of the fact that the legionary was studying her intently. "I am Jilana Augusta Basilius, first daughter of Marcus Basilius, the merchant. Our home was Venta Icenorum."

Hadrian considered repeating his offer of a chair, but decided against it. The girl before him in the dirty russet cloak had expended the last of her physical reserves and was functioning now only by the force of her will. He had seen too many men in her condition to allow her to relax now. When she had answered his questions she could collapse. "I am told that when you arrived here you spoke Briton."

"Is that a crime?" Jilana flared. "I was born on this island. I speak the Britons' tongue with the same ease I speak Latin. Since the night of the revolt I have been held prisoner by the Iceni and in order to communicate with them I spoke their language. I am guilty of having forgotten myself with your men, but I have done nothing to deserve being treated like a criminal!"

Hadrian nodded and sipped thoughtfully at his wine. "Other survivors from Venta have found their way here.

They were less fortunate than you, however; they came to us on foot."

"I stole the horse from my father's stable the night of Boadicea's feast," Jilana explained warily.

"Then you were not watched, or kept in chains?"

Jilana looked away from Hadrian's eyes. "The Iceni who claimed me sent me away when the Druid began his sacrifices."

Hadrian's eyebrows arched inquisitively. "That was kind of him."

"Aye," Jilana whispered, remembering that Caddaric had truly wished to spare her. How he must hate her for her treachery!

At the haunted expression on her face, Hadrian decided against pressing for further details of her escape. "You are the only one of your family to have survived?"

Jilana nodded, sudden tears welling in her eyes. "My parents, sister, my betrothed—all were killed the night of the uprising. I was spared because I had once shown kindness to the Queen."

Hadrian rose awkwardly to his feet and, using one crutch to support his injured leg, poured a second cup of wine and came around the desk to hand it to Jilana. "You are weary, I know. Only a few more questions and you can rest."

The wine ran smoothly down her throat and warmed her empty stomach. "Will you send me back to the jail?"

"Nay," Hadrian answered with a brief smile. "You are no Iceni spy, are you?"

Jilana shook her head and, as relief swept over her, sank gratefully into the chair Hadrian had first offered. The centurion believed her; she was safe. His smile was devastating for it was reminiscent of Caddaric's—a slight curving of lips that were more accustomed to being set in a harsh line. Jilana mercilessly drove the thought of Caddaric away and swallowed more wine. Hadrian would help her leave Britannia and she would put the nightmare and Caddaric behind her. The wine's warmth spread through her limbs, relaxing her further. Hadrian was asking questions, questions about horses and warriors. Jilana was not certain she replied, but perhaps she did for the answers she heard were in her own voice. How many did Boadicea have at her command? *A thousand, with more coming to join the war band.* Questions about the Iceni Queen. Did Boadicea plan to march? *Aye.* Where? When? *I do not known their destination.* But when? When, mistress? *Three days past.* The questions continued until Jilana's head spun. At some point the questions became amusing and she laughed, wondering that Hadrian could think she would know anything about arms and food provisions and water.

Gently, Hadrian removed the wine cup from Jilana's slender hand and placed it on the desk. Jilana Basilius was exhausted and, judging from the mixture of laughter and tears, feeling the might of the Egyptian wine. If she knew anything else—which Hadrian doubted—'twould not be learned this night. Consolingly, he ran a hand through her hair and was surprised when she raised her head to look at him.

"I have been so frightened, Centurion."

Her words were as fuzzy as her gaze and Hadrian smiled. His hand thrust through her hair and he massaged the back of her neck. "I will keep you safe, mistress."

"Aye." Jilana turned her head so that her cheek rested in the rough palm. His statement was vaguely familiar, but the effort to remember who had once said the same thing to her and why was too great, so she simply accepted the comfort his words offered.

For a moment Hadrian stood motionless, transfixed by the beauty that was visible beneath the dirt, and the trust she gave so easily. His body was hardening in response and Hadrian wished, fleetingly, that Jilana was other than what she was; that he could take her to his bed, take solace from her body and forget, for a little while, the responsibilities of his command. Ruthlessly, Hadrian killed the longing inside him and shook Jilana lightly. When her eyes opened, his face was as implacable as it had ever

been. "Tomorrow I will settle you in a civilian home, but
for tonight you will have to tolerate what the military can
offer. You may use my quarters; I will have the tribune
escort you."

Hadrian disappeared from her sight and Jilana heard
him open the door and call for the tribune. There was a
low murmur of masculine voices and then she was being
helped to her feet and led through the building into the
night air. The tribune's hand on her arm was respectful,
a vivid contrast to the way he had escorted her from her
cell. At a small, one-story building he drew to a stop,
opened the door and preceded her inside to light a lamp.
Jilana stepped inside and sagged against the wall.

"The bedchamber is through that door." The tribune
gestured toward the wood panel. "Are you hungry?"

Jilana wearily shook her head. She wanted nothing
more than to collapse into bed.

"The centurion has ordered a guard to be placed outside the door, for your protection," he added hastily at the
look of fear that crossed her face. "He will bring you
anything you may desire. Sleep well."

"My horse?" Jilana asked when the tribune was at the
threshold.

"In the garrison stable, I would imagine," the tribune
replied. "If you wish I will check."

"Please. A small, bay mare." The tribune nodded and
left and Jilana closed the door behind him.

Taking the lamp from the low table, Jilana walked
through the spartan room and opened the door to the
bedchamber. This room was equally austere, but Jilana
barely noticed. A small stand held a ewer of water and
basin and Jilana gratefully stripped off her soiled clothing and washed as thoroughly as possible. When she had
dried herself, she turned back the covers and crawled onto
the rope cot. The mattress was not as full as her own, nor
were the linens as fine, but Jilana did not care. Sleep
claimed her immediately.

JILANA AWOKE the following morning to discover she was not alone in the bedchamber. A young girl sat on the single, hard chair in the room, staring at Jilana with avid curiosity.

"Centurion Tarpeius sent me," the girl explained in a bright voice. "I have brought you a clean stola to wear while I launder your own clothes. I am Faline."

Jilana managed a weak smile and sat up, clutching the sheet to her breast. "Centurion Tarpeius?"

"You met him last night," Faline reminded her. "He said I was to let you sleep, but since you are awake, are you hungry?"

While Jilana nodded, Faline scurried off the chair and out of the room. A moment later she returned carrying a silver tray laden with fruit, fresh bread, honey, preserves, cheese and wine. She set the tray on the table beside the bed and reached behind Jilana to plump up her pillow. Jilana sat upright and tucked the linen around her as securely as possible. The tray came to rest upon her lap and Jilana was shocked to discover that she was ravenous. She sampled the bread and preserves first and then proceeded to investigate the other delicacies. Faline half-filled a cup with wine and cut it with water from a second jar while her charge ate.

"When you are finished, I will take you to the bath. Centurion Tarpeius sends his apology that he could not provide you last night with the bath you requested."

Jilana paused in mid-bite and looked into Faline's guileless eyes. Apparently the centurion had not disclosed her ignominious arrival. Jilana was grateful for his consideration.

When Jilana was finished with her meal, she dressed in her old stola and followed Faline to the public baths. There she was steamed, massaged, oiled and strigiled until the last ache disappeared from her muscles and she felt deliciously clean. The stola Faline slipped over her head was of soft, light wool dyed a pale green; its excess length was caught up by a leather belt decorated with bronze. Faline discarded Jilana's stained shoes with a disdainful wrinkling of her nose and offered in their place a pair of heeled sandals, dyed a deeper green than the stola, with low side pieces that were fastened with criss-cross thongs and tied at the ankle. It was when Faline stepped back to admire her handiwork that Jilana became aware of the muted conversations going on around her and the frosty looks sent her way. Since none of the other women in the bath knew her, indeed, had not bothered to introduce themselves, their reaction puzzled Jilana. Next, Faline took a brush and comb to Jilana's freshly washed hair and worked the snarls from its length. Faline's ministrations brought back memories of Caddaric—their lovemaking in her family's bath, his patient labor with her hair—and Jilana sought refuge in conversation with Faline.

"The clothes are from the centurion," Faline replied in response to Jilana's question. "He bought them from my mistress this morning. He will be most upset that the gown is too long."

Surprised that the centurion had gone to so much trouble on her behalf, Jilana brushed aside the matter of the gown's length. "Who is your mistress, Faline?"

The brush ceased its movement and Faline leaned down to murmur against Jilana's ear, "She is the mistress of Suetonius Paulinus."

A rush of blood warmed Jilana's cheeks and she bent her head to study the weave of her gown. That explained the reaction of the other women. No doubt they recognized Faline and had determined that Jilana was of the same ilk as Suetonius' mistress. Well let them, Jilana decided with a resurgence of spirit. She lifted her head and looked haughtily around the room until even the coldest gazes fell away. These women knew nothing of her, of what she had endured, and she would soon be on her way to the port of Londinium to take ship for Rome. Let them think what they pleased and Hades take them!

Upon leaving the bath, the two women found the street filled with people and Faline grasped Jilana's arm to keep from being separated. They stepped into the street, intending to return to the garrison but the flow of traffic was against them and they made little progress. "Where are they going?" Jilana questioned when they were rudely jostled aside yet again.

"To the temple," Faline panted. Smaller than Jilana and clutching Jilana's soiled clothing as well, she fared much worse in fighting the tide. "Every morning since we learned of the rebellion, the priests have sacrificed an ox to Claudius."

Jilana tried to force a path through the human wall in front of her. Beside her, Faline lent her slight weight to the effort but to no avail. They were firmly repulsed and Faline was in imminent danger of being trampled underfoot. "'Tis senseless," Jilana decided. Covering Faline's hand with her own, she turned back the way they had come.

Propelled forward by the crowd, they traveled to the heart of the city where the temple stood. Faline stumbled as they were pushed up the steps and only Jilana's firm grip kept her from falling. There was no gradual slowing, as was usual in a crowd. One minute she and Faline were being borne along and the next they were motionless, backed against one of the towering marble columns that rose to the ceiling and formed the colonnade. In front of her, above the heads of others, Jilana could just see the stone altar which had been set in front of the entrance to the anteroom and the fire which blazed upon it.

"Every sacrifice has been the same," Faline informed her. "The organs of all the sacrifices have been free of blemish or disease, a good sign. The augur says that is a sign that the Divine Claudius will see to it that Camulodunum will be spared the rebellion. Do you believe him?"

Jilana forced herself to nod, but secretly she harbored doubts that the late Emperor Claudius had ascended to the heights where Jupiter ruled. Her thoughts were diverted by the arrival of the priests and the highly decorated sacrifice. The ox stood docilely before the altar while the priests washed their hands with sacred water and dried them on linen cloths, and even before the herald's ritual command for silence, the only sound was the steady music of the flute. Their heads covered with the folds of their togas, the priests took up the square wooden platter that held the *mola salsa*, the sacred flour mixed with salt, and sprinkled the mixture between the horns of the animal and onto the sacrificial knife. Two attendants stripped the ox of its decorations while a third drew a knife along the animal's back from head to tail. The high priest began to chant the prayer, and as his voice rose, so did the tension of the assemblage. Jilana's fingers curled into the palms of her hands as the prayer rose to a final crescendo and she stared, transfixed, as a junior priest advanced upon the altar with a hammer in his outstretched hands and stood to the right of the animal.

"Do I strike?" The lesser priest's traditional question sucked the air from Jilana's lungs and she barely heard the high priest's affirmative reply. With a lithe movement, the priest swung the hammer high above his head and dealt the ox a well-aimed blow which stunned the animal and brought it to its knees. An image of Caddaric falling beneath her own blow replaced the scene in front of Jilana and the pain that mental image caused sliced through her heart. She closed her eyes, willing the vision away, and when she opened them again the ox's throat had been cut. A murmur of appreciation rose up from the people at the clean kill and Jilana drew a shuddering breath. She had never witnessed the sacrifice of so large an animal and she quickly averted her eyes as the priests began the task of dismembering and dissecting the ox. The internal organs were removed. They were examined and found free of disease or blemish. And, as Faline had said, the augur repeated his prediction of safety for Camulodunum. The organs and pieces of the carcass were now put into the flames for the god's consumption. The odor of burning meat spread and Jilana turned aside as it reached her nostrils and made her feel distinctly lightheaded.

Around Jilana conversation had broken out, voices punctuated with laughter as people hurried to reassure each other that they were surely safe from the Iceni rebellion. But in spite of the bright words there was an underlying despair among the Romans that made Jilana nervous. Without waiting for the ceremony to end, or to see if Faline followed, Jilana forced her way through the crowd toward the street. She ignored the angry looks and caustic insults directed her way, conscious only of an overwhelming need to get away from the temple and the death it represented.

By the time she extricated herself from the crowd and could breathe fresh air, Jilana was pale and shaken and covered with a cold film of perspiration. Remembering Faline she looked back, and was trapped in a vision so terrifyingly real that she could not breathe.

Flames rose from the roof of the temple, consuming wood with a ferocious crackling that drowned out the sounds of the dying. Bodies littered the steps of the temple, their blood staining the marble steps. At the head of the stairs, a group of men employed a battering ram against the closed double doors of the temple. As section after section of the roof collapsed, more screams were heard and the men and women who walked the street with their bloody swords dangling from their hands laughed.

"Mistress?"

Jilana gasped at the touch on her arm and she looked down at Faline's questioning face. *Faline!* Jilana jerked her gaze back to the temple and felt the earth rock under her feet. All was exactly as it had been—the temple, the crowd, the priests, the flames rising from the altar. She shivered despite the morning sunlight, the cold emanating from the very marrow of her bones. There was no refuge here, only certain death. Boadicea would come, and when she was finished the capital and all its inhabitants would be dead; Jilana knew this with the same dreadful certainty that had possessed her when she had dreamed of Mona.

"Mistress?" Faline said again and Jilana forced her thoughts back to the present.

"I must speak with the centurion," Jilana said in a hoarse voice.

"He would be with his men," Faline answered with a frown. "At work on the earthwall."

"Show me," Jilana ordered.

"Nay, mistress." Faline's eyes widened in shock. "The centurion said I should return you to your room."

Jilana shook her head and whirled away. "I must speak with him, Faline. 'Tis vital."

Wondering what to do, Faline stood uncertainly in the street as Jilana walked away. The centurion would surely be angry if she allowed Jilana to continue alone, and yet he would be just as angry if Faline accompanied Jilana to the earthwall. With a heartfelt sigh, Faline started after Jilana. She would stay close enough to keep Jilana in sight but far enough away to avoid the centurion's wrath. She was, after all, only a slave, and if she did not have a care for herself no one else would.

As Faline had predicted, Jilana found Centurion Tarpeius reviewing the progress of his defenses, and had she been less upset she would have seen his normally austere expression turn grim at her approach. Hadrian muttered a word of dismissal to his aide and sent a warning glare at three legionaries who had paused in their labors to appreciate Jilana's arrival. When the soldiers had returned to work, Hadrian allowed himself the luxury of turning his own admiring gaze toward the young woman. Last night she had been disheveled, travel-worn and badly treated by his command; he had pitied her and taken her under his protection because honor demanded it. The stola had been purchased from the governor-general's mistress for the same reason. How could he have known that the color would prove a perfect foil for the hair that now shimmered red-gold in the sunlight? At thirty-eight years of age—twenty of which had been spent in his country's service in the far-flung reaches of the Empire—Hadrian had never met a woman who stopped the breath in his throat the way this one now did. With an effort, he subdued that unexpected surge of emotion and by the time Jilana reached him, Hadrian wore his usual stern expression.

"Greetings, mistress." Though he did not unbend enough to smile, there was a soft note in Hadrian's voice.

"Centurion." Jilana inclined her head slightly. "I must speak with you."

Hadrian shifted uncomfortably on the single crutch supporting his injured left leg. "Can it wait until the noon meal, mistress? Certain details here require my attention."

"Nay, it cannot," Jilana interrupted. "Please, Centurion, 'tis important."

With a grunt of resignation, Hadrian nodded and led Jilana away from the working men to a spot of relative privacy. "Very well, mistress. Now tell me what is so urgent it could not wait."

Jilana clasped her hands in front of her, uncertain how to begin, how to convince this man that she had not taken leave of her senses. "Boadicea will come to Camulodunum."

Hadrian looked at her questioningly. "You have remembered more than you told me last night?"

"Nay." Jilana shook her head. "But I know she will come. You must evacuate the city, Centurion, or all here will be killed."

A chill presentiment raced down Hadrian's spine at her words, but he shook it off. "You are overwrought, mistress. You need to rest and in a few days . . ."

"In a few days we will all be dead," Jilana cried. Her outburst drew curious looks their way and Jilana forced herself to speak calmly. "The city is doomed, Centurion, but there is still time to save the people. Surely there are other cities nearby, perhaps even a legionary fortress, which afford more protection than Camulodunum."

Hadrian cut off her speech with an impatient gesture. "So I am to evacuate the several thousand citizens of this city because you doubt the protection it affords," he inquired angrily. "And how, mistress, am I to protect a column of that size with less than three hundred legionaries when you doubt I can use those same soldiers to protect a town that will soon be surrounded by a defensible rampart?'' Hadrian drew rein on his temper, knowing that his anger stemmed, in part, from the fear that he would *not* be able to defend the city. "Forgive my outburst, but you must see that I cannot abandon the possibility of saving both Camulodunum and its citizens simply because one young refugee thinks she knows Boadicea's mind."

"You do not understand." Jilana drew a deep breath before continuing. "I have seen the city's destruction, Centurion. In spite of your efforts, Boadicea will take the city."

"You have seen—" Hadrian frowned down at Jilana. "Are you saying you have had a vision?"

Disbelief was so clear in his voice that Jilana felt herself redden. "Aye, Centurion."

Relieved, Hadrian chuckled. "Mistress, since news of the uprising reached us, I have been besieged by citizens claiming to have had one vision or another."

"You do not believe me."

"I believe you have lived through a terrible experience," Hadrian replied gently, "and are justifiably frightened at the thought of undergoing such an ordeal again. I believe this fear is playing tricks on your mind."

Jilana swallowed her disappointment. She would never convince the centurion of the truth of her vision. "I thank you for the kindness you have shown me, Centurion, but I know what I know. If you will order my mare released from the stable, I will leave for Londinium immediately. And, if you could spare a man to accompany me…" Her voice trailed off as a grim expression settled across the centurion's face, and an instant later his hand wrapped painfully around her arm.

"Even if I could spare a man—which I cannot—I would not allow you to undertake such a journey. With the Britons traveling to join Boadicea, I doubt even a full century can travel safely."

"You have no right to keep me here," Jilana argued heatedly. "I am not your prisoner."

"'Tis my responsibility to keep you and the others safe," Hadrian growled, giving Jilana a shake. "And right now, Camulodunum is far safer than the countryside! I have sent messengers to Lindum and to the governor-general; with luck, reinforcements from the Ninth at Lindum will reach us before Boadicea does."

"Centurion—"

"I will hear no more of this. If necessary, mistress, I will place you under guard." Releasing her arm, Hadrian said in a softer tone, "I fear you must stay in my quarters until this is over; the inns are filled with refugees and citizens are wary of taking in strangers at this time." When Jilana nodded and would have walked away, he added, "I will keep you safe, lady; do not fear."

Jilana walked back into the city in a daze, resigned at last to whatever fate the gods had in store for her. For the last two weeks she had fought for her life and subdued the terror she felt only to have the centurion's misplaced sense of responsibility seal her fate. She could fight no longer.

Before Jilana was out of sight, Hadrian signaled his aide to join him. "Go to the stable; leave orders that Lady Jilana is not to be given her mount." The aide saluted and hurried off and Hadrian turned back to the preparations.

As WAS HIS NATURE, Caddaric awoke quickly at the moment of sunrise, alert to his surroundings although his eyes remained closed. An instant later he cursed his wakefulness, for a sensation akin to having a battle-axe buried in his forehead radiated pain throughout his body. The battle-axe was a perfect counterpoint to the tender lump at the back of his skull. He turned his head to the side and groaned softly at the resultant nausea. Warily, Caddaric forced his eyes to open into narrow slits and regarded the brown blur directly in his line of vision. Gradually the blur came into focus and he realized he was staring at a tree. With that realization came the knowledge that last night he had broken every one of his self-imposed rules and given vent to a fine display of Celtic temper.

It had been the sight of the leather tent in the cart that had ignited his anger and made him swing at Heall. The older man had had no way of knowing that the tent had been intended to allow Jilana and himself a measure of privacy, Caddaric reflected morosely, and Heall had been confused by his sudden attack. The tent, Heall had reminded him, had been confiscated from the small garrison supplies at Venta Icenorum by Caddaric himself. Heall had simply packed it in the cart with the rest of the provisions for the march. By the time Heall had finished his explanation, the older man's jaw was bruised and Caddaric was flat on his back on the ground beneath the combined weight of four warriors, being warned by his chieftain that fighting was now punishable by banishment. Embarrassed, Caddaric had apologized, and Heall had accepted by producing a cask of wine from his portion of the booty. The successful completion of the first six days of the march was cause for celebration, Heall had reasoned, and Caddaric concurred. With their backs against the wheel, they had broken open the cask and begun the celebration.

The afternoon had darkened into evening and others had wandered over to join them. Someone lit a fire, another cask of wine appeared, and the evening meal had been a mixture of venison, cheese and wheat cakes. The wheat cakes, however, served as another reminder of Jilana and Caddaric had hurled his into the fire and turned his full attention to lowering the level of wine in the cask. Events following the meal were rather vague. He remembered trading barbs and jests with the rest of the company, and joining in the ribald songs with unnatural exuberance which did nothing to lessen the hollow ache in his chest.

The gods curse his treacherous, red-haired witch, Caddaric thought now with a resurgence of impotent fury. She was responsible for the emptiness that gnawed at him by day and tortured him by night. She was fortunate that the march had prevented him from hunting her down and beating her senseless. His eyes burned and Caddaric squeezed them shut, denying the sadness that appeared in the wake of his rage. Why had she run? Had his promise of protection meant nothing? Surely she understood that he would never allow Lhwyd to lay so much as a finger upon her. Or, Caddaric winced, had it been not Lhwyd's touch but his own that had frightened her into that desperate escape? Caddaric knew he was not the most artful of lovers, but had he disgusted Jilana?

Caddaric was drawn from his thoughts by a rustling at his side. Cautiously, he turned his head to the other side and opened his eyes. Ede lay beside him, her green eyes wide and watchful. Above the blanket which was thrown over both of them, her shoulders were bare and Caddaric realized belatedly that he was naked beneath the blanket. With a sinking feeling in the pit of his stomach that had nothing to do with the amount of wine he had consumed, Caddaric watched as Ede pressed herself firmly against his side and began drawing idle patterns on his chest. She was as naked as he.

"How long have you been here?" Caddaric's voice grated like a rusted hinge.

Ede smiled and draped a leg across his thigh. "All night. Do you not remember?"

Caddaric dimly remembered staggering away from the campsite when his thoughts of Jilana had proved too distracting for the celebration. Had Ede followed? Aye, she had, Caddaric groaned inwardly, for now he remembered kissing her in the vain hope that she would drive the thoughts of his violet-eyed witch from his mind. Ah gods, what else had he done? Ede's leg moved in a blatant, erotic gesture and Caddaric caught at her hand when it started to disappear beneath the blanket. "Ede, nay."

Ede blinked in surprise. "But last night—"

"—was a mistake," Caddaric interrupted, aware of the flush staining his cheekbones. His physical response to Ede was growing more obvious by the moment and it shamed him. Damn, where was his tunic? "I am sorry."

"As well you should be." Ede snatched her hand away and pushed herself up on one arm to glare at him in mock outrage. "'Tis not like you to drink so much that you fall asleep during a kiss." A lazy smile curled her lips and she slid provocatively upward against his body. "In truth, I did not mind; preparing you for bed was most enjoyable. And I recalled your morning appetite is not limited to food."

"Then last night we did not mate?" Caddaric asked bluntly, and unconsciously held his breath for her answer.

"Nay, but I forgive you," Ede teased, not the least embarrassed and oblivious to the look of relief that passed across Caddaric's features. "I know you will make up for it now." Once again her hand drifted under the blanket.

Caddaric snared her hand and pushed her firmly away. "Nay, Ede. I thank you for caring for me last night but I will not repay you in this manner. Where is my tunic?"

Ede stared at him in disbelief which, as she realized that Caddaric had no intention of bedding her, turned to anger. With a low cry she kicked aside the blanket and rose to her knees. Her green eyes swept the length of him and settled upon his tumescent manhood. "Why do you deny that you want me?" she demanded, shifting her gaze to his face. "I have missed you in my bed, and 'tis obvious that you have missed me as well." When he shook his head, Ede taunted, "Your Roman did not know how to please you, did she? Did she faint at the sight of you, the Iceni barbarian? Did she threaten to kill herself if you but touched her?"

"Enough, Ede," Caddaric snarled. Despite his body's protests, he rolled awkwardly to his feet and located his clothing. "What passed between Jilana and me is none of your concern." With quick, efficient movements he wrapped the loincloth about his hips and shrugged into his tunic.

"When you hold me in your arms and call me by her name, it becomes my concern," Ede threw back at him. "That Roman bitch is the reason you will not bed me. I pray she is dead!'' The cold look Caddaric gave her made Ede self-conscious and she drew the blanket around her, averting her eyes.

Caddaric looked away also, his eyes darkening as he studied the straggling stand of trees where they had spent the night, and considered her words. Ede was right. While his body might welcome the release to be found in any woman, his mind wanted only Jilana. What kind of a spell had his Roman witch woven that he could not forget her? ''We should go back to the camp,'' he said at last.

''Go then,'' Ede spat at Caddaric's broad back, her tone not betraying the tears in her green eyes. ''With your precious Jilana for company, you have no need of me. Go and pack that stupid tent you found for her, the one she will never see. Break your fast with Heall; you can both mourn her leaving and your aching heads and forget that she did not gently bid you farewell—she hated us so much that she broke a shovel over your thick head and *escaped*!''

Caddaric whirled without a word and strode back to the camp. Behind him, Ede buried her face in the blanket and gave way to her tears. When the tears were spent, she wrapped her warrior's pride about her like a shield. She wiped away the wetness on her cheeks, dressed and folded the blanket, then she followed Caddaric, her head held high. She would allow none to see how deeply her heart and pride had been hurt by Caddaric's rejection.

She found the camp preparing to march. Caddaric stood on one side of the cart he shared with Heall and Clywd, chewing a mouthful of grain. At her approach he washed the grain down with the water with which he had refilled his wineskin and straightened. ''Ede. I—''

''You forgot the blanket,'' Ede interrupted. Avoiding his eyes she tossed the blanket into the cart and walked away, her spine stiff with pride.

She would go to Lhwyd, Caddaric guessed with a sigh, or Artair. He scooped a handful of grain from the sack in the cart and chewed it thoughtfully. He had no desire to hurt Ede, but she continually brought the pain upon herself. If only the gods would see fit to send a man who would be strong enough to take her to wife, Caddaric thought, and then he brightened. Surely in Boadicea's war band there was *one* warrior who could catch Ede's eye.

After a last drink, Caddaric slung the wineskin over his shoulders and walked to where his horse was staked. The grain had settled his stomach, and as Caddaric saddled his mount he unwillingly remembered the forced marches in the legion, when they had moved for days with grain and water their only meals. That was exactly what Suetonius Paulinus would do once word of the rebellion reached him. The thought made him impatient with the lumbering pace of the war band. Their ranks swelled every day, and with the growing numbers came the impossibility of swift execution of any maneuvers. If Paulinus ever succeeded in trapping the column, which, Caddaric admitted, was not likely, the Iceni would be cut to pieces by the legion's rapid deployment. And if Paulinus brought not only his infantry, but an *ala* of cavalry as well, the Iceni would be cut to pieces. The presentiment of danger was so unexpected and so strong that Caddaric found his hands trembling as he tightened the girth on the horse.

"Ah, gods!"

The low, agonized rumble jarred Caddaric from his bleak thoughts and he looked over his shoulder to see Heall stumbling toward him. A faint smile touched Caddaric's mouth at the sight of Heall's red-rimmed eyes and pained expression. In the face of Heall's suffering, his own headache diminished. Leaning an arm against the saddle, he nodded sympathetically as Heall leaned against the horse's shoulder and closed his eyes. "Mayhap you should ride in the cart, my friend," Caddaric suggested.

"Nay," Heall croaked. "Clywd would only try to force one of his vile potions down my throat; 'tis the disadvantage of having a healer for a friend." He drew a shuddering breath and squinted up at Caddaric. "I must be getting old, lad; a night spent lifting a drinking cup should not leave me at Annwn's gate."

Caddaric chuckled, and was only faintly surprised when Clywd's soft laughter joined in. There were times when Caddaric wondered if his father could conjure himself wherever he wished. Turning, he watched Clywd glide forward with his usual easy grace. The cart horse, Caddaric noted, meekly followed his father without benefit of halter or harness.

"So, you both survived the night," Clywd commented, his blue eyes glinting. "Heall, my friend, your face is nearly the same color as your beard."

Caddaric gave a muffled laugh. Heall's face was, indeed, a dull gray which reflected the silver of his beard. Affronted, Heall drew himself shakily upright and went to tend his horse. Caddaric grasped the reins of his mount in one hand and walked beside his father to the cart. "How do you manage that?" he asked, indicating the trailing horse. "Magic?"

Clywd laughed softly and shrugged. "Beasts trust me. 'Tis a gift."

"Like the sight."

The impatient statement made Clywd sigh as he reached for the leather harness. How had he created a son who believed only in what he could touch or see? Jilana believed, Clywd thought with a sudden pang; he had seen it in her eyes, read the knowledge in her mind. She believed because she, too, had the gift of sight; but like a fledgling she feared stepping into the world beyond her nest.

"We will reach the city by nightfall," Caddaric offered by way of apology for his brusqueness. "I want to camp well back from the battlefield."

"Why?" Clywd asked. There was great competition for the limited space just behind the front lines; everyone knew the best observation sites were at the fringe of the battlefield, and the privilege of viewing the combat was hotly contested.

Caddaric adjusted the final buckle on the harness and rounded the horse to stand in front of his father. "There is always the possibility of defeat," he answered grimly.

"Should that happen, you must flee since you will not fight."

"You want me to desert you and Heall." Clywd frowned. "I am no coward, Caddaric."

"I did not name you such," Caddaric insisted. Tentatively, he placed a hand on his father's shoulder. This was the first time he had touched his father in several years and he was struck by Clywd's frailty. "Your brothers fought because it was allowed in defence of the sacred island, but your vows forbid you to enter into battle and take a life. If the Romans break through our lines, you, a Druid, will be a great prize. I do not want to chance you falling into their hands by reason of having no avenue of escape."

A smile lightened Clywd's face and he covered his son's hand with his own. "I will do as you wish, unless there are injured who need me. Then I cannot remain safely in the rear."

"Agreed." Caddaric squeezed the frail shoulder and then self-consciously withdrew his hand. Turning away, he untied his horse from the cart and swung into the saddle with easy grace. "If you like, Heall and I will ride back and take the midday meal with you."

Clywd nodded, a pleased expression on his face. Heall and Caddaric were in the Queen's vanguard, a position of pride, and Caddaric had taken his noon meals with the advance body. Until today. Throwing a jaunty salute, Caddaric wheeled his mount and trotted off.

Caddaric joined an uncomfortable-looking Heall and together they rode toward the place where the vanguard was forming up. Approximately ten miles remained between the rebels and the city of Camulodunum and the warriors were anxious to reach their first battleground. With luck, the civilians in the column would be able to keep pace with the main body of the force and they would make camp within sight of the city long before evening. The sight of the opposing army would demoralize the civilians within; a small advantage, but important nonetheless. As Caddaric moved ahead with the vanguard his thoughts turned once again to Jilana, and where on the island of Albion she would have fled. Pray the gods Jilana had been wise enough to seek the protection of the legion garrisoned at Lindum, for if she had run south... That possibility did not bear close examination.

JILANA HURRIED ALONG the paved streets of Camulodunum, Faline close behind. A pall hung in the air that had naught to do with the stench of blood and burning carcass of the sacrifice which had just taken place at the Temple of Claudius—a pall some of the citizens sought to dispel with a forced air of optimism. Boadicea had come, as Jilana had known she would, and only now did the residents of the city realize that while Hadrian's defense allowed only one entrance to the city, it made them virtual prisoners as well.

Word of the Iceni arrival had spread like wildfire and, like the others, Jilana had been seized by a morbid curiosity to see the force Hadrian and his men would oppose. The vallation was complete now, and the raised platform which ran along the inside of the wall was crowded with soldiers and citizens alike who fell silent as they gazed at the rebels. One by one the civilians turned from the sight in front of them and left the platform. As others took their places and the process was repeated, their optimistic veneer cracked and was replaced by desperation. When her turn came to peer over the earthwall, Jilana understood the change. The cleared fields which should have held the seeds of new crops now bristled with wicker chariots, mounted warriors and well-armed infantry. Behind them, wagons were being drawn up and women and children hurried about to make camp. And in the distance Jilana could see a tremendous cloud of dust rising above the treetops, heralding the arrival of still more Iceni. The scene was duplicated as far to the right and left as she could see, as the city was encircled by an Iceni force that now numbered in the thousands.

Because her dreams and visions had prepared her, Jilana was spared the overwhelming fear that swept through her countrymen; she simply accepted the inevitable with a sense of fatalism. About to turn away, Jilana was suddenly shaken by a thought she had successfully kept at bay since her arrival. Caddaric was here! She stared at the distant warriors, knowing it was futile to think—hope?—she could distinguish him from the others, but she tried nevertheless. Behind her, impatient voices told her to move aside but Jilana ignored them. She laced her suddenly trembling hands together and willed the mind that had shown her so much in the past four days to show her Caddaric now. She needed to know that he suffered no ill effects from the blow she had dealt him. The force which tortured her with scenes of destruction, however, refused her attempts to control the nature of those visions. Nothing appeared save the prolonged arrival of the Iceni force and, defeated, Jilana turned to relinquish her place on the platform. Something touched Jilana; it was the lightest of pressures, as if an arm had been draped around her shoulders and then slowly drawn away. Startled, Jilana glanced about to see who had taken such liberties and found no one near her who would have been so gentle. And in that instant she knew who had touched her, although she did not know how. Clywd.

As Jilana made to step from the platform, a very human hand reached up to assist her and she looked down into Hadrian's stern countenance. "You should not have come," Hadrian admonished as he forged a path for them through the crowd.

Jilana remained silent, wincing inwardly when Hadrian misstepped and came down hard on his injured leg. As unobtrusively as possible she steadied Hadrian until he regained his balance and they could continue. "You should be using your crutch," Jilana told him softly.

"The citizens are skittish enough; the sight of me limping along on crutches would send them into a blind panic," Hadrian gritted.

And how will you manage in battle when your leg is not totally mended? Jilana wondered, but she kept the question to herself. Hadrian had become her protector, benefactor and friend during the course of the evening meals they had shared and she knew how heavily the responsibilities of his office weighed upon him. She would do or say nothing to upset him. They paused before one of the houses that marked the beginning of the city and Jilana gazed once more at the dust clouds that rose in the distance. "Will you dine with me this evening, Centurion?" Her invitation was formal and gracious, as if destruction did not wait beyond the vallation.

Hadrian glanced at her profile, admiring the set of her jaw and proud carriage. If Jilana was frightened, she hid it well. "If my duties permit, mistress, I would be honored."

Jilana looked at him then and offered a brave smile. He was care-worn, the lines of responsibility deeply etched in his face. She had tried to hate him for keeping her here, for confiscating her horse, but she had not been able to. Like Caddaric, Hadrian was trying to protect her, but unlike the warrior, Hadrian had ruthlessly blocked all her avenues of escape and sealed her within his protection. How could she hate a man who, though misguided, had only her welfare at heart? She could not. She accepted the situation as it was and, because Hadrian treated her kindly, she created a haven out of his quarters so that he might escape his grinding responsibilities for a time. Now she touched his arm lightly. "Whatever the hour, Centurion."

Hadrian nodded curtly and walked away, and Jilana knew he had been embarrassed by her touch. In spite of the desperate situation, Hadrian had been concerned with her reputation; when they dined together, the door to her quarters remained open and a tribune stood guard outside; and if they met in public, Hadrian addressed her as "mistress" or "lady." As she watched Hadrian melt into the crowd, Jilana knew a tremor of fear for him—and, if she would but admit it, for another.

Instead of returning directly to her quarters, Jilana skirted the garrison and walked toward the center of the city until she encountered the building she sought. It was a small temple—not on the same scale as the one of Claudius—but its workmanship was flawless. The temple of Minerva, the goddess who patronized defensive war and useful and ornamental arts. The temple was empty, although oil lamps flickered in their wall holders. The sound of her footsteps was unaccountably loud against the silence and the muted street sounds. Jilana passed through the anteroom into the *cella*, and as she walked she drew the belt from her waist. At the foot of the steps leading to the altar Jilana prostrated herself, then rose and ascended to the altar to place the belt with its bronze decorations upon it. Behind the altar stood the statue of Minerva, the daughter who had sprung from Jupiter's brain in full battle armor. She hoped the goddess would deem the belt an exchange worthy of the favor she was about to beg. Descending the steps, Jilana stretched out full length upon the floor and shivered when the cool marble chilled her skin.

"O merciful Minerva," Jilana prayed, her eyes fixed on the altar steps. "I ask your intercession with Mars for the lives of two warriors, the Iceni Caddaric and the Roman Hadrian. In return, I offer my belt and—" she drew a tremulous breath "—my own life." There was a hint of desperation in her voice when she added, "I have nothing else of value to offer, O goddess, yet I would have these two men live through Mars' most savage love of bloodshed and violence. I beg you to accept my unworthy offering and find favor with my plea."

Rising, Jilana retraced her steps through the cella and paused when she found Faline waiting at the door to the anteroom. The two women exchanged a long look. "You heard," Jilana questioned at last.

Faline nodded. "Why do you pray for the enemy?"

Jilana gave a choked, confused laugh. "Because he, in his way, also sought to protect me; because in a night of death he gave me back my life." Jilana shook her head as the memories descended. "Because in another time, another place, he would not have been my enemy." She looked through the anteroom to the street beyond where frightened people moved aimlessly or clustered in small knots, arguing. The panic Hadrian feared had not set in, not yet.

"Do you think they will attack today?"

Jilana turned her attention back to Faline. "I do not know. Mayhap."

"What should we do?" Faline's voice held a rough edge of fear.

"Do?" Jilana smiled wearily. "There is naught to be done, Faline. Later we can be of help to those who are injured but now..." Her voice caught and she was silent for a moment. "We can but wait, and pray. Go home, Faline."

The girl hesitated. "'Tis said Centurion Tarpeius sent to Lindum for reinforcements. Will they arrive in time?"

Jilana forced a confident smile. "I am certain they will. The centurion's defenses will doubtless hold the city for several days, more than enough time for the relief column to arrive." She touched the younger woman's shoulder reassuringly. "Go home now, Faline."

The two women went their separate ways. Jilana stopped at the stable on the way to her quarters to visit her mare and feed her a handful of oats. The mare would at least be spared, Jilana thought numbly. The rebels had need of horses. Once inside her quarters, Jilana swept the two small rooms and straightened the covers on the bed—all unnecessary tasks since Faline had cleaned the rooms that morning, but the work kept her thoughts from the inevitable. When that was finished, she returned to the front antechamber and sat watching the shadows lengthen against the floor. She wished that she could cook, and that the small house afforded a kitchen, so that she might occupy the time, but the garrison kitchen saw to her needs. She knew that her calm was unnatural, that she would shatter against the fear the way the glass vial had shattered against the floor, and she waited for her control to break.

When more shadows than light filled the room, Jilana struck a spark against a taper and lit the oil lamps with

steady hands. The Iceni had not attacked; Camulodunum had been given one last night of life. Her meal arrived and Jilana gratefully turned to arranging the food
on the low table in front of the couch. She sat back, admiring her handiwork, and at last allowed her thoughts to
turn to Caddaric. What was he doing? she wondered, and
immediately there arose a strong image of Caddaric sitting before a fire, partaking of the evening meal. The
firelight played over his set features and burnished his
heavily-muscled flesh so that he resembled a statue of a
god. A whirlwind of emotion swept through Jilana and
she closed her eyes against its force.

He would never be called handsome; his features were
too harshly angular to fit that word. But there was about
him a strength that was far more compelling than the su-
perficial arrangement of flesh over bone. She had felt that
strength upon their first meeting, had been drawn to it in
spite of herself. That power could overwhelm, frighten,
and it concealed his astonishing capacity for gentleness.
Had she stayed, Jilana was certain she would never have
feared Caddaric again. Had he understood why she ran?
She shook her head miserably, knowing he had not. He
had promised her his protection, and to his mind that
promise should have been enough to allay her fears.

"Mistress?"

Jilana snapped out of her reverie to find Hadrian regarding her curiously from the doorway. Oh, Juno, if only
things had been different! "Welcome, Centurion; come
in." As he stepped into the room, Jilana glanced beyond
the door. "Where is your tribune this evening?"

"In charge of the vallation." Hadrian pulled his helmet off and ran a hand through his hair. "He will send for
me if I am needed."

Jilana smiled and rose to take the helmet from him and
set it aside on a low chest. "Sit down, Hadrian; the pain
in your leg must be fierce."

"'Tis not so bad," Hadrian replied, but the sigh that
escaped him as he settled upon the couch said otherwise.

Looking at the night sky, Jilana's heart quickened. The sky was unnaturally bright with the Iceni campfires. Behind her, she could hear Hadrian pouring wine. "Will they come tomorrow, then?"

There was a pause before he answered. "Aye, tomorrow. Probably just after first light."

His voice was laced with weariness and Jilana firmly closed the door against the sight that had sent a brief pang of terror through her. The sight of Hadrian sitting stiffly erect on one side of the couch brought an indulgent smile to Jilana's lips. "You will be more comfortable without your armor," she said quietly, moving to his side. "Come, I will help you."

For a moment it looked as if he would protest, but then Hadrian simply nodded and allowed Jilana to undo the shoulder buckles that held the front and back pieces of the cuirass together. When she set the heavy armor on the floor and propped his leg on a small stool, Hadrian nearly groaned in relief. "Thank you, Jilana." She smiled, handed him a cup of wine, then filled one of the garrisons' tin plates from the food on the table and handed him that as well before taking her seat at the opposite end of the couch and preparing a plate for herself.

"How are your men faring?" Jilana asked when they had eaten in silence for several minutes.

"Well enough," Hadrian replied. "Most of my men have been blooded, so the sight of the enemy has not unnerved them." He reached for another piece of fowl and ate it thoughtfully while watching Jilana nibble at the food on her plate. "And you, Jilana, how are you faring?"

"I thought I would be afraid, but I am not," she answered quietly.

"I should have let you go when you asked," Hadrian said, and then cursed eloquently when she stared at him. "Forgive me, Jilana, for both my profanity and stupidity."

"Your language does not offend me, Hadrian, nor do I think you stupid. You have done your best for all concerned." Jilana set her plate aside and refilled their wine cups.

"But you would now be safe—"

"Safe!" Jilana laughed despairingly. "There is no safety here on Britannia. I know that as well as you. Nay, Boadicea will have her revenge."

"When Paulinus hears of the uprising, he will waste no time in returning and putting an end to the rebellion." Hadrian savored the rich Egyptian wine, unaware that Caddaric had voiced the same opinion.

"But he will not be in time to save Camulodunum, will he, Hadrian?" Jilana queried softly. "Neither will the Ninth Hispana."

"If we can hold them long enough. . . ." The words he had recited so easily to the terrified citizens who had approached him throughout the long afternoon lodged in his throat. Jilana deserved better from him than a desperate lie. Hadrian studied the depths of his cup before continuing. "I believe that Suetonius will come, but too late. In all truth, I believe the messenger I sent to him has yet to arrive at Mona. And as for the Ninth—Petilius Cerealis is a noble commander, but I fear the messengers I sent to Lindum were killed before they could reach him."

Jilana expelled her pent-up breath as Hadrian drained his wine. "Thank you, Hadrian."

"For what," Hadrian laughed bitterly. "Condemning you and this city to death?"

"Nay." Jilana shook her head. "For the truth."

"You accept your end too easily," Hadrian said angrily, "and far too calmly. I will fight to my last breath."

Sipping her wine, Jilana considered the man opposite. "I think the gods planned for me to die at Venta Icenorum; and I would have, save for the intervention of a warrior. For nearly a fortnight I have fought against and delayed my fate. This time, when the Iceni come, I will not be spared; nor do I wish to be. I am tired of the struggle, Hadrian, so tired. I feel as if I have never known peace."

Hadrian nodded in understanding and filled his empty cup in brooding silence. "Over half my life has been spent fighting Rome's avowed enemies and putting down rebellions. At the end of the year, my twenty years of enlistment would have been up. With my separation pay and the money I saved over the years, I planned to buy a farm and retire from the legion.''

"A farm?" In spite of their hopeless circumstances, or perhaps because of it, Jilana found the thought intriguing. "Where?"

"At home, a hundred miles or so outside of Rome." Hadrian smiled at the thought. "My cousin found it for me and the last time I was home on leave, I met with the present owner. We signed a contract for the sale.''

"What would you have raised?"

"Wheat and barley. And horses." Hadrian laughed when Jilana glanced at his broken leg. "Aye, horses. The cavalry alae are constantly in need of good horseflesh and they pay very well. For the profit, I could have grown to like the animals.''

Jilana laughed as well. "Is there a wife waiting for you also?"

Hadrian shook his head and gave Jilana a wry smile. "A smart woman does not marry a man to whom she must constantly bid farewell. I would have liked to marry, though, when I retired." He paused, his brown eyes shimmering as he glimpsed a future now beyond his reach. "Perhaps even had a child or two to brighten the rest of my years." He shook off the thought and looked at Jilana. "And you, Jilana; what plans did you have for your life?"

"I would have been married by now," Jilana replied, then teasingly added, "to one of those tribunes you constantly reproach. When his tour here was finished, we would have gone to Rome.''

"You did not like that idea?" Hadrian asked, alerted by the subtle change in her tone.

"I have lived on Britannia all of my life," Jilana said, her hands raised in a helpless gesture. "'Tis all I know. My sister, Claudia, visited Rome and told me of it. I suppose in time I would have adjusted to the city, but I think I would have missed my home."

"Did you love him?" Hadrian asked impulsively, and then was embarrassed when Jilana stared at his boldness. "Forgive me, Jilana, I did not mean—"

Jilana waved aside his apology. "Nay, Hadrian, I did not love Lucius, but I found him considerate." Hard on the thought of Lucius came disturbing memories of Caddaric and Jilana rose to pace the room. Opening the shutters, Jilana gazed at the star-filled sky. "Do you sleep before a battle, Hadrian?"

"Aye."

Sighing, Jilana rested her head against the window frame. "I do not think I shall sleep."

"I will send the surgeon to you," Hadrian offered. "He can give you a draught that will bring you rest." At her soft refusal, he got to his feet and went to stand behind her. In a low, halting voice he said, "Or I will stay with you." When Jilana did not reply, Hadrian wiped his damp palms against the skirt of his tunic before placing his hands lightly upon her shoulders. "Let me give you what comfort I can."

Jilana turned, a small smile playing across her lips as she looked up at him. "I will not be intimate with you."

Hadrian swallowed. "I understand; physical release is not what I seek." He hesitated. "I would like, for the remainder of the night, to pretend that I am home on my farm. That you are my wife and our children sleep in the next room. I would have, if only for a few hours, that which now will never be mine. In truth, I fear you will bring me far more comfort than I will you."

His request was so much like Caddaric's had been, revealing the softer side of their natures that both concealed, that Jilana nearly wept at Hadrian's simple wish. Caddaric had asked for a little peace, and Jilana fully understood, at last, what he had meant. Such a good man, she thought sadly; too good to have his life ended before his dream was realized. At that moment, not even Jilana could have said whether she meant Hadrian or

Caddaric. She took one of Hadrian's rough hands in both her own and walked beside him into the small bedchamber.

The chamber was lit by a single oil lamp, and in its flickering glow Jilana slipped out of the green stola and laid the garment across the chair. By the time she unbraided and brushed out her hair, Hadrian had stripped to his loincloth and eased himself beneath the covers. Jilana blew out the lamp, but when she joined Hadrian on the narrow bed and her flesh brushed his, she stiffened. Hadrian's arm curved around her shoulders and drew her to him so that her head rested on his shoulder. Hesitantly, Jilana placed her hand upon his chest but Hadrian did nothing more than draw the linen and blanket around her shoulders.

When some of the stiffness had left Jilana, Hadrian spoke, his voice barely more than a whisper. "Now, wife, tell me of your day."

It was a game of pretend and Jilana spun a tale of household duties and the antics of two children who would have brightened their father's life. When she fell silent, Hadrian took up the story, telling her of crops recently planted and foals newly born. Jilana expanded upon his stories, thought up new ones of her own for which Hadrian returned the favor, and for a time it was easy to believe the imagined was real. Incredibly, Jilana grew drowsy, her eyelids drooped and she snuggled into a more comfortable position against Hadrian. Weariness overtook ner and she fell asleep.

Hadrian smiled when her breathing took on a deep, even rhythm and he pressed a kiss upon her forehead. "It was such a beautiful dream." He closed his eyes and sleep claimed him instantly.

IN THE DARK GRAY of early morning, that time of day suspended between moonset and sunrise, Jilana awoke to the sounds of someone moving about the antechamber. Stretching out a hand, she found herself alone in the bed and knew that Hadrian had risen and was preparing to leave. Tears burned her eyes as she thought of the night past but she pressed the heels of her hands against her eyes to drive them away. Recovering a measure of composure, Jilana rose and went to the antechamber. Hadrian sat where he had during the evening meal, partaking of the fresh meal which had been laid upon the table.

Sensing her presence, Hadrian turned and met Jilana's gaze with his own calm regard. He stood and managed a slight smile as he invited her to join him. "'Tis only a cold meal," Hadrian explained when Jilana sat beside him. "I ordered the cooks to forsake their kitchen for the comfort of the vallation."

"You need not apologize, Hadrian." Jilana carved a wedge of cheese from its wheel and ate it slowly. Hadrian was ready for dawn; his plated cuirass gleamed in the light of the oil lamps, as did the apron of iron strips which hung from his waist. At the door sat his helmet with its tuft of colored horsehair and his baldric which sheathed his gladius. A dagger was suspended on the right side of his belt. "Did you sleep?"

"Aye, soundly." Hadrian finished a wheat cake and washed it down with a cup of water. "You gave me more than comfort last night, Jilana, you brought me peace and renewed my courage. Even my leg does not ache this morning." He took her free hand and held it gently within his rough one. "I can almost believe that we can save the city."

Looking deeply into his eyes, Jilana saw the truth there. "I am not afraid, Hadrian; do not seek to bolster my spirit with false hopes."

Hadrian nodded. "We can hold them for a time, with luck, until nightfall and they will break off the attack. We will have bought another day."

"Do you believe that?"

"Nay," Hadrian answered. "At best we can keep them from the city until midday, after that . . ."

"I understand."

"Mithras, I wish I did," Hadrian exclaimed fiercely, his facade shattering. He strode to the door and picked up his helmet and baldric. "These tribes have been civilized for nearly two decades. Except for an occasional trouble-maker like Caratacus, most of the trouble had been confined to the west; the Britons in this area accepted us long ago."

"Nay, they did not," Jilana said quietly. "We invaded their island, took away their priests, left their kings powerless and set up temples so that they might worship our Emperor. In our arrogance we laid the kindling for this conflagration; Boadicea is but the spark."

"Since the early days of the Republic, it has been our way to conquer. An uprising in some far-flung territory will not change policy." Hadrian muttered an exasperated oath.

"It does not matter to us, Hadrian."

Jilana's words dropped into silence and they stared wordlessly at each other for several moments before Hadrian swung the baldric over his shoulder. He pulled the dagger from his belt and held the unadorned weapon out to Jilana. "You will have need of this. 'Tis well honed; there will be little pain."

After a brief hesitation, Jilana took the dagger from him.

Hadrian took her arm and pushed back the wide sleeve. Using his forefinger, he traced a path across her wrist as he spoke. "A dagger strike to the heart is not certain; you must open your veins in this manner, with deep, bold strokes. Do you understand?" When Jilana nodded, he continued. "When my legionaries fall back you will know the defenses have been overcome. Bar the door and windows and use the dagger. Do not hesitate, Jilana; better a swift, honorable death by your own hand than what the Britons would do to you. This is the only comfort I can give you."

Hadrian kissed her lightly on the mouth and then he was gone. Jilana closed the door behind him and slowly walked to the bedchamber. She laid the dagger upon the bed, then washed and drew on the green stola and green-heeled sandals. Jilana straightened the room and the bed, reclaimed the dagger, and then returned to the antechamber and forced herself to eat a bit more of the meal. When she was finished, Jilana covered the remaining food with a cloth. From its place on the table, the dagger drew her attention and, giving in to some impulse she could not explain, Jilana used it to cut a strip from the cloth covering the food and tied the dagger securely to her inner thigh. Going to the two windows, she opened their shutters. The sky was no longer gray, but streaked with the first light of the sun. Jilana put out the oil lamps and then returned to the window.

All was silent, not even the birds trilled their usual morning greeting. Jilana stood motionless for several minutes, staring blindly across the parade field to the deserted barracks. As the silence dragged on, Jilana allowed herself to think Hadrian had been wrong. Mayhap Boadicea thought Camulodunum's defenses too strong to attack. Mayhap she sought worthier prey than a detachment of legionaries and defenseless citizens. Mayhap—

The silence was rent by three sharp blasts that Jilana identified as coming from a *carnyx*, a Celtic trumpet. The echoing sound drained the strength from her legs and Jilana slid downward until she came to rest upon the floor. Thousands of Celtic voices raised in battle cries flooded the air to assault her ears, and there followed the rumble of thunder which was in reality the pounding of horses' hooves and human feet as the Iceni stormed the vallation. A minute later came the screech of metal upon metal and Jilana covered her ears so that she would not hear the screams of the wounded and dying.

CADDARIC'S PLACE WAS in the first line of the phalanx surrounding Camulodunum. To his right and left, had he been able to look, he would have seen his fellow Iceni hurling their javelins across the vallation in the hope that their spears would find a mark. Far to the rear, the best archers loosed their arrows upon the defenders with little success. The soldiers behind the earthwall had undoubtedly been ordered to keep their shields above their heads in order to foil just such an attack. Caddaric himself was in the vanguard assaulting the legionaries who held the only land bridge to the city. The legionaries were well trained; they presented a solid wall with their shields which neither raised nor lowered although it bristled with the blades of their short swords. Those blades would thrust and withdraw, thrust and withdraw, in the time-honored tradition of the legion and took their toll on the attackers. Early on, Caddaric had tried to tell those next to him how to breach this defense: the attackers must keep their own long shields in front of them and use their swords—of greater length than the gladius—to thrust through the cracks which appeared in the wall of rectangular shields.

A few listened and were successful in their attacks; from time to time, and with increasing frequency as the battle wore on, one of the rectangular shields would fall but it was quickly replaced by another. Those who ignored Caddaric's hoarse shouts and tried to defeat the barrier with their favored slashing strokes found death at a Roman sword. Caddaric blinked the sweat from his eyes at the same moment he felt an enemy blade thrust against his leather-covered shield. In answer, he jabbed his own sword forward and felt it slither between two shields. A heartbeat later his sword encountered resistance and he heard a man cry out. The enemy shield wavered when Caddaric pulled back and though it fell completely, an instant later the gap it left was filled.

The battle had raged since dawn; it was now midday and Caddaric had been fighting the entire time. His reflexes had slowed, and the arm which held the heavy, wooden shield was trembling under the strain. He should have left the front line long ago, before his strength had been depleted to this point, but his judgment had been clouded by this joyous physical release of his inner turmoil. His control had returned, however, and now Caddaric eased himself out of the fray. The battle lines behind him were five deep and his place was immediately filled. Looking back, Caddaric was filled with dismay at the

Iceni bodies which littered the ground at the bridge. Blood turned the dirt to mud and the bodies made a firm purchase all but impossible. At the sides of the bridge, the bodies had been kicked aside into the trench, but the middle ground had not been cleared. In their battle lust, the Iceni gave no thought to the hazard the bodies caused and so did nothing to remove their fallen comrades.

While Caddaric watched, the frustration of the unbreachable Roman wall drove the Iceni mad and several hurled themselves upon the exposed short swords. The back lines surged forward in the vain hope of overpowering the wall through sheer force and Caddaric turned away, sickened. He forced his way to the rear where he dropped his sword and shield and sank onto the grass. A young boy struggling under the weight of a water bucket hurried to his side and offered Caddaric the wooden dipper he carried. Caddaric drained the bowl, poured a second cup over his head and sent the boy on his way with a gruff thanks. Similar scenes were being repeated elsewhere behind the lines as tired warriors and warrior maids retired from the front. Behind the wagons, the nonfighting women and older children were felling trees and using horses to drag them in front of the encampment. Boadicea's strategy was to clean the trunks of branches and then drop them across the ten-foot ditch to provide access for the warriors to the vallation.

The Queen's plan might have succeeded, if she had agreed to delay the attack until after the trees were felled and ready for use. Unfortunately, she had not. By now the legion commander—who, Caddaric had decided upon seeing the defenses, was a cunning veteran—had had time to assess the meaning of such activity and was undoubtedly planning ways to negate this newest assault. Caddaric himself saw Boadicea's plan as futile. *If* the Iceni managed to position the tree trunks securely, and *if* a warrior managed to cross the makeshift bridge without losing his balance—and this meant leaving his shield behind—and falling to his death, all the legionary had to do was wait until the warrior was close enough to be felled by a thrust of a gladius. Caddaric's respect for the Roman commander rose. The man had taken an indefensible city and turned it into a stronghold. Aye, Caddaric reasoned, the key to breaching the defenses lay in taking the land bridge. Once the bridge fell, with the attackers engaging the legionaries from behind, the tree trunks could be positioned and the Iceni could cross them at a greatly reduced risk to themselves. Caught between the two Iceni lines, the Roman defenders would be cut to pieces. It was vital that the bridge fall *before* the logs were positioned. Rejuvenated, Caddaric took up his sword and shield and set out to find the Queen.

THE SHARP BLARE of the carnyx followed by the reluctant withdrawal of the Iceni forces came as a surprise to Hadrian. All morning his soldiers had gradually given up possession of the land bridge inch by hard-fought inch, but even though he estimated that there were three Iceni casualties to his one, Hadrian was grimly certain that unless the Ninth Legion appeared immediately, the city was doomed. Given the Iceni reserves and the growing number of Roman dead and injured, by nightfall the Iceni would have reached the city side of the bridge. Once they reached their goal, the enemy would fan out and the city would be lost.

Hadrian had spent the morning circling his defenses, exhorting the legionaries to keep their shields above their heads. The Iceni archers were accurate, though their efforts were futile as long as the Roman shields remained in place. The leather of Hadrian's own shield was scarred where the enemy arrows had dug into the covering and penetrated to the wood beneath. Hadrian's tribune had been insulted by the slim shafts protruding from the leather and, over Hadrian's objections, had taken it upon himself to pull out the arrows or break the shafts of the ones that had penetrated too deeply. A nice boy, Hadrian reflected now as he stood on a slight rise behind the land bridge, watching the Iceni pull back, a bit too filled with the glory of Rome for Hadrian's taste, but nice enough, even so. Now the tribune lay on the other side of the city with an Iceni javelin buried in his chest. He had tried to remove the weapon, but had stopped when it became obvious that the head was of the twisted and barbed type that ripped the wound still further when it was taken out. Mercifully, the javelin must have penetrated some vital organ for the tribune had died quickly. Hail Caesar, Hadrian thought bitterly.

Of necessity, Hadrian pushed such useless thoughts out of his mind and concentrated on the scene in front of him. What was Boadicea planning? Why had she broken off what would, ultimately, have been a successful attack? He shook his head when the Iceni did not bother to protect their rear as they withdrew; his junior officers saw the advantage at the same time and shouted orders. Roman arrows and *pili* sang through the air and found defenseless targets. Hundreds of attackers fell beneath the missiles, and when their comrades turned back to drag their bodies from the field—a noble, stupid action which caused Hadrian to shake his head—they, too, were killed.

Across the field, Hadrian could just discern Boadicea where she stood in her chariot. During the battle she had done what he had, except that she circled the outer perimeter of the defences in a wicker chariot drawn by two jet black horses. Now her chariot stood in the midst of a knot of perhaps a hundred warriors—her cadre, Hadrian guessed. Hadrian watched the meeting for several minutes, curious. From the distance came the sounds of axes meeting trees; Boadicea still planned to use the trees to breach the ditch, then. Hadrian considered and discarded several reasons for the Iceni withdrawal and at last shook his head. He would know soon enough the Iceni queen's plan; until then he needed to take advantage of the respite.

Hadrian lowered his shield to the ground and slid his gladius into its baldric. He motioned to the only centurion in his ranks as he descended the rise. "My tribune is dead," Hadrian informed the officer when he had saluted. "You will take his place." He pulled the helmet from his head and ran a hand through his damp hair. Without the battle fever to mask it, the ache in his leg now grew to sickening proportions. Hadrian willed himself to ignore it. "Pick your best *decurio* and have him lead a detachment to relieve the force on the bridge. See that the men eat and drink while they have the chance." Hadrian glanced back to where Boadicea held council. Pray Mithras this meeting dragged on like other Celtic councils had been known to do. If the Iceni squabbled long enough, Camulodunum might gain another day.

"Is that all, primipilus," the centurion asked.

Shaking his head, Hadrian pressed his lips together and came to a decision. "Take ten men, go into the city and bring out every man capable of fighting. Draw their arms from the garrison armory and get back here as soon as you can."

The centurion saluted and left and Hadrian lowered himself to the ground. Immediately the ache in his leg settled into a dull throb and Hadrian forced himself not to groan in relief. Eating the food taken from the pouch on his belt, Hadrian watched as his orders were carried out. Hadrian, as well as his men, ate and drank slowly and sparingly. By the time he had finished, the centurion had returned from the city with the hastily-armed civilians. Hadrian got to his feet and explained briefly what would be expected of them.

One of the civilians—more foolhardy than the others—protested. "We are not soldiers. Tarpeius! Most of us have never handled a gladius before."

Hadrian glared at the man. "You will have to learn quickly."

"This is ridiculous," the civilian sputtered. "The armory did not even have enough weapons for all of us."

"Then go among the dead and take their swords," Hadrian ground out. "Or you can meet the Iceni bare-handed if you prefer. I care not what weapon you choose, but you will fight."

"Not I." The man threw his gladius to the ground and folded his arms across his chest. "I am a cloth merchant.

My taxes support the legions and you are paid to protect me, not drag me into the midst of the fighting!''

Murmurs of agreement rose from the men around the spokesman and Hadrian knew what he must do. The man was frightened, refused to accept the danger the city faced, and was inciting the others to mutiny. To argue with him was pointless. Hadrian's eyes hardened until they looked like polished stones as they sought out and found the two legionaries in the front ranks of the civilian escort. Raising his left hand, Hadrian crooked two fingers toward them in a deceptively careless gesture. The two soldiers stepped forward and when Hadrian nodded, each seized one of the civilian's arms. Drawing his sword, Hadrian walked to the captive. The man had just a moment to realize what was going to happen before Hadrian's gladius pierced his heart.

Hadrian pulled his blade free and, while the legionaries dragged the dead man away, fixed his gaze on the other civilians. "If the Iceni make it past our vallation you will envy your friend his death. Is there anyone else who doubts his ability to fight?''

There was no chance for an answer, because at that moment a cry went up from the guard on the bridge. "Deploy them," Hadrian ordered the centurion as he bent to retrieve his helmet and shield. Climbing the rise, Hadrian could see that the Iceni were on the move once again, but this time there was a difference. Now they advanced like legionaries, their shields interlocked both above their heads and in the front ranks, and spears, not swords, protruded from the front line. Instead of wildly assaulting the vallation, the other Iceni hung back, using their javelins and archers to advantage; but what concerned Hadrian was that the advancing phalanx was double the size of the Roman contingent it would meet on the bridge. Armed with spears, they could decimate the legionaries while remaining out of reach of the gladius, and through sheer force of numbers, they would roll over the bridge.

Hadrian's eyes narrowed as the enemy approached, wondering if the well-ordered ranks would dissolve once they encountered his men. It had happened before—the Celts were easily provoked and found more glory in individual combat than disciplined strategy. The two forces met and Hadrian knew a twinge of unwilling admiration for the enemy as his legionaries were immediately forced backward. While he watched, the Iceni formation shifted, consolidating itself into a wedge while maintaining the protection of its flanks. Alarmed, Hadrian ordered reinforcements to the bridge and drew his own sword. Someone in Boadicea's contingent had a practical, working knowledge of battlefield tactics and had persuaded the Queen to use that knowledge. Even now the wedge had forced an opening in the front Roman ranks and was worming its way forward. Reluctantly, Hadrian ordered more legionaries to the bridge and knew as he did that it was futile. More Iceni were charging forward, rolling over the legionaries left in the wake of the vanguard before they could close behind the wedge. The Iceni vanguard broke through to the Roman side of the bridge in what seemed an impossibly short time and the enemy surged through the breach in an inexorable wave. The Iceni had abandoned their spears and formations in favor of their long sword and were now engaging the legionaries in brutal hand to hand combat. Bellowing, ignoring the jarring pain in his leg, Hadrian ran to meet the rebels. He had an instant—just before his sword met that of a tall, grim Iceni—to wonder if Jilana would have the strength to carry out her own suicide, and then his thoughts were taken up in defending himself against an enemy who fought like a legionary.

FOR JILANA the day passed in a daze. She sat huddled against the wall in Hadrian's quarters, moving only once, when a group of civilians and legionaries had marched through the garrison to the armory. She had watched them leave and had known the situation was desperate if Hadrian had ordered the civilians to the defenses. When the carnyx had shrilled again she nodded to herself, resigned to her fate. When the Iceni overran the city, she would be killed. Since the garrison stood on the outskirts of Camulodunum, it would be one of the first buildings to be taken. At this point the rebels, intent upon destruction, would not think to take prisoners for Lhwyd's sacrifices. Whatever warrior or warrior maid stumbled across her would make short work of her death. Jilana was grateful for that; to her shame, she was too weak to use Hadrian's dagger.

The sounds of fighting intensified and Jilana rose shakily to her feet and opened the door of the small house. Outside, the bright spring sunshine seemed a mockery of the day's events. She was frightened, Jilana realized as her trembling legs carried her into the sunlight, but it was a numbing fear, tempered with an odd sense of relief. It would all be over soon, and she would be free of the fear she had lived with for so long. She thought of Caddaric and Hadrian, wondering if they still lived or if they had already fallen during the battle. The thought of either of them dead brought a swift pang to her heart and to ward it off, Jilana offered another prayer for their safety. The stable caught her eye and without thinking of what she was doing, Jilana walked toward it. It mattered not where the Iceni found her, and the stable was as good a place to die as Hadrian's cramped quarters. At least she would be able to say farewell to her loyal mare.

The stable was shadowed and as Jilana moved down the aisle between the stalls, the horses whickered nervously at her. She paused occasionally to stroke an inquisitive nose that was pushed over a stall door. When Jilana found her mare's stall, she leaned against the low door and wrapped her arms around the mare's neck.

"You will be cared for," Jilana murmured, pulling back so that she could pet the mare's head. "The Iceni value good horseflesh." From without came the fearsome Celtic battle cries and the sound of pounding feet and Jilana knew a moment's panic. Her hands turned icy with fear and to steady herself, Jilana pressed her cheek against her mare's strong jaw.

The stable door burst open and Jilana knew someone stood in the entrance, allowing his eyes to adjust to the shadowy interior before advancing further. The breath stopped in Jilana's throat. Charon, I come, Jilana called silently to the boatman who ferried the dead across the River Styx. Accept me as you surely accepted my family. Juno, intercede on my behalf.

With the last of her strength, Jilana pushed herself away from the stall and took a step into the aisle. Her green stola stood out against the gloom of the interior and Jilana sensed rather than saw the sudden attention of the man at the door. His large body filled most of the entrance, and with the sun at his back he was a dark, terrifying figure. He stepped into the stable and Jilana felt her heart stop. She wanted to call to him, to tell him that she was alone, that no danger waited for him here and he should end this quickly, but she was beyond speech. The sound of his footsteps drummed in her ears as he drew nearer and Jilana closed her eyes. She was suspended in time, aware of nothing and everything.

"Still so eager to die, Jilana?"

Jilana's eyes flew open at the sound of her name. The dull gleam of a bronze neck torque met her gaze and she forced her eyes upward until they collided with the cold fury burning in a pair of impossibly blue eyes. Caddaric! Jilana tried to say his name but no sound emerged.

Caddaric flicked a glance toward the mare before pinning Jilana with that icy look once again. "Were you planning to run again?" he asked with a harsh laugh. "I should let you try. You would be dead before reaching the street."

Her strength deserted her and Jilana sank to the straw-covered floor, her head bowed. The cold metal of Caddaric's sword slipped beneath her chin and forced her face upward.

"No words, no pretty pleas?" Caddaric asked caustically. "You were full of entreaties and lies at Venta Icenorum."

The accusation allowed Jilana to find her voice. "I did what I had to," she whispered. Irrationally, she was glad that Caddaric had found her. At least she would die knowing Minerva had granted a part of her prayer.

"Aye," Caddaric returned brutally. "You smiled and gave me your body and a few short hours later you lied and knocked me unconscious. 'Tis fitting that we meet again in a stable."

Jilana's eyes slid from his face to the blood-covered blade. "And that you kill me here."

Caddaric was helpless to control the tremor that ran through his sword arm at her words. Damn her for her unnatural calm! Why did she not beg and plead for her life? Why could she not throw herself upon his mercy and into his arms so that he could hold her and hold her and hold her?

Cursing, he lowered the sword, wrapped his free hand around her wrist and pulled Jilana to her feet. She rose willingly enough and stood regarding him silently. No emotion showed in those lovely violet eyes save for a faint curiosity, and Caddaric realized she was simply waiting for him to kill her. A muscle working furiously in his jaw, Caddaric turned and pulled Jilana back to the door. Angry as he had been—and still was—over her treacherous escape, as often as he had sworn that he would kill her with his bare hands if he ever found her again, the moment he had laid eyes on her again Caddaric had known his passion for this violet-eyed witch outweighed all other emotions. He was going to take her back to the Iceni camp, to the tent Clywd had insisted upon raising last night, and he was going to keep her safe because he wanted her more than anything else on this earth.

Jilana tumbled in Caddaric's wake, seeking to match his long stride and not lose her footing. The street through which they passed was free of the carnage which had littered Venta Icenorum, but when they had passed through the city and reached the vallation, Jilana could not avoid seeing the destruction there. Thankfully, she caught no more than fleeting glimpses of the bodies because of

Caddaric's furious pace. The Iceni were still pouring into the city, and Caddaric's grip on her wrist tightened so that they would not become separated.

Once, as they were passing over the land bridge, the heel of her sandal caught in the stola's hem and Jilana slipped over the edge of the ditch. Before she could cry out, Caddaric's hold had checked her fall and hauled her back to solid ground. Her thanks were abruptly cut off when Caddaric dipped and easily tossed her over his shoulder. No further impediments arose to delay their progress to the Iceni camp.

Jilana, hanging upside down over Caddaric's shoulder, had no idea what he planned, so when Caddaric dropped her roughly to the ground in front of a tent she pushed the hair out of her eyes and looked around in surprise. The sword still dangling menacingly from his right hand, Caddaric tossed back the flap of the tent and jerked his head toward the interior. "Get inside."

Some of her apathy had dissolved during the trek from the city and Jilana did so warily. The inside of the tent contained nothing more than a single pallet and Jilana turned to Caddaric in bewilderment. "Stay here," he ordered in a tone that was meant to be obeyed. The flap snapped down behind him, leaving Jilana in almost total darkness except for what little light was afforded by the gap in the tent's ceiling. The hole was meant to vent the smoke from a fire, Jilana supposed, but any further musings on her part were cut short by Caddaric's return.

The sword was safely in his baldric, which left one of his hands free for the length of rope he carried. This time he left the tent flap open and the look on his face made Jilana swallow nervously.

"Lie down."

Her heart lurched at the coldness of his voice. "What do you mean to do?" Jilana had to force the question past the obstruction in her throat.

Caddaric's gaze wandered insultingly over her slender frame and then returned to her face. "Not what you imagine," he said bitingly. "Now lay on the pallet."

Jilana lowered herself onto the pile of furs and, while Caddaric towered over her, stretched out full length. He knelt beside the pallet, dropped the rope and then his hard hands bit into her shoulders. When Jilana gasped at his touch, Caddaric merely raised an eyebrow at her and flipped her onto her side so that she faced the tent wall. He released her shoulders and a moment later, Jilana felt the bite of the rope as he coiled it around her ankles. Her arms were pulled behind her back and her wrists bound by the same length of rope which tied her ankles. In the space of a few minutes, Jilana was trussed in a manner that left her immobile. Even as Caddaric rose, Jilana could feel the strain in her muscles and joints as she was arched backward over the rope.

Caddaric tested the knots at her wrists, ankles and the small of her back and then, satisfied, he unfolded a blanket and tossed it over Jilana. She had to strain in order to turn far enough over her shoulder to see him, and when she did he smiled mockingly. "Wait for me, Jilana."

With those sarcastic words he was gone and Jilana was alone in the dark tent. *Wait for me.* Jilana laughed a trifle wildly. As if she could do anything else. The laugh changed to a choked sob and Jilana felt the hot sting of tears as they filled her eyes and trailed down her cheeks. From far away came the dying cries of Camulodunum and Jilana wept for its loss and Hadrian's. Gradually the tears subsided and Jilana took stock of her situation. The whim of some god had decreed that Caddaric find her once again, and Jilana could only shake her head over the bitter irony of her rescue. Whatever feelings Caddaric had held for her, Jilana had killed with her escape; his voice and eyes had told her that much.

What did Caddaric plan to do with her? Jilana burrowed into the fur as a shiver worked its way up her spine. In spite of his treatment of her, she did not think he planned to hand her over to Lhwyd. Caddaric was not, by nature, a cruel man, only a hard one. Had he intended her to die, he would have killed her himself. That thought comforted Jilana, although she knew that this time her treatment would be far different from what she had received at Venta Icenorum. Hadrian's dagger dug into the flesh of her thighs and Jilana felt a moment of panic. If Caddaric discovered the weapon he would be furious, but at the moment, she had no way of disposing of it. She would have to wait until he gave her a moment of privacy—he had to grant her that much, if only for her body's needs—and toss the dagger away. Or find a way to conceal it from Caddaric, some rebellious spark in her mind added. Jilana closed her eyes and waited for Caddaric to return.

Chapter 5

CADDARIC RETURNED LATE IN THE EVENING and Jilana, who had been wondering if he intended abandoning her, caught her breath when he ducked through the door with an oil lamp in one hand and a wooden chest—*kist* in the Iceni language—balanced over the opposite shoulder. He walked to where the pallet lay, at the back of the tent, and stared down at Jilana.

When he said nothing, just continued to stare at her as if he had never seen her before, Jilana swallowed and asked, "Is it all over?"

Caddaric was silent for so long that Jilana had just decided he would not answer when he said, "Nearly." He set the oil lamp down and then lightly swung the kist to the ground beside it.

"What do you mean?"

He swung back to her and Jilana noticed that he stooped slightly because the slanting ceiling would not accommodate his full height unless he stood in the center of the tent. Caddaric pulled the dagger from his belt and went down on one knee beside Jilana. "Some legionaries and civilians have taken refuge in the temple of Claudius."

As he had done earlier, Caddaric flipped Jilana over and she felt the pressure on the rope as he cut through it. Being freed from her bonds brought an exquisite agony to her abused muscles and Jilana bit back a moan when she straightened her legs and back. Caddaric left without another word and Jilana carefully sat up and rubbed some feeling back into her wrists and ankles. As she massaged the trembling muscles in her legs, her hands encountered the dagger and after a moment of indecision, Jilana raised the hem of her stola and untied the weapon. Caddaric's voice sounded from somewhere just outside the tent, and Jilana hastily turned back a corner of the pile of furs and placed the dagger on the ground beneath the pallet. She had barely replaced the furs when Caddaric returned and she self-consciously pulled the rough blanket around her shoulders.

"Stand up."

The harsh command brought Jilana's head up and her eyes fastened on the metal links Caddaric held in his hands. She rose shakily to her feet and watched him approach with open suspicion. Nodding at the chain, Jilana queried, "What is that for?"

A brief, sardonic smile flashed across Caddaric's face. "The shackles are for you, sweet wicca. To make certain that the events at Venta Icenorum will not be repeated." He let the chains dangle from one hand and reached for her with the other.

Instinctively Jilana shied away from his grasp. "'Tis not necessary, Cad—" The protest died in her throat when Caddaric's hand closed around her arm and jerked her back in front of him.

"The day has been long and I am weary. If you test what little remains of my patience I will treat you accordingly."

Shaken by the controlled violence in his words, Jilana stood motionless as Caddaric dropped to the ground and locked the shackles in place around her ankles. The cool metal burned like a brand against her flesh and Jilana could only stare in stunned disbelief at the length of chain that lay on the ground between her feet. Surely he did not mean to keep her thus! Jilana raised her eyes to Caddaric's, searching for some sign that the shackles were meant only to frighten her, but in his gaze she found only grim resolve.

"You will find them awkward at first," Caddaric noted dispassionately, "but in time you will manage well enough."

Caddaric left the tent yet again and Jilana uttered a strangled cry. The thought of being kept in chains like a criminal sent a wave of humiliation through Jilana and she pressed trembling fingers against her mouth in order to still the sob that threatened. She took a tentative step forward and cringed at the ensuing noise. The chink of the metal reminded her of the bell the Iceni would tie around a cow's neck so that the herd could be easily located.

Caddaric was absent for some time, and when he returned he found Jilana pacing experimentally around the confines of the tent. Unnoticed, he watched her for several minutes, his expression shuttered. She deserved no better than this, he told himself. She had made a fool of him; allayed his doubts and then betrayed his trust. Given the chance, she would repeat her actions; of this he was certain. At least his mind was convinced—his foolish heart was of a softer nature. Disgusted with the evidence of his weakness, Caddaric stepped into the tent and closed the flap behind him.

Jilana came to a halt and looked at Caddaric. He had bathed; his hair curled damply and his only concession to modesty was a pair of breeks. His chest, with its covering of hair, was magnificently bare. As he approached, she tore her gaze away from the sight and stared at the ground. Only when he dangled a pouch in front of her did she look up.

"Food," Caddaric said in answer to her unspoken question. "Not what you are accustomed to, but all that is available." He watched while she took the pouch, opened it, and withdrew part of the contents.

Jilana turned the hard strip over and over in her hand, then sniffed cautiously at it. It was meat of some sort, dried and seasoned, and her stomach gave a sickening lurch.

"Beef, preserved for the march," Caddaric informed her. He felt a twinge of sympathy at her reaction but pushed it ruthlessly aside. He took the pouch back and handed her a wineskin in its stead. "'Tis tough. Bite off a piece and then take some water and hold them both in your mouth."

After a struggle, Jilana managed to gnaw off a tough fragment of meat and do as Caddaric suggested. When it had softened somewhat, she chewed at it while Caddaric moved around the tent, obviously preparing for sleep. He took a fresh tunic from his kist, closed it and laid the garment on top. When his hand fell to the buckle on his belt, Jilana turned away and studied the shadows cast upon the wall by the oil lamp. The action did little to soothe her modesty, however, for Caddaric's shadow also fell upon the leather and she could clearly see his every move. Helplessly, she watched him remove and carefully fold the breeks and place them atop the tunic, and then work the knots on his loincloth. He disposed of that in the same manner as the breeks and straightened, hands resting on his hips. Jilana stiffened; she could feel his gaze as surely as if he had touched her.

"Have you finished?"

Jilana chewed frantically and shook her head.

"Do you want more?"

Jilana gave up on the meal. She could chew until sunrise and the meat would still remain unpalatable. She forced herself to swallow and nearly choked in the process when the meat lodged midway between her mouth and stomach. A generous quantity of water washed the beef down the rest of the way. "No more, thank you," she answered finally.

"Then put the water and meat away and come to bed."

His shadow moved, and from the corner of her eye Jilana saw Caddaric settle onto the rude pallet. She turned, spotted the food pouch leaning against Caddaric's kist, and carefully walked to it. The chains clinked together, but did not trip her. When she had replaced her meal and set the wineskin beside the pouch, she straightened and looked at Caddaric.

"Where am I to sleep?"

Caddaric gave her a knowing look. "Here; next to me." She had expected as much, but the blood still rushed to her cheeks and Caddaric laughed shortly. "Come, Jilana, you and I are beyond such false modesty, are we not?"

Jilana laced her fingers together and strove to keep her voice level. "I should like to wash first and attend to my personal needs."

Caddaric nodded and waved a hand toward the tent flap. "Outside. You will find a barrel of water and a basin next to the wagon. As for the other..." He raised a mocking eyebrow and smiled. "Albion is blessed with trees and bushes." She had just stepped outside the tent when he added, "Do not be long."

His warning was implicitly clear to Jilana. If she took too long, he would come after her. She tended to her bodily needs, washed as quickly as possible, and returned to the tent. The chink of her shackles as she approached the bed was the only sound in the enclosure. Caddaric lay with his eyes closed and Jilana wondered if he had fallen asleep. When she reached the pallet, however, his eyes opened and surveyed her dispassionately.

"Your gown will prove uncomfortable," Caddaric noted. "Shall I help you remove it?"

The taunting note in his voice sparked Jilana's temper. "The chains will prove even more so," she snapped back. "Will you remove these as well?"

Slowly, Caddaric raised himself up on one elbow, his expression cold. "Are you offering me a trade, Jilana? Your body for the chains?" Her hands curled into fists at her sides at the deliberate insult, and Caddaric snorted. "You betrayed me once, Jilana; I am not ignorant enough to allow you to do so a second time." With that he reached out and extinguished the oil lamp.

The tent was plunged into darkness, save for the faint pool of light coming from the vent in the ceiling. Jilana removed her sandals and stood immobile, aware of the coolness of the night air and the warm haven of the pallet. Yet her pride argued that she take one of the blankets and claim another piece of ground for her bed, regardless of the discomfort. Caddaric made the decision for her.

"Leave the cursed stola on if you must, but come to bed," Caddaric snarled. "You will be less tempted to slip away if I am beside you. And," he warned, "I sleep lightly."

Reluctantly, Jilana settled onto the pallet next to Caddaric. They lay pressed together, side by side on the narrow pallet. Jilana stared into the darkness, feeling the warmth of Caddaric's large body creep over her own chilled flesh. His breathing was deep and even, but there was a tension vibrating through him that told Jilana he was not asleep. She shifted, seeking a comfortable position for her shackled ankles and the connecting chain, and felt Caddaric stiffen.

"Caddaric?"

"What is it?" Caddaric asked wearily.

"I did not run from you, but from Lhwyd." When he did not answer, Jilana turned her head toward him. "Had our situation been reversed, would you not have done the same?"

Caddaric turned on his side, presenting his back to Jilana. "Go to sleep."

THE NEXT MORNING Caddaric rose, dressed, and then shook Jilana awake. "If you want to eat, come with me."

Dazed, Jilana struggled to her feet and followed Caddaric. Even at this time of day—shortly after sunrise—the Iceni camp was busy, although the sounds were muted. The campfires had been relit and women were stirring the contents of the cookpots that hung over them. Yawning, Jilana trudged around the corner of the tent to the wagon and washed her face and hands in cold water before returning to the front of the tent. She glanced once at Camulodunum but quickly averted her gaze from the painful sight. Caddaric was waiting for her, an impatient frown on his face, and she walked as quickly as she could to his side.

"Do you know how to build a fire?" Caddaric asked without preamble. When she shook her head, he sighed. "I thought as much. Pay attention." He knelt in front of a circle of rocks and shaved thin pieces of wood from a branch he had taken from the pile of wood beside the tent. When that was done, he pulled flint from the pouch on his belt and scraped his knife blade down it. Sparks cascaded onto the kindling and the wood caught immediately. He added small, dry twigs to the flame, and when they were ablaze, stacked a pyramid of larger pieces around the fire. Extending her hands toward the fire, Jilana offered Caddaric a tentative smile. He nodded, once, rose to his feet, and resheathed his knife. "The fire is your responsibility from now on," he said roughly, pushing the flint into her hand. "'Tis foolish to hope, I suppose, that you can cook?"

Jilana opened her mouth to respond, and promptly closed it. She had dabbled in the kitchen at home, but only to bake bread and wheat or barley cakes in the kitchen's ovens, and then only for her own amusement. What Caddaric hinted at was far beyond her capabilities. Chagrined, Jilana shook her head once again. Wearing an expression that left little doubt as to his opinion of her ignorance, Caddaric took an iron pot from the wagon and showed her how to make a porridge from crushed oats and water.

Around them more of the camp was coming to life, and Jilana tried to ignore the curious looks cast in her direction. She wondered where Heall and Clywd and the others were, but was afraid to ask. To hear that Heall, who had shown her only kindness, had fallen in battle would be too much to bear. Taking a turn at stirring the porridge, Jilana wished that Caddaric would talk to her but he did not. Even the mocking jibes he had delivered at Venta Icenorum would be preferable to the way he ignored her except to issue orders. The truth hit Jilana like an icy blast—he was treating her the way he would treat any slave. Her shackles, the chores he laid on her shoulders, his dismissal of her as anything save a servant, killed the tiny hope Jilana had harbored that Caddaric's anger would pass. Whatever gentle emotion he might have felt for her was gone, and Jilana was left with the cutting knowledge that her own treacherous heart—with a heedless will of its own—had given itself to Caddaric. Ahh, Juno, how cruelly you gods twist our mortal fates! Was my heart the sacrifice Minerva extracted in exchange for Caddaric's life?

He must never know, Jilana told herself as she trudged to the wagon for the wooden bowls and spoons Caddaric had ordered her to retrieve. The heavy ache in her chest was punishment enough for what had slipped through her hands. If Caddaric found out, her misery would be doubled, for her love would provide him a potent weapon. She would shed no tears in front of him, nor would she show any sort of weakness that would betray this vulnerability. Her anger, too, must be chained, for Jilana knew all too well that in the heat of the moment she spoke before she thought.

Jilana had just set the utensils on the ground when someone behind her called her name. She spun about; the heel of her sandal caught in the chains and spilled her to the ground. A heated wave of embarrassment washed over her cheeks at her clumsiness and then a pair of hands were lifting her to her feet with the ease of a parent performing the act for a child.

Warm, brown eyes and a rough craggy face met her gaze and Jilana smiled with pure joy and threw her arms around the man's neck. "Heall," she breathed into the shoulder of his tunic. "Oh, I am so glad!" Over his shoulder she saw Clywd standing a few feet away and smiled her welcome.

Heall lifted Jilana into a crushing hug, causing her chains to clash together. "So he found you, did he? I knew he would." The chains clanked again and Heall slowly returned Jilana to the ground. His brows knotting into a frown, he held her at arm's length, inspecting her from head to toe. A heartbeat later a low rumble issued from the depths of his chest and he rounded on Caddaric. "What are you about, boy?" The tone of his voice was less a question than a challenge.

Genuinely puzzled by his friend's behavior, Caddaric answered bluntly, "She is safe. Is that not what you wanted?"

"You have chained her. Chained her!" Heall's voice rumbled ominously and he bore down on the younger man. "She is no horse to be hobbled."

"Nay," Caddaric agreed, "she is a runaway slave to be chained." Heall's hands transformed into fists at Caddaric's words, and the young warrior took a cautious step backward. "My slave, Heall, to do with as I wish."

"'Tis a degradation," Heall growled. "She deserves better."

"She deserves naught," Caddaric rejoined. "You should be thankful 'twas I who found her; I at least took her alive! Would you rather I had killed her?"

Heall paled and ground to a halt at that final taunt. Jilana, who had been unable to take her eyes from the two men, heard Clywd's sharp intake of breath.

"Let it pass, old friend." Clywd's urgent plea was abnormally loud in the ringing silence. "Jilana is safe and Caddaric is within the law. You have no right to interfere."

A shudder spasmed through Heall as he relaxed his belligerent stare. Shaking his head he turned from Caddaric to Jilana and draped a protective arm around her shoulders. "Come, let us eat." Casting a glance over his shoulder at Caddaric, he added, "If such a simple consideration is permitted?"

Caddaric's jaw tightened but he said nothing, merely nodded sharply in reply. I will have to watch them closely, Caddaric decided; Jilana could easily twist the old man's sympathy into support for a second escape. He pulled away from that disturbing thought when Clywd approached and he raised a questioning eyebrow at his father.

When Clywd spoke his voice was low, but trembling with suppressed rage. "This is an abomination."

Caddaric shrugged and folded his arms across his chest. "Merely a precaution. Stop glaring, Father; 'tis not as if I have beaten her!"

"Nay, only humiliated her; left her without a scrap of dignity," Clywd charged. "*Why?* Why, when you have gone to so much trouble to find Jilana again, do you abase her so?"

The question had carried to where Jilana sat and now she looked at Caddaric, violet eyes wide and questioning. Caddaric met her gaze and replied, in a cutting voice, "Contrary to your belief, I did not search for Jilana this time. Finding her was a trick of fate."

All the hope that had welled up in Jilana at Clywd's words drained away and she forced down a spoonful of porridge. Of course Clywd had known she was in Camulodunum—she had felt the touch of his mind that day at the earthwall—and he had passed the information on to Caddaric. And Caddaric had not cared enough to search for her. He had stumbled across her by accident, and if he had not, his actions indicated that he would not have been troubled overmuch by her certain demise.

"You are many things," Clywd cuttingly told his son, "but I would never have thought you such a fool." He joined the others at the fire and smiled at Jilana but did not speak when Caddaric took a place across the fire from him.

The shared meal was quiet, tense. Heall defiantly asked after Jilana's well-being, and she assured him in a hushed voice that she was well. Caddaric watched the exchange silently but when the meal was finished he helped Jilana carry and heat the water she needed to clean their eating utensils. Clywd disappeared without a word and Heall left shortly thereafter, telling Jilana that he would return as soon as he could.

Jilana dried the cooking pot and carried it back to the wagon. The wagon was packed in an orderly fashion; everything that would be needed during the march or for setting up camp was within easy reach and Jilana repacked the utensils just as neatly. Caddaric stood at the side of the wagon, strapping on his sword. Jilana watched him perform this ritual and her heart tightened in fear of what his actions portended. As in Venta Icenorum, he kept his weapons well away from her; in this case, they had been stored in the wagon.

"You are going into the city?"

Caddaric paused in the act of swinging the baldric across his chest and looked at her as if he had just become aware of her presence. It was all pretense, of course; in spite of himself, he had followed her every movement. He adjusted the baldric and checked his long sword by sliding it out of its sheath before answering. "There is still a pocket of resistence that must be eliminated. Aye, I am going into Camulodunum." He looked at her. "Is it necessary for me to set a guard on you?"

Jilana lifted her head to a proud angle. "Where would I run? And how?"

"Just so you understand your position." Caddaric slipped a dagger into his belt and reached into the wagon for his battle-axe.

His careless words cut Jilana to the quick and she lowered her eyes so that Caddaric could not see the pain reflected there. "My position is very clear, Caddaric." And then, in spite of herself, she asked, "What do you intend to do with me?"

A sharp ache went through Caddaric at the pathetic bent of her question, but nothing of what he felt showed on his face. What did he intend to do with her? He knew what he wanted to do, had wanted to do since setting eyes on her yesterday. He wanted to strip off that expensive, tasteful stola she wore and the white undertunic beneath it and bare her soft body to his gaze. He wanted to kiss her until she cried out and lose himself in the drugging excitement of her mouth; cover her body with his own and feel his hair-roughened flesh slide against her silken skin until this strange hurt in his chest—and the more familiar pulsing in his loins—was lost in their mating.

The handle of the battle-axe grew slick in his grasp and Caddaric realized that his hands were sweating. He pushed the fantasy away, knowing that he could not trust Jilana enough to risk taking her as a bed partner, and answered as honestly as he could. "I intend to keep you, Jilana; 'tis that simple."

And that complicated, Jilana thought as Caddaric walked away from her. She wanted to beg him to be careful, but she did not dare. At best he would laugh at her cautioning words and at worst—at worst, he would not believe she cared whether or not he was hurt.

She had to fill the time until Caddaric returned, but had no idea how to do so. She walked around the tent, examining the structure and the stakes that held it firmly to the ground, then added more wood to the campfire. That was probably the wrong thing to do, for at other campsites some of the women were banking the fires and wandering off. There were children in the Iceni host, and they dashed about energetically in their play. A few children—as well as adults—walked past her several times and looked at her with open, but not unfriendly, curiosity. No one spoke to her before moving on, and Jilana grew increasingly uncomfortable being the object of such scrutiny. Accordingly, she withdrew to the tent, but after she had straightened the pallet, there was nothing for her to do here, either.

What she would really like to do was bathe and change into clean clothing. All of which was impossible, of course. If she used the water from the barrels in the wagon she had no way to replace it, and Caddaric would undoubtedly be furious at such a frivolous use of water. He had bathed, Jilana reminded herself, but the thought left as quickly as it had come. It was *his* water, to do with as he pleased. Just as she was his.

But clean clothing, perhaps that could be managed. And a brush or comb to work her hair into some kind of order. Doubtless her trunk remained in her chamber at Venta Icenorum, but surely Caddaric would not mind if she borrowed his comb—and somewhere in his kist there must be an old tunic with which he could part. She actually worked up enough courage to open his kist, lift out its contents and find a worn tunic that suited her needs before she sat back on her heels and gave a sigh of defeat. Only two weeks ago, after their time in the bath, she would have felt secure enough of Caddaric's feelings to borrow whatever she needed, but not now. Even his physical desire for her was gone, as dead as the fierce protectiveness he had once evinced.

Jilana refolded the worn tunic and carefully repacked the kist. She gave the wooden comb lying atop the neatly folded garments a last, longing look before closing the lid and trying to work through her tangled mass of curls with her fingers.

That was how Clywd found her, and he found the expression of gladness that flitted across Jilana's face heartrending. She came to her feet immediately, and Clywd winced at the sound of her chains coming together. To see Jilana hiding away like some frightened animal was more than Clywd could bear.

Jilana was overjoyed at the prospect of companionship. "Will you sit, Clywd? Caddaric has gone and..." Her words trailed off and she glanced helplessly around the tent.

"Nay, Jilana, I cannot stay. In truth," Clywd answered as an idea took shape in his mind, "I hoped that you might aid me in my work."

Anything, Jilana decided, was better than remaining a prisoner in the tent. "I will help in any way I can, but," she cautioned, remembering her ignorance of that morning, "there is little I can do."

Clywd smiled. "I will teach you what you need to know. Come." He lifted the flap of the tent and held it while Jilana passed through. He followed and picked up a large, rectangular box from the ground.

Jilana stared curiously at the box as Clywd placed its strap over his shoulder. The workmanship was beautiful; the wood was intricately carved with writhing scrollwork and faces so fierce as to be frightening. Clywd took her arm and led her away from their campsite.

"Where are we going?" Jilana asked.

"Where we will do the most good," Clywd replied. "You are much like me, I think," he continued in a gently reassuring tone. "Tell me, did you feel me that day you stood at the earthwall?"

Startled, Jilana did not even attempt to lie. "I felt something, like the touch of a hand upon my shoulder. But I did not know—that is, I could only guess that it was you." She shrugged. "'Twas Caddaric I searched for." And then, because it seemed right to do so, she told Clywd of the vision she had had of the temple of Claudius and the disbelief with which it had been met. "The temple still stands, of course," she concluded, "so perhaps I do not have this 'gift' after all, only terrible dreams." Even as she spoke, she knew the truth. No one had dreams while they were awake. "I do not want the sight," she exclaimed fiercely.

"The sight chooses you, not the other way around," Clywd said after a moment. "Yours is not strong—not yet—or else you would have found my son when you searched. If you wish, I can teach you how to use the sight, how to channel it."

"Nay!" Jilana burst out, horrified by the thought of being continuously assaulted by such visions. Then, more quietly, "I have no wish to know the future." Because, she thought, I could not bear to know that Caddaric was going to his death and be unable to prevent it.

Clywd drew her to a halt, his hand like a vise around her wrist. He stared hard into her eyes and Jilana knew that he read her thoughts. Unable to withstand his scrutiny, she forced her gaze away.

"So, even now you care for that foolish son of mine."

"Only because he stands between me and certain death," Jilana felt goaded into saying. Clywd's knowing chuckle did nothing to settle her turbulent emotions.

"All will be as it was intended," Clywd said cryptically. He laughed, softly, when Jilana shot him a fierce look. "The chains about your ankles work both ways; Caddaric is as securely bound to you as you are to him."

Jilana gave a snort of disbelief. "You said you needed my help," she said pointedly. Minutes later, Jilana wished she had refused to leave her tent. What Clywd intended, for whatever reason the gods only knew, was that she learn the arts of healing.

The top tray of the carved box he carried contained herbs, ointments, powders and potions whose names were as confusing to Jilana as their functions; below the first tray lay a second which held well-honed knives, an array of bone needles and stiff coils of thread which, Jilana learned, were not thread at all but fine pieces of cattle gut. Once soaked, the strands became flexible and were used to sew up gaping wounds. The explanation made Jilana faintly nauseous, and when Clywd told her that once the wound was healing the strands had to be removed, she felt herself pale. The bottom of the box contained material for bandages.

All of this Jilana learned at their first stop, where Clywd was welcomed by the family of a wounded man who lay close to the fire. Jilana took one look at the man's blood-soaked side and blanched. Clywd was apparently unaffected. He smiled reassuringly at the warrior, handed Jilana the case he had carried and told her to open it. The man's wife was instructed to bring vinegar and warm water, and their three children were sent off to play. While Clywd pulled away the bandage, he explained the contents of his case to Jilana. Jilana was ready to flee back to the safety of her tent before Clywd finished his explanation, but before she could say as much, Clywd had her cleaning the wound with the mixture of water and vinegar. The man groaned whenever Jilana touched him.

Once that was done, Jilana's legs were shaking so badly she doubted she could get to her feet, so she stayed where she was and handed Clywd whatever he needed. The sight of the exposed wound made her stomach lurch and when Clywd took a piece of gut soaked in vinegar and began to stitch up the man's side Jilana had to look away or be violently ill. At Clywd's order, she washed her hands in a bowl of clean water and vinegar, repacked his case and then rose shakily to her feet.

"You should have told me what you intended," Jilana said accusingly when they had left that family behind. "I cannot do what you ask."

"This is the hardest part of battle, I think," Clywd replied thoughtfully, as if he had not heard Jilana's protest. "The suffering is sometimes unimaginable, and there is so little that can be done to alleviate it." He sighed. "The families of the injured began calling for me yesterday and still there is no end in sight."

For the first time, Jilana noticed the purple shadows curving like bruises beneath Clywd's eyes. "Have you rested since this began?"

Clywd laughed softly. "Do you worry about me, Jilana? I thank you, but you should save your concern for the wounded. When this is ended I will rest and recover; if I do so now, many will die. That I cannot allow." He glanced at her. "I understand, though, why the lives of these people are not important to you. You need not stay with me."

"'Tis not that they are unimportant," Jilana protested, coming to a halt. "I simply do not see how my fainting or being sick will help you."

"I understand." Clywd nodded and continued walking.

Jilana watched him go. "They do not want *my* help," she called after him. "I am their enemy!" The only reply Clywd made was to raise his hand in a brief salute and Jilana grimaced. For all his height and the voluminous robes he wore, Clywd made a fragile figure. In the week she had spent with him at Venta Icenorum, she had come to know Clywd well enough to know that he was as stubborn as his son. He would work at the task before him until he dropped. Reluctantly at first, and then with as much speed as her shackles would allow, she trailed Clywd and at last caught up to him. "You are a canny old fox," she told him when he looked over at her. "And you will regret choosing me as an assistant."

Clywd merely smiled and pointed to another campsite. The wound here was less serious and Clywd took the time to explain to Jilana what he was doing and why. By midday Jilana had lost count of the wounded they had tended. Her stola was soiled with blood and bits of other things she would rather not remember; Clywd's robe was no better, but since it was black the stains did not show as clearly. Her head was brimming with hastily imparted knowledge and her body was weary. When she was about to ask Clywd if they could rest, they were hailed by a very tall, dark-haired woman and with a sigh she trudged after Clywd.

Instead of being asked to treat yet another wound, however, she and Clywd were invited to share this family's midday meal. Jilana gratefully accepted the offer of water, and after washing her face and hands she sank to the ground by the fire. The meal was simple: bread and the same dried meat Caddaric had given her the night before, all washed down with a large quantity of mead. Like Clywd, Jilana refused the fermented honey drink and drank water instead. The food settled heavily in her stomach, but she thanked the woman with the same grace she had once bestowed upon the hostess of an opulent feast. The Iceni woman smiled broadly and launched into a speech that told Jilana she had become the object of gossip once again. Word had spread throughout the camp that the Druid was accompanied by the red-haired wicca who had befriended Boadicea at the flogging, been captured at Venta Icenorum, vanished without a trace, and then magically reappeared. 'Twas hardly magical, Jilana told herself dryly, remembering how Caddaric had slung her over his shoulder like a sack of grain, but she did not disabuse the woman with the truth. Wicca—witch. Caddaric had often called her that, but no longer. He knew better than to consider Jilana magical.

And where was Caddaric? Jilana wondered with a sudden pang of anxiety. Was he safe? From Camulodunum came rhythmic pounding that she had learned was the sound of a battering ram against the iron-plated doors of the Temple of Claudius. What survivors of the city remained had taken shelter in the temple and barred the massive double doors. Had Faline made it to the temple in time? Had Hadrian? So much waste and death, on both sides, she thought sadly. Clywd gave her no time to dwell on such dark thoughts. He thanked the woman, who seemed more than a little in awe of him, and they were on their way once again.

The Iceni force encircled the city, and Jilana wondered how far they had come since morning.

"Nearly halfway." Jilana gasped aloud and Clywd smiled apologetically. "Forgive me; I do not make a habit of reading people's thoughts, but you seemed so sad."

Jilana stared at him, astounded. "You can truly look into another's mind?"

"Occasionally, and through a deliberate effort," Clywd answered. "'Tis a gift, like a sight—though I have had to work much harder at this one—and I cannot use it on everyone." Clywd returned her gaze and a slow smile curved his mouth. "Nay, Jilana, you have only the sight, not the ability to read thoughts, at least, not yet."

For a moment Jilana was too stunned to respond at this latest intrusion into her thoughts and then she laughed helplessly. "I shall have to find a way to protect myself from your powers."

"You have no need to fear me, but there is a way to hide your thoughts," Clywd said casually. "I can teach you if you like; it is part of the training for controlling the sight."

Jilana had no chance to reply, for at that moment they were called to yet another campsite to tend yet another patient. The afternoon proved a repetition of the morning. Jilana learned quickly, and soon she was able to care for minor injuries on her own while Clywd went ahead to work on the more severely wounded. In this way the work was halved and it was not until the sun was setting that Clywd called Jilana to assist him once again.

One look at the man on the ground sent Jilana reeling backward, and only Clywd's sharp command stopped her from running away. The warrior lay on his back, and from the center of his stomach several inches of a thick, wooden shaft protruded. The flesh around the wound was brightly colored, from the red of infection to a bruised purple.

"I need—*he* needs you," Clywd snapped. "I must cut the javelin head out and I cannot do it alone. In my case there is a vial of opium; bring it and a bowl of water to me." When she hesitated, he pointed out the vial he meant. "Quickly, Jilana."

Jilana obeyed mechanically, averting her eyes from the patient when she knelt beside Clywd. "Pour a bit of opium into the water; I will tell you when to stop." A nervous chill enveloped Jilana and her hand, when she raised the warrior's head so that he might drink the mixture, was like ice against his flesh. It seemed impossible to Jilana that he could have endured such an injury and remained alive and yet he was conscious, if not totally rational. His eyes watched them as she and Clywd prepared their instruments and Jilana felt like screaming under his scrutiny. At last, however, the warrior's eyelids drooped and then closed completely and Jilana gave a sigh of relief.

The man's wife—at least she might have been his wife, the Celts were notoriously careless about such formalities—had brought clean cloths and these now lay beside Jilana as she knelt opposite Clywd.

"Why do you not simply pull..." Jilana swallowed a surge of bile, "pull the javelin out?" she finished as Clywd removed a knife from the bowl of water and vinegar in which it had been soaking. While she spoke, Jilana dipped her hands into a like mixture to clean them and then picked up a length of cloth.

"The head of the weapon is barbed. If we pull the head out, the barbs will catch and tear, causing more damage." Clywd looked over at Jilana. "Are you ready?"

With a quick, silent prayer, Jilana nodded. Clywd cut into the inflamed flesh and after that Jilana was too busy to be afraid or even think. She responded automatically to Clywd's orders; soaking up the blood with cloths and discarding them, keeping the warrior still—at one point actually pinning the man's arms down when he tried to push Clywd's hands away—and making a dressing of herbs and moss that would be inserted into the wound to prevent infection and hopefully stop the blood, occupied her completely. Once the head of the javelin was removed the man quieted somewhat, although his moans betrayed his torment, and Jilana's own reaction set in. She measured out another dose of opium with hands that shook so badly that some of the priceless medicine splashed onto the ground. She barely managed to dribble the liquid into the warrior's mouth without spilling that as well. Only when Clywd began bandaging the wound did Jilana find the strength to stand. Without a word, she hurried some distance from the campsite and let her stomach relieve itself of its contents.

Bent at the waist, hands resting on her thighs, Jilana was aware of nothing but the spasms racking her body. The images her mind had blocked out only minutes ago returned in full force and she shuddered against them. How could Clywd so calmly put his hands into a man's body? The sight of blood had long since lost its aversion for her, but to see the fragile flesh and muscle so easily cut away to reveal what lay below had proved too much. At last she became aware of Clywd standing some distance away and she straightened.

Clywd approached, carrying a large basin of water. "You will feel better after you have washed," he said softly and set the basin on the ground.

Jilana looked down at her stained hands and shook her head. "I doubt I shall ever feel clean again." But she walked to the basin and washed her hands. When she was finished she sat down on the ground and looked up at the Druid. "Will he live?"

Clywd studied the ground before answering. "I have done all that I can, and I have seen men with worse wounds live." He drew a deep, ragged breath and searched the darkening sky. "I do not think he will live out the night."

"Then it was all for naught," Jilana cried, tears of helplessness welling behind her eyelids.

"Nay, Jilana, we have given him a chance, some small hope. That counts above all else." Clywd picked up the basin and started back to the camp, and after a few moments Jilana followed. She arrived just in time to hear Clywd tell the woman that he would return later than evening. Respect for the frail Druid was born within Jilana at that instant. When Clywd knelt to repack his case he found Jilana beside him, cleaning the knife he had just used and he nodded his thanks.

In the beginning, Clywd had guarded Jilana because of what he saw in the future for the girl and his son. He had come to like her and, because she was so obviously terrified of the forces which had destroyed her world, feel protective toward her. Today had shown Clywd that Jilana was more than a coddled patrician; she possessed an inner strength at which her pretty face and lithe figure did not hint. To see the chains around her ankles now was a greater affront than it had been earlier in the day, and Clywd felt anger swell within him.

Walking beside Clywd back to their encampment, Jilana continued to be surprised at the lack of animosity she created among the Britons. She was obviously a slave, and though a few sullen glances and murmurs were cast in her direction, she was more an object of friendly curiosity than hatred. Remembering that gossip had labeled her a wicca brought a tired smile to Jilana's lips. In her blood-spattered gown and wildly tangled hair, she hardly looked like some magical creature.

A flash of white seen from the corner of her eye caught Jilana's attention and slowed her pace. Lhwyd stood several yards away at the sparse edge of the forest, deep in conversation with two Iceni warriors. In the dying light of the sun, Jilana could just make out the figures of people huddled against the tree trunks. She could hear weeping and the lower, less intense sounds of moaning. Unconsciously, Jilana came to a halt and stared in the direction of the sounds. She had no need to ask Clywd who the people were; she knew. Lhwyd had somehow found living sacrifices for his goddess. Roman sacrifices.

Retracing his steps, Clywd urged softly, "Come away, Jilana."

"He has wounded there," Jilana whispered, appalled. "Have they been seen to?"

"Jilana—"

"Have they been seen to," Jilana repeated, her voice gaining strength.

The gray streak in Clywd's beard trembled momentarily. "Nay, Lhwyd would not allow it."

"Then you *did* try?"

Clywd looked down at Jilana, his blue eyes—so like Caddaric's—ablaze with indignation. "I am a healer. Last night I begged Lhwyd to let me treat the wounded and he refused. Do you believe I could see such suffering and not try to prevent it?"

Jilana exhaled a shaky breath. "Nay, Clywd, I do not. Forgive me." She turned back to where Lhwyd stood. "Mayhap Lhwyd will not refuse me." Before Clywd could stop her, Jilana walked proudly to Lhwyd.

At her approach the priest turned and a knowing smile flitted across his lips. "So the little fugitive has returned," he commented in his rich, melodic voice. "Have you come to join your countrymen?"

A shaft of ice pierced Jilana, and before she could speak she had to swallow the fear that clogged her throat. "There are wounded here," she said in a voice so steady she surprised herself. "I wish to treat them."

The laughter that rolled from Lhwyd at her words was as beautiful, and chilling, as his voice. He looked down at the chain binding her ankles and then locked his gaze with hers. "You wish to save their lives so that I may take them? A most interesting thought. Healthy sacrifices are always well received."

The blood drained from Jilana's face. She had not thought beyond the treatment of the wounds. Such calculated cruelty as Lhwyd displayed was beyond her comprehension.

"Let us see to them, Lhwyd." Clywd's gentle voice came from behind Jilana. A moment later he was at her side. "'Twill do no harm."

"You too, old priest?" Lhwyd sneered. "You have grown soft over the years, forgotten the teachings of the old ones. Tend to the Iceni wounded and leave the Romans to me!"

Clywd shook his head. "That I cannot do. A sacrifice to honor a god is acceptable, but you, Lhwyd, you enjoy the agony too much." He adjusted the strap on his shoulder and grasped Jilana's elbow. "We will see the Romans now."

"You will not," Lhwyd shrieked. "They are mine!" He turned to the warriors. "Seize this old man and this slave and take them back to their camp."

Jilana the guards would have taken without a second thought, but Clywd was another matter. All knew of his power, and it was whispered that he could slay a man with his thoughts. To lay hands on this Druid was to gamble with one's life. Of the two priests, it was less dangerous to offend Lhwyd, and accordingly the warriors backed away from Clywd and Jilana.

"Cowards," Lhwyd spat after the retreating guards. He looked back at Clywd and his eyes narrowed. "See to the Romans, then, but remember they are mine. As for you," Lhwyd drew the back of his hand across Jilana's cheek, "I promise that you will be mine one day as well."

Jilana's heart thudded painfully when Lhwyd touched her, but she forced herself to remain still. Lhwyd turned and walked away and Jilana drew a ragged breath. "You did not have to take my part," she told Clywd, "but I am thankful you did."

"Do not thank me. What Lhwyd said is true; we will heal these people only to have them die as sacrifices. I am not sure what we are about to do is right." Clywd's face was drawn as they started toward the prisoners.

There were perhaps a hundred Romans, all of them bound in some manner so that they could not escape. Knowing that the Romans would refuse to allow Clywd to treat them, she accompanied the Druid so that she might reassure her countrymen that he meant them no harm. Few of the injuries were serious; Jilana learned that the rebels had shown no mercy for the severely injured—their lives had been taken with quick dispatch. Jilana was not sure the Iceni actions lacked mercy; at least the dead had died quickly. As they moved among the people, Jilana found it harder and harder to meet their eyes when they asked about their fate. That she and Clywd were binding their wounds gave them the false hope that they might live, a hope Jilana could not bring herself to kill. Most of the survivors were women; the few guards standing watch over the prisoners were men, and the women feared rape at their hands. After asking Clywd if the women did indeed need to fear their guards—out of consideration for the captives' feelings, Clywd was using Jilana as an interpreter—Jilana assured them that they were in no danger. The women were relieved at the news, and Jilana bit back the rest of the explanation. The sacrifices must not be used in a sexual way or they would be unfit as presents to the goddess. Lhwyd had threatened to kill any warrior who took one of the Roman women.

They worked steadily through the captives, and when the sun finally set they worked by the light of torches brought by the guards. Amazingly, when the Iceni saw Clywd working on the prisoners, they brought water, vinegar and cloth for bandages without being asked. Jilana was astounded by their aid and too grateful to question their motives. For the few seriously wounded prisoners, Clywd dipped into his precious reserve of opium, measuring out the dose and administering it himself; as they worked their way among the prisoners, the groans diminished one by one and Jilana hated herself for accusing Clywd of having left these people to suffer.

The gratitude and renewed hope the Romans displayed made Jilana want to weep. Lhwyd might be cruel, but at least he had not lied to these people, which was what she, Jilana, was doing. Despising herself, Jilana at first did not hear her name called in a harsh rasping voice. Only when Clywd touched her sleeve and raised one finger in a gesture for silence did she leave her dark thoughts and listen. Her name came again and at Clywd's nod she rose to her feet, torch in hand, and walked through the dozen or so prisoners they had not yet seen.

"*Jilana.*" The raspy voice was weak, barely more than an exhalation of breath, but it was enough to raise the fine hair on the nape of her neck. Surely she was mistaken, Jilana told herself, but there was a flicker of hope in her heart that would not die.

He was here, the last figure she bent over, his arms forced behind his back and bound around a tree. "Hadrian," Jilana breathed and fell to her knees beside him. Even in the torchlight he was pale, and when she brushed a hand across his forehead it came away damp with sweat. "Oh, Hadrian, what have they done to you?"

"Taken me prisoner," Hadrian said in a voice so rich in self-disgust that Jilana gave a choked sob. He trembled as a chill took him, but his eyes never left her face. "You did not use the dagger. Oh, Jilana, I meant to keep you safe, to spare you this final indignity."

Jilana bent her head so that Hadrian would not see her tears. "Lie quietly Hadrian. I will bring someone to help you." She stood and ran to fetch Clywd.

The urgent, pleading note in her voice drew a sharp look from Clywd but Jilana did not notice. She dragged the strap of his case over her shoulder and led him back to Hadrian. Wedging their torches into the tree above the legionary, Jilana knelt beside Hadrian and opened the case. Hadrian's armor had been removed, and in the light of the torches Clywd could see that the right side of his scarlet tunic was rent and stiff with dried blood.

Jilana saw it, too. "We must cut him loose." Before she had finished speaking, she was opening the case and lifting out the trays in search of the knives.

"Jilana," Clywd warned, reaching a hand across Hadrian to stay her movements, "we cannot."

Violet eyes held a wild gleam as Jilana looked at the Druid. "He is hurt, and we cannot help him—cannot stop the bleeding—with his arms bound behind him like this." She found a knife, scrambled about on her knees and cut through the ropes holding Hadrian. A groan escaped Hadrian when his arms came free. Jilana tossed the knife aside and took his right hand in both of hers. "Hadrian, this is Clywd, a physician. He will help you." While Clywd cut the tunic and examined Hadrian's wound, Jilana clung to Hadrian's hand with one hand and stroked his forehead with the other.

"'Tis bad," Clywd announced at the end of his examination. He spoke in Iceni to Jilana. "The wound is infected and deep."

Jilana forced a reassuring smile for Hadrian, but there was nothing gentle in the eyes she turned to Clywd. "Then we will clean the wound, place a dressing in it that will draw out the infection, and bandage it. I will come back tomorrow and change the dressing myself."

Even though this legionary had given no indication that he spoke the Briton's tongue, Clywd instinctively lowered his voice. "Jilana, he is in pain; already the fever has taken him. Let me give him the opium."

"Of course you should give him opium," Jilana replied, not understanding Clywd's intent. "Then we will care for his wound. The fever will pass."

"Not in the time he has left."

"If he were Iceni, or Trinovante you would help him," Jilana accused wildly. This was Hadrian! Did Clywd not understand that she simply could not leave this man to die?

"Not if his destiny lay in Lhwyd's hands," Clywd responded. "Jilana, you know what Lhwyd intends." He glanced down at Hadrian and found the legionary's gaze fixed unwaveringly upon him. For a long moment the two men stared at one another, exchanging some silent message that Jilana did not understand, and finally Hadrian nodded.

"Let him give me the poppy juice, Jilana," Hadrian said in a weak voice that was a travesty of his usual growl. "He is offering what help he can. 'Twill be a kindness."

All the breath seemed to leave Jilana as she realized first, that Hadrian understood the Celtic language and second, what Clywd was suggesting. What Hadrian was agreeing to. She remembered the Druid measuring the opium for the badly wounded, how their moans had stopped shortly thereafter, and she held a hand to her mouth in order to hold back a cry of despair. No matter that she had been raised to believe that suicide was an honorable end, or that Clywd's deed had been a blessing; these deaths were still a tragic waste.

"Let me do it, then," Jilana said at last. "Let me stay with him."

Silently, efficiently, Clywd measured out the medicine into a bowl of water and withdrew. When the Druid was out of sight, Jilana reached into the case he had left behind and began making a dressing for Hadrian's wound. She did not spare the bowl of medicine so much as a glance. A woman brought Jilana a basin filled with water and vinegar and Jilana thanked her absently. Dipping a cloth into the basin, Jilana looked up and smiled at Hadrian.

"I will find a way to free you, Hadrian," Jilana vowed. "Your life will not be wasted here, like so many others."

"There is no escape for me, Jilana, only death. At least give me the dignity of choosing my own way." Jilana applied the cloth to his wound and Hadrian pressed his back into the tree trunk, the breath hissing between his teeth at the pain.

"You will not die," Jilana repeated fervently. "Not by opium, and most certainly not by Lhwyd's hand."

In spite of his pain, Hadrian laughed shortly at her vehemence. "And how will you accomplish this, little one?

They have untied you only to assist that Druid; once you are finished you will be bound once again. You cannot help yourself, let alone me.''

Jilana concentrated on cleaning the wound while she formed her reply. ''I am not kept with the other prisoners, Hadrian, and have some measure of freedom.'' She was finished and about to draw away when Hadrian's left hand grasped her wrist.

''Explain yourself.'' When Jilana did not look at him, Hadrian raised the hand which held her wrist and used his knuckles to force her face upward. ''Tell me, Jilana.''

''The warrior who claimed me in Venta Icenorum found me here.'' Jilana swallowed nervously at the look of pure fury that swept across Hadrian's face. ''The Druid is his father.''

''And you are of such value to this warrior that he will help me because you ask,'' Hadrian asked with a sneer. ''By the gods, Jilana, leave me my honor, at least.''

''Honor,'' Jilana echoed incredulously. ''Honor! Of what use is your honor if you are dead?'' She packed his wound and and began winding a strip of linen around his chest to hold the packing in place. ''Nay, Hadrian, I have lost everyone I held dear; I will not allow you to die as well.'' She knotted the linen and gathered her things. When her hand fell upon the bowl of water and opium she hesitated and then held it to Hadrian's lips. ''A swallow only, to ease the pain.'' He shot her an angry look, but obeyed, and Jilana threw the rest of the medicine away. ''Have you been fed?''

Hadrian sighed and tipped his head back against the tree trunk. ''A thin gruel, sometime during the afternoon.''

''When I return tomorrow I will bring food.'' Jilana called to one of the guards that hovered about. ''Tie him if you must, but carefully, with his arms in front.'' While the Iceni carried out her instructions, Jilana built a small fire near Hadrian and fired it with her torch. ''This should keep you warm tonight,'' she told Hadrian when the guard had gone. ''I will have a blanket for you tomorrow." She knelt and stroked Hadrian's forehead. "Do not be angry with me, Hadrian. I only want you to retire to your villa in the country."

The opium had begun its trek through his veins and Hadrian smiled. "You are a fool," he told Jilana gently, his words slurring. "I know what that Druid has planned for us." The thought of being tortured and sacrificed had terrified Hadrian, but now he was too tired to care. The poppy's work, he knew, but he could not resist the creeping lethargy. "How can you keep me from that, little Jilana?"

Hadrian's eyes closed and he passed quietly into sleep. Jilana remained with him, tenderly caressing his blunt features, until Clywd came for her. As they walked to their camp, Jilana wondered at her own audacity. How could she, as much a prisoner as the others, have dared to say she would find a way to keep Hadrian alive? The depth of her stupidity astounded Jilana, yet she was determined that Lhwyd not claim Hadrian for his bloody rites. The bond that had been forged between herself and Hadrian during her few days at Camulodunum was a strong one; she would do whatever was necessary to see that Hadrian lived to a ripe old age, enjoying his country villa and raising horses for the cavalry. Caddaric was her first recourse. She would beg, offer him anything, if he would free Hadrian.

Heall, Artair and Ede were sharing the fire when they returned to the camp, but Jilana barely noticed them. All her attention was focused on Caddaric. He, too, sat before he fire, but when he saw Clywd and Jilana approach, he rose swiftly to his feet. There was a certain stiffness in his movement that spoke of emotion held tightly in check and Jilana approached him warily.

"Where have you been?" Caddaric's voice was strained and his blue eyes glittered dangerously. The muscles in his arms rippled as he fought the urge to grab Jilana and shake an explanation from her.

"Jilana was with me," Clywd answered before Jilana could speak. "I had need of her."

A tic started in Caddaric's jaw. "You had better remember, Druid, that she is not free to come and go as she pleases."

"My apologies," Clywd responded, a cutting edge in his tone. "I did not realize you would begrudge the wounded Jilana's assistance."

Caddaric dismissed that with a wave of his hand. "You are lucky she did not plunge a knife into their hearts."

With a gasp of outrage, Jilana took a step toward Caddaric. He arched an insulting eyebrow in her direction, daring her to contradict him. Jilana swallowed the response she would have made in her defense. She had no wish to be further humiliated in front of Ede and Artair.

"If she causes you trouble, Caddaric," Ede purred, "you need only turn her over to Lhwyd."

Artair laughed. "What would he do with a woman, Ede? His passion is saved for the Morrigan." Jilana sent him a questioning glance and Artair smiled blandly. "If you wish, Caddaric, I will take this one off your hands. No doubt she can take the chill from my bed on a cold evening."

The words were barely spoken when Heall dealt Artair a backhand blow across his mouth that sent the younger man somersaulting backward. Jilana blinked in surprise; Heall had not changed position to deliver the blow, merely swept his arm backward, and now he did not bother to look at the fallen man.

Artair reeled to his feet, wiping a trickle of blood from the corner of his mouth with the back of his hand. "The Queen has declared there shall be no fighting," he began in a voice that shook with outrage.

Heall glanced at Artair and then returned his attention to the fire. "We did not fight. I taught my son a much needed lesson in holding his tongue. Jilana is Caddaric's, so do not growl over her like a dog over another's bone. Sit down and drink your mead."

Stunned, Jilana looked between Heall and Artair, noting finally the resemblance the younger man bore to the elder. Both their eyes were brown and the same shape, and

Heall's gray hair and beard could easily have been the same golden color as Artair's. It all made sense—Heall had raised Caddaric alongside his own son when Clywd had been taken. Small wonder Artair was jealous of Caddaric; in Jilana's eyes, Artair would never be the man, or the warrior, Caddaric was. Or Hadrian.

Remembering her friend, Jilana shook off her thoughts and turned to Caddaric. She needed his help if she were to free Hadrian. "I need to wash," she said softly. "Have I your leave to do so?"

Caddaric nodded and watched as Jilana disappeared around the side of the tent. Her hair was a wild mass of tangles, her gown streaked with blood and dirt and bits of gore, and her bearing spoke of her weariness. She needed more than a bucket of water afforded—her eyes spoke of meeting horrors with which she had been ill-prepared to deal. And he, fool that he was, wanted to take her in his arms and offer comfort. Caddaric steeled himself against that unwarranted softness and resumed his place by the fire. Jilana would receive no sympathy from him.

Jilana filled two buckets from the barrel of water on the wagon and then struggled to lower them to the ground without spilling them. The rope handles bit into the flesh of her hands, accentuating the weariness that had seeped into her very bones. After a moment's consideration to her modesty, Jilana shrugged and stripped off her stola, short undertunic and sandals. The Celts were embarrassingly unconcerned with nudity; it was doubtful anyone would be curious about her own unclad form.

The water was cool, but Jilana plunged her hands into one of the buckets and scrubbed furiously at her arms. Next she placed one foot in the bucket and washed her leg, then repeated the procedure with her other leg. The length of chain made such a maneuver difficult, but not impossible, although she had to take care with her balance. When the water hit her ankles, Jilana gasped at the ensuing burning sensation; the manacles had rubbed portions of her flesh raw. She had only her hands with which to work, and it was dark away from the fire, but when she was finished, Jilana was certain she was clean. She splashed water across her breasts and abdomen, then picked up the bucket and tilted it so that water sluiced down from her shoulders. Using the second bucket, she washed her face and then pulled her hair forward and submerged it in the water. She scooped water with her hands until all her hair was saturated and then attacked her scalp and the length of curls with her fingers.

When she was finished, her scalp tingled and her hair hung in a wet mass down her back so that trickles of water ran over her buttocks and down her legs, but she felt clean. Jilana refilled the buckets and washed out her stola and undertunic. The smell that rose from her wet clothing revolted her and Jilana scrubbed and refilled the buckets until her nose told her that her clothes were no longer offensive. As she had done with the other laundry water, she emptied the buckets some distance from the tent and then returned them to the wagon and placed the lid back on the water barrel. She draped her clothes on the bushes to dry and thought longingly of her pallet.

It was only then that it occurred to Jilana that she had no dry clothing to wear, and in her present state she could not return to the tent. Groaning softly, she sank to the ground and began wringing the water from her hair. A gust of wind hit her and she shivered with a chill. She dared not call on Caddaric for help, for he would probably parade her stark naked in front of his friends to the tent and that she could not bear. She would simply have to wait until her clothes were dry enough to wear.

Caddaric listened to the conversation swirling about him with only half an ear. Clywd had gone—the gods knew where—and the others were boldly retelling their exploits in battle and discussing the booty they had taken from Camulodunum. Artair left first, his lower lip bruised and swollen, and when Ede failed to draw Caddaric into conversation, she too took her leave. Caddaric nodded to her when she rose, but his mind was on Jilana. The splashing sounds of her bath, and the clank of her chains, had ended some time ago but she had not reappeared.

Caddaric started when a package was dropped into his lap.

"For Jilana," Clwyd explained, standing over his son.

Caddaric peeled off the wrapping and snorted in disgust. The package contained a small wheel of cheese and a loaf of bread. "I provide for what is mine, Druid."

Heall had risen and now stood beside Clwyd. "'Twill do her no harm, Caddaric; she is not yet accustomed to our fare."

"Nor will she be," Caddaric told his mentor, "if she continues to eat what we do not."

"Caddaric," Clwyd broke in, "she has not eaten since midday, and she lost that after tending a terrible wound. Surely you do not intend to starve her."

"Of course not," Caddaric growled, recalling with a twinge how little Jilana had eaten the night before. He got to his feet and faced the two men. "I give you both fair warning: do not think to cosset Jilana. She must adapt to our ways and that she will not do if you intercede on her behalf."

"She was more help to me today than any other I have trained," Clwyd informed his son. "If you wish her to *adapt*, you might try kindness."

"When last I tried kindness, Jilana knocked me senseless," Caddaric exclaimed, but he found himself addressing his father's back. Frustrated, he turned to Heall. "You understand what I must do."

Heall stroked his silver beard, then shook his head. "She is a gentle creature, confused and frightened by the violence erupting all around her—"

Caddaric laughed harshly. "Gentle! The first night she sought to bury a dagger in my heart and a week later she hit me with a shovel so that she could escape. I would hardly call her gentle!"

"She fights for her life. Why do you find that so difficult to understand?" Heall argued heatedly. "From the first you have bullied her, and you continue to do so. That is foolish—look what your treatment has brought about thus far! Think, Caddaric," he implored. "She went willingly with Clywd and helped our people. Does that not prove that she responds to kindness?''

"It proves she wants to save her own skin," Caddaric decided cynically. "See how she pits father against son—even you and Artair have come to blows. We must never forget that she is our enemy." He calmed himself with an effort. "Go now, my friend. The hour is late."

Heall departed, and Caddaric knelt to bank the fire for the night. He heard the soft clink of chains and, turning slightly, he saw Jilana peer cautiously around the corner of the tent. "If you are done hiding," he taunted, "get the lamp from the tent and light it." When she neither answered nor moved, Caddaric's brows lowered into a frown. "Did you hear me, Jilana?"

Jilana worried her bottom lip before replying, unaware that the action sparked Caddaric's temper. "Caddaric, please, may I have a blanket?"

Caddaric's head snapped up and he rose quickly to his feet. "I told you last night where you would sleep; I have not changed my mind."

"I remember," Jilana said hastily, feeling the blood creep into her cheeks. "I do not intend to disobey you but—"

"But?" Caddaric inquired in a tone that chilled her even further. To add to her consternation, he began walking toward her. "Why do you meekly obey my father all day and then seek to thwart my simplest request?"

"Nay, Caddaric, I do not." Jilana held out a hand as if to ward him off and tried to make her body disappear into the leather of the tent. A few more steps and she would no longer be concealed by the corner of the tent. Embarrassed, she blurted out, "I washed my gown and have naught to wear! Please, Caddaric, may I not have a blanket?"

Caddaric came to a sharp stop and then he was moving again, a low growl issuing from his throat as he came around the corner of the tent. "By the gods, woman, have you taken leave of your senses?" He grasped her by the shoulders and was appalled by the coldness of her flesh. She was trembling, too, but Caddaric was not certain whether that was caused by the chill or fear of him. Wordlessly, he lifted Jilana in his arms and carried her swiftly into the tent and bundled her into the furs of the pallet. He took the lamp outside to light it and when he returned he also carried the package Clywd had left.

Jilana pulled the blankets higher around her shoulders as Caddaric set the lamp beside the pallet, and tried to still the shivering that had seized her limbs. She burrowed further into the furs, watching Caddaric through wide eyes.

"There are blankets in the wagon. Why did you not search for them?"

"I did not know you had more blankets," Jilana managed to say. "And even if I had, they are yours, not mine."

Caddaric's jaw tightened. "Do you think I mean for you to freeze?"

Jilana looked away. "You have said I am your slave; I am doing my best to be obedient and keep within the boundaries you have set." Caddaric said something Jilana did not completely understand, but his explosive tone was unmistakable. She closed her eyes and waited.

The power he had wanted to wield over Jilana was now his, but Caddaric felt no satisfaction. He had wanted Jilana to depend upon him, to accept what he could give without comparing it to the life she had once known. But the fact that she was afraid to take so much as a blanket to warm herself without his permission left a bitter taste in Caddaric's mouth. A length of chain spilled from beneath the blankets to the ground and Caddaric looked away from the sight. Gently, he laid the package he carried upon Jilana's stomach. "Bread and cheese," he explained gruffly when she glanced from the package to him. He rose and began preparing for bed.

Jilana broke off a small piece of cheese and chewed it slowly. "'Tis thoughtful of you, Caddaric. Thank you."

Caddaric sat on the edge of the pallet to draw off his boots. After a long silence, he responded, "'Tis a gift from Clywd."

Her appetite fled, forcing Jilana to choke down the last mouthful of cheese. She should have known Caddaric would not have bothered with this small kindness, Jilana berated herself. She rewrapped the package and set it aside. When Caddaric asked if she had finished, she nodded and curled deeply into the pallet.

"Here." Jilana looked up to find Caddaric standing over her, a tunic in his hand. "Wear this tonight; 'twill keep you warm." When she hesitated, Caddaric extended the garment toward her. "'Tis not contaminated, Jilana," he growled. "If you can accept food from my father, surely you can accept my tunic."

"Thank you." Jilana sat up, reaching for the tunic with one hand while she held the blanket to her breast with the other.

Do not thank me, Caddaric wanted to snap, but he bit back the words. This little wicca split him in two, engendering powerful, dangerous emotions. He vacillated between wanting to punish her for running away and longing to take her into his arms and protect her from the cruelty of the world. Her gratitude for so small a thing as a garment was as offensive to him as the shackles around her ankles, but Caddaric knew no other way to insure Jilana's safety as well as her dependence upon him. He blew out the lamp and heard Jilana move to the far side of the pallet. No doubt the only reason she stopped was because the tent wall was at her back, he thought bitterly as he settled onto the spot Jilana had so recently vacated. The sound and motion of her movements as Jilana drew on his tunic evoked taunting images in Caddaric's mind and he squeezed his eyes tightly shut against the memories of the beauty of her slender body meshing with his own.

"Caddaric?"

Her voice came hesitantly, provocatively, out of the darkness and his body stirred at the sound of his name on her lips. "What?" His question came out in a low snarl and Caddaric cursed silently when Jilana pulled even further away. With an effort he drew a tight rein on his emotions and repeated, "What?"

Jilana hesitated, terrified that what she was about to do would send Caddaric into a rage. "Caddaric, I have a favor to ask of you."

"A favor, Jilana?" Curious, Caddaric rolled onto his side so that he faced her. It mattered not; the faint light filtering in through the top of the tent did not extend far enough to illuminate their features. Still, he could picture her sitting there, her violet eyes wide as they sought to pierce the darkness. He reached out and found her hand, squeezing it gently when she started in alarm. "Tell me."

Jilana drew a deep breath and gathered all her courage. "Lhwyd has taken prisoners—to be used for sacrifices." Her fingers curled urgently around his.

"I know." At the naked fear in her voice, Caddaric moved nearer. "You are safe, wicca; Lhwyd will not harm you."

"I do not fear for myself," Jilana said quietly, "but for another." Before Caddaric could speak, she hurried on, "When I arrived at Camulodunum one of Lhwyd's prisoners took me in, gave me comfort and shelter. Could you—would you—find a way to extent your protection to one more Roman?"

Caddaric smiled into the darkness. That Jilana could ask this surely meant that she trusted him in spite of his treatment. And if he found a way to grant her favor, mayhap she would forgive him the shackles. "I doubt Lhwyd will listen to me, but Clywd might be willing to speak to him." He thought for a moment. "If Lhwyd should refuse my father, Clywd could go to the Queen. She might intercede."

"Would Clywd do this for you?" Jilana asked breathlessly, her hopes soaring.

"Aye, I believe so." Imperceptibly, Caddaric shifted his weight so that his legs lightly brushed against hers. "Tell me the woman's name and I will talk with my father to-morrow.''

"His name," Jilana corrected, "is Hadrian Tarpeius. He has been most sorely injured, but he will cause you no trouble, I swear it. I can care for him and still perform the duties you assign me.'' Caddaric was motionless beside her, but his fingers were now crushing her hand. A feeling of dread crept into her heart, stilling the rest of her assurances.

"Who is he," Caddaric was finally able to ask, "this Hadrian Tarpeius?''

Jilana decided not to lie. Within a few minutes of their meeting, Caddaric would recognize the soldier in Hadrian. "Hadrian commanded the force that defended Camulodunum. He is the primipilus of the Twentieth Legion.''

"Why is he here?" Caddaric growled. "The Twentieth is at Mona.''

She was being interrogated, Jilana realized, just as she had been interrogated at Camulodunum. "His leg was broken in a fall from a horse,'' she answered stiffly. "He was forced to remain behind.''

"How fortunate for you.'' Caddaric practically threw Jilana's hand from his and turned onto his back.

Had she not been fighting for Hadrian's life, Caddaric's contempt would have driven Jilana into silence. As it was, she forced herself to continue. "Aye, it *was* fortunate. When I arrived at Camulodunum, the guard thought me a spy and imprisoned me. Hadrian freed me and took me in.''

"And in turn you laid with him," Caddaric finished tightly.

"I did not!" Jilana gasped. "No man has touched me save—'' Her words died when Caddaric grasped her wrist and jerked her against him.

"Do not lie to me, Jilana," Caddaric grated. "First me, now Hadrian.'' He made a clucking sound of disapproval that was laden with mockery. "What would your beloved Lucius say about the behavior of his pure patrician bride?''

The deliberate barb lit Jilana's anger, dissipating the hurt his words had caused. "I was pure when you took me," she hissed. "You know that! And if I had lain with Hadrian, what difference could it make to you? Your own people take lovers freely, without benefit of marriage! Is it not your wish that I *adapt* to the Iceni ways?'' Only his feral snarl warned Jilana that she had pushed Caddaric too far. One moment she was half-lying across his chest, and the next she was beneath him, his weight crushing her into the furs.

Having his own words thrown back at him was more than Caddaric could bear. Rage boiled up inside him; his fingers threaded through the mass of Jilana's hair to hold her head still for his kiss. He brutalized her mouth with his and when she denied him entrance, Caddaric bit at her bottom lip until her mouth opened in a quick gasp of pain. His tongue forged between her lips and explored the damp cavern until Jilana lay trembling beneath him. Only then did Caddaric withdraw, pulling back just far enough so that their lips brushed when he spoke. "If 'tis truth you want, then truth you shall have. You were given to me, Jilana; not by Boadicea or this uprising, but by the gods. Given to me in a dream. The purpose of this *gift* is a child. Our child, created by us." She went still beneath him and Caddaric laughed harshly. "Nay, Jilana, I will not take you now, not until I am certain you do not carry another's seed within your body." Caddaric jerked at her hair so that Jilana cried out. "Now you know what I want from you: a child, no more. Once that child is born, you will be allowed to stay with him or return to your own people, as you wish."

With that he rolled from Jilana and she could do no more than lay unmoving, hearing again and again his devastating words. Her lips were bruised and swollen, and when she moved her tongue over them she tasted the blood where Caddaric's teeth had pierced her flesh. So now she knew her fate, Jilana thought despairingly. She had mistaken Caddaric's earlier tenderness; while she had lain in his arms thinking their union to be a beautiful, rapturous thing, he had merely been taking a necessary step to fulfill his prophecy. He had taken her body, and her heart as well, but her love held no place in his dream. She was his brood mare, nothing else.

Chapter 6

THE NEXT MORNING dawned clear and bright, but neither Jilana nor Caddaric took particular note of the fact.
In a tense silence they rose and dressed, and while Caddaric tended the horses, Jilana prepared the morning
meal. Ede, Artair, Clywd and Heall shared their meal and
Jilana steadfastly ignored the questioning looks directed
toward herself and Caddaric. For his part, Caddaric
talked easily with his friends while Jilana concentrated on
devising and discarding different schemes for gaining
Hadrian's freedom. When their conversation turned to
the Iceni plans for the final assault on the temple, however, Jilana gave the warriors her undivided attention.

"We will use arrows to fire the roof of the temple,"
Caddaric was saying. "The Romans will be forced to leave
or burn to death. Once the temple is taken the Queen
plans to raze the city, so we must take what supplies are
available and replenish our water barrels before the final
assault."

Whatever else Caddaric said was lost on Jilana. Her
vision of the temple in flames and the dead and dying littering its steps returned in full force and Jilana bitterly
acknowledged its truth. With trembling hands she gathered up the bowls they had used for the meal and washed
them in the water she had set to heat earlier. Never again
would she doubt the validity of her visions, Jilana promised herself as she washed and dried the utensils.

Jilana looked up from her task when Clywd came to stand beside her. "This is for you," the Druid stated as he set a carved box—a smaller version of the one he had carried the day before—next to the wagon. He opened it to display the contents: an assortment of bandages, herbs and salves.

Drying her hands, Jilana knelt and examined each of the small pots of salves and pouches of herbs in turn before turning a questioning gaze to Clywd. "Where is the opium, the knives?"

Clywd folded his arms across his chest, his hands disappearing into the voluminous sleeves of the garment. "In time, Jilana, but not yet."

Jilana closed the box and rose to her feet. "I would use them to heal, Clywd, not to kill."

"Aye, you would; until the temptation became too great."

"How can I help the wounded, use what you have taught me, if I lack the proper tools?" Jilana demanded.

"In time," Clywd repeated. "There is still much you must learn and then, perhaps—"

"You will trust me enough to allow me opium and knives," Jilana finished in disgust. "Who do you think I will kill, Druid? Caddaric? Heall? You?"

"Nay," Clywd replied softly after a long silence. "Yourself."

Jilana stared at him for a moment and then laughed harshly. "You credit me with too much courage, Clywd. Hadrian bade me take my life rather than be captured. See you how well I carried out his instructions?" But her argument carried no weight, for Clywd was watching her through eyes that saw far more than the present, though Jilana could not know that. All she saw in the set expression on Clywd's face was that further argument would be futile. In spite of his gentleness, Clywd was as stubborn as his son. Jilana turned away to repack their eating utensils. "I thank you for the gift, Clywd."

"The box is to be used, of course," Clywd gently chided, as if she would use its deficiencies as an excuse to ignore its purpose. "Many of the Romans have bandages that need changing today and I, unfortunately, have a great many other patients to tend to."

Jilana spun back to the Druid, hardly daring to believe what Clywd had implied. "You mean I—" Her voice broke under the force of her emotions and it took a moment before she could bring it under control. "Will Caddaric allow this?"

"Aye, I have spoken with my son." Jilana's obvious happiness at the news brought a quick frown of concern to Clywd's face. She was thinking of the man, of course, that Hadrian who had looked at her with such adoration. There was a degree of danger in allowing Jilana such contact with Hadrian but the alternative—that of keeping the two apart until Lhwyd took Hadrian as a sacrifice—was far worse, Clywd thought as he lightly touched the side of Jilana's face and left the camp. And how much danger could there truly be? Clywd asked himself. The Romans were guarded and Jilana's own movements were hardly unremarked. As desperate as she might be to save her friend, he doubted she would do anything more daring than asking Caddaric or, perhaps, Heall, to intercede on Hadrian's behalf. Aye, all would be well, and when Hadrian was sacrificed, as he most certainly would be, mayhap Caddaric would be wise enough to offer Jilana sympathy and comfort. When he stopped to care for his first patient, Clywd had succeeded in stilling the nagging instinct which warned that he should not have turned a blind eye to the blatant ruse Jilana had enacted the night before.

JILANA HURRIED through the remainder of her chores, her spirits buoyed by the thought of seeing Hadrian. The gods, apparently, had ranged themselves on Hadrian's side. From the tent she removed the package of bread and cheese Clywd had left the night before and placed it in her healing box. When all was in readiness, Jilana swung the box's strap over her shoulder and approached Caddaric.

"Clywd said I have your permission to tend the prisoners," Jilana said when Caddaric finally looked up from sharpening his weapons. The idle chatter between the other three Iceni died at the bald challenge of her words.

"Did he?" Caddaric asked blandly. He stared at Jilana for a moment before returning his attention to plying the whetstone along the length of his sword.

Her heart dropped sickeningly into the pit of her stomach at his tone, but she found the courage to reply. "You did give your permission, did you not?"

Caddaric tested the edge of his blade with this thumb. Satisfied, he slid the sword into its scabbard and placed both on the ground beside him. "I will not intervene with Lhwyd, nor will I ask my father to do so. Do you understand?"

"Aye." Jilana's voice was barely audible. She had come to terms with the fact that Caddaric would not help her; she would find a way to save Hadrian on her own. But if Caddaric kept her in camp...

"Then you may go." Caddaric rose and shrugged into his baldric. "I am taking the wagon into the city to resupply our water and whatever provisions I can find. You need not concern yourself with the midday meal; the Queen plans to launch the attack against the temple at noon. But be back here at dusk."

Jilana nodded, her hands twisting the leather strap over her shoulder. "More sacrifices for Lhwyd?" she asked bitterly.

Caddaric's face hardened. "I do not think so. Those that do not die in the flames will undoubtedly meet the blades of eager warriors upon their escape."

Jilana left as quickly as her shackled ankles would allow—too quickly, for she missed the fleeting surge of pain that darkened Caddaric's blue eyes.

As Caddaric hitched the team to the wagon he thought of what lay ahead. The killing of innocent civilians had never set well with him, not in the legion and not now, when he was defending his homeland from the Roman blight. Had the Roman women been trained to fight, as many of the Celtic women were, perhaps he could have justified their deaths, but they were not. Thanks be to Clywd's gods that he had not yet had to face an unarmed woman, Caddaric thought fervently. 'Twas difficult enough facing Jilana with the blood of her countrymen on his sword. How could he meet her eyes if he killed a woman? Because the thought was unworthy of a warrior, Caddaric shoved it away. Until now, he had found the killing of civilians distasteful, but *never* had he sought to justify the deed. But now he did, because of Jilana. Because he wanted her to see him as something other than the enemy with bloodstained hands. Caddaric snarled at this latest evidence of his growing susceptibility to his red-haired witch and slapped the team into motion.

It seemed to Jilana as she walked to where the prisoners were held that the Iceni force had grown in number from the day before. The encampment spread out as far as the eye could see, and it appeared that every man and woman was busy with some task while the children played at war with wooden swords or sticks. While the camp gave the appearance of unity, in fact the Iceni and their allies had grouped themselves by their original villages and heeded only their local chieftain. As a result, the chieftains were kept busy arbitrating the disputes which arose between the neighboring camps.

After avoiding several displays of Celtic temper along the way, Jilana arrived at the makeshift stockade. The guards searched her medical box and waved her past. Jilana was suddenly grateful that Clywd had refused to allow her knives; the guards would surely have confiscated them and refused to allow her any further.

She went quickly to Hadrian and found him still asleep. Some blood had soaked through to the top of the bandage, but Jilana decided against changing the dressing until he awoke. She untied his bonds and then left him to sleep while she made her way once again through the prisoners, offering what little comfort, both physical and emotional, that she could. The prisoners had not been fed, although fresh water had been rationed out by the guards earlier in the morning. While she tended her people, Jilana assured them that they would not be left to starve. The assurances tasted like ashes in her mouth, but what else could she do? Tell them the truth? Surely that would be crueler than the faint hope she offered. Was it not worse to dwell on the manner of one's certain death than to believe that one would become a slave? For her own peace of mind, Jilana had to believe so.

Surprisingly, the guards were willing to supply Jilana with buckets of water, and even an *amphora* of vinegar when she asked. But then, Jilana realized, their attention was not centered on her or the prisoners. The guards were busy discussing the upcoming assault on the temple, and as the sun tracked ever higher, their thoughts grew less and less concerned with their charges. They were eager to be in this final action and Jilana noted that, one by one, the guards drifted away until only a handful remained around the perimeter of the prison area, as well as the guard who accompanied her. And why should they remain? Jilana reasoned. The prisoners were bound hand and foot, and obviously terrified. A glimmer of hope stirred in Jilana's heart.

As she repacked her box, Jilana risked a glance at the sky and noticed her guard doing the same. The Iceni grew more impatient with each passing minute. A plan began to form in her mind and Jilana worked to keep her hands and voice steady when she got to her feet. "I have only one more prisoner to see," she told the guard in a voice which, despite her intentions, cracked ominously. The guard looked at her sharply, and Jilana prayed that he would attribute the betraying sound to her shock of tending her countrymen. She preceded the Iceni to where Hadrian lay and gave him a weak smile when he set the amphora on the ground. "I thank you for your help, but you need not remain. This man," she gestured to Hadrian, "requires a great deal of care." When the Iceni merely eyed Hadrian and shrugged, Jilana risked a broader hint. "'Tis nearly noon and this will take quite some time. If you wish to return to your friends and partake of your meal, I will call when I am finished.''

"Lhwyd ordered that neither you nor the Druid be left alone with the prisoners," the Iceni said at last. He regarded her suspiciously. "Many of the prisoners died last night."

Gods, the opium! Clywd's kind end could prove her undoing! Jilana ignored the dart of fear that dried her mouth. "Of course they died," she said as tartly as she could. "They had been tied up and left for more than a day without care! Did Lhwyd think his goddess would see to their wounds?''

Such open criticism of Lhwyd sent the guard looking nervously about, as if fearing her words would summon the white-robed Druid. "Lhwyd's orders—"

"I would not want you to disobey Lhwyd. You can help me with him," Jilana interrupted desperately. "I have to change his bandage, and he's far too heavy for me to lift on my own."

A look of hatred swept over the Iceni's face as he surveyed the wounded legionary. "I would rather drive my sword into his belly." His hand fell to his sword, as if he would carry through his desire.

Only Jilana's knowledge of Lhwyd's order kept her from crying out. For what seemed an eternity she watched the Iceni, poised to throw herself between Hadrian and the guard if he drew his sword from the scabbard. At last the Iceni recalled himself. His hand slid from his sword and he spat contemptuously at Hadrian, the spittle landing on the hem of Hadrian's tunic. Jilana watched in silence as the man pivoted and walked away to join the other four guards.

Unable to bear her weight any longer, Jilana's legs collapsed and she sank onto the ground beside Hadrian. Shaking, Jilana grasped Hadrian's hand in both of hers and closed her eyes, willing herself not to think of what might have happened if the warrior had chosen to ignore Lhwyd's instructions. The hand she was holding squeezed gently and Jilana opened her eyes to find Hadrian watch-

ng her through half-closed lids. Of their own volition,
Jilana's fingers spasmodically wrapped themselves around
his hand.

"You should not have come back," Hadrian rasped
out.

"I could not leave you here," Jilana stated, her voice
wobbling. She carried Hadrian's hand to her face and
rested her cheek against it. "I have brought food and
bandages. And a plan for your escape."

Hadrian's eyes widened and he glanced cautiously to
where the guards stood before looking back at Jilana.
"You are mad."

"I think not." Her voice still trembled, but there was a
new note of confidence in it. She released Hadrian's hand
and searched through her medical box until she found the
bread and cheese. These she broke into small pieces and
would have fed them to Hadrian had he not stopped her.

"I can feed myself," he growled. With Jilana's help, he
shifted so that his back was braced against the tree trunk
and began to eat. Jilana dipped a cup into the water
bucket and set it on the ground beside him. "I want you
to go now, Jilana, and do not come back."

Jilana stared at him. "Did you not hear me? I have a
plan for your escape." Out of necessity, their voices were
low.

"Aye, I heard, and I tell you it is madness." Hadrian's
face was pale and he was obviously in pain, but he was
once more the primipilus of the Twentieth Legion. "The
guards would kill us before I could stand."

"There are only five guards—"

"Five too many!"

"Will you be silent," Jilana hissed. "The guards have
been leaving throughout the morning for the city."
Briefly, she told Hadrian about Boadicea's plans for the
temple. "The rest will leave also."

"They will want to be in on the kill," Hadrian mused.
Realizing that he was agreeing with Jilana, Hadrian shook
his head. "Even without the guards, you cannot get me

away from here. The entire camp will not pour into the city."

"Nay, they will not, but they will be so busy wandering about, gossiping over events in the city, that they will pay us no heed," Jilana said eagerly.

"Jilana, I am not certain I can stand, let alone walk," Hadrian countered. "Just this slight movement has set my wound bleeding again."

"Would you rather stay here and wait for Lhwyd to use you as a sacrifice?" Jilana ground out. "Is that what you wish, to die like a stupid ox upon an alter? I offer you life, Hadrian, or at least the promise of life. If we are caught, what could be worse than the fate they have in store for you now?" Jilana was angry enough to scream and it showed in the flashing purple of her eyes.

"Be reasonable, little one," Hadrian began, concerned that she would attract the guards' attention.

"Nay, I will not," Jilana exclaimed with as much force as their whispers would allow. "I have seen two cities and their inhabitants destroyed; I will *not* be reasonable when you insist upon giving up your life without a struggle when there is a chance to live!"

Sighing, Hadrian leaned his head back against the tree. "Tell me your plan."

While he ate, Jilana explained. "Our best chance will be when the attack has begun; the camp will be in an uproar and most of the warriors will be gone. I will come back for you then."

"And I will simply walk away from here?" Hadrian questioned dryly. "What of the guards?"

"I think they will desert their posts as well, but if they do not...," Jilana chewed thoughtfully at her lower lip and then nodded. "I will have to bring you a disguise—a cloak, I think—something that will hide your tunic and bandages." She looked Hadrian up and down, measuring him. He and Caddaric were nearly the same height. "Aye, I know someone about your size."

"Who is willing to lend me a cloak?"

Jilana hesitated. Caddaric would discover her theft eventually, but what were stealing and Caddaric's anger compared to what she planned? "Not precisely," she answered softly. "But it does not matter."

Hadrian broke off a piece of bread and chewed it. "What will you do if the guards stay behind?"

Jilana glanced at the guards and then turned her attention to unbandaging Hadrian's wound. "I will find another way."

There was a note of quiet determination in her voice and Hadrian gave up the battle. She would try to free him and probably they would both die in the process, but as Jilana had said, anything was better than waiting for Lhwyd to use him as a sacrifice. He winced when Jilana pulled the bandages free, but shook his head when she asked if the pain was great.

It was difficult to rebandage the wound, but Jilana managed, with Hadrian resting against her shoulder, to cause as little discomfort as possible. There was seepage from the wound, but it did not appear to be infected. Jilana pulled the length of bandage as tight as she could in hope that the binding would stop any bleeding that might occur when Hadrian moved.

"Do you need opium?" Jilana asked when Hadrian was sitting back against the tree. "I can get some if you do."

Hadrian shook his head. "It would put me to sleep, and then what would you do?" He smiled at the weak jest, but when he saw the look of pain that darkened her eyes, Hadrian took her head and carried it to his bandaged chest. "'Tis not so bad, Jilana, I swear."

Jilana succumbed to the comfort she saw in his eyes and eased her head onto his undamaged shoulder. Just for a moment, she promised herself; just for a moment she would give in to the fears and uncertainties that plagued her in spite of her brave words and then she would be strong again. Hadrian's hand gently combed through the tangled mass of her hair, drawing a sigh from her. "I will set you free," she whispered, and prayed to any god who would listen to help her fulfill the vow. She felt Hadrian stiffen and drew her head back, wondering if she had unwittingly caused him pain.

"Get up, Jilana."

The cold, hard voice was like the lash of a whip and Jilana bolted upright. Caddaric stood not three feet away, his face impassive as he took in the sight of the two of them nestled together. But his eyes. Ahh, gods, his eyes were a deep, fiery blue that threatened to burn holes right through her! Jilana saw, in that moment, that Caddaric was furious, and unless she could placate him, all hope of freeing Hadrian was lost.

Jilana came to her feet as quickly as she could. As if he could sense the danger facing them, Hadrian grabbed Jilana's hand, but she shook him off and took the three steps that brought her directly in front of Caddaric.

Before Jilana could speak, Caddaric looked her up and down contemptuously and said, "You are a faithless bitch, are you not? You would have driven your beloved Lucius to murder within a month."

Behind her, Hadrian swore at Caddaric for his words, but Jilana's arm was already in motion. Hurt and angered beyond reason, she put all her weight behind the blow, but Caddaric lazily caught her wrist before her hand could make contact with his face. As his fingers closed over her delicate bones in a crushing grip, the ramifications of her action dawned on her and Jilana's face drained of color. "You..." Her throat tightened in fear and Jilana had to force the words out. "You gave your permission," she reminded him.

"For you to treat their wounds, not lay with the men!" Caddaric tightened his grasp and took a perverse pleasure in Jilana's gasp of pain.

"I did not—"

"Your name is Hadrian?" Caddaric asked the man on the ground.

Hadrian nodded, not trusting himself to speak. He struggled to rise, to put himself on an equal footing with this towering Iceni, but the slicing pain in his side sent him groaning back to the ground.

Caddaric pulled Jilana to his side, and since her arm was still upraised, she was lifted off her feet in the process. While she was still suspended in mid-air Caddaric released her wrist and Jilana went spilling to the ground. When she gave an exclamation of pain he did not spare her so much as a glance. All his attention was riveted on Hadrian. "Tell me, primipilus, were the joys of her body worth your life?"

Hadrian's eyes narrowed angrily. His voice, when it finally emerged, was even harsher than usual. "I cannot say." His dark eyes strayed to Jilana and softened in sympathy when she barely met his gaze before burying her face in her hands.

"How tragic," Caddaric snorted. "You, however, made a favorable impression, enough so that last night she begged me to free you. Shall I tell you what she offered me in return?"

Hadrian stared coldly back at Caddaric, but a vein pulsed in his temple. "If you want to know if the Lady Jilana shared my bed, why not ask?" Hadrian taunted in a low rasp.

Caddaric's face whitened. "I rejoice that my aim was not true, primipilus. This way I have the joy of watching your humiliation at the loss of your command," he retorted. Their eyes locked and the two men stared at one another.

The lengthy silence brought Jilana's face out from the barrier of her hands and she looked on helplessly while the two men conducted their mute battle. At last Caddaric spoke and Jilana had to strain to hear him.

"Did you take her?"

Hadrian's nostrils flared and it took several seconds before he had enough control to answer. "I was not so fortunate."

Caddaric nodded, once, and turned on his heel. Without a word he took Jilana's wrist, pulled her roughly to her feet and started off.

"Centurion!"

The barked command froze Caddaric in mid-step. Beside him, Jilana could feel Caddaric stiffen in reaction. Reluctantly, he turned back to Hadrian, who gave a self-satisfied nod. "The legion leaves its mark, no matter how hard you may try to erase it. Your skill with a short sword betrayed you." His lips twisted into what might have been a brief smile. "What legion?"

"Does it matter?" Caddaric parried. "'Twas a lifetime ago, in a different world." He paused, then grudgingly added, "Were it within my power, I would give you my sword."

Hadrian inclined his head in thanks for the offer. Both men were well versed in the legion's code of death before dishonor. "I fear, I would not have the strength to fall upon its length even if it were within your power."

The antagonism faded and for a moment the two men regarded each other with mutual respect. Then, in a jerky, almost-forgotten gesture, Caddaric brought his right fist to his left breast before turning away and dragging Jilana behind him.

Stunned by all that had happened, Jilana could do little more than stumble along in Caddaric's wake. Not until they reached their campsite did Jilana have the events sorted out to her satisfaction and when Caddaric released her she stood nervously beside the dead campfire.

"Why did you salute Hadrian?" Jilana asked in a small voice.

"Because he was—is the primipilus. He has worked his way up through the ranks, taken care of his men, endured the snubs of those officers whose commissions were purchased either in gold or political favors." Caddaric's voice trailed off and he looked at Jilana impatiently. "I fought him and found him a worthy opponent, yet because I was rushed I did not make certain he was dead and now he is denied the honor of dying on the battlefield."

Jilana took a moment to absorb the knowledge that Caddaric had grievously wounded Hadrian. "Then you understand why I must try to help him?"

His brooding expression vanished and Caddaric glared at her. "You will not go near him again."

"Caddaric, plea—"

"I forbid it!" Caddaric thundered. He took Jilana by the shoulders and gave her a quick, brutal shake. "He has been humiliated enough in front of you. And if you wish to cushion a man's head upon your bosom, 'tis mine you will cushion. Do you understand?" Jilana nodded shakily and Caddaric let her go. "You will stay here today. If I learn that you have disobeyed me, gone to him, I will—" Caddaric swore feelingly and stalked away.

He would go to the city, Jilana thought as she watched Caddaric's retreating back, secure in the belief that she would do as he had ordered. Jilana tossed her head and started around the tent toward the horses. No matter the consequences, she could not leave Hadrian to Lhwyd. And it was nearly midday, the time when she would have the best opportunity to smuggle Hadrian away from the other prisoners.

The horses whickered in greeting and twitched their ears forward in interest when Jilana neared them, but they were well-mannered beasts who did not object when she paced the tether line to examine them. Of the six horses, a golden stallion caught Jilana's eye. The stallion was tall, with a deep, strong chest and a glint in his eyes that promised a spirit to match his strength, but Jilana rejected him as a mount for Hadrian. Hadrian needed endurance in a mount, but in his weakened condition, Jilana doubted Hadrian could control such a horse. Her next choice was a roan gelding. Praying that this horse had a gentle temperament, Jilana untied the tether line and led him to the wagon where Caddaric stored his saddles.

He seemed gentle enough, Jilana thought as she held the woven halter with one hand and stroked the horse with the other. He playfully butted Jilana's shoulder and she petted his soft nose, then flipped back the canvas which protected Caddaric's equestrian tack. Taking the first bridle that came to hand, Jilana slipped the bit into the horse's mouth and then slid the leather strips over his ears.

The reins trailed on the ground. Jilana took a cautious step backward, and then another, watching. The horse ignored her. His tail swished and he rubbed his jaw along a foreleg, but he made no move to run away and Jilana breathed a sigh of relief. As long as the reins trailed on the ground, the horse would remain in place. Quickly, she saddled the horse and then tied him to the back of the wagon.

The last item was Hadrian's disguise and Jilana hurried inside the tent. With none of the hesitation she had felt yesterday at touching Caddaric's things, Jilana opened his kist and searched through it until she found what she was looking for. She took out a plain, undyed wool tunic, set it aside and continued her search until she found a cloak. In fact, there were two cloaks, one bright blue and the other a subdued brown. Jilana pulled the brown cloak from the kist and carefully repacked the other clothing. With any luck, Caddaric preferred the blue cloak and it would be some time before he discovered the theft of the brown one.

Folding the cloak and draping it over her arm, Jilana set out at a leisurely pace. As she had hoped, the Iceni camp was in turmoil. People scurried in all directions, talking excitedly about what was to befall the temple and making plans to take what they could from Camulodunum before it was razed. Horses and wagons were being driven into the city, adding to the confusion. Not even a woman in chains could distract the Iceni from the satisfaction that was close at hand.

Hadrian, his back braced against the tree, watched the behavior of the prisoners through narrow eyes. All were frightened, a few wept openly. With the removal of the bodies this morning, the once proud citizens of the capital had made themselves as comfortable as was possible on the hard ground and resigned themselves to their fate. As he had. A less than glorious end to his otherwise successful military career. Hadrian gave a short bark of laughter and winced at the pain that shot through his right side. He rubbed the damaged portion of his chest, glanced idly around, and felt his mouth drop open in astonishment. Jilana was marching toward him as if her presence was the most natural thing in the world. Hadrian's eyes widened at the sight of the hideous brown garment she carried on her arm.

Jilana stopped beside Hadrian and smiled serenely. "'Tis time to leave."

Hadrian gaped up at her. "You *are* mad." But he felt hope spring back to life.

"No doubt." Jilana reached down and helped Hadrian to his feet. "Put this on." She shook out the cloak, revealing the tunic she had stolen. "Not even this cloak will hide the blood on your tunic," she prodded when Hadrian hesitated.

With a nod, Hadrian struggled out of his own clothing and knew a moment of embarrassment when he stood unsteadily in front of Jilana clad only in his loincloth. She, however, seemed unconcerned with this lack of modesty, and merely stepped forward to help him into the fresh tunic. Once he was clothed, Jilana swept the cloak around his shoulders and tied it securely at the neck. Her medicine box still lay on the ground and Jilana took a moment to close it and swing the strap over her shoulder.

"Now we go." Jilana took Hadrian's arm and led him away from the prisoners. The other captives were so lost in their own misery that it seemed none of them noticed Hadrian's odd departure. Or if they did, they gave no sign.

"The guards are gone," Jilana observed in a smug tone.

"I know, I saw them leave," Hadrian replied dryly. They were away from the prisoners now and surrounded by the enemy. Hadrian's hand fell to his side, where his sword would have hung, and encountered air.

Jilana noticed the betraying movement. "There is no danger, Hadrian. The Iceni are too busy with their own plans to worry about a prisoner escaping." Her words did nothing to dispel his nervousness and Jilana squeezed his arm reassuringly. "There is no need to hurry. Just lean on me if you grow weak; 'tis not too far."

His body was weak, Hadrian discovered when they had covered only a short distance, and the jostling he received at the hands of the Iceni who were hurrying to Camulodunum caused pain to spear through his side. Against his instincts, Hadrian found himself leaning against Jilana's lesser strength. He paid little attention to his surroundings, needing all of his energy to concentrate on the increasingly complicated task of walking, until Jilana gently pulled on his arm and led him into a campsite. He recognized the style of the leather tent at once, and so hesitated to step inside when Jilana held the outer flap open for him. With the destruction that had transpired since the uprising, Hadrian wondered if the ghosts of the soldiers who had once inhabited this tent still dwelled within it.

"Hadrian, step inside," Jilana urged.

Overcoming his superstitions, Hadrian stepped forward and Jilana dropped the flap behind him.

Leading him to the pallet, Jilana said, "Wait here," and, after setting her medicine box beside a chest, left him alone.

He could hear the soft clink of her chains as Jilana moved about outside the tent and, as his eyes adjusted to the gloom, Hadrian was able to discern the furnishings within. A large chest decorated with bold, Celtic patterns sat against one wall. The Iceni warrior's, Hadrian guessed. A small oil lamp, an earthenware pitcher and basin and the pallet, the latter neatly made and the former strictly aligned against the wall opposite the chest. Odd how the discipline of the legion spilled over into one's private habits, Hadrian mused. He lay down on the pallet and closed his eyes, surrendering to his wounds. He may have slept, but when Jilana entered the tent, his eyes flew open.

Jilana crossed the small area between the tent and the pallet and knelt beside Hadrian. "I have a horse saddled and ready, behind the tent, and food and water to last you a week. Will that be enough time for you to reach safety?"

Hadrian thought a moment, then nodded. "We will go south, to Londinium. The civilians need to be warned of the uprising." Belatedly, her words made themselves clear and he looked sharply at Jilana. "You are coming with me."

"Nay, I cannot." Jilana gave him a tremulous smile and lifted the hem of her skirt so that the chains were in plain sight. "I cannot ride in these, and even if I could, I would not."

"Why?" The single word was raw with anguish.

"If I escape, Caddaric will come after me," Jilana answered calmly, but her eyes darkened with a pain that Hadrian could not begin to comprehend. "'Twill take time for the Iceni to notice that you are gone, and once they discover your absence they will assume that you died."

"We did not escape unnoticed," Hadrian argued. "In time that priest will learn the truth and come for *you*. Jilana, you must come with me!"

Jilana concealed the fear which slithered up her spine at the thought of Lhwyd. "Caddaric will protect me," she assured Hadrian bitterly. "He has plans that not even Lhwyd can contest." Even as she spoke, Jilana knew that was not true. When Lhwyd discovered her role in Hadrian's escape—and he *would* find out, Jilana knew that with dreadful certainty—even if Caddaric were so inclined, he could offer no protection. But what was a moment under Lhwyd's ritual knife compared to the agony of lying in Caddaric's arms and knowing his desire was only for the child they would create. Jilana kept these dark thoughts to herself as she knelt and raised Hadrian's tunic so that she could check his bandage. "The bleeding has stopped," she informed him. "And the dressing should hold until you reach Londinium."

"Jilana—"

"One last item," Jilana interrupted. She insinuated a hand between the pallet and the ground, burrowing around until her hand closed around cold metal. With a triumphant smile, she extracted the weapon she had hidden and presented it to Hadrian. "Your dagger."

Hadrian shook his head in wonder as he accepted the dagger. "How did you manage this?" he asked as Jilana opened the chest and drew forth a wide belt.

"Caddaric did not think to search me." Jilana shrugged. "Come, 'tis time to leave." Jilana helped him rise, smoothed the tunic into place and waited impatiently while he buckled the belt and slid the dagger beneath it. "They have fired the temple roof."

She hurried him outside before Hadrian could protest further. When Hadrian saw the size of his mount, he groaned. "A smaller horse would be welcome," he commented weakly.

"Unfortunately, there is little to choose from," Jilana answered with a wry smile. "He will serve you well, I think, and he is not as fearsome as another I could have chosen." She brushed a kiss across Hadrian's cheek, then stepped back to hold the bridle. "Up."

Hadrian rested his arm against the saddle and stared down at her. "Jilana, you must come with me."

"There is no time to argue," Jilana snapped. "You know that I cannot, and you know the reasons. You must leave, Hadrian, or the chance will be lost. I have not gone to all this trouble only to have you caught now!"

His left leg had not completely healed. Stiff and painful, it bore his weight for only a moment when he made to swing into the saddle; then the knee buckled and Hadrian's right foot slammed back to the ground. Waves of agony ripped through his side and leg and Hadrian clung to the saddle for support.

"Try again."

Through the buzzing in his head, Hadrian barely made out Jilana's words. Automatically, he obeyed the tone of command. This time, just as his left leg was about to take his body's weight, Jilana's hands were around his knee, bracing it against the strain. He settled hard onto the saddle and took several deep breaths to counteract the swimming sensation in his head. At last he opened his eyes and looked down into Jilana's concerned face. "Come with me," he grated.

Jilana shook her head, unshed tears burning her eyes, turning them a brilliant violet as she handed the reins to Hadrian. "Cut directly through the camp and skirt the city until you reach the road. Cross it and take to the forest on the opposite side. 'Tis how I reached Camulodunum without being discovered." She took the bridle strap in her hand and guided the horse between the tent and dead fire. Releasing the bridle, she took a step backward. "The gods go with you, Hadrian, and grant you peace." Her voice cracked on the last words.

"Jilana, I beg you—"

"Go!" Jilana commanded in a desperate voice. She slapped the horse on the rump and it leaped forward. It took Hadrian a moment to gain control of the mount, and when he did he was too firmly enmeshed in the Icenic traffic to turn the steed around. He looked back once, but did not wave. Nor did Jilana. The risk was too great.

Jilana watched until Hadrian was swallowed up by the trees and the jubilant Iceni. Now she could only pray that his disguise held and, if it did, that he had the strength to make it to Londinium. She turned back to the camp, prayers to Jupiter, Mithras, Mars and any other god who might offer Hadrian protection hovering on her lips. And came face to face with Heall.

Her mouth formed Heall's name, but no sound emerged. She felt the blood drain from her face, and her heart began a slow, thrumming rhythm that echoed in her head. Heall stood as unmoving as a statue, his right hand resting on his sword. His brown eyes were bright, boring into her with a fierce intensity. How much had he seen? Jilana wondered frantically. Could she bluff her way through this, pretend that it was Caddaric who had just ridden off? Heall's words killed that hope.

"You are a foolish, foolish child."

Jilana stayed on her feet, but just barely. "What will you do?" Amazingly, her voice was calm, if breathless.

Heall sighed and his body seemed to relax. "What I should have done was stop you while I had the chance. But I did not." He shook his shaggy head. "A girl in chains and a badly wounded prisoner. Who would believe it?" Both eyebrows rose questioningly at Jilana. "How do you plan to explain the loss of the horse to Caddaric?"

"I—I have no idea," Jilana murmured, afraid of the light in Heall's eyes.

"And the clothes he wore, those were Caddaric's as well?" At Jilana's nod, Heall chuckled reluctantly. "You do not lack for courage, child, only intelligence."

The insult caused Jilana to briefly forget her fear and she bristled. "Will he be stopped, do you think?"

Heall considered that a moment before shaking his head. "Nay, not today. You timed it well."

"Except for you," Jilana pointed out. What was Heall thinking?

"Aye, except for me," Heall agreed. His expression gave nothing away.

"Are you going to tell Caddaric?"

Heall laughed shortly. "There will be no need. The missing horse and clothing will speak for themselves. He is not a stupid man, Jilana."

"I know that well enough." Jilana sank to the ground and idly smoothed her stained skirt over her manacled ankles. Her hands, she noted dispassionately, were trembling. The motion drew a frown from Heall. "I will tell him that I thought to escape and the horse bolted. He will believe that." She gave Heall a wary look. "Unless you tell him the truth."

"And the clothing," Heall asked, avoiding her unspoken question.

Jilana shrugged with a carelessness she was far from feeling. In truth, with each passing minute her nerves were stretched closer to the breaking point. "I will plead ignorance and throw myself on his mercy. Mayhap Caddaric can be convinced that he failed to pack those two items."

Heall considered this, one hand stroking his silver beard. "There was some confusion when he left Venta Icenorum," he mused. "Aye, Caddaric could easily be convinced that he left the cloak and tunic behind. So," Heall drew the word out thoughtfully, "we are left with the problem of the gelding." Jilana caught her breath as Heall's meaning became clear, and his beard twitched as he smiled. "Did you think I meant to leave you to your own devices?"

There was a hint of mischief in his voice and Jilana exhaled shakily. "You are Caddaric's friend and I have just—" She paused, searching for the right word.

"Betrayed him," Heall offered.

Jilana swallowed and nodded. "Betrayed him, and Boadicea . . . and Lhwyd. Why would you help me?"

Heall sat beside her on the ground. "Tell me about this man. What is he to you?" The query was so gentle that Jilana found herself telling Heall the entire story of her relationship with Hadrian. "Friendship is a rare gift," he said when she fell silent. "That is all this Hadrian is to you, a friend?"

Jilana inclined her head. "Only a friend, Heall, not a—" she blushed "—a lover." Something like relief seemed to pass over Heall's face, but Jilana did not see it.

"Why did you not go with him?"

"Because Caddaric would have followed us, and then Hadrian would have been lost." Jilana glanced down at the links of chain which had escaped the folds of her skirt. "And because I could not ride in these."

The truth, Heall thought, but not the whole truth. Or perhaps I choose to deceive myself with Clywd's visions. Awkwardly, he patted Jilana's hand and rose.

"Where are you going?" Panic threaded Jilana's question.

Heall looked down at her and winked. "Trust me."

Heall left, and after several minutes of pondering, Jilana gave up trying to fathom the Celtic mind. Heall had asked for her trust, and Jilana realized she had no other choice. And, for some reason, she did not believe Heall

would betray her activities to Caddaric. She watched the
sky over the city, saw it darken with smoke. The Iceni were
firing all of Camulodunum. Borne by the wind, the dark
cloud expanded, moving until it blocked the sun and settled over the Iceni camp. There was a faint, acrid smell to
the air now and Jilana sneezed several times. She thought
of Camulodunum and Venta Icenorum, of all that had
been lost, and wondered when Boadicea's thirst for vengeance would be quenched. There was no answer to that
question, and Jilana turned her thoughts to Hadrian. Was
he free, or had some curious Iceni ended his life? Jilana
pushed that dark possibility aside. She needed to believe
that Hadrian was away from Camulodunum, that he
would make it to Londinium and there take ship to Rome;
that at some point in the future he would be safely established in his country villa, breeding horses for the legion.

Jilana's eyelids dropped. The excitement of the day
combined with the lack of sleep the night before took their
toll. Too tired to retire to the tent, Jilana curled up on the
grass and slept.

When Jilana woke, dusk had fallen and Caddaric had
returned. He sat facing her, studying her face as she
moved from sleep into wakefulness. There was a warmth
behind her and Jilana sat up and looked over her shoulder. The campfire had been started and meat now roasted
over the flames, its aroma mixing with the far more unpleasant smell of the burning capital.

"How long have you been sleeping?"

Because of her actions, the simple question took on all
kinds of sinister implications. Jilana scrambled to her feet.
The chain had twisted around one of her ankles and she
bent to unwind it. When that was accomplished, she
moved as quickly as she could out of Caddaric's reach. "I
apologize for the fire," she burst out, wondering if he had
checked the horses yet. "I know 'tis my responsibility, but
I fell asleep and—"

"'Twas not a reprimand." Caddaric cut through her
explanation. "I was merely curious." His face hardened
as he watched Jilana put the fire between them.

"I shall remember the fire from now on," Jilana promised him. "And my other duties as well."

Gods, Caddaric swore. She truly believes I would beat her for falling asleep. He wanted to tell her that was not his intention, that he had tried, unsuccessfully, to find cheese or some other delicacy in the city today so that she would find the beef now roasting on the spit more appetizing. But after his treatment of Jilana this morning, she would not believe him. Instead he said, "There is bread in the wagon and an amphora of wine. Ready those while I see to the horses."

Jilana froze as Caddaric got to his feet and walked around the tent. After a moment she forced her legs to move and she went to the wagon. Her hands trembled as she located the bread and wine and moved it within easy reach. While she worked she strained to hear Caddaric. Any moment he would discover the missing horse and come tearing back to the camp. What would she say? Just the thought of Caddaric's rage caused Jilana to drop the wooden plates she had been lifting from the wagon. She thought of Hadrian, safe now if all had gone well, and tried to invent some lie that Caddaric would believe. She could plead ignorance, but since she had supposedly remained at the campsite all day, Jilana doubted Caddaric would believe that someone could have taken the horse without her hearing. And the saddle and bridle as well, Jilana thought with a flare of panic. She looked at the canvas-draped shapes near the rear of the wagon. The missing saddle seemed to Jilana to have left a glaring depression in the canvas. Caddaric had confiscated those from the imperial stable yesterday. He would surely notice those were missing. Would he believe that another Iceni would steal from him?

Jilana shook her head in answer to her silent question and began marshalling her defense, even though she doubted that Caddaric would hear her out. How could she make Caddaric understand the instinctive loyalty and responsibility she felt for Hadrian? If Ede had been in Hadrian's position, would not Caddaric have done all in his power to save her? Aye, he would have, and the knowledge stiffened Jilana's spine. What did she care whether Caddaric was angry, even furious? To him she was nothing more than a useful slave, a brood mare, a bed partner sent to him by his unfathomable gods! Nothing he could do or say could hurt her more than that. Jilana set the plates and cups on the narrow shelf that was nailed to the side of the wagon.

Caddaric was talking to the horses in a gentle voice and Jilana wondered at that. Did he not notice the loss of his horse? Or perhaps he believed one of his friends had borrowed the animal. Ruthlessly, she killed such hopeful speculation. The truth would come out and she steeled herself for that eventuality. But, as she listened to the soothing drone of Caddaric's voice while she turned the meat, Jilana could not help the foolish wish that he would speak to her in that tone.

Caddaric returned to the campsite in a better mood. Not even his years in the legion had lessened his inbred love of horses. They were fascinating creatures, much like his little wicca in that respect. Unlike Jilana, however, horses were predictable in their temperaments and he found that comforting. A mean horse did not suddenly become gentle any more than a gentle horse would try to bite its rider out of sheer perversity. How simple his life would be if only Jilana were so predictable. And how angry Jilana would be if she knew that he thought of dealing with her in terms of dealing with a stubborn mount!

Jilana was lost in thought—the gods only knew what was running through her mind—and did not notice his return until Caddaric stepped up to the fire. Immediately a wary expression came into her eyes and Caddaric felt a portion of his new-found patience slip away. "I will show you how to make wheat cakes." His voice was brusque, not at all what he had intended, and neither were the words. Caddaric cursed silently as he gathered the necessary cooking utensils. If anything, Jilana now appeared more nervous. Seizing his patience in both hands, he set about teaching Jilana how to combine the ingredients—

taken from Camulodunum, although he had enough sense to keep that knowledge to himself—and then nestle the pan into a section of the coals. Caddaric used the same tone of voice with Jilana that he used with a skittish mare, but to no avail. Her tension was a tangible thing which increased in direct proportion to his efforts to calm her. When he got to his feet Jilana started so violently that she nearly lost her balance, and Caddaric snapped, "By the gods, woman! What ails you?"

Jilana shook her head, unable to speak. What kind of game was Caddaric playing? Why did he not question her, accuse her of stealing the horse? Could he not sense that her nerves were fraying under his mocking tutelage? Wheat cakes! Her stomach was in such a state that she did not even care to think about eating, let along preparing *wheat cakes*!

Oh, he was a cruel, devious man, Jilana thought with sudden insight. Of course he knew she was nervous. 'Twas exactly his intent! No doubt he intended that she should collapse at his feet and confess her guilt, beg his forgiveness. The demon! Jilana raised her head and proudly faced those blazing, blue eyes. "Will you want me to prepare wheat cakes for every meal, lord?" She was surprised that her voice did not shake.

Caddaric's eyes narrowed. The seemingly innocent question was barbed, despite the deferential title Jilana had used. She made "lord" seem like a vile epithet. "I thought Roman women were trained in the art of running a kitchen," he shot back.

"So we are," Jilana answered in a voice so sweet that Caddaric felt his temper rise. "We Roman women may not wield swords, but we are more than competent with menus."

"But not with cooking." Caddaric could not resist issuing the blunt challenge.

Jilana knew the first stirring of anger. "You should have thought of that before claiming me as a slave, lord."

"'Tis not your cooking skill that interests me." Caddaric's tone, and the slow, lingering inspection he gave her, brought a flush to her cheeks.

"I know well enough what interests you," Jilana spat, "and I find your rutting, barbarous ways repulsive."

Unseen and unheard by either of them, Heall and Artair had come into the camp in time to hear Jilana's last words. Heall suppressed a laugh while Artair whitened. When the younger man made to interrupt the two, Heall clamped a hand on his shoulder and kept Artair firmly by his side.

"Repulsive," Caddaric echoed in a mocking tone. "You did not find me repulsive that day in the bath."

"And what else could I do? Had I resisted, no doubt you would have resorted to rape!"

Caddaric's head snapped back as if he had been slapped. "There is no need to take by force that which is freely given," he said in a low growl which should have warned Jilana that she had gone too far.

But the excitement of battle was singing in Jilana's blood, deafening her to such subtleties. "What is a good slave for, save to satisfy her master's *desires*?" Jilana asked cuttingly. "I am powerless before your might."

A wild gleam entered Caddaric's eyes and he seized Jilana. "You sharp tongued she-wolf! You found as much pleasure as I, and you know it!"

"Nay, I did not," Jilana argued, struggling to be free of Caddaric's hands and the iron grip they had on her arms. "'Tis not the lot of slaves to enjoy pleasure, so do not lie to yourself! I will not willingly share your bed again! How does that suit your deluded vision of my bearing your child! The gods' will indeed!"

Caddaric crushed Jilana's words and lips beneath his ravaging mouth. As an impulsive tactic, the kiss worked extremely well, Caddaric thought vaguely. Jilana struggled, and he countered by hauling her hard against his chest. The contact knocked the breath out of her lungs and her lips parted instinctively. Caddaric used the unexpected reaction to his advantage. His tongue surged into

her mouth, destroying any resistance in its path. Jilana
fought against the embrace until she realized that beating
her fists against Caddaric's shoulders had no effect upon
his assault. She forced herself to stand unmoving in his
arms while his mouth plundered hers. There was a faint,
traitorous stirring within her body, a result of the lessen-
ing aggression in Caddaric's kiss. With a sense of desperation, Jilana turned her mind away from what was
happening and concentrated on the wounds Caddaric had
inflicted upon her soul. Knowing Caddaric's plans as she
did, to respond would bring a shame beyond bearing.

The change in Jilana was subtle but unmistakable.
Caddaric felt the mental barrier she was erecting as surely
as if it were a stone wall. Slowly he released her, engulfed
by shame, and stared into the shadowed, violet eyes.
'Twas not his way, to force a woman. So why did this
particular woman challenge and taunt and defy him until
reason was gone and his only thought was to subdue her?

Heall noisily cleared his throat and stepped into the
camp. "Before you two start again, I would like to rescue
the meat from the spit." He gestured to the fire, where
their meal was beginning to char.

Caddaric returned to the world with a start. He heard
once again the noise of the camp and wondered how far
his voice, and Jilana's, had carried. Heall was studying
him with something akin to amusement, while Artair's
expression was coldly disapproving. Caddaric puzzled
over that, but fleetingly, for Artair had a saddle swung
over one shoulder and was walking toward the wagon.

"What is that for?" Caddaric asked when Artair set his
burden into the wagon bed.

"'Tis yours," Artair replied. He flipped the canvas over
the saddle and returned to the fire. "I borrowed it this
afternoon. Did Jilana not tell you?"

"Nay." Caddaric pinned Jilana with a hard look.

Bewildered, Jilana looked from Caddaric to Artair and
back again. Had Artair taken one of Caddaric's saddles?
Behind Caddaric, Heall frowned at her and nodded impatiently and suddenly Jilana understood. "I, ah, forgot

to tell you," she murmured inanely. The overwhelming sense of relief she felt made it difficult to speak.

"I do not care for it," Artair said easily. "Our lighter saddles are far superior." He took the dagger from his belt and poked at the roasting meat, dismissing the topic. "'Tis dead. Can we eat now, or is it your intent to burn the rest of it?"

A dull flush worked its way across Caddaric's cheekbones. He bent to the task of removing the beef from the fire and slicing it onto the plates Jilana had provided. "I would deem it a courtesy if you would ask before making free with my possessions," Caddaric chided.

Artair shrugged. "As you wish." He took the plate Jilana handed him and winked at her.

"You told Artair," Jilana accused Heall in a low voice when she took his plate to him.

Heall nodded and glanced to where the two younger men sat by the fire. "I had to; 'tis his saddle."

Jilana swallowed. "The horse?"

"Replaced with one of mine." Heall popped a chunk of meat into his mouth and spoke around it. "A mare, unfortunately, but her coloring is right. By the time Caddaric notices the switch, he will not connect it with your missing legionary."

Pray to the gods Heall is right, Jilana thought. She took her own plate and moved away from the fire to eat. Clywd arrived later, waving her away when Jilana made to serve him. The beef was strong to Jilana's palate, but she forced herself to eat half of the portion Caddaric had given her and then erased the taste with a wheat cake covered in honey. It was as she was filling the drinking cups that Jilana noticed Ede was missing. A curious absence, but one for which she was grateful. The sight of Ede eyeing Caddaric so brazenly was distressing.

Jilana distributed the wine and turned her attention to cleaning the plates. She had just finished the task when, as if in response to her thoughts, Ede appeared. Jilana's lips curled into a resigned smile as she reached for another cup. The smile disappeared when a second figure followed Ede into the camp. Lhwyd. A cold knot formed in Jilana's breast when the white-robed Druid came to a halt in front of Clywd. The wine forgotten, Jilana was drawn to the two men in spite of her instinctive urge to flee. She came to a halt a few feet behind Lhwyd.

"What have you done with him, Clywd?" Lhwyd's question was soft, almost gentle in nature. The tone made Jilana's skin crawl.

Clywd looked at the younger man from beneath upraised brows. He swallowed the last bite of wheat cake and drained his wine before speaking. "Done with whom, Lhwyd?"

"My prisoner, my special offering to the goddess," Lhwyd replied, his rich voice caressing the word *offering*. "Where have you taken him?"

Clywd shook his head. "You claimed the prisoners, all of them, as your own. I did not know one was more important than the others."

"Do not lie, old one," Lhwyd warned silkily. "The Queen herself is interested in tonight's sacrifices. 'Twill not go well with you if you tamper with her wishes."

Both Caddaric and Artair came to their feet at the thinly veiled threat and started toward Lhwyd. In the space of a heartbeat, Clywd was trapped in the center of an arc formed by three armed men who had suddenly appeared from the trees. Caddaric stopped beside Jilana, his hand resting on the hilt of his sword. Lhwyd looked over his shoulder and smiled in a way that made Jilana's blood run cold.

"This does not concern you, Caddaric," Lhwyd said reasonably.

"He is my father," Caddaric growled in return. "What do you want here?"

Lhwyd's expression twisted into an ugly mask at the challenge. "Who are you to question me?" he demanded, his green eyes burning. "You, who mocks the gods, denies them—" Words seemed to desert him. Lhwyd's mouth worked silently but no sound emerged, and he shrugged off the calming hand Ede placed on his arm.

"I do not doubt the gods," Caddaric said, "only their servants."

"As well you should." Lhwyd's mouth spasmed into a parody of a smile. "Your noble father, for example, is trained in the art of healing and yet fully half of my prisoners died under his care."

"Only because you refused to let me tend to them earlier," Clywd spoke up wearily.

"I wonder." Lhwyd fixed his gaze on the seated Druid, caught up in his own thoughts.

Jilana's heart hammered wildly, *He knows!* She laced her fingers together to hide the way her hands were shaking.

Caddaric's hand tightened on his sword. Out of the corner of his eye, he saw Artair and Heall exchange a slight nod. If Lhwyd thought to take the older Druid prisoner, he would pay dearly.

Only Clywd was unperturbed. "Why do you come here with armed guards? Do you accuse me of causing the prisoners' deaths, Lhwyd?" He tucked his hands into his wide sleeves and watched the other Druid calmly.

Lhwyd shook his head and for a moment rays of the dying sun were reflected in his blond hair, framing his face in a red halo. "I seek only one prisoner, old one. The legionary; the one you and Caddaric's slave," his green eyes brushed over Jilana, "cared for."

Clywd came to his feet in a graceful movement that belied his years. "He is not here. I have not seen him since last night."

"But she has." Lhwyd turned his full attention on Jilana. His voice became caressing. "You were with him this morn."

Lhwyd's eyes and voice invaded her mind, erasing everything else. As if her body had a will of its own, Jilana felt herself nodding. "I changed his bandage." Why are you explaining, some part of her brain called out in warning. You must say nothing! And then Lhwyd smiled, moved closer.

"Where is the soldier, Jilana?"

The question beckoned, inviting an answer. Jilana stared at Lhwyd, fascinated by the emerald depths of his eyes. "I—" Speech was difficult. "I do not know."

"Release her, Lhwyd." As he spoke, Caddaric stepped forward and placed himself between Jilana and the Druid. "She knows nothing."

Hidden by the barrier of Caddaric's broad shoulders, Jilana roused herself, as if from a dream. What evil power did Lhwyd possess, she wondered, that he could reduce her will to rubble?

"Do not interfere," Lhwyd warned. "The man was my prisoner. I am within my rights to question all who saw him."

"And your little slave did see him," Ede put in triumphantly. "The guards admitted her this morning."

"I know." Caddaric informed them simply. "Did your guards not tell you that I was there as well? That Jilana left with me?" He cocked an eyebrow at Ede's surprised expression. "Nay, I can see they did not."

Lhwyd was not to be defeated so easily. "But she returned, Caddaric. One of the other prisoners swears that your slave returned and took the legionary away."

The laughter which burst from Caddaric surprised them all. "How did she accomplish such a feat?" he inquired when his mirth had subsided. "Did she work some spell that turned them invisible to the eyes of your guards?"

Lhwyd stiffened and his voice lost some of its melodic quality. "The guards were gone."

"Gone?" Caddaric reiterated in a chuckle. To his side, Artair laughed softly and Heall could not control a grin.

"Aye, gone," Lhwyd hissed. "They went into the city when the temple was fired."

Caddaric nodded wisely. "So the only witness you have is a prisoner? Tell me, Lhwyd, what would you say or do if you thought there might be a way to save your life?

Surely you would not *lie* to the man who holds your life in his hands?''

The mockery was more than Lhwyd could bear. ''I would tell him anything. Even the truth.'' His eyes glittered. ''Your father deprived me of thirty sacrifices—I cannot prove his deed, but I know his weakness. No doubt he thought to be *merciful*.''

''A quality which is foreign to you,'' Artair noted blandly.

Jilana stared at him in surprise. Artair's allegiance had always lain with Ede. Why had he changed? What forces were at work here that she did not understand?

''Artair,'' Ede gasped in dismay.

The young man shrugged. ''Gods, Ede, have you not seen enough blood since Venta Icenorum?'' Artair asked fiercely.

''The Morrigan demands—'' Lhwyd began.

''Nay, Druid, *you* demand,'' Artair interrupted. '''Tis not even an honorable death you grant your captives. 'Tis butchery.''

Lhwyd's face hardened until the skin was stretched taut across his cheekbones. The effort he made to keep his temper was visible to all. ''The legionary's tunic was found where he lay. The trees around the prisoner compound have been searched.'' His voice assumed a reasonable tone. ''While Clywd may feel duty bound to offer the wounded a painless death, he would not help one of my sacrifices to escape. Neither would any Iceni or our allies.'' He stared at Caddaric's shoulder, as if his gaze could pierce the other man's flesh and see Jilana. ''Only one person in this camp would have a reason to do such a thing.''

Caddaric gave a snort of disgust. Reaching behind him, he caught hold of Jilana's wrist and pulled her to his side. ''Look at her, Lhwyd. She is chained; as much a prisoner as your helpless sacrifices. If she were Iceni, I would admit to the possibility of what you say, but *she is Roman*.'' Caddaric did not see the look that passed between Artair and Heall at his words.

Lhwyd slowly shook his head. "You are a fool, Caddaric. Why do you not see what is so plain to others?"

"Then ask her yourself." Caddaric, impatient, nearly shouted the challenge. "We will see which of us is the fool!"

Jilana stared at the ground, consumed by dread. She would not look into Lhwyd's eyes again, for that way lay destruction, not only for herself but for Heall and Artair as well. Heall had not prevented Hadrian's escape, and then he and his son had taken risks to conceal her deed. Ahh, gods, if Lhwyd ever learned of their actions....

"Do you know where the primipilus is, Jilana?" Caddaric prodded.

Jilana swallowed convulsively. "Nay." That, at least, was partially true. She knew only his destination, not his path.

"Did you help him escape?"

Lhwyd's question settled over Jilana like an icy cloak. Her fingers were laced so tightly together they were numb. "Nay."

"Look at me!"

Jilana glanced at the Druid, but her eyes quickly skittered away. She was wiser now; to do as Lhwyd commanded was the first step in subjecting her will to his. Her eyes came to rest on Clywd and she saw the concern in his face. He, too, knew the dangers; but worse, Jilana had the feeling that Clywd also knew her guilt. "I will give you your answers," Jilana told Lhwyd in a trembling voice, "but not my soul."

"You dare," Lhwyd cried, his expression murderous. With an oath, he started forward.

In a blur of movement, Caddaric whipped his sword from the sheath and slapped the flat of the blade against Lhwyd's chest. From all around Jilana came the sound metallic hiss of other swords being drawn and readied and her stomach gave a sickening lurch. "Keep your distance," Caddaric warned Lhwyd in a steady voice. "She was given to me by the Queen. Not even you dare to touch a royal gift."

Jilana looked around. Heall and Artair stood poised for battle, the sun reflected on the naked blades of their swords. Lhwyd's guards were similarly prepared. A discreet distance from their camp, the curious had gathered to witness the confrontation. More blood would be shed, someone would be wounded—or killed—if something was not done. Jilana forced the muscles in her throat to work. "I did not help Hadrian." In the heavy, charged silence, Jilana wondered if they had heard her. "I did not help Hadrian escape," she repeated, her voice growing stronger. "Caddaric dragged me back to camp and ordered me to stay here."

"And did you?"

Damn Lhwyd, Jilana thought angrily. Why could he not simply accept her lie? The sudden rush of anger enabled Jilana to bring her head up and glare at the Druid with a certain disdain. "Aye. Thus far he has placed me in chains. What would he do if I disobeyed him?" She felt the pull of Lhwyd's will and quickly looked away before she could fall under his spell again.

"Are you satisfied?" Caddaric asked a heartbeat later.

"Nay," Lhwyd retorted. Ignoring the threat of Caddaric's sword, he moved toward Jilana. He stood close enough that his breath brushed her cheek when he spoke. "You have won this time, slave. The next time will end differently; then I will welcome you to the Morrigan's bed." Lhwyd turned and motioned to his guards. Jilana wrapped her arms around her trembling body in the wake of his departure.

It took forever before the three men relaxed enough to sheath their weapons. Artair moved first and Heall and Caddaric followed his lead.

"You have my thanks," Caddaric told Artair when the other resumed his place by the fire. "There was no need for you to make Lhwyd your enemy."

Artair stared into the flames. "One of the men I killed today had never held a sword before; his grip was wrong and he nearly dropped it before he swung at me. I imagine he was a merchant, mayhap a shopkeeper. I had to remind myself that he was as much a threat as a legionary." He took up his cup and drank deeply. "Where is the glory in such an act?"

"We do what we must in order to be free." Ede spoke up, attracting their attention. "Have you forgotten the outrages committed against us and our Queen by the Romans? 'Twas shopkeepers who screamed the loudest when the Queen was scourged."

"We know, Ede," Heall said quietly. "But that does not make the killing easier."

Ede turned to Caddaric. "Is this how you feel? Are you as weak as this old man and his braggart son?" She eyed him contemptuously.

"I do not revel in death as your brother does," Caddaric replied. "I serve my Queen and Albion as I must, where I must, and wait for the destruction to end. One day, when you are glutted on the sight and sound and stench of the battlefield, you will understand."

"Never," Ede declared, her eyes glittering. "Every Roman I kill eases the indignities I suffered under Rome. Only when Albion is ours once again and every enemy slain will I be truly free."

Jilana watched Ede leave and wondered how the other woman could be so hard. She turned back to the campsite and resumed the task of putting the plates away. Given Lhwyd's accusation, Jilana was not surprised to find herself shaking so badly that she lacked the strength to lift the amphora of wine back into the wagon. The handles slipped from her hands, and the jar would have fallen had not a pair of strong hands miraculously appeared and curled around the narrow neck. She recognized the long, blunt fingers and the heavy bracelets which circled his wrists. Caddaric!

"Lhwyd will not bother you again."

Jilana nodded, keeping her eyes on the amphora. What irony that Caddaric should choose to believe the only lie she had ever told him! And, Juno, if he ever discovered the truth— "The sacrifices will keep him busy," Jilana said bitingly. Caddaric's silence forced her to look at him, and the expression on his taut features told her the truth. "He is going to do it," she breathed, horrified. Until this moment, she had not truly believed Lhwyd capable of such an act. "Lhwyd is going to murder those poor people."

Caddaric nodded reluctantly. "Tonight, at moonrise."

A sound between a laugh and a sob escaped Jilana and she turned away. Had she not aided Hadrian this morn.... She shook her head to remove the vision.

"We have to attend," Caddaric continued. He knew what she was thinking, feeling, and he longed to gather her into his arms and hold the horror at bay. But she would reject his comfort, just as she rejected everything about this life he had forced upon her.

"Must I go with you?"

Her question was like a physical blow. Caddaric straightened slowly, aware only now that he had been bending toward her. "I never intended you to do so." He pivoted and headed for the tent.

Jilana put the plates away and went back to the fire. As she gazed into the flames, Artair came to stand beside her.

"By tomorrow Lhwyd's accusations will be forgotten," Artair assured Jilana. "Do not dwell on it."

Jilana nodded. "I want to thank you for what you have done," she said tentatively. "I know the risk both you and your father are taking."

"Do you?" Artair watched her with shadowed eyes. "We have betrayed our Queen and our friend."

The cold words cut Jilana's heart. "I did not ask you for your help—or Heall's."

"What should we have done?" Artair demanded hollowly. "Left you to Caddaric or Lhwyd?"

"You are not responsible for me!"

Artair stared at Jilana as if he had never seen her before. "So I keep telling myself." He nudged a log deeper into the flames with the toe of his boot. "You can return the favor my father did for you today by remembering who and where you are. The next time you might not be so lucky."

Tears stung Jilana's eyes and she ran blindly for the safety of the tent. She knew as well as Artair that she had placed the three of them in terrible jeopardy and the knowledge was like a stone on her heart. She had had no right to involve Heall, and through Heall, Artair.

Jilana came to a halt just inside the flap. Clad only in his loincloth, Caddaric stood in the center of the tent, his gaze fixed on his kist. At her entrance, he looked up and when their eyes met Jilana knew that something was wrong. Thinking that he desired privacy, she groped behind her for the tent flap.

"Stay where you are."

The command was issued in a deadly, controlled tone that turned Jilana to stone. The oil lamp flickered, casting ominous shadows across Caddaric's face.

"Where were you today?"

"Here," Jilana whispered, unable to force any volume into her voice.

"All day?"

Shakily, Jilana nodded. Caddaric simply stared at her. Jilana's hands curled into fists and she swallowed to ease the lump in her throat. "You heard what I told Lhwyd."

"Aye, I heard." Caddaric settled his hands on his hips and regarded her coldly. "You never left the camp?"

"Nay."

"Not once?"

Jilana's nerves tightened. He was probing for something. But what? "Nay." When anger darkened his eyes, she added, "I mean...I did leave, but only for a moment." If she had thought to placate him, she had been mistaken. If anything, his expression grew darker.

"Why?"

Jilana bit her lip. "To relieve myself." She blushed, though whether from the lie or discussing such a private act she was not certain.

"We all have bodily functions," Caddaric mocked at her blush. "Other than your, ah, natural needs, did you have cause to leave the camp?"

"Nay," Jilana snapped, her nerve destroyed. "Why must I repeat to you what you heard me tell Lhwyd?"

In answer, Caddaric took the one step that was necessary in order to bring him within reach of his kist. He lifted an object from the shadow of the chest, closed the distance between them, and dropped the object at Jilana's feet. Jilana tore her eyes from his face and looked down at the ground.

"Do you know what this is?" Caddaric's voice fairly vibrated with suppressed emotion.

"Aye, 'tis the box your father gave me." Jilana stared at it, uncomprehending.

"How did it get inside the tent, Jilana?" Caddaric demanded in a tone like ice.

"You know the answer to that," Jilana replied with a defiant lift of her chin. "Your father gave it to me." Her voice trailed off as a horrible thought occurred to her.

"And you took it with you this morn," Caddaric finished for her. "I know because I remember it lying on the ground when I found you with the primipilus."

"Aye." Jilana's answer was little more than an expulsion of air.

"And you did not have it with you when we left the prisoners. I did not give you the chance to pick it up."

It was a statement, not a question, but Jilana shook her head in reply. The beautifully carved box lay at her feet, an eloquent condemnation. Save for the frantic beating of her heart, she felt numb. Looking down, Jilana could see that her skirt was moving and she dimly realized the motion was caused by her shaking legs.

"You had no intention of obeying me, did you, Jilana?" Caddaric felt the rage swelling his chest and welcomed it. 'Twas better than the pain of knowing she had lied to him.

"Nay." Jilana had to force the word through frozen lips. "I had no choice, Caddaric—"

She never had the chance to finish her explanation. Caddaric's palm caught her across the cheek, sent her reeling into the tent wall to land in a crumpled heap on the ground. Her cheek stung and she instinctively pressed icy fingertips against it, shocked at Caddaric's violence. Tears swam into her eyes and she fought them back. Ridiculous though it was, Jilana's one thought was not to cry in front of Caddaric. Slowly, she levered herself upright, afraid of triggering another explosion.

Caddaric, his massive chest heaving with the effort of keeping his temper under some scant control, towered over Jilana. "Where is he?"

"Gone." Jilana's jaw twinged when she spoke and her tongue explored the cut inside her cheek where flesh had met teeth.

"When?" Caddaric snarled the question. "How long did you wait before betraying me?"

"Just after noon." Jilana drew a finger across the corner of her mouth and stared in surprise when it came away colored with blood. A sense of inevitability settled over her. "I took one of your tunics, a cloak." She raised her eyes to his grim face. "And some food."

"What else?"

Jilana shook her head. The truth about Heall and Artair would prove too costly for all three of the men. "And a belt," she added. "I had forgotten." Caddaric growled, deep in his throat, and reached for her. An instant later Jilana found herself suspended in mid-air, his hands wrapped around her upper arms.

"You should have gone with him," Caddaric warned. He shook her with such menace that in spite of herself, Jilana cried out. "Why did you stay?"

Jilana gasped and tried to catch her breath. "Be-because I was afraid th-that you would follow us."

Caddaric's eyes blazed. The scar on his face turned white as he lowered her to the ground and then tunneled his fingers painfully through the tangled mass of her hair.

"Caddaric?"

Artair's voice sounded from outside the tent flap and Caddaric's face underwent a terrifying transformation. His every feature was stamped with barely controlled rage. "Get out," he shouted. "All of you!"

"Cad—"

"Leave me!" Caddaric didn't notice that Jilana cried out in pain when his fingers tightened. "Artair, I think of you as a brother, but I swear I will kill you if you say another word."

There came the sound of retreating footsteps and Jilana offered a brief prayer of thanks. She wanted no one's blood on her hands. Caddaric held her motionless, looking as if he could flay her alive. Gathering up the tatters of her courage, Jilana asked, "What are you going to do with me?"

Caddaric's nostrils flared. "I should give you to Lhwyd." Jilana's heart stopped, resuming only when he said, "But I cannot. Damn you!" His mouth descended and possessed hers with the full force of every wild emotion ravaging his soul.

When he broke away, Jilana looked away from the sight of her blood staining his lips. "What will you do?" she repeated, as if nothing had happened.

Feeling a sticky wetness on his mouth, Caddaric dragged the back of his hand across his lips and was startled to see the crimson trail against his flesh. A fierce satisfaction burned in his blood. Good! The pain he had inflicted could not possibly match what he was experiencing. His mouth curled into a sardonic smile. He raised a hand and deliberately placed it over the swell of Jilana's breast. "You can temper your punishment."

His meaning was clear. Jilana caught her breath. If he took her now, in anger, the lingering memories of his first possession would be forever tainted. And perhaps that would be best; she would have no more illusions to carry in her overburdened memory. "Do as you wish. I cannot stop you."

A muscle worked in Caddaric's cheek and he jerked his hand away as if she burned him. "You beg me to save the primipilus and when I will not, you risk your life to free him. You steal from me—*for him!*" He grasped her shoulders and dug his fingers into the tender flesh until he saw the flash of pain in her eyes. "Why not do something that will ease your own lot?"

"Hadrian was helpless—"

"And you are not?" Caddaric laughed harshly. He turned and searched out a clean tunic and breeks. "Well, little witch, you will soon learn how helpless you truly are," he warned as he dressed. "You will learn what happens to those who betray me."

Chapter 7

THREE DAYS AFTER Hadrian's escape, Jilana watched Caddaric saddle his golden stallion. It was barely dawn and the air was chilly. A light fog blanketed the camp, isolating their site from the others. Jilana shivered and stretched out her hands to the fire. Caddaric wore a cloak and seemed immune to chill; she had no such luxury, nor would she ask for it. Conversation now was limited to Caddaric issuing orders and her "Aye, lord." Caddaric had not abused her further, not physically. In fact, aside from giving her orders, he ignored her. He no longer taught her to cook. That task was divided between himself, Artair and Heall, with the other two men teaching Jilana how to roast meat over the fire or make soup. As they explained what they were doing, Jilana would glance at Caddaric, hoping that her willingness to learn would lessen the tension spun between them. He ignored her overtures with the same supreme ease with which he ignored her presence in his bed.

The one question she had dared had been in regard to their sleeping arrangements. Jilana had asked if she should make up a different pallet for herself. Caddaric's answer was typical. His eyes had traveled slowly over her and in a voice rich with scorn he had asked, "Why?" She had not raised the subject again.

Now he was leaving. At the end of the wagon lay the saddlebag Jilana had packed, as Caddaric ordered, with dried meat, oat cakes and grain. Caddaric, along with two thousand other warriors, was leaving the war band to turn north to meet elements of the Ninth Hispana Legion under the command of Petilius Cerealis, the legate. The action had been decided yesterday, when allies from the north had brought the news to Queen Boadicea that elements of the Ninth Legion had left their fort and were on the march. The war council had decided to split their forces. Caddaric's force would veer north while the remainder of the war band continued south toward Londinium. Caddaric had been one of the first to volunteer, despite the greater danger, and Artair had volunteered as well. Clywd was going also; as a physician his abilities would be needed at the battle site. The southbound contingent did not expect to encounter any resistance. The news the forward scouts brought back to camp was that the Romans were deserting their *coloniae*—the settlements for veterans—and their rural villae rather than face the Iceni. No battles were expected until Londinium.

Around Jilana the camp had come to life. She could hear the usual morning stirrings even though the inhabitants and their actions were concealed by the fog. She added another piece of wood to the fire and bent to stir the oatmeal porridge. Only yesterday Caddaric had ordered her to ration their supplies more carefully, but she could not send him—or the others—on their way without a decent meal. Jilana knew they would ride hard, eating in the saddle and stopping only when the horses required a rest. This might be their last warm meal for days.

One by one the others materialized out of the fog. Jilana welcomed all of them, save Ede, with a fleeting smile. Artair and Clywd tied their horses by Caddaric's and then came back to the fire for their bowl and the warm, spiced wine Jilana had prepared. Heall and Ede would remain with the main force, and while Heall seemed not to mind, Ede was clearly annoyed.

"Why must I remain behind?" Ede demanded of Caddaric when he came to sit before the fire. "I ride nearly as well as you—and certainly as well as Artair!"

"'Twas our chieftain's decision,'' Caddaric replied. He took the bowl Jilana brought to him without so much as looking at her. Irrationally, for Jilana had expected nothing else, his dismissal hurt more this morning than it had the past two days. She turned quickly away and concentrated on her own meal. "You are needed here, Ede," Caddaric added when the woman continued grumbling.

"To do what, drive a wagon?" Ede sneered.

Caddaric nodded. "Between us we now have two wagons. Heall will drive one and you will take the other. Food is as important as fighting."

"Mayhap," Ede conceded. Her eyes fell upon Jilana. "But do not expect me to care for your pet Roman, Caddaric."

"You will not be bothered," Heall growled before Caddaric could answer. "Perhaps you should take your meals with your brother if the sight of Jilana bothers you. I will care for Jilana."

The grateful look Jilana bestowed upon Heall faded with Caddaric's next words.

"That is something we must discuss," Caddaric said in a cold voice.

"You need not worry." Heall, misunderstanding, hastened to reassure the younger man. "I will care for her as if she were my own."

"I do not doubt that," Caddaric replied steadily, "but while I am gone I do not want you treating her as anything but a slave." He set his empty bowl on the ground and gave Heall a hard stare. "In my absence you need not put up the tent."

"But—" Heall tried to protest.

"She can sleep under the wagon or next to the fire, but she does not need the tent." Caddaric's words trampled Heall's. "And I do not want her riding in the wagon."

"Caddaric, you cannot—"

"She is to be treated as befits a slave, Heall," Caddaric warned, "not a princess. She has chosen her path." As soon as the words were out, he wished them back. He had shared with no one Jilana's betrayal and a statement like the one he had just made was sure to stir up suspicion.

When Heall would have argued, Jilana broke in softly, "Let it be, Heall, please."

Heall closed his mouth with an audible snap and studied the depths of his bowl. Instinct told him that Caddaric had learned of Jilana's part in Hadrian's escape and it would take some time before his anger was appeased.

Caddaric's temper soared at Jilana's interference. How it rankled that Heall would accept her word on this matter and not his own! "And you will chain her to the wagon during the march. I will not have her attempting to escape again." The momentary satisfaction Caddaric derived from his pronouncement was overpowered by the taste of ashes when he saw the look on Jilana's pale face. Damn her! he thought savagely. How dare she look so wounded when she had deliberately betrayed him? He had the right to treat her as he chose—as she deserved. Was he not entitled to humiliate Jilana as she had humiliated him?

Clywd rose and swept his gaze across the others. "'Tis time." He went to Jilana and pulled her to her feet. "You are a foolish, foolish child," he told her in a hushed voice.

"I could do nothing else," Jilana replied, but her thoughts were on the chains.

A troubled frown drew Clywd's brows together. "I know." One hand reached inside his black robe and withdrew a sprig of mistletoe, which he brushed across Jilana's brow in blessing. "Heall will watch over you while we are gone. Be careful, my daughter." His lips whispered across her forehead and then Clywd was walking to the horses.

"Take care," Jilana murmured to his back and then she forced a smile for Artair. "And you also, Artair."

Artair grinned jauntily and paused beside Jilana. "I look forward to meeting the legion." The grin faded at the look in her eyes. "You cannot mean that you are worried about me?"

Jilana shrugged. In truth, she had grown accustomed to Caddaric's father and friends. Watching them leave now was akin to losing her family a second time. "I will miss your stories—filled with bragging though they are."

Artair nudged at the ground with the toe of his boot. "I treated you badly at Venta Icenorum. I am sorry." When Jilana looked at him in surprise, he cleared his throat self-consciously. "Caddaric and I have been rivals from childhood. He was always stronger, the better warrior. Even my father was prouder of Caddaric than his own son. I thought that if I could claim to have killed the Procurator..." Artair shifted uncomfortably. "I want you to know that I regret my action."

Jilana understood. Had she not suffered the same conflicting emotions with Claudia? The two men had been raised as brothers; 'twas only natural that such strong bonds fostered jealousy as well as love. Artair had wanted her to prove—to himself and Heall—that he was as great a warrior as Caddaric. "I forgive you, Artair."

The grin flashed back into place and with a wink Artair was off. Jilana stood quietly, hoping Caddaric would say goodbye as well. He did not. Instead, as Artair and Clywd had done, Caddaric embraced Heall and bid Ede farewell. Jilana he brushed past as if she did not exist. With tears choking her throat, Jilana watched the three men ride away until they were enveloped by the fog. No matter how indifferent she tried to be, Caddaric's slights hurt.

"Come," Heall said at last. "We will break camp and load the wagons. Ede, you will drive my wagon and I will take Caddaric's."

By the time the sun had burned the fog away, the tent had been struck and neatly stored in the wagon. A young boy from a neighboring campsite would take care of the horses during the march, returning them to Heall at the end of each day. Jilana had carefully packed away the eating utensils, wedged the sacks of grain tightly together so that they would not fall during the journey, and used rope to secure the small casks and amphorae against the side of the wagon to prevent spillage. A length of chain lay coiled like a snake at the back of the wagon and Jilana tried not to see it.

"Are we ready?" Heall asked, striding into the camp.

"Aye," Jilana answered. "You should check the wagon, though. I have never done this before."

Heall inspected her work and nodded. "You did well." He smiled, pleased, checked the harnesses of the team that would pull the wagon, and motioned Jilana to the side of the wagon. "Climb up and we can get started."

Jilana looked at the seat and then at Heall. "You heard what Caddaric said."

"Aye, and I choose to ignore it."

"Heall, you cannot," Jilana argued.

Heall's beard thrust forward belligerently. "And why not?"

"Because Caddaric will find out. I do not want to cause trouble between you." Jilana laid a hand on Heall's massive forearm. "You replaced the horse and Artair the saddle. You have done more than enough."

"It might have gone easier with you if you had told Caddaric about my part," Heall mused.

Jilana shook her head. "The fewer who know about your part, the safer you and Artair are. I am not ignorant, Heall. I can imagine what would happen to you both if the Queen learned of your actions." Heall shrugged, but the careless gesture did not fool Jilana. She knew the risk Heall and his son had taken for her.

"I cannot put you in chains," Heall said gruffly.

"I am in chains now," Jilana reasoned. "A chain that attaches me to the wagon makes no difference." Heall stubbornly shook his head and she added, "If you do not follow Caddaric's orders, Ede will certainly tell Lhwyd. Would you spare me a length of chain only to bring Lhwyd down upon my head?"

It was the most convincing argument Jilana could have used. Knowing that Lhwyd was looking for some petty excuse to bring Jilana under his power was enough to make Heall swallow his distaste for the deed. Stoically, he closed the manacles around Jilana's slender wrists and threaded the end of the chain through the ring on the wagon. It galled him, tying Jilana to the place where the horses had once been tethered, but he had no alternative. To ignore Caddaric's instructions would only worsen Jilana's situation. As he climbed into the wagon, Heall wondered if Clywd was correct in assuming that Caddaric and Jilana regarded each other as anything but the enemy.

OUT OF NECESSITY, the wagons kept to the paved Roman road while the rest of the war band flanked the slower-moving vehicles. People laughed and sang as they marched. Energetic children darted among the trees which lined the road. The creak of leather and the steady clop of hooves against stone filled the air. The charred remains of Camulodunum fell behind the column, glimpsed only through dust, then through trees, and finally obscured by distance. A door closed on another room of the charnel house Boadicea was constructing.

Along the route, eager Celts flocked to join the war band. Farmers, villagers, former slaves, all came to Boadicea's standard, some carrying only the clothes on their back, others with their possessions piled into carts or wagons. The column swelled, and its progress slowed accordingly.

For the most part, the new arrivals had obviously traveled for days to join the column, but dirty and travel-worn though they were, they were eager to explain that word of Boadicea's rebellion had spread across the length and breadth of Albion. The Queen's success had inspired other, smaller, revolts. Stories were told, and quickly passed along the column, of the destruction of coloniae and villae and the Romans who inhabited them. Iceni spirits soared. No longer were they alone in their fight. True, the puppet-kings of the other tribes might not have joined Boadicea, but their people had and numbers were what counted in this battle. By the time they met the governor-general, the Iceni would crush him and his legion easily. Provided, of course, that he stood his ground and fought. He might simply show himself to be the coward Boadicea had named him, and turn tail and run. This last possibility was greeted with jubilant, victorious laughter.

Jilana heard the stories as they were passed throughout the column, but she did not dwell upon them. She was far too busy concentrating on her own survival. Her sandals, with their delicate heels, were not meant for walking any distance. Before Camulodunum was hidden from sight, she had stumbled and twisted her ankle. While the ankle pained her, it was only one of Jilana's worries. The manacles chaffed her ankles and wrists, leaving raw patches on her delicate skin. The muscles in her thighs began to tense, then ache, as she followed the wagon in its slow, relentless pace. As the time passed, she glanced at the sun, marking its progress. Soon it would be midday and the column would stop for the noon meal. Jilana set her teeth against the various pains of her body and waited for the sun to reach its zenith.

Just when Jilana was certain she could not walk another step, Heall pulled the wagon to the side of the road and brought it to a halt. Jilana walked up the six feet of chain that led from her hands to the wagon and collapsed. Heall was rummaging through the wagon and Jilana leaned against the wheel with a sigh of relief.

Heall jumped from the wagon and came to where Jilana was sitting. "I should have remembered the food this morning," he explained, handing her two strips of dried meat and a full wineskin.

"Thank you." Gratefully, Jilana took the food and raised the skin to her mouth. The water was warm, but she could not remember when it had tasted better. The liquid washed the dust from her parched throat and she sighed again. Not even the meat was offensive, Jilana thought as she gnawed off a sizable piece and chewed it with relish. Which proved just how hungry she was.

"Do not become too comfortable," Heall warned when Jilana adjusted her back against the wheel spokes.

Jilana looked at him blankly. "What do you mean?"

Heall nodded to the still-moving column. "We have to leave."

"Now?" Jilana was incredulous. "But we just stopped."

"Only to get the food," Heall said patiently. "We eat while we march." At her dismayed expression, he went down on his knee beside her. "Can you make it?"

Jilana swallowed the beef and washed it down with a large draught of water. Her hand, she noticed, was trembling. As were the muscles in her legs. How could she possibly get back on her feet and keep moving? She was a woman, not a horse! And then she thought of Caddaric, remembering how adamant he had been that she must walk, not ride. He had known exactly how weak she was. No doubt he thought to bring her to heel with this treatment! Jilana drew a deep breath and forced a smile. "Just give me a moment, Heall, and I will be ready."

"I am sorry, Jilana," Heall apologized and, looking into his sad, brown eyes, Jilana knew he truly regretted what he was doing.

"I am fine, Heall," Jilana reassured him. If she complained, Heall would force her to ride. That she would not risk.

With a nod, Heall climbed back into the wagon. A moment later, Jilana forced her protesting muscles to move and soon they were back in the column.

The food and water helped, but as the day wore on Jilana's strength slowly diminished. Eventually she grew numb to the pain the manacles caused, to the blisters that developed on her feet. Her steps grew less certain; more often than not she stumbled, whether from the chains or her own weariness she was not certain. The muscles knotted in her legs and she fell. The paving scraped her hands and bruised her knees. Heall, who glanced back at her from time to time, immediately brought the wagon to a halt and ran back to her.

"Jilana!" Heall slipped one arm around her waist and the other under her knees and carried her back to the wagon. "No arguments, now," he told her sternly. "You cannot walk any further, and I refuse to drag you along behind the wagon.''

Jilana experienced a brief flash of guilt over the fact that Heall was once again running a risk because of her, but she was too tired to argue. They both knew she could not walk another step. They had not seen Ede since the column had moved out that morning, so perhaps the risk was not so great. Jilana closed her eyes and leaned against a sack of grain. In her bruised condition, it was the softest of pallets and the swaying of the wagon soon put her to sleep.

Night had descended when Jilana awoke. Heall had a fire going and was bending over it, stirring the contents of the cook pot. Ede was nowhere to be seen. Jilana pushed herself upright and groaned at the pain assailing her body.

Heall looked up from his task and regarded her solemnly. ''I was just going to wake you. Are you hungry?''

Food was the farthest thing from Jilana's mind and she shook her head. How she longed for a warm bath to soak away the ache and grime of the journey.

Heall came to the wagon and unchained her wrists. ''I will get you water and a basin.''

''Can we spare it?'' Jilana asked, recalling Caddaric's admonition about rationing their supplies. Heall grinned at the question, and in that moment he looked very much like his son.

''Can you not feel the weather?'' Heall chuckled. '''Twill rain tonight. We will uncap the barrels. Aye, Jilana, we can spare the water.'' He moved to the side of the wagon to fill the basin from one of the barrels strapped there.

Jilana slid to the ground, the breath catching in her throat at the pain that shot through her when her feet touched the ground. Wincing, she sat and unstrapped her sandals. The soles of her feet were covered with blisters, some of which had burst to expose the tender skin beneath. She would have to treat them with an ointment from her medicine chest tonight and hope they would heal by the morning. Her wrists would have to be treated the

same way, and her ankles, if she could reach beneath the
manacles. The flesh was raw and starting to ooze. She
could bind her wrists and feet with strips torn from her
undertunic and protect them, but not her ankles. They
would have to heal as best they could. Heall brought the
basin and Jilana quickly rose to her feet and pulled the
sleeves of her tunic over her wrists.

"Wash now and then come to the fire," he ordered
gruffly. Silently cursing Caddaric, Heall retreated to the
fire and dished out two bowls of stew.

When she was relatively clean and had treated her various injuries as best she could, Jilana followed.

"What is wrong with your feet?" Heall asked when she
eased herself down to the ground.

Jilana glanced at her bandaged feet, draped her skirt
over them and shrugged. "A blister or two; 'tis nothing
to worry about." She dug into the stew with what she
hoped was appropriate enthusiasm.

A blister or two, Heall thought, his eyes narrowing. If
it would not go worse with Jilana once Caddaric returned, he would happily disregard Caddaric's orders. A
burst of pride swelled Heall's heart as he watched Jilana
across the fire. No one could say she lacked courage, he
thought fondly. And when Caddaric returned, Heall
promised himself, he would tell that young man how
wrong his actions were.

When Jilana started to nod, Heall took the bowl from
her and lifted her in his arms. She stirred and opened her
eyes. "'Tis time you were abed," Heall said gently. "I
prepared a pallet beneath the wagon."

Jilana smiled and, when Heall placed her on the
ground, crawled gratefully between the blankets. "Where
will you sleep?" she remembered to ask drowsily.

"In the wagon," Heall replied, pulling the blanket over
her shoulder.

"But the rain—"

"I have a canvas, and you should be dry enough under
here." Heall brushed the hair away from Jilana's face.
"Sleep well."

Jilana awoke to the roll of the thunder and a dream that she was lying in a cold bath. When she came fully awake, however, Jilana realized that the rain was falling in torrents and she was soaked to the skin. She crawled from beneath the wagon to find that Heall had broken the camp and was hitching the horses to the wagon. Heall, too, was soaking wet, as everyone else must be, Jilana thought. In this downpour there was no point in trying to keep dry.

"There is water and a pouch of dried meat at the back of the wagon," Heall called over the thunder. "Keep it with you. We will not stop today."

Jilana nodded to show that she understood and went to the back of the wagon. She tied the pouch to her belt and slung the skin over her shoulder. Her sandals were wet and with a shrug, Jilana sat on the ground to put them on. She could not get any wetter. To her dismay, Jilana discovered that her feet had swollen and the ball of her foot could not be forced into the sandal. Which meant she would have to walk barefoot. Jilana groaned and threw the sandals into the wagon. Then, thinking better of it, she rose and tossed the sandals into the underbrush. They were not fit for walking and it made no sense to leave them where Heall would find them. She would simply go barefoot and hope that Heall did not notice, for if he did, he would insist that she ride, and it was suddenly, vitally important to Jilana that she show Caddaric she could take whatever punishment he decided to mete out.

Jilana's resolution lasted throughout a day which was a repetition of the previous one, but her body constantly threatened to betray her. Beneath the wrappings on her feet, Jilana could feel new blisters form and break and the chaffing at her ankles and wrists grew to such intensity that she had to clench her jaw to keep from whimpering. The rain-slicked paving made her footing treacherous and eventually she fell. This time Heall did not see her fall and Jilana recovered as quickly as possible. The rain lasted throughout the night, so the evening meal was more dried meat. Heall had covered the wagon with canvas to keep the provisions dry, so he built a sputtering fire beneath the

relative protection of a tree and he and Jilana huddled
there. They were not dry, but unless a gust of wind came
along, they were out of the chilling downpour. Jilana
closed her eyes, pulled the damp blanket around her and
wondered how she would get through tomorrow.

THE ICENI WAR PARTY had been on the move for three
days. All the warriors were mounted, lending speed to the
force, and they stopped only to rest the horses. For a time
it had seemed their information was wrong, that they
would have to ride all the way to Lindum to engage the
Ninth, but last night the advance party had rejoined the
main body, bringing with them the news that elements of
the Ninth Legion were encamped five miles ahead. The
chieftains had hurriedly called for a council and it was
decided that the Iceni would stay where they were and
prepare an ambush. Horses were taken into the depths of
the forest, out of sight and hearing of the road, and the
warriors ranged themselves along either side of the road.
The two lines were five deep, spread back south for a mile.
Everyone was in place by moonrise. No fires could be lit,
but that meant little since there was no fresh meat to roast
and the warriors had their cloaks to ward off the chill.
This night, at least, they would sleep, and when the legion marched at dawn, they would be ready to spring their
trap.

Caddaric drew his cloak around him and stretched out
on the ground. A light drizzle had dampened his clothing
earlier in the evening, but he was impervious to it. On his
right side lay his sword and Caddaric turned on his side to
draw his fingers thoughtfully over the plain hilt and down
the intricately worked scabbard. Battle fever was heating
his blood, he realized; that was why he did not feel the
cold. He wondered if it was the same with the others.

Sighing, Caddaric rolled to his back and stared at the
few stars which were visible, his mind reviewing tomorrow's battle strategy. He was at the southern end of the
line, which meant engaging the legion infantry, whose
number the scouts had estimated at a thousand. The

northern end would deal with the cavalry ala, about five hundred men. Once the ambush was sprung, it would be vital to surround the Roman force and prevent any of the legionaries from escaping. If the Iceni annihilated this detachment, perhaps the Ninth would stay in its fortress and wait for help to arrive. Then, if—when, Caddaric corrected himself—when Boadicea's rebellion was successful, the Iceni could turn north once again and destroy the fortress at Lindum at its leisure.

If, Caddaric thought with a stifled groan. *If* Petilius Cerealis, the legate of the Ninth, had accompanied this force, and *if* he fell in battle, then mayhap the Ninth would be panicked enough to sit tight in its fortress. But what if they did not? What if the acting commander of the legion decided to avenge the legate and his men? What would happen if Boadicea found herself waging a battle on two fronts? And what *if* Paulinus marched his elements of the Fourteenth and Twentieth legions from the west coast of Albion to meet Boadicea? Now they were faced with a battle on three fronts. And as dark as that possibility was, it grew even worse when Caddaric remembered that the Second Augusta was still in its fortress at Glevum. He swore softly into the night. The one thing he knew about Suetonius Paulinus was that the governor-general was a master strategist. If Suetonius was given time to gather his forces . . .

"Caddaric?" Artair raised his head to peer through the darkness at his friend. "What is wrong?"

Caddaric shook his head, then, realizing Artair would not see him, answered, "Naught."

"That is why you toss about and swear," Artair grumbled. "I have been without sleep for three nights. At least have some consideration for me."

In spite of himself, Caddaric smiled. "I beg your forgiveness, Artair."

"As well you should." Artair rolled to his side and propped his head on one hand to look at Caddaric. "Will the legionaries fight, or do you think they will run when they see the size of our force?"

"They will fight," Caddaric said with great certainty. "The legion teaches that one legionary is worth ten men." He let out his breath. "Nay, they will not run—not until the order is given."

"We outnumber them," Artair mused aloud.

"Not by much." Caddaric touched the scabbard; his fingers caressed the engraving.

"Will it be enough?"

"Who am I to say?" Caddaric snapped, and immediately regretted the harsh retort. By way of apology, he explained, "As long as our surprise is complete and we do not allow them to get into formation the odds are in our favor."

Artair was silent a moment. "You have faced battle before; true battle, Caddaric, not the overpowering of a sleeping garrison and the killing of unskilled civilians. I have not."

"Are you afraid?" Caddaric's voice was barely audible. The fear of death was natural, he knew, although he had never experienced it himself. When a man had nothing in his life that he cared about, what did it matter if his life ended?

"Not afraid," Artair replied at last, "at least, I do not fear death." He paused. "I wonder, though, how well I will fight, knowing that we are alone here."

"You will fight the better for that knowledge," Caddaric assured his friend. "When there are no replacements, men find strength and courage that they once thought beyond them. I have seen it happen."

"How does it feel, facing the legion?" Artair asked hesitantly.

"Strange," Caddaric admitted. "At Camulodunum, I heard one of the officers yell an order and I found myself obeying it." He raised his left hand a few inches from his chest and let it drop. "You see, Artair, this is new to me as well. The last great battle was Claudius' invasion, and we were but children then. For the first time in our lives we find ourselves facing the enemy as true Iceni, but for the older men, like Heall, this is only a continuation of a battle that is eighteen years old. They find nothing strange or frightening in facing the legion because they have done it before.''

Artair nodded. ''My father fought like a man half his age.'' His tone was rich with pride. ''He was upset when you said he should remain behind.''

''He may have fought like a man half his age, but that does not change his years. You see how worn we are after the ride. Heall would be in worse shape, and he knew it. That is why he agreed to remain with the column.''

''And to care for Jilana.''

Caddaric's jaw tightened, although Artair could not see the telltale sign. ''Aye.''

''You were harsh with her.''

Caddaric cursed softly. ''I had reason.''

''Aye, I know.''

The quiet statement was like a physical blow. ''You know,'' Caddaric repeated, torn between rage and disbelief. ''What do you know, Artair?'' He could feel the other man shrug.

''I know that Lhwyd was right; that in the middle of an enemy camp Jilana managed to spirit away Lhwyd's prize captive before he could be sacrificed.''

Fear stabbed at Caddaric. ''Are you going to tell Lhwyd?''

Artair gave a hushed laugh. ''Nay, I am glad she outwitted that mad Druid.''

''How long have you known?''

''Since my father told me.''

''Heall knows!'' Caddaric's voice rose, and with an effort he brought it under control. ''How?''

Artair reached out and placed a hand against Caddaric's shoulder. ''He wandered into camp just as Jilana was helping Hadrian mount the horse she had taken.''

''And he did not stop him?'' Caddaric was incredulous. ''I am surrounded by traitors!''

Artair's hand tightened warningly. ''If he had stopped Hadrian, the truth would have come out. 'Twas wisest to allow the man to escape and hide the evidence of Jilana's involvement. We thought we had done well. How did you find out?''

Numbly, Caddaric recited his discovery of the medicine box and Jilana's subsequent confession. "How is it you overlooked the box?'' he asked bitterly.

"We did not know Jilana had left it with Hadrian.''

"What evidence, precisely, did you hide, Artair?''

Artair took a deep breath. "Jilana took your roan and the saddle you had taken from Camulodunum. Father and I replaced them.''

"Gods!'' Caddaric breathed. "Ede was right, I have been played for a fool.''

"Nay, Caddaric—''

"And betrayed by the men I thought of as my own family!'' Caddaric spat out the words. "Why, Artair? *Why?*''

"Because my father asked it of me,'' Artair replied simply.

Caddaric snorted. "And you, of course, have always been the most obedient of sons.'' When Artair did not reply, he added, "Why did Heall feel it necessary to protect Jilana?''

Artair considered the question for a long time before he answered. "He had his reasons, Caddaric.''

"What?"

"He is fond of Jilana.'' At Caddaric's muttered expletive, Artair sighed. "We did not betray you, Caddaric, nor think to make you a fool.''

"The little, red-haired bitch!'' Caddaric exclaimed. "She did not say a word!''

"Of course not.'' Artair sounded smugly pleased. "No doubt she felt that she owed us her loyalty and silence.''

"But she owes me nothing? I have kept her alive, fed her—'' There was a horrible tightening in Caddaric's throat, something he had not felt since the day he saw his sisters and mother killed.

"What would you have done, Caddaric, had you been in Jilana's place and either my father or myself were captured, awaiting the kind of death Lhwyd had in mind? By all the gods, I hope you would think your first responsibility was to set us free. 'Tis all Jilana did, my friend; in truth, I doubt she thought in terms of betraying you or playing you for a fool.''

Caddaric barely heard Artair, he was too busy fighting off the treacherous softness that had crept into his heart since he had met Jilana. He had not cried since childhood, so certainly those were not tears stinging his eyes. He could not—would not!—cry over a woman, or the fact that his two oldest friends sympathized with her. Jilana was a woman, nothing more, in spite of the turmoil that had followed her into his life. So then why was the knowledge that she cared enough for Hadrian to risk her life, to steal for Hadrian when she refused to ask for so much as a blanket for herself, like a barbed spear in his heart? Deliberately, Caddaric rolled onto his side, away from Artair. Gods, what a mess his life was! All his careful plans of what would happen once he made Jilana his were destroyed—as tangible as the ashes in the bottom of Clywd's copper bowl. Why was nothing going as he had planned it would?

"Caddaric?" When there was no answer, Artair said softly, "Father and I did only what we thought best, for you and Jilana."

Caddaric remained silent. *This night the world cracks apart for both of us.* How prophetic those words, spoken to Jilana the night of the rebellion, had proved to be. He closed his eyes and waited for the dawn.

MORNING CAME, and with it ground fog that blanketed the base of the trees and the road in a gray shroud, an additional concealment for the Iceni force. The warriors moved silently into position and ate a light meal of dried meat and grain from their pouches. When they spoke, they did so in whispers which blended with the sighing of the wind through the tree tops. Cloaks had been tossed aside so that the bright colors would not betray their ambush, so that now, lying belly down in the underbrush and

grass just behind the treeline, tunics and breeks were wet
with dew.

The scouts returned with the news that the legion had
broken camp and was on the move. The message was
whispered up and down the lines and Caddaric felt his
muscles tense. He forced himself to relax; battle demanded fluid, coordinated movement, how often had he
drilled that fact into raw troops? The body must be alert
but not tight, ready to respond to any threat perceived by
the senses. You can see, hear and smell the enemy, he had
lectured his recruits, but that is not enough; you must be
able to feel their presence as well. It was an acquired skill
which Caddaric had spent a lifetime perfecting. He eased
the white-knuckled grip on his sword and concentrated on
drawing deep, even breaths.

Beside Caddaric, Artair was all too aware of the
pounding of his heart and the film of sweat on his sword
hand. Nervously, he wiped his hand on the seat of his
breeks, wet his lips and said a quick prayer to Andrasta,
the goddess of victory. Caddaric had ignored him since
they awoke and Artair wondered if things would ever be
the same between them. Perhaps he had been wrong in
telling Caddaric what he had, but it pained Artair to see
the way his friend was treating Jilana. Artair sighed inwardly and took a firmer grip on his sword. When the
battle was over, he would speak with Caddaric again and
explain why Heall . . .

The tramp of booted feet, muffled in the dense morning air, and the vibration in the earth warned that the legionaries were drawing near. Artair leaned closer to
Caddaric and murmured, "The gods be with you, my
friend." Caddaric gave no indication that he had heard
and then there was no more time.

The first legionaries rounded the bend in the road. They
came at a quick march, five abreast. The Iceni waited until the first line was even with the last of the warriors and
then gave the signal, one prolonged blast of the carnyx, to
spring the ambush. Iceni war cries rent the air and before
the soldiers had a chance to carry out the centurion's or-

der to form up, the warriors were swarming over the unprotected lines.

It was a fierce, bloody battle in which the legionaries were doomed from the outset. Unable to close ranks and outnumbered, the Romans were forced into the individual battle at which the Iceni excelled. Caddaric was right; even with the odds against them, the Romans did not retreat. They stood their ground, conceding it only with their deaths.

Death there was, aplenty. The sight of it filled the eyes; its stench assailed the nostrils. Neither side asked for mercy and neither side granted such. The need to kill or be killed filled the senses, inuring those who lived to the grisly spectacle around them. There was only the combat, the whirring of sword and battle-axe through the air and the exultant, horrible fever of battle that sang in the blood.

The sun rose to burn away the fog and the men fought on, oblivious. Bodies fell; their blood soaked the greedy earth, and the living stepped over the dead, or straddled them, and continued the battle. Sweat assaulted eyes and dampened clothing. The universe narrowed to surviving the enemy's next thrust.

Caddaric's opponent fell beneath his blade and he pivoted, seeking the next adversary, and his eyes fell upon the *aquila*, the eagle of the legion. The gilded bronze eagle, its wings partially unfurled as if ready to strike, surmounted a tall pole; it was protected by a special guard and carried into battle by the *aquilifer*, a senior centurion. It was a source of Roman pride, as well as serving as a rallying point. To allow the aquila to fall to the enemy was unforgivable, and every legionary would willingly give his life to prevent such a shameful event.

Some of the remaining legionaries had fallen back to the aquila and, while Caddaric watched, the standard now moved toward the trees, secure within its guard. Caddaric blinked and looked at the sky. The sun was in its descent; they had been fighting for the better part of a day. Up and down the road, the Romans were retreating, scattering into the forest with the Iceni hot on their heels. Since the cavalry ala had not appeared, the warriors at the northern end of the line must have dispatched them. Caddaric hefted his sword and followed his countrymen into the trees to hunt down the survivors.

It was nearly dark when Caddaric paused again, surrendering to the needs of his overtaxed body. Ahead of him, deeper into the forest, came the occasional sound of battle and the scream of a dying man. He had long ago lost sight of the aquila. The battle was over, and the Iceni dared not pursue the Roman survivors any further. Boadicea needed their strength to the south. Turning, Caddaric began the long walk back to the road.

When he first became aware of the presence, Caddaric could not truly say. One moment he was trudging along, lost in his fatigue, and the next he was conscious of a presence off to his right. Thinking another Iceni was walking some distance away, concealed by the foliage, Caddaric called out and halted, waiting for a response. There was none, save the sound of his own breathing and the rustling of the leaves in the wind. Was it only his imagination?

Caddaric slid his sword from its scabbard and continued walking. The forest was devoid of life—the birds and animals had been driven away, along with the legion. There was movement on his right and Caddaric spun toward it, his sword raised. "Who is there?" His throat was dry, Caddaric discovered, and it hurt to speak. His voice was little more than a tortured whisper.

"Caddaric?" A voice as harsh as Caddaric's emerged from a large tree trunk.

Caddaric took a firmer grip on his sword. "Aye." A tall, graceful figure appeared from behind the tree and one of the last rays of the sun struck the gold hair. "Artair!"

"Aye." His sword tipped to the ground and Artair leaned against the tree.

Relief trembled through Caddaric and he started toward his friend. "What are you about, Artair? Why did you not answer when I called out?" Gods, but Artair was a sight, Caddaric thought wearily. Blood and gore clung to his face, his clothing and his sword. But then, Caddaric reasoned, he probably looked no better.

"I did not hear you." Artair lifted his sword and slid it back in its scabbard with a tired sigh. "I swear, I have covered half the forest this day, and the thought of spending what is left of this day—"

Artair's voice stopped abruptly and he made a gasping sound. Caddaric laughed, in spite of his tiredness. "Ever the clown, Artair. Come along; I will help you back to the road." To Caddaric's everlasting horror, Artair groaned and sank to the ground. "Artair!"

Before Caddaric could reach his friend, another figure detached itself from the tree and stepped over the motionless body. The helmet of the legionary was unmistakable, as was the sword he held in one hand. The man was a centurion. "Come along, Briton; 'twill give me great pleasure to dispatch you as well before I die."

The centurion was gravely wounded, Caddaric could see that now as he drew near. And there was something else about this soldier, something... Then Caddaric knew. He had served with this man in Judea.

As the distance between them lessened, recognition came to the centurion as well. "'Tis you, Caddaric." He smiled, but the effort merely produced a grimace and he gestured to the forest. "'Tis a long way from Judea." He raised his sword. "Your old century is here; they transferred the entire cohort. Somehow fitting, is it not, for a deserter to die at the hands of his comrade-in-arms?"

In answer, Caddaric swung his blade. The sound of sword meeting sword echoed through the still forest, drawing others who were on their way back to the road. Caddaric was oblivious to the silent audience; he fought with deliberate cruelty, seeking to assuage his maddening loss by inflicting as much pain as possible upon the other man. The centurion was weak, no challenge for the tall Iceni. Caddaric played with the Roman, inflicting painful, nuisance wounds that weakened the man further, until he was beyond pressing any attack and could only parry

Caddaric's thrusts and calculated swings. The end, when it finally came, was a mercy for the centurion. He was bleeding from the myriad wounds Caddaric's blade had inflicted and so lost in the pain of those wounds that he barely felt the mortal blow.

The centurion toppled to the ground and a moment later Caddaric fell to his knees beside Artair. A dark froth foamed at Artair's lips; his eyes stared sightlessly skyward. In the center of his chest was the exit wound of the centurion's sword. Caddaric assimilated these facts even as he reached out to close Artair's eyes. A low sound rumbled in Caddaric's chest and found its way upward to his throat and mouth. His keening, feral cry split the eerie silence and the watching Iceni stepped back, alarmed. Caddaric gave vent to his rage and anguish until there was no more breath in his lungs and, exhausted, he slumped forward across Artair, heedless of the fresh blood that was added to his already stained tunic. A hand touched his shoulder and Caddaric violently shrugged it off.

"We must leave," a disembodied voice reminded him. "The hour grows late. We will carry him—"

"Do not touch him," Caddaric snarled. In an instant his sword was in his hand and brought to bear on the intruder. "He was my brother; I will care for him!"

The warrior backed away, his arms upraised in a placating gesture. One by one the others disappeared and when he was alone, Caddaric slowly sheathed his sword. Bending, he carefully lifted Artair in his arms, as a father might hold a child. Cradling his dead friend against his chest, Caddaric made the seemingly endless journey back to the road. He should have known it was not Artair he had heard, Caddaric berated himself. Like the other warriors, Artair had been trained to move silently—he should have known that only a Roman would move so carelessly through the forest. He should have warned Artair of the danger! Where had his much-vaunted training been when Artair's life hung in the balance? A cry rose in his throat but Caddaric refused to give voice to it again. What good would it do to scream and rail against fate? Gods, all the screams in the world would not alleviate his guilt!

Clywd met Caddaric when he emerged from the trees. One look at his son's face told the Druid of the burden on the younger man's soul and Clywd longed to take Caddaric in his arms and offer some measure of comfort. Instead, Clywd tucked his hands into his sleeves and moved to Caddaric's side. "Pyres have been prepared. We will honor our dead before riding south."

Caddaric closed his eyes, unable to bear the thought of Artair's body consumed by flames. Artair should be standing at his side, a grin threatening to split his face, not lying in his arms, growing steadily colder. He should have told Artair that he forgave him his part in Jilana's treachery, that they were still friends.

"Caddaric," Clywd gently called, "I ache for your loss, but we have no time in which to mourn. We must bless our dead quickly and leave."

Gods! Why had he not told Artair he was not angry, that all was forgiven?

"Caddaric!"

The urgency in Clywd's voice penetrated Caddaric's despair and he nodded. Following his father to a clearing, Caddaric became aware that others had been lost. The pyres filled the clearing and a single fire burned brightly in their center. Caddaric lifted Artair to the bed of dried wood, folded his arms across his chest and took the sword from his scabbard. A warrior's sword accompanied him to Annwn, but Caddaric would bear Artair's weapon back to his father. Caddaric's heart wrenched; how was he to tell Heall of his son's death?

Clywd blessed the dead in clear, proud tones and called for the family to come forth and receive the torch which would light the pyre. A few had some family member present, but most did not, so friends and acquaintances—and occasionally total strangers—took the responsibility of acting as family. Caddaric took his torch and paced stoically back to Artair's pyre. There had not even been time to prepare the body, Caddaric thought irrationally as the flame illuminated Artair's features. Behind him, Caddaric heard his father extolling the virtues of the dead to the appropriate gods. As if in a dream, Caddaric watched his hand reach out and touch the flame to the wood. The tinder caught and with a *whoosh* the pyre was engulfed in flames.

Caddaric took a step back, out of reach of the greedy fire. "Goodbye, my friend." He tossed the torch into the pyre and walked away without a backward glance, Artair's sword gripped in his left hand. He would not remember Artair as a monster of charred flesh and bone.

During the hard ride south Caddaric rode beside his father, not speaking, the reins of Artair's horse wrapped around his saddle horn.

FOR JILANA, the march took on all the aspects of torture. Despite her care of them, Jilana's feet were blistered and cut each day, and eventually they became infected. Where the manacles chafed, her flesh fared no better, and she was hard pressed to keep the sores from Heall. The rain had lasted four days before abating, and by then Jilana was wracked with fever. That she managed to stumble along behind the wagon without crying out her weakness to Heall was due to the streak of stubbornness that seemed to increase even as her physical strength diminished. Blessedly, Heall insisted upon preparing their evening meals, so Jilana had some time to herself to clean and bind her injuries and gather the strength to pick at her food. At night she would roll into her blanket and fall into unconsciousness.

When the sun finally emerged, Jilana was gripped by a feverish chill that the sun did nothing to abate. On the sixth day, Jilana woke to the discovery that her body had one more act of treachery to play upon her. Walking some distance from the wagon, Jilana fought back tears while she tore what remained of her undertunic into several strips and tended to her body's needs. Wrapping a blanket around her shoulders, she left Heall harnessing the horses and sought Ede. Ede was engaged in the same task as Heall and Jilana waited until she had the horses hitched to the wagon before she spoke.

"Ede, I need a word with you."

Ede whirled around. A biting retort rose to her lips, but the sight of Jilana stopped the words. The Roman looked terrible! Ede had seen neither Heall nor Jilana since the first day of the march, preferring Lhwyd's company to theirs. One of Lhwyd's guards—less conceited than the others—had taken an interest in her, and Ede had found herself, unwillingly at first, returning that interest. Now, she discovered, her jealousy of Caddaric's Roman mistress, which had once burned so hotly, had been all but extinguished. Ewan's attention was a balm to Ede's wounded pride.

Ede's stare was so intense that Jilana had to force herself to speak again. "Please, Ede; just a moment of your time."

Ede nodded and watched Jilana approach. Her first instinct was to tell the smaller woman to sit down, but Ede stopped herself. 'Twas none of her concern that Caddaric's slave looked to be on the brink of death. "What do you want?"

Jilana nervously wet her cracked lips. What she was about to ask was embarrassing, and before she could change her mind, Jilana blurted out the request. "I have need of rags or strips of cloth. Can you give me some?"

Ede frowned. "Why?"

A dull flush tinged Jilana's pale cheeks. "'Tis personal, Ede."

"Then ask Heall; he is your watchdog, not I."

"I cannot!" Jilana gasped. "I—the cloth—" She dropped her eyes to the ground. "'Tis my woman's time, Ede," she confided on a barely audible note, "and I have no provisions for..." Her voice trailed off in numbing embarrassment.

Ede found herself blushing as well, something she had not done since she first learned of the differences between men and women. "I understand; bide a moment." She went to the wagon and rifled through one of the kists until she found what Jilana needed. Jilana's heartfelt thanks when Ede handed her the cloths shamed Ede and she hesitantly offered the Roman a clean tunic.

"Oh, nay, I could not," Jilana answered, aware of the stains on her stola and its frayed hem. "But thank you."

Ede noted the overly bright eyes and the blanket Jilana clutched about her. Obviously Caddaric's Roman was ill. "I have a spare cloak," Ede said gently. "'Twill keep you warmer than that blanket."

Jilana shook her head. "Caddaric would not want you to interfere. Thank you again, Ede."

It was on the tip of Ede's tongue to say that Caddaric would not want her dead, either, but Jilana was already walking away. Shaking her head, Ede went back to the wagon. The Roman had courage, no doubt of that, but it was sorely misplaced. She should talk to Heall, tell him that Jilana was ill, but the column was starting to move. She would tell Heall tonight.

Heall was waiting when Jilana returned to their camp, and as unobtrusively as possible, she placed her bundle of cloth in the wagon. Heall, for all that he had never married, was no stranger to women and their needs. He understood what Jilana needed the cloth for and made no comment about it. Instead, he peered intently into her face.

"You do not look well."

Jilana forced a tiny smile. "Only a chill from the rain, Heall. May I keep the blanket today?"

"Of course." Heall placed the back of his hand against her forehead and frowned. "You have a fever."

"A small one." Jilana stepped away from Heall's touch and extended her arms. "We should leave."

"No chains," Heall decided in a voice that brooked no argument. "Not today. I think you should ride in the wagon."

"But Caddaric—"

"Caddaric be hanged," Heall swore. He had had enough of inflicting the punishment Caddaric had dictated. "You will ride with me."

Jilana was too weak to argue. When Heall picked her up in his arms and laid her on the grain sacks in the wagon she did nothing more than murmur her thanks.

"What is this?" Heall demanded.

Jilana opened her eyes and looked at Heall. Her skirt had ridden up, exposing her bandaged feet.

"Where are your shoes?"

Jilana sighed. "I threw them away after the first day; they were not made for walking. 'Twas easier to go barefoot."

"And these?" Heall touched one of the ankles she had managed to bandage.

"The manacles chafe my skin," Jilana explained wearily.

Heall gave an angry growl. "Why did you not tell me?" When Jilana merely shrugged, his eyes narrowed. "Do you think I would have made you walk had I known this?"

"Nay," Jilana whispered.

"Tonight when we make camp, we will see to these." Heall gestured to her feet. "From now on, you will ride." At Jilana's meek nod, he grunted in satisfaction, went to the front of the wagon and swung into the seat. "Go to sleep."

Jilana needed no further urging. She slept throughout the day, waking only when the column stopped for the night. When Heall had helped her down from the wagon, Jilana took two of the cloths from the bundle Ede had given her and looked uncertainly about.

"Come, there are some bushes a short distance from here." Heall took Jilana's arm and led her away from their campsite. She made no move to avail herself of the relative privacy and he understood her hesitation. "I will wait for you by the wagon. Call me when you are ready to return."

Heall was as good as his word. When Jilana was finished, she called out softly and he hurried back to her. Another time she might have found such doting behavior amusing in such a gruff man, but now she was grateful for his assistance. She felt weaker than ever, despite her day's rest, and when they reached the fire, she barely had the strength to stay on her feet. Heall settled her on a blanket on the ground, tugged a second blanket securely around her shoulders, and poured the water he had set to warming over the fire into a basin.

His gentleness was amazing, Jilana thought as Heall unwrapped her feet and ankles and washed them. Much like Caddaric... She drifted off during his ministrations and came to much later. She was still lying by the fire, but Ede and a man had joined Heall. Jilana tried to make her eyes focus properly, but the effort was too great. She gave up and closed her eyes again.

"Jilana, are you awake? Are you hungry?"

Jilana shook her head and instantly regretted the movement, for it increased her dizziness. Heall ignored her answer and ladled broth from the cooking pot into a small bowl. With Ede's assistance, he lifted Jilana so that her back was against his chest and brought the bowl to her lips. "Try to drink some of this."

With her eyes closed, allowing Heall to bear her weight, Jilana managed to swallow a bit of the broth he had prepared. When he brought the bowl to her mouth again, Jilana weakly shook her head. She heard him set the bowl aside and, with a small sigh, Jilana nestled her head in the hollow of Heall's shoulder. Sleep claimed her immediately.

Heall gazed at the figure in his arms and his beard twitched as he frowned slightly. Jilana appeared to have lost weight in the past week, but that was easily remedied. What was of greater concern was the infection in her injuries. Her feet were the worst. By all the gods, why had she not asked him for a pair of shoes? Even as he asked himself the question, Heall knew the answer: her stubborn pride would not allow it. Foolish child, he thought, shaking his head. And her ankles and wrists were more than chafed; the flesh was scraped raw and oozing. No doubt the infection was contributing to her fever. How he wished Clywd were here; the Druid would know how to

care for Jilana. Heall brushed the hair away from her face
and studied her features. Such a pretty, delicate creature,
he thought with a smile. Who would have thought... He
looked up to find Ede regarding him curiously. Heall
lowered Jilana back to the ground and covered her with
the blanket.

"Will you ride with me tomorrow?" Heall asked Ede.
"I need someone to watch over Jilana."

After a moment's hesitation, Ede consented. "Ewan
will take my wagon, will you not?" she cajoled the warrior at her side. Ewan nodded and was rewarded with a
lingering kiss. The two rose and, after bidding Heall good
night, walked to their own camp.

Heall checked the fire and then rolled into a blanket
near Jilana. Before falling asleep, the old warrior entertained himself with visions of the tongue lashing he would
give Caddaric upon his return.

THREE DAYS LATER, at nightfall, the war band returned,
and while the chieftains immediately made their report to
Boadicea, the warriors spread out through the column to
find their kinsmen. Word of their arrival spread like
wildfire through the column. Heall and Ede talked excitedly as they prepared a stew from the rabbit Heall had
killed that afternoon, while Jilana brought bowls and an
amphora of wine from the wagon. The resiliency of the
young, Heall thought, watching her. She moved slowly,
but the fever had broken and a few days in the wagon had
done much toward healing her feet and ankles. Much as
he had wanted to, Heall had not dared remove the shackles around her ankles, but he had made padded bandages that kept the metal from irritating her flesh. Her
wrists were healing as well, and were without bandages
since she was no longer chained to the wagon. The raw
areas were scabbing well and would leave no scars; of that
Heall was proud. Not even Clywd could have done better, he thought proudly.

Jilana had laid a second fire and now water heated over
it. When news of the warriors' return had reached them,

Jilana had helped Heall and Ede erect the tent. Caddaric's kist and the oil lamp had been placed within. He would be able to wash, change into clean clothes and dine on fresh meat. Surely that would mitigate his anger, Jilana thought hopefully. She had no thought of explaining—or trying to—why she had helped Hadrian. If he did not understand the bonds of friendship, she could not explain it to him.

Had Caddaric been wounded? Jilana wondered as they waited impatiently for their three friends. She should wish that, Jilana knew; she should want him to suffer as she had suffered at his hands, but she could not bring herself to hope that he was hurt—or dead. The thought sent a chill through Jilana and she moved closer to the fire. Ede greeted her with a smile, which Jilana returned warily. Though the Iceni warrior maid had been nothing but kind during the past three days, Jilana still did not trust her completely. Ede was, after all, Lhwyd's sister, and Jilana did not doubt that the Druid's attitude toward herself had remained unchanged. Aye, the sooner Caddaric returned, the better.

Caddaric and Clywd rode slowly into camp. They barely had time to dismount before Ede and Heall were upon them. Jilana hung back, not wanting to intrude on the reunion, but an unseen smile of relief curved her lips when she noted how easily Caddaric moved. So he had not been injured after all!

"The stew is nearly ruined," Ede laughed, hugging first Caddaric and then Clywd. "What has taken you so long? Were you successful? What of the Roman legion?"

"The Ninth is defeated," Caddaric answered slowly, allowing the reins to trail on the ground. "A few survived, including Petilius Cerealis, the commander. He has fled to his fortress."

"Another victory!" Heall laughed and embraced the two men. "We will hear of it while we eat." He peered into the shadows beyond the camp. "And where is Artair? What has he found that is more important than greeting his father?'' Heall grinned and looked expectantly at Caddaric and Clywd.

Clywd came forward and rested a hand on Heall's shoulder. The gentle, reassuring movement drove a spear of dread into Heall's heart and he shook his head slightly. In the heavy silence, Jilana closed her eyes and waited.

"He is in Annwn," Clywd told his friend. "Artair died in the battle."

Ede cried out once and then there was silence. Voices and laughter echoed from the neighboring campsites, a vile intrusion that seemed to mock Clywd's quiet announcement.

"How?" Heall's question was barely audible.

Caddaric looked to Clywd for guidance, and when his father nodded, Caddaric explained the circumstances of Artair's death. "'Tis my fault, Heall," Caddaric concluded grimly. "I should have warned him—"

"My son..." Heall cleared his throat. "My son fought bravely?"

"Aye, my friend; he did." Caddaric turned to his horse and took from the saddle an object wrapped in what was plainly Artair's cloak. He handed it to Heall.

With trembling hands, Heall reached out and took the burden from Caddaric. He unwrapped it slowly, knowing what he would find. When at last Artair's sword was revealed, Heall clutched it to his breast and bowed his head. His eyes were tightly shut, but even so the tears streamed down his cheeks. The cloak fell unheeded to the ground.

Jilana felt the wetness on her own cheeks and knew that she wept for all of them: for Artair, who had lost his life, and his father and friends who had loved him. Mutely, she offered up prayers to her own gods for Artair's spirit. Without speaking, Heall stepped away from Clywd's hand and left the camp. The shadows swallowed him and for a moment the four who remained stood motionless, trapped in the depths of their loss. Ede was the first to recover.

"I will see to the horses," Ede said briskly, although sorrow lent her voice a husky quality. "Jilana, serve the stew before it burns."

Jilana picked up Artair's cloak, folded it, and placed it in the wagon before returning to the fire. As she handed Caddaric his bowl, she noticed the weariness that etched his features, but otherwise his face betrayed no emotion. Was it possible that he did not feel Artair's loss?

"Shall I make you a pallet here?" Jilana asked when she served Clywd. Before, Clywd had spent the night with Heall and Artair at their camp but Heall had not made a separate camp for himself since taking charge of Jilana.

"Nay." Clywd smiled as he accepted the stew. "I will go after Heall and we will spend the night in the forest."

Jilana glanced at Caddaric and then knelt beside Clywd. "Did you know this would happen," she asked in a whisper. "Did you see Artair's death?"

Clywd shook his head. "I saw pain for my son, but I did not know its cause. I suspected—" He broke off and stared at his food. "The sight can be illusive and my suspicions were wrong."

Jilana did not press him further. They finished the meal and when Ede offered her help in cleaning up, Jilana thanked her but refused. Clywd had gone in search of Heall and with Ede's departure, the campsite seemed unnaturally quiet. Jilana finished her task and returned to the fire.

"I have water warmed," Jilana said at last when Caddaric made no move to leave the fire, "and your kist is in the tent."

Caddaric nodded that he had heard, and poured more wine into his cup.

"I am sorry about Artair."

Caddaric looked at her then, the first time he had looked at her since his return, and Jilana caught her breath at the pain pooled in the blue depths of his eyes. "You barely knew him."

Jilana thought of the night Artair had carried his saddle into camp to replace the one she had stolen. "Does that mean I cannot mourn his passing?"

Shrugging, Caddaric returned his gaze to the fire. "Nay, I suppose not." He drained the cup and refilled it. "Go to bed, Jilana; I will see to the fire."

Dismissed, Jilana took care of her needs some distance from the camp. When she returned, Caddaric was stripped to his loincloth, washing with the water she had heated. His tunic and breeks lay discarded on the ground and Jilana reached for them.

"Leave them," Caddaric ordered in a voice so harsh that Jilana froze.

"I—I was only..." Jilana faltered at the look on his face. "They need laundering—"

"I said leave them," Caddaric ground out. In two steps he was beside her and snatched the clothing from her hands. "'Tis not laundering they need, but burning."

"Oh, nay," Jilana protested unthinkingly. "I can wash them clean—"

"Clean?" Caddaric gave the clothing a vicious shake. "What can you do that will wash Artair's blood away?" With that he hurled the clothing into the fire.

Jilana swallowed and backed cautiously away from Caddaric. "As you wish." His mood was violent and she had no wish to displease him.

Ignoring her, Caddaric went back to the basin and continued washing. Jilana took the lamp from the tent, lit it from the fire, and slipped back inside the leather walls. The lamp showed the two pallets she had prepared earlier and she walked to the smaller one. Would Caddaric be angry with this also? she wondered. She looked down at her stained gown and ran a hand over her wildly tangled hair. She had not bathed properly since Hadrian's escape; surely Caddaric would understand her reluctance to share his bed in this condition. Sighing, she sat on her pallet and tried to comb her hair with her fingers.

When Caddaric entered the tent and stood silently watching her, Jilana tried to quell her rising alarm. He

said nothing, however, simply watched her while he drank
from a wineskin. The flickering light played over his
bronze chest with its wedge of brown curls and danced
down the length of his legs. Her body responded to the
sight with a will of its own, and Jilana quickly folded her
hands in her lap before they could betray her by reaching
out to touch him.

"You look awful."

Jilana looked down at her hands and said nothing. She
could not dispute the truth of his statement.

Caddaric walked to his own pallet and sat down. When
he had taken a long drink from the wineskin, he added,
"You are pale. Have you been ill?"

"I—a chill, nothing more," Jilana answered uneasily.
She tugged at her sleeves, making certain they covered the
scabs on her wrists. As unobtrusively as possible, she
tucked her feet beneath her skirt.

Caddaric glanced between the two pallets. His was
cushioned with furs while Jilana's was nothing more than
a blanket laid upon the ground. "You will be warmer
here."

Jilana's cheeks flamed and she looked over at Caddaric. "My woman's time is here." Despite the blush, she
bravely met his gaze. "You wanted to know, did you not?
So you could be certain of my fidelity?"

"Aye," Caddaric answered in a hushed tone. "I wanted
to know." He blew out the lamp and settled into his pallet after another long pull at the wineskin.

Jilana waited in the darkness, listening to his breathing. When she was certain Caddaric was asleep, she slid
under the top blanket and rested her head upon her forearm. She thought of Heall and his pain and wept silently.

It was Caddaric's groan that woke Jilana, though she
did not realize that he had made a sound until he groaned
again. A dream? Jilana wondered, frowning into the
darkness. Caddaric was silent for so long that she thought
the dream had passed, but then he cried out, a sound so
full of pain that it brought Jilana to her feet. Groping her
way through the darkness, she found Caddaric's pallet

and knelt beside it. Harsh, gasping sounds came from just in front of her, and Jilana's hand searched for a moment before it encountered bare flesh.

"Caddaric?" Jilana shook him hesitantly. "Caddaric, wake—" An iron fist closed around her wrist and she gave a soft cry.

"Artair!"

The name was a hoarse croak and Jilana felt tears sting her eyes. "Nay. Caddaric, 'tis Jilana." She tried to relax against the painful grip. "Caddaric, 'tis but a dream."

Caddaric came awake, aware at first only of the cold sweat that bathed his body. A moment later he realized where he was, that he had been dreaming, and then he realized that he was holding Jilana's wrist in a grip that threatened to crush her bones. Reluctantly, he released her. "Go back to bed."

Jilana did not move. Her hand, resting upon the bulge of muscle in Caddaric's upper chest, felt the sweat that dampened his flesh, "'Twas but a dream," she repeated soothingly. "About Artair."

Caddaric groaned and rolled away from her touch. More a curse than a dream, to see Artair's death again. "Leave me." He felt Jilana's hesitation and then heard the clink of her chains as she moved back to the side of the tent. She deserved the chains, he told himself stubbornly, but his heart spoke a different truth. Jilana deserved a better fate, as had Artair.

THE NEXT MORNING Caddaric rose early, dressed, and slipped silently from the tent. Around him, the camp slept. The Queen had decided to break the march for three days, in order to prepare for the festival of Beltane, the fire of god. A foolish decision, Caddaric thought as he wandered away from the camp. The war host needed to move swiftly; Beltane could be celebrated without elaborate preparation—the tribes had been without the Druids and their celebrations for nearly two decades, after all; they would be happy simply to have the fire kindled again—and those who had ridden north could recover during the slower-paced march of the column. Suetonius Paulinus would not rest; he would drive his men unmercifully. And therein lay the difference between the two leaders, Caddaric mused as he unconsciously headed toward one of the groves which dotted the surrounding land. One was a commander accustomed to battle and the winning of wars; the other was an untutored civilian depending upon the advice of chieftains whose last battles were over twenty years in the past and who may have confused boastful dreams with reality.

He entered the grove and gazed curiously about. Accustomed to the dense forests of his home, Caddaric found the grove a mean substitute, but it offered the privacy he craved. He found an oak tree whose branches were laden with buds and sat beneath it, awaiting the sunrise while sorting through his emotions.

In his life, Caddaric had seen many deaths, but none had shaken him as Artair's had. The feeling of guilt would not leave him, even though he knew, logically, that the fault was not his. The guilt, Caddaric discovered with a start, stemmed partially from the fact that they had argued before Artair's death. Had his friend died thinking that Caddaric hated him? Caddaric closed his eyes and rested his head on his upraised knees. Gods, he hoped not. And Heall; poor Heall. Alone now, childless. Would he ever be able to look upon Caddaric and not see Artair? For so many years he and Heall and Artair had been a family—stronger than most natural families because of the circumstances which bound them together—that now the loss of Artair and the possible loss of Heall was threatening to tear Caddaric apart.

"Caddaric."

At the sound of his name, Caddaric's head snapped up and in a blur of motion he was on his feet, his right hand reaching for the place where his sword usually hung. His hand encountered air; he had left his weapon in camp. Even as he discovered this lapse, his mind assimilated the fact that he was in no danger. His father's voice had called to him, and now Caddaric leaned against the tree and waited for Clywd to reach him.

"You have risen early," Clywd observed as he moved through the lightening shadows. When he reached the tree, Clywd halted and studied his son. "I have disturbed you; forgive me. I will leave."

"Nay, there is no need," Caddaric protested. "Sit with me a moment, Father."

A brief smile touched Clywd's lips. Nodding, he sank to the ground and made himself comfortable against the tree trunk. Caddaric followed, and they sat in silence, watching the sun chase the gloom from between the trees until the branches stirred in dappled sunlight.

"A new day," Clywd murmured, as if in awe of the sunrise. "No matter our sorrow or happiness, there is always a new day."

"Aye," Caddaric agreed, although his thoughts followed a different path from Clywd's. "Another day to be endured."

"Is that how you see life," Clywd asked, astounded, "as some loathsome task to be undertaken?" When Caddaric did not answer, he considered the idea for a few moments, then said, "Aye, of course you would. What little joy there has been in your years has been taken from you. First our family, then your life here on Albion, and now Artair. Always the pain to follow the joy."

"It does not matter," Caddaric lied. "I am happy enough with my life."

"Do not lie to me," Clywd softly chided. "I am your *father*, Caddaric. No matter your opinion of my road in life, you are my flesh. I see the way you close yourself away from those who care for you. Because an ending is inevitable, you refuse to allow a beginning."

Caddaric sighed. "'Tis easiest that way, old one. You have only to look at yourself and Heall. You took your beginning and lost a family—save for a son who mocks your gods and does not pretend to understand you. Heall lost his entire family. What is left to either of you?"

"Memories," Clywd replied. "Bright, warm memories. When I think of your mother, your sisters and brothers, 'tis a welcome visit from past loves."

"How can you have forgotten the pain?"

"Forgotten?" Clywd's eyes grew bright with tears. "I have never forgotten their loss, but I have accepted it."

"And you have me," Caddaric said sarcastically.

Clywd blinked at his biting tone. "You think I am not grateful that you were spared?"

Caddaric shrugged and stared at the tree tops and in that moment Clywd glimpsed the uncertain adolescent that he had never seen. "I know I am a disappointment to you. I lack the gift of sight and the art of healing which you have. I am a soldier, and even in that I am more Roman legionary than Iceni warrior." He shook his head. "You must wonder how you could have sired such a changeling."

"I have never wished you differently," Clywd began, carefully feeling his way, as if he were removing a twisted blade from a vital organ. "On occasion—frequently— your actions mystify me, and that is when I challenge your judgment, but never, *never*, have I wished you other than yourself."

"When we first returned to Albion, I used to watch you with Artair," Caddaric confessed, "and be filled with envy."

"Why?" Clywd was stunned.

"Because he made you laugh. And because you always seemed to approve of his actions," Caddaric admitted.

"Ah, gods," Clywd breathed. "Do you not know that it is always hardest for children to win approval from their parents than it is for another child, someone else's child?" He hesitated before adding, "Artair was the happy one; he found the laughter in life and helped everyone else find it, too, but he could never equal your skill as a warrior, no matter how he tried. And that was the source of his envy."

"I know." Caddaric's voice was strangled. That aching lump was back in his throat and he could not dislodge it. "I used to tease him over his lack of skill."

"Just as he used to tease you about your serious nature," Clywd countered. "'Twas natural, Caddaric; it did not alter the bonds between you."

Caddaric clenched his jaw and swallowed, hard. "I shall miss him."

"We all shall, but as long as we remember him, Artair is not really dead."

Caddaric did not mock the statement. Instead he asked, "How is Heall?"

"Sad, grieving." Clywd closed his eyes. Would the gods forgive him for being grateful that the centurion's blade had not found his son's heart as well? "He wishes to be alone for a time."

"When he returns, the two of you will make your camp with me," Caddaric decided.

"A generous offer," Clywd replied, the gray streak in his beard twitching with concealed amusement, "but I think the two of us would rather not intrude."

"There would be no intrusion," Caddaric said grimly, his mind turning to Jilana. Had it been the wine and his weariness, or had Jilana truly looked ill? Aye, she said she had taken a chill, but would that account for the odd way she had moved?

"How is Jilana?" Clywd inquired blandly, knowing well where his son's thoughts had fled. "Heall said she has been ill."

Caddaric frowned and turned to look at his father. "Heall spoke of Jilana?"

Clywd spread his hands. "He is fond of the girl, and concerned over your treatment of her."

"Why do you and Heall think you know how I should treat her?" Caddaric asked through clenched teeth.

"Because we are older and wiser," Clywd said with a chuckle. Then he sobered. "To put her in chains, Caddaric—"

"If you knew what she has done, you would not think me harsh," Caddaric interrupted.

"*If* I knew?" Clywd lifted an eyebrow and stared pointedly at his son.

Caddaric's eyes narrowed and he came to his feet. "My plan for Jilana is simple enough... or it was, before you and Heall decided to meddle in it. The two of you are born troublemakers."

"Aye, it has always been thus," Clywd agreed, rising. "When we were young, Heall and I were the despair of our families. Between them, our fathers killed a score of trees in their search for switches for our backsides."

A smile tugged at Caddaric's mouth. "I find that hard to believe."

"Oh?" Clywd smiled in return and stepped past his son. "On a dare I kidnaped your mother, one of the fiercest warrior maids in our village. Within a month we were wed. A scant eight months later your eldest brother was born."

"You jest!" Caddaric shouted at the retreating figure.

"Ask Heall," Clywd called over his shoulder. A moment later he was gone; only his laughter remained, floating on the air.

Caddaric mulled over his father's parting words on his way back to camp. 'Twas hard to believe his father could ever have been that impetuous, yet on the other hand, Caddaric had never known his father to lie. But to kidnap a woman? It happened occasionally, if the woman was overly coy or the suitor impatient, but Caddaric found it hard to reconcile the image of his father as an impassioned suitor with the calm Druid he had become. And yet...

Jilana scrambled to her feet as soon as Caddaric set foot in their camp. The fire was going and Caddaric saw a pan of oat cakes baking over the embers on one side of the fire. All was in readiness for the morning meal and Jilana stood waiting to serve him. The sight should have pleased him, but it did not. Instead he had the impression that something precious had been lost.

"Will the others be joining you?" Jilana asked when Caddaric settled before the fire.

Not *us*, but *you*, a verbal acceptance of the boundaries he had set forth. Caddaric flinched inwardly. "Not Heall and Clywd; I do not know about Ede."

Jilana doubted Ede would appear—Ewan had seemed to command most of Ede's time the last few days—but she kept her thoughts to herself as she set out a small pot of preserves, sliced cold meat upon Caddaric's plate, and took the oat cakes from the coals. The oat cakes were dark brown on the bottom, but edible, and Jilana could not help the tiny rush of satisfaction she felt when she served Caddaric the meal. Even the fact that Caddaric did not comment upon her accomplishment could not dispel her satisfaction in the task. When Caddaric had been served, Jilana took an oat cake, spread it with preserves, and sat down across the fire from Caddaric to eat.

His appetite surprised Caddaric, as did the fact that when he made to refill his plate, Jilana anticipated his actions, took the tin plate from him, refilled it, and returned it to him. All without a word; the only sound she made was the clinking of her chains when she walked. The perfect servant, anticipating her master's wishes. His heart squeezed painfully and he suddenly found it difficult to finish his meal.

Caddaric set his empty plate aside and drank the last of his mead. He started to rise but before he could complete the motion, Jilana was at his side, gathering his dirty dishes. Obviously, she did not want his help. He cleared his throat uncertainly. "I will tend to the horses."

"'Tis done," Jilana told him as she walked carefully to the wagon. Her feet and ankles were still tender, but if she walked slowly, the discomfort was minimal. "I will pack the wagon."

"There is no need," Caddaric said, watching her scrub the dishes. He approached the wagon cautiously, aware that Jilana kept as much distance as possible between them. When she looked up warily, but did not move away, he leaned against the wagon and explained, "The Queen has declared a three-day respite so that Beltane may be celebrated tomorrow night."

Three days, Jilana thought, nodding. In three days she would be recovered sufficiently to resume the march.

Caddaric's eyes swept her from head to toe. The red-gold hair was an untamed mass of curls; her gown was frayed and stained and bare feet peeped from beneath the hem. Her hands were rough, and the long, oval nails he remembered were gone, broken or bitten to the quick. Outwardly, nothing remained of the gracious Roman patrician he had met at Venta Icenorum and the knowledge saddened him.

Jilana wiped the last dish dry and placed it in the wagon, then picked up the bucket of water she had been using and walked some distance from Caddaric to empty it. Frowning, Caddaric watched her return.

"Has the march been difficult for you?" Caddaric asked in a surprisingly soft voice.

Not for the world would Jilana admit her weakness to him. She shook her head, stepped around Caddaric, and dipped clean water into the iron pot from one of the barrels on the wagon. She made to grasp the handle of the pot, found Caddaric's hand there and jerked away as if burned.

Caddaric's face hardened as he straightened, the heavy pot in one hand. "Where do you want this?"

"Over the fire," Jilana managed to say. When she was sure Caddaric was indeed headed in that direction, she half-filled a pail with cool water and carried it, a wash basin and an empty pail into the tent.

"What are you going to do?" Caddaric asked when she emerged from the tent.

"I need to wash my gown and—" Jilana stumbled over the words, unable to tell Caddaric that she also needed to launder the cloths from her woman's time "—and if you need anything washed..." She allowed the words to trail off and knelt to add more wood to the blaze.

The perfect slave, Caddaric thought again, tending to his creature comforts but remote, untouchable. He studied her gown and appearance and frowned. Did she think that by making herself unattractive she would be spared his attentions? Or had she dressed this way deliberately, thinking to stir his guilt over his treatment of her and thus manipulate him? Conveniently, he pushed to the back of his mind the fact that his conscience had already pricked him on that point.

From the corner of her eye, Jilana watched Caddaric gather his sword and whetstone and settle by the fire to hone the blade. 'Twas strange to be alone with him now, with all that lay between them. Had he forgiven her for Hadrian, or was he pleased with the effectiveness of his punishment? His expression gave nothing away and Jilana did not care to broach the silence that had fallen between them, so when the water was hot, using a scrap of cloth to protect her hand, Jilana lifted the pot from the fire and carried it into the tent.

Caddaric heard her retreat, and a moment later heard the sounds of splashing water from the tent. Laying aside his sword and whetstone, he uncoiled his large frame from the ground and strode to the wagon. Tossing back the canvas covering, he studied the contents that sat at the front of the wagon and frowned. Did Jilana think he would believe that she had not taken advantage of his absence to go through the wagon? Grasping the handle of the chest which claimed his attention, Caddaric lifted the chest from the wagon and considered it as it dangled from his hand. Jilana had said she planned to wash her gown. How, then, was she going to hang it out to dry when her change of clothes was in his possession?

In her eagerness to clean both her clothing and herself, Jilana had not considered that minor flaw in her plan. Mixing water to the correct temperature in the spare pail, she did her laundry first, then filled the basin and bathed, paying special attention to the sores and abrasions. The bandages on her feet and ankles were the worst; in spots, the cloth had stuck to the raw flesh and Jilana had to soak them free. The bite of the warm water on the open sores made the breath hiss between Jilana's teeth, but she continued until all the wounds were clean. Only then did she discover that she lacked a towel and fresh bandages. There was nothing to be done about the bandages, but for a towel, Jilana used the top blanket from her pallet, and then she turned her attention to her hair.

After adding the last of the cold water to the hot water in the pot, Jilana knelt and dunked her head into the water. When her hair was thoroughly drenched, she scrubbed her fingers over her scalp and down the length of the heavy mass, stopping only when her scalp tingled and the hair squeaked beneath her fingers. She wrung the excess water out of her hair, rose, and, after a moment's hesitation, wrapped herself in the blanket.

Surveying the mess in the tent, Jilana smiled wryly. Bathing had been much simpler at home, where one had only to go to the bath house, and as for the laundry—such menial labor had been the purview of the servants. With a sigh, Jilana picked up the pails and carefully made her way from the tent. She would have liked nothing better than to sit beside the fire and bring some kind of order to her wet hair, but that luxury would have to wait.

The moment Jilana stepped from the tent, she felt Caddaric's eyes upon her and she glanced warily about. He stood by the wagon, one booted foot resting on a chest, and Jilana hurriedly looked away and went about her chores. She avoided his gaze as she emptied the dirty water and replaced the pails, basin and iron pot in the wagon, but when she left the tent for the final time, her wet laundry in her hands, she realized that their campsite was out in the open. There were no trees or bushes on which to hang her gown. Which left the wagon. Swallowing her uneasiness, Jilana walked to the wagon and began draping the clean cloths over the wagon's slatted sides.

Caddaric viewed her actions through narrowed eyes, his hands clenching into fists at the sight of the bare expanse of her shoulders and the way the blanket was folded around the swell of her bosom. Desire, hot and unbidden, flowed through his veins only to be shot through with guilt when Jilana moved and the clink of her chains fell upon his ears. Caddaric had to force himself to remem-

ber that she had betrayed him twice before; he would be
a fool to remove the shackles and give her a third opportunity. He noticed the hasty, skittering glances Jilana directed his way and ground his teeth together. By the gods,
one would think he had beaten her the way she shied
away! The punishment he had decreed had been lenient,
mayhap too lenient, since she so obviously thought to
foster his guilt and play upon it. With that thought in
mind, Caddaric rounded the wagon and lifted the clean
stola from its resting place.

"This gown is little better than a rag," Caddaric noted.
He cocked an eyebrow at Jilana, waiting for her to agree
and ask him for a new gown. To his surprise, Jilana said
nothing, merely stared at the stola in his hand as if it
might disappear. "It should be burned."

His observation produced a reaction in Jilana. "Nay!"
The single word was a cry of despair and she reached for
his arm, as if to prevent him from carrying out his threat.

Her hands grasped his wrist and that was when Cad-
dric saw the abused flesh which circled her own wrist like
a bracelet. Catching her forearm in his free hand, he demanded harshly, "What is this?"

Jilana caught her breath at his tone and bruising grip.
The stola was temporarily forgotten as she sought both
to answer and subdue her fear. "P-please, lord, let me
go."

"Nay." Caddaric's eyes narrowed, his grip tightened.
"Not until you answer."

"I...'tis from—" While Jilana fought to control her
stumbling tongue, she wondered, fleetingly, why Caddaric seemed so angry. "'Tis from the shackles, lord," she
managed at last.

A muscle jumped in Caddaric's jaw; he stepped back a
pace but did not release his hold. He dropped the stola
and touched his forefinger to the ugly scabs. "The shackles," he murmured and his eyes grazed the length of her
until they came to rest upon her leg irons. Jilana stood
motionless, afraid to move. "And your ankles?"

"I did not hold Heall back," Jilana answered on a quavering note. "You can ask him if you do not believe me."

"That is not what I asked," Caddaric said warningly.

Her voice froze and Jilana closed her eyes as Caddaric crouched in front of her and pulled the trailing edge of the blanket away from her legs. She felt his hands lift the leg irons up, away from her ankles, and drew a shuddering breath. Now he would laugh, delight in the physical evidence of his punishment and her own weakness. She bit her lip when Caddaric forced her to raise one of her feet so that he might inspect the sole. Like a lamed horse, Jilana thought tearfully.

The raw sores circling Jilana's ankles made Caddaric catch his breath, but at the sight of her torn foot he cursed explosively. All thoughts of her treachery were forgotten as he digested the ravages his orders had wrought. "Did Heall know of this?" he questioned roughly. Caddaric felt the muscles in her leg tense at his question.

"Aye." The word was barely audible.

"And he did nothing?!"

"He did," Jilana burst out in Heall's defense. Violet eyes glared at the top of Caddaric's head. "He bandaged my feet and ankles and insisted I ride in the wagon, although I told him you would be angry."

Caddaric released her leg and got to his feet. "That much damage was not done in a single day." Her eyes fell away from his and a low growl issued from Caddaric's chest. "What kind of sandals were you wearing?"

"None. The sandals Hadrian gave me were impractical for marching, so I threw them away." Jilana lifted her chin and faced Caddaric defiantly.

"Heall would have found you a suitable pair—"

Jilana gave a very unladylike snort of disbelief. "I am a *slave*, lord, not a guest to be cosseted. Is that not your wish?"

Something clicked in Caddaric's brain. "So you went barefoot in that ragged gown to teach me a lesson," he demanded angrily.

The accusation was too much for Jilana. "Of course," she jeered. She swept a hand down her side. "I placed myself in irons, rubbed my flesh raw against my bonds, blistered and cut my feet, all to make you feel guilty!" The gold flecks in her eyes blazed into angry life. "You stupid, odious barbarian!" With that, she curled one tiny hand into a delicate fist and swung.

Her fist connected with his jaw only because Caddaric was not expecting the blow. His head snapped to the side beneath the force of her swing, but otherwise he did not move. Jilana, however, cried out at the moment of impact, and when Caddaric turned back to look at her, she was cradling her hand against her breast and massaging her knuckles.

Jilana glared at him. Hitting Caddaric had been like hitting a rock; she was certain every bone in her hand was broken. Still, there was satisfaction to be derived from seeing Caddaric experimentally wiggle his jaw from one side to the other and touch the lump that now sprouted just to the left of his chin. And then she realized what she had done. Uttering a silent prayer to Juno, Jilana awaited Caddaric's retaliation.

Caddaric was silent, not because he meant to intimidate Jilana, but rather because he was uncertain how to deal with the situation. He rubbed the lump on his jaw and nearly laughed aloud; to think he had feared that her spirit had been broken! His temper had abated and now he considered his course of action. "You did not know about the kist," he asked slowly.

"What chest?" Perversely, Jilana chose to reply in Latin. Juno, but the man was exasperating, and she had had enough of being accused and questioned and tormented at every turn.

"Your kist," Caddaric replied.

Jilana folded her arms across her chest and favored Caddaric with a belligerent glare. The man was as bad as his father; both spoke in riddles. "My chest is in Venta Icenorum, in my father's house," she ground out.

Caddaric shook his head. "'Tis here, on the other side of the wagon." He motioned for Jilana to accompany him. After eyeing him suspiciously, she followed, well out of his reach. Caddaric stopped in front of the chest, opened it, and then stepped to the side. "You see?" He watched her expectantly.

The suspicious look remained as Jilana looked at the chest and its contents. Why was Caddaric showing her this? Jilana wondered, and the next moment she had the answer. He wanted something, of course, but what? What did she have that he could not take?

Some of Caddaric's good humor faded when Jilana did nothing more than stare at the kist. "Well?"

Jilana drew her eyes from the chest to Caddaric. The top garment was a snowy white stola which made Jilana loathe the very thought of putting on the worn green gown again. And lying atop the stola was her comb. Jilana forced herself not to think of either of those. "What are you planning to do with the clothes?"

"Do with—" Caddaric ground his teeth in frustration. "I *plan* to have you wear them."

Jilana considered that for a moment. "Why?"

Caddaric barely stopped himself from echoing the word. "Because you obviously cannot continue wearing that green rag," he gritted.

"I see." Jilana nodded and took a step backward. "And what will your generosity cost me?"

"Cost you? *Cost you?*" Caddaric's anger soared into full-blown rage. "Naught! I am trying to make amends!"

Frowning, Jilana asked again, "Why?"

"Because I never meant for you to be hurt; because I am responsible for you," Caddaric ranted, past rational thought. "Because you run from me and betray me and still you haunt me until I want either to break your pretty neck or kiss you senseless even though I know you are not to be trusted!" He drew a deep breath; his hands clenched into fists at shoulder level and he shook them as if railing against fate. "And all of that, my little Roman wicca, does indeed make me a stupid barbarian!" Caddaric whirled and stormed out of the camp, leaving Jilana to stare after him in shock.

"Gods," Jilana breathed when Caddaric was out of sight. His absence was like the calm after the storm. The trembling in her legs slowly passed, and when she was capable of movement, Jilana went to the open chest. Hesitantly, she touched the white gown, assuring herself that it was real. She glanced around, expecting Caddaric to reappear as unexpectedly as he had left, but he was not in sight. She considered the chest a few seconds longer and then, with a slight shrug, she closed the lid and dragged the chest into the tent. Caddaric might change his mind when he returned, but until then she would avail herself of the clothing and her comb.

Caddaric returned at midday, having exhausted both his anger and his friends' hospitality during the course of the morning. A stew bubbled over the fire and Caddaric sniffed its aroma appreciatively before greeting Jilana with a short nod. She nodded curtly in return and went to the wagon to pour the mead. Caddaric watched her, noting the white gown and the neat braid of her hair. Her feet were bandaged but she wore the sandals from her kist. Caddaric's eyes narrowed critically; the sandals were an improvement over her bare feet, but they would not withstand the rigors of the march. He would have to solve that problem before the march resumed.

Jilana handed him the cup of mead and a jar filled with the same liquid, then returned to the fire and ladled out a generous portion of the stew. She placed two wheat cakes along the edge of the plate as well as a wooden spoon and handed the plate to Caddaric.

"Thank you."

This quiet civility nearly made Jilana trip over her chains; when she dared a look at Caddaric from the safety of the other side of the fire, his attention was directed to his meal and there was no trace of mockery on his features. Jilana served herself a smaller measure of stew and ate thoughtfully, seeking to fathom his changed attitude. Her recently acquired suspicion warred with her gentler side and, eventually, she responded to his overture. "The clothes are most welcome." Her eyes darted to his and then returned to her plate. She could not bring herself to thank him for the return of what was rightfully hers.

Caddaric ate in silence for a while longer before responding. "'Twas not my intention to dress you in rags."

Jilana said nothing. She wanted to believe him, but the memory of his anger was too recent and too strong. Setting her plate aside, she sipped at the sweet mead.

Caddaric did the same, but studied her face while he drank. "Why did you hide your injuries from me?"

Jilana hesitated before answering, her hands tightening around her cup. "I did not want you to laugh at me, to mock my weakness." Her shoulders lifted in a slight shrug. "And I was afraid you would think I had held Heall back and be even more angry with me."

"I see." Caddaric looked to where his sword and whetstone lay, undisturbed. Jilana had not touched them during his absence. It seemed a good omen. Perhaps this was the time to clear the air between them. "Your actions with Hadrian put us all in great danger."

She had to speak quickly, before the courage to do so deserted her. "I realize that now, but at the time," Jilana sighed softly, "at the time, I thought only of getting Hadrian safely away from Lhwyd."

"And Heall and Artair helped cover your trail," Caddaric added. When Jilana looked at him in surprise, he nodded. "Artair told me."

"Do not be angry with Heall," Jilana pleaded. "He did what he did in order to protect me, not to betray you. I never meant to involve either of them in Hadrian's escape."

Caddaric finished his mead and poured another measure from the small jar beside him. "You said that you did not escape with Hadrian because you feared I would follow. Was that the truth?"

Only part of the truth, but Jilana would not admit that, in spite of everything, she felt bound to Caddaric. Instead, she answered, "Aye. And when you found us, you and Hadrian would have fought—his pride and honor would have demanded no less—and Hadrian would have died. I wanted him to have a fair chance at life, not a postponement of death.'' Her voice dropped. ''I did not mean to betray you, only to save my friend. Can you understand?''

Caddaric's heart twisted. She had stayed behind to save Hadrian, to offer herself up like a sacrifice so that he would not pursue the legionary. A grim thought indeed and his voice was harsh with it when he spoke. ''Aye, but that does not change the fact that I cannot trust you.''

Violet eyes met blue. ''Nor I, you,'' Jilana replied. ''Twice you saved me from death, and what have your actions wrought? Misery for us both.''

Caddaric rose. His face settled into grim lines while his gaze turned toward the sky, as if searching the heavens for an answer. ''I did not intend for it to be thus,'' he said finally. ''I dreamt of you so often...'' He gave a short, humorless laugh. ''No doubt 'tis the gods' revenge for my mockery of them, to put my dream within reach and then watch it sift through my fingers.''

''I do not understand.'' And Jilana discovered that she wanted very much to understand this man who was her captor.

''Neither do I,'' Caddaric muttered. He shook his head to clear it and picked up his sword and whetstone. ''A hunting party from my village is going out this afternoon. We need fresh meat in order to conserve our other supplies.'' From the wagon he took his bow and a quiver of arrows and a throwing spear. ''If my father or Heall return, tell them I will be back at nightfall.''

Jilana nodded and got to her feet. Knowing that the change in conversation meant that Caddaric would share no more of himself with her, she said, ''We could use fresh water as well.''

Caddaric paused long enough to check the barrels. ''There must be farms, and thus wells, nearby. I will check the countryside this afternoon. With luck, at least one well will not be poisoned.''

"P-poisoned," Jilana stammered.

"Aye." Caddaric looked surprised at her reaction. "'Tis a common enough practice to poison the wells so the enemy is denied their use."

"Oh."

"You did not know this?"

Jilana shook her head. How could she know such things? "But you drew water from the wells at Camulodunum."

"They were not poisoned; the primipilus had to supply the city's civilian population," Caddaric explained. "These farms—whether Roman or Trinovante—will be deserted. The owners will have taken as much water as they could carry and then poisoned the well when they left."

"I see." Suppressing a shudder at such actions, Jilana gathered the plates and worried about Hadrian making his way through the hostile countryside.

As if reading her thoughts, Caddaric snapped out, "Your primipilus is safe. He did not reach his age or rank without knowing the most basic of tactics."

They parted on that note. Caddaric rode out on his golden stallion and Jilana was left to pass the afternoon in the camp. She was not to spend the day alone, however. Clywd stopped at the camp shortly after Caddaric left, and soon thereafter Ede came by, with Guendolen in tow. If possible, Guendolen's hair was even blonder than it had been when Jilana had met her at Venta Icenorum, and while Jilana wondered why Ede had brought her to the camp, the reason became clear. Guendolen, it seemed, had a knife wound which was infected and needed treating.

Using the preparations for Beltane as a reason, Clywd excused himself and Jilana had no choice but to treat Guendolen's wound herself. When the warrior maid's arm was cleansed and dressed, the three women sat around the fire and Guendolen and Ede began a lively discourse on everything from the rebellion to the best way to prepare a haunch of venison. Jilana found herself drawn into the conversation when Guendolen announced that the tunic she hoped to wear to the Beltane fire was too long but that she was incompetent with a needle and thread. Before Jilana could think better of it, she had offered her services and Guendolen had accepted with a glad cry.

"Guendolen likes you," Ede said when the other woman left to get the tunic.

Jilana shrugged off the compliment. "She needed me to tend her wound and hem her gown."

"She wanted to see you again," Ede snapped, and immediately apologized for her tone. "I am sorry. Guendolen has asked about you repeatedly since Caddaric found you at Camulodunum. She would have come before, but we were afraid Caddaric would not like it."

Jilana was forced to agree with Ede's conclusion. "Then why did she come today?"

"Is it not obvious?" Ede grinned. "Caddaric is gone."

In spite of her wariness, Jilana smiled in return. "So it is safe to visit his slave."

Ede's grin faded instantly. "I do not like to hear you call yourself that."

"I am what the rebellion has decreed," Jilana answered quietly. "'Tis not your doing."

"Nay," Ede replied sharply, "'tis Caddaric's."

Jilana laughed at the other's fierceness. "He saved my life; in his eyes, I should be grateful."

Ede snorted. "Aye, he would expect your gratitude." She shook her head. "He is a fine warrior, the strongest I have seen, but in his dealings with women he is exceedingly clumsy."

"I am hardly a woman in his eyes," Jilana said thoughtfully. "His slave and his property, aye, but not a woman."

Ede gaped at Jilana, recalling the night Caddaric had drunk himself into a stupor over the Roman woman and the following morning when her memory had kept him from easing his body's hunger with a willing Ede. Ede picked up a twig and trailed it aimlessly through the dirt.

"I think," she said slowly, "that Caddaric sees you too much as a woman."

Jilana laughed aloud in disbelief, but her laughter died when Ede fixed her with an intent glare. "You cannot be serious."

"But I am. Caddaric runs from you," Ede pointed out. "Have you not noticed?"

"Only because he will strangle me if he remains," Jilana tried to jest, "and if I am dead, who will fix his meals?"

"You frighten him," Ede argued. "I wonder why?"

Guendolen returned and the matter was set aside by tacit agreement. The afternoon passed with Jilana hemming the gown and the two Iceni women telling stories of their youth and battle prowess, some of them so blatantly embroidered that Jilana laughed until tears welled in her eyes and blinded her. Their laughter drew attention from the rest of the camp, and little by little, other Iceni joined them. By dusk, a dozen people were ranged about the fire, entertaining themselves with stories. Jilana was, by turns, entranced, horrified, and amused by the tales. The sewing lay forgotten in her lap while she listened as a young man, not much older than herself, recounted his daring in a raid against one of the neighboring villages near his home.

'Twas a new world these people opened for Jilana and she hung on every word, trying to imagine herself in their place. Would she have been like Ede, Jilana wondered, had she been raised an Iceni? The thought of holding a sword—aye, even using it!—was not as abhorrent as it would have been a month ago. Oh, the freedom with which Ede had been raised, Jilana thought enviously, remembering her own furtive, cherished, morning rides alone. Ede did not have to bow to her father's wishes, no matter how well-intentioned they might be. She could choose her fate, rather than accept a decision that was made for her. Jilana thought of Lucius and her attempts to please him, attempts that required forfeiting her own wishes and desires.

With a start, Jilana realized that, had the rebellion not come to pass, she would have married Lucius and spent the remainder of her life bowing to his will. She would have been, virtually, his slave, a possession for him to arrange and order about. She would have lacked the chains, Jilana admitted, glancing at the hateful iron around her ankles, and she would have been called Lucius' wife, but she would have been a slave nonetheless. At least with Caddaric, her position was honest—if painfully so.

Jilana's attention returned to the storyteller just in time to hear him say, "'Twas different at Venta Icenorum, of course, for great stealth was required to enter the houses..." His voice trailed off and when he looked at Jilana, his gaze was filled abject apology.

Jilana smiled her forgiveness, and her thanks for his regard for her feelings. She was still too raw to hear this particular tale. "You must have another tale to tell," she gently encouraged when the young man made to leave. His reply was stilled when another voice intruded.

"I think there have been enough stories for today."

Caddaric's voice came from behind Jilana and she scurried to her feet to the accompanying rattle of chains. "Lord," she acknowledged breathlessly, her arms crushing the red gown into a bright splash of color against her chest. "I did not hear you return."

Caddaric grunted and paced toward the group, a blanket-wrapped object slung over his shoulder. "The hunt was successful."

As if the statement were a command, the visitors rose as one, said their goodbyes, and drifted away. As Caddaric approached the fire, Jilana nervously wet her lips and clutched the gown more tightly. "I did not shirk my duties, lord," she hurried to explain the lack of an evening meal. "Ede said you would undoubtedly want the fresh meat tonight." The strange look Caddaric gave her sent Jilana back a step. "Truly, lord, had I known—"

"Jilana," Caddaric interrupted gently, "I am not angry with you."

Jilana swallowed convulsively. "Oh." It was all she could think of to say and Jilana felt extremely foolish for her outburst.

Caddaric's face centered on the red tunic. "Where did you get the gown?"

Blinking, Jilana looked at the tunic, as if surprised to find it in her hands. "'Tis not mine. I am hemming it for Guendolen." She looked at him inquiringly. "I did not think you would mind."

Her explanation sent relief through Caddaric and he shook his head. "Nay, I do not." He set down his burden and gestured to Jilana. "Come, see what the hunt yielded."

Jilana had no desire to view the kill, but she dared not refuse, so she edged closer.

"You see?" Caddaric opened the blanket with a flourish and viewed its contents with pride. "A fine stag. We will carve part of it for tonight and roast the rest tomorrow for Clywd's celebration."

Averting her eyes from the sight, Jilana struggled to subdue her protesting stomach. She had adjusted to the dried and cured beef, but the raw venison in front of her was a different matter.

Caddaric saw the look on her face and understood immediately. "I will cut the meat and teach you how to season it."

Jilana nodded weakly and backed toward the tent. "I will just put Guendolen's tunic away." Inside the safety of the tent, she drew several deep breaths as she folded the tunic and placed it atop her chest. She would manage this next trial, she told herself fiercely. She *would*! She would show Caddaric that her strength was equal to any Iceni maid's.

"You dropped the thread."

Jilana gasped and spun around to find Caddaric standing just inside the tent, the twist of matching red thread lying across his open palm. He closed the distance between them and extended his arm. Jilana snatched the thread from his hand and turned back to place it on the tunic. Caddaric sighed inwardly. The set of her shoulders bespoke her nervousness, a nervousness that had been absent when she sat with the others around the fire.

"Did you enjoy the afternoon?"

Smoothing nonexistent wrinkles from the tunic, Jilana nodded. "Ede's friends were most kind. I liked their stories—they reminded me of the ones Artair used to tell."

"Artair would have made a good bard," Caddaric agreed. "Come now, help me prepare the meal."

Reluctantly, Jilana followed Caddaric from the tent and watched while he carved a portion for the evening meal and explained how they would prepare the remainder. "Tomorrow morning I will spit the venison; and while I dig a roasting pit, you will rub the seasonings into the meat. Then we will lower the meat into the pit, *smoor* the fire and let the meat roast all day. We will feast when the ceremony is finished." He thrust an iron skewer through the small roast and ordered, "Build up the fire."

Jilana obeyed. "How is Beltane celebrated?"

Caddaric paused in his work for a moment, considering his answer. "Outside of my village there is a sacred mound—built many years ago, long before Albion had heard of Rome or Caesar—with a wide, stone altar upon which the Druid would build the fire of Beltane to honor the god Be'al."

"Be'al," Jilana repeated, frowning as she sought to translate the name. "The life of all things?"

"That is close," Caddaric nodded. "The fire welcomes the return of the sun after the cold desolation of winter. There are songs and dancing and offerings to Be'al."

"Offerings?" Jilana's blood ran cold and her next word ended the tenuous truce between herself and Caddaric. "Sacrifices?"

Caddaric's eyes snared hers across the blaze. "My father, in case you have not noticed, does not hold with living sacrifices. He believes that Be'al holds all life sacred and frowns upon blood offerings. Clywd's offerings to the god take the form of grain and wine."

"I did not mean to offend."

"Lhwyd is in love with death," Caddaric snapped as he settled the spit over the fire. "Do not judge us all by that priest."

"I try not to," Jilana said defensively. "Just as you do not judge all Romans by the actions of Caesar and his Procurator."

The barb drove straight into Caddaric's heart. His eyes darkened with sadness as they stared at one another and silently acknowledged that the chasm which yawned between them was unbridgeable. "Do you hate me," he asked at last.

Jilana rose and went to the wagon to gather the ingredients for wheat cakes. "I have no feelings for you at all," she brazenly lied, "just as you have none for me. Your Queen's rebellion has thrown us together and when the war is over, whether you win or lose, we will not see each other again. You have said as much."

"So, you can endure my presence because you know it is only temporary?"

"Aye."

Caddaric mulled that over. "If Boadicea loses, your world will return and you will be able to forget all that has happened."

"Aye," Jilana answered again.

"You can forget me so easily?"

Jilana's fingers tightened around the wooden spoon she was using. "Nightmares are to be endured and quickly forgotten."

Caddaric stiffened at the verbal slap and barely managed to hold on to his temper. "And if Boadicea wins?"

"You have said you would release me."

"Not precisely. There was a condition," Caddaric reminded her silkily. "A child."

Jilana whirled on him then, the spoon grasped like a weapon in her hand. "If Boadicea is victorious, why would you want a child who was only half Iceni," she demanded bitterly.

Caddaric sorted through several answers before deciding upon the truth as he knew it. "Because the gods have so ordained," he answered simply.

"Your gods, perhaps, but not mine," Jilana retorted hotly. With a shrug of his massive shoulders, Caddaric dismissed her objection. The action infuriated Jilana, and before she could stop herself, she hurled the spoon at his head. The weapon was ill-balanced and wildly thrown, so only the purest chance—or the intervention of the gods—allowed it to land with a solid *thwack* against Caddaric's forehead. Wheat batter splattered into his hair and dripped down his nose and he roared in outrage. Jilana completely ignored his outrage in favor of her own. "I will cook for you, launder your clothes and follow behind your wagon like some chained dog, but I *will not* bear you a child. *Never*, do you hear me?"

Caddaric blinked owlishly at her, admiring the beauty her anger brought forth even while he wiped the wheat batter off his face. "Why?"

"W-why?" Jilana sputtered in wide-eyed disbelief. "Why?" Her voice rose to a high, carrying pitch. "Because I am no brood mare for the continuation of my owner's line!"

"That you are not," Caddaric heard himself concur. "You are the other half of myself."

The quiet assurance in his voice took Jilana aback. "You are mad," she said breathlessly when she finally found her voice. "As insane as Caligula."

"Mayhap." Caddaric came forward until he stood directly in front of Jilana so that she was forced to tilt her head upward in order to see his face. "If so, then you are the source of my madness. Have you considered that?"

He leaned forward, his arms on either side of Jilana, crowding her back against the wagon until her breasts brushed his chest. Her breathing stopped, her knees went weak and she closed her eyes, awaiting his kiss. And knew, in that instant of waiting, that she was as mad as he, for she *wanted* the touch of his mouth. The metallic rattle from the wagon snapped her eyes open and she discovered that Caddaric was pulling back, the basin dangling from one hand and a faint smile hovering on his lips.

"I need to wash."

Jilana stared, open-mouthed, while he poured water into the basin and proceeded to wash his hair and face. Caddaric had had no intention of kissing her! She spun away, a hot blush suffusing her cheeks, to finish the wheat cakes and remembered that she had thrown her spoon at Caddaric. She stomped over to where the offending utensil lay and scooped it into her hand.

"I think you lied," Caddaric said goadingly when her back was turned. "You feel something for me, little wicca."

Uttering a shriek that fairly split Caddaric's eardrums, Jilana whirled and threw the spoon at him once again. This time, however, her aim was far from true. It sailed harmlessly past the side of his head, across the wagon and struck the black-robed figure who had chosen that unfortunate moment to step into camp.

Clywd grunted in surprise and peered down at the splotch of dirty wheat batter on his chest. Leaving a sticky trail in its wake, the spoon slid slowly downward for several inches before letting go of the fabric and falling to the ground.

Ahh, Juno, I have struck a Druid, Jilana moaned silently. Her fingers pressed against her lips in an attempt to hold back a groan. What was the punishment for such a transgression?

Caddaric stared in disbelief. Jilana's aim was either incredibly good or incredibly bad, depending upon one's point of view.

Clywd's bewildered gaze traveled first to his son and then to Jilana, both of whom were frozen in place, before retrieving the spoon. "What else are we having for the meal?"

Caddaric's great shout of laughter echoed across the campsite. Jilana gave a cry that was half embarrassment, half thwarted rage, and fled into the tent.

"Were I you," Clywd intoned as he walked around the wagon, "I would see that Jilana never has access to a knife."

The advice sent Caddaric into another bout of laughter that finally ended when he was sitting on the ground, his back braced against the wheel for support. "Sh-she was aiming at m-me," he managed to say.

Clywd raised an eyebrow at his son. "Her aim is poor."

Caddaric grabbed his sides and bent forward until his forehead touched his upraised knees. "Father, if you could have seen the look on your face..."

"Thankfully I was spared that indignity," Clywd said dryly. He dropped the spoon onto the wagon ledge, brushed at the stain on his cloak, and gave in to the smile he had been repressing. "Never before have I been attacked with a spoon."

"Nor I," Caddaric grinned. "She nearly broke *my* nose."

Clywd chuckled then and gestured at the tent. "Will she come out, do you think?"

"Eventually, when she is done putting rocks under my pallet." Grinning hugely, Caddaric pulled himself to his feet and finished the wheat cakes Jilana had started. When they were seated by the fire and Caddaric had poured them each a cup of wine, he confided, "She confuses me."

"Of course she does; that is a woman's purpose in life."

Caddaric shook his head impatiently, his expression serious. "Is it possible that my dreams were wrong?"

"In what manner?"

Caddaric took a bracing sip of wine. "The dreams were straightforward enough: I would meet Jilana and she would bear my child; a child who would reflect the best of both our worlds. But now—" He sighed and stared glumly into the fire.

"Now," Clywd prompted. "What, my son? You no longer wish the child?"

"Nay—I mean aye, I do wish the child but—" Caddaric ran a hand through his hair, searching for the words. "I thought it would all be so *simple*, Father!"

"And it is not?"

"'Tis anything but," Caddaric answered in a low roar. "I am a reasonable man, would you not agree?" Before Clywd had a chance to reply, Caddaric continued, "Aye, I am most reasonable. I am not given to fits of temper or melancholy, I am honest in my dealings with those around me, but she—she," he pointed an accusing finger at the tent, "she does not believe me when I say I will protect her. Nay! She runs away! I forbid her to see a Roman prisoner and she not only defies my order, but helps him escape." This was said in a low voice for, in spite of his steadily rising ire, Caddaric was still aware of the danger in such an admission. "I clap her in irons—for her own sake as well as mine—and she dares to look at me like a wounded doe! And when I punish her for her misdeeds," he drew a shuddering breath. "Gods! 'Tis as if the shackles are around my soul as well."

Ahh, the satisfaction to be derived from Caddaric's confusion, Clywd reflected with a hidden smile. 'Twas as if he could see the bricks fall one by one from the wall Caddaric had built around his heart. Amazing, the havoc one small Roman had managed to wreak in his too-rational son. "What is it you wish from me?" Clywd asked.

'Answers," Caddaric replied harshly. "How do I rid myself of these complications?"

"'Tis simple enough." Clywd took a sip of wine. "Rid yourself of Jilana and the complications will disappear."

The implications of the answer fell like lead upon Caddaric's heart. "But without Jilana, the dream dies," he protested.

"And it is alive now?" Clywd probed. "I told you once, Jilana is your destiny. To continue as you are is to throw that destiny away."

Caddaric pondered his father's words throughout the evening and acknowledged the truth of the matter. To continue like this would serve no purpose. He did not want Jilana afraid of him, shying away at his every word or gesture, but rather accepting, both of him and their circumstances. She would bear his child—aye, she would!—but he wanted her to do so willingly. Caddaric did not bother to examine *why* it was important to him that Jilana be willing; the reasons were secondary to his knowledge.

Jilana stayed within the security of the tent for the remainder of the evening, despite the protests of her stomach. She was embarrassed to see Clywd after what had transpired, but the embarrassment was unimportant compared to the fear that coursed through her whenever she thought of Caddaric's softly spoken goad. *You feel something for me, little wicca.* She fought that truth until, sighing, she admitted defeat. Even though she wore his shackles, Jilana could not forget that, once, things had been different between them; that she had fallen in love with him. Oh, Juno, if he ever guessed how *much* she cared there would be no defense left to her. She fell asleep listening to the quiet voices outside the tent, and wishing with all her heart that she and Caddaric were not sworn enemies.

THE NIGHTMARE STRUCK Caddaric again that night. His cries woke Jilana and for several moments she lay motionless, vowing she would not go to him as she had the night before. Her resolution lasted until his cry of anger turned into a choked, masculine expression of wordless sorrow and then she threw off her blanket and hurried through the darkness to Caddaric's side.

"'Tis the dream again, Caddaric," Jilana whispered urgently as she shook his shoulder. Beneath her hand the iron muscles trembled, and compassion swamped her.

Caddaric came awake feeling the tremors in his body and the soothing hand upon his shoulder. *"Artair."*

"I know." Jilana felt sympathetic tears well in her eyes. "At least he was consecrated to your gods. I do not have even that small comfort for the loss of my family." She felt his muscles contract at her words and wondered at his tension.

"'Tis cold comfort," Caddaric grated at last.

Jilana felt him relax and breathed a sigh of relief. "I would take it, cold or not."

Caddaric moved his hand until it found and covered Jilana's. "The rebellion has taken much from both of us, even the time to mourn our dead."

"Aye," Jilana softly agreed, and made to rise. Caddaric's hand kept her firmly in place.

"Stay," Caddaric ordered in a low voice. And then, because he wanted her to choose freely, he released Jilana's hand and said, "Please stay, just for a few moments."

Sighing, knowing it was madness but rendered helpless by the entreaty in his voice, Jilana settled back into her position beside the pallet. "If you wish."

"So agreeable," Caddaric teased, his fingers lightly stroking her hand.

Bristling, Jilana inquired, "That is what you wish, is it not?" His fingers stroked higher, raising gooseflesh along the length of her arm, and she shivered in reaction.

"Once I did." Caddaric cupped his hand and slid it up and down her arm. Feeling her reaction he asked, "Are you cold?" As he spoke, his knuckles brushed the material covering her breast.

"N-nay," Jilana stammered on a quick breath, and it was the truth. Where he had touched her the stola seemed to burn against her flesh.

"Of course you are," Caddaric contradicted. He swept back the blankets with his free hand. "Come, lie next to me."

"Nay." This time there was no hesitation in her reply. Jilana pulled her arm free and backed away before he could reach for her again. "I am no fool, Caddaric."

Caddaric listened to the sounds she made returning to her own pallet and cursed silently. His impetuous action had driven Jilana away, but finding her crouched beside him once again had seemed too good an opportunity to let slide through his fingers. In the future he would have to tread more carefully, Caddaric lectured himself as he flipped the blankets back into place.

SHE LIKED IT BETTER, Jilana decided late in the afternoon of the next day, when Caddaric absented himself from the camp. Except for two brief absences, he had been in their camp the entire day and his presence was a strain on her nerves. Not that he did anything to make her wary; his actions were quite the opposite. While Jilana baked successive batches of wheat cakes for the night's feast, he tended the roasting venison, for which Jilana was mutely grateful, for even had she been able to raise the slab of turf which covered the pit to check on the coals, she was certain she could not endure the initial odor of cooking meat that rose from the pit when the turf was removed. Caddaric sharpened his sword—again, Jilana thought, as the whetstone rasped the length of the blade and set her teeth on edge—and he cut wood for the fire and he helped her with the chores and through it all *he watched her.* 'Twas his still, innocent, blatant gaze that distracted her so. She did not trust it for a moment.

Only the passing visits from Caddaric's friends kept Jilana from retreating to the tent and staying there. The tasks which had occupied so much time when she was first learning them were now easily accomplished and time hung heavily on her hands. The visits provided her with an excuse to bustle about, pouring out wine and mead for the guests. Guendolen stopped by to pick up her gown but stayed all too briefly, despite Jilana's urging. By the time the afternoon shadows had lengthened, the last visitors had departed and she was alone with Caddaric.

Jilana stood uneasily by the wagon and Caddaric walked toward her slowly, aware, and puzzled, by the tension he sensed in her. Throughout the day he had behaved impeccably—not threatening or shouting when her edginess sparked his temper—while he sought a way to recapture what they had known at Venta Icenorum, before the mistrust had grown between them. But nothing he did seemed to have an impact upon Jilana; instead she grew increasingly nervous in his presence, and he could see no reason for it unless . . .

"Are you planning another escape?" Caddaric demanded when he was less than a foot from Jilana.

Startled, Jilana dropped the jar she had been holding. It crashed to the ground and shattered, showering wine over both their feet. "Oh!" The cry was a mixture of embarrassment and consternation. "See what you have made me do?" Jilana would have picked up the shards of pottery, but two strong hands closed around her upper arms and lifted her bodily from the mess. Instinctively, her fingers curled around Caddaric's muscular forearms for additional support and, dismayed, she looked directly into Caddaric's eyes. "P-put me down." Her voice was sadly lacking in both command and dignity; indeed, it sounded more like a whimper.

"When you answer," came Caddaric's blunt reply. "Are you planning to run again?"

Jilana shook her head vehemently. "I am well and truly beaten, lord. Now will you put me down?"

He did, but kept a hand around one of her arms. "I found a pure well yesterday. We will take the wagon and fill our water barrels."

"N-now?" Why could she not seem to rid herself of the stutter?

Caddaric quirked an eyebrow. "Everyone will be in camp, preparing for Beltane. We can be assured of privacy, and an unlimited supply of fresh water." Jilana's frown showed her confusion and Caddaric clarified, "I would like to bathe; I thought you might as well."

She would have dearly loved to refuse, but the offer was too tempting. Tomorrow, after the noon meal, they would march again, and the thought was enough to make Jilana feel as though she were once again covered with dust. "As you wish," she replied calmly. Caddaric's eyes turned cold, but Jilana was too relieved that he had dropped her arm to notice.

The ride to the farm was accomplished in silence and Jilana was only too happy to drop down from the seat without waiting for Caddaric's assistance. The site of the well was a small, deserted farmstead and while Caddaric set about building a fire, Jilana looked about in dismay. The buildings consisted of a byre with a rudely-fenced pen and a house. The house was small, timber-framed, covered with daub and capped with a wattle roof—it came as a shock to Jilana, accustomed as she was to the buildings of two or more stories of Venta Icenorum. It dawned on Jilana then that, despite having spent her life on Britannia, she had taken no notice of how the Iceni lived. The door to the house stood ajar and she entered the structure.

There were no separate rooms as she knew them. The door opened directly onto a large room which held a table and two stools, both of which lay on the dirt floor. Jilana unconsciously righted them as she passed by on her way to examine the fire pit in the center of the room. Looking up, she could see the smoke-hole cut into the roof. The windows had wooden shutters, but they gaped open now, admitting the afternoon sunlight. To her left, two curtains were suspended from the ceiling rafters and she cautiously pulled back the first. Inside was a small bedchamber containing two mattresses which, Jilana guessed from their scent, had recently been filled with fresh straw. The second curtain revealed another bedchamber, just slightly larger than the first, but here, instead of the straw-filled pallet residing on the floor, it reposed on a bed with roped framework. The adults' bedchamber, Jilana thought; the other would have been for the children. With curtains in place of doors, there would be little privacy. Jilana grimaced at the thought. Where was the family now? Had they joined Boadicea or had they fled before the onslaught of the rebellion? Their ghosts seemed to haunt the structure.

"Jilana?"

Jilana cried out in alarm and spun around. Caddaric stood silhouetted in the doorway. "You startled me."

Caddaric ignored the accusation as he stepped into the house. The door frame was low and he had to stoop to enter. "What are you doing?"

"Only looking at the house."

Blue eyes traveled around the interior before coming to rest on Jilana. "Seeing how we barbarians live?" Caddaric could not help the mocking taunt; the look on Jilana's face spoke eloquently of her distaste for her surroundings.

Fighting down the blush that was an answer in itself, Jilana countered, "I was wondering what had happened to the family who lived here."

"They left." Caddaric raised an eyebrow, telling her that the fate of the family was obvious.

"But where did they go?" Jilana persisted, thinking of the two small pallets in the first bedchamber. "Do they fight with your Queen or against her? They had children; where are they? Are they safe or—"

"Jilana, stop this." Caddaric's voice cut across her questioning with the surety of a knife. He prowled the perimeter of the house, pausing to look inside the bedchambers, and came to a halt in front of her. "They are gone. They loaded their possessions into a wagon, took their horse and cow and drove away. 'Tis that simple." He threw her an impatient look and strode from the house.

Jilana followed slowly, carefully shutting the door behind her. Seeing the courteous action in a world turned upside down, Caddaric shook his head and began drawing water from the well.

"The house will be burned," Caddaric informed her when she reached the well.

Jilana stared at him, horrified. "Why?"

"The Romans will assume the occupants were rebels and the war host will assume they were Roman sympathizers." Caddaric shrugged. "Either side will destroy the house in order to teach the owners a lesson in loyalty." He poured water into one of the three buckets that rested at his feet. "Start filling the barrels."

They worked in silence for a long time before Jilana dared a question. "Is your home like this one?" She glanced over her shoulder as she spoke and the breath caught in her throat. Caddaric had removed his tunic. The breeks that clung to his narrow waist and hips served to emphasize the broad wedge of his chest and shoulders. As he hauled on the rope that lowered the pail into the depths of the well, his muscles bunched and relaxed beneath the bronze flesh. Like an awe-struck mortal in the presence of god, she forgot the bucket in her hand and admired the sight of him.

Caddaric laughed harshly. "Nothing so grand. My father and I share a *bothie*." He straightened, turned slightly to fill another bucket, and found her looking at him. "What is it?"

Dazed, Jilana could only shake her head and stumble forward. When Caddaric turned back to the well, she found her voice. "Bothie?"

"A hut—about the same size as our tent—with a turf roof."

"Oh." Jilana filled the barrel mechanically, unable to drag her eyes away from Caddaric. Praise Juno he did not look at her again! Every time she turned for a full pail of water she could see the tiny beads of perspiration that formed between his shoulders and trickled down his spine to disappear into the waistband of his breeks. She felt hot and cold all at once and her lungs were not functioning properly. She forced her eyes away but it brought no relief, for now she could hear his deep, even breathing and catch the faint scent of sandalwood which clung to him. And, worse, she could remember the taste and texture of his skin beneath her lips, the feel of his chest hair as it abraded her breasts.

"Jilana!"

Jilana screamed, the bucket she had been holding went flying, and she would have jumped as high as the wagon had Caddaric's hand not been on her shoulder, holding her firmly to the earth. She looked down and found rivulets of water running around and under her feet, soaking the ground. The rivulets were caused by the steady stream of water from the wagon which was caused, in turn, by the overfilled water barrels. Ahh, gods, you have no mercy at all!

"Jilana?" This time Caddaric's voice was softer. He used the pressure on her shoulder to turn her so that she was facing him, puzzled by her labored breathing and the flush that suffused her face. And then he cursed under his breath. "Your feet; I should have remembered how tender they are." He swept her into his arms and carried her to the back of the wagon where he slipped off her wet sandals.

"Nay, Caddaric, you need not—" Jilana's protest ended abruptly when Caddaric caught the calf of her right leg in his hand and raised it to rest on his left thigh so that he could unwrap the bandage.

"Hold still," Caddaric ordered when Jilana tried to squirm away.

Jilana closed her eyes and endured his touch. Endured, she mocked herself. His hands were callused, yet gentle, and she loved the way they felt against her flesh. Inadvertently, her toes curled into the material of his breeks in response to the pure pleasure of his touch.

Caddaric nearly groaned aloud at the small, kneading motion. How glorious if he could replace her foot with her hand...images of her long, tapered fingers splayed against his thigh sent a shaft of desire through his groin and Caddaric nearly bent double under its force. As if in a dream, he lifted her left foot to his right thigh to unbandage it. She had lovely legs, strong but not corded with muscles; and her thighs, revealed by the creeping hem of her gown, were slender but well-formed. He remembered their strength when they had closed around his waist, drawing him deeper.... A sharp pain sliced into his knee. Astounded, Caddaric looked down and found a link of Jilana's chain crushed between his knee and the wagon. He had been gradually lowering himself toward her—only the chain had stopped his descent. Straightening, he released her legs. "The day grows short." His voice was thick with desire, but there was nothing he could do about it. Offering Jilana his hand, he helped her down from the wagon. "The water should be heated by now."

In fact, the water was boiling. They tempered it with fresh water from the well and then reveled in the indulgence of an unlimited water supply. Caddaric had prepared everything, down to the presence of old blankets which had been cut into rectangles to serve as towels. Jilana washed her hair first and wrapped it in one of the towels. Caddaric had washed his hair as well, and now, from the corner of her eye, Jilana saw him strip off the last of his clothing. Her ingrained sense of modesty was offended, but not enough to prevent her gaze from traveling the length of his back and legs before turning her attention back to her own bath.

Caddaric's actions were correct, Jilana decided after she had mentally struggled with the problem of how to bathe without removing her clothes. Modesty between them at this point was ridiculous. She slipped out of her stola, folded it carefully, and placed it out of harm's way.

Caddaric covertly watched Jilana as he went about his ablutions. He nearly smiled when she shed her gown—nearly. The sight of the chains drowned his pleasure. He scrubbed at his skin until it hurt.

Jilana hurried through her bath. The brush of wind against her wet skin set her teeth to chattering, a condition that was not relieved until she wore her stola once again. Caddaric, of course, seemed impervious to the discomfort and Jilana shook her head in disbelief as he sluiced pail after pail of well water over his shoulders. He must be made of stone to endure that, Jilana concluded, and then turned quickly away before she was caught spying.

They left the farm in gathering darkness and once again the ride was accomplished in silence. Caddaric seemed lost in thought and the lack of conversation did not bother Jilana. She was growing accustomed to the fact that Caddaric did not make idle small talk or partake in the wild storytelling that passed the nights around the campfires.

Such pursuits were not in his nature. His was a quiet personality; even in a gathering of his friends, he seemed a little apart, isolated, sharing his thoughts and himself only with his father and Heall. His trust was not easily given, nor won, but once it was, he would be loyal unto death itself.

The camp was controlled chaos when they reached it. People hurried this way and that in preparation for the evening's celebration, and a hushed expectancy hung in the air. Caddaric cared for the horses while Jilana prepared a light meal. When they had eaten, Caddaric unexpectedly gave Jilana first use of the tent so that she might change in privacy. At first she had argued against attending Beltane, but Caddaric had been adamant and Jilana had capitulated. Besides, her curiosity about the celebration outweighed her trepidation at being the cynosure of Iceni eyes. Jilana was ready and waiting when Caddaric emerged from the tent. The bright blue cloak she had seen in his kist now swung from his shoulders; beneath it, his black tunic and breeks were a solemn contrast. The bronze torque at his throat glowed in the firelight.

Caddaric admired Jilana's appearance as silently as she admired his. She had changed into her remaining white stola and brushed her hair dry by the fire. Now the redgold mass hung in shining waves down to her waist, trapping his gaze. The only discordant note was the clanking of those damnable chains as she rose and moved toward him. A beautiful woman, Caddaric thought when Jilana came to a halt beside him; the man who claimed her loyalty would be truly blessed.

They left the campsite and joined the river of people flowing to the east. Half the distance had been covered when Jilana felt an unfamiliar pressure at her waist. Caddaric had settled his arm around her. It meant nothing, Jilana told herself; he meant only to keep them from being separated in the crush. But her heart was not convinced and gave an elated thump against her ribcage. As the press of people grew heavier, it seemed only natural to move closer to Caddaric until her shoulder was comfortably ensconced beneath his arm. Was it only her imagination, or had Caddaric's hand squeezed her briefly when she moved nearer? As they walked, Jilana noted that the cook fires were extinguished as the people left their camps, just as Caddaric had extinguished theirs.

Clywd had found a low, broad hill for his ceremony. Two days of work by his army of volunteers had flattened the top of the rise so that it could accommodate the rough, stone altar that had been constructed under Clywd's watchful eye. Now the surface of the altar was covered with brush and overlaid with small logs; unlit torches were piled around the foot of the hill. It took Clywd fifteen paces to cover the distance from one end of the altar to the other. When the Beltane fire was lit, it would be seen for miles around. Beltane! Clywd's spirit leaped proudly as he surveyed his altar and the people gathering at the foot of the hill. For nearly two decades his people had been denied the presence of Druids for this celebration; for the past weeks they had lived with bloodshed and death but now they would celebrate life and the coming year. If they died tomorrow, or next week, or next month, they would have the memory of their own gods and their own ceremonies to comfort them before the final darkness closed their eyes.

Caddaric cleared a way for the two of them to the front of the crowd. No one objected; he was the Druid's son and a fierce warrior, deserving of a place of honor. Jilana gazed upward and found Clywd in the flickering light thrown by the torches which stood at intervals around the sides and back of the altar. He paced back and forth in front of the altar, the silver streak in his beard moving as he spoke to himself. Was he rehearsing his prayer? Jilana wondered, and she smiled at the thought. It seemed that Clywd was forever mumbling to himself, as if in constant communication with his gods to the exclusion of this world. She caught sight of Lhwyd some distance away, unmistakable in his robe of pure white, with Ede at his side. She quickly averted her eyes and fought the chill which crept up her spine.

Caddaric felt the tremor. Bending down, he asked, "Are you cold?"

"Nay." Jilana met his eyes and tried to smile. To her surprise, his lips twitched briefly in what might have been a like response, but the movement was gone so quickly that Jilana could not say for certain. "Lhwyd is here."

Caddaric glanced around until he found the Druid. In a protective gesture, he pulled Jilana in front of him and wrapped both his arms around her waist. His lips brushed her ear as he murmured, "So am I. When will you believe that Lhwyd will have you only over my cold body?"

There was no need for Jilana to reply, nor did she protest the embrace for three reasons. First, held fast as she was, Caddaric's arm blocked the sight of Lhwyd; second, Caddaric's body blocked the cool night air and warmed her with its heat; and third—ahh, third—it was wonderful to be held in those strong arms. It was all Jilana could do not to sigh aloud her pleasure.

"We are gathered to celebrate Beltane!"

The voice rolled down from the hilltop like gentle thunder, surprising Jilana with its force. Looking up, Jilana saw that Clywd had moved behind the altar and now stood with both arms upraised and a warm smile on his face. His expression was far different from the one the Roman priests usually wore on such solemn occasions.

"The snow and cold of winter are past; the earth warms and buds appear on the trees. Soon will come the time to till the fields and watch the mares foal their young." Clywd's face sobered. "But not this year. This Beltane we celebrate the rebirth of our tribes, our nations, and ourselves. This year we sow not the seeds of wheat but of independence; seeds that, by the grace of the gods, will ripen and be reaped by our children." The shout of approval that went up from the assemblage forced Clywd into momentary silence. When the cheering died, he resumed. "Our offering to Be'al this year is in thanks for our vic-

tories and his continued beneficence as we seek to reclaim what is rightfully ours.''

Clywd lifted a large copper bowl from beside the altar
and raised it high above his head. ''Accept the sacrifice of
this wheat, O mighty Be'al; 'twas grown in the earth you
warmed and nurtured by the rains you sent. As you give
us the means of sustaining life, so do you give us life. Do
not turn from us, we beg of you, even though we must
take the lives of your other creatures in order to bring
freedom to our land.'' He placed the bowl on top of the
log-filled altar and touched one of the torches to the grain.
The grain took fire, the breeze freshened, and where Jilana stood, she could smell the sharp odor of burning
wheat. While Jilana watched, the smoke from the bowl
turned from gray to purple to red, and then burst into a
rainbow of bright colors that shot skyward. The torch
flames bent and flickered with the force of the wind.
Around them, the Iceni murmured in awe and Jilana
gasped at this obvious sign of Be'al's acceptance of the
sacrifice.

Of the crowd, only Caddaric and Lhwyd were unmoved, although Caddaric's mouth twisted in appreciation of the phenomenon his father had created. No doubt
Clywd had added some of his special herbs to the wheat
in order to generate the colors, but how he had managed
to force the smoke straight up when the wind so obviously eddied about the altar was a mystery. Jilana's head
moved against Caddaric's chest, and he looked down. Her
face held a rapt expression of awe as she watched the
spectrum of colors burst against the night sky. Caddaric
chuckled silently and then sobered. 'Twould be nice to
believe in the miracle of such things, even for a few moments.

Lhwyd stood stiffly at the front of the crowd; the only
hint of his disgust were the bright points of light that
danced in his eyes. To ask forgiveness for the slaying of
the enemy, Lhwyd thought with an inward sneer. They
should be celebrating Beltane with a sacrifice of Roman
blood, complete with thanks to the Morrigan! The god-

dess had made the victories possible, not Be'al. Were it
not for the fact that the old man was respected and admired by the people, Lhwyd would have stayed away from
this celebration—as Clywd so pointedly avoided those in
honor of the Morrigan—but he dared not. While the
people enjoyed his living sacrifices to the goddess, their
enjoyment sprang only from seeing their enemies killed,
not in the honor thus paid to the Morrigan. Lhwyd had
only a few devoted followers; before he could challenge
Clywd's position, he needed to expand his power and this
could not be done if he directly insulted Clywd.

If only I could have remained on Mona, Lhwyd thought
as he watched the older Druid through hate-filled eyes,
and learned the different arts that Clywd has at his command. But the chief Druid on the island had stumbled
upon Lhwyd during one of his private sacrifices to the
Morrigan and, upon seeing the pain the young acolyte
inflicted before allowing death to claim the sacrifice, had
exiled Lhwyd from Mona. Now, remembering, Lhwyd's
mouth curled in contempt for the chief Druid and all
those—such as Clywd—who worshiped at the altar of the
soft gods. *His* spirit demanded devotion to a harsher de-
ity.

Clywd began the song of praise and thanks to Be'al, a
song that had not been heard in this land for nearly twenty
years. One by one, hesitantly at first, and then with
greater assurance, other voices joined Clywd's as words
long unused sprang from the depths of memory. As the
song rose in strength and emotion, Clywd removed the
bowl from the altar, took one of the torches from its
holder and walked with stately grace the perimeter of the
altar. Just as the song ended, Clywd touched the torch to
the center of the altar.

The dry tinder caught; the fire raced from the center
outward, visible to those below only as a glow that illuminated the Druid's face. Then, with an audible *whoosh*,
the split logs caught as one and the flames rose, obscur-
ing Clywd from sight. In the ensuing tumult, Lhwyd
turned and elbowed his way toward the rear of the cheer-

ing crowd; he would not be missed. The flames died down and one by one, the people moved forward to take one of the torches from the pile stacked around the foot of the hill.

At first the movement of the crowd frightened Jilana, for it was impossible to resist and she was torn from Caddaric's arms and swept along in its tide. Just as she started to panic, Jilana felt a strong arm go around her waist and a quick look over her shoulder showed that Caddaric was right behind her. She relaxed and observed the ritual going on around her. Two lines had formed, each making its way up one side of the low hill to the ends of the altar. The two lines met in the center of the altar where Clywd stood. The Druid blessed each person and passed a sprig of sacred mistletoe across their forehead; then the worshiper lit his torch from the altar fire and descended the hill. Twenty years past, the torch the Iceni carried would have lit the fires in the hearth so that every house would know the blessing of Be'al. This night, Be'al's hallowed flame would have only lowly campfires to grace.

I should not be here, Jilana thought as her turn came to receive Clywd's blessing. I do not know this god, have not worshiped at his altar. But retreat was impossible, so she swallowed and gave Clywd an apologetic look. "Forgive me, Clywd; I do not mean to profane your god."

Clywd smiled gently. "All are Be'al's children." He brushed the mistletoe across Jilana's brow saying, "The blessings of Be'al go with you this night," and then raised his eyes to his son. "You should no longer doubt the power of the gods, especially Be'al's, for through his magic, here you are, awaiting the blessing." Before Caddaric could reply, Clywd murmured the blessing, touched the mistletoe to his brow, and then presented his back to his son in order to receive the next supplicant.

Jilana started to move down the hill but Caddaric's hand upon her wrist stopped her. Caddaric handed Jilana the torch and then wrapped his large hand around hers and together they dipped it to the sacred flame. "So the blessing will extend to all in our camp," Caddaric explained when she gave him a curious glance.

It seemed to take forever before they were free of the gathering, and as they walked back to their camp, Jilana could see fires springing up as other worshipers returned to their camps. The torch lit their path, and as they turned into the campsite, Jilana saw a lone figure sitting in front of the dead fire. It turned at the sound of their approach and the light from the torch fell upon familiar features.

"Heall!" Jilana broke away from Caddaric and hurried to her friend. Without a moment's hesitation, she threw her arms around the older man's neck in a joyful embrace. "Welcome back."

"Thank you, child." Heall held her with one arm and extended the other to Caddaric.

Caddaric grasped Heall's forearm. "'Tis good to see you once more, old friend."

"And you." Heall pulled Jilana's arms from his neck so that he could peer down into her face. "And you, little one. Are you well?"

"Aye." Jilana studied Heall's face just as intently, her hands framing his jaw through the graying beard, and wanted to weep at the sorrow reflected in his eyes. "You will stay with us?"

"I will make my camp with Clywd," Heall replied, "but this night I would welcome your company—and a piece of that venison I smell cooking."

"In a moment," Caddaric broke in. "First we have one last ritual to attend to." Handing the torch to Jilana, he knelt and laid fresh wood and kindling. Hesitantly, Caddaric spoke the words he had heard his father say in private for so many years. "The blessing of Beltane enter our home. May Be'al find favor with us and see us safely through the coming year." He looked at Jilana. "Put the torch into the wood."

Heall had to bite back the cry of surprise that sprang to his lips at Caddaric's order. Tradition held that the man of the house laid the fire but his mate, if he had one, placed the Beltane fire upon the hearth. It was an honor not lightly taken, but Jilana was obviously ignorant of that fact. While she appeared pleased to have been included in the ritual, she placed no special significance upon the act.

Jilana thrust the torch into the pyramid Caddaric had created out of wood and smiled as first the kindling and then the logs caught fire. Being included in the festival of Beltane had brought a rare peace to her heart. And, from the laughter and singing that issued from the surrounding camps, it seemed to Jilana that the peace extended to everyone. There was a gay air to the Iceni host tonight that had not been present after Lhwyd's ceremonies. Humming softly, Jilana went to the wagon and laid out the wine, honeyed mead, wheat cakes and preserves which would be served along with the venison to their guests.

No sooner had Jilana completed this task—and Caddaric declared the venison roasted to perfection—than the night's revels began. People stopped by the campsite and, after the exchange of greetings and blessings of Be'al, helped themselves to the food and drink. They had brought their own drinking cups and cut the venison with their own daggers and when Jilana made to serve them she was gently, but firmly, refused. Confused, she went to Caddaric and, after timidly pulling him away from a conversation, asked what she should do.

"There is nothing for you to do, save to converse with the guests," Caddaric explained. "In time we will leave and visit other camps; there we will be expected to wait upon ourselves, even as they do here."

Jilana started to protest that such behavior was improper for a slave, but Caddaric had already rejoined his friends. Shrugging, she wandered around and greeted the strangers who made themselves at home in the camp. Soon she was caught up in the celebration and forgot her status, as did those around her. High spirits and laughter reigned; wine and the fermented mead flowed freely and the bards told stories of great battles and sang of the glory of Albion and her people.

Jilana poured wine for herself, sipped it, and then cut the wine with water until it was the proper consistency. She saw Heall standing apart from the rest and went to him. "This must be difficult for you, Heall. I am sorry."

Heall shook his shaggy head. "The sadness I feel is only because Artair did not live to see the old ways publicly celebrated, but I do not mourn him any longer. Annwn, so the priests tell us, is a happy place. If I close my eyes, I can hear his laughter."

Jilana smiled and squeezed his arm. "You have Clywd and Caddaric."

"Aye." Heall nodded. "Neither is of my blood, but they are still my family." He draped an arm around Jilana's shoulders. "And there is you, my little friend. You help the heartache."

Jilana dropped a kiss upon his bearded cheek. "Come, Heall, you must be thirsty," she teased affectionately. "Let us get you a cup of mead."

Shortly thereafter, Caddaric came to claim Jilana and, together with Heall, they took their turn at going from camp to camp. Wherever they went, Jilana was warmly greeted, although some admonishing looks were directed at Caddaric. They ate, drank and talked until Jilana's head was fairly spinning. Even Caddaric unbent far enough to join in the dancing at one of the camps and Jilana stood back to watch Caddaric and Heall complete the dance. For such large men, they were incredibly graceful, Jilana thought as she sipped at her wine. No sooner had the thought crossed her mind than Caddaric stumbled and only the firm grip Heall had on his belt kept him from sprawling full-length upon the ground.

Jilana giggled, swung around to refill her cup, and found Lhwyd standing not two feet behind her. Her automatic reaction was fear, but Caddaric's words of earlier this evening—and perhaps the wine that was working its way through her system—calmed her.

Nodding, Jilana greeted the Druid politely. "The blessings of Beltane upon you, Lhwyd."

Lhwyd's mouth curled into a smirk. "And to you, slave."

Jilana paled at the verbal slap, but she was determined not to ruin the peace of this celebration. She would have walked away, but Lhwyd was suddenly right in front of her, blocking her escape.

"Make no mistake, slave, I will have you. Caddaric cannot protect you forever and I am a patient man." Lhwyd would have said more, but a glance over Jilana's head stopped him. "Another time, slave, when your guard dog has no further use for you."

Caddaric did not need to ask what had transpired between the two. When he had seen Lhwyd talking to Jilana, he knew the Druid was baiting her. He was not quick enough to catch the Druid, but that was just as well. In his present mood, Caddaric was tempted to do Lhwyd bodily harm.

"Caddaric, nay," Jilana implored when she turned and saw the violence on his face. "'Tis Beltane."

The fingers of his right hand flexed, as if curling around the hilt of his sword, but Caddaric finally nodded in agreement. He took Jilana's arm and they continued their rounds, but their manner was much subdued.

The celebration wore on and, amidst the high spirits of the others, Jilana was able to push all thoughts of Lhwyd away. Caddaric's attitude toward her helped. He was attentive, if not talkative, spending most of his time at her side. Acquaintances from his village were introduced to Jilana and she found herself firmly drawn into the Iceni community. It was impossible not to laugh at the jokes and broadly exaggerated stories of courage, and the smallest smile was encouragement enough to set off another round of tales or another song from the bards. The songs were beautiful, sometimes eerie things which ran the gamut from the love between a man and woman to the feats of the mystical heroes of Albion. The words swept Jilana into a world long past where she witnessed the glory of the tribes of Albion. When the songs ended and she returned to the present, she sadly acknowledged the injustice that Rome had committed against the Celts. And she—and other civilians—were no less guilty than the legions, for they had continued the work of the soldiers in a far more subtle manner.

By the time the three made their way back to their own camp, Jilana was pleasantly exhausted. A few revelers still remained, grouped about the campfire, and Heall went to them, but Caddaric drew Jilana toward the wagon.

"You are weary, I know, but there is one last task I would do before you retire."

Jilana blinked away her drowsiness and looked at Caddaric. "Aye, lord."

Caddaric took a hammer and iron chisel from the wagon and turned to Jilana. "'Tis my Beltane gift to you. Lift the hem of your gown." When she hesitantly did as he asked, Caddaric went down on one knee and placed the chisel against the lock of her leg iron. One blow of the hammer shattered the lock. Caddaric repeated the process on the other ankle, then spread the manacles and took them from Jilana's ankles.

Jilana stared at him in disbelief. "Am I free then?"

"Nay." Caddaric shook his head as he put the manacles and tools back into the wagon. "Only the Queen can grant you freedom."

"Then, why?" When he did not answer, Jilana took hold of his sleeve and tugged gently to gain his attention. "Why, lord?"

Caddaric faced Jilana, but could not meet her gaze. "Because I wish it," he replied gruffly.

His answer was puzzling, but Jilana did not press further. Whatever his reasons, she was grateful for the small freedom. She smiled and touched his hand. "Thank you, Caddaric."

"This changes nothing," Caddaric felt compelled to remind her. "You are still mine."

More so than you can know, Jilana thought, but she merely nodded. "That does not alter my thanks, Caddaric. You cannot know how wonderful it feels to be free of those chains."

With that she turned and made her way to the tent, her step light. Caddaric watched her go, torn between happiness and despair.

Chapter 8

BOADICEA TURNED HER ARMY to the southwest, toward
Londinium. Most of the countryside was deserted, its
loyal inhabitants having fled either to the safety of Roman fortified cities or legion outposts. Those who remained added their number to Boadicea's war band. As
Caddaric had predicted, the farms—and in some cases,
entire villages—were put to the torch. If the missing owners were known to be sympathetic to Rome, the Celtic
force burned the buildings by way of a lesson in loyalty.
In some cases, the farms had already been razed and the
animals slaughtered by those loyal to the Empire, in order to deny Boadicea's army supplies. Few crops had been
planted, and those that had showed signs of abandonment as weeds overran the soil. Jilana saw the way Caddaric's face hardened at the sight of such destruction, and
later she heard him tell Clywd and Heall that the coming
winter would be a lean one with so little grain available.
The next day, Caddaric began a strict rationing of their
grain.

The war band moved slowly, covering a scant ten miles
a day. The vanguard usually stopped to make camp at
mid-afternoon, but the rear of the column did not arrive
until nightfall. When the entire force was camped, it
blanketed an area of two square miles. Progress was made
at a snail's pace. It soon became obvious, even to Jilana,
that the column was unwieldy and far too slow, but the

Celts refused to abandon their wagons piled high with household goods. Neither would they agree to send the women back home with the wagons and children. So they plodded on, inching their way across Albion.

Meanwhile, Suetonius Paulinus, encamped on Mona, received word of the uprising. Leaving part of his forces to complete the Romanization of Mona—when the legion left the island, no evidence would be left to suggest it had once been a Druid stronghold—Paulinus took the cavalry alae of the Fourteenth Gemina and Twentieth Valeria legions and turned them toward Londinium. The Twentieth's marching camp at Deva was sixty miles from Mona. Paulinus and his alae covered the distance in two days, and attached five infantry cohorts, of one thousand each. Deva was left with only a token force for defense, and the governor-general prayed to his gods that the detachment on Mona would return before the rebellious western tribes could take advantage of the fact. To Paulinus, it was a calculated gamble: Boadicea and her allies posed a greater threat than the unorganized western tribes. Paulinus swung his legion southeast and sent an order to Poenius Postumus, camp-prefect of the Second Augusta's Fortress at Glevum, to strip the fortress down to a skeleton force and march. They would meet at Verulamium, one hundred and sixty miles southeast of Deva. Paulinus drove his men mercilessly; those who could not keep pace were left where they had fallen and their horses, if they were cavalry and their mounts were still useful, confiscated. With luck, they would make it back to Deva before the bands of rebels scattered through the western mountains found them.

Once out of the mountains, Paulinus set a killing pace. Men and horses alike dropped from exhaustion, but the governor-general was a man possessed. He had stripped the east of its defenses for his expedition and thus it was easy prey for Boadicea. If Britannia fell, Caesar would have Paulinus' head on a platter.

The reported size of Boadicea's army worried Paulinus briefly, until he decided the numbers had been vastly exaggerated by terrified civilians. He sent scouts ahead and comforted himself with the thought that the Second Legion would bolster his own number by nearly six thousand. More than enough to defeat a rag-tag band of rebels. Thus, the reply from Glevum sent Paulinus into a rage. Poenius Postumus had received word of the uprising and decided that his superior's daring plan was also quite mad. His legion would be best utilized in keeping the west secure in order to serve as a base for the counter-offensive which would be launched when Paulinus failed. It took three men to restrain the fifty-year-old general when he read the mutinous reply. Postumus would, Paulinus vowed in his rage, be executed for his seditious act. In fact, Paulinus would see him crucified in the same manner in which Pilate had dealt with that Jewish upstart sixty years earlier. Paulinus contented himself with visions of the slow, torturous death in store for the camp-prefect and plans for the dissolution of the Augusta. No legion that had mutinied was allowed to remain together. Elements of it would be transferred to other legions in exchange for fresh troops, the officers either transferred away from their command—if they were found innocent of culpability in the crime—or executed—if their guilt was evident. If the mutiny had extended into the enlisted ranks, examples would be made of a *decade*—a unit of ten men—from randomly chosen *centuriae*.

Paulinus pushed his men to the brink of exhaustion and beyond but when one hundred miles had been covered, he was forced to slow his pace. His command had covered the distance in four days; only sixty miles remained between them and Londinium, but the forced march had taken its toll. Men and animals could no longer sustain the grueling pace. Paulinus ordered a half day of rest and for the first time since leaving Mona, campfires were lit and the men erected their leather tents for a full night's sleep. Londinium was another three days' march away.

THE ICENI MARCH to Londinium was far different for Jilana than the previous leg of the journey. Free of her chains, she would have gladly walked the distance, but Caddaric would not allow it. Instead, she rode in the wagon beside Heall, jumping out occasionally when she needed to relieve herself or when her muscles became cramped from the enforced inactivity. Caddaric was in the vanguard of warriors, but he rode back during the day to see how they fared. Of Clywd there was little sign during the day, although he always managed to turn up beside the wagon when they were about to make camp. Clywd, Jilana later learned, roamed about the war band, treating the sick and injured, and making his presence known. A few days later, when Ede had had her fill of driving the second wagon, Clywd took up the reins. Children descended upon the Druid's wagon and he kept them enthralled with stories and songs.

Two days into the march, Heall taught Jilana to drive the team. By the time they made camp that night, her hands were swollen and blistered and her arms ached, but nothing could erase the grin from her face as she helped unhitch and tether the team. Caddaric said nothing about her accomplishment, but that night he carried the water to the fire for her and later, when they were alone in their tent, he applied balm to the palms of her hands. They were back to sharing a pallet, Caddaric having said, rightly, that there were not enough furs for two. Still, Jilana was uneasy with the enforced intimacy, but the look on Caddaric's face had stilled any protest she might have made. Now, Jilana sat nervously on the edge of the pallet while Caddaric knelt on one knee in front of her.

"You will have calluses," Caddaric stated as he wrapped her hands.

Jilana studied the top of his bent head. "It does not matter."

Caddaric stroked his fingers down one bandaged palm. "Your hands were beautiful at Venta Icenorum," he said thoughtfully, almost to himself. "So soft and lovely."

The touch of his hand sent a flood of warmth up her arm and Jilana snatched her hand away. "But now I can drive a wagon," she reminded him briskly. "'Tis much more useful than having pretty hands."

Caddaric stared at her for a long moment, his eyes clouded, and then he nodded curtly. "As you say."

He blew out the lamp and Jilana hurriedly crawled to her side of the pallet so that Caddaric could get under the blanket. Earlier, she had changed into the tunic Caddaric had given her as a nightdress and now she turned onto her side, away from Caddaric, and listened to the sounds he made as he prepared for bed. She felt his weight on the pallet, the movement of the blanket as he tugged it around his shoulders, the warmth of his body. The nights were still cool and his heat was a temptation to Jilana. She burrowed into the furs, waited, and heard his breathing change into the rhythm of sleep. Cautiously, she rolled onto her back and then her side. Her nose grazed his shoulder. Catching her lip between her teeth, Jilana eased herself closer, until she was pressed comfortably along his warm length. Exhaling a soft sigh, Jilana closed her eyes and drifted into sleep.

Beside her, Caddaric smiled into the dark and rested his cheek against the top of her head.

Jilana awoke the following morning to the feeling of something heavy across her stomach. She stirred, seeking to dislodge the weight, but when it refused to move she opened her eyes. She was laying on her right side with the back of the tent directly in front of her. She bent her head to look down at her stomach and came fully awake. A hard, brown arm was draped around her waist, as if anchoring her to the pallet, and against her back was an equally firm cushion. And not only her back, she realized with a hot blush, but against her buttocks and legs as well. Caddaric. She was curled into him and he around her and she could feel . . .

"'Tis dawn." The soft pronouncement stirred against her ear and Jilana shut her eyes on a wave of embarrassment. Caddaric watched the color fade from her cheeks and surge back a moment later when he moved against her. "Have you no greeting for me, wicca?"

Jilana swallowed hard and found her voice. "Greetings, Caddaric." No sooner had the words left her lips than she was being turned onto her back.

"Open your eyes," Caddaric ordered gently. He waited patiently until she obeyed, and when she looked at him, his expression softened. "Greetings, Jilana." He touched his lips to hers, lingered a moment, and then withdrew. Jilana's eyes widened at the contact and one hand crept up to touch his cheek. Encouraged, Caddaric dipped his head and found her mouth again. This time her lips softened under the pressure of his and when his tongue traced the line where her lips met, they parted for him. With a low growl he plunged into her mouth and sought her tongue.

Forgetting her previous embarrassment, Jilana gave herself up to the kiss. Her arms wrapped themselves around Caddaric's neck, pulling him down, and her tongue measured the length of his. She wanted his heaviness, welcomed it, and tried to tell him so. All that she managed was a choked little moan, but it was enough. The kiss went wild and Caddaric's hands were beneath her shoulder blades, lifting her, crushing her breasts into the hard wall of his chest while his mouth worked feverishly on hers. When Jilana sensed some of Caddaric's control returning, she dug her fingers into his neck and teased his mouth with the tip of her tongue. The kiss exploded again and this time Jilana explored the damp interior of Caddaric's mouth until she was drunk with the taste of him.

Their lips parted gradually and the tent was filled with the sound of their labored breathing. Caddaric laid his head beside Jilana's and waited for the ache in his loins to abate. His body was on fire and the rise and fall of her breasts beneath his chest was both pleasure and torment.

He opened his eyes and saw the tear that trailed forlornly down Jilana's cheek. Wonderingly, Caddaric caught it on his forefinger and then raised himself up on one elbow to look into her face. "Did I hurt you, wicca?" When she shook her head, he ran his finger along her jaw until she opened her eyes. "Then why are you crying?"

How could she explain? Jilana wondered miserably. In a cracked voice, she asked, "What am I to you, Caddaric?"

Caddaric's brows came together in a frown and he sat up. "What do you mean?"

"What am I?" Jilana insisted.

"You are mine," Caddaric growled, uncomfortable with the question and his own unsatisfied body. "Have I not said it often enough?"

"Exactly," Jilana replied. "I am yours—your slave, to do with as you will. I will not be a convenient body for you."

"Convenient?" Caddaric echoed, and though he tried not to allow it, his temper flared. "Convenient, by the gods! Woman, you are many things, but I would not call you *convenient*!" He sprang from the bed and began dressing, jerking on his clothes with such violence that Jilana was certain the seams would rip. "If I wanted a body upon which to slake my desire, there are many in camp that would serve the purpose. And gladly! They would not cry after a simple kiss!"

"I was not crying about the kiss!" Jilana raged.

"Then why?" Caddaric bellowed. "Have I not made amends for the way I treated you? Do you want for anything?"

"Aye, you have made amends, but that does not change the fact that I am still a *slave*," Jilana exclaimed. When Caddaric flipped back the tent flap she cried, "I have no control over my own life."

Caddaric hesitated and then, slowly turned back to her. "I have told you before, I cannot free you," he said ominously.

"I know."

"Then what are you seeking?"

The knowledge that I am more than a slave to you, she answered silently, but she could not say the words aloud.

"My touch does not displease you," Caddaric stated with absolute certainty, "so you must be shamed by the fact that I am no Roman patrician, but a barbarian. A barbarian who can set fire to your passion.''

Jilana shook her head but said nothing, and a moment later Caddaric left the tent. Jilana rose and dressed, her heart aching. If Caddaric had said that he cared for her, she would have thrown herself into his arms and never let go. His kindness to her over the last few days was no comfort; indeed, the care Caddaric took with her only made the pain worse, because she knew his heart was not involved.

During the next two days barely a word passed between Caddaric and Jilana. Jilana was proficient enough with the team that Heall took to his horse to ride with the vanguard, and now Caddaric did not check on her progress during the day. Only when he had found a campsite did Caddaric return to the wagon. At night, they slept as far away from each other as the pallet allowed.

The next morning they packed the camp and, after laying out the harness, Jilana led the horses to the wagon. The space to the back of their camp had been occupied by Heall and Clywd, but the older men were already gone. Caddaric doused the fire while Jilana harnessed the team. When he was finished, he came around to the team and checked the buckles.

''Can you get the wagon onto the road by yourself, or would you like me to do it?'' Caddaric asked. It was, to him, an olive branch. He did not like the coldness that lay between them.

''I can manage,'' Jilana answered steadily. They drew the reins back to the wagon and Jilana climbed onto the seat. ''We are running low on water and Clywd said his barrels are nearly empty as well.''

Caddaric hid his disappointment in her answer by handing the reins to Jilana. ''I will look for a well or stream today.'' He met her eyes and momentarily lost himself in the violet depths. ''Wicca, about the other morning—''

"You should go," Jilana interrupted. She looked into the distance where she knew Boadicea had her camp. "The vanguard will be forming."

A muscle worked in Caddaric's cheek and he swung onto his horse without another word. Jilana watched him go with tears burning the back of her eyes. Could he not see what it cost her to keep the wall of indifference between them? If he would utter only one loving word, give her some sign that he saw her only as a woman, not as a possession bought and paid for—

"Greetings, Roman."

The melodious voice scattered her thoughts and Jilana looked down to find Lhwyd standing beside one of the horses. Jilana's hands tightened around the reins, but she managed a polite nod for the Druid. "Caddaric is not here," Jilana informed him, and immediately wished she had not.

Lhwyd smiled, but his eyes remained cold and hard, like polished gems. "I came to see Clywd." He glanced toward the remains of Clywd's fire. "But I see I am too late."

Knowing of the animosity between the two priests, Jilana doubted Lhwyd's words. "I will tell Clywd you were looking for him."

Lhwyd nodded, his cold gaze surveying her. "I see Caddaric removed your chains." His lips pursed thoughtfully. "I had heard rumors that he had done so, but I did not believe them." His hands moved to stroke the horse nearest him.

Jilana was snared by his gaze. She had only to snap the reins and the horses would move and take her to safety, but her hands lay unmoving in her lap.

"What did you promise Caddaric, I wonder? That you would not run again? Or that you would share his pallet?" Lhwyd smiled and something twisted deep inside Jilana at the sight. "But then, you have shared his bed since the beginning, have you not?"

The answer to Lhwyd's taunt trembled on the tip of Jilana's tongue, but before she could give voice to it, the

Druid looked away and the spell was broken. Jilana was left weak and trembling when Lhwyd bade her farewell and walked away. Around her, wagons moved out, but it took Jilana some time before she felt strong enough to handle the team. As the day progressed, Jilana put Lhwyd out of her mind and concentrated on driving the team and the countryside.

The land flanking the road had been cleared of trees, but a mile away the forest loomed again. It was a welcome sight, reminding her of home, and banishing the memory of the open lands just south of Camulodunum. At noon, Jilana took a piece of dried beef for her meal and wondered if Caddaric had remembered to take food with him for his own meal. Of course he had, she chided herself. Caddaric was a soldier first, with a soldier's eye toward what was necessary to sustain a body during a march. She took a sip of water from the skin and held it in her mouth, savoring it. Had Caddaric found a source of water for them? How pleasant it would be if there were a stream close by when they made camp for the night. Despite the chill in the night air, she would dearly love to submerge herself in a stream and wash away the grime of the march.

Shortly after noon Caddaric and Heall were successful in their search for a stream and rode back along the column to tell the others their news. They found Clywd's wagon first and spent a few minutes talking with him. They decided to leave the war band now to replenish their water rather than backtrack once they had made camp. Accordingly, Clywd pulled his wagon out of the column and eased it down the grade of the road while Heall followed. Caddaric swung back down the column to find Jilana.

Jilana saw Caddaric before he caught sight of her, and she felt free to gaze at him. Seated upon his golden stallion, he presented an imposing figure. He rode easily, with the air of control that was second nature to the Iceni, and even without the weapons that hung from his belt there would be no mistaking the fact that he was a warrior. Nor

was he the handsomest of men, Jilana thought as he rode
in her direction, but the hard planes of his face were
dearer to her than any other. He was strong and proud; he
could be fierce or gentle, and in that moment, Jilana knew
she would give her life to hear him say he loved her.

"We have found a stream," Caddaric announced
without preamble when he drew abreast of the wagon, "a
mile or so to the east. Clywd and Heall will meet us there.
Drive the wagon off the road and follow me."

He swung off the road before Jilana had a chance to
reply. Taking a firmer grip on the reins, she guided the
team to the edge of the road and approached the grade at
a cautious angle. Heall had warned her about taking the
grade straight on and though she had managed very well,
going down the incline always made her nervous. They
had almost reached the bottom when one of the reins went
slack in her hands. The horse on the right immediately felt
the easing of tension on the bit, panicked at the lack of
direction, and lunged forward. His teammate followed
suit and the wagon lost its gentle angle of descent and
plunged straight down.

The change bounced Jilana around on the seat and a
vision of being pitched forward, to land between the
horses' hooves and the wagon's wheels, swam before her
eyes. Jilana braced a foot against the low board in the
front of the wagon, prayed that the wagon would not
overturn, and gave the horses their head. The descent took
only a few seconds, but for Jilana, it seemed hours. When
the wagon was firmly on level ground, she pulled back on
the reins to bring the horses to a stop and found, to her
horror, that they were beyond her control. Once they were
free of the grade the horses broke into a trot and then a
gallop and no matter how she sawed at the reins they refused to slow. One of the wagon wheels hit a hole and Jilana flew into the air. For a terrifying moment, her only
attachment to earth was the death grip she kept on the
reins, and then she was slammed back onto the seat. The
wagon hit another hole and Jilana was thrown forward
only to be brought up short by the vertical board that

separated the driver from the horses. The wood caught her just below her ribs, knocking the air out of her lungs. Over the sound of the hoofbeats and her own pounding heart, Jilana thought she heard someone yelling. She slid to the floorboard, unable to breathe. Her last rational thought, before fear overrode all else, was that when the wagon tipped—as it surely must—it would create a terrible mess and Caddaric was going to be angry with her.

Caddaric had watched proudly as the wagon began its gentle descent. Jilana had learned a great deal in the past month and he thought that tonight he would tell her so. He found it hard to compliment her but, the gods knew, she deserved that much from him. When the wagon had veered and plunged straight down the grade, Caddaric had only stared at first, and then grown angry. She knew better than that! And then the wagon hit the level ground and Caddaric's heart stopped. The team was out of control— why or how, he did not care—and he caught a glimpse of Jilana's pale face as the wagon shot past him. For a stunned moment, he sat watching the team bolt for the trees and then he dug his heels into the sides of his stallion and raced after the wagon. He saw Jilana fly off the seat once, twice, and then disappear. Sheer terror swept through him and he yelled her name.

He drew even with the team and saw the bit dangling beside the horse's jaw. The treeline was approaching fast and Caddaric hoped he had enough time to do what had to be done before the team smashed the wagon into one of the trees. Keeping the reins of his horse in one hand, he bent low over the horse's neck and reached for the halter with his free hand. His fingers brushed the horse's jaw and the animal shied. The contact was lost. The stallion stretched out, increasing his pace and following the other's lead until he was even with the team once again. They moved closer. This time Caddaric grasped the bridle. The runaway tried to shy again, but Caddaric grimly hung on. From his peripheral vision, Caddaric could see the forest was dangerously close. He slowed his stallion and hauled on the bridle with all his might. The team slowed—fractionally, but it slowed—and he pulled again. He could feel the strain in his arm, the burning heat as his muscles were worked past their endurance. *Jilana,* he thought and strength flowed back into his arm as he hauled against the bridle. It was not going to be enough, because the other horse was still running flat out.

Caddaric filled his lungs with air and bellowed, *"Ji-lana!* Stop the team! Do you hear me, woman? *Pull on the reins!"*

Jilana heard and struggled to obey. She could barely breathe and the wagon tossed her about like so much flotsam in a heavy sea, but she managed to get to her knees. Dust swirled around, nearly blinding her, but she did not need to see. She drew back on the remaining reins with all her strength and tried to yell "Whoa," but all that emerged was a strangled croak. She could just see Caddaric, leaning so far out of the saddle that she was sure he would fall at any moment, and pulled even harder.

And then, miraculously, it was over. One moment the team was charging recklessly toward the forest and the next they had settled into a trot, then a sedate walk and then, blessedly, they had stopped altogether. Jilana slumped back against the seat and began to cry quietly, the reins still wrapped around her hands.

Caddaric leaped from his horse and found that his legs were shaking. He ran to the wagon, tore the reins out of Jilana's hands, and dragged her to the ground. His legs turned to water and he slumped to the ground, his hands digging into Jilana's shoulders. "Are you hurt?" he demanded harshly. When she buried her face in her hands and shook her head in answer, he shook her, hard. "By all the gods, woman, what possessed you to take the grade that way? Have you no sense at all?" He shook her even harder when he remembered his own fear and his voice rose until he was yelling. "If you cannot drive the wagon, I will call Heall back or I will do it myself!"

"'Twas n-not my f-fault," Jilana tried to say between her own sobs and the punishment he was inflicting.

"You were the driver," Caddaric yelled with such force that she tried to shrink away. "You would have crashed into the trees. The horses would have been killed—"

"'Tis all you care about, your precious horses," Jilana sobbed, shaking with the aftermath of fear, but angry now as well. "No d-doubt you would have kicked my b-b-body aside and c-cursed me for the lost of sup-p-plies and the w-wa-wagon!"

Abruptly Caddaric wrapped his arms around her shoulders and gathered her against his chest. Cursing, he crushed Jilana against him, one hand destroying what was left of her braid as he cupped the back of her head and pushed her against his shoulder. "You could have been killed," he muttered into her hair. "Gods, how could I have borne losing you?" The thought frightened him more than the runaway team. He had dragged his red-haired witch kicking and screaming into his life and now, inexplicably, he discovered she was firmly embedded in his heart as well. How had he allowed such a thing to happen?

Jilana cried brokenly into his tunic, beyond caring if he saw her weakness and her tears. This new life was alternately fascinating and terrifying and she knew now that she would never be as strong as Ede or Guendolen. No doubt they would laugh at her inability to handle the team, her stupidity in dropping one of the reins. Her sobs died as that last thought struck home. She had not dropped the rein; one had gone slack in her hand! "Caddaric?" She tried to push away from him, but he held her in place and continued to stroke her hair. "Caddaric," she said more forcefully and pushed at his chest.

"Hush, Jilana; 'tis over now," Caddaric murmured.

Dense man! Jilana hit him in the shoulder with her fist to get his attention. Surprised, he relaxed his hold and she was able to pull back far enough to look up into his face. "Caddaric, the rein broke."

He frowned at her, as if he did not understand. "What?"

"The rein broke," Jilana repeated patiently, "when the wagon was coming down the grade."

"Impossible. I checked the harness myself only last night." Caddaric pulled her back into his arms. "You are frightened and imagining things."

This time Jilana hit him harder and struggled out of his arms. "I may be frightened, but I have not lost my wits!" She meant to run to the wagon to show him her evidence, but her legs were so weak that she managed no more than a stagger. "Here." She fished the broken rein out of the tangle on the floorboards and triumphantly held it aloft. "You see? 'Tis not my imagination."

Caddaric followed slowly and took the rein from Jilana. He turned it over and over in his hands, examining it from every possible angle. Without a word he went to the team—standing quietly now, exhausted from their flight—and examined the length of rein which dangled from the useless bit. His first suspicion, that he had caused Jilana's accident by missing a crack in the leather, gave way to a second, more alarming one. The ends of the rein were not cracked and discolored as they would have been had the leather broken from wear, but were neat and several shades lighter than the outside of the leather. An invisible hand tightened around Caddaric's heart and the bile rose in his throat. The rein had been intentionally cut. He would stake his life on it. But 'twas *Jilana*'s life which had been placed in jeopardy.

The look on his face frightened Jilana. "What is it?" she whispered, moving next to Caddaric to look at the two parts of the rein.

Caddaric remained quiet for a moment and then shook his head. "Naught. I missed a crack in the leather." He squeezed her shoulder reassuringly and drew her back to the wagon. "I will fix the rein and then we will go to the stream." He lifted Jilana onto the wagon seat and she stayed there while he took tools and a length of leather from the wagon and replaced the rein. When he was finished, Caddaric tied his horse to the wagon and swung onto the seat beside Jilana.

"I can drive," Jilana protested, stung by his obvious lack of trust.

"Tomorrow," Caddaric assured her and clucked to the horses.

Heall and Clywd were curious about the delay and, within Jilana's hearing, he described the accident as "a small mishap." Taking clean clothing from her kist, Jilana bathed upstream, where the low limbs of a tree granted her some small privacy. She could hear the men talking as they filled the water barrels and then splashed noisily into the stream. Shivering, she washed her hair in cold water and scrubbed at her skin until it reddened. Cold or not, she knew this was one of the rare chances she would have on the march to be truly clean and she was determined to make the most of it. It was just as Jilana decided her nails had taken on a distinctly blue tinge and she should get out of the stream that she felt eyes upon her. Slowly, shaking with more than just the cold, she returned and faced the bank. Caddaric sat beneath the limbs, watching her, his sword on the grass beside his leg.

Instinctively, Jilana crossed her arms over her breasts and sat down in the water. "How long have you been there?" Her tone lacked the indignation she felt because her teeth were chattering.

"Since you stepped into the water," Caddaric replied easily. "You should come out before you freeze."

Jilana clenched her teeth together and shook her head.

"Jilana," Caddaric sighed, exasperated. "I have seen you naked before. You are being foolish."

Despite the chill, Jilana's face warmed at the memory. "Will you turn your back?"

Caddaric gave a short bark of laughter. "Nay, but I will close my eyes."

When he had done so, Jilana scrambled from the water and snatched up the piece of blanket she had brought for a towel.

"Gods!"

The single word was a low hiss of air and Jilana swung back to catch Caddaric looking at her. "You promised!"

Caddaric's face was drawn as he rose and came toward her. Jilana wanted to back away, but the stream was directly behind her. There was no place to flee. "Caddaric, please, I do not want—"

But Jilana's fear was misplaced. Caddaric drew the towel away from her, but only to examine her body. Looking down, she saw what held his attention. There was a faint bruise on her hip and another, longer one on her thigh. When he touched them she winced. Beneath her breasts was a large, angry welt where the board had caught her. When Caddaric touched it, she caught her breath and flinched away.

"Nay, wicca, I will not hurt you." Tenderly, Caddaric wrapped her in the blanket and dried her. Then he helped her into her gown and led her back to Heall and Clywd. From his kist, Caddaric removed his cloak, draped it around Jilana's shoulders and led her to the small fire that had been built. "Stay here and warm up."

"But there are clothes to be washed—"

"I will do it." The look on Caddaric's face brooked no further protest.

Jilana huddled in his cloak by the fire while Caddaric bathed and washed their clothing. When he was finished they secured the wagons, put out the fire and headed back to the column—Heall and Clywd in one wagon, she and Caddaric in the other. They regained the road without difficulty and Jilana turned to Caddaric. "Will you not rejoin the vanguard?"

Caddaric shook his head. "We will make camp soon. I will stay here."

Jilana nodded and turned her eyes forward. By the time the wagon was turned back off the road for the night and she crawled down from the seat, Jilana found she was stiff and sore. She set her teeth and helped prepare the camp. She had proved today how incompetent she was; she would not compound the error by complaining. She made the meal from their rationed grain and roasted the last of the fresh meat. To the men she served large portions of each and took the remainder for herself—as she had done since seeing the concern in Caddaric's eyes when he had strictly apportioned the grain. They were larger than she and thus needed more food, Jilana reasoned, and they would need to fight at the end of the march; she would not.

"Is that all you are eating?" Caddaric asked sharply when he saw her plate.

Jilana met his gaze without wavering. "I am not very hungry." He frowned but said nothing more, and Jilana concentrated on eating the venison without choking. When the meal was finished, she cleaned their dishes and then sat by the fire beside Caddaric while the men talked. Her eyelids grew heavy and her head nodded. The next thing she knew, Caddaric was lifting her into his arms. She looked at him drowsily.

"'Tis time you were abed," Caddaric murmured as he carried her into the tent. He undressed her as if she were a child and slid her between the blankets on their pallet. "Sleep now, you are going to be sore tomorrow and will need your strength for the march."

She was sore now, but there seemed no point in telling him that. "Are you coming to bed?"

"Soon." Caddaric smoothed the hair away from her face and tucked the blankets around her shoulders. "I must smoor the fire and see to the horses one last time."

Jilana nodded and closed her eyes. She heard Caddaric leave, heard him talking to the others and then she was asleep.

"No accident," Clywd agreed when Caddaric had told them the whole story about the runaway. He took the piece of rein Heall offered him and wrapped it around his hand.

"Nay 'twas not an accident." Caddaric poured mead for the three of them and handed a cup to each.

"But who?" Heall wanted to know. He took a mouthful of mead and savored it before continuing. "Who would want to kill Jilana? The people from our village have come to accept her as one of us."

Caddaric shook his head. "It could have been anyone. You know how the camp is. People move about at all hours without arousing suspicion."

"The cut would have been noticed when the horses were harnessed," Heall pointed out.

"Mayhap." Caddaric shrugged. "Jilana is not experienced enough to notice a small cut in the rein. I inspected the harness last night, however; there were no breaks or cracks or cuts then. Nor did I see any when I checked Jilana's work this morning."

"Let us assume that the harness was intact when it was put on the horses this morning," Clywd put in. "What does that mean?" The two men looked at him in confusion. "It means," he clarified, "that the rein was cut once the horses were harnessed." He looked at his son. "Did you escort the wagon to the road?"

"Nay," Caddaric answered. "Jilana was in the wagon, ready to drive to the road when I left to join the vanguard."

Heall nodded thoughtfully. "Then someone was by the horses after you left but before Jilana joined the column."

"But who?" Caddaric asked again. "The only one I know who would want to harm Jilana is Lhwyd, but this is hardly his way. He wants her as a sacrifice for his goddess." He swung his gaze to his father. Clywd sat with his eyes closed, his fingers running the length of the rein. "Well, wise one? Is your precious gift of any use to us?"

Clywd's eyes opened, but he seemed unaware of the taunt. "There is naught." His voice was so frail that Caddaric reached for him. "Naught," Clywd repeated hollowly.

The look in Clywd's blue eyes stopped the sarcastic comment Caddaric had been about to make. "Father?"

Clywd blinked and looked about him, as if awaking from a deep sleep. With a convulsive movement, he hurled the rein into the fire. Without speaking, the Druid rose and disappeared into the night. Clywd struggled with the dread which assailed him. He had not lied to Heall and

Caddaric; when he held the rein, he saw nothing. 'Twas like stepping into an emptiness where nothing existed, save for an invisible presence of overwhelming evil. Cold sweat covered Clywd's body and only when he was deep within the womb of the forest did he become calm once again. Pausing, he gathered kindling and brought forth the battered copper bowl and the herb pouch.

"What is amiss?" he muttered to himself as he set about building a small fire. "I should have seen something...*someone*. I always have in the past, why not now? What is different this time?" He measured herbs into the bowl and nestled it into the side of the fire. "Be'al, help me," he intoned. "The girl is in danger, but from what quarter?" Sparks of white light appeared in the bowl and Clywd studied them while they danced around the metal and changed color. "Be'al, I implore you, help me! There is evil around the girl, around all of us. How can I fight it if you do not help me?"

This evil will not take her life, my child.

Clywd closed his eyes and let the peace wash through him. "But the danger—"

She will not die at its hands. Be content with this.

Clywd swallowed at the warning, but was compelled to press further. "Will you not show me from whence the danger comes, Father?"

So that you might shed another of my creature's blood?

"Nay, I would not."

There is another who would, and I cannot permit that. The evil will not take her, faithful one. Ask no more.

When Clywd opened his eyes, the copper bowl was empty. Using a twig, he removed the bowl from the fire. He wrapped himself in his cloak, curled up on the ground and watched the fire die. Shortly before dawn, Clywd rose, scattered the dead ashes, and returned to camp.

Heall was awake as well and together they added wood to the campfire and made the morning meal. By the time Caddaric and Jilana rose, the two men had packed away much of the camp and the meal was ready.

They ate in silence, although Jilana did not notice anything unusual. She was so stiff and sore that it was agony to move. Caddaric and Heall struck the tent but when Caddaric made to harness the team, she made a token protest.

"I will drive today," Caddaric interrupted and she said nothing more.

Nor did Heall ride with the vanguard. He and Clywd shared the second wagon.

"Go into the back and rest," Caddaric said an hour into the march when he saw Jilana wince.

Jilana was too miserable to argue. She crawled over the seat and settled herself as comfortably as she could. I will never sleep, she thought, but the next moment she did. Caddaric glanced back at her from time to time, and when he did, his face softened. While he stared at the wagon in front of him, he wondered how he could protect Jilana every minute of every day. When Jilana woke, shortly before noon, Caddaric helped her climb back onto the seat. From beneath the seat she took the leather bag containing their meal and a skin of water.

"I can drive while you eat," Jilana suggested softly.

Caddaric glanced at her. "Do you feel up to handling the team?"

Jilana nodded and smiled slightly when Caddaric handed her the reins.

Caddaric took an oat cake from the bag and chewed it thoughtfully. "How do you feel?"

"Sore," Jilana replied with a wry face. She peeked at him from the corner of her eye. "Thank you, Caddaric."

"For what?"

"For saving my life," Jilana snapped. "It may not mean much to you, but it does to me!"

Caddaric choked on the oat cake and had to take a healthy swallow from the skin before he could speak. "Why are you angry?"

"I am not angry," Jilana hissed, her eyes throwing sparks at him.

"Yes, you are," Caddaric argued. He eyed her curiously. "Are you going to throw something at me again?" Jilana ground her teeth together and stared at the road ahead. He ate another oat cake and a piece of dried meat before speaking. "I will keep you safe, Jilana. Why do you not believe me?"

Jilana lifted her shoulders, not deigning to look at him. At last she said, in a small voice, "I have never been this far from home before. All of this is strange to me."

Caddaric lightly touched her arm. "Are you frightened, wicca?"

"Aye," Jilana admitted. "Had your Queen not rebelled, I would have seen all this with Lucius, when we traveled to Londinium to take ship to Rome."

Caddaric ran a finger up and down her arm. "Do you think of him often?"

Jilana looked at him in surprise. "Lucius?" Caddaric nodded and Jilana said, "Nay, I have not thought of him in weeks."

"And your family?"

Jilana sighed. "I think of them sometimes, when I wake at night and forget where I am."

"And who you are with," Caddaric added gruffly.

The violet eyes softened and Jilana smiled slightly. "I never forget who I am with, Caddaric."

The corners of Caddaric's mouth lifted fractionally. "I wish we could have met earlier, wicca, before the rebellion."

He said it so softly that for a moment Jilana thought she imagined the sentiment that so echoed her own. He took the reins from her hands and she stared at him for a long time before she took an oat cake from the bag and nibbled at it. At last she asked, "How long before we reach Londinium?"

"Five days at least, at the rate this column travels," Caddaric answered with a trace of disgust. "The legions will make better time."

Jilana's mouth went dry. "They will come for Boadicea then?"

"Aye, they will come." Caddaric's hands tightened on the reins. "Paulinus will not flee from Albion like a dog."

"Can Boadicea win?"

"Mayhap, but it will not be an easy victory."

But his voice lacked assurance and Jilana wondered why.

That night, as they sat around the fire after the evening meal, Ede and Ewan came to their camp. Their news shocked Jilana.

"We would like you to marry us," Ede told Clywd when the pleasantries had been exchanged.

Apparently the others were as shocked as she, for it took some time before the men stood to grasp Ewan's forearm and congratulate him.

"Are you sure?" Clywd asked the couple when the commotion had subsided. "Your brother would undoubtedly want this honor."

"No doubt," Ede said, a trifle coldly. "But these days he has no time for anything save the Morrigan and those who are equally dedicated to her." She gave them all a brilliant smile as she pushed thoughts of Lhwyd away. "I want our marriage to be a joyful occasion."

"This calls for a celebration," Caddaric announced. He went to the wagon and lifted up a small cask of wine he had been saving.

"You need not sound so relieved," Ede chided and everyone laughed, even Ewan, who gave his betrothed adoring looks throughout the evening.

Jilana sat with them, listening to the plans for the marriage. The wedding would take place in three days, leaving enough time for all the people of their village to be told.

"There will be some discrepancies, of course," Clywd mused when the wine was nearly gone. "No white oxen to pull the chariot." He fixed Ede with a bleary, accusing, stare. "And there has been no feast."

Ede looked embarrassed and Ewan shifted uncomfortably upon the ground. "Surely, wise one, given the circumstances..." Ewan's voice trailed off when Clywd's gaze fixed on him.

"Some things," Clywd pronounced solemnly, "must be done correctly, or not at all."

At that, a belligerent expression settled on Ewan's normally placid features. A Druid's word was law and Clywd was intimating that the marriage might not take place.

"What feast?" Jilana asked innocently and nearly dropped her wine when five pairs of eyes swung in her direction.

"The woman's family gives a feast for all the young people in the village. When everyone is present, the woman chooses the man to become her husband by offering water to him so that he might wash his hands."

"Oh." Jilana thought about that for a moment. "And this is what bothers you, Clywd, that Ede has not offered Ewan a bowl of water before witnesses?" When Clywd nodded gravely, Jilana said, "With the shortage of supplies, a great feast is impossible, but we can observe the form nonetheless." She rose and, motioning for Ede to join her, made her way to the wagon.

"What are you doing?" Ede asked when Jilana climbed into the wagon, hunted through the supplies until she found what she wanted, and then dragged a copper bowl from its resting place.

"Satisfying Clywd's need for tradition." Jilana handed the bowl to Ede and climbed off the wagon. "Fill it with water." She grinned at Ede and after a moment the other woman returned the look. She left Ede to the task and, keeping her right hand behind her back, returned to the fire.

"Clywd, do you agree that we cannot have a feast?" Jilana questioned the priest.

"Aye, I do."

"And would you agree that, next to Lhwyd, you and Heall and Caddaric are the closest thing Ede has to a family?" Clywd nodded and Jilana brought her hand from behind her back. In her hand was a cloth which she carefully unwrapped to reveal a small wedge of cheese. "Caddaric, may I have your dagger?"

Had the wine not affected him, Caddaric would have protested such usage of a fine weapon, but the tone in Jilana's voice hinted that it would be to his advantage to do as she asked. He handed the dagger to Jilana without an argument.

Jilana carefully cut the cheese into six sections and gave one to each. "Now eat," she ordered, and popped the cheese into her mouth. The other five followed suit. Jilana sat down and nodded at Ede. Ede rose, picked up the bowl, and placed it in front of Ewan.

"I choose you," Ede said in a clear, sure voice. For a long moment her gaze locked with Ewan's and then he plunged his hands into the bowl. He washed his hands with more vigor than was necessary and when he was through, he grabbed Ede by the nape of her neck and pulled her across the bowl and onto his lap for—to Jilana's mind—a thoroughly indecent kiss.

Heall and Clywd exchanged smugly satisfied looks and Jilana ducked her head to hide her embarrassment. Beside her, Caddaric gave a noncommittal grunt and drank the rest of his wine. No doubt Ede had insisted upon marriage, Caddaric thought, although why Ewan seemed just as enthusiastic as his betrothed was puzzling. No man in possession of his senses would take on a wife now, in the middle of a war. He kept his thoughts to himself, however, and poured the last of the wine.

THE NEXT MORNING, Jilana awoke before Caddaric and she worked the soreness out of her muscles by adding wood to the fire and caring for the horses. She set the oatmeal porridge to cook over the fire and ventured back into their tent to wake Caddaric. Not an easy task, she decided as she bent over the pallet and shook him by the shoulder. The wine made Caddaric sleep like the dead and to add to her troubles, her hand kept slipping from his shoulder to the broad expanse of his chest. Not exactly slipping, Jilana admitted to herself. She liked the way the hair on his chest felt under her fingers and her hands ached to explore the soft hair and the hard flesh beneath it. Warmth suffused her body and Jilana pulled her hand away just as Caddaric's eyes slitted open.

"Morrow." Caddaric's voice was a hoarse croak and Jilana was unable to suppress a smile.

"Good morrow," Jilana replied, straightening. "The meal is nearly ready."

Caddaric groaned, sat up, and groaned again, both hands going to his head. "Are the others awake?" The words were muffled, since his hands covered his mouth.

"Not yet." The blanket had fallen to his waist and Jilana's eyes roamed avidly over the exposed flesh. "Shall I wake them?"

"Aye." Caddaric slowly got to his feet and the blanket dropped away.

He turned away from Jilana and she stared at the ridges which marred his back. "Caddaric," she breathed, "what happened to your back?"

Caddaric glanced over his shoulder at her, frowning because of the hammer behind his eyes. "My back?"

Instinctively, Jilana glided forward and touched the hard scars with her fingertips. The marks were old, but that did not lessen their impact upon her. 'Twas obvious that Caddaric had once been beaten, severely, and anger surged through Jilana. "Who did this to you?"

Caddaric moved away from her touch and drew on his tunic. "'Twas a long time ago, Jilana," he answered, as if that was the end of it.

"Who?"

Slowly, Caddaric pivoted so that he was facing Jilana. "When I first joined the legion, one of the *decurioi* was outraged that a Briton had been assigned to him as a replacement. When I did not follow one of his orders as quickly as he thought I should, he made an example of me."

Tears welled in Jilana's eyes at the thought of Caddaric being so mistreated, and she turned quickly away. "I will wake Heall and Clywd."

There was little conversation during the meal—the god Bacchus was having his revenge upon those who overindulged, and breaking the camp took more time than usual. Even gentle Clywd wore a pained expression and spoke more softly than was normal for him. Heall groaned whenever he moved too quickly, and as she loaded the wagon, Jilana could hear his low sounds of agony as he packed the second wagon. That day Jilana drove, and after a few minutes of swaying next to her in the seat, Caddaric mumbled something about checking their supplies and climbed back to the wagon bed. When she glanced over her shoulder later, Jilana found him asleep, with his head pillowed by the grain bags.

The next day, Caddaric took charge of the team. Jilana wanted to ask why he no longer rode with the vanguard, but she did not. She enjoyed riding next to him, even though they exchanged few words. And too, she was grateful for the free time, for she had offered to sew Ede's wedding gown when she saw the hopeless mess the warrior maid was making of it. Ede's talents, apparently, did not extend to sewing, although she had cut the material correctly. Thus, Jilana sewed on the gown while Caddaric drove the wagon.

"You need not labor so for Ede," Caddaric told Jilana the day of the wedding.

They were in the wagon and Jilana was finishing the hem of the gown. When that was done, she planned to add a design to the hem of the sleeves. Beneath her fingers, the bone needle flew through the material. She would have to hurry in order to embroider the sleeves by moonset. "I do not mind," Jilana protested, not looking up from her work. "Every woman should have a beautiful gown for her wedding."

Caddaric snorted. "Not so long ago, you and Ede could not bear the sight of one another."

"Things change," Jilana said philosophically. She glanced at Caddaric from the corner of her eyes. "Maybe you are jealous of Ewan."

Caddaric laughed shortly. "I have been too long among foreigners; I prefer my women more biddable than Ede."

Jilana knotted the thread and bit it off. From the notions Ede had given her, she took a twist of green thread and measured a length of it for the sleeves. "Lucius, too, liked biddable women. I hope you have better luck than he."

Caddaric considered that for a moment and then asked carefully, "Meaning you were not biddable?"

"I fear not." Intent upon her sewing, Jilana failed to notice the odd note in Caddaric's voice. "I was forever angering him with my actions." She sighed and shook her head. "Poor Lucius. He could never understand why I preferred riding my horse through the forest to riding in a litter to the market."

"But you would have married him?"

"Oh, yes," Jilana said dryly. "'Twas a good match; my father was well-pleased with it."

Caddaric shook his head in disbelief. "Did it never occur to you to challenge your father's dictates?"

Jilana stared at him. "To what end? I had not the freedom of your Iceni women, Caddaric. I could either remain in my father's house or marry, at his discretion. 'Tis the way of things."

"Did Lucius meet with your approval?"

"Aye." Jilana gave him a slight smile. "He was young, sound of body and mind, and not unpleasant to look upon. We would have had a satisfactory marriage."

"You make it sound like a dose of one of Clywd's medicines," Caddaric commented acidly. "Had you no thoughts of your own?"

"Of course I did," Jilana bristled. "I agreed to Lucius as my husband. 'Twas far better than journeying to Rome and allowing my father's father to choose a husband for me! I thought that Lucius—oh, what does it matter? You cannot possibly understand!" She bent back over her sewing, glaring at the material.

Caddaric watched her for a moment. "You are right—Lucius would not have found you biddable." He turned to the road, a hint of a smile softening his lips.

That afternoon, when the camp had been set up, Jilana gathered all her courage and told Caddaric he would have to stay with Heall and Clywd until the ceremony.

"Why?" Caddaric growled, rising from the fire he had just started.

"Because we need the tent, and the privacy."

"We?"

"Ede, Guendolen, three other village women and myself," Jilana replied, eyeing his fierce expression.

"Jilana, I am weary," Caddaric began to explain with what he thought was admirable patience. "I had hoped to wash and rest before the evening meal."

"You can do that in Heall's camp," Jilana pointed out.

"I planned to rest on *my* pallet," Caddaric clarified. "Not the ground or the wagon bed."

"Caddaric, have you no heart?" Jilana pleaded. "Ede and Ewan have already lost so much because of the war, they should have this one night, at least."

Caddaric eyed her suspiciously. "Have you given them our tent for their wedding night?"

"Of course not," Jilana exclaimed. "But I promised Ede a warm bath and the privacy in which to dress."

"You promised? Without asking me?"

It was like a slap in the face. Caddaric was reminding her that she was only a slave, without any authority of her own. Jilana swallowed back the hurt and studied the toes of her shoes. Caddaric had bartered a portion of their cured meat for a pair of leather slippers for her the day after Beltane. They were more comfortable than her sandals and would wear better. She had been touched by his thoughtfulness, but he had curtly brushed aside her thanks. Had he not said he would take care of her?

"I am sorry, Caddaric," Jilana whispered, "I had no right—"

"Jilana," Caddaric interrupted roughly, "I was teasing." Jilana's head snapped up and she stared into his brilliant blue eyes. "You can give them the damned tent if you wish; I do not care. Just remember that it would mean sharing a pallet made beneath the sky."

He brushed the knuckles of one hand over her cheek and, with an exaggerated sigh, went into the tent to gather a change of clothes. When he emerged, Jilana still stood where he had left her. Grumbling under his breath, Caddaric walked the few feet that separated their camp from Heall's, tossed his clothes into the wagon and then joined the two older men at their fire. When he was settled with a cup of mead, Caddaric looked up and winked at her.

An explosion of tender warmth burst within Jilana's breast and she turned away so that Caddaric could not see the expression on her face. How could he be so cold and remote one moment, and so kind the next? He was a puzzle that fascinated her and Jilana had to constantly remind herself that she was only his slave, no matter how considerately he treated her. She had only to look at the fading scars on her wrists and ankles to remember how quickly he could turn on her. But when the women arrived and they began preparing Ede for her marriage, Jilana still had not succeeded in quashing the pang that stabbed her heart when she thought of Caddaric sitting only a few feet away.

Laughing, the women bathed Ede and dressed her in the gown that Jilana had finished only minutes earlier, and then brushed her hair until it dried and fell down her back like a shining waterfall. One of the women brought a vial of jealously hoarded perfume and it was generously applied to the bride. Ede's marching sandals were exchanged for a delicate pair with low heels and then the cosmetics were brought forward. Ede's cheeks were rouged, her eyelashes and brows darkened, and kohl generously applied to her eyelids. When they were finished, Jilana nearly gasped aloud. Although the cosmetics were more heavily applied than was fashionable for a Roman woman, there was no doubt in Jilana's mind that Ede was the most strikingly beautiful woman she had ever seen and for a moment Jilana was secretly relieved that Ede had chosen another. She could never compete against Ede for Caddaric's affection. As soon as she had the thought, Jilana chastised herself for being so foolish, but the feeling remained just the same. The women ate a light meal—to which they had all contributed—and then retired to their own camps to prepare for the ceremony. Ede and Jilana were left alone.

"The gown is beautiful," Ede murmured, running her fingers over the embroidery on the sleeves.

Jilana smiled. "So are you." She sighed and opened her kist. "And now, I must change and rebraid my hair."

Ede left the pallet, where she had been sitting so carefully in order to remain unmussed, and peered over Jilana's shoulder as she pulled out her other white stola. "Why do you not wear these tunics?" Ede inquired.

Jilana shrugged. "I am uncomfortable in them."

"Are they too small?"

Jilana shook her head and a faint blush rose in her cheeks. "I used to wear them at home when I rode, but here...they expose most of my legs," she finished lamely.

Ede rolled her eyes. "Jilana, most of the women wear short tunics."

"I know, but..." Jilana raised her hands in a self-conscious gesture. She was not about to tell Ede that she had put a tunic on one morning and Caddaric had done nothing but stare at her while she did her chores. Before the tent had been struck, Jilana had ducked back inside and changed into her stola. She had never forgotten the feeling of his eyes lingering upon her. Jilana turned her back on Ede and stripped off her stola in order to wash.

"What is this?" Ede exclaimed.

Jilana turned and saw the length of saffron in Ede's hands. "My wedding veil," she replied shakily. She presented her back to Ede and washed quickly in the cool water.

"'Tis very pretty." Ede shook out the gauzy material and held it up in front of her eyes. "It gives everything a golden appearance."

Jilana shrugged into her gown. "You may have it if you wish." She knew of the Celtic love of color, and Ede was obviously fascinated with the garment. "I have no use for it."

"Oh, do you mean it?" But Ede was already drawing the veil over her head. It provided a vivid contrast to the white gown with its green decoration.

"Of course." Jilana smiled at the rapt expression on Ede's face. The child-like enthusiasm—common among Ede's people—was endearing. "I will certainly have no need of it."

At moonset they emerged from the tent and both women stopped dead at the sight awaiting them. A wicker chariot stood in the camp, and it was drawn by a team of snow-white horses.

"Oh!" Ede made a sound that to Jilana sounded suspiciously like a sob, and walked slowly forward. Caddaric stood at the horses' heads, holding the bridles while Heall stood in the chariot. "Where did you—" Ede's voice broke as she reached out to stroke a white neck.

"They are from the Queen, so that you might be properly taken to your wedding," Caddaric explained gently, although he was frowning. "The Queen said—and my father agreed—that the gods would not be offended by the substitution of horses for oxen."

"They could not be offended by such beauty," Jilana agreed. She followed Ede and placed a hand upon one of the velvet-soft noses. The horse accepted her immediately, butting its nose against her shoulder when she tried to show the same attention to its teammate.

"Heall will drive you," Caddaric told Ede, although his eyes were fixed upon Jilana.

"Aye," Heall put in. "Whenever you are ready, Ede."

"I am ready now." Ede smiled and raised the veil in order to place a kiss on Caddaric's cheek. "Farewell, Caddaric."

Caddaric's eyes glowed with remembered affection. "Farewell, Ede." Both knew their camaraderie of the past would be forever changed by her marriage, but neither had any regrets.

Jilana, Ede took in her strong arms and hugged warmly. "Who would have thought we could be friends?" she murmured. "I will return your veil to you—I think you may find a use for it." With that she left them and stepped into the chariot.

"What did Ede say?" Caddaric wanted to know when the chariot was nearly out of sight.

"She thanked me." Jilana brushed at the betraying wetness in her eyes.

"Are you crying?"

Jilana chuckled weakly. "I am afraid so."

Caddaric took her chin between his thumb and forefinger and tilted her face up to his. "Why did you give Ede your bridal veil?"

"Because she admired it so," Jilana replied softly. His hands framed her face now, and his thumbs were brushing away her tears. "'Tis not proper for a Celtic wedding, I know, but mayhap my gods will bless the union as well."

"Mayhap." Before he could think about the consequence of his actions, Caddaric lowered his head.

Jilana's eyes fluttered closed as Caddaric's lips touched hers. The kiss was a soft, questioning thing and she responded in kind. When his tongue at last followed the seam of her lips, she opened willingly and took him inside. Her hands went to his chest and the kiss lengthened into a gentle, erotic exploration that left her aching when Caddaric finally lifted his head.

"Come." Caddaric offered Jilana his hand and after only a slight hesitation, she took it. He twined his fingers with hers and they walked to the site of the wedding.

The ceremony was unlike any Jilana had witnessed, but she found it beautiful nonetheless. Or perhaps it was the fact that Caddaric kept a firm grip on her hand throughout the ritual that colored her perception. To Jilana, it mattered not. Along with the rest of their village, as well as Queen Boadicea and her retinue, Jilana watched as

Ewan stepped into the chariot beside Ede and took the reins from Heall. Clywd blessed the couple and recited their lineage, and the *filid* listed the property that they brought into the marriage. Clywd invoked the blessing of Be'al and the lesser gods upon the couple, calling for their health and prosperity in the coming years. Garlands of mistletoe were set upon the heads of the bride and groom and Heall sacrificed to the gods the wine and handful of wheat the couple had offered.

The men had erected a bower for the couple—far enough away from the main camp to allow privacy, but close enough for safety—and when the ceremony was finished, the village surrounded the chariot and escorted the bride and groom to it. Ribald jokes mingled with good wishes as the couple ducked into the shelter made from branches. The blanket which constituted the door was flipped into place amid loud cheers, and after drinking a toast to the couple with the mead the bride and groom had left outside the bower, the wedding guests withdrew, leaving the newlyweds alone.

That night, when they were settled into their pallet, Caddaric drew Jilana into his arms and kissed her again. In spite of all the warnings that flashed through her mind, Jilana melted in his arms, returning his passion. Reality spun away. She did not even think to protest when his hands cupped her buttocks and drew her into the hard evidence of his desire. When the kiss ended, she knew a longing so intense that she forgot to be embarrassed, but Caddaric tucked her against his side with the soft admonition, "Sleep now," and, to her surprise, she did.

PAULINUS AND HIS CAVALRY ESCORT reached Londinium. Like Camulodunum the city was unwalled, indefensible. From the two centuriae based in the city, Paulinus sent out mounted scouts to find the Iceni war band. Then he turned his attention to provisioning his exhausted troops and making plans for the defense of the city. Two days later, Paulinus' infantry staggered into Londinium. By the time his infantry arrived, Paulinus had come to the hardest decision of his long and distinguished career. Londinium could not be defended, at least not with the troops available to him; if he tried and was defeated, he would lose his troops, his life, and the entire province. Once he was dead, Boadicea would turn her war band to the west, join with the unruly tribes there, and the legions he had left in the west would be overwhelmed. Rome would be forced to mount a major offensive in order to retake Britannia, if it could. Londinium must be sacrificed in order to save the island. Still, knowing all that he did, Paulinus hesitated to announce his decision to the city.

When the scouts returned and reported that the rebel force was encamped some twenty miles to the east of the city, Paulinus could delay no longer. He summoned the civil leaders and priests and announced his decision to evacuate the city—in effect, turning it over to the rebels. But first the soldiers would strip it of as much food as they could carry; what could not be transported would be burned. The civilians were invited to join his column the following day when it withdrew from Londinium.

Word of Paulinus' decision spread through the city like wildfire. Men and women alike wept at the news, and they gathered at the temples to offer sacrifices to their gods and learn what their friends and neighbors intended to do. The staunchest and wisest of the citizenry opted to pack what household goods they could and join the legion. The price of wagons quadrupled in half a day; the cost of those few horses the legion had not confiscated for its own use increased tenfold. The strongest and greediest fed upon the stricken city. By midday, a horse, mule, wagon or cart could not be purchased by coin, only blood. People died fighting for possession of a lame pony that would die during the forced march the following day.

The legionaries opened the granaries—both those belonging to the city and those belonging to the temples. While guards, their weapons drawn in order to keep at bay the citizens who gathered there as well, stood watch over the doors, other legionaries filled their carts with the much-needed grain. Once the military needs had been met, the civilians were allowed to draw as much as they wished. The guards stayed. When Paulinus and the rest of the legion were safely out of the city, those left behind would fire the granaries and then take to their horses to join the Roman column.

That night, the altar fires in the temples burned continuously as the citizens flocked there in search of favorable omens and comfort. What they found only added to their panic: the temples had been stripped of all their trappings; all the sacred valuables, right down to the gold-covered cult statues, had already been packed into wagons for transport. Before daybreak, the faithful were unceremoniously shoved through the cella and out onto the steps. The wide temple doors were barred from the inside while the priests and attendants made ready to flee with Paulinus.

By dawn, the city streets were choked with traffic; movement was all but impossible. Paulinus had camped the night before with his men beside the road to Verulamium, and as the sun spread its golden fingers over the city, he swung into his saddle and gave the order to move out. The legion, already in formation, moved forward. It was noon before the last of the citizenry passed out of Londinium's gates. Shortly thereafter, dark plumes of smoke spiraled into the sky, mute evidence that the granaries had been torched.

The city was not entirely deserted. More than half of the populace had stayed behind, either because they were physically unable to make the march or because they foolishly believed, in spite of all Paulinus had told them, that Boadicea would not make war upon non-combatants. Few of the Romanized natives had remained in the city; they held no such illusions concerning their brethren. The Romans rushed to the granaries to battle the flames. Perhaps if they offered the rebel queen what remained inside the granaries, she would be even more willing to overlook their once-vaunted Roman citizenship. All day and long into the night they fought the flames. By the dark, cold hours of early morning, the fires were out but there was little grain left. Discouraged, the people trudged to their homes and barred their doors. A few brought out swords and daggers, long unused, and sharpened them, but most simply sat and waited for the rebellion to touch their lives.

JILANA DID NOT SEE THE SMOKE, but when they camped for the night she smelled it. 'Twas a strange, bitter odor carried on the night breeze, and she sniffed it curiously. It flavored their meager meal, and when she finished washing their plates, she walked some distance from their campfire and turned her face into the breeze.

"You smell it, too." Caddaric had followed and now he stood behind her in the dark.

"Aye." Jilana turned her head slightly so that she could see his face. "What is it?"

Caddaric drew a deep breath and considered. "I would guess it is wheat. The Romans have fired the granaries."

Jilana was aghast at the waste. "Why?!"

Caddaric smiled mirthlessly, his teeth flashing whitely in the starlight. "In order to deny us supplies."

"Oh." Jilana nodded. The action made perfect sense. "That will not stop us, of course."

"Nay, it will not stop us."

It dawned on Jilana then exactly what she had said and she took several steps away from Caddaric. What was happening to her? Where were her loyalties?

"You said 'us,' wicca."

"I know what I said," Jilana snapped, her mind in torment. "I meant..." Her voice trailed off. What exactly had she meant? She nervously smoothed the skirt of the short tunic she had put on that morning. She had told herself she wore the garment only because the weather was growing warm and her longer stolae were uncomfortably hot—not because she liked the way Caddaric's eyes followed her or the myriad freedoms of movement the short tunic allowed her. And most certainly not because wearing the garment made her look and feel like the rest of the women around her.

Caddaric had stopped wearing his breeks now that the warmer weather was upon them and Jilana found it nearly impossible to drag her eyes away from the sight of his long, heavily-muscled legs. Juno help her, but she found him the most attractive man she had ever seen! He rarely raised his voice to her now, and it seemed he was always underfoot, ready to help her with a heavy pail of water or some other chore that she was perfectly capable of handling. They were constantly together, constantly brushing each other. His presence filled her days and nights and Jilana felt the weakening within herself. When he had ridden with the vanguard, she had had time to harden herself against him, but now—ahh, gods, now she was on the brink of throwing herself into his arms and giving him anything he wanted—including a child!—if only he would promise not to cast her aside afterward.

Caddaric's hands settled on her shoulders and Jilana started. She tried to move away, but he held her fast. "What did you mean, wicca?"

Jilana swallowed, fighting the traitorous softening of her foolish heart. When he shook her gently, mutely demanding an answer, she sighed. "In truth, I do not know what I meant." She turned so that she could face him and summoned a glare. "Are you satisfied now, *lord*? I am confused; I no longer know to which world I belong. In two days the Queen will attack Londinium. I should be worried for the Roman citizens! I should be praying to my gods to bring defeat and ruin down upon the rebels' heads! I should be hoping that Paulinus is there, that his forces will slay every rebel that attacks the city. I should—" A sob tore from her throat and Jilana buried her face in her hands. "Instead, I pray that my gods will keep you safe! Damn you, Caddaric, what have you done to me!?"

Caddaric's hand wrapped around her braid and tugged her head upward, while his free hand circled her wrists, pulling her hands away from her face. Scarcely daring to believe what she had just admitted, he answered softly, "Made you Iceni."

Jilana reacted violently to his statement. She jerked away from him and he let her go. She faced him an arm's length away—angry, defiant, tormented, and, to Caddaric, incredibly beautiful. "I do not want to be Iceni," she spat at him. "'Twas not my wish."

"But you are, nonetheless," Caddaric said gently. "Do not fight so hard against the truth. You cannot escape it, wicca."

"Stop calling me that!" Jilana cried. "I am not a witch and I am most certainly *not Iceni*!"

"Look at yourself, Jilana," Caddaric urged, sweeping his hand from her head to her toes. "You speak my tongue, you dress like an Iceni woman, you even act like one. You help Clywd care for the sick and injured—*Iceni* sick and injured. You can drive a wagon, light a fire, and cook a meal over it. You eat the food *I* provide and you share my bed. If you are not an Iceni woman, if you are not *my woman*, then what are you?"

Jilana stared at him, horrified, hearing his words and knowing they were the truth. How had she changed so radically in three short months? "Nay," she denied. She shook her head vehemently and held up a hand as if to ward him off, though he had not moved. *"Nay!"* She whirled and fled back to camp.

She ran past Heall and Caddaric and straight into the tent, her heart hammering in her breast. Oh, gods, what had happened to her? What was to become of her? What would happen to her if the Iceni won and Caddaric took her back to his village? Worse, what would happen if the Iceni lost and Caddaric was killed? Juno, it would be beyond bearing! How could she go on, knowing he was dead? How could she not? What kind of a loyal Roman was she if she prayed for a life with Caddaric? Jilana threw herself onto the pallet and indulged in the fit of crying she had denied herself since Venta Icenorum.

Outside, Heall and Clywd heard the heart-rending sobs and exchanged a puzzled look. Heall would have gone to her, but Clywd shook his head and Heall subsided once again by the fire. When Caddaric returned to camp, both men eyed him with a large measure of hostility.

"What did you do to her?" Heall growled when Caddaric glanced at the tent and then settled himself by the fire.

"Naught," Caddaric replied. He poured himself a cup of mead and tasted it.

"If you have hurt her—" Heall began.

"I have not," Caddaric interrupted his friend. "Rest easy."

The three men sat quietly, listening as the sobs slowly subsided. When several minutes had passed without a fresh outburst of tears, Caddaric drained his cup and rose. "Will you smoor the fire for me?" Without waiting to see if either man responded, he stepped into the tent.

Jilana heard him enter and every muscle in her body tensed. The lamp had not been lit and the only illumination inside the tent came from the starlight falling through the smokehole in the roof. Jilana was grateful Caddaric could not see the ravages her crying had had upon her face.

"Jilana?"

"Please, Caddaric, no more." Jilana drew a shuddering breath. "I can bear no more *truths* this night."

Caddaric knelt on the pallet and reached for her. When she stiffened at his touch he murmured, "As you wish." With quick, gentle fingers, he undressed her and tucked her under the blanket. He shed his own clothes and joined her, drawing her protesting body into his arms. "Sleep now, wicca, just sleep."

Jilana held herself rigid in his embrace, trying not to give in to the comfort he was offering. She was his slave, she reminded herself, *only* his slave. She told him as much in a trembling voice.

Caddaric chuckled warmly and pulled her hard against his chest. "You are my woman, Jilana, my own little red-haired, Roman witch. How can you believe differently?"

Gently but firmly, he pushed her head into the hollow of his shoulder. "Now go to sleep, wicca."

Their meal the next morning used the last of their grain. Jilana served the men the thin oatmeal porridge along with a piece of dried beef and then began to pack the wagon for the day.

"Are you not eating?" Caddaric followed her and watched as she scrubbed out the pan and dried it. He held his steaming bowl in one hand but made no move to eat.

"I ate earlier." Jilana sidled around him to place the pan in the wagon.

"Do not lie to me, Jilana."

Caddaric's voice was hard but when her eyes flew to his, there was a softness in their blue depths she had not seen before. "I—I am not lying."

"Jilana," Caddaric said warningly.

Jilana folded the bag which had contained the oats and placed it with the others. "I have no appetite this morn."

"You seem to have lost your appetite for several days now." Caddaric eyed her sharply. "We are short on rations, yet to see the portions Heall, Clywd and myself receive, one would not know it." He stepped up into the wagon and went down on one knee beside her. "The rations are for all of us, Jilana."

Irritated that her little ruse had been discovered, and even more irritated that Caddaric did not understand why she had felt it necessary, Jilana snapped, "I am only a slave. Certainly I am not entitled to eat like the rest of you."

Caddaric's face turned fierce and he leaned forward until he could feel the touch of her breath across his mouth. "I have never known a woman so infuriating. I swear, Jilana, there are times when I could—" He choked off the words and drew a deep breath. "You are the one who labels yourself a slave. No one from my village thinks of you thus."

"Do not deceive yourself," Jilana retorted. "All remember the day Boadicea stood before them and gave me to you. 'Tis forever burned into their minds—and mine."

In reply, Caddaric took her hand and wrapped it around the bowl. "Eat this, or by all the gods, I will—"

When he could not find the words to continue, Jilana supplied helpfully, "Strangle me? Beat me? A fitting punishment for a slave."

Something flamed in Caddaric's eyes and he speared his hands through her hair, drawing her closer until his lips brushed hers. "I will take you back inside the tent and make love to you until you are too weak to stand." He watched her eyes widen in shock, then darken to deepest purple with remembered passion.

"Y-you would not."

"Aye, I would," Caddaric contradicted her breathless statement. He covered her free hand with his and placed it on his chest. Under his guidance, her hand drew circles over his chest and trailed down his stomach. When she tried to resist, he forced her hand still lower, until it covered the hard evidence of his desire. "I want you, Jilana, as a man wants a woman, not a slave. I want you willing in my bed, soft and warm and welcoming. The ache I feel for you is enough to drive a man mad, so do not tempt me with your wild defiance."

He released her hand and Jilana snatched it away, her face bright scarlet. "Now eat." Jilana obeyed, not daring to look at him.

Today Caddaric and Heall would ride in the vanguard and Jilana and Clywd would be left alone with the wagons. Jilana told herself she was glad Caddaric would be gone all day, but the truth was, she missed him the moment he rode out of camp. Clywd pulled out of camp just as Jilana finished packing her wagon. She filled her wineskin with water from one of the barrels and placed it under the seat, then went to the back of the wagon for a small pouch of dried meat for her midday meal. As she came around the wagon, she came face to face with Lhwyd.

"Greetings, Roman," the Druid said, and smiled.

Jilana straightened her shoulders and nodded briskly. "Good morrow. As you can see, you have missed both Caddaric and his father."

Lhwyd inclined his head slightly. "Today, however, 'tis you I wish to see."

Fear swept through Jilana and she edged away from him. There was some comfort to be taken from the fact that other people were not too far away, but she had no intention of getting too close to Lhwyd. "What is it you want?"

"Only to return this." Lhwyd reached inside his cloak and drew out Jilana's saffron veil. "From my sister, with her thanks."

Hesitantly, Jilana reached out and took the veil. "How is Ede?"

Lhwyd shrugged. "Well enough, though I see little of her or Ewan these days. Ewan, I fear, has fallen from favor with the Morrigan."

Which means he has displeased you in some manner, Jilana thought, but she said nothing. She waited impatiently for Lhwyd to leave, but he seemed in no hurry.

"Today will be a short march," Lhwyd was saying when Jilana turned her attention back to him. "And then we will reach the city."

The wild glint in his eyes made Jilana shiver. She knew well enough what intrigued him about Londinium. The citizens. His last sacrifices had been made at Camulodunum; after that, the Iceni had looked to Clywd as their priest.

"You know what will happen then." Lhwyd's voice was soft, caressing, and filled with such greed that she was certain he was mad.

Jilana gave him a cold look and climbed back into the wagon bed. With shaking fingers she opened her kist and folded the veil into it. She lingered over the task as long as she dared, her head bent, and when at last she looked up, Lhwyd was gone. Breathing a sigh of relief, she crawled onto the seat and clucked softly to the horses.

The column moved more swiftly than it had in the past
and they reached Londinium by midday. Jilana found
Clywd and pulled her wagon off the road to join him and
prepare the camp in the city's shadow. Heall and Caddaric would be gone most of the day, checking on the defenses of the city. As they unloaded the wagons, tethered
the horses and set up the camps, Jilana studiously avoided
looking south toward the city. Once the camps were prepared and the tent erected, Clywd wandered off to visit
other camps and pick the wild herbs he would need after
the coming battle. Jilana built a fire and sat beside it to eat
her meal. She was hungry enough to eat two of the pieces
of dried beef and she smiled at herself when she thought
of her initial reaction to the meat. It left her thirsty, however, and she drained the skin, though the water left a
bitter aftertaste. She carried their belongings into the tent
and sorted through their meager supplies to see what she
could prepare for the evening meal. There was mead, and
some dried fruit, but that was all. Her frown lifted, however, when she recalled that Heall and Caddaric had
mentioned going hunting before returning to camp. *You
eat the food I provide.* Caddaric's words brought back the
frown and with an exclamation of disgust, Jilana jumped
off the wagonbed. It seemed to take forever before she hit
the ground, and when she did her legs folded beneath her.

For a stunned moment Jilana lay in the grass, wondering what had happened, and then she realized she had
fallen. When she looked up, the sky with its fleecy white
clouds spun wildly and she closed her eyes against the
sight. When she opened them again, the spinning had
stopped and, using the wagonbed, she pulled herself upright. Her stomach lurched, then settled back into place,
and her strength gradually returned. Puzzled, but not
alarmed by the strange occurrence, Jilana considered lying
down for a few minutes but then rejected the idea. She
needed to water the horses before she did anything else.

Halfway to where the horses were staked, her stomach
lurched again and the buckets she carried slipped from her
numb fingers. She fell to her knees just as her stomach

emptied itself. Drained, Jilana struggled to her feet but she managed only a few more steps before the nausea claimed her again. When the last spasm passed, she spat, wished fleetingly for some water with which to rinse her mouth and tried to rise. Her legs refused to obey and she pitched head-first into the grass.

Panic curled through Jilana. She tried to call for help, but all that emerged was a pitiful whisper. Her eyes focused on the trees only a few feet away and all the stories her father had told of the wild beasts which lived in Britannia's forests came back to haunt her. She needed help, needed to get back to camp. Cramps gripped every muscle in her body and she moaned in protest, knowing she was terribly ill. Her head spun giddily as Jilana raised it to see where she was. Grimly, she thrashed around in the tall grass until she faced their camp and then, setting her teeth against the pain, she began to crawl.

She would be found, of course, Jilana reassured herself as she measured her progress by inches. Caddaric would check on the horses and find her. *If he took the same path she had.* Even if he did not, he would certainly search for her! *As he had before.* He would know she had not run away again. *Or would he?* Oh, Juno, why had she ever run from him?

"Caddaric," she whispered, tears running down her face. "Help me."

Four miles away, in the heart of the forest, Caddaric abruptly reined in his mount and sat stiffly erect, listening.

"Caddaric, wha—"

Caddaric sliced a hand at Heall, silencing him. The two men sat unmoving for a long time. The sudden tension in Caddaric communicated itself to his mount; the well-trained horse stood as if carved out of marble. At last Caddaric reined his stallion in a tight circle, surveying the woods. His eyes probed every shadow, seeking . . . something.

"Did you hear?" Caddaric asked Heall, the question a mere breath of sound on the air.

Heall shook his head, his hand falling to his sword. Across his saddle lay a brace of rabbits they had snared earlier. They had been on the trail of a deer when Caddaric had suddenly halted. "I heard nothing." He eyed the younger man worriedly. "What did you hear?"

"My name. Or I thought I did." A cold chill ran up Caddaric's spine and he shuddered. "Let us find our camp."

Heall had relaxed at Caddaric's answer but now he frowned. "Now? Caddaric, we need that deer—"

Caddaric shook his head. "Not today. 'Tis important we find my father and Jilana." How he knew it, Caddaric could not say, but at this moment he did not need a logical reason. Every fiber of his being was crying out a warning he could not fathom, but he knew it was urgent that they return to camp. Without another word, he kicked his mount forward, guided by some unseen hand.

Behind Caddaric, Heall grumbled, but he followed. When they emerged from the trees, Caddaric recognized their camp a short distance to their left and he galloped the rest of the way there.

"Jilana!" Before his horse had come to a complete stop, Caddaric had thrown himself out of the saddle and was racing for the tent.

"Perhaps she went with Clywd," Heall said when Caddaric emerged from the tent, his face rigid with fear.

"I should hope my father would have the sense to take her with him," Caddaric ground out, but he found no comfort in Heall's words.

Heall dismounted and walked around the campsite. "Mayhap they are watering the horses."

"Mayhap." Caddaric walked around the tent and spied the tethered beasts. Clywd had selected an area with tall grass, ideal for grazing. Unable to shake his feeling of dread, Caddaric strode toward the horses. The same force that had guided him unerringly through an unfamiliar forest brought him directly to where Jilana lay, unconscious.

His breath froze in his lungs as he dropped to his knees and rolled her gently onto her back. Her face was pale, her flesh clammy. Shaking, he held a hand in front of her mouth and nose and gave a choked sob of relief when he felt her exhale. "Jilana." Desperately, he touched her arms and legs, checking for broken bones, and then ran his fingers over her scalp. He could find nothing wrong. He gathered Jilana in his arms, stood, and hurried back to camp.

"Find my father," Caddaric snapped when Heall ran to meet him.

"The girl—"

"She is alive. Hurry!"

Inside their tent, Caddaric stripped Jilana, checked her from head to toe, and then covered her with a blanket. There were no wounds, no lumps from a fall, nothing! He chafed her hands in his and called her name in the hope that she had fainted. Jilana did not respond. Nothing he said or did brought so much as a flicker of an eyelid.

When Clywd entered the tent, he was accosted by a man he barely recognized as his son. "Where have you been?" Caddaric snarled, his hands gripping the front of Clywd's black cloak. "You knew you were not to leave her alone! You knew!"

"Caddaric, let him go." Heall was beside him, prying his fingers away from the material.

"Damn him! He knew. All of us knew! We agreed Jilana was not to be left alone—" His voice broke and Caddaric jerked backward, away from the two men. He pointed a trembling finger at his father. "If she dies, old man, I will never forgive you. Never."

Clywd's face was the color of bleached linen as he knelt beside Jilana and examined her. Heall crouched at Jilana's head while Caddaric, his face a stony mask, watched the proceedings from the door. "Well?" He grated when Clywd rose.

"I need my case." Clywd walked to where his son stood and tried to brush past him. An iron fist around his arm stopped him and Clywd looked into his son's stormy eyes.

"What is wrong with her?"

Clywd swallowed, berating himself for his own stupidity. What had he cost them all by believing so deeply in Be'al? When he spoke, his words fell like stones into a dry well. "She has been poisoned." The fingers around his arm fell away and Clywd stepped out of the tent. When he returned scant moments later, Caddaric had not moved. Heall was crying quietly and stroking Jilana's hair. Clywd had opened his case and was searching for the proper herbs when Caddaric spoke again.

"Can you save her?"

Clywd carefully crushed the herbs and stirred them into a cup of water. "I can try."

Caddaric stared at his father and then turned his gaze to Jilana. He wanted to go to her, take her in his arms and kiss her until she wakened. He wanted to feel the silk of her hair against his skin and the warmth of her body curled against his in the middle of the night. There was so much he wanted—and now he doubted if he would have any of it. The pain in him grew until he thought he would go mad with it. "So much for your gods and your prophecies, old man!" He swung on his heel and stalked out of the tent. The thought of losing Jilana seared white-hot through his heart and drove him through the Iceni camp. Some distant part of his mind screamed that he was out of control, but he ignored the warning. Perhaps being out of control would drive the pain out of his heart.

Those who saw him stepped out of his way, and when he stopped at one campsite to ask direction, the old woman he accosted stammered out her answer. The black look on his face reminded her of years past, when a blood feud was about to be declared. Although, given the question he had asked, a feud made no sense. When Caddaric was gone, she ran to the adjoining camp to tell her friends what had happened. Caddaric found the camp he wanted and when two of the guards made to stop him, he tossed them aside as if they were nothing more than kindling. Before other guards could come to their aid, Caddaric was upon the man he wanted.

"Lhwyd," Caddaric growled.

The Druid was kneeling at the altar he erected every night. Before he could rise, Caddaric had seized him by the shoulders and thrown him a good ten feet, into the outer edge of the fire. Dazed, Lhwyd scrambled to his feet. When he saw the hem of his cloak smoldering, he tore it off and tossed it aside.

"What are you doing, warrior?" Lhwyd asked tauntingly. "You, above all others, know it is death to lay hands upon a Druid."

"Aye, death," Caddaric agreed with a feral grin. "But whose will be first, Druid, yours or mine?" Before the guards could step between them, Caddaric charged across the space that separated them and clamped his right arm around Lhwyd's neck. The Druid made a harsh, gasping noise. "Stay away," Caddaric warned when the guards drew their swords and edged closer, "or I will snap his neck like a dry branch right now."

"Caddaric," Lhwyd managed to croak. "Release me!" His long, thin hands clawed frantically at Caddaric's arm.

"Afraid to die," Caddaric jeered, tightening his arm fractionally. "Do you not long to join your Morrigan, priest?" Lhwyd tried to reply, but Caddaric increased the pressure again. Lhwyd's hands fell to his sides and dangled helplessly.

"Caddaric, nay!"

Caddaric's eyes flickered up briefly to see Ede and Ewan running toward him. Ignoring them, he dragged Lhwyd back to his altar. "Let us see how the Morrigan takes the offering of your blood, priest!" His left hand released his right wrist in order to draw his dagger, but the pressure on Lhwyd's throat never wavered. There was a savage motion of his left arm and Lhwyd's tunic was slit open from neck to waist and the dagger was pressed just under the Druid's breastbone.

"Caddaric, nay," Ede cried again and stumbled forward, Ewan on her heels. "Caddaric, he is a *priest*!"

"A murdering priest," Caddaric threw back fiercely. "He poisoned Jilana."

All the blood drained from Ede's face and she fell back against Ewan's chest. Part of her denied the words, but another part, the one which was sickened by her brother's fascination with death, knew instinctively that it was true. "L-Lhwyd?"

Lhwyd could not speak but he managed to move his head from side to side. His movement stopped when he felt the tip of the dagger bite into his flesh.

Ewan took a hard look at the two men in front of him and came to a decision. He pushed Ede behind him and walked forward. Unnoticed, Ede whirled and ran from the camp. "Caddaric, even if what you say is true, you cannot kill him. The Queen will have no choice but to have you executed. That is the law. You know it as well as I."

"My woman lies dying," Caddaric snarled back, "because of this pathetic excuse of a man. Think you I care about the law?!"

Ewan shoved his hands beneath his broad belt and considered what Caddaric had said, looking for all the world as if their discussion was of no great importance. At last he said, "Are you certain she is dying?"

Caddaric hesitated. "She has been poisoned; my father confirmed it."

Ewan nodded solemnly. "I am sorry; Jilana is a good woman."

"Aye." Inadvertently, Caddaric flexed his arm and Lhwyd's tongue lolled out of his mouth.

"But that does not mean she will die," Ewan pointed out. "If Clywd is with her, I would wager that she will live. What will her life be like if you are dead?"

Some of his rage faded and Caddaric drew a shuddering breath. "Even if she lives, it will not change what *this*," he gave Lhwyd a nasty shake, "has done."

"You will put down your weapon this instant and release the Druid." The command was delivered in a strong, feminine voice that demanded attention.

Caddaric's gaze shifted to the source of the voice and pure shock eased his hold on Lhwyd's neck. Not enough so that the Druid could escape, but enough so that he could speak.

"My Queen," Lhwyd rasped. "This man has gone mad."

Boadicea flicked a contemptuous look at the Druid. "You are not a wise man, priest. Never call the man who holds your life in his hands mad." She looked back at Caddaric and her eyes softened. One of her chieftains had rushed to her tent with news of the impending murder and she had arrived just in time to hear Caddaric's reasons. If what the warrior said was true, Boadicea believed he was well justified in his actions, but she could not allow a Druid under her protection to be coldly murdered—no matter how much she personally disliked him. "Caddaric, you know I have forbidden fighting. You sat at council when I made the edict."

Caddaric nodded. "I know, my Queen, but—"

Boadicea silenced him with an upraised hand. "I have heard your reasons. That does not change the fact that you are about to break the law." Her voice filled with sincere regret, she continued, "I cannot allow that." She nodded once to the imperial guards and the four of them drew their swords. The Queen looked back to Caddaric. "Do what you must, warrior, and so will I."

"So be it." Caddaric stepped over the low wooden altar and dragged Lhwyd across it.

"Nay, Caddaric!" Clywd's voice floated across the campsite and Caddaric's head jerked up. His father was running—running!—past the onlookers, Ede at his side.

Caddaric's only thought was that Clywd had come because Jilana was dead and his face darkened again.

Accurately reading his son's thoughts, Clywd came to a halt only a few paces away and held out his hand. "Jilana lives," he panted. "I swear to you, Caddaric, she lives."

Caddaric's eyes narrowed and he flashed a look at Ede, who nodded. "He is telling the truth, Caddaric. I have seen her with my own eyes." She smiled tremulously. "I have never lied to you."

"Nay, you have never lied," Caddaric agreed. He looked down at the man dangling in front of him. "Why did you do it, priest?"

"I have done naught!" Lhwyd protested hoarsely. "Why would I try to kill your slave? In time she will come to my altar, when the rest of the island is free of the Romans. Our Queen has sworn that not a single Roman will remain alive on Albion!" He looked triumphantly at Boadicea.

Anger stained Boadicea's cheeks until they were the same color as her flaming red hair. "Druid, you are under my protection, but lie thus again and I will see you delivered to Paulinus!" She sighed and stepped closer until she was even with Clywd.

Caddaric watched his sovereign approach. "Is it true, O Queen?" he asked softly. "Have you promised Lhwyd Jilana's life?"

Boadicea slowly shook her head. "I promised him nothing of the sort, warrior. I gave the woman to you—yours she will remain."

Caddaric considered her answer for a long time before coming to a decision. "I would ask a boon of you, my Queen."

The corners of Boadicea's mouth twitched with unwilling amusement. "You dare much, warrior, to assault a Druid, break my edict and then ask a favor." Dull color flooded Caddaric's face and Boadicea laughed aloud. "Release the priest, Caddaric, and I will hear your request." When he hesitated, Boadicea said, "A promise given under duress need not be honored."

Everyone held their breath for the space of several heartbeats until, with a snarled oath, Caddaric sheathed his dagger and shoved Lhwyd away to sprawl in the dirt at Boadicea's feet.

"My Queen, arrest him," Lhwyd shrieked as he rose to his feet. "He has broken your edict and threatened a member of the priesthood."

Boadicea looked down her nose at the Druid. "My edict forbade fighting; it did not seem like much of a fight to me." Some of the onlookers snickered, for indeed, Lhwyd had done little more than croak and be tossed about. "As for threatening a member of the priesthood," Boadicea continued, "the law demands that the murder of a Druid is punishable by death. It says nothing of threats."

"Majesty, if you will not punish this upstart I will have my guards—"

Boadicea glared at him. "If you try to harm this man, Lhwyd, I will disband your guards and forbid your sacrifices. I leave it to you to choose."

Lhwyd's face contorted in rage. With a jerky bow he left the Queen and stood among his guards. One of them offered him a cloak and he rudely snatched it out of the man's hands.

"Now, Caddaric," Boadicea said with a sigh, "what is your request?"

The royal guards sheathed their swords and Caddaric breathed easier. The danger had passed. Boadicea did indeed plan to hear his request, and, just as obviously, she did not plan to have him arrested. Caddaric cleared his throat and went down on one knee before his Queen. Boadicea hid a flash of amusement and touched his shoulder lightly. "Rise, Caddaric, 'tis too late to appear humbly beseeching."

Caddaric met the Queen's gaze and held it. "Majesty, I ask permission to free the slave you gave me."

Of all the things she might have guessed Caddaric would ask for, Boadicea had never thought of this. "Free her," she repeated questioningly. "Why?"

"Because she has proven herself," Caddaric answered steadily. "With my father, she cared for our wounded after Camulodunum, and she has proven her loyalty to me in many ways." He inclined his head toward Lhwyd. "If I should die with Jilana still a slave, this one would no doubt claim her. She deserves better."

Boadicea's gaze slid to Lhwyd, considering. The Druid had come to her with a wild tale, accusing the Roman slave of aiding one of his sacrifices to escape. Boadicea doubted the validity of the tale, but what was important was that Lhwyd believed his own accusations and was determined to see the girl punished. His obsession was like an ugly canker, growing and festering inside him. She did not doubt that Lhwyd was fully capable of poisoning the girl if the act would relieve his madness. And Caddaric was right; for her services to him, and her kindness to the Queen, the Roman did not deserve to die at Lhwyd's hands.

"Very well, you may free the girl. For a price," Boadicea added before Caddaric could express his gratitude. She had to exact some punishment for his wild actions. "You will give me a horse, one broken to the saddle, for the disruption you have caused."

"Thank you, Majesty." Caddaric bowed.

"Do not be so quick with your thanks," Boadicea said tartly. "Your chieftain may exact a higher penalty for your behavior, and I will not intervene." She swung away, her guards following.

"This is not over yet," Lhwyd snarled when Caddaric—flanked by Clywd and Ede—walked past him.

Caddaric paused and fixed the Druid with an icy stare. "Harm Jilana, or any of my family, or even attempt to do so, and I swear you will pay. I am a patient man, priest; I can wait years to have my revenge, and you, in the meantime, will never know a moment's peace." He strode off, leaving Lhwyd to fume impotently.

Caddaric walked silently, listening to Clywd's explanation of the poison and the measures he had taken to counteract it. When they reached the camp, Caddaric went straight to the tent and entered. A small fire had been built within the leather walls and in its light, Caddaric saw Heall sitting beside the pallet, one of Jilana's hands clasped in both of his. The older man looked up at Caddaric's entrance and managed a smile.

"She will live, Caddaric."

"Aye, so I was told." Caddaric bent down to brush the damp hair from Jilana's face. "Has she awakened?"

"Twice." Heall placed the delicate hand beneath the blanket and tugged the material higher around her neck. "Clywd says 'tis best to let her sleep." Caddaric grunted noncommittally and Heall studied the younger man. "He saved her life, Caddaric."

"After nearly causing her death," Caddaric replied caustically.

"He thought she would be safe," Heall argued. "How could he know—"

"He could not," Caddaric flared. "None of us could. That is why we agreed that one of us would remain with her at all times."

"Caddaric, he has checked all of our provisions; none of them are poisoned." Heall cleared his throat. "Did Lhwyd admit the deed?"

"Nay, but he is guilty."

"Then we will have to warn Jilana. Mayhap if we had told her our suspicions, this could have been avoided." Heall rose. "I will dress the hares and prepare a stew."

Once they were alone, Caddaric moved to Jilana's side and tenderly drew his fingers over the fine bones of her face. He could delude himself no longer. The pretense of keeping her only for the child was only that—a pretense. She had found a way into his warrior's heart and built a place for herself there. He had not realized, until her death seemed imminent, how great a part she had come to play in his life. The thought of life without her was enough to drive him mad, as was the thought that she was anyone's slave, even his. So he had asked for her freedom and been granted his request. A pang of fear stabbed at him. Once she learned she was free, Jilana would have the freedom of remaining with him or leaving, as she chose. Many of the Iceni would welcome her into their camp, adopt her; and the young, unmarried warriors would be free to vie for her hand. Would she go? Caddaric wondered sadly, and then answered his own question. Why would she not? Whenever she looked at him, she saw the death of her family and the beginning of the end of her world.

Kissing her gently on the forehead, Caddaric left the tent and strolled to where the horses were tethered. From the six, he selected a mare whose coat was black as ebony for the Queen. She was a spirited horse, but well-trained; the Queen would be pleased. He returned to the camp with the mare and found his chieftain sitting beside Clywd by the fire.

"This one is for the Queen," the chieftain demanded, rising.

Caddaric nodded and handed the rope to the man.

"I should punish you. To break the Queen's law about brawling was bad enough, but to assault a Druid and try to kill him!" He shook his head. "Lhwyd wants your head on a pike, young Caddaric."

Caddaric folded his arms over his chest. "Are you going to give it to him?"

The chieftain frowned blackly. "Have a care, young pup, or I may consider it!" Caddaric nearly laughed at being called a young pup, but he caught himself in time. The chieftain, however, had seen the glint in his eye and now shook his head in exasperation. "Lhwyd is forbidden to enter your camp uninvited, and you are forbidden to enter his. I have no liking for Lhwyd, but you have left me no choice in the matter." He extended his hand and wiggled his fingers. "Another horse, Caddaric, that is my fine. One I choose myself."

Caddaric had no choice but to agree and led the man to the horses. The chieftain inspected all of them, but he lingered over the golden stallion and Caddaric's heart sank. Resigned, Caddaric stepped forward to untie the stallion.

"Nay, not this one." The chieftain pointed to one of the mounts that held no interest for Caddaric. "That one."

Trying not to show his relief, Caddaric untied the horse and handed the rope to his chieftain.

"Let this be a lesson to you," the chieftain admonished as he took the rope. "Do something as stupid as this again and the Queen will not be so generous. And never forget that I could have taken the stallion."

Clywd was emerging from the tent when Caddaric returned to the camp a second time. They met at the entrance to the tent and for a long time neither spoke. Behind them, the fire crackled and the sounds Heall made as he prepared the meal were muted.

"I thought she would be safe," Clywd said finally, his voice low. "Lhwyd's camp was far away—" The words died; his eyes fell away from Caddaric's. He spread his hands helplessly and started to walk away.

"Wait." Caddaric stared at the tent flap. "I should not have spoken to you as I did."

Clywd laid a trembling hand upon his son's arm. "I would cut off my arm before I would hurt you. In truth, I do not know what I was thinking of. We set up the camps and then I remembered that I had bandages to change and I needed to replenish some of the herbs and roots in my medicine case and I..." He shook his head sadly. "I am so sorry, Caddaric."

Caddaric covered his father's hand with his and squeezed roughly. "I understand, Father. I did not mean the things I said; but I was so afraid for her." Clywd nodded and moved away. Caddaric went into the tent to sit with Jilana.

As the sun set, Heall brought a pot of stew, bowls and spoons into the tent and gave them to Caddaric. "Do you want me to stay with her?"

Caddaric shook his head. "I will care for her."

Heall looked as if he might argue, but then thought better of it. With a slight nod he left them alone. Caddaric took a portion of the stew and ate without really tasting it. He nestled the pot into the coals to keep it warm and then rolled into a blanket on the ground beside Jilana's pallet. The camp quieted earlier than usual, anticipating the battle tomorrow. With a start, Caddaric realized that he had not spared a thought for the coming battle, nor sharpened his weapons. He started to rise and then fell back wearily. There would be time enough in the morning.

JILANA AWOKE in the cold, dark hours of early morning. Her body and head ached, but she recognized immediately the emptiness in the pallet. One hand crept over to where Caddaric normally lay, and when it did not encounter the familiar warm body, she weakly called his name. Why did it hurt even to speak, she wondered, and then gasped when Caddaric loomed over her.

"What is it, wicca?"

Jilana blinked, trying to bring his face into focus. "Thirsty," she whispered.

"Wait." Caddaric fetched a skin and held it to her lips while his other arm supported her head. "Drink, but only a little." When she would have emptied the skin, he firmly removed it from her mouth and returned her to the furs.

The water eased the parched ache in her mouth and throat and Jilana turned her head to the side. The tent looked different and it took several moments before she realized why. "Why did you light a fire inside?"

"Because Clywd said you should be kept warm."

Remembering what had happened, Jilana sighed. "I fell ill. Have I been a terrible burden?"

Something between a laugh and a sob escaped Caddaric's throat. He shook his head and took her hand. "Nay."

"I am glad." Jilana searched his face. "Are you angry with me?"

Caddaric closed his eyes and shook his head again. When he opened them, Jilana was still staring at him. "Are you hungry? I have kept some stew warm."

Jilana's stomach revolted at the thought. "A bit more water?" Caddaric brought the skin to her lips and this time allowed her to drink a bit more. "Is this fresh? It tastes much better than the water I drank at midday."

"Nay, 'tis from the barrels." Caddaric studied her intently. "What was wrong with the water in your skin?"

Jilana shrugged. "It left a bitter taste in my mouth."

"But you took it from the barrels?"

"Aye." Jilana's brows drew together when Caddaric abruptly released her hand and started out of the tent. "Caddaric, what is wrong?" He did not bother to reply and Jilana was too tired to repeat her question. She closed her eyes and when she opened them again, Caddaric was once more beside her. "Where did you go?"

"To talk to my father." Caddaric stroked her cheek with his forefinger. "Would you like to try some stew now?"

"Nay." Jilana frowned at him. "What is it, Caddaric? What is amiss?"

Caddaric pursed his lips together, as if considering his answer. "Did you see Lhwyd yesterday?"

"Aye," Jilana answered slowly, a prickle of unease running through her. "Before we marched. But—"

"Did you fill your skin before or after you saw him?"

"Before."

"Did he touch the skin?" Caddaric demanded.

Her unease blossomed into pure dread. "I do not think so, but—he could have, I suppose. I left the skin under the wagon seat and he was standing next to it when I put away the veil that Ede had sent him to return." A terrible thought formed in Jilana's mind and she asked softly, "I did not take ill, did I?" When Caddaric answered, she closed her eyes.

"Nay. You were poisoned; by Lhwyd."

"Juno," Jilana breathed. Swallowing, she told Caddaric, "Lhwyd came to our camp the day the rein broke. To see Clywd, he said, but Clywd was gone and Lhwyd was standing by the team the entire time." She looked at him with wide eyes, her fingers fearfully curling into his arms. "The broken rein was no accident, was it?"

"He will not bother you again," Caddaric soothed. "He has been forbidden by our chieftain to come to our camp."

That was welcome news, but Jilana sensed Caddaric had not told her everything. She started to ask what else had happened but his next words stopped her.

"I gave you my word that I would keep you safe and I did not," Caddaric stated harshly. "I would not blame you if you never trusted me again."

For a stunned moment, Jilana could do nothing more than stare at him, and then she placed her hand upon his cheek and turned his face toward her. "'Twas not your fault, Caddaric. The poison was Lhwyd's doing, not yours. How could you think I would blame you?'' She hesitated before adding, "Caddaric, I would trust you with my life.''

The light seemed to come back into Caddaric's eyes. "Would you?'' A beautiful, masculine smile curved his lips.

In reply, Jilana moved over and lifted the corner of the blanket. Caddaric needed no further invitation. Stripping out of his clothes, he slid in beside her and took her in his arms. Moments later they were both asleep.

Jilana awoke alone the next morning. The fire had gone out, and through the hole in the roof, she could see the gray fingers of light which signaled early morning. She stretched, cat-like, feeling the ache that lingered in her muscles—the ache Lhwyd had caused. Jilana shuddered. She had proof now of how deeply Lhwyd hated her, and so did Caddaric; the Druid would not catch them off guard again. Muted sounds drifted into the tent from the camp and Jilana recognized the distinctive grate of iron against whetstone. Fear darted through her. The Iceni were preparing to attack Londinium. She rose and dressed as quickly as she could, then wrapped Caddaric's cloak about her and left the tent.

The three men around the fire rose when she appeared and Heall hurried to meet her. "You should remain in bed,'' he chastised her.

"Nay, Heall, I am well." Jilana took his hand and they walked to the fire. The contents of Clywd's medicine chest had been emptied and were strewn about the Druid as he sorted through them. Caddaric's sword and battle-axe were propped against a log and he held the whetstone in one hand. Heall's weapons were also being readied. Her eyes came to rest on the fire and the pot suspended over it. "Is that porridge?"

Her words seemed to release the three men. Heall and Caddaric seated her on a log while Clywd filled a bowl for her. "Heall bartered for the oats," Clywd explained as he handed her the food. She smiled at him, but his eyes slid away. "I have a potion for you to drink when you have eaten." He walked back to his place, sat down, and continued sorting through his supplies.

Clywd's actions worried Jilana, but she had no chance to ponder them with Heall and Caddaric hovering over her. She raised the wooden spoon to her mouth and, looking up, found both men's eyes upon her. She ate slowly while the men watched her like a pair of hawks. When she was finished, Caddaric took her bowl and Heall poured a cup of water for her. Clywd brought his potion and the three of them watched while she drank it and took a large swallow of water. Jilana found their watchfulness amusing. "I feel much better," she announced when they showed no intention of leaving her alone. "Have the three of you nothing better to do than watch me?"

The older men went back to their tasks but Caddaric sat by Jilana and resumed honing his sword. "Clywd will remain with you," he informed her. "You are not to leave the camp."

"You cannot ask Clywd to stay here," Jilana protested. "He must see to the injured."

"He can tend them once Heall or I have returned," Caddaric said.

"But that may be too late for many of the wounded." Jilana laid a hand on his arm. "I will go with Clywd."

"You will not," Caddaric growled. "Gods, woman, have you no sense at all? I will not allow you to place yourself in danger."

A spark of anger flared inside Jilana, but she tamped it down. "Caddaric," she said reasonably, "where is the danger in accompanying your father?"

Caddaric's jaw set stubbornly. "Have you forgotten that Lhwyd tried to kill you? You need to rest."

"I am not at death's door," Jilana retorted.

"Yesterday you were!"

Struggling to keep her voice level, Jilana said, "I am stronger than I look, Caddaric." His answer to that was a snort of disbelief. "Why will you not allow me to help where I may?"

Caddaric stood. "'Tis nearly time. I will see to the horses."

Jilana gaped at him as he strode away and then, with a strangled cry she was on her feet, following him. He heard her, Jilana knew, but he did not wait. Instead he lengthened his stride and she had to run to catch up with him. "Why are you acting this way?" she demanded, struggling to keep pace. "At least I am asking your permission. I could simply agree to obey your order and then do as I please when you are gone."

"Aye, you have done that often enough in the past," Caddaric agreed grimly.

Jilana opened her mouth to argue further and then gasped. "Someone has stolen your horses!" Tears flooded her eyes and she failed to see the odd look that flashed across Caddaric's face. "Caddaric, the black mare is gone. And the brown gelding. Who could have done this?"

Caddaric untied the remaining four horses in order to move them to fresh grazing. "The horses were not stolen, Jilana, I gave them away."

"Gave them—" Jilana stared at him. "Why? Were they what Heall traded for the grain?"

Caddaric turned his attention to retethering the horses. "'Twas the fine imposed upon me."

"Fine!" Jilana waited until the last horse was tied, then grasped the short sleeve of Caddaric's tunic and pulled with all her might until he turned to face her. "What fine?"

Caddaric cleared his throat and stirred restlessly beneath her violet stare. "The fines imposed by the Queen and my chieftain."

Jilana's eyes widened. "What have you done?"

"I tried to kill Lhwyd," Caddaric retorted with a shade of defiance. "And I would have, except that the Queen intervened!"

"Because of what Lhwyd did to me?" Jilana questioned breathlessly.

"Aye," Caddaric admitted, his chin lifting.

"Oh, you fool," Jilana screeched. "You *fool*!" She gave him a shove that knocked him back a step and burst into tears.

Caddaric watched silently, dumbfounded by her reaction. He could not tell whether she was angry or sad, but either way she certainly was not pleased by the action he had taken in her defense. "I did it for you, Jilana," he tentatively explained.

"For me? For *me*?" She was screaming through her tears. "And what would have happened to me when you were executed for killing a priest?!"

"My father and Heall would have cared for you. Jilana—" Caddaric extended his hand to her.

Jilana batted his hand away. She wanted to throw herself into his arms and cry out that she did not want him to die for her sake; that she loved him and wanted him safe. But she did not, because even slaves had some pride. "You did it for yourself, because someone had dared to hurt your slave and damaged your pride in the process. Gods! You men with your silly pride and your childish need for vengeance." She looked up at him, imagining what would have happened had he succeeded and grew even angrier. "Are all men this stupid?"

"Only me, apparently," Caddaric said coldly. He swung on his heel and walked away. She had called him stupid, a fool. No doubt he was, compared to the Roman men she knew. Something withered in his heart. He should have ignored the dream, should have known it was impossible. And above all, he should have guarded his heart more closely. In camp he paused only long enough to gather his weapons, then headed to join the vanguard, Heall close behind. When Jilana did not return to the camp, Clywd put away his medicines and went in search of her.

He found her sitting on the ground near the horses, Caddaric's cloak wrapped tightly around her. Silently, he sat beside her and watched the horses graze. When Jilana made no move to leave him, Clywd said, "They are gone."

"I know." Jilana's voice was thick with tears. "If Caddaric is wounded it will be my fault. We argued." When Clywd said nothing, only watched her calmly, she poured out the story to him.

In turn, Clywd told Jilana the details of what had happened, ending with, "Did he tell you that he asked the Queen for your freedom, and she granted it?"

"Nay. I did not give him a chance." Jilana's lower lip trembled and she felt the tears spill down her cheeks again. "Why did he do such a thing?"

"He told the Queen it was because you had proven your loyalty to him." Clywd hesitated before adding, "And that he wanted you a free woman, safe from Lhwyd, should he die."

"Oh, Juno, what have I done?" Clywd opened his arms to Jilana and she went into them without hesitation.

"Forgive me for leaving you alone," Clywd murmured. "I should have been here when you needed me."

"You were—Heall told me yesterday how you cared for me. I thank you for my life."

When her tears subsided, Clywd helped Jilana to her feet and they returned to the camp. The morning dragged by and they filled their time with packing their medicines. Cloth that they would use for bandages was boiled in water and vinegar and hung over the ropes they had suspended between the wagons to dry. Jilana noticed that Clywd's gaze often strayed to the city in the distance, as hers did. At midday they shared a meal of the last dried fruit and washed it down with water, saving the grain for the evening meal.

"Caddaric said that when we took the city he would forage for supplies," Jilana mused when Clywd noted their lack of provisions.

Clywd nodded. "And Heall says the hunting is good in the forest." He smiled speculatively. "A good haunch of venison would not be amiss now."

Jilana chuckled, but she could feel her nerves fraying as time passed. "How do you bear the waiting, Clywd?"

The old man sighed heavily. "The fighting is a way of life for us, Jilana. Before we fought the Romans, we fought each other."

"Surely you fear for them?"

"I fear the pain their passing will cause," Clywd admitted, "but they are both warriors. 'Tis a fact I have accepted, and you must as well, if you are to be Caddaric's woman."

Jilana nodded, but in her heart she knew she would never be able to accept such a violent life as normal. She turned to the city, blocking out the sounds that were borne back to the camp by the breeze. Within the maze of buildings was Caddaric, and she prayed to every god she knew to keep him safe.

By MIDDAY, Caddaric was covered with dirt and blood and sick at heart at the slaughter of unarmed civilians. The soldiers and most of the civilians had been evacuated; the only opposition to the Iceni came from poorly armed men who had rarely—if ever—handled a sword. He shook his head as, in front of him, a Roman was cut down before he could so much as lift his weapon. All around him were the sounds of the dying and the Iceni battle cries. Caddaric saw no need to yell out his victory or scream a challenge at his poor opponents. He did what was necessary, as swiftly and as mercifully as was possible.

Disconcertingly, his mind kept turning to Jilana. His anger over her words had long since burned itself out until now he felt only the pain. He had to force himself to concentrate on fighting, and when he turned away from the sight of yet another enemy falling beneath an Iceni battle-axe, Caddaric knew he could not continue. There were warriors enough to deal with the city's population. Some of the other warriors had dropped back in order to begin looting and he decided to do the same. They needed supplies, and if he waited until the enemy was totally annihilated he would not find them.

Bodies lay everywhere, both in the streets and sprawled across the thresholds of the houses. Caddaric turned a blind eye to them, knowing that he would find more when he entered the Roman homes. Survival was what mattered now, and none of them, Jilana included, would survive if he did not find provisions. Keeping his sword in his hand, Caddaric retraced his steps and began a methodical search of the houses in his path. From one he took a large square of material; in the next he found several clay pots of preserves and freshly baked wheat cakes. These he wrapped in a small piece of linen torn from the material he had found, placed them in the center of the square and knotted the ends together to form a handle. In another home he discovered several casks of wine. He tucked one cask under either arm and walked back to the street.

Caddaric turned onto one of the broader streets, knowing that it would eventually lead to the temples. After crossing several intersecting streets, he found what he sought. The temple was large, the columns ornately detailed. Above the doors was carved the name of the god— or goddess—to whom the temple was dedicated, but Caddaric could not read. In any case, he was less interested in the god's name than in finding the temple's storerooms and granary. Caddaric found the double doors barred from the inside so he followed the colonnade around the building until he came to the temple garden. A stone path led through the garden to a low door, which stood ajar. Stooping, Caddaric entered the temple.

The only light was from the open door. Caddaric set his burdens on the floor and edged around the perimeter of the room until his hand encountered a wall bracket and a torch. He lit the torch with his flint and advanced farther into the room. A small silver statue winked in the flickering light, and further on the torch revealed a jeweled cup lying on the floor. The room was apparently one of those used for storing the temple treasures, and the two Caddaric had seen had either been overlooked or dropped in the haste to flee the city. He did not bother to pick up either one; jewels and silver would not feed a hungry stomach. Opening the door in the far wall, Caddaric found that it opened onto the cella. Caddaric entered, the torch held high in front of him. The flickering light cast eerie shadows throughout the deserted room, as did the hole in the ceiling that allowed the smoke from the sacrifices to escape, and, in spite of himself, Caddaric felt his skin crawl. The Roman god would not be pleased with his intrusion. He slowly paced the width of the cella, past the empty altar, his footsteps echoing hollowly, until he came to a second door.

He pushed the door open, allowing it to swing all the way against the wall, and drew his sword. He entered cautiously, braced for an attack. This room, too, was deserted but a triumphant light came into his eyes when he saw that he had found the storeroom. Sacks of milled grain lined one wall; along the far wall were barrels of what Caddaric assumed were wine. To his right stood tall amphorae, and above them were shelves holding clay jars of various shapes and sizes. Other shelves held bolts of material and spindles of thread and in one corner were stacked coils of rope. Caddaric put the torch into the wall bracket, sheathed his sword, and investigated the sacks of grain. All the sacks he opened contained wheat and Caddaric grinned. Using his knife, he cut a dozen lengths of rope from one of the coils and tied each end to one of the grain bags. When all twenty-four bags were secured, he turned his attention to the jars and amphorae. The amphorae contained olive oil, but the jars yielded dried figs, dates, honey and preserves. Caddaric grinned again, thinking of Jilana's pleasure when he returned with such delicacies. Leaving the torch in the wall, he went back to the entrance to retrieve the goods he had left there, and then returned to the storeroom.

'Twas his good fortune to have found these stores intact, ahead of someone else, Caddaric thought as he filled his bundle. Tomorrow, he and Heall would hunt rather than stay with the column, and if their luck held there would be meat enough to dry and cure. Still smiling, he draped the ropes containing the wheat around his neck and stood. The grain was heavy but he could manage easily enough. However, with the additional weight of the wheat and other supplies, he could not carry both casks of wine. Regretfully, Caddaric tucked one of the casks under his left arm and lifted the bundle with his right hand. He left the torch where it was. He would return later, for one of the bolts of material had been of a color that would match Jilana's eyes.

A movement close by the altar caught his eye and Caddaric stopped. "Who is there?" he asked, his eyes narrowed against the gloom. Only later would he realize that he had spoken in Iceni. There was no answer but he took a step closer to the altar.

"Come no closer!" A frightened, feminine voice ordered him from the shadows. When he ignored the challenge, the voice came again. "Stay away. I have a weapon."

"I will not harm you. Come out where I can see you." A slender shadow detached itself from the altar and moved just far enough for Caddaric to see that he was facing a young woman about Jilana's age but without her beauty. "Are you alone?" The poor thing was terrified; he could see the sword she held tremble in her hands, and Caddaric knew that he could not kill this girl even though the hatred she held for him was plain on her face. He would take her back to Jilana, Caddaric decided suddenly. Meaning to reassure the girl as to his intentions, he turned his back on her. "Come with me—"

Caddaric felt a crushing pressure begin in his back and continue through to his chest, accompanied by a grating sound. Then came the searing pain. The wine cask and

bundle dropped to the floor and Caddaric stared down
stupidly at the sword point protruding just below his right
collarbone. She had stabbed him. This poor, frightened
child had stabbed him! While he watched, the sword point
disappeared and he felt the blade grate against his ribs as
it was withdrawn. Blood coursed down the front of his
tunic, soaking the material, and he instinctively pressed
his fingers over the wound as he pivoted to face his as-
sailant. His head grew light and the girl seemed to dance
from one place to the other.

"I would not have hurt . . ." Caddaric's eyes rolled up
into his head and he crashed to the tiled floor.

"Stupid barbarian!"

The epithet rang in his ears just as he was kicked in the
side, and then he heard her retreating footsteps. Little
fool, he thought distantly, she was running straight to her
death. A welcoming void loomed in front of him and
Caddaric floated into it.

How long he was unconscious, Caddaric could not say.
When he woke, the torch still burned and light still came
through the smoke hole in the ceiling. His wound burned
like Hades and he felt weak, but Caddaric forced himself
to his feet. The wheat hung like millstones around his neck
and when he tried to lift his bundle of provisions with his
right hand, white-hot pain seared through his chest.
Stubbornly, he shifted the load to his left hand and
lurched toward the barred double doors at the front of the
cella. He had to set the bundle down in order to lift the
bar, and when he did, he nearly fainted from the pain the
action caused. He leaned his weight against the doors and
it was enough to swing them open. Sunlight poured over
his face, blinding him, and Caddaric staggered backward, nearly falling over his provisions. Grabbing the
bundle, he reeled through the doors and stumbled down
the first flight of steps leading from the temple. Poised on
the edge of the landing between the two tiers of steps,
Caddaric dimly heard someone call his name. Turning, he
tried to find who had called to him, but black spots leaped
in front of his eyes and the ground beneath his feet tilted

precariously. He felt himself falling, felt his shoulder strike the edge of the step and then he was tumbling downward.

On the street below, Heall watched in horror as Caddaric rolled down the middle flight of steps leading from the temple. With an agility that belied his age, Heall raced up the bottom tiers of stairs and reached Caddaric just as the younger man hit the second landing.

"Gods, Caddaric," Heall cried when he saw the blood soaking his tunic.

Caddaric's eyes forced themselves open. "I found... the... grain."

Tears brightened Heall's eyes. "Damn the grain! We have to get you to Clywd." He tried to lift the grain from Caddaric's neck, but Caddaric curled a hand around his wrist and groaned loudly in protest. Heall left the sacks where they were. Taking Caddaric's good arm, he lifted the younger man to his feet and draped his arm around his neck.

"The bundle," Caddaric gasped, fighting the weakness in his legs.

"I will come back for it," Heall said grimly.

"N-nay. I found... dates and... figs. For Jilana." Caddaric's head lolled forward and when next he opened his eyes, Heall was half carrying, half dragging him along the street. "The bundle."

"I have it," Heall snapped. "I only wish I could find a cart as well."

Caddaric laughed shortly and knew the taste of blood in his mouth. "No-no use. The Romans took their carts... with them."

"Save your strength," Heall ordered curtly. "I do not intend to carry you all the way to camp."

But, in the end, that was exactly what Heall did.

The wounded had started returning to the Iceni camp shortly after midday, and after much arguing, Jilana had persuaded Clywd to tend to the wounded while she remained in camp. In the end, he had agreed only because so many were asking for him and Jilana swore that she would not leave their camp. Before he left, however, Clywd gave Jilana a dagger for protection and she had kept it at her side throughout the afternoon. Jilana was adding wood to the fire and wondering whether or not to prepare oat cakes for the evening meal when she saw Heall and Caddaric.

A scream caught in her throat and she raced toward them. When she was close enough to see the blood covering Caddaric's right side, her face paled in horror. "What happened?" she gasped as she reached them.

"Can you not see he has been stabbed," Heall snapped at the girl, but Jilana was too shaken to be offended. He shoved the bundle at her. "Take this while I get him into the tent."

Jilana ran back to camp, threw the bundle into the wagon, and followed Heall into the tent. Together they took the grain from around Caddaric's neck and then Heall cut his bloodied tunic up the middle while Jilana took the weapons from his belt and removed it.

"Juno," Jilana whispered once the tunic had been stripped away. When Heall rolled Caddaric to his side in order to expose both wounds, she covered her mouth with her hand in order to stop the cry which sprang to her lips.

Heall glared at her. "Can you help him or should I find Clywd?"

A strange calm seemed to come over her and Jilana forced herself to examine the wounds. Blood bubbled from his mouth, a bad sign, and the wounds themselves showed no sign of clotting. "Stay with him," Jilana ordered in a soft voice and left the tent to get her medicine box. She returned with her case, a bowl, a jar of vinegar, and set about cleaning the wounds.

Since the injury went through from front to back, Jilana could neither sew it closed nor sear it. Instead, she made a thick pad out of one of the cloths to place over the wound, and, with Heall's help, bound it tightly in place with a long strip of linen. Caddaric remained blessedly unconscious throughout the entire ordeal. When Jilana left the tent to wash, Heall followed her.

"Will he live?" Heall demanded as Jilana poured water into a basin and washed her hands.

"I have done all that I can," Jilana answered, trying to still the quaver in her voice. "The blood in his mouth means the lung has been punctured, but I do not know how badly. The wound itself is clean, but there is always the danger of infection."

Heall watched Jilana for a long time, wanting to offer her comfort but uncertain how to go about it or how such an offer would be received. If Jilana and Caddaric were each other's destiny, the gods were certainly taking a perverse delight in keeping them apart, Heall thought. Feeling helpless, he at last busied himself with carrying the sacks of wheat from the tent to the wagon.

Jilana stared at the red-tinted water and forced back a scream. This was her fault, she knew. The gods were punishing her for the way she had treated Caddaric this morning. See what your pride has wrought, she bitterly chastised herself. Once his anger over Hadrian had passed, Caddaric had taken such care with her, shown her many small kindnesses which, as a slave, she had no right to expect. She had worked, to be sure, but so did every other woman in camp. And when her fears regarding Lhwyd had been realized, Caddaric had retaliated in the only way he knew how; as if, as he had often said, she was truly his woman, deserving of his protection. A foolish act, one that jeopardized the life she held more dearly than her own, but in Caddaric's eyes, he had had no choice.

Jilana emptied the basin, filled it with clean water and carried it into the tent. Caddaric lay on his left side, unconscious. Carefully, Jilana bathed the dirt from his face and body and covered him with a blanket. She laid a fresh fire inside the tent to ward off any evening chill and then sat quietly beside him, watching, occasionally touching his cheek and wiping away the blood that gathered in the corner of his mouth.

That was the scene that greeted Clywd when he hurried into his son's tent late in the afternoon. For a moment,

Clywd felt his heart stop, and when it started again its rhythm was painfully erratic.

"The bandage needs changing," Jilana said when Clywd knelt beside her, "but I was afraid to move him."

Clywd nodded and examined his son. Together, they removed the soiled dressing and replaced it with another. Clywd fashioned a pillow from blankets and pelts and, with Jilana's help, placed it on the pallet and moved Caddaric so that he lay on his back upon it. "'Twill help him breathe," Clywd explained when she directed a questioning look at him. From his medicine case he took a small vial of opium and handed it to Jilana. "He will need it when he wakes."

Trembling, Jilana took the vial, placed it in her own case and asked the question she was terrified to ask. "Will he live?"

"His lung is punctured and the bleeding must stop." Clywd touched his son's hair and Jilana saw that his hand was shaking also.

There was no more to be said, and the two of them sat in silence as evening fell. Heall entered quietly. "Forgive me, Clywd, but there is a lad outside who says you are needed. Shall I send him away?"

Clywd hesitated, clearly torn between his duty as a healer and his duty to his son, until Jilana told him, "If he worsens I will send Heall for you."

Clywd nodded and rose. "Change the bandage often. If—when he wakes, give him a dose of opium." He picked up his medicine case and cast one last look at his son. "If he needs me—"

"I will send Heall for you," Jilana repeated. "I swear it."

It was hours later that Caddaric swam slowly back to consciousness. He lay with his eyes closed, feeling the pallet beneath him and the tearing pain in his chest that made every breath an exercise in torture. Someone groaned and he forced his eyes open, wondering if Heall had been wounded as well. To his surprise, once he was able to bring his eyes into focus, he saw Jilana and his father bending over him and he was able to make out the leather ceiling of the tent. So he had made it back to camp after all. Clywd nodded to Jilana and she moved out of Caddaric's sight, and in her absence he could dimly make out Heall seated beside the small fire. Caddaric smiled weakly, trying to convey his relief at finding his friend safe, but his lips barely moved.

"Drink this."

Jilana was beside him, holding a cup to his lips. Caddaric obediently opened his mouth and swallowed the sweet liquid, his eyes clinging to Jilana's face. When he tried to speak, she laid a finger over his lips and shook her head warningly.

"Do not talk; save your strength." She placed a hand on his right shoulder and even her gentle touch sent waves of agony through him. "Your bandage needs changing but it means rolling you onto your good side. We will wait until the opium has taken hold." She smiled at him and reached for something on the ground. A moment later she was blotting his face and neck with a warm, wet cloth.

"Hate...changing my...ban-dage," Caddaric managed to say and Jilana felt her throat tighten.

It must be the effect of the opium, Caddaric thought, that made her eyes seem to fill with tears. He felt her fingers tremble when she laid them against his mouth again.

"Oh, Caddaric," Jilana whispered, "you are such a foolish man."

And then, miraculously, he felt her lips first upon his brow and then lightly upon his mouth. Her action stunned him, but the opium was spreading a warm glow through him and he gave himself up to the sensation. He was floating on the soft pallet and his eyes closed as he felt himself turning. The pain of the movement seemed far away, an insignificant thing, and he wondered why someone was groaning again.

It was all she could do not to cry out when Caddaric moaned as they turned him. Clywd was as shaken as she, but neither could give in to their emotions. They removed the old bandage and replaced it with a fresh one as quickly and efficiently as possible and eased Caddaric back onto the pallet. Clywd pulled the blanket away from him and shook him gently. Caddaric's eyes flickered open in response.

"Breathe for me, son," Clywd ordered. "As deeply as you can." He put his ear against the right wall of Caddaric's chest and listened.

Pain which not even the opium could master mushroomed through him when he obeyed his father's command, and this time Caddaric realized it was he who groaned so loudly. Sweat broke out on his forehead and was immediately replaced by a warm cloth against his skin. He pried his eyes open and looked directly up into Jilana's pale face. Ridiculous to think she could be worried about him, but just for a moment he allowed himself the fantasy. He lifted a hand toward her and she smiled and took it in hers.

"You must rest now," Jilana said, appalled at the way his muscles trembled. She dropped the cloth back into the basin, took his hand in both of hers and stroked it.

His eyelids were growing heavy and Caddaric fought against the blackness which threatened to engulf him again. He felt his lips moving and tried to force the words out of his throat. " . . . go . . . do n . . . go . . . ."

Jilana's heart lurched painfully and she bent closer. "Do you want me to go, Caddaric?" She held her breath until Caddaric slowly turned his head to one side.

"N-no."

Jilana gripped his hand fiercely. "I will never leave you, Caddaric. Never."

She stayed with him throughout the long night, as did Clywd and Heall, refusing to leave his side. Together she and Clywd changed his bandages and when he awoke, hers was the hand which held the cup containing the admixture of opium and water to his lips. When the pain caused the sweat to pop out on his face and chest, she bathed it away. Near dawn the bleeding stopped and they all breathed a little easier.

"You must rest," Heall admonished her as they ate the wheat cakes he had prepared. "Clywd and I managed to sleep during the night, but you did not."

"I will sleep later, when Caddaric is well," Jilana replied steadily.

"Heall is right," Clywd put in. "'Twill serve no purpose to have you fall ill as well."

Jilana's eyes traveled to the man sleeping a scant foot away. "Later." Her voice was filled with such resolve that neither man tried again to dissuade her.

Later that morning Heall joined the other men from his village to hunt while Clywd went to those who had need of him. Jilana took advantage of their absence to wash and change into a clean tunic. The one stained with Caddaric's blood she burned. She understood now why Caddaric had burned the clothes which had carried Artair's blood—Caddaric still lived, but even so she could not bear the sight of her stained tunic. She prepared a thin oaten gruel, and when Caddaric awoke for a few minutes, she managed to feed him a little before dosing him with the opium. Blood no longer trickled from his mouth and Jilana knew that was another good sign. Some of her worry faded.

Heall returned bearing a side of venison, several hares and, best of all, the news that they had found some cattle wandering in the forest that had escaped their fate when the Romans withdrew from Londinium. Each of the hunting party would receive a quarter of a side. While Heall and Clywd moved about the camp, dressing the game and making the necessary preparations for smoking the venison and beef, Jilana washed Caddaric with warm water and gently dried him. Clywd held that clean surroundings aided healing, though why he could not say, and Jilana had taken his words to heart. The cloths she used on Caddaric were used only once and then tossed aside. Clywd would launder them in water and vinegar this afternoon.

It was as she drew a fresh blanket over Caddaric—the one from the night before, drenched with Caddaric's sweat and spotted with blood would be washed along with the cloths—that Jilana noticed his skin felt unnaturally warm. Frowning, she touched her lips to his forehead and then, as her mother had taught her, held one of his hands between hers. His hands were warm and, worse, dry. Her heart in her throat, Jilana rose and called Clywd.

"He seems warm," Clywd agreed when he touched Caddaric's brow. "Help me remove the bandage."

When Jilana saw what lay beneath the dressing, her stomach revolted. The skin around both wounds was red and swollen, and a foul odor emanated from it. "The wounds were not like this when I changed the bandage last," Jilana cried softly. "What did I do wrong?"

"Naught, naught, child," Clywd soothed. "It happens like this sometimes." His face turned grim. "Now we must fight—and so must he."

The rest of the afternoon was a nightmare. The wound had to be thoroughly cleaned and, even in his drugged state, Caddaric would surely thrash about. Clywd and Heall would hold him down. To Jilana fell the task of spreading the edges of the wounds apart and probing as deeply as she could with a vinegar-soaked cloth. First, however, the dead skin from the wounds had to be cut away and Jilana did this under Clywd's instruction while the two men held Caddaric still.

"You are not strong enough to hold him motionless," Clywd had said when Jilana had begged him to trade places. "If he should move when the knife is against him..."

Clywd had not had to argue further. Jilana knew well enough that even in his weakened state Caddaric could easily throw her aside. Throughout the ordeal, Jilana's throat ached with unshed tears while Caddaric groaned and then screamed under her hands. When it was over and the men had left the tent, Jilana laid her head upon the pallet and let the tears come. At least the nightmare was over.

But it was not. The process was repeated that night and three times the following day. Jilana stayed beside Caddaric while the fever raged, trying to soothe him when he grew agitated and sponging him with cool water to try and bring his temperature down. At first he was quiet, but then he grew restless, kicking off the blanket or trying to tear the bandage from his chest until they were forced to tie his hands together so that he could not injure himself further. Then his ravings began—at least, in the beginning, Jilana thought they were nightmares, but when she listened more closely, she found that Caddaric was reliving old battles fought when he was a legionary.

As the fever rose, his nightmares took him deeper into the past, to his adolescence and then, to his childhood. From Caddaric's lips fell the story of his father's abrupt appearance in his life, a stranger to the son he had left behind. All the hurt and confusion felt by the boy poured forth while Jilana held the man's bound hands and offered comfort that would not be heard. The worst, however, was the destruction of Caddaric's village by the Roman invaders. In horror, Jilana listened and learned that Caddaric had hidden in the trees and seen his brothers carried off to meet their fate in the Roman auxiliary. He had also seen his mother and sisters cruelly raped and then killed by the legionaries while he had watched helplessly from his place of concealment. Tears scalded Jilana's cheeks and she cried for the boy who had lost so much in his life.

He spoke of Jilana as well, alternately cursing her and calling brokenly for her. She discovered how deeply she had hurt him by calling him a barbarian and a fool. And she learned how badly he wanted her and how badly his own desire frightened him. He hid his battered and scarred heart from her, afraid that one day she, too, would leave or, worse, reject him.

"I did not mean it," Jilana told him, her hands lovingly stroking the planes of his face. 'Twas foolish, of course, he neither heard nor understood her, but she drew some small comfort by talking to him. She rested her cheek against his. "Oh, Caddaric, all I wanted was for you to care for me." Raising her head, she looked at

Caddaric's face and discovered his eyes were slitted open, watching her. They still bore a fevered glaze, but there was no mistaking the recognition in them.

"Ji...lana," Caddaric said on a thread of sound. "You stayed."

"Of course I stayed," Jilana responded, straightening. Flustered, she set about sponging his face. "Where else would I be?"

"Water?"

Jilana hastily poured a cup of water and held it for him while he drank.

Caddaric's eyes surveyed the tent. "Have we kept up with...the war band?"

"We have not moved, nor has the rest of the column," Jilana quickly assured him. "The Queen has decreed that we stay here a week in order to gather provisions."

Caddaric sighed and relaxed against the pillow. "Stay with me," he whispered just as Jilana had decided that he was asleep again.

"Aye." Jilana covered his bound hands with hers and watched sleep claim him.

The third day after the battle Caddaric awoke and his fever was gone. He was weak, scarcely able to move, but his eyes were clear and when he demanded they untie his hands, Jilana knew he would live. She hovered over him, feeding him the beef broth Heall had made, bathing him. He seemed to enjoy the attention she lavished upon him until she brought him a battered basin and reached for the blanket.

"What are you doing?" Caddaric demanded, retaining a grip on the covering with his good arm.

Jilana blushed to the roots of her hair, but she was not about to be deterred. "I thought you might, ahh, that is, you must need to—umm—relieve yourself."

Caddaric looked amused. "I do, but I can manage on my own." He nodded toward the tent flap. "Out."

"Do not be ridiculous, Caddaric," Jilana retorted. "I have seen everything you possess—more than once, I might add—and you are still weak. It will not embarrass me—''

"Did you stop to think that it might embarrass me?" Caddaric questioned with a mocking lift of his eyebrow. "Out, Jilana. If I need help I will call for my father or Heall."

Which was exactly what he did. Jilana was allowed back inside the tent only after all his bodily needs had been seen to.

Caddaric greeted her return with, "Heall tells me you have not slept in three days."

Jilana stared at him. Had it been three days? She frowned, counting, and agreed, "Aye, it has been three days." Strange, but she did not feel sleepy. In fact, she was filled with such energy that she felt positively giddy.

"You need to sleep," Caddaric stated decisively. "Now."

"In a moment." Jilana gathered up the soiled cloths for laundering and took them outside to Heall. Next she straightened the tent, filled an ewer with water and placed it where it would be within easy reach for Caddaric, brought a small bowl of figs and dates and set them beside the pallet, and laid fresh wood for the evening fire.

As she straightened, Caddaric reached out with his good arm, grasped the hem of her tunic and pulled. "Rest, Jilana. Now."

Jilana twisted so that she could look at the hand holding her hostage. "I will get a blanket—"

But Caddaric had guessed her thoughts. Another tug of his hand brought her heels against the pallet. "Now. Here. With me."

"But, Caddaric, you are hurt and—"

"I will take the risk that you will injure me further," Caddaric informed her dryly. "I will not have you sleeping on the ground when there is room enough for us both on the pallet. Come to bed."

With an exasperated sigh, Jilana sat on the edge of the pallet and took off her shoes. "You will wake me if you

need anything?'' she worried as she carefully slid in beside him.

"I swear it," Caddaric promised as her head came to
rest beside his shoulder.

"You had better," Jilana admonished. "I really am not
the least bit tired, Caddaric."

"Close your eyes." He watched as she did so, and a
smile touched his mouth. When he softly called her name
a few minutes later, her response was a deep sigh. His
smile slowly faded as he realized that she was now a free
woman. She had cared for him because she believed she
was his slave, and a slave had certain duties to her master. When she learned she was free what would she do?
Certainly not share his pallet again, Caddaric grimly
concluded. It never occurred to Caddaric to withhold the
truth from her; nor did it occur to him that Jilana might
already know she was free. He closed his eyes and let sleep
overtake him.

JILANA AWOKE late in the evening to the feel of something tugging at her hair. Still half asleep, she smoothed
a hand over the back of her hair and was startled when it
met warm flesh. Turning, she saw that Caddaric was
awake and the tugging she felt was her braid being undone. She did not mind the small intimacy in the least.

"How do you feel?" Jilana asked, one hand smothering a yawn.

"Better." Caddaric allowed his gaze to skim over her
before returning to the business of unbraiding her hair.
"Heall made soup for the evening meal. Are you hungry?"

Jilana shook her head and settled more comfortably
onto her back. "You should be resting."

"I am," Caddaric protested innocently. "I am flat on
my back, in bed. What could be more restful?" Finished
with the braid, he lifted the heavy mass of hair onto his
chest and began combing the fingers of his left hand
through the red-gold length. "You have beautiful hair,
Jilana. Did I ever tell you that?" When she shook her

head, he sighed. "Of course I did not. There are many things I should have said that I have not, beginning with how sorry I am that I placed those cursed manacles on you."

"You were angry—"

"That did not give me the right to treat you the way I had sworn never to treat another human being!" Caddaric interrupted. "Gods! When I think of how I treated you—"

This time it was Jilana who interrupted. "I forgive you, Caddaric." She laced her fingers together and studied them. "When you first put the irons around my ankles, and then later, when you ordered me chained to the wagon, I hated you for it. But I do not hate you any longer."

"Truly?"

Jilana raised her eyes to his. "Truly. I am very lucky that Boadicea gave me to you."

Caddaric looked away from her trusting expression, remembering how he had manipulated the events of that night so long ago. "You are not mine any longer," he informed her gruffly. "Boadicea has freed you."

"I know." The startled look on his face brought a smile to Jilana's mouth. "Clywd told me the day of the battle."

His hand stilled on her hair. "Then you know you do not have to stay here."

"Aye, I know." Raising up on one elbow so that their faces were level, she asked, "But, Caddaric, how could I leave you?" His eyes, so dark a blue they were nearly black, bored into her, and she slowly brought her mouth to his. They kissed with their eyes wide open, watching, seeking, and when Jilana withdrew she said quietly, but with pride, "I love you."

Caddaric could not reply to her declaration. He cared for her as he had cared for no other woman, but to give voice to his emotions now, when he held his dream in the palm of his hand... Perhaps the gods were, even now, watching; waiting for him to open his heart so they could brutalize it yet again. He had mocked the gods so often in the past that, if they in fact existed, surely they would be waiting to take their revenge. With his good arm he pulled Jilana against him so that her head rested against his shoulder and said nothing, knowing himself to be a coward.

Jilana lay quietly, understanding his silence. By his actions he showed his love for her, even if he could not bring himself to say the words. It was enough for now; later—the gods willing, years from now—he would feel secure enough to give her the words as well, but she would not press him.

Long minutes later, Caddaric heard the faint chanting and the screams that came to their camp on the evening air. He stiffened, as did Jilana, but 'twas she who broke the silence.

"'Tis Lhwyd," Jilana told him when she felt the tension tightening his frame. "He claimed the survivors from the city."

Caddaric remembered the girl who had wounded him and hoped that she was not among the captives.

The week following the fall of Londinium the war band rested. Hunting parties roamed the countryside; the rivers and streams abounded with fish which provided a distraction for those too young to hunt; those who still had livestock slaughtered it, and meat was plentiful once again. Caddaric's recovery was, in Jilana's eyes, nothing less than miraculous. Once his fever had broken, he chafed so at remaining in the tent that Jilana capitulated and fixed a place for him by the fire. From there he could watch as she and Heall went about the business of preserving as much meat as they could. Clywd doted on his son with a fierceness that both amused and touched Jilana, but Caddaric seemed not to mind.

Visitors to their camp laughingly commented that the wound seemed to have improved Caddaric's disposition, but the way Caddaric's eyes followed Jilana's every movement did not escape their attention. Neither did the fact that when Jilana sat, her place was at Caddaric's side.

The week's respite grew into two and though Jilana enjoyed the rest, Caddaric did not. The war band was losing the urgency which had possessed it after the fall of Venta Icenorum. Women longed for their homes; children grew querulous now that the sense of adventure had worn off; and men fretted over what they would find upon returning home. The war band had to march, and soon, before desertion weakened both the morale and the number of Boadicea's force. Even though he knew it would be difficult for him to travel, he also knew that delay now could prove fatal. Suetonius Paulinus was no longer safely tucked away on Mona. When the word was passed through the host that Boadicea had ordered a resumption of the march, Caddaric breathed a sigh of relief.

"But surely there is no reason for your concern," Jilana asked. It was late and she was engrossed in bathing from the basin while Caddaric lay upon the pallet, watching.

"The governor-general is no coward," Caddaric replied. His eyes wandered over the enticing swell of her breasts as she washed first one and then the other, and his loins tightened uncomfortably. "He evacuated Londinium because it was indefensible. I do not doubt that even now he is marshalling his forces and picking a battle site that will favor the legion."

Jilana rubbed the cloth over her stomach, considering. "Boadicea has nearly seventy thousand warriors and warrior maids. Does Suetonius Paulinus have that many legionaries at his disposal?"

While Caddaric watched, the linen cloth dipped between her thighs and he felt the sweat pop out on his forehead. Her shyness with him was gone, but he was not certain if that was a blessing or a curse, for she was constantly warning him to take care lest he open his wounds again. If she only knew where his thoughts were wandering....

"Caddaric?"

At the sound of his name, Caddaric wrenched his eyes up to hers. He had not answered her question and now she was frowning at him as she rinsed out the cloth. "Aah, Paulinus. Nay, I doubt he can command an equal number in the field."

Jilana smiled and shrugged into the tunic she wore to bed. His tunic. "Then there is no need for concern, is there? Boadicea will defeat him easily enough." Blowing out the lamp, she slid onto the pallet beside him and settled into the crook of his arm. "Good night, my love." She reached up to kiss him gently on the lips.

The kiss she planned upon was not the sort he wanted. When Jilana would have withdrawn, Caddaric cupped the back of her head in his hand and held her fast. His tongue probed achingly at her mouth and, after a moment's hesitation, her lips opened on a soft sigh. He explored her mouth at leisure, sometimes bold, at times gently questing, until he felt her body press against his and her fingers curl into the hair on his chest.

"Caddaric," Jilana protested when his lips left hers in order to explore the line of her throat. "Your wounds . . . ahh. . . ." This as his hand closed around her breast.

"Hush," Caddaric admonished, his fingertips seeking her nipple through the material and teasing it awake.

Fiery sensations danced through her breast and arrowed down through her stomach. His mouth reclaimed hers, and Jilana boldly plunged her tongue into his mouth. Caddaric's hand drifted downward from her breast to cup her and her hips instinctively arched against the palm of his hand. Their mouths mated wildly while his hand slid beneath the hem of her tunic and caressed the soft flesh there.

"Take off the tunic," Caddaric ordered when he pulled his lips from hers. She hesitated and he slowly dragged her hand down his chest and stomach until it grazed his manhood. "I ache for you, little wicca; do not deny me again tonight." And with that he closed her hand around him and showed her all the desire which had been building in him.

He was as vulnerable as she, Jilana realized as she stroked him. A tremor ran through his strong frame; his hand fell away and he groaned while she explored that mysterious part of him. Emboldened, she rained kisses along his jaw, and when he tugged at the hem of her tunic, she struggled out of it and tossed it aside. Caddaric rolled to his back and watched Jilana return to him through heavy-lidded eyes. Her skin was a pale blur in the moonlight and when he reached out to run a finger from the hollow in her throat to her belly he felt her tremble.

"Wicca," Caddaric murmured, cupping her breasts. "You are everything I have ever wanted."

Resting her hands on his shoulders, Jilana bent and kissed him with all the love in her heart. His hands moved, stroked the length of her back and the firm mounds of her buttocks, then clasped her thighs and drew her upward so that her breasts were positioned above his mouth. Drawing each nipple into his mouth in turn, Caddaric laved the hard buds with his tongue and sucked gently on them. His long fingers teased the curls at the juncture of her thighs and, above him, Jilana cried out softly.

I want you, Caddaric, Jilana thought deliriously, or perhaps she said the words aloud; she did not know. All she knew was that his touch set fire to her blood and she wanted to be consumed by the flames. Sanity returned briefly when he gasped in pain and Jilana realized that she had rested her weight against his wound. "Caddaric, wait."

"Nay," Caddaric said thickly. His head tipped back and even in the moonlight, she could see the fierce glitter in his eyes.

"But your shoulder—" Jilana faltered. "How—"

"Watch." Caddaric drew one of her legs over his hips so that she straddled him. "Take me inside you, wicca."

She gasped when he entered her, but his lips were upon hers, swallowing the sound. His hands held her hips, lifting, guiding, teaching, and Jilana felt the world fall away.

The veil of her hair fell around them, touching Caddaric's thighs with a sensuous brush that threatened his sanity. He felt the change in Jilana when she took control of their embrace and he gave himself up to the riotous sensations she was creating. Her fingers dug into the hard muscles of his waist, and above the heavy thud of his own heartbeat, he could hear her softly cried endearments as she reached for her own fulfillment. With a wildness he had not known he possessed, Caddaric thrust violently upward and at that moment Jilana cried out and went rigid above him. A hoarse moan was torn from his throat when his own release came a heartbeat later.

Jilana collapsed upon his chest in a trembling heap, dazed but pleasantly sated. Caddaric's hand was tangled in her hair, holding her close, and she pressed a kiss onto the damp flesh over his heart. "I love you, Caddaric."

His hand tightened on her hair in response. "You are mine, Jilana. Nothing can take you from me now." He felt Jilana's smile against his skin and knew the strength of the magic between them.

Reluctantly, Jilana eased herself away from her love so that they were lying side by side. "What will we do when the rebellion is ended?"

Caddaric laced the fingers of his left hand with hers and silently studied them in the moonlight.

When he did not answer immediately, Jilana asked fearfully, "Caddaric?"

Sensing the path her thoughts had taken, Caddaric said, "We will be together, little wicca, do not fear."

"That is not an answer," Jilana pointed out, but inwardly she was relieved. Their changed relationship was still too new for her to be totally confident of it.

Caddaric sighed. "To think beyond the war," he said slowly, "is to tempt the Fates."

"I thought you did not believe in the gods, whether they be Roman or Iceni," Jilana could not resist teasing.

Caddaric gave her a fierce look that dissolved into a gentle, lingering kiss when she smiled at him. "The time to consider the future is when the final battle has been won, not before." Even as he said them, the words left a cold spot of fear in his heart.

"But we will be together," Jilana persisted, smoothing away the lines that suddenly appeared between his brows. "Always."

"How could you think otherwise?" He drew the blanket over them and settled her more comfortably against his side, effectively ending the conversation.

WITH HIS COLUMN of weary cavalry and terrified civilians, Suetonius Paulinus reached Verulamium two days after Londinium fell to Boadicea. Though he deplored the slow pace, the evacuees were his responsibility and he could not leave them behind. Word of the uprising had spread to Verulamium and Paulinus found the city in a panic which seemed to subside when the citizens saw the legion. Their relief was to be short-lived. Verulamium was as indefensible as Londinium had been, and even though news of the uprising had reached the city a month earlier, no effort had been made to fortify the city. The Romans on this accursed island were no better than sheep, Paulinus railed at his officers. Did they honestly believe there were enough men in the legions to protect every city and outpost? His officers stood silently during his tirade, knowing no response was expected—or wanted. When the initial rage had passed, Paulinus swallowed his bitter frustration and summoned the city's leaders and priests. The city was to be evacuated; the people could take whatever they could carry without slowing down the column. The legion would accompany them as far as the road to Glevum; the civilians should be able to reach Augusta's fortress unescorted. Verulamium, Paulinus announced, would be razed in order to deny the enemy comfort and provisions. The citizens had twenty-four hours.

The following morning was a repetition of the evacuation of Londinium, with one notable exception. This time the century that brought up the rear fired all the buildings before withdrawing. The taste of smoke lingered in the mouths of all who traveled in Paulinus' column. The taste would follow the governor-general to his deathbed. Wherever the column traveled, they razed farms and slaughtered the livestock. If the owners were present, they were allowed to gather their belongings before watching their homes burn to the ground, but in his wake, Paulinus left destruction.

When the civilians were safely on the road to Glevum, Paulinus set about selecting a battleground. He would retreat no further—his men were weary and demoralized and his supplies were running out. Unlike the Celts, his men would not eat venison or the occasional head of cattle they stumbled across until they faced certain starvation. For better or worse, he would take on the rebel Iceni queen. His search took three weeks, but in the end he found a place that suited his needs.

The site was approached by a narrow defile which opened onto a plain. To its flanks and rear rose heavily wooded hills. Paulinus rode over the sight a dozen times with his senior centurion, debating and weighing the odds. The grassy plain was well-suited for a pitched battle, and the narrow defile meant that Boadicea would have to funnel her forces through it to the plain, but even better, she could not make an organized withdrawal if the tide of battle went against her, as Paulinus fervently prayed it would. The wooded hills made escape—and retreat—impossible. The legion would be boxed in with no direction to go except forward. But that would work to the legion's advantage. With their backs to a wall, the legionaries would fight with mindless ferocity. And if Boadicea had even half the estimated number of warriors, the Iceni would be hard-pressed to maneuver in such a confined area. Paulinus made his camp on the plain and sent messengers northward to guide his infantry to the battleground.

"JUNO," JILANA BREATHED. Caddaric had chosen today to ride instead of staying in the wagon, and she had eagerly accepted his invitation to accompany him. Before her lay the remains of what had once been a city but was now nothing more than charred timber and crumbled mortar. The wind had not been able to disperse the pall of ashes and burned animal hides which still hung in the air.

Beside her, Caddaric kept a steady hand on his stallion's reins. The bloated Iceni column had taken six days to travel the thirty miles from Londinium to Verulamium, and the sight that awaited them at the end of the trek now sent a wave of dismay through them. They were seeing the work of an enemy who gave no thought to destroying a city and the animals that could not be evacuated.

"Paulinus." Caddaric said the name in a stark, flat voice.

Jilana did not have to ask why the governor-general would do such a thing. She had learned much of tactics from Caddaric. "It does not matter," she said quietly. "Once the rebellion is ended, the Catuvellauni will rebuild the city."

"If any remain. Most of the Catuvellauni are now more Roman than Celt." Caddaric reined his horse around. "Let us find Heall and Clywd and make camp for the night."

When they had found the two men, they set up their camp and took stock of their supplies. Thanks to Heall and Caddaric's avid scavenging, the two wagons were filled with grain, wine and meat. "We are better provisioned than many," Clywd said when the last bag of grain had been packed back into the wagon. "A sack of wheat is selling for ten gold pieces and a haunch of venison—" He shook his head. "Boadicea must end this quickly, so we can return home."

Caddaric sent his father a hard look. "And what will we find there? Granaries that were emptied when we began the rebellion and unsown fields."

"The cattle and horses were turned loose before we left," Heall reminded him. "It may take time, but we can track them down."

"Aye. Now they can graze, but how will we feed them during the winter when there is no grain to be harvested?'' No one had an answer for him, and Caddaric absently massaged the ache in his right chest. "We cannot worry about what will happen; the present is what matters." He drew a deep breath. "And for the present, we must stringently ration our supplies." He looked into the deep purple of Jilana's eyes and smiled slightly. "No more wheat cakes."

Jilana shrugged and dredged up a smile for him. "I had lost my taste for them."

"Liar," Caddaric mocked, but when he helped her down from the wagonbed, he kissed her lovingly. Jilana melted against him, oblivious to Heall and Clywd standing not far away. When he released her, the loving expression on her face tripped his heart. "Jilana, I wish the circumstances were different, that I could provide you with all the comforts you knew in your father's house."

"You are all the comfort I need," Jilana said with a shake of her head.

Still, it ate at Caddaric that she had lost so much that he could never replace. While Jilana prepared their meal, Caddaric took from the wagon the section of sapling Heall had cut and stripped for him. The wood was as long as a sword—though not as heavy—and as thick as his wrist, and each night Caddaric used it to practice the thrusts, slashes and parries of which swordplay was comprised. Jilana had been horrified when he had begun the exercises, fearing he would do further damage to his shoulder and chest, but he knew the importance of exercising the weakened muscles. Left alone, they would stiffen and his usefulness as a warrior would be ended. Tonight he drove himself even harder, dodging and twisting away from an imaginary opponent while his arm constantly extended, slashed and withdrew until he was covered with sweat.

"'Tis nearly time for the meal," Jilana informed him when he finally came to rest, panting, against a tree trunk. Walking to him, she raised a critical eyebrow. "And you need a bath. Come, there is a stream not far from here." Taking his hand, she led him away from camp.

Caddaric followed docilely, massaging the deep ache in his chest with the heel of his hand.

"You worked too hard," Jilana scolded when she spied his action.

"Not as hard as I work at night," Caddaric said with a wicked grin, delighting in the blush that stained her cheeks.

"Caddaric," Jilana exclaimed, darting an anxious look over her shoulder.

"Everyone knows you share my bed," Caddaric teased.

"I know, but—"

"Are you afraid someone will overhear me and think you too demanding?" Caddaric stepped from the grassy bank to the rock- and tree-littered shore and helped her down.

Jilana sent him a scathing look. "Certainly not."

Laughing, Caddaric came to an abrupt halt and yanked Jilana against him. "I do not think you are too demanding, either."

"That is not what I meant," Jilana began furiously.

"In fact," Caddaric continued as if she had not spoken, "I think we are well-suited." He dipped his head and captured her mouth.

Jilana struggled for a moment before surrendering to his hungry kiss. Pleasure arrowed through her and when she wrapped her arms around his neck he crushed her against his chest. Even through the layers of clothing separating them, Jilana felt his rising desire and grew warm with anticipation. She rose up on her toes and wantonly rubbed herself against him. His tongue plunged into her mouth and his hands slid to her buttocks, cupping them and holding her in place until they were both aching with need.

Jilana's eyes opened, revealing their deep purple color and dilated pupils. "Your bath." Baring her teeth in a wild, primitive smile, she stripped the tunic from him and pressed kisses across the expanse of hair-roughened chest she had exposed.

"Aah, Jilana," Caddaric groaned. "Here...let me...."
He cupped the back of her head in one hand and guided
her lips to the left side of his chest. She hesitated only a
moment and then he felt her tongue flick experimentally
against his nipple. Her teeth found it next, and then she
drew it into her mouth with a sweet suction that threatened to make his knees buckle.

Jilana drew back to stare at the flesh that had turned
pebble-hard under her ministrations. She brushed it
wonderingly with a fingertip and looked up when Caddaric shuddered in response. His eyes were open, watching her. "'Tis as sensitive as mine."

"Aye," Caddaric grated, the breath rasping in his
throat. "Again, wicca, I...." His words dissolved when
her mouth turned to his burning flesh.

Someone could stumble upon them at any moment, but
when Jilana glanced up at Caddaric's face, that caution
fled. Caddaric's head was thrown back, exposing the twin
cords in his neck, and his eyes were tightly closed, as if he
found the pleasure unbearable. And she was the source of
that pleasure. With hands that trembled ever so slightly,
Jilana undid his loincloth and pushed the material off his
hips. Her hands worshiped him, loved him, and his groans
mingled with the wind stirring the trees and the tumbling
sound of water cascading over the rocks in the stream bed.

"Jilana," Caddaric moaned when she ended the twin
torments of her hands and mouth.

"'Tis time for your bath."

Caddaric forced his eyes open as Jilana grasped the hem
of her tunic in both hands and slid it upward with deliberate slowness. When she was as naked as he, she held out
her hand and he took it mindlessly, willing to follow
wherever she would lead. At midstream, the water came
to their thighs. Jilana knelt and urged Caddaric down beside her. The cold water should have shocked him, but
Caddaric felt only heat, and when Jilana cupped her
hands and began to lave water over his head and shoulders, he caught his breath at the wild glitter in her eyes.
Her hands caressed his shoulders, his arms, his chest,

washing away the sweat and grime. When he was clean, she washed herself as well, and he followed every movement of her hands as they traveled over her body.

Jilana moved so that the tips of her breasts brushed his chest. After the nights they had spent in each other's arms, she knew the signs that heralded his impending loss of control. "Now, Caddaric," she purred, "do you still think we are well-suited?"

In answer, Caddaric grasped her shoulders and pulled her into his arms for a wild kiss. Her arms circled his neck while his tongue plundered the sweetness of her mouth.

"Love me," Jilana murmured when his mouth released her.

"I do, wicca," Caddaric responded, and then he gasped as her thighs brushed his and she lowered herself onto his manhood. "Gods, Jilana, not here—" His desire to take her in privacy gave way to a more pressing need when her hips slowly rotated and he shuddered.

"Love me," Jilana repeated breathlessly, her body humming as she absorbed his strength. His hands fell to her buttocks, lifting her, steadying her, and she felt the first pulsings of ecstasy deep in her belly.

Her neck arched and she cried out softly, her fingers burying themselves in his hair. "See how perfectly we fit together," Caddaric whispered against the hollow of her throat. His mouth found her breast and his tongue lashed at the pink crest.

"Caddaric!"

He felt the storm take her, felt the spasms where she sheathed him so tightly, and greeted his own release with a hoarse cry. For what seemed an eternity they remained locked together, their heads cushioned upon each other's shoulders, heedless of the water coursing around them.

"You amaze me, wicca," Caddaric murmured when she stirred in his arms. She kissed him lingeringly and rose from the water and he reluctantly followed.

Her hair was soaked and Jilana undid the braid and combed her fingers through the heavy mass while the breeze dried their bodies. "I am a fine one to talk about discretion," she said wryly, eyeing the discarded clothing strewn upon the rocks. Turning to Caddaric, she mockingly accused, "'Tis all your fault, tempting me so."

Caddaric shook his head and grinned. "I meant only a kiss; you did the rest."

"So I did." Jilana grinned in return and dropped the tunic over her head. "Next I suppose you will accuse me of making you miss your meal."

"Even so." Caddaric knotted the loincloth around his waist and patted his stomach.

Jilana sighed dramatically. "'Tis a woman's lot to satisfy her man's need only to have another take its place." She teasingly patted his stomach as he had done, but he caught her wrist in his hand and the hard expression on his face brought an abrupt end to her play. "What is it, Caddaric?"

"Is that how you think of me, Jilana," Caddaric asked carefully, "as your man?"

"Aye," Jilana answered, her voice as steady as she could make it. "Should I not?"

Caddaric drew a deep breath and tempted the Fates. "I love you, Jilana." While he watched, her eyes widened and filled with tears. "I want you beside me, always. My father was right: you are the other half of myself, my destiny."

"Oh, Caddaric," Jilana choked out just before she threw herself into his arms. "You captured my heart so long ago, I cannot remember when it did not belong to you."

Caddaric's heart took wing and he lifted Jilana and swung her about. How alive he felt, and how wonderfully free! As if he could dare anything, battle any foe, and emerge victorious knowing that his woman would be waiting for him. Jilana was in his arms, proclaiming her love while alternately laughing and crying and he knew— *knew*—that he had been right to risk his heart this one last time.

His heart swelling with love for the woman in his arms, Caddaric willingly broke his own rule. Setting her back on

the ground, he vowed, "When the war is over we will go
north, back to my village. We will build a life there, wicca,
perhaps not as comfortable as the one Lucius would have
given you, but a good life nonetheless."

Jilana smiled and shook her head. "All I want, my
fearsome warrior, is a life with you. A bothie will be a
palace as long as we share it."

Caddaric twisted a strand of damp, red-gold hair
around his fingers and brought it to his lips. He cleared his
throat and when he spoke, he was touchingly uncertain.
"I would like it very much if we shared the bothie as husband and wife."

For a moment, Jilana was too stunned to answer and
when she found her voice it shook. "I understand your
ways, Caddaric, and accept them. I will be content to live
as your woman, knowing you love me. You need not
marry me."

"Are you refusing?" Caddaric asked mildly, running
his lips up and down the side of her neck. "For if you are,
know you that I come from a line of men who think
nothing of kidnaping a woman and holding her until she
agrees to wed." When she laughed, he nipped warningly
at her earlobe. "Besides, little wicca, your Roman conscience would not be comfortable with anything less than
marriage. And neither would mine."

Jilana's head fell back against his arm and she lost herself in his blue, fathomless gaze. "Ahh, well, if you are
going to threaten me..." The words trailed away as he
claimed her mouth, and when she surfaced a long while
later she murmured, "I think I will enjoy being your
wife."

Before she could change her mind—not that she would,
Jilana indignantly told him—Caddaric dressed and hurried her back to camp where he announced their betrothal to Heall and Clywd. Clywd looked smugly
pleased—as if he had planned their marriage from the
start—and did not insist that she offer Caddaric water
with which to wash when he pointed out, to Jilana's embarrassment, that they had just bathed and were surely

clean enough. Nor, since their supplies were rationed, did Clywd mention even going through the motions of a feast. Heall, to Jilana's great surprise, both laughed and shed a tear over her, then set off to announce the wedding to their village.

They were wed the next night, Jilana in her best white stola and her head draped with the saffron veil, and Caddaric resplendent in black tunic and breeks and his blue cloak. The chariot in which Jilana rode to the ceremony, with Heall driving, as well as the magnificent pair of white horses, had again been loaned by Boadicea for the festive occasion, and the Queen herself attended the ceremony.

Ensconced beside Heall in the wicker chariot, Jilana was the last to arrive. The chariot moved slowly through the crowd while Clywd offered up the ancient song of praise and joy which accompanied the bridal procession. Clywd welcomed the witnesses to the marriage and then placed wreaths of mistletoe upon Jilana and Caddaric's brow. He called upon Be'al and the attendant gods and goddesses to bless the union and protect any issue that might result from it. When the blessing was finished, Heall stepped down from the chariot and Caddaric took his place. Caddaric's lineage was recited by Clywd, as was Jilana's, although hers was, perforce, not as lengthy as his. Caddaric's chieftain and the filid—the man who, Jilana remembered from Ede's marriage, was responsible for the histories of the village's families—took their places on either side of Clywd and the filid asked Caddaric what wealth he brought to the marriage. Jilana's heart sank as she listened to Caddaric recite the number of horses and cattle which made up his portion of what was to be their joint fortune. Unlike Ede, she had nothing to contribute. The villagers would understand, Jilana told herself when the filid repeated his question for her. Nervously, she wet her lips and opened her mouth to respond.

"The bride brings thirty gold pieces to the marriage."

Heall strode forward and Jilana gaped at him, as did the rest of the village. He carried a leather purse in one hand and, for the benefit of all those assembled, he

opened it and counted the contents into the filid's hands.
When the filid was satisfied, the coins were poured back
into the purse, which Heall then delivered to Jilana.

"Heall, 'tis most generous of you but—"

Heall smiled at her and pressed the purse into her hand.
"Now you are a proper bride, child. No self-respecting
Iceni woman would enter into a marriage without a
dowry."

Jilana clutched the purse in both hands as Clywd solemnly informed the bride and groom of the responsibilities marriage entailed and made the sacrifices of the grain
and mead Caddaric had placed upon the makeshift altar.
The gold was a mere fraction of the dowry her father
would have paid Lucius upon their marriage, but to Jilana, its size made it no less important. She had no doubt
that Heall had just sacrificed all of his wealth for her, so
that her marriage would be as valid as any other, and her
eyes filled with tears for the old man. As she repeated the
vows that bound her to Caddaric, Jilana silently welcomed Heall into her heart as well. She had lost her family, as Heall had, so perhaps the gods had meant for them
to find and adopt one another. It comforted Jilana to believe so.

Their tent had been set apart from the rest of the wagons, and when the ceremony was ended, the villagers surrounded the chariot and accompanied them back to their
shelter. Caddaric had set out three kegs of wine earlier,
and in their absence, two large fires had been lit. Caddaric lifted Jilana from the chariot and, keeping a firm
hand around her waist, led her through the laughing,
cheering crowd to their tent. When they reached the tent
flap, he slanted her a wicked gaze and then proceeded to
kiss her thoroughly in front of the villagers. To his surprise, she threw her arms around his neck and kissed him
back with the same fervor he had displayed. When the
laughter of the crowd broke them apart, the grin on his
face was belied by the passion flaring in the depths of his
eyes.

"Long life," Clywd said, embracing his son and then Jilana.

Heall did the same, and Jilana embraced him warmly. "How can I ever thank you?"

Heall drew back and smiled at her. "I think I would like to see that one," he inclined his head toward Caddaric, "surrounded by children as stubborn as he." He gave a satisfied nod. "Aye, half should be sons who will be as stubborn as he and the other half should be daughters who will lead the boys of the village a merry chase."

Jilana chuckled, even though her cheeks pinkened, and then Caddaric was drawing her into the tent. A small fire had been lit, and the tent was filled with a warm, golden flickering light. Outside they could hear the toasts being offered in their honor and they smiled at one another.

"What did Heall say to you?" Caddaric asked as he lifted the saffron veil from her hair. She had left her hair unbound, in the Iceni tradition, and now he combed his fingers through the tumbling length.

"That you deserved children who would turn you as gray as he," Jilana laughed. "'Twould fulfill the rest of your prophecy."

Caddaric's hands left her hair and moved to frame her face. "A child was but the means to bind you to me, like the chains I forced you to wear. The prophecy was fulfilled when you gave me your heart—I need nothing else, my love."

"Nor do I." Jilana laid her head upon his shoulder and touched her lips to his neck. "Yet, 'twould give me great pleasure to bear your child, Caddaric."

"'Twould please me as well," Caddaric admitted, one large hand falling to her abdomen, "but later, when he— or she—" he conceded with a laughing glance at her, "can be raised in peace."

"As you wish, lord," Jilana teased, her fingers slipping under the neck of his tunic to caress his warm flesh.

Caddaric closed his eyes, savoring the familiar heat that flared in his blood. "Most of my life has been spent in war. I am so weary of battle, sweet wicca."

Jilana raised her face to his and met his descending mouth with feminine greed. His hands roamed over her body, lighting fires wherever they alit, and she returned touch for touch, eager to please him and—for this night at least—protect him from the violent part of the world.

Clothes fell away beneath eager hands; each newly-exposed area of flesh was touched with fingers and mouths until Jilana's legs gave way and she sank into the soft furs. Under Caddaric's guidance, she stretched full length upon the pallet, the furs sensuously caressing her back. Caddaric towered above her; the fire at his back shadowed his face, but she could feel the masculine desire radiating from him and her eyes fluttered shut. He came down beside her a moment later and she lifted her arms, anticipating the crush of his body against hers. Instead, a finger began drawing concentric circles around her breast and her eyes opened.

Caddaric knelt beside her, a cup of wine in his right hand. While she watched, he dipped his forefinger into the wine and resumed the intricate tracing of her breast. Her skin grew damp with the liquid and he paid particular attention to the pink crest which stiffened achingly when he touched it. Satisfied, he withdrew his hand and Jilana gasped when his mouth followed the same path his finger had taken.

"Your skin is so soft, so sweet," Caddaric murmured. He teased the stiff crest of her breast with his mouth and then his tongue curled lovingly around it. When her arms raised, he whispered, "Nay, not yet. Let me love you first. We have all night."

His words dissolved into throaty coaxings and endearments and he lavished the same care on her other breast. Jilana's fingers curled into the furs as Caddaric deliberately seduced every part of her body with his tormenting magic. She arched and twisted, longing to touch him, but her every attempt was gently, but firmly, repulsed. When he flavored her womanhood with wine, she would have protested but his mouth was there before she could voice the words and then she was incapable of speaking. Pleasure exploded through every part of her and she cried out and sank her fingers into his arms.

Dazed, she felt Caddaric raise himself above her and she slowly opened her eyes to meet his gaze. A pleased smile lay upon the hard line of his mouth and she raised a languid hand to trace the curve of his lower lip. "How—"

Caddaric's smile grew at the unformed question. "How I learned is not for your ears, wicca." He kissed the palm of her hand and then teased her mouth until her lips were parted and glistening with his moisture. He rubbed the callused pad of his finger over her bottom lip, then caught his breath as her tongue laved the tip and tentatively drew it into her mouth.

A violent shudder ran through his massive frame and Jilana seized the advantage to push Caddaric onto his back. Remembering the pleasure he had given her, she explored him just as thoroughly, though she scorned the wine. She loved the taste of him upon her tongue, the feel of his flesh against her lips. She rubbed her cheek against the pelt of fur covering his chest, then roused the flat, masculine nipples from their protective whorls of soft hair.

"Not yet," she taunted when his hand tangled in the wild length of her hair. But it was more a plea than a command. They both knew her desire was growing apace with his, and she would be helpless to stop him if he chose to end the torment. Reluctantly, his hand fell away and she expelled a small, grateful sigh.

The plane of his stomach with its arrow of curls seemed oddly vulnerable, although she could feel the muscles jump beneath her lips. Her hair flowed over him, sensitizing his skin, and she felt it twine with the thick wedge on his chest. Her fingers raked down his sides and slid beneath him to clench daringly into the resilient flesh of his buttocks and then, allowing love and instinct to guide her, she took the heart of his passion into her mouth. The intensity of his reaction first stunned, then enraptured her and she gloried in the wild contraction of his muscles and the loving phrases that were little more than groans when they fell from his lips.

Caddaric felt the breath rasp in his throat and knew he was at the limit of his control. Her fingers were scoring his inner thighs now and his entire body was pulsing heavily at her ministrations. He loved the feel of her skin against his, the sight of her in the golden light as she bent over him, loving him. 'Twas the cruelest of torments—and he wanted it to go on forever. His tongue flicked out to moisten his dry lips, tasted her essence lingering upon them and reason deserted him. With arms that trembled, he reached for Jilana and hauled her upward along his length, savoring the sensation.

Jilana went willingly, desperately wanting the fierce warrior who flipped her onto her back and rose above her, his face intensely savage in the wavering light. Caddaric stared down at her, his nostrils flaring, admiring her wild, barbaric mien and knew in that moment that she possessed not only his heart but his soul as well.

She cried out at the driving impact of him, and wrapped him in her legs and arms. He stroked and teased, driving them straight into the tempest. They merged so completely that he could no longer tell where his flesh ended and hers began and then it no longer mattered. The completion was violent; the leather walls muted their cries and he caught his breath with each long, slow pulse that filled her with his seed.

Caddaric rolled to his side with Jilana locked firmly against him. He could not bear to leave her, not yet, and they lay intertwined while their hearts gradually slowed. Brushing the wild curls away from her cheek, he looked down and willed the lovely, violet eyes to open. When they did, he kissed her gently and settled her damp body more comfortably against his.

"Caddaric—"

He laid a cautioning finger over her lips. "No words, not tonight. Just let me show you how much I love you."

Wide-eyed, she nodded, and he began the magic all over again. They filled the night with their love, ignoring the inevitable approach of dawn in favor of creating a lifetime of memories. When Jilana finally slept, Caddaric held her close, watched the dying embers of the fire and knew fear. Love brought the inherent promise of life and he cursed the gods for allowing him to find love in the midst of war, when death was more certain than life. Aye, he admitted to himself, he feared the next battle, for now he had Jilana and he wanted nothing more than to return to her. He had mocked his father's gods, cursed them, even denied them, but now Caddaric silently, hesitantly, offered a prayer to Be'al. Surely, after all the gods had taken from him, they could grant him this one wish.

The morning brought a resumption of the march. Verulamium and the land surrounding it were barren; no purpose would be served by remaining. Though she had slept little the previous night, Jilana went about the business of breaking camp with a light step, supremely at peace with the world. Her contentment was shattered, however, when Heall and Caddaric saddled their horses and brought them to the wagons. Clearly, her husband intended to rejoin the vanguard.

A chill invaded Jilana's heart, but she bit back the protest that sprang to her lips. Instead, while the men filled their skins with water from the barrel, she took a sack of grain and one of dried venison from the wagon.

"Do not forget to eat," she admonished Caddaric, handing him the provisions. "And do not tax your shoulder."

Caddaric nodded and hung the bags from the saddlebow. Odd how he had come to know her so well, he thought, turning back to Jilana. She looked calm, but he could sense the tension in her and knew that she was against his decision to return to the Queen's vanguard. "I am well, wicca."

"Aye." He reached for her and Jilana went up on tiptoe to kiss him lightly. She had left her hair unbound, and his hand tangled briefly in its length before he released her. She did not question why this parting, which had been a part of the normal routine before their marriage, was so different now; she merely accepted the fact that it was. But when she watched the two men ride away, a proud smile touched her mouth. Perhaps she was, in fact, becoming a warrior's woman. With that thought, she climbed into the wagon and swung the team to the north-west.

Two days later, Caddaric volunteered to lead one of the night patrols that roamed the countryside in advance of the Iceni column. While Jilana drove their wagon, Caddaric slept in the back, waking only when they stopped to make camp for the night. Jilana prepared the evening meal and, while the men ate, she fixed Caddaric's provisions.

"I can do that, wicca." Though his footsteps had been silent, Jilana had sensed his approach and he smiled when she did not start, simply turned to smile at him.

"It gives me something to do," Jilana countered.

Caddaric nodded and leaned against the wagon while she worked. The sight of her sent a pang through his heart. She consistently wore her hair down now, and part of their evening ritual upon retiring to the privacy of their tent was for him to comb the tangles out of its glorious length. It was an exercise that soothed both of them, creating an air of intimacy that brought them even closer and allowed Caddaric to open his heart and mind to her.

To think he had once wondered how to talk to a Roman lady like Jilana! They were so greedy to know one another that the words spilled out as they shared their lives, their thoughts, and he smiled fondly, remembering the night past when she had taken a branch and carefully scratched a series of lines in the dirt. He had been shocked when Jilana had proudly announced that the lines were her name and that she could read and write and do sums as well. Having had no sons, her father had decided to educate his daughters. Claudia had shown no interest or inclination in anything other than the traditional feminine disciplines of music and dance, but Jilana had gloried in the learning. And she had promised to teach him how to read, beginning last night when she had taught him to print his name. There was, Caddaric discovered, no shame in admitting that Jilana was better educated than he.

"What are you thinking?"

Caddaric drew himself away from his thoughts and smiled at his bride. "That I should teach you to wield a sword in exchange for my lessons?"

To his surprise, Jilana's eyes lit up. "Would you?" she asked excitedly.

Caddaric chuckled and shook his head. "What has happened to my proper Roman lady?"

"She is Iceni now, or as much so as she can possibly be," Jilana responded tartly, shoving his food at him. "When can we begin?" she prodded. "How long will it be before I am as proficient as Ede?"

Laughing, Caddaric gave her hair a gentle tug. "Such a bloodthirsty little thing! Ede has trained since she was a child—'twill be years, if ever, before you are as capable as she." At her crestfallen expression, he pulled her into his arms. "Understand, my heart, an Iceni woman is free to choose her path; no one thinks less of a female who chooses not to become a warrior maid."

"I want you to be proud of me—"

He tipped her face up to his and gazed into her wide violet eyes, seeing the uncertainty there. "I will be proud of you whether or not you can wield a sword or battle-axe; it does not matter to me. You must do what you want to do."

His sincerity was obvious and Jilana smiled. "Then I would still like to learn."

"Then I will teach you, once we have the time." Caddaric kissed her tenderly and then, regretfully, moved away. "Let me raise the tent for you before I leave."

Jilana shook her head. "The night is warm. I would prefer to sleep beneath the stars." In truth, she did not think she could bear to be alone in the tent they shared.

Caddaric guessed her reasons for wanting to sleep in the open and did not argue. Their separations, even for so short a time, cut him as well. Before he could weaken further, he saddled his golden stallion, gave Jilana a swift, hard kiss and left the camp.

That night the nightmares came again. Jilana awoke, her throat aching with a silent scream, and tried to calm the frantic beating of her heart. Rolling from beneath the wagon, she poured water into the basin and rinsed the cold sweat from her face and neck, seeking to rinse away the bloody images as well. Only a dream, she tried to tell herself, brought on by her conversation with Caddaric. But she knew better. This dream was similar to the ones in which she had seen Mona's destruction, but this time her vision was populated with people she had grown to know and care about. And Caddaric was in the dream.

"Come, daughter, share a cup of wine with me."

Jilana whirled around to find Clywd standing a few paces away. Behind him Heall snored, oblivious to all else. Clywd spread his cloak on the ground and, shuddering, Jilana sank upon it while he poured each of them wine.

"Now," Clywd said when he had handed her one of the cups and settled himself beside her, "what troubles you?"

Jilana swallowed half the wine before replying. "'Twas a dream, one of destruction, of a place I have never seen."

Clywd covered the delicate hand that rested upon her knee and felt her tremble. "Show me."

"Show—" Jilana looked at him in confusion. "How can I show you?"

Clywd's hand lifted and his fingers drifted lightly over her eyes, closing them. "'Tis not so fearsome. Take a deep breath, release it, and allow yourself to remember."

Jilana did as he asked, but as soon as the first image appeared behind her closed lids, her eyes flew open. "I cannot."

"Drink your wine," Clywd commanded gently. "Now, try again."

When she did as he asked, a strange lethargy descended upon her, and Jilana felt as if she were adrift in the tepidarium of her father's bath. Her tension and fear dissolved and she wondered, fleetingly, if Clywd had drugged her wine. "Remember, Jilana." Clywd's voice seemed to come from a great distance. "Show me what you have seen."

It was absurdly easy to do as he bid. Now that the terror was gone, she allowed her mind to return to the dream, but this time there was a startling difference. Now she and Clywd stood side by side in a dense forest which grew on a hill. Although the world was bathed in sunlight, there was a chill to the air where they stood beneath the shelter of the trees. Below them two great armies did battle, and the sounds of the engagement fell harshly upon her ears. To her right, Jilana could see the aquila of the Roman legion and on the left were the wicker chariots of the Iceni and the tall, regal figure of Boadicea. Clywd's hand was upon her shoulder and she forced herself to look into his eyes.

"You must show me the rest."

Strange, but though Clywd's lips had not moved, she heard him clearly. Nodding, she turned back to the sight below them and concentrated on one place in the line where the armies met. The next instant, she and Clywd were there, but apart from the carnage that was taking place. Combatants fought around them as if unaware of their presence, and Jilana watched as the Iceni fell beneath the unwavering line of legionaries who advanced with their shields locked. The smell of blood and death assaulted her nostrils, and, helpless to prevent it, the horror grew within her again. Caddaric's face swam into view and Jilana was nearly strangled by a sob. Beneath the blood and dirt and sweat, his features were incredibly weary and etched with pain. From time to time, whenever the lack of opponents permitted, his gaze would flash to the hill on his right, and his jaw would tighten grimly just before another legionary came at him. She could not touch him, she knew, yet she ached to take him into her arms and lead him from this place of death. Since she could neither touch nor speak to any save Clywd, it was the Druid's arm she clutched when she saw the legion form into a wedge, the point of which drove forward and split the Iceni force apart.

Screams of rage and frustration from the Iceni, of the dead and dying on both sides, rent the air and Jilana thought the sound would drive her mad. Caddaric and the men around him fought doggedly, but little by little they were forced to give ground, to try and retreat against the solid wall of their countrymen who, by their sheer number, made retreat impossible. The colors, the sounds, all seemed more vivid than was natural, and Jilana felt the scream claw at her throat when a sword flashed out from between the Roman shields to drive through Caddaric's side. He did not cry out, only gave a surprised gasp, and sank to his knees when the blade was withdrawn. In a moment, he was trampled by the relentless Roman advance. She tried to go to him, but her legs would not move, and the hammering thud of her heart seemed to beat out, "My love, my love my love my love...."

"Enough!"

Jilana blinked and came back to reality, drained. She looked around, startled to find that she had not moved from the spot—at least not physically. She expelled her breath in a shaky sigh and looked straight into Clywd's eyes. "You were with me," she said, more than a little afraid. "But I was alone the first time."

Clywd nodded and patted her hand reassuringly, but even in the moonlight his face was unnaturally pale. "You were afraid to go alone, so I traveled with you."

Jilana retreated ever so slightly. She had thought she feared Lhwyd, but that emotion was insipid compared to the awe Clywd inspired. She knew this man to be gentle and loving and kind and yet the power he wielded was formidable.

"Do not be afraid." Clywd withdrew his hand. He rose and refilled their cups.

Jilana suspiciously eyed the cup he offered her. "What is in it?"

"Only wine." He pressed the cup into her hand and resumed his place beside her.

"Did you drug me?" From whence came the courage to ask that question, Jilana could not say, but her own daring amazed her.

Clywd studied her, debating his answer. "Why are you afraid of me, child? I am no different than I was yesterday, or the day before."

Jilana swallowed nervously. "To speak of reading my thoughts is one thing; to actually enter my mind—" She gestured weakly with her free hand.

"I understand." Clywd nodded. "I did add an herb to your wine," he told her, deciding upon the truth. "Not this cup, but the first one you drank. Your fear stood between myself and your vision, yet I sensed 'twas important for me to see it."

"And to think I once feared Lhwyd," Jilana murmured. "You have no need for a weapon, have you, wise one? You can destroy your enemies with your thoughts."

Clywd lifted his shoulders and locked his gaze with hers. "Whether I could or not, I cannot say. Such a thing is forbidden, so I have never tried it."

"If Lhwyd had your power—"

"The gods did not gift him with it, and the priests on Mona refused him the training that would grant him even the portion of the gift you have received." Clywd smiled wryly. "Be'al chooses his servants carefully."

"Thank the gods," Jilana said in such a heartfelt manner that after a moment they both laughed softly. They sobered quickly, however, and her hand went to Clywd's arm. "Is my vision true?"

Clywd bowed his head and studied the depths of his wine. "I believe so." His voice was little more than a whisper.

Tears spilled down Jilana's cheeks. "Then I have lost him!"

"Perhaps not," Clywd intervened. "We saw him wounded, not killed. Did your dream take you any further?"

"Nay." Jilana brushed at her eyes.

"Then there is hope."

Jilana cast desperately about for a solution, but, in the end, could think of only one way to save Caddaric, for she could not risk his being injured. "He must not fight." Clywd fixed her with a disbelieving stare and Jilana hastily explained, "He has been wounded once, and still weak, though he would argue the point; to go into battle again would be madness! When the battle comes—as we both know it will—I will drug him." She leaned forward excitedly. "A measure of opium in his drink and he will never reach the battleground—"

"Nay, Jilana; I will not allow it." Clywd's voice held the note of finality.

Despair tore through Jilana. "And what of me? Have I not been robbed of enough? Must the gods also cheat me of my husband?" Angry, she left Clywd to his wine and escaped to the security of her bedroll. With her back to him, she let the tears come again and cried herself to sleep.

Feeling incredibly old, Clywd returned to his own blanket and found Heall watching him. "How long have you been awake?"

"Long enough." Heall nodded toward Jilana. "How odd she should have the gift."

"Not so odd, perhaps," Clywd sighed. "My son became a warrior."

"Aye." Heall was silent, studying his old friend. "I will guard him, Clywd. Regardless of my age, I have forgotten more tricks than Caddaric has learned. If necessary, I will drag him from the field. We will not lose another of our children."

Clywd nodded, his eyes dark pools of pain. "You are a blessing, my friend."

Heall took a deep breath and asked the question so many had put to Clywd over the years. "How will it end?"

"I wish I knew," was the tortured reply.

Five nights later, Caddaric's patrol returned early to report that the Roman legion was encamped on a plain barely a half-day's march to the north. Boadicea gathered her chieftains and gave them first the news, and then her decision.

"We will march tomorrow and engage Suetonius Paulinus and put a quick, victorious end to our war."

"Should we not wait, my Queen?" one of the chieftains asked. "Our warriors will be tired after the march—"

"We have waited long enough," Boadicea snapped. She gestured wildly at the darkening landscape visible from the open pavilion which had been erected for her. "The land through which we travel has been decimated; nothing grows, the livestock has been slaughtered—even the wild game has fled from the Roman destruction! My people must have food, and there is none to be found here. We must end this, and quickly, before the people lose heart."

Caddaric sat behind his chieftain, in silent agreement with Boadicea, although he had a bad feeling about fighting the Romans on a site of their choosing. Listening with half an ear to the arguments raging between the chieftains and advisors, he wondered exactly what Suetonius Paulinus had in mind. The first rule of war, he reminded himself, was to never allow the enemy the advantage of field position; and if you could not adhere to the first, you made certain you obeyed the second: a clear path for retreat.

The thought of retreat had occurred to several of the chieftains as well, and when they put it to the Queen that their forces would effectively be boxed in, she waved aside the concern.

"If we cannot retreat, then neither can the Romans. We are seven to their one—our war band will roll over them! Caddaric, you have seen the Roman force. What say you?"

Caddaric scanned the faces turned upon him and answered slowly, "That we outnumber the Romans is plain, but 'twould be better if we could draw them into the open. There we could use our chariots and the sheer weight of our numbers to advantage. In an open area, with room to maneuver, we could surround and crush them."

Boadicea nodded, but her mouth twisted into a mocking smile. "And of course Paulinus will happily leave his encampment if we but ask. Or have you a strategy learned at the hands of our enemy that will bring him to us?"

Knowing that his Queen was desperate did not lessen the cutting edge of her words. Caddaric felt the blood spread along his cheekbones and he said, "Nay, my Queen, I have not."

"Then you agree that we should meet the governor-general?"

The taunt bit deep, as it was meant to do. The council knew that whether he agreed or disagreed would make no difference. Caddaric's thoughts touched briefly on Jilana, on the supplies in their wagons that would be enough to get them home but would not stretch much further. "I agree that you have no choice," he said finally.

Boadicea nodded curtly and turned to Clywd, who sat at her side. "You will offer sacrifices here tonight, at moonrise, both to Camulos and Andrasta. Lhwyd will assist you. The people will be heartened by the sight of my two priests united, and by the favorable omens you will divine from the entrails." With a slight inclination of his head Clywd assented and Boadicea rose. "Speak to your people," she ordered the chieftains, "tell them what the morrow will bring. I will address them myself, tonight, after the sacrifices."

Caddaric reclaimed his mount and waited for his father outside the pavilion. "Will you do as the Queen asks?" he demanded when they were walking to their camp. "Will you read the omens as favorable, even if they are not?"

"Aye," Clywd replied softly.

Caddaric's mouth tightened. "Why? Why would you betray the gods just because the Queen asks it? Has it all been a lie, your devotion to your gods?"

"I will do as she asks because, no matter what I say, she will do battle tomorrow." Clywd crossed his arms and buried his hands in his sleeves. "Should I deny my friends the comfort of a favorable omen to carry into battle?" With that, he veered away from his son and was soon lost to sight.

Caddaric sighed heavily. He had meant neither to insult his father nor to argue, but he had succeeded in doing both. Clywd was right, of course. Believing their gods favored the battle would give the Iceni confidence. That confidence might even be the difference between defeat and victory. It would not matter if they knew, as Caddaric did, that the Roman priests would be offering identical sacrifices, with identical omens, for exactly the same reason.

Word of the pending battle had not had time to spread along the Iceni grapevine, but Jilana had only to look at Caddaric's face to know what had transpired. When he held out his hand to her, she took it and walked with him to tether his horse.

"Paulinus has been found," Jilana stated woodenly as he unsaddled his mount while she held the reins.

"Aye." Caddaric removed the bridle and tethered the stallion before devoting his attention to her. "He and the legion are camped a short march from here; we will meet them tomorrow."

She went light-headed with fear and struggled to conceal the emotion. "Will it be over then?" Jilana was amazed at how calm she sounded.

Caddaric placed his hands on his hips and studied her. "The worst will be over. If we defeat Paulinus, the western tribes will take care of the remainder of the troops Paulinus took to Mona. Then we will be free to return home."

Jilana swallowed, thinking of the men who would be trapped. "What about the Ninth Legion at Lindum?"

"They are alone, isolated, with no hope for reinforcements." She closed her eyes and Caddaric cursed softly. "I am sorry, wicca, I should have thought—" He pulled her into his arms and kissed her hair. "We must go. The Queen has ordered sacrifices made and all are ordered to attend. Nay," he said quickly when she stiffened in his embrace. "My father is in charge of the sacrifice, not Lhwyd, though he will be there as well."

In fact, Lhwyd had been put in charge of procuring the sacrifice and attending to its sacred demise. In the light of the torches, Jilana watched the animal being led to the hurriedly erected altar and felt an unexpected sympathy with it. Like the animal, her life was racing forward, out of control. She would give anything to have a few more days with her husband before the coming battle.

Caddaric had chosen a place for them well back from the pavilion. He stood behind Jilana, with his arms wrapped securely around her waist, and when the moment came for Lhwyd to draw the knife across the poor beast's neck, Jilana bowed her head, unable to watch. Caddaric's arms contracted gently, seeking to lend her strength, and her fingers bit into his arms in return. How would Caddaric react if she asked him not to fight? Jilana wondered as Clywd removed the entrails and read the favorable omens to a cheering crowd. Dare she ask him? She was his wife, did that not give her certain rights where his life was concerned? With all the warriors Boadicea had at her command, what difference would it make if Caddaric fought?

Boadicea rose to address the hosting and Jilana pulled herself away from her thoughts.

"My people, you have heard the divinations," Boadicea shouted. She raised her sword skyward. "The gods are with us. On the morrow we will meet and defeat the army that has held us in bondage for so long—the same army that took our lands, our sons, our daughters. We will crush them beneath our might!" A deafening cheer went up and the Queen waited until it died away before continuing.

"We are seven to their one," the Iceni Queen asserted. "The Roman general has chosen as a battleground a plain with forested hills to their flanks and to their rear. Surely

Andrasta blinded Paulinus when he picked that spot, for they have no place to run! Our chariots will attack first and scatter their front lines, and then, my brave warriors, then we will drive our attack straight into the heart of their ranks! We know how useless the legionary is when he cannot cower behind a wall of shields; we know how they fear an honorable fight! Neither our resolve nor our swords must falter—we cannot take pity upon our enemy when he falls at our feet and begs for his miserable life. Let Camulos guide your sword arm; remember what the Romans have done to the land through which we have passed. The moment of our revenge is near!''

Jilana felt the muscles in Caddaric's arms tighten beneath her fingers as the crowd around them went wild. Boadicea's frenzy was contagious and Jilana watched as familiar faces took on the crazed look of battle lust.

"All will be avenged," Boadicea screamed, her voice barely heard over the tumult of the hosting. "All the Romans will die! The sacred soil of Albion will drink the blood of her enemies and grow strong once again! Through the guidance of our gods and the strength of our resolve, WE WILL BE FREE!''

Savage tension beat in the air when Boadicea retreated to her tent and the Iceni made their way to their own camps, reminding Jilana of the day after the fall of Venta Icenorum. She tried not to be afraid of the madness, to be the woman a warrior such as Caddaric should have at his side, but she had been gently reared and clung desperately to his hand until they were safely inside the leather walls of their tent.

Caddaric felt the tension in her and sat beside her on their pallet. "'Twill be over soon.''

Jilana nodded, not wanting to think of the coming battle, or what her vision had portended.

"You are one of us, my wife. The anger, the hatred, is not directed at you," Caddaric told her, his hands gripping hers.

"I know." Jilana drew a deep, calming breath. "You must think me such a coward.''

Caddaric smiled and drew her against his chest. "Never." His lips brushed over her forehead and down her cheek until they fastened on her mouth. When she sighed softly, he nuzzled at her ear and coaxed, "'Tis late; come to bed."

In moments, they were free of their clothing and lying face-to-face beneath the blanket. Jilana buried her face against the hard column of his throat and touched her lips to the pulse there. He was so warm, so alive; she could not let him go without a fight. "Caddaric?"

"Mmm." One of his arms was around her shoulders and the other was busy shaping her waist.

"Will you fight tomorrow?" The hand on her waist stilled instantly.

"What else would I do?"

From his tone, it was plain that he had never considered otherwise. Jilana offered a quick prayer to Juno, gathered her courage, and blurted out, "Your shoulder is not healed. I do not think..."

Her words trailed off as Caddaric levered himself up on one elbow and looked down at her in the darkness. "What are you saying, Jilana? That I should remain behind?"

Jilana swallowed the lump in her throat and reached up to push back the hair that had fallen onto his forehead. He flinched away from her hand and she nearly cried out at his withdrawal. "You have been wounded," she reminded him in a whisper.

"So have many others," Caddaric told her curtly. "No Iceni has ever avoided a battle as long as he could raise a sword."

"I understand," Jilana said despairingly, knowing her cause was lost, had been lost from the beginning. "But they are not my husband."

"What is it you want me to do, Jilana?" Caddaric asked bitingly. "Should I sit in the wagon? Mayhap I should sleep while my countrymen fight for my freedom."

"Nay, of course not." If she told him of the dream, Jilana thought desperately, perhaps he would listen to her.

At the barely audible denial, Caddaric tunneled his fingers through her hair, forcing her head up. "I am a warrior, my heart. 'Tis not the same as being a merchant or a farmer—a warrior is what I am, all that I am. Of what use is a warrior who will not fight?" When she shook her head in quick, silent negation of his words, he held on to his patience. 'Twas important for both of them that she understand. "My life has been spent learning the art of soldiering; 'tis as much a part of me as breathing. If that is taken from me, I have nothing."

"And after the rebellion," Jilana asked tightly. "What will you do when Boadicea runs out of cities to destroy?"

Caddaric sighed. "There is always a need for soldiers, Jilana, if not to wage war, then to train those who might have to do battle one day. I can help build Albion's defenses against the day when the Romans—or some other power—seek to take my home away."

His words drifted into the darkness and Jilana bowed to the inevitable. She might be able to convince him to stay out of the battle tomorrow by telling him of her dream, or keep him safe by drugging him until the battle was over, but in doing so, she would endanger their love. His life or their love—which could she bear to lose? And she knew she could not choose, for the loss of either would prove an unending torment.

"I will take care, little wicca," Caddaric whispered against her mouth, sensing her thoughts. "You will lie in my arms tomorrow night. I swear it."

Jilana clung to him, willing the night to go on forever. And when the dawn came and the march resumed, she clung to his promise.

Shortly after midday, the Iceni column drew to a staggering halt and Jilana climbed down from the wagon seat. They had passed through the narrow defile and onto the broad plain Caddaric had described to the Queen. The excitement and tension of the rebels hung in the air like heavy perfume and the women laughed and chattered as if they were about to visit an exotic bazaar. In truth, the

Iceni were so certain of victory that their wagons, three and four deep, now ringed the far borders of the plain. The warriors were making their way back to their wagons in order to gird themselves for the coming battle, and the Iceni end of the plain was a scene of chaos compared to the neatly arrayed Roman field. She could see the precise rows of leather tents in the distance, along with the larger tent with its aquila and standards. That, Jilana assumed, was Paulinus' headquarters. Looking back the way they had come, Jilana could see the narrow pass was now clogged with abandoned wagons; the wives and children in the rear of the column had left their vehicles in order to gain an unrestricted view of the battleground. Worry and fear had assailed her all morning until now, Jilana felt almost numb as she went about the business of unhitching the horses as Caddaric had instructed her earlier.

By the time Heall and Caddaric returned to the wagon, Jilana had filled their skins with water and laid out a cold meal of dried meat. A full belly, Caddaric had told her, was a hindrance during battle. Jilana could not understand how they could eat at all, for her own stomach rebelled at the thought of food.

"Where is my father?" Caddaric wanted to know as they ate the light meal.

"Boadicea summoned him," Jilana answered, unable to drag her eyes away from her husband. She stared at him, memorizing every line, angle and curve of his face and form.

Caddaric swore under his breath. "I wanted him here, not offering up prayers to his gods so close to the Roman lines." He rose and began saddling two of the horses that had been tied to the wagon during the march.

Jilana's spirits rose a bit. Her vision had not seen Caddaric fighting on horseback. "I thought you intended to fight on foot."

"I do." Caddaric's back was to her and he did not see the color drain from her face. "These are for you and my father. I want you to pack these two and the two Heall and I rode this morning with blankets, food and water." He tightened the cinch under the second horse's belly and drew Jilana around to the opposite side of the wagon. Pointing to a spot high on the hill he ordered, "Take the horses there, just below the rise. Tie them to the trees so they cannot bolt and wait."

"Wait?" Jilana stared at him dumbly. "For what?"

"For Boadicea to lose the battle," Caddaric told her grimly. "If that happens, we surely cannot retreat through the defile." He looked back to the narrow pass, saw the wagons massed there and gave an imperceptible shake of his head before turning back to Jilana. "I will try to find my father and tell him where you will be."

"You think we will lose?"

Caddaric draped an arm around her shoulders and her head came to rest against his chest. "I know not whether we will win or lose, but a wise man plans for the worst. If we are forced to retreat, I do not want you trapped here, with no means of escape."

"But the others—"

"Let the others do as they wish. *You* will do as I say." Caddaric smiled to take the bite from his words. "If the Queen's plan is successful, then all these preparations will have been unnecessary, and we can laugh at them this night. But now, 'twill be easier for me to fight if I know you are safe, out of harm's reach."

That convinced Jilana as none of his other arguments could have. Above all else, she wanted his concentration solely upon the battle and emerging from it alive. She nodded and dredged up a smile.

Caddaric's face hardened and he spoke quickly and quietly. "If the worst happens, we will come to you as quickly as we can, but under no circumstances must you stay if the legionaries begin to search the trees. The moment you see the Romans heading for the treeline, take one of the horses and leave. Do not hesitate, do not delay, not for anything or anyone. Do I make myself clear? Go west, for there are Roman settlements there that will take you in. We will follow you when we can." He frowned at her until she nodded to show him she understood. "There is a sword in the other wagon; take it with you as well and use it if you must."

"There will be no need," Jilana managed to say. "You will ride with me."

Looking down into the wide, violet eyes, Caddaric felt the love he held for this woman pour through him, just as he felt her love reach out for his heart. "Aye, I will ride with you."

No purpose would be served by further delay; there would be no comfort for either of them until the battle had been won—or lost. Releasing her, he slipped a battle-axe onto his belt and readjusted his sword and baldric. He checked the dagger in his belt and strapped a knife in its sheath around the calf of his leg. When he straightened, his eyes locked with Jilana's and Caddaric wished he could give voice to assurances, no matter how false, that would erase the worry lines between her brows.

Jilana summoned up the dregs of her courage and went up on tiptoe to place a gentle kiss upon Caddaric's lips. There was no passion in the kiss, only love and concern, and when he pulled her into his arms for a quick, hard embrace, she whispered, "I love you, my husband. The gods go with you."

"And with you." Gently, Caddaric set her away from him. After a slight hesitation, he added, "Put on a stola, my heart."

Jilana was about to ask why when the reason blazed into her mind. Dressed as she was, in a short tunic with her hair unbound, she was certain to be mistaken for a Celt. A stola would not identify her as a Roman, but it might give a legionary pause if her escape was unsuccessful. "I will wait for you." Heall was standing beside Caddaric now and she wrapped the older man in a tender embrace. "For both of you," she promised when Heall released her.

They had run out of words and time. Caddaric swung away and Heall followed an instant later. Although her eyes followed the two until they were swallowed up in the hosting, neither man looked back. Jilana's breath escaped in a shudder and she set about following Caddaric's final orders. In her blanket, she wrapped a stola; there would be time enough later to change if it proved necessary. She waited as long as she dared for Clywd to return, and when he did not, she swung into the saddle and rode into the trees.

Jilana had just reached the rise in the hill when the first blast of the carnyx echoed through the trees. The horses snorted and tossed their heads in alarm. Jilana quieted her own mount and then slid from the saddle and tied the four steeds securely. It was chill within the forest, and Jilana took Caddaric's cloak and wrapped it around her shoulders while she listened to the oddly muted sounds of battle rising from the plain. She could see next to nothing from where she stood, but farther down the hill, she spotted a small clearing. After an agonizing deliberation, she checked the horses' tethers and began a careful descent until the battlefield came into view. The baldric cut into her shoulder and the sword swung painfully against her hip, but Jilana barely felt it. Her breath caught involuntarily in her throat at the spectacle below.

Paulinus had ranged his troops so that the infantry formed a center wedge with archers and cavalry on the wings. Contrary to Boadicea's battle plan, the Iceni infantry broke ranks and charged across the field separating the two armies, rendering their chariots useless. The gods alone knew how much courage it had taken for the legionaries to watch the Celts—some naked, their bodies painted blue with *woad*, their battle cries reverberating across the plain—roll toward them like some demonic wave. When the two armies collided, the clash of sword against shield was enough to cause the governor-general—mounted, at the rear of his army and surrounded by the standard's guard—to wince. For good or ill, the battle was joined. Messengers ran from the lines to their commander and Paulinus weighed the reports his officers were sending. The trap he planned had to be sprung at exactly the right moment or all would be lost.

A cold horror seeped through Jilana as she watched the engagement. At first glance, it looked as though the Iceni should trample the legion beneath their feet, but it soon became evident that such a thing would not happen. Even to her untrained eye, it was obvious that the Iceni were crowded, too crowded. Those in the rear lines were howling madly at being denied this chance at the hated Roman legion and pushed forward while those in front were literally thrown against the sword points which bristled from the wall of Roman shields. Numerical superiority, in this case, was not an advantage.

The wicker chariots chased wildly behind the Iceni lines, useless. They needed room to maneuver, and none existed. Now there came the sound of a Roman battle horn and suddenly a torrent of arrows poured from the sky to fall upon the Iceni force. The screams that reached Jilana were mercifully dampened, but she understood what had happened. A second volley of arrows followed the first and those in the rear of the Iceni lines lost all patience. They surged forward in an unstoppable wave and at the same moment the Roman wedge moved. The wedge sliced neatly into the center of the Iceni, splitting them apart. There came a second blare of the legion's horn and the cavalry, held in reserve at the base of the hills, pranced forward. In place of arrows, lances now menaced the unprotected flanks of the Iceni. There was no protection; the lances kept both horse and rider well out of sword's reach while retaining the ability to pierce through Celtic shields. Those caught on the flanks fought valiantly and died calling upon their gods; those who tried to flee never saw the instruments of their death. The Iceni collapsed back on themselves, the wedge moved forward yet again, and the chaos began.

Instinctively, forgetting the danger she was in, Jilana had edged ever closer to the battlefield until she stood only a few feet behind the place where the cavalry had so recently waited. Now she could smell the battle as well as see it, and her stomach lurched sickeningly at the mixed odors of blood and sweat and fear. Dust clouded the plain now;

the earth was churned into clods by horses' hooves and vibrated beneath her feet. The Romans were advancing steadily and the first Iceni bodies were becoming visible Hopelessness swept through Jilana and she began to pray to every god and goddess she could remember, Roman a well as Celtic.

"So this is where Caddaric has hidden you."

Somehow the voice, and the hand that came to res upon her shoulder, did not surprise Jilana. She turned beneath the pressure of the hand and met the green star of Lhwyd. Hopelessness was replaced by a savage fury that glittered in Jilana's violet eyes. Juno, but she hated this Druid! The emotion burst into her breast and swep aside all her fear. Caddaric was out there, trapped, per haps *dying*, and this imitation of a man could think onl of one last sacrifice for his goddess, of his need for ven geance.

"If you want to kill," Jilana said in a voice that shool with disgust, "go out there and help your countrymen!"

Lhwyd smiled. "Afraid, Roman?"

"Not of you," Jilana spat, and it was true.

"You should be." Lhwyd glanced at the battle and ther looked back at Jilana. "'Tis forbidden for a Druid to kill."

"You do so readily enough when your enemy i bound," Jilana goaded, soaring in a tempest of emotion "What a coward you are, priest. You slay helpless pris oners and then incite those braver than you to face th enemy while you cower behind your vows."

Lhwyd's face blanched and then flooded with color "Roman bitch," he hissed. "When I offer your heart to the Morrigan, she will see us victorious."

There was laughter and Jilana, staring at Lhwyd's thi mouth, realized that the sound came from her. Lhwyd' hand moved inside his robe and reappeared an instan later with a dagger. Jilana glanced contemptuously at th long, thin blade and took a step backward. Before Lhwy could follow her, she flipped back the left side of her tuni and pulled the sword from its baldric. Lhwyd was incred ulous at first and then, when he saw the effort it took for her to raise the weapon, he grinned evilly.

"Too late, Roman. You have not the skill, or the courage."

In one sense Lhwyd was correct, she had no skill with a blade; but as Caddaric could have told him, she did not lack for courage. The Druid's mistake was in underestimating his opponent and overestimating the power of his spells. Just as her fear had hidden her thoughts from Clywd, so now did Jilana's rage protect her mind from Lhwyd. He began a soft, hypnotic chant and, while Jilana watched in disbelief, advanced upon her.

"Stay away, priest," Jilana warned him quietly, backing away. The sword was too heavy for her wrists, and the tip dragged on the ground as she retreated. Hate Lhwyd she did, but she had no desire to kill him.

Lhwyd's answer was to chant louder. His pace never faltered, nor did his eyes leave hers. The carpet of leaves muffled the sound of their steps and Jilana felt the gentle rise beneath her feet give way to flat ground. A heartbeat later, her back came up against a tree trunk and Jilana knew she could retreat no further.

"You are mine, Roman." Lhwyd smiled, seeing her trapped. "Just as the Morrigan promised."

Jilana never remembered raising the sword. One minute Lhwyd was several feet away, the dagger held high in his hand and a mad gleam lighting his eyes, and the next he gave a breathless, almost feminine gasp and looked down at the space between them. Jilana followed his gaze and saw the sword held at an upward angle in front of her. Lhwyd was impaled upon its blade.

"Bitch," Lhwyd cursed her with his final breath and in a last, convulsive movement, pulled himself off the blade.

Jilana watched in horrified fascination as her enemy fell. When he came to rest, his arms were outstretched, his eyes wide open. Save for the spreading red stain on his white robe, he might have been watching the clouds pass overhead.

"Juno, forgive me," Jilana prayed, and dropped the sword. What appalled her the most was that she felt no guilt at having taken a life. Keeping an eye on Lhwyd's corpse, she moved some distance away until the body was hidden from her sight and then she turned her attention back to the battle. She was totally out of the concealment of the trees now, but that was a small consideration compared to the mayhem in front of her.

More than a few Iceni bodies were visible now and Jilana stood frozen in place by the sight, sound and smell of war. *Caddaric,* her heart cried when she heard the Iceni curses rise above the tumult.

The battle had turned into a rout. Caddaric, buried in the midst of the Celtic force, felt the shock wave when the Roman wedge advanced. Experience told him what was happening even before the first Roman shield came into view. His sword was free, but there was no room to wield it, and he spared a thought for the short sword he had left for Jilana. The long sword he held was made for slashing, not stabbing, and with his neighbors' elbow jammed into his ribs, he was sorely lacking in maneuvering room. The second shock wave rolled through the warriors and Caddaric grabbed Heall's wrist.

"Here they come," he shouted over the din. "If we become separated, remember where the horses are."

"I will not leave without you, boy," Heall shouted back.

"You will do what is necessary, my old friend," Caddaric said in a voice that once brought eighty Roman legionaries to heel. "And that includes seeing my father and Jilana to safety. Do you understand?"

Heall was given no chance to reply, for at that moment the wedge broke through to where they were standing, separating the two men that had been as father and son.

"Remember," Caddaric screamed as Heall disappeared from sight, and then he raised his own shield just in time to deflect the menace of the Roman short sword that jabbed from the wall of interlocked shields.

At first, his small world of battle went well. The men around him followed Caddaric's example and used their swords in short, stabbing motions rather than killing their own people by seeking to swing their blades in the time-honored way of their fathers. A few Romans fell, but always any breech in the wall of shields was immediately filled. Sweat dripped down Caddaric's face, burning his eyes and lips. His arm began to ache from the strain, and when his thrust met a particularly effective parry, he felt something give in his shoulder, followed by a sunburst of pain. His wound had broken open, and he confirmed that guess a moment later when he glanced down and saw the shoulder of his light brown tunic turning a rusty color. But there was nothing he could do about it now. He forced the pain away, willing it to the back of his mind until there was time to deal with such trivialities. With all his attention focused on avoiding a mortal blow, Caddaric barely noticed the bothersome wounds inflicted upon him, both by the Roman swords and those of his own people. His arms and legs bled in dozens of places where honed iron had slipped against his flesh. Like his shoulder, the stings of the razor-like wounds were ignored.

With the third flight of arrows, Caddaric knew they were doomed. The Iceni were being relentlessly forced back toward the defile. The Iceni had fought bravely, but they were helpless as babes against the superior Roman strategy. To stay was madness, for only certain death waited on the battlefield. They could move neither forward nor to the sides, only backward. Already he could hear the screams of women and children as the Romans reached the wagons. He thought of Jilana and wondered if he could fight his way to the perimeter. From there he might be able to bludgeon a path through the cavalry. He managed to withdraw from the front rank, using brute force and his shield to push his countrymen out of his way and then he felt the earth tremble under his feet. Straining to see above the heads of those around him, Caddaric looked to the rear and what he saw brought forth a string of curses from his mouth.

Enraged by the obvious failure, and frustrated beyond endurance, the famed Celtic temper had overridden strategy once again. The chariots, which had been helplessly milling back and forth for several hours, now tried to charge through their own ranks in an effort to reach the Roman cavalry, and leading them was Boadicea. For just a moment, Caddaric's spirit rallied at the sight of his Queen, a spear in one upraised hand, charging toward him, and then he realized what would happen and that was when he cursed. More screams—these of fear and anguish—rent the air as Iceni infantry was crushed beneath the hooves and wheels of Iceni chariots. Caddaric turned away and doubled his efforts to reach the perimeter. The chariots would never reach the Roman lines; instead they trampled their own people.

There came a sound like the buzzing of maddened hornets and Caddaric felt himself reel when something slammed into his left shoulder. The shock numbed his arm; his shield dropped from his hand and Caddaric looked down to see an arrow shaft still quivering where it was embedded in his shoulder. There was no pain. Instinctively, Caddaric reached up with his right hand, wrapped his fingers around the shaft and yanked the missile from his flesh. The fount of blood which followed the extraction left him light-headed, but Caddaric could not have fallen if he had wanted to. The crush of bodies held him upright.

Pitilessly, he pushed and shouldered his way through the ranks until the Roman cavalry came into view. Shifting his sword to his left hand, he took a moment to wipe his bloody right hand against his equally bloody tunic and then grasped the hilt in both hands. With a feral cry, he burst through the last two lines of Iceni, his sword held high above his head. He saw the shock in the cavalryman's eyes as he avoided the lance and arched his blade into the man's neck. The man fell, adding his body to those already heaped underfoot. Raw power pulsed through Caddaric, and he charged forward, his blade singing through the air above his head. The wild charge took the cavalry by surprise and the horses were reined aside to avoid the madman. He was nearly through them when one of the rearing horses came down squarely in front of him. This man held no lance, though Caddaric could not think why, and then he saw the distinctive helmet of a centurion. In place of a lance, this man wielded a sword and Caddaric had just a moment to wonder why the shadowed face beneath the helmet looked familiar before the blade bit deeply into his side.

"Jilana," Caddaric cried as the sword was withdrawn. He felt the hot rush of blood as his life drained away and cursed the gods one last time. His world went up in flames and then he plunged into a welcoming darkness.

Jilana heard his voice as clearly as if he had been whispering in her ear. An unworldly chill enveloped her, and she stepped onto the plain. Some force she did not understand set her feet upon an unseen path, and she was mercifully blind to the carnage surrounding her. The pace of battle was quicker now as the Iceni threw themselves upon lances and swords in a mad scramble to escape defeat in any manner that presented itself, and the Romans followed relentlessly. Though she was plainly visible, neither the cavalry nor the archers paid her any heed as she picked her way over Roman and Iceni bodies. Which was friend and which was foe, Jilana wondered madly, and then her thoughts focused once again upon finding Caddaric.

High above the battlefield, Clywd reached the tethered horses and his heartbeat faltered when he could find no sign of Jilana. Not daring to call out, he plunged downward through the trees, praying. In his haste, Clywd nearly tripped over Lhwyd's body. The sight of the dead priest gave him pause and when Clywd was able to force his gaze from the body, he saw Jilana step onto the battlefield. Clywd drew a deep breath and started to call her name.

Nay!

The breath was locked in his lungs and though he struggled to follow the slender figure in the blue cloak, his legs would not obey. "Father, I beg you," Clywd prayed desperately, "let me go after her."

Nay. You are the last of my priests. You must live to tell the children of me.

"There will be no children," Clywd sobbed. "The Romans will kill them all. I beg you, Father, spare me the agony of being separated from my child a third time."

Remember the children.

Clywd felt his legs move, but they were carrying him deeper into the forest, away from the battle. When he sought to change direction, his legs refused to work. Tears streamed down his cheeks as Clywd found his way back to the horses. There he gathered his cloak about him and waited, praying that one of his family would escape.

Heall's sword arm grew weary and an unfamiliar ache blossomed in his chest. Bodies pushed and twisted against him, and there was a humming in his ears that sapped his strength. A Roman sword skittered off his shield and when he made to drive his blade through the opening that had somehow appeared in the Roman wall, his foot slipped on the ground turned muddy with blood. The fall stunned him and then he felt the smothering weight as another body landed on top of him. A tear squeezed its way out of his eye. Clywd, my old friend, Heall thought fleetingly, I have left so much undone. Then there was a roaring in his ears that brought peace.

Jilana stopped by a body which, to another, would have borne no resemblance to her husband, but her heart knew. She dropped to her knees, her fingers reaching out to trace the blood-stained features she had come to know so well. With the hem of her cloak, Jilana wiped away the blood and then she gently took him in her arms. Cradling Caddaric's head against her breast, she brushed the hair away from his forehead and began to cry silently, rocking him as she would a babe. His blood soaked her cloak and tunic and soon she began to sob, then wail. At last she threw back her head and a high, keening sound ripped from her throat. The lamentation filled her ears just as the man in her arms filled her world. She did not see the cavalry centurion wheel his mount around and stare at her in disbelief. She finally realized that she was not alone with her beloved when a pair of hooves pranced nervously only a few feet from where she sat.

Tears clouding her eyes, Jilana slowly looked up until she could make out the armor-clad figure of the legionary. "You shall not have him," she choked out, drawing the cloak around Caddaric's chest in a protective gesture and clutching him tighter. "You shall not."

The man was in the process of dismounting when he suddenly shouted, "Nay!" and held up his hand in a warning gesture that caused him to lose his balance and sent him tumbling to the ground.

Jilana's head exploded in a shower of stars. Her last thought was: I did not have to choose after all.

Suetonius Paulinus turned away from the carnage to address his second-in-command. "Light the fires and have the torches brought to them. 'Twill be soon be dark and we will need the light in order to track down these rebel dogs." As the officer hurried away, Paulinus turned back to watch the massacre, a satisfied smile on his hard lips. Above him, a mute witness to the carnage, the Roman eagle glinted victoriously in the last rays of the sun.

JILANA AWOKE TO AGONY so intense she knew at once she was alive. Charon had not ferried her across the Styx to the promised paradise of the afterlife. Her head pounded with a thousand hammers, threatening to beat itself apart. A sweet, sickening smell assaulted her nostrils and she weakly turned her head, gagging. A hand was behind her head, holding her, as her stomach emptied itself.

"Drink this."

Jilana tried to pry her eyes open, but the effort was too great. She felt the rim of a cup pressed against her lips and obediently opened her mouth. Wine, she thought, but something else as well that left an aftertaste. There were hands on her body, and then she felt the cool air against her skin. She should protest such a liberty, but speech was beyond her. A blanket was drawn over her and she drifted away.

When Jilana awoke next, she was able to open her eyes. Three braziers illuminated her world. The surroundings were familiar; she recognized the leather walls of the tent Caddaric had brought for her. So it had all been a dream then, Jilana thought, denying the crawling tendrils in her belly that told her differently.

"Drink this."

A hand bearing a cup appeared in front of her and Jilana shrank away from it, her eyes going to the unfamiliar face above her. "Who are you?" The words emerged in a throaty whisper and the man's jaw set.

"None of your heathen tongue." He pushed the cup roughly against her mouth, jarring her teeth.

Jilana cried out as the small pain triggered the larger one in her head, and then she swallowed hastily to avoid choking as the wine was poured down her throat.

"Why he bothers with one of you I do not know," the man said in disgust, wiping droplets of spilled wine from his hand with a towel. "Our own lie wounded while I waste my time on you."

"I can waste even more of your time," threatened a harsh voice from somewhere behind Jilana's head. "You may be assigned to the surgeons' staff, but that can be remedied. How would a transfer to one of the western marching camps suit you?" The voice had come further into the tent during the speech, until now it was so close that Jilana started at the lash in the question. "How is she?"

The man paled and swallowed convulsively. He had come to attention, but his legs were trembling. "Awake, sir, but I dosed her again."

"Get out."

The man obeyed with alacrity and when he was gone, the owner of the rough voice moved so that Jilana could see him. Her eyes wandered up the thick, heavily mus-

cled body and widened in disbelief when the man removed his helmet.

"H-Hadrian!" And then Jilana remembered the legionary who had fallen from his horse while shouting a
warning. "'Twas you this afternoon."

"Yesterday afternoon," Hadrian corrected, drawing up
a camp stool beside the cot. He took one of her hands in
his own hard paw. "Jilana, you must speak Latin."

The gentle reminder was like a slap in the face and it
brought back all the memories Jilana had managed to
hold at bay. "'Tis over, then." She found her native
tongue strangely awkward.

"Aye." Hadrian met her gaze. "All that remains is to
track down those who scattered into the hills."

Jilana closed her eyes, feeling the first effects of the
opium the soldier had forced into her. The poppy juice
lent a dream-like quality to their conversation—or perhaps it was only that her mind refused to accept what
Hadrian was saying. "Where am I?"

"In my tent." When she opened her eyes and frowned,
Hadrian said, "Oh, I see. We are still on the battlefield.
Paulinus will not march for another week or so."

Jilana wet her dry lips. "There is something I must
do—"

Hadrian was ahead of her. "Nay, Jilana, there is not.
The bodies are being seen to."

The thought of Caddaric being pushed into a mass
grave brought a choked sob from Jilana. He deserved a
decent burial, one in accordance with his own ways, Jilana wanted to argue, but it was far easier to drift into the
world the opium offered.

"Sleep now," Hadrian told her as he watched the tears
seep from beneath her closed lids. "Just sleep."

The next time Jilana came to it was morning. The massive throb in her head had receded to a dull ache behind
her eyes. She could smell the dew on the grass, hear the
birds singing their morning hymns in the trees and, just
for a moment, she was grateful to be alive. And then the
memories came crashing back and she turned her face

away from the light streaming through the open tent flap.
Now she had to learn to live without Caddaric—if she
could.

"Jilana?"

Hadrian's voice came from outside the tent and Jilana
roused herself enough to reply.

"I thought you might be hungry." Hadrian ducked inside the tent, a tray in both hands. "Can you sit up?"

Jilana started to, but the scratch of the blanket against
her skin brought her up short. "I . . . Hadrian, I cannot."
Blushing to the roots of her hair, she gestured helplessly
at the blanket.

Hadrian looked equally embarrassed. He set the tray on
a small table and opened a chest. Dragging forth a crimson tunic, he handed it to her. "I will wait outside." He
did not return until Jilana told him she was decently at-
tired.

The meal had been carefully prepared in order to tempt
her appetite, but it tasted like ashes to Jilana. Hadrian
watched her nibble at the bread and cheese until she finally sighed and shook her head. He took the tray from
her and sat beside the cot. "How do you feel?"

"My head aches." Jilana carefully lifted a hand to inspect the large knot on the back of her head. "What happened?"

"One of Paulinus' guards saw you. Luckily, he was able
to turn his blade at the last minute." Had he not, Hadrian thought again with a shudder, Jilana would have been
beheaded. Seeing the legionary charge down upon her, his
sword drawn, had been the worst moment of his life.
Looking at her now, seeing the garish purple bruise that
bled from her scalp onto her forehead, dissipated any
sense of victory he might have felt. Aware that she was
watching him, Hadrian cleared his throat self-consciously
and continued, "I ordered you brought to my tent and
one of the surgeon's assistants cared for you."

Jilana nodded, remembering the man's animosity. "Is
he the one who undressed me?" The thought of a stranger
stripping her made her feel violated.

"Nay; I did so upon my return."

Jilana gave a soft sigh of relief and leaned back against the pillow. They sat in silence for a long time before she asked, "Did you go back for Caddaric's body?" In answer, Hadrian rose to pour them both a cup of wine. After handing her the drink, he turned his own round and round, watching the liquid slosh from side to side. "Forgive me, Hadrian, I should not have asked that of you."

Hadrian's mouth thinned. "There were—are—thousands of bodies, and there were the survivors to be pursued. By the time I returned the burial parties were already at work—"

"I understand," Jilana hastily interrupted, not wanting to think about the aftermath of the battle. Her eyes remained dry—the agony she felt was too deep for tears. She took a sip of wine to moisten her dry throat. "How is your leg?"

Hadrian glanced down at the left limb stretched stiffly in front of him and gave a short bark of laughter. "It hurts like Hades. Now that I do not need to sit a horse, the surgeon is going to splint it again this afternoon."

Jilana nodded. "You made it safely to Londinium?" Though she had been worried about him, now Jilana asked the question more from a polite need to make conversation than curiosity.

"And from there to the marching camp at Deva. I arrived the day before General Paulinus came from Mona." Hadrian exhaled loudly. There were things she had to be told and no purpose would be served by delaying any further. "General Paulinus knows of you, of course. He wants to see you when you feel strong enough."

She was surprised by the commander's interest, but that emotion died quickly, leaving her numb once again. "I am at his disposal." What other choice did she have? She could hardly ignore what amounted to an order from the governor-general.

Hadrian tossed down his wine. "He wants to question you, Jilana. In spite of my explanations, he suspects you of treason."

Jilana's eyes widened incredulously and for a moment she was too stunned to speak. *Treason?* She caught her breath; perhaps she was a traitor, for in her heart she had hoped that Boadicea would succeed. "Tell the governor-general I will see him this afternoon." Whatever the man had in mind, she wanted to finish it quickly.

"As you wish." Hadrian rose to walk to the tent flap and now Jilana saw the limp he tried to minimize. "I will find you some clothes."

Jilana did not ask Hadrian where he found the clothes he brought to her along with the noon meal. She could guess well enough. She had dozed on and off throughout the morning, but the snatches of conversation she caught from outside the tent told her that the Romans had set out not only burial parties, but looting details as well. In the time-honored tradition of soldiers, the legion was stripping the dead and raiding what remained of the wagons. At least she did not recognize any of the clothing Hadrian brought her. 'Twas ironic, she mused as she smoothed the pale blue wool stola over her hips. The gown had undoubtedly been part of the plunder taken by some faceless Iceni from a Roman dwelling, and now it was in Roman hands once again. As were the brush and comb he had given her.

The governor-general was not the only one who was curious about Hadrian's guest. The minute she stepped from the tent with Hadrian, conversation among the surrounding legionaries died. Jilana avoided their gazes and walked beside Hadrian to the large tent she had seen at a distance two days earlier.

Suetonius Paulinus was seated behind a campaign desk. A map lay open upon the desk and he and several of his officers were studying it. When Hadrian announced them, Jilana felt six pair of hostile eyes drill into her. Unconsciously, she lifted her chin and met their stares. There was utter silence in the tent, and Jilana knew she was being judged. Like their commander, these officers thought her a traitor.

"General," Jilana said at last. "I was told you wanted to see me." She was proud of the calmness of her voice.

"Indeed, indeed." Suetonius Paulinus rolled up the map. The officers took the action as dismissal and strode from the tent and all the while the governor-general stared at the woman in front of him. "You also, Centurion."

There was no need for Paulinus to give the order a second time. Hadrian saluted and followed his brother officers.

"Centurion Tarpeius saved your life," Paulinus began without preamble. "You are very lucky."

Jilana could have argued the point, but instead she nodded. "The centurion and I are old friends."

"Aye, so he has said." Paulinus leaned back in his chair, his eyes narrowing as he studied Jilana. Her hair fell to her hips in a glorious riot of curls and Paulinus disliked the barbaric appearance it gave her, despite her dress. "Why did you not go with the centurion when he escaped?"

Obviously she was not going to be invited to take one of the chairs ranged in front of his desk. Jilana folded her hands in front of her and replied, "I would only have held him back."

"Yet Tarpeius says you can ride." Paulinus' fingers tapped against the desk's surface.

"Aye, I can ride," Jilana admitted, "but not in chains."

"You were not in chains the day of the battle," Paulinus stated icily. "You were quite capable of running onto the field and throwing yourself upon one of the dead rebels." He cocked an eyebrow at her sudden pallor. "Did you think I did not know? Tarpeius is a primipilus; he knows where his duty lies. As you apparently do not."

Which meant, Jilana thought bitterly, that Paulinus had questioned Hadrian until her friend had had no choice but to answer truthfully. "I am well aware of my duty, General."

"Are you indeed?" Paulinus smiled coldly. "Then suppose you tell me your story, beginning with the fall of Venta Icenorum."

Jilana did as she was ordered, but she gave the general only the barest of facts. She told him nothing of her life with the Iceni; that she kept closely guarded in her heart, and his dissatisfaction with her answer was plainly written on his face.

"But the rebel did unchain you?" Paulinus probed.

"Aye." On Beltane, Jilana thought, treasuring the memory she would not share with Paulinus.

Paulinus' fist slammed against the desk, startling Jilana. Pleased with her reaction, he rose and stared daggers at her. "Why, mistress, did you not run the moment you were freed?"

Jilana returned his stare and gave a most unladylike snort of disbelief. "And where, pray, should I have run? You and your vaunted legion were nowhere to be found and the Iceni—" her voice cracked on the word but she continued doggedly, "the Iceni were laying waste to everything in their path. Tell me where I could have run and been assured of safety, General!"

She was actually snarling at him, Paulinus realized. Stunned, he sank back into his chair. "I was on Mona," he began, though for the life of him he could not understand why he should explain himself to a female civilian.

"Aye, slaughtering priests and women and children," Jilana retorted hotly.

"They are a threat to the Empire!"

"Like the children you murder now?" Jilana flung back at him, undaunted by the rage sweeping across his features. "And we dare to call the Britons barbarians! You are no better than Boadicea."

Paulinus was choking on his anger now. "And you, mistress, are a traitor!"

Once, months ago, she would have quailed before such an accusation, but no more. She had lost everything in life dear to her; life itself no longer mattered. "Prove it," Jilana challenged.

Paulinus actually went white with rage. "You dare—"

"I dare a great deal, General," Jilana replied. "What is left that can be taken from me? What can you do to me that has not already been done, save take my life?" She took a deep, calming breath and checked the wildness singing in her blood. "Have I your permission to withdraw?"

"Not yet," Paulinus ground out. "I have questions to put to you regarding the rebels. Living with them as you have, you undoubtedly know where they will go into hiding. I am particularly interested in where Boadicea would have fled." He raised a compelling eyebrow at Jilana and waited.

"I cannot help you," Jilana replied steadily.

"Cannot, or will not?" Paulinus asked cuttingly.

The most powerful man in Britannia was now her enemy, Jilana realized. Not that his animosity mattered. Her family was dead, her husband was dead, and she did not particularly care what fate Paulinus had in store for her. "Cannot," she said at last. "But even if I knew, General, I would not tell you."

The retort Paulinus was about to make was stopped by the appearance of his aide. "Your pardon, General," the young man said hastily, "but a messenger from Lindum has just arrived. I thought you would want to see him at once."

"I do." Paulinus rose and paced across the area separating him from Jilana. "Hold yourself in readiness, mistress. This is not yet ended."

Jilana bowed slightly in acknowledgment of the dismissal and turned on her heel. Just outside the tent, she collided with the dust-covered messenger. The man's hands gripped her upper arms to keep her from falling.

"Your pardon, Tribune," Jilana said, taking a hasty step backward to rid herself of the man's touch. "I—" The rest of her apology died in her throat when she met the shocked, dark eyes above her. She could feel the blood drain from her face, the abrupt, cold tingling in her hands and the weakness in her legs. The world spun madly on its axis and she collapsed at the feet of Lucius Quintus.

Chapter 9

THE ICENI REBELLION WAS ENDED. In the space of four months, three major cities and countless villages had been razed. The island's population had been reduced by sixty thousand, both Roman and Briton. Albion fed upon the blood and bodies of its sons and daughters and upon the scarred earth, grass grew thick and lush over the burial mounds. At the last, the Queen of the Iceni had cheated Suetonius Paulinus of his revenge. Boadicea and her daughters, protected by the royal guard, had fled the final battleground before they could be captured. In a place safe from prying Roman eyes, the Queen had given her two children an easy death and then followed them to Annwn. Some said she fell upon her sword, in a manner befitting a warrior maid; others said poison had been her end. The royal guards had buried their bodies before fleeing north and try though he might, Paulinus could neither find the graves, nor induce any of the captured royal guards to betray the Queen's final resting place.

Autumn was late in coming to Britannia, as if granting a reprieve to the island's inhabitants. Even now, in early September, the days were pleasantly warm, although the evenings were chill. Inside the villa of Marcus Basilius, every room was ablaze with lamps, and the courtyard and garden, too, were well lit by torches. On the opposite side of the courtyard from the garden was a door to another path, but that was not lit, for it led to the slave quarters.

The slave quarters themselves—a collection of huts—were hidden from view by a high wall. It was in the garden that Jilana Augusta Basilius sat now, watching the villa. The reason for her father's extravagance was that this night they would entertain Governor-General Suetonius Paulinus, the man who had put down the Iceni rebellion.

Since his victory over Boadicea, Paulinus had been single-minded in his determination to see the native tribes brought to heel. His first act had been to burn Venta Icenorum to the ground and forbid any resettlement within a thirty-mile radius of the former capital. His second act had been to order every legionary who could be spared into the countryside to track down the survivors of the final battle. Paulinus was as merciless in his victory as Boadicea would have been in hers. Iceni rebels who survived being captured were either sold into slavery—with the money they brought going into the Imperial Treasury—or, if they were healthy specimens, turned over the the Imperial Navy, to spend the remainder of their lives as galley slaves. Lovers were torn apart, children forever separated from their parents, and still Paulinus' thirst for vengeance was not slaked. All Iceni land was confiscated and sold to those who could claim Roman citizenship. The Iceni horses that had been left behind were found and now wore the brand of the Roman cavalry. The governor-general planned to erase the Iceni from the collective memory of Britannia, and it seemed as if he would succeed.

Jilana sighed, touching the necklace at her throat. How strange that she should be living in such a grand place while her homeland was systematically impoverished. This villa was ten miles from Londinium and had been spared the worst of the sacking. The villa as well as the outlying buildings had remained intact; all that had been necessary was to furnish the rooms, which her mother had done, magnificently. There was even a complete bath, on a larger scale than the one they had had at Venta Icenorum. A high wall enclosed the building site, with gates opening to the south, east, north and west. For Jilana, brought to this place by Lucius, it was as if she had stepped backward in time. She had been stunned to learn her family was alive. *Alive!* And from Lucius' description of him, the man who had saved her family was Caddaric. The night of the rebellion, her family and Lucius had been overpowered and taken to the stable. There, Caddaric had given them horses and sent a man—Jilana deduced it was Heall, for Caddaric would have entrusted her family's welfare only to him—to guide them out of the town. The reason they were to be spared, they were told, was because of Jilana's aid to the Queen. In gratitude, Claudia had raked her dagger across Caddaric's cheek, leaving him with the scar Jilana remembered so well. Caddaric had clipped Claudia on the jaw, tossed her across her saddle and ordered them to flee while they still could. They had reached the safety of the fortress at Lindum a few days later, grateful to be alive, but left with the impression that Jilana had been killed.

Jilana had almost smiled when Lucius had related the story. How like Caddaric it sounded! By allowing her family to believe her dead, he had forestalled any search they, or Lucius, might have been tempted to make. They had grieved and then turned to each other, just as she had grieved when she believed her family dead, and then built a new life with Caddaric. *Ever the strategist, my love,* Jilana had thought. Tears had been shed at the reunion, but not by Jilana, though she was overjoyed to see her family alive. Her family treated her gently, assuring her that she would soon forget the nightmare of her past months, and tried to comfort her; Jilana had not been able to bring herself to tell them that their comfort was useless now that her love was dead. They would think her mad, and perhaps she was.

Time had yet to heal the wounds left by the rebellion, but the Empire was pouring material and people into the tiny island at an astonishing rate. Nero had ordered the legions reinforced, and with the promise of additional security, people were willing to leave their homes for this less civilized frontier. Her father's business was flourishing;

the populace needed food and clothing and household furnishings, all of which the house of Basilius imported. Jilana knew how well her father was doing—at her request, she had been allowed to keep his books in order to alleviate the long, boring hours that stretched in front of her. He had added to his fleet of ships and purchased, or built, warehouses along Londinium's riverfront. The house of Basilius was now wealthy indeed.

Jilana sighed again and rose to walk the paths through the garden. From the kitchen came muted Celtic voices and the sound brought a stab of pain to her heart. At least she was able to help some of Caddaric's people, she thought, remembering that her first visit to the slave market had come about quite by accident. She had been on her way to her father's office in the city when she had seen a group of ragged Britons being led through the street. Their hands and feet were chained, and all wore iron collars through which ran a chain, connecting them one to the other. She could not drag her eyes away from the terrible sight, and when one of her attendants—all Romans traveled well-protected these days—asked if she wished to attend the slave auction she almost said nay, but then she met the eyes of one of the prisoners. Was it only her imagination, or was his face familiar? Jilana could not be sure, and that uncertainty compelled her to visit the auction. Her litter had joined the rest of the traffic and Jilana had closed its curtains until they reached the marketplace.

She loathed the place immediately; hated the auctioneer for treating human beings as if they were animals, hated her countrymen for their smug, self-satisfied comments when they viewed what was for sale and debated whether this one was better suited to the fields or the stable or if that one would serve better in the kitchen or the bedchamber. When the man who had caught her eye was pushed up the steps to the raised platform, Jilana was certain she had seen him. She did not remember his name, but she knew he was of Caddaric's village. She had motioned to her bodyguard and ordered him to bid on the man. When she returned to her father's villa six hours later, three slaves were carried in a wagon behind her. They had stayed for two weeks, recovering their health, and then Jilana had written out their papers of manumission, given them an additional set of clothing as well as a small purse, and offered them the choice of remaining as a servant or leaving. They had chosen to leave and were soon replaced by four others.

Jilana's face became well-known at the slave market and she was the object of a great deal of speculation, but she did not care. For the first time in a very long time she felt useful, needed. She kept none of the Britons as slaves; as soon as they were well enough to travel, they received their freedom. Some stayed a few days, others a few weeks; some Jilana knew from her time with Caddaric, others were strangers, all were in desperate need of assistance. They gave meaning to her life. To save the pathetic remnants of Caddaric's people, she ignored her father's words of caution and her betrothed's angry remonstrances. What was she thinking of? How *could* she free the same people who had held her a slave, whose marks she still bore upon her wrists and ankles, and who had undoubtedly abused her vilely? Jilana let the words pass; she did not discuss her time with the Iceni with anyone. Reluctantly, her father continued to supply her with funds, much to Claudia's loud objections. Her mother, Augusta, said nothing, only watched her daughter with sad eyes.

"Lady Jilana?"

At the hesitant summons, Jilana drew herself away from her musings and looked over her shoulder at the young woman who stood some distance away.

"The governor-general is here, lady."

"Thank you." Jilana turned and walked back to the villa. At the door, she paused to make certain her toga was properly draped and touched a hand to her hair. She had allowed Claudia's slave to dress her hair for tonight, and now the red-gold mass was pulled sternly back from her face and secured with combs. The length of it had been oiled and tortured into tight curls in what Claudia said was the height of fashion. Jilana badly wanted nothing more than to wash the oil and perfume from the tresses, but tonight she had to look her best and so she took a deep breath and walked into the house.

Marcus had just finished introducing Paulinus to his family when Jilana entered the *triclinium*. The banquet hall was three steps lower than the rest of the first floor and Jilana took the tiled steps gracefully, halting directly in front of Paulinus. The general wore his dress uniform and the sight of it repulsed Jilana.

"You know my daughter, of course," Marcus said, a trifle nervously.

"Aye." Paulinus' eyes did a thorough inspection of Jilana as she curtsied before him. "You look much different than you did at our last meeting, Lady Jilana. More...civilized."

Jilana bared her teeth in a brief smile. "But then, General, I had no slaves to dance attendance upon me." How she hated this man who so relentlessly pursued the defeated rebels. Paulinus was set upon, and would settle for no less than, the complete destruction of the Iceni and those who had been foolish enough to ally with them.

Paulinus' eyes narrowed dangerously. "From what has been related to me, that is not the case now."

Jilana arched an eyebrow at the bite in his words. "You above all, General, should know how difficult it is to find good slaves among the native population. They are so...intractable."

"Jilana," Lucius broke in with a warning look. "I am sure the general does not care to discuss the slave situation with you."

"I am sure he wishes to discuss nothing else," Jilana countered blandly. Reluctantly, she let the subject drop. This night, of all nights, she could not risk baiting Paulinus. Her situation was precarious enough. "Was your journey a pleasant one, General?"

Paulinus eyed her suspiciously, but followed her lead. "Pleasant enough, thank you, lady. Oh, I had almost forgotten. Your friend Tarpeius is in Londinium." He offered Jilana his arm and led her to one of the couches ranged in a circle in the center of the room.

Marcus and Augusta exchanged a relieved look and followed the general, leaving Lucius to escort Claudia.

"Hadrian," Jilana inquired as she settled herself into a half-reclining position upon the pillows. Paulinus took one of the couches next to hers while Lucius took the other. Claudia took the couch on the other side of Lucius. Slaves hurriedly pushed low tables in front of the couches as soon as they had been seated.

"He has retired from the legion," Paulinus replied. "He is staying in the city, awaiting passage on a ship bound for Rome."

"We cannot allow that," Augusta put in from the couch she shared with Marcus. "We owe him Jilana's life, not once, but twice. Where is he staying, General? I will send a servant to fetch him at once."

Paulinus coughed discreetly. "I think, mistress, 'twould be best if you sent a message to him tomorrow. This is his first night of freedom, if you will, and I doubt he will return to his inn until morning."

Augusta colored attractively. "Of course, General. As you say."

"General," Claudia joined in. "I understand the Emperor has ordered more men to Britannia in order to finish the rebels. Is this true?"

"Aye, it is." Paulinus looked up at Claudia and smiled warmly. How his host and hostess had managed to produce two such different daughters was beyond him. "Two thousand legionaries, a thousand cavalry, and eight cohorts of auxiliaries have recently arrived from Germania. With them, I will see to it that the Iceni never raise so much as a finger against Rome again."

Jilana's appetite fled, and she pushed listlessly at the poached fish on her plate.

"I have also heard that Poenius Postumus committed suicide when he learned of your victory over the Iceni rabble." Claudia leaned forward eagerly. "Is that true?"

All of the warmth left Paulinus' face. "Aye, and 'tis fortunate for him that he fell on his sword before I could reach him. At least he spared his family the dishonor of a court-martial and summary execution." That he had been denied his vengeance sat like a stone in the general's soul, and he forced himself to smile again. "But surely a beautiful creature such as yourself can have no interest in military matters."

Claudia beamed and the conversation wandered onto safer topics. Course after course was served and disposed of and Jilana watched her tongue and behaved as correctly as she possibly could. The rich food, however, upset her stomach, and at last she simply waved away the servants when they brought the trays to her table and sipped at a goblet of wine. Musicians played from behind a curtain and Jilana paid more attention to the music than she did to the conversation until, having partaken of the confectionary and fruit served as dessert, Paulinus apologized for the lateness of the hour and rose.

"You are welcome to stay the night, General," Marcus offered politely.

"Much as I am tempted, I fear I must refuse your generosity," Paulinus declined. "There is business in Londinium that requires my attention tomorrow morning, but I thank you for the offer." He gave his hand to Marcus and then to Lucius. "In his last report, Petilius Cerealis told me your time with the Ninth Legion had expired and that you were planning to return to Rome."

"That is correct, General," Lucius replied.

"You plan to work with your father, the senator, I take it?" When Lucius nodded, Paulinus clapped him on the shoulder. "When you inherit his seat, young man, remember the legion. The legion protects the Empire, but it cannot do so without funds."

"I will certainly remember, General."

"And Cerealis also informed me that you are to be wed before leaving Britannia." Paulinus graced Jilana with a cold smile. "Your choice in wives is puzzling, but mayhap you can turn her into a proper Roman wife."

Lucius sent a dark glance at Jilana. "I shall certainly try, sir."

The general bade farewell to the women, who remained in the triclinium while the men saw Paulinus to his escort. When Marcus and Lucius returned, the younger man's temper showed in his flushed face and he went directly to Jilana's couch.

"You do realize, do you not," Lucius said, "that you have just been privately reprimanded by the governor-general, the Emperor's representative here?" When she nodded, he added, "Now will you give up this mad scheme of yours involving the Iceni slaves?"

Jilana carefully sat her cup on the low table. "Nay."

Lucius caught his breath at her answer. "Jilana, this is not Venta Icenorum; you are no longer living in a small town close to the frontier. Your actions here are noticed and remarked upon, that is why Paulinus came here tonight. You are buying and freeing his slaves as fast as he runs them down."

"That is not humanly possible," Jilana said bitterly. The next moment she gasped as Lucius' hands bit into her shoulders.

"Listen to me," Lucius ordered fiercely, his dark eyes fairly glowing with anger. "Paulinus hates the Iceni, and all those who allied themselves with Boadicea. He means to destroy them, Jilana. Do you understand? He will destroy them utterly, and if you stand between him and his heart's desire he will destroy you as well! I want to protect you, but I cannot if you persist in freeing those accursed Britons!"

"You may not want to protect me in any event," Jilana said after a long silence.

Lucius sighed. "Of course I want to protect you, Jilana, you are to be my wife."

Jilana cleared her throat nervously. "Perhaps not."

Lucius took her hands in his and sent a pleading look to her parents. "Marcus, Augusta, how can I convince her of my intentions?"

Augusta looked from her daughter, to Lucius and back again. With a feeling of dread, she answered, "I do not think Jilana doubts your intentions, Lucius. Do you, Jilana?" Her hand grasped Marcus' when Jilana shook her head.

"What are you talking about?" Claudia asked impatiently. "Of course Jilana is going to marry Lucius."

Summoning up her courage, Jilana pulled her hands away from Lucius and announced, "I am with child."

The silence that fell in the triclinium was deafening. Claudia's mouth fell open in astonishment; Augusta closed her eyes and leaned against her husband. Lucius tilted his head to one side and frowned at Jilana, certain he had not heard correctly. "What did you say?"

"I am with child." Jilana carefully folded her hands in her lap and waited for the storm to engulf her. She did not have long to wait.

"With child!" Lucius sprang to his feet, staring at her in disbelief. "Whose—Jupiter! 'Tis an Iceni bastard you carry in your womb!"

Jilana bit back the denial that rose to her lips. No one—not even her parents—would recognize the validity of her marriage to Caddaric, and now she had to consider the welfare of her child.

"Juno, the scandal," Claudia breathed, her eyes glittering. "Jilana, how could you? What will my friends say?"

"Be silent, Claudia," Augusta snapped. Shakily, she rose and went to sit beside Jilana. "How long have you known?"

"I have been certain for about a month," Jilana replied softly. "Until then I thought—" she gestured helplessly "—I did not know what to think."

"Why did you not tell us that you had been raped," Lucius demanded. When Jilana did not answer, his face grew grim. "It was rape, was it not?"

"I hardly think it matters, Lucius," Augusta answered tartly. "We must deal with the babe now." She stroked Jilana's hair. "What are you planning to do, daughter?"

"She will get rid of it, of course," Lucius announced before Jilana had a chance to reply. "There are physicians who will rid her of the brat and keep their mouths closed."

Jilana's head snapped up and she glared at her betrothed. "Do not presume to tell me what I will do!"

"You cannot intend to have the child," Lucius cried, outraged.

"Of course she does not," Claudia screeched. "My sister may cosset those filthy beasts because she has a soft heart, but she would not give life to one of them!"

Jilana looked at her mother and then her father. Lucius and Claudia she ignored for the present. "I want the babe," she said simply.

Augusta nodded. "Aye, I thought you might. Marcus, I am taking Jilana to her chamber." The sounds of Lucius' outrage followed them up the stairs to the second floor. Jilana's maid was waiting when they reached her chamber. "Ede," Augusta said, "Lady Jilana has had a trying evening. Help me undress her and put her to bed."

Ede took one look at Jilana's pale face and her green eyes darkened in sympathy. Without a word she took one of Jilana's bed gowns from her chest and helped Augusta strip off the younger woman's toga. The shadows cast by the lamps helped to conceal the livid red scar which ran down the side of Ede's neck and disappeared into the neckline of her wool stola. When Jilana was abed, Ede retreated to a shadowed corner of the room and waited.

Augusta had not missed the look the maid had bestowed upon her daughter. "Shall I send Ede away, Jilana?"

"Nay." Jilana turned her head on the pillow so that she could see her friend. "Ede knows." In fact, it had been Ede who had told Jilana why her woman's time had stopped.

"That does not surprise me." Augusta patted Jilana's hand. "Much as I hate to say this, I must. Coming as it does on top of everything else, your bearing a child now will surely bring about a monumental scandal." Word of

Jilana's ordeal had spread through the Roman city, though Augusta had doubted that "ordeal" was the correct term. The sorrow she sensed in her daughter had not been caused by the death of a hated enemy.

"And a scandal would ruin you and Father, as well as Claudia's hopes of making a good marriage," Jilana added listlessly. "I know. But I cannot seek out a physician and rid myself of this new life, Mother. I cannot. If only you knew..." Her voice trailed off and she looked beseechingly at Augusta.

"I understand," Augusta told her daughter, her own eyes clouding with tears and remembrance. "'Tis just that, by your actions, you have focused so much attention upon yourself."

"I could go away," Jilana suggested. "Ships leave every day from Londinium for different parts of the Empire. Ede would come with me."

"I will not allow you to run away to have this babe," Augusta decreed. "Since you mean to have this child, you will have it here, where I can keep an eye on you." She kissed Jilana warmly on the forehead. "We will work it out, do not fear. Sleep now, and we will discuss the situation in the morning, when everyone's temper has had a chance to cool."

When Augusta was gone, Ede came to the bed and settled into the chair at its side. "Your news was not well received, I take it?"

The wry note in her voice brought a hint of a smile to Jilana's mouth. "Claudia screamed and Lucius looked like he was going to strike me."

Ede made a face at the mention of Lucius. "He is eaten up by the fact that you do not love him. All this fuss over the birth of a child! What difference does it make who the child's father is?"

Ede was so truly bewildered that, in spite of herself, Jilana laughed softly. "'Tis hard for you to understand, I know, but my people frown upon children being born without the benefit of marriage. And then, my family has guessed that the father of my child was not Roman. That makes all the difference—as it would with you, Ede.''

Ede shrugged. ''It would not matter to me if the father of my child was not Roman.'' She gave Jilana a wink and the two of them chuckled briefly and then Ede sobered. ''You are right, however. Not even my people would easily accept a child fathered by their hated enemy.''

''Oh, Ede, what am I going to do?'' Jilana asked fearfully. ''My parents will allow me to have the child, but once it is born—'' She swallowed the painful lump in her throat. ''I am certain they will make me give it away, and I cannot bear to do that.''

Ede chewed thoughtfully on her lower lip. ''Have you spoken to Clywd?''

Jilana shook her head. ''He is still so frail that I am afraid to burden him.''

''Burden him!'' Ede hissed. ''Jilana, you carry the flesh of his flesh. How could knowing that be a burden to him?''

''You have seen him, Ede, you know how weak he is.''

''He is weak because he refuses food; instead he feeds on his grief for Caddaric and Heall.'' Ede shook her head. ''I believe all Druids are mad.''

Jilana looked away from her friend. She had expected the manner of Lhwyd's death to turn Ede against her, but Ede had accepted it with more equanimity than Jilana could have managed under similar circumstances. ''He was mad,'' Ede had told Jilana. ''Had you not defended yourself, he would have killed you.'' Then Ede had wept for the brother of her youth and, when she had calmed, asked to remain with Jilana. Jilana had readily accepted, for Ede was a tie to Caddaric. They soon became closer than most sisters. And then they had found Clywd in the slave market.

''Your mother was right, you need to rest,'' Ede said upon seeing the pinched look to Jilana's features. ''I will see you tomorrow.'' She blew out the lamps and silently made her way from the chamber. Tomorrow, she promised herself as she walked past Clywd's hut in the slave quarters, she would convince Jilana to speak with the Druid.

Augusta and Marcus were up half the night, discussing Jilana's situation. The next morning, they summoned their eldest daughter and Lucius and told them of the decision they had reached. They agreed that Jilana would be allowed to bear the child.

"You cannot be serious," Lucius burst out when Marcus had finished speaking. "I demand that Jilana abort this thing!"

"You demand," Marcus repeated quellingly. "You are not in a position to demand such a thing, Lucius. She is not yet your wife."

"I will not raise a bastard as my own," Lucius said in a voice shaking with rage.

"We have not asked you to," Marcus said calmly, and Jilana knew that they had not yet heard the entire decision. "When the child is strong enough, it will be given away."

"Nay," Jilana cried. "Father, you cannot do this!"

Marcus frowned at his daughter. "What has happened is tragic, but we—your mother and I—will not allow it to ruin the rest of your life. The babe will be placed with a native couple, to be raised as their own."

"Nay, Father, I beg you—"

"Be silent," Marcus roared, his fist slamming against the table in front of him. His composure was destroyed and the look he gave Jilana was filled with anger and pity. "Do you know what your life would be like were you to keep this child? Decent society would be closed to you forever; you would both be outcasts! And do not think that you could remain here, in my house. The stigma would stain the rest of the family as well. Is that what you want for your mother and sister? Do you want them to be gossiped about when they enter the city?"

"Nay, of course not," Jilana whispered, appalled.

"And what of the child?" Marcus persisted. "What kind of a life would he or she have? How would you support the two of you? What kind of work could you find?

Even if you could find a way to live—and I am certain you can well imagine the kind of positions that would be open to you—what of the child himself? You know how cruel people can be, Jilana. Do you want your child to be taunted and bullied whenever he steps foot outside the door? Is that what you want for your child?''

Jilana shook her head and felt tears sting her eyelids.

Marcus sank back in his chair and when he spoke again his voice had gentled. ''There are many Britons working for me. I will find a good home for the babe. The people he is given to will never know of his mixed heritage; he will be totally accepted by the natives.''

''Aye, Father,'' Jilana said brokenly.

''It is for the best, Jilana,'' Augusta put in, her eyes welling with tears. ''Surely you can see that.''

''Aye.'' She understood, but it was a knife in her heart to think of her child being raised by strangers, never knowing his true father and mother.

Next Marcus turned his attention to Lucius. ''If you wish to break your betrothal to Jilana, we will, of course, understand.''

Lucius turned to Jilana, considering. She was beautiful, intelligent, and wealthy—everything he could have wanted in a wife. She stirred the fires in his heart as well as his loins. ''If we marry, this must forever remain a secret. I cannot allow scandal to touch my family.''

Lucius' hands were clenched into fists and Jilana stared at them. ''Perhaps you should find another, Lucius,'' she managed to say. ''I do not think I will adapt well to Rome.''

''Once we are away from this wretched island all will be well,'' Lucius replied. Jilana raised her eyes to his and Lucius felt his anger drain away. Once they were married, he would see to it that she was kept so busy managing his house and raising their children that she would not have time to get into trouble. ''I love you, Jilana,'' he said truthfully, for her ears alone. ''Do you know how rare that emotion is in marriages among our class?''

Jilana knew, all too well. If she did not marry Lucius, her father would find another candidate, for it was a father's duty to make advantageous alliances for his daughters. Unmarried women were held in contempt and pity by Roman society. The freedom she had known so briefly with Caddaric was gone and the remainder of her life stretched endlessly in front of her. She had to survive those years. Forgive me, my love, Jilana thought as she slowly nodded to Lucius. "As you wish."

Lucius rose. "I will write to my father, telling him that our departure has been delayed, and send it on the next ship leaving Londinium." He cleared his throat in embarrassment. "When shall I tell my family that we will leave Britannia," he asked Jilana.

Jilana's cheeks flushed. "The child is due in early *Martius.*"

"How fitting," Lucius said cuttingly, "that the brat should be born in the month dedicated to our god of war." He watched the blood drain from Jilana's face and hardened himself against the rush of pity. By demanding to have the child she had brought this trouble upon herself. He turned to Marcus. "Under the circumstances, I believe it will be best if I stay in the city. I am sure the general can find some use for me over the next six months." He left without another word.

Alone with her parents, Jilana asked, "Does Claudia know?"

"Not yet," Marcus answered.

"I want to tell her." Jilana rose on shaky legs. "I would ask one final indulgence, if I may." When her father nodded she continued, "I would like to choose the family that will raise the babe."

Augusta exchanged a long look with her husband and when it ended, Marcus nodded. "Only keep in mind what I have said. Not a breath of dishonor must touch our family."

"The people I have in mind will see to it that your reputation remains intact, Father."

"Jilana," Augusta gasped in dismay.

"I am sorry." Jilana apologized immediately, regretting her outburst. "But this is *my* child as well, and everyone is treating the babe as if he or she is a piece of soiled linen to be quickly disposed of!" She felt sobs choking her throat and ran from the room before she could pour out the entire story to her parents.

"Oh, Marcus," Augusta breathed. "What have we done?"

"What is necessary," Marcus replied, but his hand, when he reached for Augusta's, was trembling. "My heart goes out to her, my dear, but what else can we do? She will marry Lucius and lead a good life, and in time, the pain she feels now will pass."

Augusta shook her head. "I wish I could be as certain as you. Marcus, you forgave me all those years ago. Why can you not forgive Jilana now?"

"'Tis not a matter of forgiveness," Marcus said firmly. "I love my daughter and will see her safe, in spite of herself. If that means that I must rule her with an iron hand, then I will, for I will not see her made a prostitute or, at best, some man's mistress, were this scandal to be known." He pressed a kiss upon his wife's forehead. "Now I must go to the city. Obviously, Jilana can no longer come to my office with me, so during her confinement, you can teach her how to manage a household."

"People will think it strange if she is not seen for so long a time," Augusta mused.

"Nay, they will not. She has been through a terrible experience; I will drop a few hints that she desires seclusion in order to recover. That should be sufficient to satisfy any curiosity. I leave it to you to break the news to Jilana."

So IT WAS that Jilana, with the best of intentions, was kept in exile at her family's villa, but the restriction had little impact upon her life. She accepted her father's edict without protest and then calmly explained that she would send Ede to the slave market in her place. Reluctantly, Augusta agreed and, to Jilana's amazement, so did Marcus. It was then that Jilana realized that her parents were as saddened over the treatment of the defeated Iceni as she. Revenge, her father had said, was an empty quest which would only deepen the native hatred for the Romans. He defended her actions to all detractors, including his youngest daughter. Claudia rarely spoke to Jilana once she had been told of the unborn child's fate, except to say that Jilana was bringing shame upon the family and that she, Claudia, would never forgive her. Jilana accepted Claudia's reaction and refused to be drawn into futile arguments. Neither of them would change their minds. Thankfully, Lucius joined Paulinus' staff as a civilian advisor and was frequently gone from Londinium, and during his brief visits they discussed everything but the child. Jilana often wondered if Lucius loved her as much as he claimed.

There were two great comforts to Jilana. The first was the expression on Clywd's face when she told him of the babe. He was awed, at first, then overjoyed. And then Jilana told him of her parents' decision.

"But do not fear," Jilana hastened to reassure him when the faint spark went out of his eyes. "Ede has agreed to take the child as her own and go north, on the condition that you go with her to help raise the babe." Jilana grasped the frail hands between her own. "Think of it, Clywd, you will have the joy of raising Caddaric's child—you can tell him of his father, of his proud ancestry—and I will have the comfort of knowing that my child is loved. Please, Clywd, you must agree."

Clywd raised his eyes to Ede, who stood in the background by the door of the hut. "You have agreed?" he questioned, almost fearfully.

"Aye, old one," Ede assured him. Coming forward, she knelt by his bed. "Once Jilana is sent to Rome, there will be nothing to bind me here, and her betrothed will not allow her to take me along. Think of it, Druid," she said encouragingly. "There will be others like us. We will find a village, safe from the Romans, and raise the child there.

Mayhap the child will take after you and inherit the sight—both the priesthood and your line will continue."

Clywd nodded slowly and looked back at Jilana. "It would fulfill Caddaric's dream."

Jilana caught her breath as pain swept through her. "Aye, wise one, that it would. But you cannot continue as you have been; you must grow stronger, for the sake of the child."

The child gave Clywd back his reason for living. Under Ede and Jilana's watchful eyes he began eating and his strength grew with each passing day. Thank the gods Clywd had not been recognized as a Druid, Jilana thought once when she helped him walk the paths through the slave quarters. He had been captured and beaten, but because he had been unarmed, as were most of the scattered Iceni, the soldiers had spared his life. The Empire could always use more slaves.

The second comfort was Hadrian's arrival. He came to pay his respects and, at Jilana's insistence, remained at the villa rather than returning to his inn. Since her father went to the city daily, Marcus promised to book passage for Hadrian on the first available ship. Hadrian accepted Jilana's situation without comment and Jilana nearly wept in gratitude. He offered no advice, did not lecture her, merely *accepted* and remained her friend. The tall, gruff ex-centurion became, for all intents and purposes, a member of the family—much to Claudia's chagrin. A month later, when Marcus informed him that a ship had arrived in port and was bound for Rome, Hadrian announced that he did not intend to return home. Instead, he said, he would send a letter, instructing his cousin to sell the farm he had purchased for his retirement. Hadrian had decided to remain in Britannia.

Jilana was not surprised. The first time Hadrian had set eyes on Ede, he had been dumbstruck, and he found the most absurd reasons to seek out the warrior maid, including escorting her on her daily trips to the slave market. Ede had suffered as much as Jilana; she too had seen her husband killed in that final battle, so whenever Hadrian hung too closely to her heels she sniped mercilessly at him, protecting herself from further hurt. Hadrian, however, was immune to such tactics and persevered. Ede, at first wary and abrasive, softened toward the former primipilus and soon, where there was Hadrian, there too was Ede. The sight of her two friends together brought Jilana as much joy as it did pain.

Hadrian and Ede were married on the first of *Novembris* in a Roman civil ceremony; the day was also the festival of Samh'in for the Celts, so that night, in a private ceremony in the slave quarters, their vows were repeated before Clywd.

That night, the tears Jilana had held so long at bay broke through, and she wept for all that she had lost and all that she had yet to lose. When her sobbing ended, she felt a tiny flutter in her abdomen and placed a hand lightly over the area where the movement had occurred. When it happened again, she smiled, aware of a fierce protectiveness welling in her heart. She was doing all she could for her child; he or she would be raised in love and freedom, and since Hadrian could read and write, he had promised to send word of her child to Jilana whenever he could. She would have to be content with that, she told herself, for her life was decided. But in her heart, she longed to make the trip north with her friends.

Heall was found the following day. He was half-starved, his arm had been broken and his color was ashen. Jilana tended him herself and when he awoke, they both wept with the sheer joy of having found the other alive. He accepted Hadrian immediately, and the two warriors passed many hours in Heall's quarters while the older man recuperated. Heall's heart was weak, Clywd told Jilana when he had examined his friend. He needed total bed rest in order to recover. So in the evenings the little circle of friends met in Heall's quarters, remembering better days with laughter and tears.

"'Twill be nice to raise a grandchild," Heall said one night, his eyes resting fondly on Jilana. She gave him an odd little smile and he realized what he had said. Nervously, his eyes dropped to the cup of mead he held. "I mean—"

"I know what you mean," Jilana said, touching his arm in a gesture of understanding. "You helped raise Caddaric; 'tis only natural you think of this babe as your grandchild. In truth, you honor me."

The brief autumn gave way to winter, and Jilana spent much of her time inside the villa, not wanting to risk the icy paths as her balance grew more precarious. From Augusta she learned how to manage the villa with its many intricacies. She planned the evenings in which her parents entertained their friends, from planning the menus to overseeing the servants. She did not, of course, attend the feasts, but that did not matter. It was enough to know that she was learning the skills that would hold her in good stead once she was in Rome. During the evenings, her friends would gather in Jilana's bedchamber and she and Ede would sew small things for the babe—Ede was growing quite skilled with a needle under Jilana's tutelage— while the men talked or diced.

It was on one such evening that Augusta came to Jilana's chamber bearing a tray of confections. "I thought you might like some of these," Augusta said brightly as she sailed into the room. "They are truly excellent—" Her voice died when she saw the group. "I am sorry, Jilana, I thought 'twas only you and Ede and Hadrian."

"You need not apologize, Mother," Jilana assured her, rising to take the tray from her hands and set it on a low table. "Come, let me introduce my friends to you." She pulled Augusta toward where the others sat or reclined on cushions, chairs and couches. "This is Clywd," she said, touching him on the shoulder, "and this is Heall. They were most kind to me, Mother, both treated me as if I were their daughter. They are very dear to me."

The two men had risen when Jilana introduced them, and Augusta gave them a weak smile. "I remember Heall, of course," she said in a voice that sounded oddly choked.

"Oh, of course," Jilana exclaimed, smiling. "He led you out of Venta Icenorum. Thank you for my family's lives, Heall." And with that she kissed him soundly on the cheek and smiled up at him.

"I must go." Augusta, always the most polite of women, whirled and all but ran from the room.

Puzzled, Jilana watched her go, and then shrugged. "She is probably afraid one of the guests will wonder where she is and come searching for her." With a mischievous smile, Jilana patted her burgeoning stomach, settled back in her chair and reached greedily for the sweets her mother had brought. She was oblivious to the strained look that passed between Heall and Clywd.

THE NEW YEAR brought another visit from Suetonius Paulinus. The governor-general met briefly with Marcus in his office and departed without seeing anyone else. Shortly thereafter, Jilana was summoned to her father's office.

"Sit down, Jilana," Marcus ordered when she arrived. His face was white and strained, and when Jilana was seated he said bluntly, "Your activities with the Iceni are at an end."

Jilana's heart gave a wild thud against her ribs and then seemed to stop beating altogether. "Why?"

"Why?" Marcus echoed, fury lending an edge to his voice. "Because Suetonius Paulinus, in his capacity as governor-general, has ordered it stopped."

Jilana sighed. She had expected something like this. "And if I do not?"

"Then he will arrest you," Marcus informed his eldest daughter, "and confiscate my business and property."

Fear ran the length of her spine. "Gods!" Paulinus was utterly ruthless; Jilana did not doubt for a moment that he would do as he threatened, and not even for Caddaric's memory could she place the life of their unborn child, or her family, in danger.

"My feelings exactly," Marcus said grimly. Distractedly, he shuffled the scrolls and parchments littering his desk. "I love you dearly, Jilana, but not even for you will I place my family in jeopardy." His hands ceased their restless movement and he looked sadly at Jilana. "You have found and freed nearly two hundred of the rebels; be content with that."

"Have I a choice?" Jilana asked bitterly. "Nay, Father, I do not blame you," she added when his mouth thinned. "I blame our glorious Empire, which is built upon the backs of slaves and controls our lives so completely." She shivered and knew the coldness came from within her, for the room was heated with the hypocaust as well as braziers. "Ede is in Londinium."

"I told Paulinus as much," Marcus replied. "You will put an end to it when she returns." The order, softly spoken though it was, fell like a barrier between them.

Jilana nodded, defeated. "How will I survive Rome, Father?"

Marcus' expression softened. "'Tis for the best. Away from here you will have time to heal, forget the past, something you cannot do when you constantly surround yourself with reminders of the rebellion. Lucius will make a good husband." He hesitated. "You will have other children, daughter, to replace this one."

Jilana shook her head. She might bear other children, but none could replace Caddaric's child, for this one had been conceived in love, not duty.

"I have never asked about the time you spent away from us," Marcus said, his attention focused on the parchment in front of him, "nor will I now. But I want you to listen to me and try to understand. 'Tis obvious you cared a great deal for the man who fathered your babe, but that part of your life is over, finished. That you know this man is dead is also plain." His voice lowered. "I grieve for you, for your pain, but you must remember that, even without the rebellion, there would have been no future for the two of you."

"I do not believe that," Jilana protested.

"Believe," Marcus replied intently. "In the normal course of events, how long do you think you could have lived with this man without the comforts our ways afford? How long could you have gone before you found yourself longing for the comforts of a true bath, or the feel of a gown made of fine linen or silk? How long before you missed the companionship of your own kind?''

Jilana gazed at her father with tears glazing her eyes. ''I could have lived forever without those things—had he lived.'' She cleared the constriction in her throat. ''Did you give Hadrian this same lecture?''

''Hadrian is a man,'' was Marcus' answer, as if that explained everything. ''You are a woman—my child. I want the best in life for you, and that does not include living in some mean hut in some squalid village.''

Jilana rose and left the room without another word. Her father would not believe that, for her, Caddaric had been the best in life.

Hadrian burst through the double doors of the entrance hall just as Jilana had taken the first stair leading to the second floor. He shook the dusting of snow from his cloak with a massive shake, and Jilana smiled, for his action reminded her of some bear recently awakened from hibernation.

''*Salutatio*, Hadrian,'' Jilana greeted him, stepping back to the hall. ''You have returned earlier than usual.''

Hadrian stared at her, his dark eyes running worriedly over her rounded form. He loved Ede, but this woman would always hold a special place in his heart, and the news he brought would shatter the world her family was so carefully building around her. ''Ede wants you to come to the slave quarters, Jilana.''

''How many did she find this time?''

''Ten.''

Jilana sighed. ''I am glad she found that many. Paulinus has ordered,'' she gave a derisive stress to the word, ''me to cease.''

''Jilana, you must come,'' Hadrian said impatiently.

''Can you not see to their quartering?'' Jilana asked with a grimace. ''I do not like to leave the house now.''

''I know, but Ede feels it is important.'' Hadrian smiled weakly. ''Please, Jilana.''

''Very well. I will get my palla.''

Minutes later, Jilana was carefully negotiating the paths to the slave quarters with Hadrian's hand firmly beneath her elbow. "Are they badly hurt?" she questioned her silent escort.

"One is," Hadrian answered and then lapsed into silence.

Jilana shrugged inwardly. Clywd was more than capable of dealing with the wounded, but if Ede felt her presence was necessary...

The slave quarters were laid out in three parallel rows, each row containing twenty one-room huts. Hadrian pushed open the door of the last hut in the second row and allowed Jilana to precede him. A brazier had been lit to aid the newly-laid fire and had taken some, but not all, of the chill from the room. Jilana pushed the hood of her palla from her face and advanced toward the cot where Heall, Clywd and Ede stood.

"What is it, Ede?" Jilana asked softly. "Or should I say who? Did you find someone from your village?"

In answer, Ede stepped away from the cot. Her hands were locked so tightly together that the knuckles were white. Jilana wondered briefly at her friend's agitation and then turned her gaze to the pallet. The man laying there was streaked with dirt; his face was covered with a thick, brown beard and his hair, a shade lighter than the beard, lay in matted tangles against his scalp and nearly brushed his shoulders. His breathing was labored and an awful smell emanated from him.

Frowning, Jilana moved forward and placed her hand upon his forehead. His skin was hot to the touch and, looking down, she saw that his tunic had been stripped from him. An angry gash, barely healed, lay like a brand upon the left side of his hair-roughened chest, and the flesh was so tautly stretched that she could count his ribs. "He has a fever," she said, breaking the heavy silence, "and has obviously been half-starved...." Her voice trailed off as her eyes tracked upward and found the purple scar on the man's right shoulder. Memories flooded her and a vise seemed to squeeze her chest. It could not be! she thought wildly. Her eyes were playing tricks upon her mind. Jilana gave a choked gasp, trying to force air into her starved lungs. 'Twas impossible that now, after so much time had passed—

And then his eyes fluttered open, bright with fever, but recognizable nonetheless. Blue, a brilliant blue; the color was forever seared in her memory. "Caddaric." Jilana's voice was little more than an exhalation of air. His eyes ran wildly around the room, and he strained against his bonds to the accompanying jingle of the manacles. And then, mercifully, he lost consciousness.

Jilana pressed her cold fingers against her mouth, holding back the cry that rose in her throat. Oh, my love, what have they done to you?!

"I am sorry, Jilana," Ede said, lightly touching her shoulder. "But I thought it best not to announce this in the villa."

"Nay, nay, you were right," Jilana whispered with a jerky shake of her head. "Juno, what has happened to him?" Abruptly, she brought herself under control. Her voice gained strength and there was a harsh note to it when she spoke. "Get these chains off of him. Clywd, fetch your medicines. Heall, we need to clean him, so set water to heat. Ede, go and tell my parents where I am and gather fresh linens and towels from the house." When Ede turned, Jilana grabbed her arm. "And please, act normally! If they so much as suspect—" Ede nodded curtly and ran out of the hut.

The remainder of the day passed in a blur of activity and prayer. Clywd poured medicines down Caddaric's throat and then Jilana set about cleaning the filth from his body. He was covered with fresh scars that brought tears to Jilana's eyes while she tormented herself with questions that only Caddaric could answer. How had he survived? Where had he been all these months? Had he been free or had he been held in some horrible cell, tormented by his Roman jailers? When he was clean and lying between clean linens and a warm blanket, he regained consciousness and she managed to spoon broth down his throat before his eyes closed again. Her worry was abated somewhat when Clywd told her that he did not think the fever was life-threatening. Caddaric was weak, but with time and proper attention he would survive. All of them breathed a little easier at Clywd's words. Hadrian took Ede back to the house at midday. If she remained here, he pointed out, her absence along with Jilana's would certainly raise suspicions.

Jilana perched on the edge of the cot, ignoring the strain on her lower back. She held Caddaric's hands in hers, pressing kisses upon the strong, blunt fingers while she prayed as she had never prayed in her life. Once he opened his eyes and breathed her name in a cracked whisper and she brushed her lips against his. "I am here, my love. You are safe now."

"Searched . . . for you."

Tears spilled down Jilana's cheeks. "And you have found me. Rest now, dearest."

When darkness fell, Ede came for her. "Jilana, you must return to the house." Jilana shook her head in violent refusal and Ede knelt beside her. "Jilana, Lucius is here."

Jilana closed her eyes. "I do not care."

"Ede is right, child," Heall said. "You have spent the day here; you must leave now, before Lucius comes for you."

Looking at the three, familiar faces around her, Jilana saw the same thing in each of their eyes. Fear. They had been beaten, conquered; and now, even though they were free, their lives were held in Roman hands. How they lived, *if* they lived, depended on their enemy's whim. Reluctantly, she nodded, and then she suddenly felt as if a stone had been lifted from her shoulders. Jilana rose and excitedly drew her friends around her. "Do you know what this means?" she asked them, her eyes shining with life. Not waiting for them to reply, she continued, "I am free of Lucius. How can I marry him when my husband lives?" She grinned and clapped her hands together in pure joy. "We will be together, all of us, wherever Caddaric chooses to live. I will not have to give up my babe!"

Heall and Clywd exchanged a worried look and Heall counseled gently, "I do not think it would be wise to tell your parents about Caddaric. Your father—"

Jilana waved his objection aside. "I do not plan to tell them. I meant that, when you leave, I will leave with you. 'Tis so simple! I will just—" she snapped her fingers, "—disappear."

The three Iceni avoided her gaze. If she disappeared, either Marcus or Lucius would come after her and, if necessary, drag her back. But none could bring themselves to spoil Jilana's dream.

"Lucius is waiting," Ede said at last.

Jilana kissed Caddaric tenderly on the forehead and then returned to the villa with Ede. That night, although she said little, her family noticed the change in her. She was more like the Jilana of old; her eyes sparkled, she smiled easily and, much to her mother's delight, her appetite was voracious. For Marcus, expecting her to be sullen and withdrawn after their discussion that morning, the sudden change was troubling. He knew his daughter too well to believe that Lucius' unexpected visit was the cause for such change.

Lucius stayed for a week and Jilana fretted under his presence. Strange as their circumstances were, she was his betrothed, and as such she could hardly abandon him for hours on end, particularly after he made it quite clear that he intended to spend time with her. How she managed to converse with him she did not know, for her thoughts were with Caddaric, worrying over him, longing for the sight of him. Her only consolation was that Ede faithfully reported upon his progress. One night, when the others had retired and she could bear the separation no longer, Jilana made her way to the slave quarters. She slipped once on a patch of ice in the courtyard and gave a startled shriek as she landed on her bottom. Biting her lip, she struggled to her feet and looked over her shoulder toward the villa, watching for a sign that someone had heard her. When several minutes had gone by and she remained alone, she continued on her way.

Caddaric was asleep, Clywd seated beside the cot on a stool, and when she touched his forehead, she was relieved to find it warm, but not with fever.

"He is better."

Clywd nodded. "Aye. The fever has been gone for a day now; all he needs is rest and food."

Jilana smiled and eased herself onto the edge of the cot so that she could touch her husband at will. "Have you told him about me? Does he know I am here?"

"We have told him. How much he has understood I do not know."

"And the babe? Have you told Caddaric about our child?"

Clywd looked away from her avid gaze. "Not yet."

"I am glad. I want the pleasure of that for myself." Jilana ran a hand through the waves of Caddaric's hair. The strands were clean, soft to the touch; someone had washed his hair since she had seen him last, and trimmed his beard. "He needs his hair cut."

"That would not be wise, not while he remains here," Clywd said quietly. "Nor should he shave the beard. Ede overheard Lucius talking with your father." He sighed heavily. "Although you have said nothing, the two of them have reasoned that Caddaric is the father of your child. Lucius is mad for you, Jilana, if he should learn that Caddaric is here, alive, the gods know what he would do."

Privately, Jilana thought that Clywd worried about nothing, but she did not want to upset him by arguing. "Lucius is returning to Londinium tomorrow morning. I will have Ede bring Caddaric to me when he is gone."

Her expression of love and hope pained Clywd. "Jilana, do not expect too much from him."

Jilana frowned and gave him a puzzled smile. "I expect nothing, Clywd."

"You know how much pride my son has," Clywd hesitantly continued. "He may be angry at finding himself here, under these circumstances."

"You are speaking in riddles," Jilana murmured, shaking her head. "What circumstances? He is here, alive; we are together. What else is there?"

Clywd held his tongue and Jilana left shortly thereafter. Jilana was right—their reunion should be a joyful thing, but Clywd knew his son well enough to fear that Caddaric would not see it in that light.

The next morning, Jilana waved farewell to Lucius. As soon as he passed through the gate, she returned to the villa and asked Ede to bring Caddaric to her father's office. She sat behind her father's desk and wrote Caddaric's papers of manumission. When the ink was dry, she melted wax onto the bottom of the parchment and pressed her father's seal into it.

Lucius believed she had dressed to please him, but in truth, Jilana had labored over her hair and arrayed herself in her best stola in order to please Caddaric. She had even applied kohl to her eyes, making them appear even larger. Now, her heart drumming wildly, Jilana bit color into her lips and waited. Even though she had been expecting it, the knock at the door made her jump. She touched a hand to her hair, swallowed, and called out her permission to enter in a shaky voice.

Caddaric paced into the room and froze when he saw Jilana. Behind him, Ede tactfully withdrew and closed the door behind her.

It seemed only natural to address her husband in his native tongue. "Caddaric." Jilana found herself unable to move as she drank in the sight of him. Had she not been seated, she would have collapsed in a heap at his feet; as it was, her legs were shaking.

Caddaric returned her stare, a dagger twisting through his guts. For months he had been mad with grief, believing her dead. Nothing had mattered, especially not his life. He had prayed for death, but his body had been stronger than his will; it had fought off the infections and eventually healed. When the Roman patrol had finally found him, he had fought them barehanded, waiting for the blow that would end his life—the blow that never came. Instead he had been captured and herded into a pen with other survivors. He would have been sent to the galleys had he not been labeled a troublemaker. The Imperial Navy needed strong men, but not mutinous ones. Instead, he was to be sold as a household slave. When he had learned that, he had stopped eating the miserable food the Romans brought into the pen. Eventually, he hoped, he would starve, but even that had been denied him. When his captors discovered what he was doing, he was force-fed.

And now, here he was, looking at his wife. *His wife!* By the gods, what a cruel jest! He was her slave and she—she had never looked more beautiful, or more Roman. He wanted to either kiss her or kill her, but, for the life of him, he could not decide which. Trying to check his temper, Caddaric surveyed the room. The shutters and drapes were drawn across the windows so that the light in the chamber came from lamps scattered upon the desk and tables. And he could feel the heat from the hypocaust. After the chill of his hut, this room was stifling.

Jilana could stand the silence no longer, could not bear the way his gaze roamed disinterestedly around the chamber. "Please, Caddaric, you must be tired. Sit down." That brought his eyes back to her, and she caught her breath at the anger in those blue depths.

"Is that an order, Lady Jilana?" Caddaric mockingly inquired. Gods, why did she look at him that way, as if he had struck her?

"Nay," Jilana replied, bewildered. She tried to smile, but succeeded only in increasing the trembling of her mouth. "Please, Caddaric, sit down. There is so much we have to talk about."

"I can imagine." Caddaric shrugged out of the cloak he had been given and sprawled leisurely in one of the chairs in front of the desk. "Shall we begin with your family's miraculous return from the dead?" He cocked an

insolent eyebrow at her but his hands, out of her sight on
his lap, balled into fists.

This time Jilana did manage a small smile. For now, she
would follow his lead. "I should be angry with you.
Would you ever have told me the truth?"

Caddaric's eyes narrowed. "I never lied to you, Ji
lana. Never!"

"That is true," Jilana said carefully. "But you al
lowed me to believe the worst, that my family was dead."

"And Lucius," Caddaric added in a drawl. "Let us not
forget Lucius."

"I know why you did it," Jilana told him, her love
shining in her eyes. "You wanted me to come freely to
you." When he said nothing she prompted, "Did you
not?"

Caddaric shrugged. "My reasons no longer matter."
His eyes bored into her. "I hate your hair that way."

Jilana's hand flew to the braids so artfully draped on
her head and her heart sank. In truth, she had thought the
style most becoming. "I only wore it this way because I
thought it would please you."

"Please me," Caddaric burst out. "Why are you con
cerned with pleasing a slave?"

A chill crept over Jilana, and when she spoke, her voice
was filled with dread. "You are not a slave, Caddaric."

Caddaric laughed mirthlessly. "You bought me, did
you not? A few coins in exchange for a body? That makes
me a slave, *lady*."

"You are no more a slave than your father or Ede or
Heall," Jilana flared, goaded by his stubbornness. "Did
they not explain what we are trying to do?"

"Aye, they explained," Caddaric said harshly. "Does
it ease your conscience to free a few, pathetic souls who
were once proud people?"

"Why are you doing this?" Jilana whispered. "Why
are you treating me like an enemy? I am your wife, Cad
daric."

"My wife?" Caddaric sent her a look of such con
tempt that Jilana drew back in her chair. "My *wife* would

not have resumed her betrothal so soon after my death, not if she had truly loved me."

"I did love you—I still do," Jilana protested.

"But then, I had forgotten," Caddaric went on as if she had not spoken, "the Roman magistrates do not recognize a wedding celebrated in an oak grove by a renegade priest of an outlawed religion. Nor, apparently, do you." His temper was threatening to flare out of control and he firmly reined it in. "I made it back to the horses that day, Jilana. I had to crawl on my belly and I kept passing out, but I made it back to where I thought you were waiting. There were three horses left. Did you even stay long enough to see if I survived, or did you run to Paulinus' camp before the first blow was struck?"

"Is that what you believe?" Jilana breathed, stricken.

Caddaric smiled coldly. "What other explanation is there?"

Jilana closed her eyes, unable to believe the cold, hard man across from her had once held her and made sweet love to her. "I—I saw you fall," she said falteringly. "I thought you were dead."

"A conclusion you are all too eager to reach," Caddaric threw at her.

Slowly, Jilana opened her eyes and carefully folded her hands on the desk. "I love you, Caddaric."

Caddaric stoked his beard, studying the drawn set of her features. His people were the conquered; hers the conquerors. His people were forbidden weapons, save for those needed to maintain life, which meant he was no longer a warrior. He was nothing, while she had her family, a splendid villa, wealth and social position. Whatever had been between them had ended with the rebellion, he knew that, but he wanted her still, with a ferocity that left him raw and bleeding on the inside. No matter what she had done, he wanted her, and he hated her for having made herself so great a part of his life. "You need not hide behind such polite phrases, Lady Jilana. If you want me in your bed again, just ask." Her eyes flew to his, enormous in her pale face, and he dropped his gaze to the swell of her breasts. His next words crucified her heart. "What is it, Lady Jilana? Can your polite, Roman betrothed not satisfy you the way a barbarian can?"

A strangling noise came from her throat and Jilana levered herself to her feet. Caddaric's gaze dropped lower as she rose and he opened his mouth to let fly with another barb but the words never came. His eyes came to rest on the swell of her stomach and he felt the blood drain from his head. "Gods!"

Jilana barely heard his curse. Tears streamed out of her eyes, ruining the outline of the kohl, and she dashed frantically at them with one hand while she reached for the paper of manumission with the other. "You are free," she said in a cracked voice. Unable to bear the thought of being near him, she threw the parchment at him. "Ede will tell you the rest."

Caddaric had sprung to his feet and he stood across the desk from her, his eyes wide with disbelief. The parchment struck his chest and dropped, unseen, to the floor. "You are with child."

"There is no need for you to see me again." Jilana stumbled around the desk and blindly made her way to the door. Her hand had barely reached the latch before her arms were caught in a pair of strong hands and she was swung around.

"Is the child mine?" Caddaric demanded, his fingers biting into her flesh, bruising her. "Answer me!" He punctuated the command with a none too gentle shake.

"I think we would all like the answer to that."

Caddaric raised his head and found Marcus and Lucius regarding them from the doorway. Behind them, he could see a very frightened Ede standing with Hadrian. "Get out," Caddaric snarled, forgetting himself.

Lucius went for his dagger and only Marcus' hand on his arm stopped him from attacking the man who still held his betrothed. "Close the door, Lucius," Marcus ordered calmly, then turned his attention to Caddaric. "Release my daughter."

A muscle ticked in his jaw, but eventually Caddaric did as Marcus asked. The moment his hands were removed, Jilana swayed and would have collapsed had Caddaric not caught her again. Without asking anyone's permission, Caddaric lifted her in his arms and carried her to the couch the room afforded.

"Release her," Marcus repeated when Caddaric knelt beside the couch, chafing her hands. "If you do not obey, I will, regretfully, have you removed from my home and placed in irons."

The threat made its impression, as Marcus had intended, and Caddaric moved stiffly away from the couch. Jilana's eyes darted between the three men like those of a small, hunted animal. Her tears had streaked the kohl around her eyes and now she brushed ineffectually at the dampness.

Marcus sat next to Jilana on the couch, but there was no sympathy in him. His face was a study in outraged, Roman parenthood. "You have refused to answer any questions regarding your time with the Iceni or about the babe's father. This time is now at an end." He inclined his head toward Lucius. "Lucius saw you leave the house last night and go to this man's hut." Marcus' hard, brown eyes glared at Caddaric. "Why?"

Jilana swallowed, unable to form a coherent thought. Instinct told her that she must protect Caddaric in spite of what had just passed between them. "He was ill."

Lucius snorted. "He seems to enjoy the best of health today."

"I—he . . ." Jilana faltered.

"Do you know him, Jilana?" Marcus' tone demanded an answer.

Jilana's eyes flew to Caddaric. "A-aye." When her father stared pointedly at her, she tried to think of a plausible explanation. "He is Clywd's son." It was as close to the truth as she dare come. When Caddaric frowned at her, she hastily looked away.

Lucius had been staring at Caddaric and now the air hissed between his teeth. "I know you. You were in the stable that night at Venta Icenorum."

Caddaric watched Jilana struggling like a fish on a hook and could bear it no longer. She was with child and he knew suddenly, with every fiber of his being, that the child she carried was his, and that child had to be protected at any cost.

"I am the babe's father," Caddaric said, his voice rich with pride. "Jilana is—was—my wife."

At his words, a merciful blackness descended and sucked Jilana into its depths.

When she recovered, Caddaric was gone. Her father was seated in a chair that had been pulled beside the couch and Lucius stood at the far side of the room, a goblet of wine in his hands.

"Where is he?" Jilana barely had the strength to force the question past her lips. She heard Lucius curse but her attention was all on Marcus.

"I sent him away. Nay—" Marcus said when he saw the fear in her eyes. "Only to his hut, no further, and he took his paper of manumission with him." He sighed heavily. "He wants the child, of course. I have said he can remain until the babe is born and old enough to travel. And then, daughter, that is the end of your traffic with the Iceni." Marcus did not raise his voice; there was no need. Jilana was totally broken.

"I would like to go to my room, please," Jilana whispered.

Ede was summoned and the two women were at the door when Lucius' voice stopped them. "Your father has said you may see this barbarian, Jilana, and I cannot interfere with his orders. But I swear to you, if you think to run away with him, I will hunt him down and kill him. Are my words plain enough?"

Jilana nodded and allowed Ede to lead her away. Lucius would never have reason to make good his threat. Caddaric wanted no part of her now, he had made that painfully clear. His love for her was as dead as the rebellion, or perhaps it had never existed. Whatever the explanation, they were back to being enemies and this time the gap between them was too wide to be bridged.

Jilana kept to her room after the confrontation, seeing only Ede, and it was Ede who told her that Lucius and her father had laid the trap in which she and Caddaric had been so neatly caught. Jilana simply nodded and refused to be drawn into conversation. Caddaric had torn her heart apart and now she withdrew herself, caring for nothing save the fragile life she carried inside her.

Seeing her friend so completely defeated first saddened, then angered Ede. After two weeks she could stand no more and, with a militant gleam in her eye, she burst into Caddaric's hut. "The gods curse you, Caddaric," she shouted at him before Caddaric could say a word. "What have you done to her?"

Caddaric, who had stripped to his loincloth in order to wash himself, glared at her. "Close the door, Ede."

Ede complied with a force that rocked the wooden structure. "I should throw you outside and let you freeze to death, you bastard! She will not talk, will not even leave her bed. I can barely get her to take food." Ede stalked up to Caddaric and hit him solidly in the chest with her fist.

Caddaric reeled backward from the blow. "This does not concern you, Ede—"

Ede advanced a step and delivered a second whack to his shoulder. "It does concern me, you ass. She is dying from the inside out and it—is—your—fault!" She punctuated each of her last words with a punch.

Caddaric caught Ede's wrists and shoved her away. "Enough! Why do you care what happens to her, a Roman?"

"She is my friend," Ede spat. "Can you understand that? Do you know what she has done for me, for us? Do you have any idea of the risks she has taken on our behalf, the threats that have been made against her?" Sobs tore from Ede's throat and she sank to the dirt floor. "Gods, Caddaric, what have you done to her?"

Caddaric folded the towel away and donned his tunic and breeks. He had forbidden anyone to speak to him of Jilana and until now they had obeyed. The truth was, he did not want to know what had happened to her or what her life had been like without him, and, perversely, part of him hungered to know what she did with every minute of every day. He lifted Ede to her feet, settled her upon the pallet and sat beside her. "Tell me," he said in a hollow voice. And Ede did.

Night fell before Ede finally made her way back to the villa and the room she shared there with Hadrian. Caddaric sat upon the cot, his back braced against the wall, and watched the fire while he considered all that Ede had told him. Shame burned through him when he remembered the things he had said to Jilana. She was undeserving of his hatred, of the bitterness he carried in his heart. Did he still love her, Caddaric asked himself? He supposed he did, but the love was buried in some distant part of himself, unreachable. And even if they had the love, what could he offer her now save back-breaking labor and poverty? Whatever they might have had was lost now, as dead as his nation. Nay, there was nothing between them now, except the child, and he was determined to have his child. He would raise their child the way he had been raised and, in time, he would forget his violet-eyed, Roman witch and the love they had shared.

How well you lie, Caddaric taunted himself. He would still be thinking of Jilana when he drew his last breath, and he knew it. But his injured pride was a goad. She had bought him. *Bought him.* He and his people were no more than animals now, to be purchased and discarded at their owners' whim. All that had made him a man had been stripped away, but his child would not know that. He would never look at his child and fear that he might see pity in his eyes, as he would with Jilana. More than anything else, Caddaric feared that, if Jilana remained with him, she would look at him one day and think of all she had given up in the name of love.

JILANA AWOKE the following morning to the sound of someone moving about her bedchamber. Listlessly, she rolled onto her back and ground the heels of her hands into her gritty eyes. Her tears had been spent days ago and now she felt hollow, empty. She could not even summon up pain. Regretfully leaving the sanctuary of sleep, she opened her eyes. And stared at the apparition at the foot of her bed.

"Good morrow." Caddaric returned her look dispassionately, even though he longed to gather her into his arms and lose himself in her.

"W-what are you doing here?"

"Ede says you are not eating." Caddaric moved to the side of the bed and lifted a tray of food from the table there. "You must eat, for the child's sake, if not for your own."

"Get out." Jilana meant to hurl the words at him, but they emerged more as an entreaty than an order. She averted her eyes, knowing all the yearning of her soul was mirrored in them.

"Nay, I will not," Caddaric replied calmly.

Incredibly, she felt fresh tears burn her eyes and Jilana hated herself for such a blatant display of weakness. "I— hate you!" What was he doing here? Had he not done enough? Did he need to hurt her even more?

Not yet, Caddaric thought sadly, but you will. "The sooner you eat, the sooner you will be rid of me."

Anything, she decided, she would do anything to be free of his presence. Avoiding his gaze, she pushed herself upright and reached for the tray. No sooner had she taken it in her hands than he was sitting beside her on the bed, plumping pillows behind her back. "You may leave now," she told him, her eyes fixed on the slices of freshly baked bread.

"When you have eaten."

Unable to argue, Jilana spread a layer of jam on the bread and obediently bit into it. She kept her eyes firmly on the tray, but she could feel the warmth of his thigh as it lay alongside hers on the bed. Her stomach twisted into one large knot and she carefully set the bread back on th tray.

"Now some of the milk." Caddaric lifted the goble from the tray and curled one of her hands around it.

Jilana jerked away from his touch as if scalded, an milk spattered both of them. He took the napkin from th tray and soaked up the milk that had landed on his breel and the bed. "Nay," she frantically ordered when h started to dab at the bodice of her gown. With her fre hand she snatched the linen from him and blotted up th liquid herself. When she was finished, she needed bot hands to lift the goblet to her mouth without spilling it.

"Try some of the cheese," Caddaric coaxed. The mil had dampened the material of her gown just enough s that it clung to her breasts, and he found it hard t breathe.

Jilana took one bite of the cheese and then returned to the tray. "Now will you leave?" When he did not a swer she looked up and caught him staring at her. "Sto it!"

Caddaric's eyes jerked back to hers. "Your breasts ar larger." Color flooded her face and receded just a quickly, leaving her unnaturally pale, and Caddaric s lently cursed himself for blurting out his thoughts.

"Go away," Jilana said through stiff lips.

To her surprise, he picked up the tray and left th chamber without further argument. When she was ce tain she was alone, Jilana got out of bed, washed, an drew on a clean stola in case he had the audacity to r turn. She passed the morning in the comfort of he chamber, sewing a small garment for the babe. At mic day, her door opened again and Jilana felt the hair on th back of her neck stand straight up. She did not have t turn around to know who had entered.

"May I come in?"

Jilana bent her head more deeply over her sewing. moment later she heard his footsteps and then a pair o boots were standing in front of her. "I brought yo something to eat."

Jilana concentrated on keeping the trembling in her body from reaching her fingers as she made another stitch. "I am not hungry. When I am, I will summon Ede."

"Ede is gone," Caddaric informed her easily. "Hadrian has taken her to the city for a few days." Jilana's head whipped up in disbelief and he nodded. "Now will you eat?" When she simply looked at him, he placed the tray on the low table and took the chair across from her.

"Why are you doing this?" Jilana dredged up the courage to ask when it was obvious he had no intention of leaving. "You made it very clear how you feel about me."

Caddaric poured milk into a goblet while he answered. "You carry my child, Jilana, and I want my child more than I have wanted anything else in my life."

Jilana felt as if he had hit her. "I see." The babe chose that moment to land a particularly violent kick against her ribs and Jilana winced and absently rubbed at the ache.

"What is wrong?"

Startled at the vehemence of his question, she retreated to the depths of her chair. "'Tis naught, only the babe moving."

Caddaric's gaze dropped to her stomach, and, as if sensing his regard, the child stirred more vigorously. The cloth across Jilana's abdomen moved and jerked and she felt herself blushing. His jaw clenched, Caddaric jumped from the chair and strode to the chamber door. "Eat your food. When I return, I will take you for a walk."

"I do not go—" Jilana protested, but the door closed on her words.

Her resolution to the contrary, she did go with Caddaric when he returned; he gave her the choice of coming willingly or being carried through the villa in his arms.

"I did not think you would like the alternative," he mocked when he saw the fear come and go in her eyes.

He walked with her through the courtyard, an arm firmly around her back. Jilana bit her lip to keep from crying at the warm touch of his hand upon her hip. 'Tis for the child that he does this, she reminded herself

constantly, but she could not help the tiny spark of hope
that came to life in her heart when he remained with her
throughout the day. Surely he would not do that if his
only concern was for the child.

"I will be back in the morning," Caddaric informed her
when the hour grew late and he caught her stifling a yawn.

And he was. He brought her meals to her and took her
for walks and sat by her while she sewed until Jilana
thought she would go mad. When Hadrian and Ede returned, Caddaric firmly refused to allow Ede to resume
her duties as Jilana's maid. With nothing to do, Ede and
Hadrian returned to Londinium and began the involved
process of purchasing what they would take with them on
their journey north. Before they left, they sat down with
Caddaric and Jilana to make a list of their provisions.
Working in Marcus' office, Jilana wrote out the list while
the three of them debated what was necessary and what
was not. Participating in the preparation brought her
misery back in full force and when Ede and Hadrian left,
Jilana was hard-pressed to keep the tears at bay.

"Is it the babe?" Caddaric questioned, glimpsing her
pained expression.

Jilana shook her head. "Nay, not the babe." She turned
the quill round and round in her fingers, studying its
movement. "You are going far to the north, are you not?
I mean, further than Venta Icenorum."

Caddaric frowned. "Aye. Why? What does it matter to
you?"

Jilana shrugged, longing for the courage to ask Caddaric to take her with him. "'Tis my child you are taking,
Caddaric. Is it odd that I should wonder where he or she
will be raised?"

Caddaric rose and paced the perimeter of the room.
"By the time we reach our destination," he said at last,
"you will be safely on your way to Rome with your betrothed. Aye, I find it odd that you should be concerned
with the welfare of a child that is proving such an embarrassment to you."

Tears flooded Jilana's eyes. Throwing the quill at him, she hurried from the room to the sanctuary of her bedchamber. Once there she locked the door and collapsed on the bed, where she cried her heart out. Downstairs, Caddaric retrieved the quill from the floor and laid it carefully on the desk. If he did not move carefully, he feared he would fly apart. The strain of being with Jilana, yet separate from her, day after day, was beginning to tell. He did not try to see Jilana again that day; instead he went to his hut and opened the flagon of wine that had appeared there one day. A gift from Jilana, no doubt, for Heall and Clywd had received one as well. He poured a cup of the rich, red wine, silently toasted his wife and proceeded to drink himself in to a sweet stupor that was haunted by Jilana.

He woke late the next morning to a head that felt as if a battle-axe were buried in it, and when he entered the villa his mood worsened at the sight of Lucius sitting with Jilana in one of the chambers on the first floor. They both looked up when he entered, and the sight of Jilana twisted his heart. Her eyes were red and swollen and for just a moment, Caddaric longed to gather her into his arms and erase all the pain he had caused her. He ruthlessly killed that desire and, pivoting on his heel, he left the two alone. Later that day, he saw them walking together in the garden. He watched them for a few minutes and was just about to turn away when he saw Jilana stumble and fall. Before her cry could reach his ears, Caddaric was running, and when he reached her, he thrust Lucius aside and knelt beside her.

"Get away from her," Lucius ordered in a cold fury. "Do not lay a hand on her."

"And leave her to your tender care," Caddaric growled. "Never." He slipped his arm under Jilana's knees and shoulders and stood. She curled against him as if he were a fortress in a storm and his hold tightened. Lucius was forced to stand aside and allow Caddaric to return to the villa.

"'Twas not Lucius' fault," Jilana haltingly explaine as Caddaric carried her through the halls. "I slipped."

"He was supposed to be caring for you," Caddar snapped. "He should have been holding you so you cou not fall."

"I can walk," Jilana protested, suddenly aware of ho good it felt to be nestled against him. "Please, put n down."

"I will, when you are safely in your chamber."

Wisely, Jilana decided not to argue and, against he better judgment, she rested her head against his shou der. His beard tickled her nose and mouth and she reache up to push it out of her way. Once her fingers touched t beard, however, they lingered in the surprising softness it and moved gently in discovery.

"What is it?" Caddaric asked sharply, turning his hea so that the beard slid away from her hand.

Jilana swallowed. "Your beard, I like—it tickled Caddaric grunted in reply and a moment later he settle her on her bed.

"Are you hurt?" he questioned as he removed her pal and tossed it onto a chair.

"Nay."

"And the babe?"

The warmth in Jilana's heart seeped away. "The ba is fine." She pressed the palm of her hand against the si of her abdomen. "See, he moves." Her breath caught Caddaric's hand came to rest upon her distended ston ach.

Something jerked against his hand, and he looke sharply at Jilana, the question clear in his eyes. She no ded shakily and he closed his eyes, willing the moveme to come again. It did, with astonishing force and rapidi and Caddaric's mouth twitched into a smile. "Is it li this all the time?" he asked in awe.

Jilana's mouth was dry. "Not—not all the time," s finally answered. "Sometimes it is worse."

"Worse?"

Caddaric's brows knit into a frown and she quickly explained, "Not worse...I mean, he does not cause me pain, only...at times he is very impatient." Jilana gave a breathless little laugh. "I think he wants more room." She ran out of words when his other hand joined the first. She simply sat motionless, watching the play of expression across his face, savoring every moment.

"I had no idea—" Caddaric began, and then he merely shook his head. He did not have the words to describe what he felt. Overcome, he bent and pressed his mouth to the cloth covering Jilana's stomach.

Of their own accord, Jilana's hands reached up and her fingers curled into his hair, holding him in place.

That was how Lucius found them. With an inarticulate cry, Lucius flung himself at the other man, tearing him away from Jilana. Jilana screamed but the two men did not hear her. They rolled across the floor, scattering chairs and breaking one of the little tables.

"Stop it!" Jilana screamed as they came to their feet and Lucius' fist connected with Caddaric's jaw. "Please, stop!" Caddaric delivered a blow to Lucius' midsection that caused the other man to double over in pain.

Her cries brought one of the maids who, after one look into the bedchamber, ran to get Augusta. Augusta, in turn, sent the woman to the slave quarters and a few minutes later Augusta, with Heall and Clywd flanking her, ran into the bedchamber. Neither man hesitated. Heall grabbed Caddaric while Clywd took Lucius' arms and twisted them behind his back.

Augusta, her arms protectively around Jilana's shoulders, lost her temper. "This is neither a tavern nor an arena," she hissed at the two bruised and bleeding men. "I will not tolerate such conduct! Has my daughter not suffered enough that you must subject her to such a brutal display? Get out, both of you." When Lucius started to protest, she spat, "That is an order!"

Claudia, watching the proceedings from the doorway, looked at her sister in disbelief when Jilana began to cry. Claudia shook her head. If she had two men fighting over

her, she certainly would not ruin it by crying! She eye
Caddaric speculatively when he brushed by her and the
sighed regretfully. The man was handsome in a barbari
sort of way, but she simply could not take someone lik
that into her bed. At least, not now.

"Darling, I am sorry," Augusta crooned against Ji
lana's hair. "I will speak with your father about thos
two."

"'Twas not Caddaric's fault," Jilana sobbed. "Luciu
attacked him."

"Shh," Augusta soothed. "Do not upset yoursel
'twill do the babe no good." She eased Jilana onto th
pillows and brushed the stray strands of hair away fror
her face. "'Twill all be over soon."

Jilana nodded, misery tightening her features. "An
then he will leave and I will never see him again. Oh
Mother," she cried softly, "how will I bear it?"

August had no answer. She could only stroke he
daughter's hair until she fell into a troubled sleep. Wit
each day that passed, Augusta grew more convinced tha
the decision she and Marcus had made was a mistake, bu
Marcus had closed his ears to her arguments. Augusta wa
left with no recourse save the purse of coins she had give
to the temple of Juno with instructions to offer daily sac
rifices on Jilana's behalf.

Caddaric did not return to the villa until his black ey
had faded. Contrary to Augusta's opinion, he had no de
sire to upset Jilana, but he still remembered with grea
satisfaction the feeling of his knuckles loosening severa
of Lucius' teeth; if he encountered the Roman again, h
would happily break his jaw. Jilana was not in her bed
chamber and none of the servants knew where she ha
gone, so Caddaric went from chamber to chamber i
search of her. When he finally found her in the sma
storeroom on the second floor, his patience was spent.

"What are you doing in here?" he demanded when h
saw her pulling bolts of material from the shelves.

Jilana spared him a glance and then returned her at
tention to the shelves. "My mother wants me to choos
the material for my wardrobe," she said tonelessly.

What she left unsaid, Caddaric knew, was that the material was for the clothing she would take to Rome. His breathing stopped at the thought, and he looked around the room, watching the shadows cast by the lamps flicker and jump against the walls.

As if driven to fill the silence that hung between them, Jilana went on, "My father is adding a ship to his fleet. Her maiden voyage will be to take us to Rome." She lifted a bolt of emerald green wool and moved closer to the lamps. "I have never been to sea before. Do you suppose I will be sick?" She glanced up at him and then shrugged, as if to say he need not bother to answer, and then her eyes returned to his face. "Your beard is gone!"

Caddaric nodded and ran his fingers along his jaw. "It itched."

Jilana nodded and turned away, not daring to comment upon the fact that his hair had obviously been freshly cut as well.

"Where is Lucius?"

"Back in Londinium I imagine," Jilana answered distractedly, as if it did not matter.

Which, in truth, it did not, but Caddaric did not know that. "Jilana, I am sorry, but I could not stand there and let him hit me."

"I know that," Jilana said, surprised.

Caddaric moved a hand idly across one of the bolts of silk. "I did not mean to cause trouble between the two of you."

Jilana stared at him and then gave a humorless laugh. "Oh, there will be no trouble. Have you not heard? Lucius believes that once he gets me to Rome all my troubles will be ended."

"You will have a good life there," Caddaric offered. "Much better than you would have found here."

"Juno, I am sick of hearing those pious words," Jilana spat at him, her heart bleeding. "Everyone seems to think they know what is best for me, but no one has asked what *I* want. Roman men do not believe in giving their women choices, but I expected better of you!"

Caddaric met and held her gaze for an eternity. "Wha
do you want?"

Jilana caught her breath and then, her love for hir
glowing like a beacon in her eyes, she answered, "To g
with you, to love you, be your wife."

"That," Caddaric said, his words falling like a deat'
knell upon both their ears, "is impossible." He swun
sharply about and left her to her misery while he deal
with his own private hell.

FOR THE NEXT SIX WEEKS, Caddaric was in constant at
tendance, and neither knew which was worse: not seein
each other or being together but neither touching no
speaking of anything personal. Even the touch of Cad
daric's hand when they walked was impersonal, and h
was quick to release her as soon as they returned to th
safety of the house. Since the fight with Caddaric, Lu
cius had not returned to the villa and Jilana was gratefu
for his absence. Her moods grew more precarious wit
each passing day, while her body grew heavy and slug
gish. Often Caddaric found her weeping and at thos
times he retreated quietly, sensing she would not wel
come his presence.

In order to pass the time, Caddaric taught Jilana to dic
and they passed many evenings gambling for imaginar
fortunes. This evening, however, as she had throughou
the day, Jilana found it difficult to sit still. The chair wa
uncomfortable, even with a cushion pushed into the sma
of her back, and soon she was up and pacing the con
fines of her bedchamber.

"My being here serves no purpose if you do not wish t
dice or talk," Caddaric pointed out when she left her chai
for the fourth time.

"Then leave," Jilana snapped, unable to control he
frayed emotions any longer. "Just leave. I am not beg
ging you to stay!"

Stunned by her attack, he raised both hands in a pla
cating gesture. "I did not mean to offend you."

"Why not?" Jilana inquired waspishly. "All you care about is the child—surely my feelings cannot matter to you in the slightest."

Exhaling in a silent whistle, Caddaric picked up the dice and got to his feet. "I think you need to rest—"

"Do not think for me!" Jilana rounded on him, her hands absently massaging the cramp in her stomach. "I am tired of you telling me when to eat, when to sleep, when to walk! Juno! I am so very weary of everyone thinking for me, making *my* decisions—Oh!" Her eyes grew wide as her midsection was engulfed in such unexpected pain that she gripped the back of a chair for support.

"Jilana!" Caddaric was beside her in two long strides, one arm going around her waist. "What—"

"The babe," Jilana whispered when the pain receded. "Oh, Juno, I think the babe is coming."

Caddaric went cold with shock. Without conscious thought he whisked Jilana into his arms and deposited her on the bed. "I will get your mother."

Jilana's fingers dug into his forearm. "Clywd. Bring me Clywd."

Caddaric nodded and all but ran from the room. By the time he had informed Augusta and brought Clywd to Jilana's bedchamber, his forehead was bathed in cold sweat and his heart was pounding so hard he was certain it would burst.

"Stay out here," Clywd ordered when Caddaric made to follow his father into the room.

"But Jilana—"

"Does not need to see you this way," Clywd interrupted. "Go tell Heall what is happening and then come back." Gently shutting the door in his son's face, Clywd turned with a smile and went to Jilana. "So," he teased when he reached the bed, "you have finally decided to present me with my grandchild?"

Panic-stricken, Jilana reached for Clywd's hand and held on to it with all her strength. *"Clywd, I do not know what to do."*

Clywd smiled, patted her hand, and settled on the edge of the bed. "There is very little you need to know, is there, Lady Augusta?" he inquired of the woman standing on the other side of the bed.

Augusta shook her head. "'Twill come naturally, dearest, as it did with me. Just relax and do what your body tells you to."

Jilana nodded, trying to relax until the next contraction hit her and then she grew as taut as a bowstring.

"Hush now," Clywd soothed. "Ignore the pain, child, push it away."

When the next contraction came, Jilana took a deep breath and tried to do as Clywd said. She summoned up pleasant memories, lost herself in them, and was surprised when Clywd tapped her on the arm and she discovered that the pain had passed.

"Very good," Clywd applauded. "Now, before the next contraction, let us get you into something more comfortable than this gown."

Caddaric was returning to the villa with Heall in tow when they encountered Marcus on the path to the slave quarters. Marcus halted abruptly at the sight of them, and then he nodded curtly.

"I was just coming to tell you that Jilana is about to give birth."

Caddaric thought it strange that Marcus should be informing him of that fact, and then he realized that Jilana's father was addressing Heall.

"You are both welcome to wait with me, inside," Marcus invited, gesturing to his home.

The curious look Caddaric directed to the two older men was ignored as they made their way to the villa.

The house was ablaze with lights and Marcus led the way into the triclinium. A sealed amphora of wine and three goblets had been set out on one of the tables, while another held an assortment of food. "Men," Marcus said as he broke the seal and poured the wine, "are useless at times like these. I know that from experience." He handed Heall and Caddaric each a goblet and then raised his own.

"For this night, let there be no animosity between us; let us join together in celebrating the birth of my first grandchild."

"A grandchild you will never know," Heall felt compelled to add. "I pity you."

Two pairs of brown eyes locked as the older men regarded one another. "Aye, I know you do, but I must do what is best for my daughter."

Heall nodded and the three men raised their goblets in salute and drained them.

"Please, be seated." Marcus swept a hand toward the couches. "We have a long night ahead of us."

They had emptied three goblets of wine before Caddaric found the courage to ask, "Have you sent word to Lucius?"

Marcus blinked. "Nay. He has no part in this; his role in my daughter's life will come later."

"Jilana will not be happy with him," Caddaric stated with conviction, and then was appalled by his presumption.

One corner of Marcus' mouth twitched. "She will learn to be happy." He splashed wine into all of their goblets before continuing. "Do not even think of taking my daughter with you, boy," he warned. "She deserves to live in Rome, in a magnificent villa with every comfort. What can you offer her?"

"Nothing that can rival Rome," Caddaric said honestly. "Do not fear, Lord Marcus, I have no designs upon your daughter. I am as anxious for her to leave Albion as you are to take her away."

"Aye," Marcus nodded. "I almost believe you." He turned his gaze on Heall. "And you, have you nothing to add?"

Heall shook his head. "I have no say in the matter."

Marcus was so absurdly pleased with that response that he called for a second amphora.

Augusta descended the stairs near dawn and found the men reclining on their couches, discussing, of all things, Marcus' business. Judging by the sight of the amphorae, they had passed the night in drinking and Augusta only hoped that Caddaric was not too drunk.

"Excuse me," Augusta said in a voice that brought the three of them upright like naughty boys. "Caddaric, Jilana wishes to know if you want to be present at the birth of your child."

The pleasant glow brought on by the wine evaporated into thin air. Caddaric rose on legs that suddenly shook and made his way to the staircase. Behind him, he heard Augusta say, "I will tell you as soon as the babe is born," and then he heard her footsteps on the stairs.

Additional braziers had been lit in Jilana's bedchamber but Caddaric was not conscious of the heat. His eyes went immediately to where Jilana lay on the bed, her eyes closed. She was so still that, except for her breathing, she might have been dead and Caddaric nearly cried out at the thought. Instead, he moved to the foot of the bed where his father stood, his hands moving in circles over Jilana's stomach.

"Sit by her head," Clywd ordered without looking at his son. "When she tells you, lift her upright and hold her there."

Caddaric swallowed heavily when he caught sight of the blood staining the linens and did as he was told. Jilana's eyes flickered open when the bed sagged under his weight and he smiled shakily. "Thank you," he whispered.

Jilana nodded weakly. "Clywd told me—'tis your right, as the babe's father." She went tense in his arms and gritted out, "Lift me."

Caddaric obeyed immediately. Jilana seemed to vibrate in his arms and a feral sound emanated from her throat. Caddaric could do nothing more than hold her, wonder how bad the pain was, and wish he could take it from her. As suddenly as it had begun, it was over and she was lying limply against his chest, her eyes closed.

"Good, Jilana," Clywd said encouragingly. "Not much longer now."

Clywd had barely finished speaking before Caddaric felt the vibrations begin again. No sooner had that contraction ended than another began and suddenly Jilana's groan changed into a screech of agony. Caddaric's stomach turned over and he swallowed down the bile that rose in his throat.

"Wait, wait," Clywd ordered. Caddaric saw his arms move and then he said, "Again, child, once more."

Jilana seemed to come apart in his arms and then she collapsed, gasping for air. Before Caddaric had time to realize that it was finished, over the sound of her labored breathing came the mewling sound of a newborn babe. Caddaric's eyes flew from Jilana's pinched face to his father.

Clywd straightened, a mass of red, wrinkled humanity held in his hands. "A son," Clywd announced, smiling. "You have a son."

Tears clogging his throat, Caddaric bent his head to Jilana. Forgetting their circumstances, he whispered thickly, "Did you hear, my heart? We have a son." The corners of her mouth twitched in response and Caddaric surrendered to his emotions and kissed her tenderly.

"Love you..." Jilana murmured as she was lowered back to the pillows. She felt a warm, hard hand cup her cheek and turned her mouth against its flesh before exhaustion claimed her.

The others had gathered at the far end of the room to examine the child, and they stepped away from the cradle when Caddaric joined them. The babe was squalling at the top of his tiny lungs and a smile tugged at Caddaric's mouth as he pulled the blanket away and studied the small, perfectly formed body. Small, so small, he thought in wonder. His hand easily spanned the shoulders.

"Like this." Augusta stepped forward and showed him how to hold his son.

Caddaric copied her actions and held his son in front of him, one hand bracing his back and head while the other cupped his buttocks. "He is perfect," Caddaric said with such awe that the others chuckled.

"I sent for the priests when Jilana's labor began," Augusta told her husband. "They should be here by now. I will give them the offering."

Marcus nodded. "Wrap the babe in his blanket, Caddaric, and we will take him below."

"Why," Caddaric demanded, feeling abruptly possessive over the bit of life he held in his hands.

The men grinned, understanding the feelings that held Caddaric in their sway.

"The priests are here to bless the babe," Marcus explained, reaching out to touch the cap of brown hair on the child's head.

"I will stay with Jilana," Clywd offered, and then he helped Caddaric wrap the babe securely in the tiny blanket.

At the front door stood three men, their faces hidden behind masks representing the gods Intercidona, Pilumnus and Deverra; they held, respectively, an axe, pestle and broom. Augusta and Marcus stayed in the shadows, leaving Caddaric to face the priests alone.

"Who presents this child to be blessed?" One of the men intoned.

"I—I do," Caddaric stammered. Apparently, his answer was correct, for the three began to beat the threshold with the symbols they carried. The noise was unnerving and when they began to chant, the babe began to cry. Over his son's cries, Caddaric could make out the words to the chant: the priests were cutting, crushing and sweeping away any evil spirits which could attack a helpless, newborn babe. Augusta and Marcus closed the double doors on the priests' chants and Caddaric found himself smiling at them. They might not be able to claim their firstborn grandson, but neither had they rejected him out of hand.

"Precious child," Augusta whispered, brushing a kiss on the babe's cheek. She looked up at Caddaric, her eyes brimming with unshed tears. "If things had been different—" Her voice broke and she fled up the stairs to the sanctuary of her chamber.

"Women," Marcus scoffed. "They think all babes are precious." But the longing look he cast the babe before he followed his wife belied his words.

Caddaric, Heall beside him, returned to Jilana's bed-chamber and found Jilana awake.

"Let me see him," Jilana said eagerly, her arms out-stretched the moment she saw the babe in Caddaric's arms.

"Hold his head," Caddaric instructed as he turned the babe over to her care.

Jilana gave him an exasperated look. "I know how to hold a babe, Caddaric."

And, from what Caddaric could see, she was telling the truth. She held the babe snugly in one arm while her free hand made short work of the blanket and she made her own inspection of the body so recently separated from her own. Satisfied, she rewrapped the blanket and then, with her forefinger, lifted the babe's chin ever so slightly. "Oh, see, he has blue eyes!" She looked up at Caddaric and smiled. "What shall we name our son?"

Reality intruded with jarring abruptness and Caddaric's euphoria vanished. Gods! what was he doing? An icy chill settled around his heart and he knew, by the way Jilana's smile faltered, that his withdrawal was mirrored on his face. When he spoke, his tone was gentle, but unmis-akably final. "I will name him Artair."

Jilana ducked her head and blinked rapidly to clear away the tears. The babe nuzzled at her breast and she said in a small, broken voice, "I must feed the babe. Will you leave us please?"

Ede returned the next day and resumed her duties as Jilana's maid. Jilana did not see Caddaric again. He saw Artair several times throughout the day, but Ede always brought the babe to him. If it had been torture for Jilana to see Caddaric every day, it was even worse not to see him at all. No one spoke of Caddaric in her presence unless she questioned them directly.

"Do not torture yourself so," Ede implored her one night when she brought Artair back from his time with Caddaric. "Please, Jilana, you know it is futile."

Jilana nodded and reached for her son to nurse him.

Lucius returned to the villa four weeks after Artair's birth. He ordered the babe taken from Jilana's chamber during his visit, and then announced that their ship would depart in three weeks.

"So soon," Jilana cried, dismayed. "Lucius, I cannot possibly leave yet. Artair is still so small—"

"He is a month old, Jilana," Lucius said coldly. "I have already told your rebel lover to find a wet nurse for the child."

The ability to speak deserted Jilana and she sank back against her pillows, barely hearing Lucius tell her about the plans he had made for their journey. It is ending, she screamed silently, unable to accept the truth even though she felt the pain slashing through her. Just months ago she had thought she could leave the babe with Ede and Clywd and sail away, comforted in the knowledge that he would be well cared for and loved, but now, it was not enough. He needs me, her soul shouted. *I* am his mother. And she knew, then, that she would do anything to stay with her child.

She would go to Caddaric, on her hands and knees if necessary, and beg him to take her north. Though he did not want her as a wife, he would have need of a wet nurse, so she would go with them in that capacity. She would make no demands of Caddaric, she promised herself. If he wished, he could even take another wife. An Iceni wife. Jilana relaxed ever so slightly and planned how she would make her appeal to Caddaric.

All Jilana's plans came to naught, for from the day she left her bed, Caddaric was forbidden to come to the villa and she was forbidden to step foot into the slave quarters. Her father had even posted guards by the courtyard gate, to ensure she followed his orders. Panicked, Jilana sent word to Caddaric through Ede and the others, but there was no reply to her entreaties. A week before Ji-

lana, Augusta, Claudia and Lucius were to sail for Rome,
Ede told Jilana that Caddaric had found a wet nurse for
Artair. He was claiming his son now, this instant, and
leaving the villa. Jilana watched them take the cradle, the
clothes she had sewn, and the child she had borne and the
bottom dropped out of her world.

Her last week on Britannia passed in a blur, though Jilana was immune to the excitement whirling around her.
No one save Augusta seemed to notice her distraction.
Certainly Lucius did not. He was full of stories of Rome,
of the life they would build, the feast that would follow
their wedding, and Jilana was his passive audience.
Whenever she thought of her coming marriage, it was
with revulsion and she began to question her own sanity
when she discovered that thoughts of her own death
brought her comfort.

The day before they were to sail, Clywd came to see her
and he was stunned by the change that had overtaken her
since he had seen her last. She had lost the weight gained
while carrying Artair, and more. The skin was stretched
over her cheekbones and her eyes held a haunted look.

"Have you come to bid me farewell?" Jilana asked
with a pale smile.

"Aye, I have." Clywd took the chair next to her. "I
shall miss you."

"That is nice to hear." Jilana's gaze drifted to the window, which was open now to the spring breezes. "Have
you seen Artair?"

"Aye, he is well," Clywd said, thinking to allay her
fears.

A gust of air came through the window and Jilana
closed her eyes, savoring the feel of it against her flesh.
"Clywd, I have a favor to ask of you."

"Jilana, nay," Clywd pleaded. "He will not take you
north."

The ghost of a smile flitted across her lips again and
then was gone. "Nay, I know. What I ask now I think
Caddaric will agree to." She paused, then said on a thin

thread of sound, "I want to see Artair once more, before I leave."

"Jilana—"

"Please, Clywd," Jilana begged. The violet eyes opened wide and her thin fingers wrapped around his wrist with surprising strength. "'Tis such a small thing. I want only to see him, hold him. Surely Caddaric will not refuse."

Clywd considered a moment before nodding. "I will ask him. If he agrees, I will send word to you."

Jilana nodded and then rose and wandered out to the colonnaded gallery that ran around the front and sides of the villa. Clywd watched her for several minutes, his eyes dark with concern, before quietly letting himself out of the bedchamber.

Caddaric's reply came by messenger late in the afternoon, disguised as a letter from Hadrian. Her fingers trembling, Jilana broke the wax and unfolded the paper. In Hadrian's hand were the directions to a deserted house not far from the docks. She memorized the directions and then burned the message in a brazier. Jilana's ship sailed on the noon tide; Artair would be at the house at mid-morning.

Jilana did not sleep that night.

When dawn broke, Jilana rose and finished packing the last of her possessions. Then she left her bedchamber by way of the gallery and availed herself of the bath. As she soaked in the tepidarium, her mind turned to the first bath she had shared with Caddaric, but instead of pain, the memory brought her a kind of serenity. Returning to her chamber, she dressed in her finest toga and then, with the help of Claudia's servant, swept her hair up into an artful arrangement of braids. The meal she shared with her parents and Claudia was a light one, but Jilana did not taste it. Claudia left the hall first, leaving Jilana alone with her parents.

"I have an errand in Londinium," Jilana said quietly, her eyes fixed on the view of the garden the windows afforded. "If you have no objections, I will leave ahead of you and join you at the dock."

Marcus frowned. "What is the errand?"

"I am going to see Artair," Jilana replied with a dreamy smile. "I will be at the dock, Father, I swear it."

"I will go with you—"

"Nay, I want to go alone." Jilana gazed at her father, a distant look in her eyes. "Please."

"You must, at least, take a servant with you," Marcus countered, concerned with her safety.

Jilana nodded. "As you wish."

She and the man chosen as her guard left shortly thereafter in one of her father's wagons. Jilana's mind was blank during the trip; she thought only of seeing her son again, not of the parting that would so swiftly follow the reunion. Following her directions, the servant soon pulled the team to a halt in front of a small house and helped Jilana from the seat. No sooner had her feet touched the ground than the door opened and Ede and Hadrian stepped forward to greet her.

"We will talk later," Ede said as she embraced Jilana. "I know you are eager to see Artair."

Jilana nodded and with a faint smile for Hadrian she stepped into the house. She pushed the hood of the palla off her head and closed the door behind her. It took a moment for her eyes to adjust to the dimness after the morning sunshine, but when they had she saw her son lying on a blanket in the center of the empty room. Smiling, she walked forward and knelt beside him.

"*Ave*, Artair, my son," Jilana murmured as she took him into her arms. The babe gurgled happily and she tickled him beneath one of his chins. "How you have grown!" She nuzzled his cheeks and cooed to him, loving the feel of his body and the smell that told her he had just been bathed. "How are you faring with your wet nurse, mmm? Does she treat you well? And your father, does he hold you and play with you as I used to do?" She laid Artair back on the blanket and rubbed the soles of his tiny feet.

From the shadows of the adjoining room, Caddaric watched their play, his gut wrenching. Even from here he could smell her perfume, the light scent of roses reaching out to tease his senses. Nearly two months had passed since he had seen her last and, if anything, she was more beautiful than he remembered. Clywd had warned him that she was painfully thin, and while that worried Caddaric, it also lent Jilana a fragile air that made him want to sweep her into his arms and protect her. Caddaric shook himself mentally. No purpose would be served thinking of things that could never be. She was leaving today, as was he. They had been fated to come together briefly, then part; they could not change their destinies. But, oh, how he wished it were otherwise!

Holding such treacherous emotions at bay, Caddaric took the step that would bring him into Jilana's vision. He watched her slowly raise her head until their eyes met; she seemed neither surprised nor dismayed at his presence, merely accepting, but she gathered Artair back in her arms as if afraid he would snatch the babe away.

"Good morrow, Lady Jilana." Caddaric heard his voice as if from a great distance, and he wondered at its hollow ring.

"Good morrow, Caddaric." Jilana carefully came to her feet and offered him a hesitant smile. "Thank you for letting me see Artair."

Caddaric shrugged, a nebulous feeling of unease forming when he saw how empty those beloved, violet eyes were. "You are his mother."

"Aye, I am." Jilana tilted her head to peer into Artair's face. "Will you tell him of me when he is old enough to understand?"

The blunt question took Caddaric by surprise; he turned away from her and went to stand by the window. "I had not considered it."

Misunderstanding, Jilana said, "You may tell him I am dead if you wish, only—only let him know that I did not willingly abandon him, I beg you."

"Gods, Jilana!" Caddaric's hands curled into fists and he felt his breathing grow ragged.

"Lucius will never allow me to return to Britannia," Jilana continued, "so you need not worry that I will suddenly appear and take Artair away. Is it so much to ask that you tell Artair that I loved him, that I wanted to stay with him?"

"Nay." Caddaric shook his head.

Artair nuzzled at her and Jilana stroked his hair. "They bound my breasts when you took Artair away," she told him softly. "My milk is gone. Even if you had agreed to take me along as Artair's wet nurse, I would be of no use to you now."

Caddaric squeezed his eyes shut against the burning there. "Stop it, Jilana," he ordered thickly. Somewhere, no doubt, the gods were laughing at the trick they had played on these two lowly mortals.

Jilana looked at the man who was her world and slowly walked to his side. "I have had a great deal of time to think about us, Caddaric, to wonder why all of this is happening." She ignored the impatient shake of his head and plunged forward, spurred on by the demons which had haunted her during the long, empty nights. "Had the Iceni won, would you have cast me aside?"

Caddaric forced himself to open his eyes and gaze down at her. "Nay."

"And if you had found me with the horses?" she asked, her eyes clinging to his.

Shaking his head, Caddaric tenderly drew his forefinger along her jaw. It was agony to touch her, knowing that soon she would be out of his life, but he could not resist the impulse.

"Then why cast me aside now?" Jilana demanded bitterly. "Why?"

"Your father—"

"You are no more afraid of my father and his threats than Caesar is!" Jilana bit her lip and brought her voice under control. "Was your love for me a lie, Caddaric?"

She was tearing him apart and she did not even realize it. Caddaric pressed a lingering kiss against her forehead before he found the strength to answer. "It was not a lie," he murmured against her hair. Pushing her away, he held her at arm's length, feeling the sharpness of her bones even through her toga and palla. "I told you once that I was a warrior. Now what am I, Jilana? A freed slave."

"So was I!"

"Aye, but it is different for a woman." When she would have protested, Caddaric laid a finger across her lips and shook his head warningly. "My village is gone, my nation is gone. All I have left is my son and my pride. Can you understand that? I could take you away, we could hide where your father and Lucius would never find us, but what then? What can I give you? I have no money, no land, not even a bothie to take you to."

Jilana wet her dry lips. "Neither does Hadrian."

"It is different with Ede and Hadrian."

"Why?" Jilana cried.

"Because it is," Caddaric snapped, drowning in his own sorrow. "Look to how you were raised, the villa you left just this morning. How can I compete against the life Lucius will give you?" He jerked his gaze back to the window.

"Oh, Caddaric," Jilana whispered brokenly. "'Tis you who do not understand. What I need, only you can give me. I am not whole without you, can you not see that?" She held Artair securely in one arm and laid her free hand upon Caddaric's forearm. "Take me with you, Caddaric, please. I beg you, my love, do not send me away."

The muscles in Caddaric's jaw worked and he shook his head. "I cannot." His decision was immutable.

Without another word, Jilana stepped away from him and carried Artair back to the blanket. She sat with him there, talking to him, playing with him, while the time flew by. Much later, she looked up and found Caddaric standing over them.

"'Tis time you left." Caddaric offered her his hand and, with a final kiss for their son, Jilana took it.

As soon as she was on her feet, Jilana reclaimed her hand. "This is for you." She untied a purse from her belt and offered it to Caddaric.

"I cannot—"

"For my son then," Jilana burst out. When Caddaric did not take it, she dropped the purse onto the dirt floor. She stared at him for an eternity, memorizing his face, wondering how she could bring herself to leave. "Will you kiss me farewell?"

Caddaric could have died from the pain her question aroused. "Do you want to see me bleed," he demanded, cursing softly.

"Do you hurt, Caddaric?" Jilana wanted to know. "I do. I am dying inside, did you know? Dying—"

And then Caddaric's lips were upon hers, silencing her torment. Their mouths brushed and clung in a kiss that spoke only of love, not passion. The hardest thing he had ever done in his life was end the kiss and hold Jilana to him one last time. "You must go. Now."

With the last of her strength, Jilana pulled away and carefully draped the palla around her head and shoulders. She walked woodenly to the door and went out without looking back. Caddaric watched the door close and felt his heart shatter.

Hadrian and Ede were waiting. Jilana allowed herself to be embraced by both of them and then she climbed into the wagon. "Be happy," she told her two friends.

Ede nodded and Hadrian stepped forward and laid something in her lap. "Not a proper gift for a lady, I know," Hadrian said sheepishly when her eyes dropped to her lap. "But it will remind you of us. I wanted you to have it."

In her lap lay a dagger in its sheath. Jilana picked it up and then looked at Hadrian. "The same one you gave me at Camulodunum?" When he nodded, she reached down and squeezed his shoulder. "You are a better friend than you know." Placing the dagger in one of the folds of her palla, she nodded curtly to the driver.

The servant slapped the reins and the wagon jolted forward. By the time they reached the docks, Jilana felt as if she were moving in a dream. She watched Lucius lead her up the gangplank and onto the ship, saw herself smile in greeting to Augusta and Claudia.

"I will sail in two weeks," Marcus was reminding his tearful wife. "Take care of our daughters."

Jilana watched her parents kiss each other tenderly and then she was enfolded in her father's arms.

"You completed your errand?" Marcus asked, concerned by Jilana's vacant gaze.

"Aye," Jilana heard herself reply. "I love you, Father."

"Do not worry," Marcus reassured her, misunderstanding. "I will be in Rome before you have time to settle in."

Jilana watched him walk down the gangplank and, after raising her hand in a final wave, she turned to Lucius. "I am tired. Will you show me to my cabin?"

"Of course, my love," Lucius agreed. "Your mother said you did not sleep well."

Jilana embraced her mother and sister, startling them both, and then followed Lucius below deck. The cabin to which he led her was the one she was to share with Claudia during the voyage. Their chests were in the cabin, and someone had propped open the wood cover of the porthole so that the fresh air could fill the cabin.

"Are you certain you want to stay down here when we cast off?" Lucius queried. "You will miss all the excitement—"

"I am sure, Lucius."

After a moment's hesitation, Lucius shrugged and left her to return to the deck. She could hear muffled sounds coming from the deck below her feet and then she remembered that this ship had not only sails but slaves as well, so that they would not be dependent upon the wind to see them quickly to Rome. Undoubtedly there were Iceni slaves, chained to the benches. Jilana tugged off her palla and folded it on one of the beds before taking the bench beneath the porthole. She could see the docks and the people milling about and, if she tried, she could just make out the house she had so recently left.

There was a shouted command from the upper deck and Jilana watched the ropes holding the ship to the pier fall away. A moment later there came a rhythmic drumming from the lower deck and the oars slid outward from the sides of the ship and dipped into the water. Slowly Jilana pulled the pins and combs from her hair, letting the heavy mass fall freely down her back. She was going to Rome.

Jilana stretched out a hand to the bed nearest her, picked up the dagger Hadrian had given her, and turned it idly about in her hands as the pier slipped out of sight and the window afforded her a lovely view of the landscape of Britannia. She would never return; as she had told Caddaric, Lucius would see that she was kept far away from her beloved island. The serenity she had felt in the bath that morning returned and Jilana smiled faintly and dropped her gaze to the dagger she held. The first time Hadrian had given her the dagger, it had been to save her from a fate worse than death. She had not had the courage to use it then, but now her life was no longer precious.

Suicide was an honorable deed, undertaken for many reasons. Even a person who had brought disgrace upon himself and his family in life could redeem himself by the manner of his death, and the gods knew she had brought a great deal of shame to her family. It would put an end to the torment she had endured for so many months as well, and Caddaric would be telling Artair the truth when he said Jilana was dead.

Frowning, offering a final prayer to Juno for guidance, Jilana turned the blade and laid the tip of it against her left wrist.

WHAT DROVE CADDARIC to follow Jilana he would never know, but when he stepped from the house, a sleeping Artair tucked safely in his basket, he knew that he could not leave Londinium without seeing Jilana's ship sail. 'Twas useless to torture himself in such a manner, but he was helpless to resist the compelling need to see Jilana leave his life as suddenly as she had entered it. Ede took Artair and, with Hadrian, the four of them made their way to the docks. By the time they reached the pier the galley was already free of its moorings and had pulled out into the center of the river. The side of the ship facing him bristled with oars and as he watched, they dipped into the water and propelled the ship forward. Scanning the crowd, Caddaric could see Marcus, alone, and his heart sank. Fool, Caddaric chided himself, did you really think she would not go?

Jilana was gone, out of his life. Bitter defeat rose in his throat. He should have stopped her; he should have defied her father's orders and his own common sense and taken her north with him. But no, his pride had risen to the fore—cold, useless pride—and he had sent her away. Ahh, gods, Caddaric mourned silently, feeling the gaping hole her absence had left in his heart, what have I done?

"Look!"

Ede's hand was on his arm and Caddaric looked to where she was pointing. The galley had neared the bend in the river that would take her out of their sight but now, inexplicably, she had reversed course and was lumbering back toward the pier. Momentarily, Caddaric's spirits soared but then, as he watched the galley, a sense of foreboding swept through him. There was no good reason for a ship to return.

When the galley was in hailing distance and her captain called, "Bring out the gangplank—we have an injured man aboard," Caddaric tensed.

The galley was close enough now so that Caddaric could make out Augusta and Claudia standing at the railing; behind them was Lucius, a bundle of white cloth in his arms. It seemed to take an eternity before the galley was docked and Lucius finally came down the gangplank, but when he did, Caddaric saw that it was Jilana the Roman held.

Augusta and Claudia fell weeping into Marcus' arms, but Caddaric had eyes only for the burden the Roman carried, and as Lucius approached, Caddaric stepped in front of him. Jilana's head was arched across Lucius' arm, the rich length of red-gold hair falling in a cascade that shimmered with every step he took. The snowy linen of her toga was marred by a rich crimson stain and Caddaric could now see that the bandages which had been hastily tied around her wrists were turning red as well. It was all Caddaric could do to stop the scream of denial that rose in his throat.

"She needs a physician," Lucius, dazed, said to no one in particular.

An awful agony ripped through Caddaric and he wordlessly took Jilana from the Roman. "Find my father," he told Hadrian. Clywd and Heall were to have met them at the deserted building where he had met Jilana, and Hadrian turned to bull a path through the crowd.

The weight of Jilana in his arms threw Caddaric headlong into a nightmare. Vaguely, he heard Marcus send for a Roman physician, and then Augusta's voice rose above the others, insisting that Jilana be taken back to the villa. Suddenly Clywd was in front of him, tearing strips from his tunic and using them to tightly bind Jilana's wrists. Claudia was near hysteria, wailing something about disgrace and gossip that the family agreed was to be avoided. Over Clywd's strenuous objections, Jilana was to be taken home, but when they made to take Jilana from him, Caddaric refused to relinquish his precious burden.

"You will not take her from me again," he told a furious Marcus. "Never again."

He held Jilana during the endless ride to the villa, held her so close that he could feel the beat of her heart. He remained in her bedchamber when an argument broke out between Clywd and Marcus over Jilana's treatment.

"You cannot wait for the physician," Clywd insisted. "Her wrists must be closed now."

"Not by you," Marcus argued. "She is Roman—"

"She will be dead if you do not act soon," Caddaric interrupted harshly, coming to himself. "Do it, Father. I will deal with him if he tries to interfere." There was a wild glitter to his eyes that rendered Marcus immobile and then Caddaric's nostrils were assaulted by the stench of seared flesh as his father drew red-hot iron across the openings Jilana had made in her wrists. Unnoticed, Marcus left the bedchamber.

Though he stayed with her until late afternoon, Jilana did not regain consciousness. Repeatedly, Caddaric touched her throat, needing to feel the reassurance of her pulse. At last, when Clywd could no longer bear his tortured expression, he sent Caddaric to tell the others of Jilana's condition. The first sound Caddaric heard when he left the chamber was angry voices coming from the first floor and he slowly made his way toward them.

"Why would she do such a thing?" Lucius was asking the others when Caddaric entered.

Apparently it was not the first time the Roman had asked such a question because Heall leaped to his feet, upsetting the low table in front of him.

"Why?" Heall asked in an angry rumble. "You can ask that after all that has happened?"

Caddaric looked at his friend and was stunned by the anger burning in the older man's brown eyes. "Heall, we have no right—"

"Do not speak to me of rights," Heall thundered. "Do all of you know her so little that you could not see what losing her son would do to her?" He gave Caddaric a look of pure contempt. "And you, allying yourself with them, forcing her into a corner from which there was no escape. Could you not see that you were tearing her apart?"

"Caddaric had no say in the matter," Augusta said, a trifle coolly. "We did what was best for Jilana."

"Aye, just as you did what was best for you eighteen years ago," Heall raged, turning on Augusta with a savage oath. "You took my child from me once before, with the promise to love her, and look at the end she has come to!''

Augusta reeled under the attack, grasping her husband's arm for support. The stunned faces Caddaric and Lucius turned to her went unnoticed. "You swore—" she said weakly.

"I swore never to interfere," Heall agreed fiercely, his beard quivering in outrage. To Caddaric, he had never looked more dangerous. "I swore never to be a part of her life, to allow you to raise her in your ways. I went away; I raised a son of my own. But never, *never*, did a day pass that I did not think of my other child, the child you carried and kept apart from me!"

Caddaric placed a restraining hand on Heall's arm only to be flung angrily backward when Heall rounded on him.

"For you I have no words," Heall growled. Then, suddenly, his eyes filled with tears. "How could you treat her thus? She is your wife!"

The loathing in Heall's eyes was no less than he deserved, Caddaric acknowledged. So much suddenly became clear now: Heall's attraction toward Jilana, the risks he and Artair had taken to protect her when she had helped Hadrian to escape, the dowry he had given her. The signs had been ridiculously plain, but he, Caddaric, had been too blind to see them. How the gods must have laughed at his interpretation of his dream, for the child of their union was more Iceni than Roman!

"Jilana may be of your seed, but she is my daughter," Marcus told the other man haughtily.

"Aye, and see how you treat her," Heall retorted. "She should have been given to me!" He dashed his tears away and stamped from the room, unable to bear the sight of any of them a moment longer.

"Jilana is *his* daughter?" Lucius stared at Marcus incredulously. "You would have allowed me to marry her without telling me—"

The appalled expression on Lucius' face sent a wave of rage through Caddaric. "What does her blood matter?"

he demanded of Lucius. "Jilana is no different now than she was yesterday or six months ago."

Lucius laughed coldly. "It makes a great deal of difference, Briton. I can trace my lineage back to Julius Caesar; to taint it with that of a barbarian—" He never finished the aspersion. Caddaric's fist crashed into his jaw and sent him sprawling on the tiled floor. He started to rise, saw the fury in Caddaric's eyes and remained where he was, raising a hand to his injured jaw. "Why are you so affronted?" he taunted rashly. "Have you forgotten that you do not want her either?"

Caddaric's face whitened. At that moment he was not certain who he hated more, himself or Lucius. "You are wrong, Roman," he said when he was calm enough to speak. "I never stopped wanting Jilana; I only stopped being a man." He turned to Marcus and Augusta. "When next I leave this place, my wife will go with me."

"Your marriage is not valid." Marcus' face was rigid. "I will not allow—"

"Whether you allow it or not," Caddaric said softly, warningly, "I will take Jilana with me, by whatever means are necessary."

Three pairs of eyes watched in disbelief as he walked from the chamber; Caddaric could feel the stares boring into his back and he wondered if Marcus would choose to fight him. Under Roman law he had fewer rights than Jilana, and yet, Caddaric swore to himself, he would do everything in his power to keep Jilana with him. If, please the gods, she lived.

It occurred to Caddaric, as he opened the door to Jilana's chamber, that today was the first of May. *Beltane.*

A SOFT RAY OF SUNLIGHT filtered through the leaves of the sacred oak trees, clothing the woman who knelt beside the stream in a mantle of light. A doe and her fawn, having drunk of the refreshing water, approached the woman and trustingly accepted the grain she held in her outstretched hand. She laughed—a sound which she had not voiced in many months—and the gentle sound floated through the

rove and brought a smile to the lips of the man who
tood watching her from the concealment of the trees. He
tepped from behind the oak and walked toward her qui-
tly, utilizing the stealth which had been handed down
rom his father and his father's father. The woman did
ot hear him, did not sense his presence—not until he
tood directly behind her and grasped a handful of the
oose, flame-colored hair which lifted in the breeze.

She turned and regarded him through wide, violet eyes.
The doe and her fawn scampered away but she appeared
ot to notice. "Briton." Her voice was soft, musical and
eartbreakingly uncertain.

"Roman." The word should have been a curse, but in-
ead it fell lovingly from his lips. Her gaze skittered ner-
ously to the hand threaded through her hair and
addaric released his hold only to settle upon the ground
eside her. His eyes strayed to the bandages around her
rists and darkened in pain. "'Tis good to hear you laugh
gain."

Self-consciously, Jilana tugged the sleeves of her stola
ver the bandages, afraid to be drawn into conversation
nd just as afraid that to remain silent would drive him
way. "Lucius has gone."

"Aye, I know." The corners of Caddaric's mouth
ugged upward in a brief smile. "I have spies in your
ousehold."

Jilana allowed herself to smile in return. "Your fa-
er—and mine."

Caddaric hesitated. "Does it disturb you that Heall is
ur father?"

"Nay." Jilana shook her head and the sun danced
rough her hair. "Now I know from whence my wild-
ess comes." She pulled her eyes from his to watch her
ands nervously pleat the material of her gown. "Thank
ou for bringing Artair to me."

Caddaric nodded, remembering those awful days when
e had hung between life and death. He would never
rget the moment she opened her eyes and saw him sit-
ng beside her bed. She had raised a shaking hand to his

face to touch the tears dampening his cheeks and said, "I want only a little peace." He had brought Artair to her then, speaking to her of the need both father and son had for her in their lives. Whether his actions had done any good, he did not know, but gradually the scales had tipped in favor of life. Artair still resided with his mother while Caddaric occupied the hut he had used when he had first come to the villa.

He pulled himself away from the awful memories. "What will you do now?"

"Now that I am not to be a correct Roman matron," Jilana asked, a trifle mockingly. "In truth, I do not know."

Caddaric's palms suddenly went damp with apprehension and his mouth was unaccountably dry. "I have a suggestion, if you care to hear me out." From the instant he had known she would live, he had been hard-pressed not to order her life and inform her that she was his wife and that he intended to take her with him. Lucius had quickly broken their betrothal and her parents had, reluctantly, agreed to abide by whatever decision Jilana made. If they—and he—had learned anything from the near-tragedy, it had been that Jilana must make her own choices.

Jilana glanced at him and then quickly looked away. She had seen very little of Caddaric during her recovery, and then he had been careful and courteous, almost a stranger. 'Twas obvious, even to a blind woman, that he no longer wanted her, that he pitied her, but she could not help but hope. Drawing herself back to the present, she said, "I welcome any advice."

Caddaric nodded and cleared his throat. "I... Do you..." He sighed, abandoning all hope of presenting a clear, persuasive case, and blurted out, "How strongly do you feel about remaining here?" Now it was his turn to study his hands as he fitfully plucked out blades of grass by their roots.

Jilana considered the question for a moment before answering honestly, "My family is here, of course, but it

ou mean am I attached to the villa or Londinium, the
nswer is nay." When he did not respond, she prompted,
"Why do you ask?"

"The north country lacks the cities," Caddaric an-
wered obliquely. "And the winters are colder; but,
roperly built, a bothie can be warm."

The tiny spark of hope in her heart grew and Jilana
urned so that she could look directly at Caddaric. "Pau-
nus has not been able to extend his vengeance that far.
A measure of safety is to be found in the north." The
reath locked in her throat when Caddaric's brilliant blue
yes found hers.

"Aye. Safety... and peace." At a loss for words, Cad-
aric held her gaze and reached for her hand. "I want you
o come with me, Jilana."

"I—I cannot, not if you are asking because you pity
e."

"Pity you?" Slowly, Caddaric smiled and the smile ig-
ited an answering blaze in his eyes. "Oh, my heart, I feel
any things for you, but not pity." He cupped his free
and around the back of her head and brought her to his
ps. "I love you, Jilana; love you, need you, want you."
Vhile he spoke, his head narrowed the distance between
em and his last words were spoken against her lips.

Liquid fire seared through her and Jilana murmured,
Caddaric." Their mouths met and she sighed softly.

"Come with me," Caddaric urged, drawing back
ightly. "I was a fool to think I could let you go and still
ake a life for myself, and I was a greater fool to believe
at I was less of a man because the rebellion failed. My
ride nearly destroyed us, and I beg your forgiveness for
e things I said and did, but, my heart, I never stopped
ving you." He kissed her tenderly but intensely. "Come
orth with me, Jilana. Be my wife; make me whole
gain."

The joy singing in her blood brought tears to her eyes
nd her hand lifted to stroke his scarred cheek. This
roud, arrogant, fearsome man who had burst into her
ell-ordered world was her life; to know that his feelings

ran as deep as hers was almost more than she could bea[r]
"Caddaric," she said in a husky voice, "I love you mo[re]
than life."

The blue gaze heated as Caddaric drew her to her fee[t]
"Wicca, I have waited overlong."

"As have I." She rose and was willingly enfolded by h[is]
arms. He drew her against him and kissed her deepl[y]
hungrily; when they parted, her eyes, now a fathomles[s]
purple, trapped him and held him prisoner while time fle[w]
past unheeded.

From the wicker basket a few feet behind them cam[e]
the cry of their son as he awoke. They smiled into eac[h]
other's eyes, feeling their wounds begin to heal.

Prophecy.

EPILOGUE

THE EIGHTY, heavily-armed men marched along the rutted path which wound its way through the dense wood. Upon their backs they carried the usual forty pounds of equipment as well as a cloak and blanket. They wore their helmets, and aprons of iron strips were belted around their waists. Such precautions were necessary, for the land through which they traveled was not entirely friendly toward Romans, armed or otherwise. Farther to the south, from whence they had come, the land of the Iceni was only now recovering from the devastation the former governor-general, Suetonius Paulinus, had wreaked upon it. Forts had been built throughout the Iceni holding so that those who resettled the land could be constantly under the eye of the military. It had been good duty, for Paulinus had allowed his men free rein when dealing with the civilians. The Roman memory was a long one; it did not quickly forget that it had been Celtic civilians who had risen in revolt and nearly succeeded in breaking the Empire's grip on Britannia. The legionaries, many of whom had marched with Paulinus during the revolt, avenged themselves by taking from the settlements anything they wished. Those days were now at an end. Paulinus' successor, Pretonius Turpilianus, had decreed that the days of vengeance were finished. To be of any use to the Empire, the province must export its goods, and that could not be done while a state of undeclared war prevailed.

Turpilianus wanted peace, with both the conquered Icen and the elusive rebels who seemed to spring up ever where, and now an uneasy truce lay across the island. Fa to the south, Verulamium was being reconstructed, fi teen years after the end of the rebellion. Venta Icenoru did not enjoy the same fate. It remained the charred pi of rubble to which Paulinus had reduced it, inhabited onl by ghosts.

None of that occupied the minds of the legionarie however. Their concern lay with the woods they we traversing. The forest closed around them, blocking th bright summer sunshine, and the rustling of creatur came constantly from the underbrush. Sweat that ha nothing to do with physical exertion, and everything to d with fear, trickled between their shoulder blades as the sensed eyes upon them, watching, waiting. At the front of their column walked their centurion, a tribune at his side and the men grumbled beneath their breath. Why ha they been ordered so far to the north simply to purcha forty horses when there were mounts aplenty to be had i the areas where Roman might was undisputed? The morale dipped even further as they recalled stories of pa trols disappearing without a trace. Peace might exist in th reports Turpilianus sent to Rome, but here on Britanni no Roman traveled unarmed throughout the country side.

The centurion stepped into a clearing and blinked, un able to believe the vision in front of him. A stockade— nay, a fortress—rose in the clearing, flanked by fields an pens for sheep, cattle and horses. The logs which forme the outer wall had been chiseled to end in sharp teeth ca pable of impaling any attacker foolish enough to try t scale the walls. The centurion could see four watchtow ers, presumably set at the four corners of the fortress, an there was an open gate facing him. The path they we following crossed the clearing only to change into a ram part within one hundred feet of the gate. The construc tion bothered the centurion, for he had been expectin simply another collection of rough huts, especially this fa

rom civilization. With a certain amount of trepidation he
;ave the order to enter the fortress through the open gate,
or clearly visitors were welcome. He also ordered the men
o enter with their swords drawn; he would not be caught
mprepared.

Inside the walls, more surprises awaited the centurion
nd his legionaries, and as they walked through the streets
he centurion was struck by a sense of familiarity, as if he
ad been here before. Buildings that seemed neither Ro-
nan nor Celtic but a melding of both lined neat, arrow-
traight dirt streets. His nose told him a bakery was close
y and, glancing around, he saw the building sitting
omewhat apart from the others. So that if it burns, he
hought, the fire will not spread. And then he knew why
his place was so familiar; incredibly, it was laid out so
hat it resembled a legionary camp. All Roman camps
vere laid out in an identical pattern, so that any legion-
ry could walk into any camp and be immediately at ease.
)ne- and two-story homes sat side by side, in perfect
armony. To judge from everything he was seeing, this
ettlement had thrived and was prosperous. The centu-
ion removed his helmet and, gesturing for his men to re-
nain behind, followed the street that paralleled the front
vall of the stockade. The expanse was bare, save for a
olumn of sharpening stone. The centurion frowned at it,
trickle of fear running down his spine at the thought of
he inhabitants of this fortress possessing weapons.

He could hear the laughter of children, and the breeze
arried faint gusts of conversation to him. So the place
vas not deserted, despite the fact that he had yet to see any
f the inhabitants. As if in answer to his thoughts, a
oman came around the corner of the street, a child held
 her arms. Seeing him, she set the child on the ground
nd, with a little slap on its buttocks, sent the child back
e way she had come. Then she continued toward the
enturion and when only a few feet separated them, she
alted and said in a cultured, melodic voice, "Salutatio,
'enturion."

"S-salutatio," the centurion managed to reply. A braid
of red-gold hair curved over the woman's shoulder to fall
to her hip and wide, violet eyes regarded him curiously as
he stared at her. She wore a green stola, which clung to the
curves of her lithe form, but she was barefoot. His eyes
wandered up to her face, where they lingered. She was
past the first blush of beauty, and there were faint lines at
the corners of her eyes, but she was an arresting woman
nonetheless.

"How may we be of service to you?" the vision asked
when he simply stared at her.

"You speak Latin." It was the only reply that came to
the centurion's mind.

"Aye." Jilana's lips curved into a smile. "What is it you
wish, Centurion?" A sudden gleam came into the man's
eyes and, as he glanced around the settlement, her smile
faded.

"Where are your men?" the centurion inquired,
thinking that perhaps the long march would yield more
than a few horses.

"Do not even consider such a thing, Centurion."

The man started at the low, but unmistakable warning
in her voice. How had she known what he was thinking?
The centurion barely managed to suppress a shudder at
the violet eyes which now regarded him without their
previous friendliness. "We have been sent to purchase
horses," he said at last, setting the helmet back on his
head.

"I am Jilana. You will wish to speak with my husband
and Hadrian regarding the horses. They will return soon."

While the centurion watched, Jilana raised her hand
and the street was soon filled with the citizens of the fortress. "You have no need of your weapons," she told him.
"No harm will come to you here unless it is by your own
hand." She smiled slightly when he sheathed his sword
and his men followed suit. "Come, I will introduce you
to our elders."

The centurion followed her obediently and greeted several old men—two of which she introduced as her hus-

and's father and her own—and women. The children
ere present now and they surrounded the Roman infan-
y, gazing at them with wide eyes.

"We see few legionaries here," a woman called Ede
xplained to the centurion. "They are a novelty for the
hildren." Her Latin was heavily accented, but correct.

The children spoke Latin as well, and when the centu-
on commented upon the fact, Jilana laughed. "Nearly
veryone in our village speaks both tongues."

The centurion stared at her. "You are not Celtic."

Jilana looked at him in surprise. "But I am, Centu-
ion, and Roman as well." She swept a hand around her.
We are each part of the other; Roman or Celtic, it does
ot matter."

The centurion opened the pouch at his waist and ex-
racted several sealed pieces of parchment. "These are for
ilana Basilius."

Jilana took them eagerly, her eyes alight. "Thank you,
Centurion."

"You *are* Jilana Basilius," the centurion insisted. "The
laughter—" his voice trailed off and he glanced in con-
usion at the grizzled man with the look of a warrior
bout him who had been introduced as Jilana's father.
"The daughter of Marcus Basilius, the merchant?"

"Aye." Understanding his confusion, but not caring to
nlighten him, Jilana merely smiled. Her gaze went to the
ate and an expression so loving it tugged at the centu-
ion's heart fell across her features. "Here is my hus-
and."

The centurion turned and watched the column of men
coming through the gate. The two men who led them were
oth large and powerfully built, though he noticed that
he one on the left walked with a slight limp. And then the
centurion knew what else had been bothering him—the
illagers were friendly, but there had been no men of
ighting age here. He remembered the feeling of being
vatched as they came through the woods and knew that
hey had been watched for several miles. To his relief,
one of the Celts carried weapons.

The column dispersed as soon as it passed through the gate as the men sought out their families. The men in the lead and a tall youth came to where they were standing.

"You must be here for the horses," Hadrian greeted the centurion and then bent to kiss his wife.

"Aye." The centurion watched the man and the youth flank Jilana.

"Centurion, this is my husband, Caddaric." Jilana indicated the towering, fierce-looking man on her left. "And my son, Artair." She glanced at the other man who had draped an arm around Ede's shoulders. "That is Hadrian." She stepped away from her family and linked an arm through Ede's. "Come, Ede, let us leave the men to their business."

THAT NIGHT, Caddaric closed the door of their bedroom and watched Jilana prepare for bed. Their house was small, two-storied, a melding of his culture and hers, but for the first few years they had lived here, their home had been a bothie. Jilana had not minded, but he had insisted upon building this present structure when the stockade had been completed.

Jilana looked up and found Caddaric's eyes upon her. "Did you hide the weapons?"

"Of course, my heart," Caddaric replied with a grin. "Artair helped me."

Jilana raised an eyebrow at that. "No doubt he helped you only because Cymbre told him *she* was helping Hadrian."

"No doubt." Caddaric sat beside her on the bed. "Shall I brush your hair?"

"Aye, I would like that." Jilana hesitated. "I should check on the children."

"I have already done so," Caddaric assured her. "They are all asleep."

"All six of them?" Jilana grinned, considering the possibility of such a thing at this early hour.

"The excitement exhausted them." Caddaric's eyes darkened and, taking the brush from her and tossing it side, he drew her into his arms. "What did Marcus say in his letters?"

"That he wants to see us."

"Us?" Caddaric tilted her face upward. "Or you?"

"All of us this time," Jilana said firmly. "You may read the letter yourself if you do not believe me."

"So the gods have at last worked a miracle." Caddaric chuckled dryly. "What else?"

"That Lucius and Claudia have had another child—their eighth." She slanted her husband a teasing look. "I fear we have fallen behind, my love."

Caddaric snorted. "I think Lucius is trying to keep your sister from dabbling in politics."

Jilana smiled and rubbed her hands against the tunic covering Caddaric's chest. "Allyce is nearly three, my love. Mayhap we should give her a playmate."

As ever, her touch stirred him, and Caddaric eased them both back onto the bed. "Mayhap," he whispered against her lips.

JULIE ELLIS

author of the bestselling
Rich Is Best rivals the likes of
Judith Krantz and Belva Plain with

THE ONLY SIN

It sweeps through the glamorous cities of Paris, London, New York and Hollywood. It captures life at the turn of the century and moves to the present day. *The Only Sin* is the triumphant story of Lilli Landau's rise to power, wealth and international fame in the sensational fast-paced world of cosmetics.

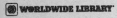

Sarah

MAURA SEGER

Sarah wanted desperately to escape the clutches of her cruel father.
Philip needed a mother for his son, a mistress for his plantation.
It was a marriage of convenience.
Then it happened. The love they had tried to deny suddenly became a
blissful reality... only to be challenged by life's hardships and brutal
misfortunes.
